Andrezj of Hollywood

a postmodern epic in eight parts

David Schulze

David Schulze Books | davidschulzebooks.com

Cover design by shommy
Published in the United States of America

ISBN-13
eBook: 978-1-7370378-4-2
Paperback: 978-1-7370378-3-5
Hardcover: 978-1-7370378-5-9

Andrezj of Hollywood is a work of exaggerated fiction loosely based on true events. 30% actually happened. 15% easily could've happened. The rest are lies. Any similarity to any real persons, living or dead, is completely coincidental and does not represent the intentions of the author.

It is highly recommended, though not required, for the reader to have finished *The Sins of Jack Branson* before staring *Andrezj of Hollywood*. Spoilers are incoming.

There are not enough words,
not enough phrases,
not enough ways I can properly express
just how much you've changed my life.

So I wrote this book as a consolation,
immortalizing a world in which you hadn't.

It's a sadder world. A colder world. A lonelier world.
It's the world you saved me from.

And now, thanks to you,
it's only fiction.

To Howie Schulze,
the best thing that ever happened to me.

“Why did I ever say no to Charles? Everything could’ve been so much better.”

— Ms. Diana Spencer, RN to herself
as she waits in a McDonald’s drive-thru

August 31, 1997

PROLOGUE

Did You Know Him Well?

Drew clutches the practically full 750mL bottle of Domergue by its slender neck and chucks it across the conference room. Upon deafening impact the glass shatters into a million microscopic pieces, a razor-sharp mist floating down the air like a cloud of gnats. Poisoned Scotch spatters across the slamming door and ricochets onto the carpet. Vibrations of the collision echo throughout the room, shaking the overturned chairs, shimmying across the carpet, crawling up Drew's legs and rattling his bones.

The metaphorical smoke clears from Drew's elongated 80 proof baseball. A single unsmeared handprint reveals itself on the conference room door, a beautiful, seemingly phosphorescent scarlet stinging Drew's eyes. Frankie was gone, racing down the stairs if not already outside. But did he really leave that room? Even if he had pushed the door with his left hand, the one covered in sweat instead of blood, could Drew really forget what just happened? What Frankie said? What he tried to do?

Nevertheless, Drew was alone.

Truly, utterly alone.

Here, at the end of his story, Drew Lawrence is forty-three years old. Black Armani suit custom-fitted to tastefully accentuate his Mike Trout proportions, from the curve of his objectively impressive biceps down to his toned thighs, the physique he spent twenty years and thousands of dollars manufacturing. Elephant gray Brooks Brothers dress shirt ripped under his right arm. Cut upper lip. Bleeding gums. Bloodshot eyes. Welted cheek. Bruises on both sides of his neck. Why is he hotter because of it? How is a bruised and battered exterior more alluring, more masculine?

Drew takes in short, jagged breaths, his muscles unbinding, the threat finally neutralized. He crouches to inspect the overturned chair. Lifts his eyes. Freezes, his lungs tightening with recognition.

Sitting on a coaster on Drew's twenty-man mahogany conference table is a half-empty Waterford crystal tumbler. Drew's poisoned glass of 22yr Domergue Single Malt Scotch whisky. The venom survived, even after Drew overhanded Frankie the Traitor his farewell present. But so did Drew. Theo didn't plan on that. He'll take it out on Frankie, won't he? Even though the botching wasn't Frankie's fault. It was the smell.

Theo managed to get poisoned whisky literally and figuratively under Drew nose, but even he underestimated how powerful that nose was. Even with a deviated septum and fifteen years of cocaine abuse, Drew could tell something wrong in that tumbler. Throughout the whole fucking bottle as it turned out. He was never one of those fickle winos whoring his tongue along the top shelf, palette abused by a myriad of flavors. Drew was a loyal son of a bitch. Practically a Domergue brand ambassador. He'd make a good one too. He had the scent fucking *memorized.*

Drew stands, his eyes fixed on that unmolested glass. The poisoned Domergue glances back, resting comfortably in its octagonal abode. Clear ice ball still geometrically intact. Waterford crystal condensing with oblivious tranquility. Did he underestimate Theo in return? Did he mean for Drew to spot the poison in time? Maybe it was never a true assassination attempt. Just a message. "Look what you made me do," or something like that. That and "See what you've done to your friend?" He did choose Frankie of all people, not some Compton junkie. Or maybe Drew's still in denial about it. Theo really truly tried to kill him.

And Frankie. His best friend. He just got here. Drew was hugging him just a few minutes before. They were catching up. Frankie even came bearing gifts. "A peace offering," he said. He said a lot more after that. Too much.

Drew looks back at Frankie's bloody handprint, gravity ushering amber streaks of Domergue across the crimson palm and thumb. What if Drew hadn't noticed the poison in time? Would Frankie have stayed? Would he have watched?

Drew combs a tender hand across his hair, fingers mopping up a pungent, sticky mix of sweat and American Crew Pomade (an admittedly copious amount, just enough to keep his high shine life at medium hold). Tired. Hurt. Sad. Drew flips his Florentine leather chair right-side up and sits. Sits and stares. Stares out that window wall of his. That view of the Hollywood Sign. The nighttime view worth its weight in gold.

Four hours pass. Ephemeral Pictures' newly refurbished, newly shabbied conference room is still the same. The shattered tumbler on the carpet. Frankie's bloodied handprint shining on the door. The fine remains of his "peace offering" on the carpet below, soft glass ashes. The pile of old screenplays on the conference table, whisky ravaging through them like a bushfire, dissolving the paper into a shriveled, spongy pulp. A crime scene without a body. For now.

Drew slouches in his chair, face hard and cold, replaying that fight with Frankie in his mind, silent as a GIF. He holds up his tumbler of poisoned Scotch. He hasn't dumped it out yet. Why hasn't he dumped it out yet? Why does he like looking at it? Why does it flatter him? Because he's actually somebody worth assassinating. Who else can say that? And not with a paper knife, with Excalibur no less. What a way to go.

What if he drinks it anyway?

Drew's throat closes up. He blinks. Looks up at the unrisen morning light. What's more fucked up? The fact that he thought that at all? Or the fact that he's still thinking about it?

It's not just Frankie, is it? It's everything. Everything's gone so wrong. He used to be so loved. So popular. So respected. What happened? When did it all begin? So scary. He did the right thing. He kept doing the right thing. And yet here he is. No money. No prestige. No hope. He thought the era of spite was over. That awful time. All that hate. Those chickens coming home to roost. Snipping at his fingertips. Clawing at his kneecaps. Pecking his eyes out. He thought it was finally over. And now this. Is Frankie's betrayal the climax? The Second Act Break? The First Act Break?

Oh fuck, it's the cold open, isn't it? The fucking prologue. This is never going to end.

It's not even a misunderstanding. He earned it. He deserves it. It's nobody's fault but his. No one to pass the buck to. No one to cry to. No one to talk him down this time.

Drew stares into space. Thinks it over one last time. Lifts the octagonal tumbler like Yorick's skull. Stares through the amber fog. That dark brown abyss obfuscating his view of Griffith Park. If the sun was rising, he wouldn't have known. He takes a deep breath. Closes his eyes. Makes his choice. A few seconds pass. The crystal tumbler slips out of his fingers. Falls to the floor. Bounces away, ice and poisoned Domergue flying everywhere. Drew jolts up, stares at the mess, his strong body trembling with instant regret. It's too late, isn't it? He can't change his mind now. He just has to wait. Prepare. Endure.

Drew Lawrence watches the morning light stroll down Sunset Boulevard frame-by-frame, on the edge of his seat, scared shitless of what's gonna happen next.

PART ONE

Not Minding That It Hurts

INT.	Interior
EXT.	Exterior
I/E.	Interior *and* Exterior
V.O.	Voiceover
O.S.	Off-screen
CONT'D	Continued
CUT	Simple change of scene
DISSOLVE	Fade to next scene
JUMP CUT	Skip ahead in time
SMASH CUT	Abrupt, disorienting cut
MATCH CUT	Visual or audial similarities between cuts
INSERT	Cut to a clip

JACOB

Choose Your Own Adventure

FADE IN:

INT. AIRPLANE - DUSK

JACOB ANDREZJ (21) stares at the back of the seat in front of him, his mind in another realm. A pair of THIN BROWN FRAMES rest atop his monstrous honker of a nose, magnifying glasses for lenses. He's wearing an absolutely gorgeous RED LEATHER JACKET. Noticeably unkempt dark brown hair. Pimples on his forehead and cheeks. Awful posture showing off his fat, bouncy belly. To a stranger it would appear Jacob doesn't care what he looks like. In reality he simply doesn't know what he looks like.

PILOT (V.O.)
(British; over intercom)
Ladies and gentlemen, we are about to begin our descent into Boston. The sound you've just heard is our landing gear locking into place. The weather is clear, temperature seventy-two degrees. We expect to make our six-hour forty-minute flight on schedule.

Jacob slides the window shade up, the burnt sun barely hanging onto the western horizon, and a mix of emotions swirl across his face. Relief. Anxiety. Sadness. At what he's not quite sure. Nothing. Everything. Both at once, if that was possible.

PILOT (V.O.)
Thank you for flying British Airways. We enjoyed having you on board and look forward to seeing you again in the future.

Jacob faces forward and closes his eyes.

CUT TO:

EXT. LOGAN INTERNATIONAL AIRPORT - NIGHT

Jacob waits in the car pickup zone. Nervously puts his iPhone to his ear. The dial tone rings three times and gets cut off.

VOICEMAIL (V.O.)
Please leave a message for… SIX. ONE. ZERO. NINE--

Jacob hangs up with disappointment.

JACOB
(breaking fourth wall)
You believe this shit? I thought I was supposed to be the child.

HONK-HONK! A pair of headlights turn onto the terminal's drive, a BLACK HYUNDAI ELANTRA blasting "Lone Digger" by Caravan Palace, bass heavy electro-swing, and getting louder. Jacob pockets his phone, smiling with recognition.

RIAN HOFFMAN (21) pokes his head out of the Elantra's front passenger window. Yellow flannel shirt. Large black glasses. Light gray Newsies cap. Charcoal hair the same shade as his mustache and scruff.

RIAN
There he is! Jacob!

NICH HOLSTEIN (21) sticks his head out of the rear passenger window. Short fuchsia hair spiked like Sid Vicious. Enough earrings to hang a shower curtain. Thick nose ring fit for a Minotaur.

NICH
Jake!

JACOB
You're fucking late!

TJ MASON (21) puts the car in park. African American. Plaid burgundy button-up. Black necktie. Slim fit khakis. Wheat Timberland boots.

TJ
C'mon everyone, hurry up.

All three doors open at once, the young men pouring out like a NASCAR pit crew. Jacob's already overwhelmed.

RIAN
(hugging Jacob)
Hey buddy! How was Italy?

JACOB
Unbelievable.

NICH
Love the jacket, dude!

JACOB
Thanks. Just got it.

Nich tries to grab the bag's handle out of Jacob's hand.

NICH
Someone pop the trunk.

JACOB
No, I'll get it.

TJ bro-hugs Jacob long enough for Nich to roll the bag away. Rian pops the trunk. Nich lifts the bag, buckling.

NICH
Mother-FUCKER!

TJ runs over to help Nich.

TJ
Lift with your legs.

The two of them heave the bag into the trunk.

NICH
What the fuck do you have in here, Jake?

JACOB
Four months of clothes, some souvenirs--

RIAN
Think that was rhetorical.

JACOB
Course it was.

CUT TO:

INT. TJ'S ELANTRA - NIGHT

The lights of Boston streak by as TJ speeds down the highway. The Elantra's interior is trimmed with custom LED strips, soothing blue raspberry light being the only other source of illumination. Rian sits in the passenger seat. Nich and Jacob sit in the back.

RIAN
How're we doing on time?

TJ
We'll hit King of Siam's around 7:00. Should make it back to LB by 8:15.

RIAN
Perfect.

JACOB
Who's coming?

RIAN
Pretty much everyone on Film Immersion. Max Ellis is bringing their MT buddies from the Weird One.

NICH
Trevor wanted to bring his roommate Matty. I said it was alright.

JACOB
That's fine. I like Trevor.

TJ
Carter Jackson's running late, but he said he'd stop by.

Jacob can't help but smile from the name alone.

JACOB
Carter's coming? I didn't know that.

Rian and TJ give each other knowing looks. Jacob catches this. Self-consciously drops his smile.

NICH
What are you doing this summer, Rian?

RIAN
Nothing much. Just hanging around Savannah, avoiding my folks, same as last year.

JACOB
(to Nich)
You're still doing the Battle of the Bands?

NICH
(proud)
Semifinals! Which is surprising, cause we suck without Jeremy.

TJ
What are you doing over the summer, Jake? Going back to your mom's in Conshohickon?

JACOB
ConshoHOCKen, and no. I'm doing the janitor thing up here.

TJ
What janitor thing up here?

RIAN
Someone didn't read Jacob's Facebook post this morning.

TJ
Who does?

Everyone laughs except Jacob. Nich notices.

NICH
(to Jacob)
TJ can't read. He just wikes to wook at the wittle piwctures.

TJ
Go fuck yourself.

Jacob smiles with gratitude at Nich.

JACOB
But to answer your question, TJ, Whitman's paying me to stay behind and clean up the dorms.

TJ
That's a thing?

JACOB
Every year apparently. Trevor did it last summer. He's the one that told me about it.

NICH
Isn't that really hard to get?

JACOB
They had a last-minute cancellation. Carter emailed me a couple months ago and asked if I wanted to do it.

RIAN
Did you tell your mom yet?

Jacob's face hardens.

JACOB
Yeah. In London.

TJ
Seems a bit harsh, waiting till the day before move-out.

RIAN
You don't know his mom.

TJ
What does that mean?

NICH
(to Jacob)
You never told him?

JACOB
It was two years ago.

NICH
You tell everyone!

TJ
Tell me what?

Jacob throws a look at Nich.

JACOB
(to TJ)
You know my parents got divorced, right?

TJ
Yeah.

NICH
Tell him where you were when they had that big--

JACOB
I'M telling it!
(pause)
My family went to Disney World right after I finished high school. Melanie's graduation gift.

TJ
Where were you?

JACOB
Ireland. Eagle Ridge school trip.

RIAN
They went to Disney without you?

JACOB
They got the dates mixed up. It's okay. I didn't mind. I've been there enough. It's not like I was missing anything.

NICH
Except--

JACOB
Nich, I swear to God!

NICH
Fine-fine-fine!

JACOB
(to TJ)
My parents had a huge fight down there and Mom asked Dad for a divorce. Karen overheard Mom talking on the phone with her lawyer and told Melanie about it before I got back from Ireland.

TJ
When did you find out?

JACOB
Six months later.

TJ
Six months?! Fuck! Why didn't anyone tell you?

Jacob hesitates.

JACOB
Does it matter?

NICH
She sold the house too.

TJ
What house?

JACOB
The house in Phoenixville. Mom couldn't afford it on her own.

TJ
How long were you there?

JACOB
Since I was six. Mom didn't tell me until Christmas in the car on the way home from the airport.

TJ
Told you what?

JACOB
That she and my dad were getting a divorce and the house was already sold.

TJ
BOTH?!

NICH
Captive audience. Pretty ballsy of her.

JACOB
That's one word for it.

Awkward silence. Rian looks back at Jacob.

RIAN
Well?

JACOB
Well what?

RIAN
When you told her about the janitor thing, how'd she take it?

JACOB
Not good.
(pause)
Not good at all.

No one talks.

NICH
Let's get some music going, huh?

TJ
Absolutely. Jacob?

JACOB
Sure.

TJ hands back the AUX cord. Jacob plugs it into his iPhone. Scrolls through his Apple Music library. Looks out the window at you.

JACOB (CONT'D)
(breaking fourth wall)
Nich always picks something like Slipknot or Megadeath, and TJ's gonna balance it out with some indie rock like Mumford and Sons or Fleet Foxes, so I should really pick something different.
(pause)
I'm really into Billy Joel at the moment, but I think that's a bit too vanilla for these guys. Simon and Garfunkel too. I really should stick to 70s progressive rock. I know they like that. But the problem with Zeppelin is that their songs are either too mainstream, too weird, or just shit. And I know they all like Pink Floyd, but all the songs I like by them are twenty minutes long. They're more of an album group anyway. I gotta think of something else.
(pause)
They don't know much George Harrison.

Jacob scrolls through the track listing of <u>All Things Must Pass</u>.

JACOB (CONT'D)
(breaking fourth wall)
"Isn't it a Pity" is really the best choice but it's over seven minutes long. So it's between "Wah-Wah" or "Art of Dying."
(pause)
"Art of Dying" might be a bit too disco-y for Nich. "Wah-Wah" it is.

Jacob taps "Wah-Wah." The strange guitar intro makes Nich raise his brow. The sudden joining in of the rest of the instruments perplex TJ and Rian.

NICH
What is this?

JACOB
"Wah-Wah." George Harrison.

TJ
Don't know it.

RIAN
You like the Beatles, don't you Nich?

NICH
Don't get me started.

TJ
They formed the foundation for all modern music.

NICH
The Velvet Underground & Nico did more for modern rock than Sgt. Pepper and I will die on that hill.

RIAN
Their popularity was what ushered the changes. No one outside Warhol's inner circle even heard of the Velvet Underground until the 80s. And where would your band be without "Helter Skelter"?

JACOB
(meek)
"Helter Skelter" is on The White--

NICH
That is a BULLSHIT argument!

TJ
No yelling in my car.

RIAN
Did it not invent heavy metal?

NICH
NO! "Helter Skelter" is what mainstream normies THINK heavy metal sounds like! The Beatles are like Target. Just a bunch of different songs in a variety of styles and nothing beyond the surface. They should've just picked a lane and done it right!

Jacob tries his hardest to tune out the bickering and listen to the song.

TJ
So you're saying "Revolution 9" is just avant-garde 101?

NICH
No way! "Revolution 9" is the only good thing they've ever done!

RIAN
Oh, you WOULD like "Revolution 9!"

Jacob closes his eyes with a lamentful sigh.

NICH
And let me tell you something else!

CUT TO:

INT. KING OF SIAM LIQUOR STORE - NIGHT

Jacob wanders down the whisky aisle, right hand grazing the bottlenecks like Maximus and the wheat in Gladiator. He can hear Nich, TJ, and Rian the next aisle over.

NICH (O.S.)
We really should get handles.

TJ (O.S.)
We gotta get going. The gas station closes at 8.

RIAN (O.S.)
Let's just get seven and leave the rest for Jacob. He's not going anywhere.

NICH (O.S.)
Make it an even eight then.

Jacob rounds the corner to see TJ and Rian holding FOUR HANDLES OF ROMANOFF VODKA each and Nich pulling out his wallet.

JACOB
Romanoff? Really?

NICH
You're not buying.

JACOB
I'll chip in if that means we can get the good stuff.
(crouches down)
Look, we can get a handle of Ultimo for...

Jacob bugs his eyes at the price tag.

JACOB (CONT'D)
What the FUCK?!

TJ
$35 for a handle? That's actually not bad for Ultimo.

JACOB
You know much that would cost in Florence? Fifteen euro.

NICH
What is that?

JACOB
I dunno. Seventeen, eighteen dollars.

NICH
Oh. Cool. We're not in Italy.

TJ stops in front of a locked case.

TJ
I don't believe it! Guys, look at this!

TJ points up at a LARGE PARCHMENT BROWN BOX on the top shelf, the brand name handwritten in red cursive: "DOMERGUE 15"

TJ (CONT'D)
It's the Scotch my dad drinks. He smuggles it out of Canada to avoid the tariffs.

Nich raises his brow at the price tag: "$1,199.99"

NICH
Does it give him an orgasm?

TJ
It probably tastes like shit.

NICH
Yeah, well some people are into that.

RIAN
I sure hope it tastes like shit.

JACOB
Can you imagine being able to afford a $1,200 bottle of shit just to be able to say you can afford a $1,200 bottle of shit?

NICH
I can barely afford eight $17 bottles of shit.

Jacob sighs, tracing the red cursive with his blue eyes.

JACOB
Don't think we'll be able to afford one of those for a while.

TJ
Speak for yourself.

Nich, TJ, and Rian head to the checkout counter. Jacob looks to the door. Wanders toward the exit.

NICH
Where're you going?

JACOB
Just wanna get some air.

Jacob pushes the door.

CUT TO:

EXT. KING OF SIAM LIQUOR STORE - NIGHT

Jacob sits on the curb. Stretches out his legs. It's quiet. No cars. Decaying Allston businesses across the street.

Rian comes out of the liquor store and plops down next to Jacob.

RIAN
Your mom got you all upset, huh?

Jacob nods softly.

JACOB
I called her to apologize just before you guys pulled up. She sent it to voicemail.

RIAN
What do you have to apologize for?

JACOB
She's my mother.

RIAN
I definitely can't relate to that.
(pause)
Why do you want to stay up here anyway?

JACOB
Ever since the divorce I've been bouncing place to place. Four months here, three months there, eight months here, three months there, four here, four more in Italy. I just wanted to stop.

Jacob looks at Rian, helpless.

JACOB (CONT'D)
That's it. That's all it was.
(pause)
And she didn't believe me.

Rian frowns.

JACOB (CONT'D)
She thought I did it to get back at her for canceling her flight out there.

RIAN
Out where? To Italy?

JACOB
That was the plan. She was gonna meet me in Florence after classes were over and spend two weeks roaming the rest of Italy with me.
(pause)
We'd still be there right now.

RIAN
You really weren't upset about that?

JACOB
Of course I was. But what was I gonna do? It's her money. And she did just lose her job.

Jacob looks off, thinking.

JACOB (CONT'D)
Maybe it was revenge. Unconsciously. The timing of everything...

RIAN
What was the reason she didn't want anyone telling you about the divorce? I don't think you ever told me.

Jacob hesitates.

JACOB
She thought I'd be so distraught that I'd drop out of college.

Rian chuckles.

RIAN
She thought YOU would drop out?

JACOB
I know.

Rian leans back, shaking his head.

RIAN
She doesn't know you at all, does she?

JACOB
(frowning)
That's what I'm trying to get used to.

RIAN
You shouldn't be blaming yourself. You're a fucking adult. You're not always going to be there at her beck and call.

JACOB
But didn't I just prove her right?

RIAN
Huh?

JACOB
She thought it was in-character for me to get so emotional that I'd drop out of school. Didn't I just prove her right?

RIAN
You're staying on campus for an extra three months and getting paid for it. That's not the same thing at all.

JACOB
But it wasn't the plan. I made trouble when there wasn't any.

RIAN
So?

JACOB
So that's something Karen would do. That's something Karen DID do.

RIAN
You've never disobeyed your mother? Ever?

JACOB
Not when I was living with her. I was always the amenable one. I liked it.

RIAN
And look how they repaid you.

Jacob wraps his arms around his legs. Rests his chin.

JACOB
This is probably the first real decision I've ever made. What if I just fucked up my life and don't know it yet?

RIAN
Dude, it's one summer.

JACOB
Mom had absolutely no idea when she got married that she'd end up regretting it in thirty years. She always said it was the happiest day of her life. What if this is one of those? How would I know?

Rian looks off, unsure how to respond.

RIAN
Does it feel right at least?

JACOB
No, it really doesn't. No thanks to her. GOD, she really just...!

Jacob shakes his head.

JACOB (CONT'D)
Why can't she care about my feelings just as much as I care about hers?

They sit in silence. Rian sits back up, wiping his hands together.

RIAN
We're gonna be fine, man. Just think. This time next year we'll be in LA, living it up and making our dreams come true. They're just four people you used to live with. Don't let 'em weigh you down.

JACOB
It's not that simple.

RIAN
Make it that simple.

JACOB
Those people were my entire life for eighteen years. What, am I'm supposed to just move on from that?

RIAN
Why not? They did.

Jacob goes quiet.

JACOB
(whispers)
I just want it all to have been worth it.

RIAN
You didn't have them in Florence. Fuck, you didn't have anyone! Every person you ever met was 4,000 miles away. You were on the complete other side of the world.

Jacob doesn't speak. Thinks.

RIAN (CONT'D)
It wasn't so bad, was it?

JACOB
Suppose not.

RIAN
Look what you had out there. Homemade pasta. Cheap booze. Priceless paintings. Museums. Gigantic buildings. You wrote a couple more features.

JACOB
Fucked around.

Rian chuckles suggestively.

RIAN
Oh yeah.

JACOB
Watched a man die.

Jacob looks at Rian with pursed lips. Rian simmers down. Jacob looks away, suddenly self-conscious.

JACOB (CONT'D)
I'm over it. Really I am.

Rian sighs.

RIAN
My point is, why should you have to stop now that you're back? Keep living your best life up here. Write another movie. Blast your records. Fucking streak through the halls.

Jacob laughs. Smiles at Rian.

JACOB (CONT'D)
I really missed you, man.

RIAN
I missed you too, buddy.

Rian puts a hand on Jacob's shoulder.

JACOB
I wish we didn't have the party tonight.

RIAN
How come?

JACOB
I only get you guys for one night. It really should be just the four of us.

RIAN
We're hanging out now, aren't we?

JACOB
Rushing around doing errands isn't really the same thing.

Rian thinks.

RIAN
How about we get really fucked up tonight and at four in the morning we all go to South Street Diner for some pancakes?

JACOB
You really wanna stay up that late?

RIAN
Nich and I aren't flying till noon.

JACOB
TJ's driving to Michigan.

RIAN
He slept all day. C'mon, it'll be great.

Jacob thinks it over.

JACOB
I'm not gonna drink.

RIAN
C'mon, dude! We're celebrating. Who cares if it's cheap vodka?

JACOB
It's not that.
(pause)
I don't want to drink. It's my last night with you guys till Labor Day. I want to remember everything.

Rian takes a deep breath with a hint of a smile.

RIAN
Dude... Do whatever the fuck you want.

Jacob grins.

WHALE

Waiting for Rapture

Normally Whale sleeps like a rock, even before busy days or in anticipation of all-or-nothing emails, but today's different. Can't still be jet lag. He's been acclimated to Pacific Time for two weeks now. Yet there he was, lying on his back, staring up at the ceiling of that North Hollywood ranch house, the sun at an angle he seldom sees.

Whale slides out of bed, slips on a pair of silk pajama pants, knots the little tassels just enough to prevent another Alex pantsing, and slides open the glass door. His bare feet crunch the cold dew-drenched grass. He lowers his butt to the ground, lies on his back, and stares up at the light blue sky.

The shade's colder than Whale had anticipated, his shirtless torso goosebumping, but he powers through it. Wraps his big arms under his head for support. Just lays there, a slight smile cropping onto his face. He's got plenty of time. Nothing to do besides dress, eat something, and head out. He can even make eye contact with God without that pesky sun blinding him, melting his eyes like the wax wings of Icarus. And he gets to notice the silence. The beeping of a garbage truck far away. The soft whisper of commuters on the 405.

Whale takes in a slow, long waft of warm California air, holds it in, and slowly lets it out.

```
                    WHALE
              (whispers)
       Thank you.
```

The morning sun finally pokes its face over the fence, a burst of light hitting Whale's lean chest and toned shoulders, a sudden warmth he can feel in his pits. Anyone else might see the timing as just coincidence, but Whale knows what it really is. Doesn't matter if it's true or just narcissistic projection, it's what he chooses to believe. He doesn't need to prove it to anyone else.

Whale instinctively reaches down for his phone, hitting flat pocket instead. If only he had the foresight to bring it out with him. Some Pet Shop Boys would be perfect right now. Was it really worth getting up, racing back into the house, grabbing his phone, and lying back down on the cold wet grass just to have a soundtrack? Whale thinks that over for a few seconds. Yes. Yes, it was. He hops up, waddles back inside, unplugs his iPhone, dashes back onto the grass and plops down in the same spot. He flips through his exhaustive PSB collection and picks the song most sonically appropriate for laying on morning grass: "Was It Worth It?," one of two previously unreleased singles on their 1991 greatest hits album *Discography: The Complete Singles Collection*. He has the CD now. And how fitting he play this song today of all days, considering—

Whale jolts up. It happened again. It's been happening a lot lately. Whale's actually getting used to it. But this was different. This one actually freaked him out.

"You're not one of those tai chi freaks, are you?"

Whale sees Alex standing at the open backdoor, eating a bowl of cereal in an orange bathrobe stinking of weed. Or maybe it was CBD cereal, the kind dispensaries craft out of low-profit desperation. Oh who was he kidding, the smell was Alex. Even an NFL ref could see the dude was a human bong.

```
                    WHALE
       No. Not a morning person at all, actually.
```

Alex wipes a bit of milk from the edge of his mouth. "Why start now?"

Because God is real and talks to Whale through a series of loosely connected and easily explainable coincidences, *dumbass.*

```
                WHALE
      Couldn't sleep.
```

"Oh shit," Alex says, realizing. "It's today, isn't it?"

```
                WHALE
      Last I checked.
```

Alex rolls his eyes. "Your internship."

```
                WHALE
      I know what you meant. Just roasting ya, boy.
```

Whale stands, taking his time. He catches Alex staring at his chest. He doesn't know if that flatters or grosses him out.

```
                WHALE (CONT'D)
      What?
```

"What's that music?" Alex murmurs.

```
                WHALE
      The Pet Shop Boys.
```

Alex doesn't react.

```
                WHALE (CONT'D)
      Remember? The gay British group from the 80s?
```

"Oh yeah. Right." Alex swirls his cereal around with his novelty *Toy Story* spoon, his unfocused eyes staring at Whale's upper body. "You have unbelievable shoulders. What the fuck."

```
                WHALE
      Pull ups, my dude. Best workout in the world.
```

"I can see that." Alex nods ambiently for a few moments. He abruptly turns and wanders back toward his kitchen.

Whale takes a shower. American Crew Daily Cleansing Shampoo. American Crew Daily Moisturizing Conditioner. Every Man Jack Cedar + Red Sage 3-in-1 All Over Wash. He steps out to shave. Gillette Foamy Sensitive Skin shaving cream. Gillette Fusion 5 razor (fresh refill of course). Aqua Velva. Degree Ultraclear Black + White 72hr Dry Spray Antiperspirant. Dermatologica Intensive Moisture Cleanser. Dermatologica Skin Smoothing Cream. He blow dries his hair. Runs a brush over the clumps. American Crew Forming Cream. Spritz of Unpredictable Pour Homme by Glenn Perri. Done. Only took two hours.

Whale dons a periwinkle button-up in his room, a slim-fit Oxford collar with stretch technology. He gazes at his handsome self in the full-length mirror. The *Pulp Fiction* poster behind him moves, catching his eye. The bottom left-hand corner's curling up again.

```
                WHALE
      Darn it.
```

Whale approaches Uma Thurman and pushes the corner with one finger as hard as he could, the Command strip squeezing against the wall. He steps back. Waits. Nothing. Good.

Whale returns to the mirror. Unbuttons his Oxford collar. Ties his silk tie, a beautiful blue one with black and silver stripes. He looks out the door at Alex assembling another bowl of cereal, studying his roommate from afar. His curiously alien habit of milk-first, cereal-second. The way his long hairless legs hog the chair next to him. The fact that his stained orange bathrobe hasn't left his sweaty body since Whale first moved in. What a loser. All his fault too. Whale asked for his story early on and Alex gladly divulged everything.

Alex Avery was once a third-generation Ivy Leaguer with a lawyer daddy and CFO mommy, full of privilege, promise and potential to thrive in such a capitalist, mutual back-scratching society. But what did Alex do? He dropped out of Yale, flew out to LA, and used his trust fund to buy a ranch house to lie around all day, drink booze, smoke copious amounts of weed (and sometimes meth), party every night with his yuppie friends, play Xbox Live for hours on end, watch *The Wolf of Wall Street* on repeat, and use his desktop computer exclusively for jerking off to yaoi. And that's not Whale passing judgment, that's literally what Alex told him. The dude was *bragging*!

Whale wanders into the kitchen, fully dressed and ready to go. He checks his phone. The closest Ridr is 15 minutes away. Just enough time for coffee. Whale pops in a dark roast pod and lets the Keurig do its thing. Whale watches Alex clip each toenail with one-and-done precision. As he reaches for his right pinkie toe, Alex readjusts his ass, a sharp little jiggle, his genitals shamelessly flopping out of his bathrobe. Whale discreetly looks away.

"I used the last of the almond milk," Alex mutters, his eyes fixed on his toes.

```
                    WHALE
Don't worry, I take it black.
          (smirks)
Like my men.
```

Alex scoffs. "Very original."

```
                    WHALE
Ah, but I wasn't trying to be original. 'Twas an
homage.
```

Alex looks up at Whale, his brows together. "You're fucking weird, you know that?"

The Keurig sputters, its job done. Whale holds the steaming hot cup, processing Alex's jape.

```
                    WHALE
Because I said 'twas?
```

"That, and you're a grown man that can't curse."

```
                    WHALE
I actually can curse, I just choose not to.
```

"La-dee-fuckin-da."

Whale blows the top of his coffee. Puts the mug down to roll up his sleeves.

"How're you doing on time?" Alex asks.

Whale checks his watch.

```
                    WHALE
All good.
```

"Where is it?"

```
                    WHALE
Century City. You know where that is?
```

"Of course. You know, you'd get there faster if you took the Metro."

```
                    WHALE
I'll get around to that. Wanna be above ground for a
while. Soak it all in.
```

"I get that."

Whale sips his coffee. Looks up at Alex.

```
                    WHALE
Hey, I don't wanna get weird or anything.
```

"Uh-huh," Alex says, amused.

WHALE
Just... Thanks dude, you know, for...

Whale gestures around at Alex's house.

WHALE (CONT'D)
You have no idea how grateful I am.

"Don't sweat it, bro."

WHALE
Is there anything I can do to...? As long as it's legal. I don't mind you doing drugs in the house, just don't expect me to buy any.

"You can stop at Trader Joe's and get some more almond milk."

WHALE
I don't know when they're letting us out. It might be closed by the time I get there.

"Doesn't have to be Trader Joe's. There's a Gelson's at the Westfield out there. I know they don't close till 10."

Whale chuckles awkwardly.

WHALE
I'm sorry, I don't...

"The grocery store at the mall," Alex clarifies. "I don't care what size you get. Just make sure it's unsweetened vanilla."

WHALE
Unsweetened vanilla. Got it.

"The Gelson's under the Westfield."

Whale chuckles.

WHALE
Is that the only grocery store in the mall?

"Pretty sure."

Whale nods, finally sipping his coffee.

WHALE
You going out tonight or staying in?

"My buddy Mason's got this thing down in La Brea." Alex pauses. "Wanna come along?"

Whale downplays his excitement.

WHALE
Sure. Why not.

"Cool." Alex stands, refolding his bathrobe. "I gotta piss, so... See you whenever."

WHALE
Yeah. Seeya.

Whale watches Alex wander off, amazed by that unexpected display of human nuance. The dude might've been a pitiable burnout, but what Alex lacked in ambition he sure made up for it in social graces.

Whale opens the blue Prius door parked on Calvert Street, scooting all the way over to the other side.

WHALE
Darryl?

"Yup." Darryl officially accepts the ride request and puts the Prius back into drive. As he turns onto Ethel Avenue toward Oxnard, Darryl gets another look at his passenger. Clean shaven. Early twenties. Wide-eyed. Too interested in the palm trees. Definitely a tourist. Lots of East Coast energy. "Century City, huh?"

WHALE
Yup.

"Locals don't normally Ridr to Century City," Darryl says, turning onto Coldwater Canyon Avenue. "It's faster if you take the Metro."

WHALE
So I've heard.

"Didn't know there was a subway out here, huh?"

WHALE
No, I knew.

"Really."

WHALE
Yeah. Really.

Darryl shrugs it off. "Cool." He pauses. "How long you in town for?"

WHALE
Forever, I guess. Hopefully.

Darryl looks back at Whale. "First time in LA?"

WHALE
Yup.

"Thought so."
Whale looks at the back of Darryl's headrest. Why would he say that?

WHALE
I snagged a paid internship with The Professor.

"The Professor, huh?"

WHALE
You know The Professor?

"Of course. The guy who did *Rant*."

WHALE
And others.

"Anything I've heard of?"

WHALE
Alabaster King.

"I didn't know he did *Alabaster King*."

WHALE
Dust Storm. You ever see that?

"I think so. It was probably one of those free On Demand movies."

WHALE
What did you think of it?

Darryl shrugs. "Has he done anything in the last twenty years?"

WHALE
You ever see Something Original?

Darryl hesitates.

```
                    WHALE (CONT'D)
          That's the name of the movie.
```

"Oh. No, should I have?"

```
                    WHALE
          It won Best Picture.
```

"Oh, I remember it now. He wrote it?"

```
                    WHALE
          And produced it.
```

"Gotcha." Darryl nods. "Funny title, considering it's a blatant rip-off of *The Odd Couple* and *All About Eve*."

```
                    WHALE
          He produces full-time now.
```

"Oh, that's a relief."

```
                    WHALE
          My internship's at his development company, The
          Factory.
```

"Cool," Darryl murmurs, zooming through Mulholland Drive. "Never heard of it."

```
                    WHALE
          It's only for recent college graduates. He gets
          15,000 applications a year and only picks four. I'm
          one of the four.
```

"How's it going so far?"

```
                    WHALE
          Don't know yet. It's my first day.
```

Darryl nods broadly.

```
                    WHALE (CONT'D)
          So how long have you been driving for Ridr?
```

"Long enough."

```
                    WHALE
          You must like it a lot.
```

"No." After a moment Darryl adds, "I'm not as lucky as you in the internship department."

```
                    WHALE
          Is this what you wanted to be growing up? A Ridr
          driver?
```

Darryl chuckles bitterly. "An actor."

```
                    WHALE
          You can still be an actor.
```

Darryl weaves through the Beverly Ridge Estates. "The older I get, the more I realize it's just you turning off your mind and renting out your body for bureaucratic assholes to say stupid lines in stupid costumes." He looks up at Whale's reflection. "What's your contribution to the machine? Directing?"

```
                    WHALE
          Writing.
```

"A writer!" Darryl says, mock impressed. "The next Tarantino or the next Sorkin?"

Whale doesn't answer.

Darryl shrugs. "Maybe you'll reroute and become the next Stephen King instead. Or the next J.K. Rowling. The next Tennessee Williams."

Whale looks out the window.

Darryl sighs pleasantly, turning onto Sunset Boulevard. "I've driven hundreds of guys like you over the last ten years. You know how many of them actually become the next Martin Scorsese or Bill Gates or whatever? None." He looks up at the rearview mirror. "I hope you do though. That way I can tell the next guy, 'Hey, guess what, I drove so-and-so back when he was a nobody, before he started that internship with The Professor that started it all.'"

```
                    WHALE
      I hope so too.
```

"What will you do if The Professor doesn't give you the job? What's the backup plan?"

```
                    WHALE
      Don't have one.
```

"No family?"

```
                    WHALE
      Not one I'd go back to with a tail between my legs.
```

"Doesn't sound like much of a cushion."

```
                    WHALE
      Which is why I need the job.
                 (pause)
      And just might be why I get it.
```

Darryl gets on the 2, quickly exits onto the Avenue of the Arts, and parks outside a harmless looking two-story office building. "This it?"

```
                    WHALE
      Think so.
```

Whale steps out of the Prius, softly closing the door behind him. Darryl doesn't waste time driving off. Whale watches the Prius fade into the distance. Pulls up the Ridr app. Rates Darryl 5-stars. Adds a $20 tip. He imagines Darryl's phone ka-chinging and his shocked eyes and his audible laugh as he grins his way onto the 2.

Whale locks his phone with a soft smile. All day he's said only the right things, easily managing himself in the face of strangers like Alex and Darryl, not letting his first impulses ruin his fresh start. And it all came so naturally. He looks up at the sky. Yes, to answer your question. Yes it was.

Whale whips open the door and marches into The Factory.

JACOB

Rotten Tomatoes

INT. WHITMAN UNIVERSITY - LITTLE BUILDING - SUITE 710 - NIGHT

Jacob steps out of his single room and quickly shuts the door.

The entire suite is packed with COLLEGE STUDENTS of all genders, races, nationalities, body types, sexualities, and hair colors (natural or not). "Uptown Funk" by Mark Ronson feat. Bruno Mars blasts from a bass-heavy Bluetooth speaker somewhere.

Jacob soaks in the loud, chatty menagerie of familiar faces. His smile slowly disappears.

CUT TO:

KITCHENETTE

Jacob leans against the cheap countertop. YAN PARK (22), a Korean Publishing Major with an Americanized accent and a Jane Austen T-Shirt, talks to him.

YAN
Love the jacket.

JACOB
Thanks.

YAN
It's very Star-Lord.

JACOB
That's more burgundy, but... Yeah, thanks. I just got it.

YAN
In Florence, right?

JACOB
Yeah.

YAN
Didn't know we had a program in Florence.

JACOB
Oh, we don't. I did the whole external program thing. I was the only Whitman guy there. Everyone else was either from University of Pittsburgh, UC Boulder, or University of Indiana. And a semester in Florence's cheaper than a semester in Boston apparently.

YAN
Not shocked.

JACOB
Yeah.

YAN
God, it must've been so amazing over there.

JACOB
Oh my God, yeah. I walked past the Duomo every day to get to class. The coffee is just out of this world. Everything's all old-world, you know? No subways or public transportation. And there's tourists and all,

but actually living there, I really got to see the real Florence.

Yan's already losing interest.

YAN
You got any pictures?

JACOB
They really don't do it justice. It's not about resolution, it's really about scope. Cameras can't even capture just the sheer sense of puniness you feel standing among those things. The David is, like, eleven feet tall.

YAN
Excuse me.

Yan wanders away. Jacob's smile drops, suddenly self-aware.

JACOB
Dammit.

CUT TO:

BY THE BATHROOM MIRROR

Jacob fills up a RED CANTEEN in one of the twin sinks. Standing by the other is Nich and TREVOR MILLER (21), a long-haired Post Malone fan with an oversized camo jacket and black Sharpie nail polish. They're taking hits from a geeb carved out of an empty 1L Pepsi bottle. Jacob watches them, impressed by the contraption.

Blowing out smoke, Trevor meets eyes with Jacob.

TREVOR
(holding out geeb)
Wanna hit?

JACOB
I'm good, thanks.

NICH
Jake doesn't smoke.

TREVOR
Oh. Sorry.

JACOB
It's okay.

Nich and Trevor wander back to the living room. Jacob watches them go, frowning slightly.

CUT TO:

IN THE HALLWAY

Jacob stands across from MATTY KLEIN (20), a clean-cut redhead drinking an IPA.

JACOB
You're a Screenwriting Major too, right?

MATTY
Yeah.

JACOB
Working on anything lately?

MATTY
Not really. My suitemate's friend Tim asked me to write a short for him, but I don't know... I don't think I'm very good at it.

Jacob forces a laugh. Matty nods, looking off. Jacob takes a deep breath.

MATTY (CONT'D)
What about you? You working on anything?

Jacob hesitates.

JACOB
Kinda.

MATTY
What is it?

Jacob scratches the back of his head.

JACOB
A feature.

MATTY
A feature. Wow.

JACOB
I know. It's not my first either.

MATTY
How many have you written?

Jacob hesitates.

JACOB
This would be five.

Matty coughs on his beer.

MATTY
Five? Shit.

JACOB
Yeah.

Matty and Jacob stand awkwardly.

MATTY
What's it about?

JACOB
A dark comedy set in a Beef 'n' Fries. I'm going for Clerks meets Black Swan.

MATTY
Clerks meets Black Swan?

JACOB
Not as silly as it sounds.

MATTY
How does Black Swan fit in?

JACOB
It's a bit complicated.

Matty nods awkwardly.

JACOB (CONT'D)
I used to work there. That's where I came up with the idea.

MATTY
Fry cook?

JACOB
Drive-thru.

MATTY
Ah.

JACOB
That's what it's called, actually. Drive-Thru.

MATTY
What's it like working there? Pretty shitty?

JACOB
On principle it kinda sucked, but the location was good for traffic and it wasn't too dirty. Most of my co-workers sucked, but all the ones I really hate aren't there anymore, so it probably wouldn't have been so bad going back.

Matty bursts out laughing.

JACOB (CONT'D)
No, really, it probably wouldn't have been.

MATTY
No, just the way you said it was so...

Matty laughs some more.

JACOB
I wasn't trying to be funny.

MATTY
I don't know. I thought it was funny.

Jacob nopes out of there.

MATTY (CONT'D)
(calling after him)
Oh, c'mon! You're really funny!

CUT TO:

INSIDE JACOB'S ROOM

Jacob buries his face in his hands, his frames resting atop his hair, door closed and locked, the crowd chatter and music significantly muffled.

Jacob's single room is just as he left it back in January. Movie posters on the walls (Pulp Fiction, 2001: A Space Odyssey, Cloud Atlas, The Lord of the Rings Trilogy). Criminally small bed raised three feet off the ground like a top bunk without a bottom. Gorgeous microfiber comforter in red, black and elephant gray. Extra wide computer monitor on the desk with an HDMI cable hanging out. Papers, textbooks, and Snickers wrappers on the floor. Black mini-fridge under the bed.

Jacob takes deep, uncomfortable breaths. He rips off his red leather jacket and throws it on the floor.

CUT TO:

INSIDE TJ'S ROOM

Jacob pours a shot of Romanoff into a cup. Tops it off with orange juice. Takes a sip. Smacks his tongue around. Adds more vodka.

KYLIEE MARIE (20) and CLEM WANAMAKER (21) gab behind him. Kyliee's a short Production Design major with luscious curls and an emerald dress. Clem's an overweight Directing Major with mermaid-blue hair in a heather gray tank top, My Neighbor Totoro pajama bottoms, and rose-gold Harry Potter glasses.

CLEM
You hear back from Comic Con yet?

KYLIEE
I got in!

CLEM
No way! That's great!

Jacob invites himself into the conversation.

JACOB
How did that happen?

KYLIEE
I told them I was a contributor for Whitty Entertainment and that was it. They're sending me a press pass and everything.

JACOB
Oh wow. That's great, Kyliee.

KYLIEE
(to Clem)
And guess who's having a meet and greet Day One? Hayley Atwell.

CLEM
Ah! You're so lucky!

JACOB
Who's Hayley Atwell?

KYLIEE
She plays Peggy Carter, Cap's girlfriend.

JACOB
Oh.
(pause)
I don't like the MCU.

Clem and Kyliee nod dismissively. Look at each other. Jacob frowns.

CLEM
You gonna cosplay as Peggy when you meet her?

KYLIEE
I don't know. Wouldn't that be a bit hokey?

Jacob looks out into the hall. His jaw slacks. "Dream Weaver" plays in his mind.

Walking toward him in warm, misty slow-motion is CARTER JACKSON (21), Directing Major and Film Immersion's RA. Slim-fit button-down with the sleeves rolled up. Rugby physique. Hairy forearms. Scruffy jawline. Bright blue eyes. Blond fauxhawk. Bold white teeth. Natural smile.

CARTER
Hey Jake. Welcome back.

Carter wraps an arm across Jacob's shoulders. The warmth of his athletic body and the smell of his woodsy cologne instantly makes Jacob hard.

JACOB
Thanks.
(clears throat)
Saw the trailer for <u>Smashers</u>. Looks really good.

Kyliee stops talking at the sight of Carter, her smile gone. Carter looks back.

CARTER
(to Jacob; distracted)
Thanks. It was a lotta fun.

Clem whispers to Kyliee.

CARTER (CONT'D)
Hey, Kyliee.

Kyliee heads out, bumping into Carter. Clem awkwardly squeezes past Carter and follows her.

JACOB
What's all that about?

CARTER
She's just weird, bro.

JACOB
I don't mind Kyliee. She's really nice.

Carter shrugs. Drinks from his cup.

CARTER
You looking forward to caretaking the Overlook, Mr. Torrance?

JACOB
I don't really know what to expect.

CARTER
It's not that bad. If you need anything I'll be just down the hall.

Jacob's face goes numb.

JACOB
You're staying behind too?

CARTER
Yeah. I always do.

Jacob smiles. Takes a big sip.

JACOB
You wanna hang out sometime? I got a whole chest of Blu-Rays. We can watch something.

CARTER
I'd love to, man, but I got a whole bunch of RA shit to do.

JACOB
Whenever you want.

Carter looks down the hall with concern.

CARTER
I gotta ask Kyliee something.

JACOB
Yeah. Sure.

CARTER
Great talking to you, bro.

JACOB
Yeah. You too.

Carter claps Jacob's shoulder and wanders off. Jacob watches every second, a quivering horny mess.

CUT TO:

BY THE FRONT DOOR

Jacob's halfway through his second screwdriver and talking to MAX ELLIS (21) and TABITHA MACLEAN (21). Max is a twinkish Cinematography Major with a light brown bowl cut, sharp shoulders and noticeable vitiligo on their arms. Tabitha is a black Marketing Major in a denim jacket with large hair and a nose stud.

MAX
The nuclear family was never about cultivating happiness. It's just a way for privileged white guys to justify their world as the social standard.

JACOB
But what's wrong with a standard every now and then? In this country, everyone has the ability to do whatever the fuck they want with their lives--

TABITHA
Not everyone!

JACOB
I know that, but our society is literally based on choices. We don't have to go to school if we don't want to. We don't have to believe in a bearded man in the sky granting wishes and bribing us into being good people.

TABITHA
Some of us don't even have to pay taxes.

JACOB
Exactly, we do whatever we want. But how do we know what we want? Isn't everything just a reaction to how we were raised? Everything is groups in Italy. You don't go out to eat in a restaurant, you go home and eat with your family. And bars aren't places to meet strangers, they're places you go with your friends. Honestly I kinda like that better. It's so exhausting DIY-ing everything all the time.

MAX
Do you actually want your parents to get back together?

JACOB
I dunno. Mom wasn't really happy with him. But on the other she single-handedly destroyed our family unit, literally throwing away my childhood home in the process. And she doesn't stop talking shit about him. It's awful. She has no idea how much damage she's causing just to make herself feel better.

TABITHA
But that's exactly Max's point. You feel incomplete without a nuclear family. THAT'S the problem.

MAX
It's not a problem, it's fucking evil! It's a racist, classist, homophobic social construct that straight white men have been using to marginalize people like us for centuries!

JACOB
So what, I'm supposed to feel guilty I had a normal upbringing?

MAX
SEE? You just called it normal. My dad forces me to use male pronouns when I come home. He gets away with it because I depend on him financially. How is that normal?

JACOB
I didn't mean it like that.

TABITHA
This is such a first world problem. I never knew my dad and I turned out fine.

MAX
Some people don't even have a family. Consider yourself lucky.

JACOB
Oh yes, I'm so lucky to have a family of Trump supporters.

Max and Tabitha GAG simultaneously.

CUT TO:

INSIDE RIAN'S ROOM

Jacob finishes his third screwdriver on Rian's stripped bed. Rian plops down next to him with a handle of Romanoff.

RIAN
Want another?

JACOB
We're out of OJ.

RIAN
So?

JACOB
I told myself I'd drink until I ran out of OJ.

RIAN
It's still early. Are you even buzzed?

Jacob shrugs.

RIAN (CONT'D)
(taking Jacob's cup)
We're doing a shot.

JACOB
Not a big shot.

RIAN
We'll take it slow.

JACOB
Are we still going to South Street after this?

RIAN
Of course.

JACOB
You promise?

RIAN
Promise.

Rian hands Jacob's cup back. They toast. Drink. Rian rolls his throat. Jacob doesn't.

JACOB
Another.

Rian pours two more. They down it fast.

RIAN
Fuck!

Jacob laughs, wiping his lips.

JACOB
Yeah, I think that's it for me.

CUT TO:

INSIDE NICH'S ROOM

Jacob pours another shot, mid-conversation with Max and ARELI SANCHEZ (21), a snarky dark-skinned Latina Musical Theatre Major with a long black ponytail and dimples.

JACOB
Physical media just means more to me, you know? Blu-Rays are so affordable now.

ARELI
I'm really into vinyl.

MAX
Me too.

JACOB
Me too. I've got a whole record collection in my room.

ARELI
Ooh! What do you have?

JACOB
Everything. Beatles, Pink Floyd, Led Zeppelin, Eagles, Elton... I'm trying to find a good Billy Joel greatest hits but there doesn't seem to be one with all the songs I like. He's got so many.

MAX
Got any Gaga?

Jacob hesitates.

JACOB
No, but I've got all three Adeles, a couple Andrea Bocellis, all of Evanescence, Postmodern Jukebox, Red Hot Chili Peppers, Simon and Garfunkel, Peter, Paul and Mary, ABBA, Meat Loaf--

ARELI
Childish Gambino?

JACOB
No. You know what's funny, I didn't realize Childish Gambino and Donald Glover were the same person until last year.
(pause)
That's not racist, is it?

MAX
I could really do for some <u>Hamilton</u>.

ARELI
Oh my God, I LOVE <u>Hamilton</u>!

JACOB
Haven't seen it yet.

MAX
Neither have I. Just listen to the album. It's the whole show.

Jacob scrunches his face. Shakes it.

JACOB
No. I don't think I'd like it.

ARELI
It's a hip-hop musical.

JACOB
Exactly. And the hype doesn't help.

MAX
It won the Pulitzer for a reason.

JACOB
That doesn't help either.

ARELI
Do you have anything from the 80s?

JACOB
No way. I hate the 80s.

MAX
(scoffing)
What DON'T you hate?

Jacob blinks.

JACOB
I already told you. Do you want me to list it again?

CUT TO:

IN THE HALLWAY

Jacob pleads with an irate Tabitha. They're both drunk.

JACOB
I wasn't trying to be offensive.

TABITHA
Doesn't matter, you should never use that word!

JACOB
I have autism. I don't find it offensive.

TABITHA
Just because you don't doesn't mean other people don't. It's incredibly derogatory.

JACOB
I have more of a right to say it than you.

TABITHA
That doesn't matter. It's about creating a safe space for people whose disabilities aren't obvious.

JACOB
When I hear someone say...
(whispers)
...retarded...
(normal volume)
...I don't think of it as a slur because to me it's just a word.

TABITHA
To the rest of the autistic community it's not just a word.

JACOB
Well I AM autistic and I'm saying it's not! If you take the meaning away from the word, it stops being a slur! Autistic people get that! We have way thicker skins than you think we do!

TABITHA
I understand you're upset, but you have to remember that there are hundreds of disabilities and plenty of people without the privilege you have.

JACOB
I'M privileged? I'm the one with the autism here!

TABITHA
You're very high functioning.

JACOB
It's a fucking spectrum!

Tabitha sighs.

TABITHA
Just consider a world where no one calls people with disabilities the r-word. That would be pretty good, wouldn't it?

JACOB
Of course.

TABITHA
We have a duty to tell other people to change their actions so they don't cause marginalized people harm. Derogatory jokes at their expense, slurs, outdated ways of thinking. The key is to make a safe space for everyone to feel comfortable, right?

Jacob hesitates.

JACOB
But I don't like telling people what not to say.

TABITHA
I know it feels like that, but remember the big picture. Silence is the reason we have these problems in the first place. Doing nothing makes you part of the problem.

Jacob sighs.

JACOB
You're right. I'm sorry.

CUT TO:

INSIDE JACOB'S ROOM

Jacob bites his nails. Notices a HANDLE OF ROMANOFF on his desk. Spits out some cuticles.

He grabs a new cup. Fills it halfway with vodka. The smell alone gives him pause. He looks into the cup. Swishes it around.

JACOB
Fuck it.

He clogs his nose. Gulps the cup down. Coughs up a bit. Wipes the drips off his chin. Shakes his head around. Chuckles.

CUT TO:

IN THE LIVING ROOM

Trevor smokes his geeb and passes it to Jacob. Jacob immediately passes it on to TJ. Nich sits in a side-chair.

JACOB
(sloshed)
If you have to explain to me why I'm watching a twelve hour one-take of the Empire State Building, it's not art.

TJ hits the geeb. Passes it to Nich.

NICH
Just because there isn't a story doesn't mean it isn't art. The three-act structure wasn't in Aristotle's <u>Poetics</u>, it was invented in '79 by Syd Field. He figured out the perfect psychological formula to keep as many eyes on screen as long as possible, and Hollywood labeled it the standard so they could teach it to film students and keep the cycle going.

Nich hits the geeb. Passes it to Trevor.

JACOB
That's bullshit.

NICH
Wake the fuck up, Jake. We've been programmed to idolize fast-paced movies because corporations want us under their control. Look what Hollywood is famous for. Product placement. Wartime propaganda.

JACOB
What about auteurs? They don't have producer oversight. They can do whatever they want.

NICH
They're still putting their personal views in our faces. That's more dangerous. The brainwashing is our idea.

TJ
You're giving Hollywood way too much credit, Nich. It's the laziest industry in the world. Blockbusters

are safe investments, that's all. "Art" is just another word for what's selling.

JACOB
And arthouse doesn't sell.

TJ
Neither do auteur films. True creativity's impossible to achieve when you throw profit in the mix.

JACOB
What about Oscar films? Those are some of the best of all time.

TJ
Maybe in the beginning, but they're certainly no good now.

JACOB
I wouldn't have seen half the movies on my Top 100 list if they weren't highlighted during Oscar Season.

TJ
The very concept of For Your Consideration campaigns makes the whole ceremony a farce.

NICH
Fuck the Oscars!

TJ
And I'm not even talking about how pretentious it is that they televise that shit.

NICH
Circle-jerking motherFUCKERS.

Trevor passes the geeb to Jacob. Jacob stares at it.

JACOB
You're all crazy.

Jacob reluctantly hits the geeb. Coughs. Hands it to TJ

TJ
(to Nich)
That being said, arthouse films are too up their own ass to function as entertainment--

NICH
That is fuckin bullshit!

TJ
--which film has to be! We might like them but no one else does.

TREVOR
Since when is money such a bad thing? Did we not grow up on blockbusters? I can't stand hearing so many people describe Hollywood as if it's the absolute worst thing in the world. Why the fuck are we in film school for then?

TJ
No opinion isn't an opinion, Trevor.

JACOB
No, he's got a point. We're not experts. We're not even done college. Big executives don't make money because they're playing us or following a lazy set of guidelines, they made a name for themselves. We might not understand their world yet, but we sure know how difficult it is to break into it. They made it that way, to weed out the idiots and lazy copy-and-pasters. Executives aren't evil stooges or greedy pigs, they're artists just like us and they know what they're doing.

DREW

Sunset King

Drew Lawrence snorts a line over breakfast and another with his coffee, his head still splitting from the raucous night prior. Or is it because of the messy day to come? Drew can't tell the difference anymore. How long has it been, three days? Two weeks? Larry knows. Gotta get to Larry.

Drew collapses halfway through his morning push-ups. Instinctively looks around for Shayne to explain. Where is he? Oh right. He's not at work yet. He's at home. Oh boy. Drew stands, his large hairy pecs glistening with sweat in the morning light. Turns to the mirror, full-length and extra wide. Yup, still muscled. Unless the mirror lying's to him too. Everyone lies to the CEO. Or so logic would dictate. The same logic that says a built man with 10% body fat could do sixty push-ups no problem. Yet there he was.

Here, at the beginning of his story, Drew Lawrence is forty years old. A tuft of hair atop his head, sides buzzed down. Dark scruff to cover his adult acne, a loathsome Tren side effect Shayne swore was temporary. He keeps his mustache longer than the rest.

Drew jerks off into his toilet. Slides on a $3,000 suit. Snorts one last line of the good shit before he has to settle for the blockbuster junk in the sugar bowl on his desk, house coke quite possibility cheaper than actual Coke. Speak of the devil, Drew finds a goodie bag of passable coke in the Acting CEO care package waiting for him in the company car. Great guy that Larry. Attached is an itinerary typed on official Not That Nutty stationary. Guess the coke's less of a gift and more of a dog biscuit of sorts, the kind you give to Fido no matter if he'd been a good boy or a very very bad boy, just to get his attention, but Drew's too fucked up to pay attention to tiny words typed by Asian fingers, and Larry should've known that, or maybe he did but just wanted to try out anyway, or perhaps he's a fucking liar too and he knew all of this and still did it because of plausible deniability when Mr. Landreth gets back from China and sees what Drew did and hears how he fucked up and what a mess he's made and this is why he'll never get a chance to be CEO again God dammit Drew you fucking piece of shit you finally got your chance and you already fucked up you God damned faggot you can't do this what were you crazy you can't even push-up anymore fuck fuck fuck it fuck it fuck it he snorts another line and his breaks get slammed and it's like he's sliding on ice what's that called again oh yeah hydroplaning and he hates the goodie bag coke where the fuck did Larry get this shit and woah watch that turn driver and fuck he's here.

Larry Lin opens the door. Late thirties. Korean. Pudgy. Big smile. "How are you doing today, Mr. Lawrence?" he asks like a fucking preschool teacher.

"Fucking marvelous, Larry!" Drew declares, the voice ringing through his ears distorted like John Lennon's on "Tomorrow Never Knows."

Larry leads the way to the elevators. Discreetly waves his finger under his nose. Drew gets the hint. Rubs the dust off his mustache. Steps into the shiny chrome box that zooms up up up fast fuck too fast and too bright in here oh fuck that's a rough stop Larry sees him and they're all gonna see him and he's gotta play it cool now now NOW.

The doors open. Dozens of faces greet him. Drew instinctively waves with a smile. No, Larry's shooing the leeches away. "Don't look at them" he says to Drew before shouting, "Leave your resumes with Doris in the front! Mr. Lawrence is very busy! He does not accept unsolicited applications! If you don't comply, you will be escorted out by security!"

Drew blanks a bit. Snaps back in his office, Larry handing him a cold glass of Domergue 15. Drew slurps up half in one go, his coke-numbed throat reacting off the burning Scotch in a cerebral mindfuck of a way, one of the few nonsexual sensations worth planning a whole day around. He can taste the whisky when he breathes.

"Mr. Lawrence?"

Drew looks up, only now realizing Larry had tried thrice now to regain his attention. "Larry!" Drew cries back with a laugh. "God, you need to calm down. I'm not deaf."

"Did you read the itinerary or not?"

"Yes!" Drew lies. "God! Yes! Of course!"

"I don't write them for my own amusement."

"I read it!" Drew lies again. "What more do you want me to say?"

Larry sighs. Grabs his notepad. Flips through it.

Drew eyes him suspiciously. He couldn't have bought it. No way. Why doesn't he say anything?

"You ready to go?" Larry asks. "Or do you wanna look over your notes first?"

"Read 'em off." Drew takes another huge sip.

Larry skims his notepad. "You didn't like the new cut of *Have We Met Before?* because... 'It was too confusing.'"

"What happened again?"

"Tobey Anderson's character is revealed to be the killer all along."

Drew furrows his brow. "How is that confusing?

"You weren't confused by that. You were expecting, based on the title, that it was gonna be revealed that Dirk and Janet had, in fact, met before, and when that didn't happen, you told me to add, 'Change the ending to match the title or change the title. It'll confuse the audience.'"

Drew nods. "Oh yes. I remember now. What else?"

"Note-wise..." Larry skims. "Nothing crazy. Except for that fight scene you wanted between two elephants."

"Yes! Elephants. Elephants are cool."

"Whatever you say, Mr. Lawrence." Larry flips a page. "And Merv Shandt—"

"You like the elephants, don't you Larry?" Drew asks, testing him.

Larry hesitates. "I think everyone expects elephants to show up at some point."

"But you do understand why it's cool, right? It's not hard to figure out or anything? If it's stupid, feel free to tell me. Seriously."

"I understand."

"No, but do you actually think it's cool?"

Larry shrugs. "It's a motif. Motifs are cool."

Drew blinks. Sits back. "What about Merv?"

"He said he was able to lock Anna Schmidt down for *Joshua Tree*, which means we gotta break the news to Gordy Benson at 9:30."

"Who?"

"The screenwriter. Now that it's a comedy, he's gonna have to rewrite it himself or let us take over. Either way, Anna's contract requires her to have a co-writing credit. She likes to improvise on set."

Drew takes another sip. "What was *Joshua Tree* before?"

Larry flips to the back of the pad. "Logline says, 'A psychedelic, gritty *Scarface* for the R-Rated demographic.'"

"That's sounds badass! Who's fucking idea was it to make it a comedy?!"

Larry looks up, confused. "Yours."

Drew laughs. "What?"

"You saw Anna Schmidt in *Up Yores* last Christmas and laughed your ass off. Said you wanted to make her a lead in something."

"Which one was she? The fat one?"

"The sarcastic mom, remember? The one Twitter went nuts over? Focus groups said she stole the show."

Drew looks desperately at Larry. "It *is* a good idea, right?"

"You know what you're doing."

"Just tell me the fucking truth, Larry."

"Merv's a fantastic director. Anna's an up-and-coming comedian. Audiences love her. What could go wrong?"

Drew sighs, not entirely assured. Checks his watch. "Let's get going."

Drew's new confidence holds tight through his 9:00 meeting with *Have We Met Before?* line producer Stephen Kaffer, the message of third-act coherence delivered and accepted without a hitch. But during Drew's 9:30 with Gordy Benson, in the middle of Drew's passionate defense of Anna Schmidt's budding comic prowess and how Benson's feature debut, if properly rewritten, would cement her future as a bankable star of big-budget action-comedies, he notices Benson's eyes sag, a complete contradiction to his verbal acceptance. Drew spends the entirety of his 10:00 pitch meeting and 11:00 dailies screening replaying Benson's brown-eyed reaction over and over to the point of questioning if it even happened. If Benson didn't like the idea of *Joshua Tree* being a comedy now, why didn't he say anything? Was he just processing the news, knowing he had to accept because this is Hollywood and that's showbiz and all that jazz and real art doesn't sell and how dare he assume otherwise? Or was that eye-sag the only honest feedback Drew received all day? Was the coke fucking up Drew's instincts or were they really all lying to his face? Maybe Drew just fucking sucks and they all know. Or maybe Drew's the one who's wrong and he's actually really really good as Acting CEO and he's gonna be co-CEO again when the trial's over. Or what if this is all totally normal and average and he's not even remotely ready to handle it because he's so stupid and easy and doesn't know what he wants and how could he if all he does is say yes to everything?

Drew storms out of the screening room mid-screening. Ignores Larry calling after him. Runs around the corner. Picks an empty conference room. Locks the door. Grabs a vase. Smashes it on the floor. Grabs another one. Throws it against the wall, blood pumping across his massive arms, all through his veins, running up and down his body, down his leg, up his cock, strong and tough, and rips a painting off a wall, an original Renoir he bought at auction, and knees its fucking French face in, and then a hefty postmodern statue with a bulb base of authentic bronze, two feet long before he snaps it in half and tosses it away and grabs the TV mounted on the wall and rips its tough black arms off and kicks its face and throws the whole bookshelf down and chucks knick-knacks at the window that shatter in the light falling and shining like a beautiful rainbow and he dumps the coffee bar onto the floor and stomps on the cups and rips the ceiling fan's ugly hazelnut spokes and throws them across the room and then the chairs next heavy tough wheelie chairs he grabs one by its back and slam on the floor and lift and snap even louder now the plastic cracking so loud he could feel it in his dick and smashes it to pieces beyond recognition with no indication it once held a producer's fat ass and another chair the same way slam lift snap crack crash no more butt-holder and once more with feeling Drew he grabs it and fuck that window wall with that bulletproof glass and Sunset Boulevard seven floors down there with all that hustling and bustling and no help to him and so happy maybe and get him out he wants out go get out and he swings the chair into the glass hard as he could he needs to get out again blam again again harder you pussy you roid raging faggot harder fuckin harder and crash again crash again crash it's working keep going crash crash crash CRACK the chair breaks and Drew backs up and he sees what he did, that large shatter in the industrial glass, the midday sun illuminating the room, the glistening spider web prisming the UV waves in two dozen tiny little ways, uncountable individual shards barely hanging on. Perhaps only one thin layer of glass away from a breached hull. Drew's satisfied. He adjusts his tie. Leaves the room. Closes the door behind him.

Thirty seconds go by. Six don't-ask-don't-tell custodians push 32-gallon trash bins into the trashed conference room. No emotion. No personality. They sweep pieces of glass. Vacuum all they can. Roll in new chairs. Replace panels of glass. Quarantine the $7 million Renoir, the TV, and a half-dozen other objects too damaged to repair on site. Takes them three hours to restore the room to its default state. Longer than average. Quite a bit more work. Nothing they haven't done before.

WHALE

Four Horsemen

Whale signs the NDA without reading it and hands it back to The Secretary. Thirtysomething. Spitting image of Léa Seydoux. "Your phone."

```
                    WHALE
        Oh. Sorry.
```

Whale hands The Secretary his iPhone. "Any Bluetooth devices? AirPods, speakers, wireless headsets?"

```
                    WHALE
        Nope.
```

The Secretary scoots her rolling chair back, bends down, and unlocks the bottommost drawer with a tiny steel key. Slides it open, revealing a cushioned chamber wrapped in signal-blocking insulation. She lays Whale's iPhone on top of the pile and slams the drawer shut.

```
                    WHALE
        That's not gonna be every time, is it?
```

"I'm afraid it is," The Secretary responds with flight attendant cordiality.

```
                    WHALE
        Does that mean we're expected to work without
        computers?
```

"Oh no, of course you will!" The Secretary says with a laugh. "The Professor will explain everything in his orientation." She gestures to a row of chairs. "Please take a seat until the others arrive."

```
                    WHALE
        Ok. Thanks.
```

Whale plops down and checks his watch. 10:35. Twenty-five minutes early. His mom worked in offices her whole life, managing a few interns of her own. She said a good intern was expected to do everything their supervisor told them to do, to keep their head down, to grin and bear it, to always offer to do more even if there wasn't anything more to do, to never ask for time off or use their sick days, to always arrive a half-hour early and clock out an hour late. That last part always confused him. If he was expected to do everything his supervisor told him to do and his supervisor told him to come in at 11 and leave at 5, why wouldn't he come in at 11 and leave at 5? How does that make him a bad intern?

10:45. The lobby door opens and Cashew moseys in, 5'5" at most with premature baldness and huge glasses, a bite-sized George Constanza with an unusually circular head and furry forearms. He nods awkwardly at Whale. Whale nods back. Cashew reads the entire NDA before signing and very reluctantly hands over his phone.

10:47. Bumps hurries in, out of breath. Very short blonde hair. Bit of a belly. Tasteful stud in her left nostril, the same shade as her navy-blue pantsuit. She politely waves to Cashew and Whale. They wave back. Bumps hurriedly scratches her signature on the NDA and tosses The Secretary her phone. She sits next to Whale and smiles. Whale smiles back. They both face forward, their smiles gone.

10:55. Whale, Cashew, and Bumps sit in silence when Peabrain finally arrives. Vaguely British features. Brows too high up his face. Eyes just too far apart. Black hair naturally growing vertically before bending with gravity like unmowed grass. Whale watches Peabrain talk to The Secretary. He came in so calmly, why was he so out of breath? Upon further listen Whale realizes Peabrain is in fact stuttering, always at the beginning of his sentences. Peabrain immediately hands over his phone, slowly signs his NDA, and sits in the last empty chair.

The four interns sit silently for five minutes, every second felt. Whale wonders why no one's talking, too afraid to break the ice himself.

The Secretary's phone rings, startling the young quartet. "Yes," she mutters into the mouthpiece. "I'll send them in." She hangs up the phone. "Follow me, please."

The Secretary leads the foursome down the hall into an open concept office full of natural light. Glass doors everywhere. A consistent blue/gray/silver color scheme on the decor. Cathedral ceiling. Whale's eyes stop on a freestanding cylindrical staircase encased in glass, a crystal spine all the way up to a floating office on the second floor, an incredibly modern and architecturally impressive cube made entirely of frosted glass, the staircase leading to a black door on the far side of the cube.

The Secretary stops before a whiteboard in the center of the room. "This is The Classroom. Please sit." The Secretary gestures to four desks in a 2-by-2 arrangement. "The Professor will be with you shortly." She struts back to the lobby. Cashew watches her go, looking at Whale with a randy smirk. Whale doesn't react, simply sitting at the front left desk. Bumps sits to his right, Peabrain behind him, Cashew behind her. Whale looks at Bumps. Opens his mouth to compliment her suit.

SLAM!

The interns flinch, their heads whipping up to the cube like meerkats. An older man in a royal blue jacket and light gray dress pants stands on the landing, looking down at them and — Wait, THE CUBE'S TRANSPARENT NOW! Oh my God! That's SO cool! — and he slowly descends the spinal staircase, brown shoes scraping each rung. The Professor is fifty-seven according to Wikipedia but he really doesn't look it. He's in fantastic shape, specifically in the shoulders and abs. His Rolex has one link too many though. It keeps jangling. Back and forth, back and forth, up and down past his wrist with each step. Whale has to force himself to stop looking at it.

"Okay," The Professor mumbles in the deepest voice Whale's ever heard, stepping off the staircase, "Let's get started." He grabs a chair from behind the whiteboard and plops down, facing the group. "You all know who I am, you all know why you're here, so I'll get straight to the point. This is not a 'dream internship.' That term is fragrant and fucking pretentious as hell. It doesn't matter what I've done. This program is no different from any other. I expect each and every one of you to prove yourselves. Yes, you've all been selected from a very, very long list. But if you want to make it in this industry, you're gonna have to give it your all now. I don't mean how much you respect the craft, or how you saw a movie when you were twelve and ever since then wanted your name on the big screen, I mean you have to work. That's all I care about. That's all anyone cares about. Hollywood does not run on dreamers, it runs on fighters. It is a shit ton of work to make a movie. It takes drive. It takes sacrifice. You will never be able to enjoy a movie ever again."

Whale's stomach drops.

The Professor looks at each of them coldly. "That's the price you've paid. Accept it." He pauses. "Grow from it." The Professor stands. Paces around the desks. "You four were chosen because of your portfolios, whether it be a short film or a feature script. You showed me you know how to write, how to direct, how to put hours and hours of work into something that ultimately is worthless. You are twenty-two years old. You have not lived long enough to have a unique or nuanced perspective of the world. No one on Earth wants to pay ten cents, let alone twenty dollars, to see anything you've created at this point. But you know more than nothing, which is why you're here. You are finished with college. There are no more classes hogging your time, no more juvenile distractions, no more exams, no more papers." The Professor stops in front of Whale's desk. "Which means no more excuses. I only expect more from you than what you've already given me. Do you understand?"

Whale nods. The others nod too.

The Professor smirks. "But therein lies the problem. I know you all want a job here. You've been wanting it your whole lives. Because when you're young, you consume. You consume television. You consume pop music. You consume social media. Your generation was the first in human history to consume more media in a single year than anyone could realistically produce in that time. You're absolutely addicted to content. You live and breathe it. What's good and what's not is a natural instinct for you. You know what sells because you've spent your whole lives buying." He shrugs. "So why are Millennials such shitty workers?"

Whale shifts in his seat.

The Professor raises a finger. "One word: expectations." He resumes pacing. "Because you've spent your formative years consuming media, you feel the only way to be seen is to make media of your own. That's what's driving you. Not money or responsibility but yourselves. And with that comes expectations, expectations that never existed twenty years ago. Mental health days. Preferred pronouns. Safe fucking spaces. Instead of changing to fit the world you were born into, you want the world to change for you, because you can't handle someone else having a bad opinion of you, or making a joke at your expense, or treating you like everyone else. Because you are obviously the most interesting person in the world."

Whale doesn't move. He can hear everyone else breathing just as uncomfortably as he is.

The Professor shakes his head. "And because you're the target demographic, you're winning. And the country is getting softer because of it. The industry is getting softer. But contrary to what you'd expect—as always—I don't see that as a bad thing. There is now a void of fighters in Hollywood. You will have more opportunities than I ever had." The Professor returns to his seat. "So, in order for you to be the best fighters you can be, you need to stop thinking about how you see yourself and start accepting how everyone else already sees you. This is a competitive industry. No one likes you at the start. And you are a spoiled generation, so that just makes the vitriol worse, but you need to hear it. This is the real world. No one gives a shit what PC standards you had in college. What they see is what you are. If you really want to be a successful filmmaker, let alone a full-time member of my staff, you will fight through that and prove those fuckers wrong. Because if you fail, you only prove them right." The Professor takes a deep breath. "Let's start in the back." He points to Cashew. "You. Stand up."

Whale turns his head. Cashew stands, his body shaking slightly.

The Professor smirks. "God, you're a pipsqueak aren't ya?" He laughs. "I can't believe you're twenty-two."

Cashew looks down, his lip tight.

The Professor shakes his head. "I see boys like you all the time. You waste your life getting beat up and jerking off to hentai until one day you realize you're just a little bitch, and Daddy might love pussy but he sure don't respect his kid for being one, so you do everything you can to make up for the fact that you were born with a penis the size of a cashew. And it's so painfully obvious too. So stop pretending you're packing a forearm down there, Cashew, and fucking grow a pair."

Cashew doesn't budge.

The Professor laughs. "This is how it works. I'm gonna call you Cashew, and everyone else here is going to call you Cashew, because that is what you are. And if I hear someone call you by any other name, you'll both be fired." The Professor looks at the others. "Everyone get that?"

Whale, Bumps, and Peabrain uncomfortably nod.

The Professor nods back. "Good. Cashew, sit back down." Cashew sits. The Professor sighs. "Alright, who's next." He looks at Bumps. "Let's get the token girl out of the way." Bumps starts to stand. "No, you don't have to stand. They already know."

Bumps sits back down.

"Now let me see," The Professor murmurs, scanning her with his eyes, sitting on her desk. "You're one of those that never had an older sister. No one to idolize. No one to dress like. The boys didn't like you. They liked the pretty ones. The girly ones. And for while you never understood. But then you got into college and you found out how to blame society for your faults. You didn't do anything wrong, it was the patriarchy! White cis male blah-blah-blah. Not you. Never you." The Professor leans in closer, Bumps avoiding eye contact. "But underneath all that feminist rhetoric, you still wanna be one of those pretty girls, those models on Instagram. All those men looking at you. Wanting to do things to your body. Sure, you fight for all the right causes. Boycott the things you like to stay on the right side of history. Never accept a job unless you're hired for your resume and your brain. But when your bills pile up, and your unemployment check is late, and there's nothing left for you to do... at least you'll have your sex to fall back on, right?" The Professor looks down at her chest. "But you don't even have that. Just goosebumps for tits. Bumps for short."

Bumps simply closes her eyes. Whale can't believe her composure. He wants to vomit just listening to that.

Peabrain angrily stands. "Y-y-y-ya-y-y-y-y-yo-ya-ya-ya-ya—"

The Professor widens his eyes, laughing hysterically. "Oh, wow! I did not expect that!" He approaches Peabrain's desk. "What is it, boy? Huh? I shouldn't mock the girl because she's a girl? That's pretty suh-suh-suh-suh-sexist of you." He cackles.

Peabrain's eyes sag as he strains. "St-st-st-st-sta-st—"

"This is hilarious," The Professor tells the others. "He can't say anything, no matter how gallant he tries to be, because his mom couldn't stop smoking and fucking while she had him and now he's retarded for life." He waves a dismissive hand. "Sit back down, Peabrain. You're an easy one."

Peabrain lowers his head in shame. Plops down.

The Professor makes eye contact with Whale. Whale stares back. Watch him make a comment about his muscles, accusing him of being a popular kid in high school, a jock with lots of friends, and now he has to coast on his good looks. That would actually be a well-earned compliment.

The Professor's brows bend, almost like he was straining, but then they snap back to place. "Are you really wearing a slim-fit shirt with those shoulders?"

Whale looks down at his babies. Did he call it or what?

The Professor studies Whale's body. "You certainly look like you work out. Which is why you wore that, no doubt. You want people to know you work out, but you want to be subtle about it." The Professor looks Whale in the eye. "But you don't know how. Because they're new."

Whale's heart pounds.

The Professor grins. Checkmate. "Bulked up just in time, haven't you? Let me guess. Lifelong wallflower, no friends, all alone in your room writing script after script because no one bothered to invite you to the party, whining on social media how unhappy you are to an audience of none. No followers. No likes. No one that gives a shit."

Whale stubbornly maintains eye contact, his lip trembling in the process.

"You're trying to start over out here," The Professor continues. "A new city, a new man. Maybe you can pass for a native. That would be great, wouldn't it? All that work worth it?" He leans in, his nose touching Whale's. "Hate to break it to you," he whispers, his warm breath minty fresh, "but we can smell the newbies. The posers. There is nothing you can do to hide the fact that you're just a beached whale, crying, whining, 'Someone look at me. Someone pity me. Someone save me.' But no one will. We still don't give a shit. Because you did it to yourself. And we know it's only a matter of time before you give up and relapse."

Whale finally looks away.

The Professor doesn't budge. "You can't change who you are, Whale. You were born soft." He pauses. "Look at me."

Whale tentatively looks up.

The Professor stares blankly. "And when you jump off a bridge three weeks from now, you're gonna die soft." He holds his gaze. "So stop wasting your fucking time."

Whale uses every muscle at his disposal to keep from crying.

The Professor nods softly, a question mark.

Whale softly nods back.

The Professor steps back. Grabs a dry-erase marker. "This is what I need from you all over the next five months." He scribbles on the board. "I have three hundred feature submissions you can pick from, that's seventy-five each, I want no less than two pages of coverage for each one. I have five novels that need coverage as well, given out on a first-come-first serve basis. You read here, you type here. No homework. I do not allow smartphones or laptops in the building, but you will have Internet access on any computer in The Classroom. I expect all documents completed that week given to me via email every Friday at 10 o'clock exactly. Anything arriving too soon or too late will get buried and I will not hunt them down. I'll simply assume you did nothing that week, which will greatly affect your final review. In addition to the coverage, I want a list of stats on the notable films at the festival level, specifically Locarno, which starts in two weeks, and Venice at the end of—"

```
                  WHALE
            (raising his hand)
Excuse me?
```

The Professor turns, surprisingly calm. "Yes, Whale?"

Whale hesitates. The dude wasn't kidding about the nicknames.

```
                  WHALE
You want two pages of coverage for each script?
```

"Yes."

```
                  WHALE
Why?
```

The Professor stares, uncharacteristically dumbfounded. "Why what?"

```
                  WHALE
What's its purpose here, the coverage?
```

The Professor blinks. "Do you not know what coverage is?"

```
                  WHALE
I know what coverage is. I just wanna know what YOU
use it for.
```

"How do you not know that already?!" The Professor exclaims. "What the fuck did they teach you at that school?"

WHALE
```
They--
```

"They what?! Spit it out!"

WHALE
```
Well, I--
```

"What?!"

Whale's breath quickens.

WHALE
```
I don't--
```

The Professor chucks the marker at Whale's face, hitting him hard. He cries out. The Professor huddles over Whale. "What else don't you know, huh? Hm? Do you know how to edit?"

WHALE
```
Yeah.
```

"On Premiere?"

Whale hesitates.

WHALE
```
A little.
```

"How many hours of set experience do you have?"

Whale trembles in his chair.

WHALE
```
I don't know. I never...
```

The Professor laughs bitterly. "You don't know how to edit. You don't have any set experience. Do you even have a film degree? What's the difference between a line producer and a supervising producer?"

Whale looks at the others. They all look back with stone faces. That only made Whale feel worse.

"Well?!" The Producer cries.

WHALE
```
What was it again?
```

"Un-FUCKING-believable!" The Professor hollers.

WHALE
```
Just tell me the question again!
```

"Why should I?! What did you think was gonna happen out here, huh? You'd go straight from being an intern to writing features? Did you not take business classes at your school?"

WHALE
```
Why would I?! It wasn't my major!
```

The Professor goes silent. "You didn't take Hollywood business classes because it wasn't your major?"

Whale doesn't respond.

The Professor scoffs. "You were one of those movie watchers weren't you, Whale? Just do what Tarantino did, huh? And what, you thought because you had so much passion and love for film that it would be enough? That it would just make up for the fact that you have no skills or training at all?"

WHALE
```
No. That's why I'm here.
```

The Professor nods, faking understanding. "That's why you're here, huh? I get it now. You thought you'd be one of those coffee run interns in the big city, and you'd just happen to bump into the CEO in the elevator and comment a little blurb about movies, and I'd stop my meeting and I'd say, 'Who's that guy?' and someone would say, 'Oh, he's just the intern,' and I'd call you into my office and make you my personal assistant on the spot, and even though I'm hard on you and push you to your limits, you see a human side of me, and that helps you grow as a person, and you get promoted to executive before you're thirty? Is that what you actually fucking thought was gonna happen?"

```
                    WHALE
        No, I--
```

"THIS IS NOT *THE DEVIL WEARS PRADA*!" The Professor screams in Whale's face. "I AM NOT MERYL CUNTING STREEP!" He looks at Bumps. "No offense."

Tears form in Whale's eyes, his lip trembling rapidly.

The Professor shakes his head with disgust. "You just don't know how to stop, do you?"

```
                    WHALE
               (through tears)
        I'm fine.
```

"Oh, you're fine? This is your definition of fine? Crying on your first day?"

```
                    WHALE
        I have allergies.
```

The Professor points at Bumps. "Look, LOOK! She's not crying. Cashew's not crying. Fucking Peabrain's not even crying! He has more to cry about that any of us with that Easter Island head of his!"

```
                    WHALE
        I'm not--
```

"It doesn't matter how much work you do now, Whale. I've never hired an intern that was stupid enough to cry on their first day."

```
                    WHALE
        I'm not crying!
```

"Don't fucking lie to me."

Whale looks straight in The Professor's eyes.

```
                    WHALE
        I am not crying.
```

The Professor stares back. Whale maintains his gaze.

```
                    WHALE (CONT'D)
        It's allergies.
```

The Professor stares. Nods a bit. Picks up his marker. Whale looks at Bumps. She avoids eye contact. He turns around to look at the others. Peabrain and Cashew avoid him too. Whale faces forward, his head fuzzy, his eyes red.

The Professor returns to the board and uncaps the marker. "Alright. Where were we?"

DREW

Take Your Medicine

"We were talking about the..." Drew says, shooting a finger gun at his butt. "You know."

Shayne Parker pockets his AirPods. "Oh, right. Sorry, bro. Very busy time of year. Beach bods and all."

"It's alright." Drew slips off his tie. Starts to unbutton. Stops. "May I?"

Shayne casually flaps a hand. "Of course, dude."

Drew rapidly unbuttons his shirt. Slips it off. Lifts his white tank top. Shayne snaps on white latex gloves. Inspects Drew's pecs. Left. Right. A bit of squeezing. A bit of touching. Mainly searching.

Drew exhales roughly. "Well?"

Shayne scours through his black leather bag open on Drew's desk. "Nothing."

"Bullshit. I know something's wrong."

"You're just adjusting to the Tren."

"It's been three fucking months! What's taking so long?"

Shayne pulls a syringe from the bag, the one marked LAWRENCE, D. "Don't do the push-ups for a while. Let your body tell you when it's ready." He injects an extra half-dose into Drew's ass. Drew can't even feel it anymore.

"What about stacking?" Drew asks, re-buttoning his pants. "Would that help?"

Shayne shrugs. "I'll get some Stan from my guy. We'll start you on Monday, but we gotta start small to avoid any crazy side-effects."

"As long as it works, I don't give a fuck." Drew puts his shirt back on. "Hey Shayne, do I...?" He sighs, realizing how pathetic it is.

"What?"

Drew looks at Shayne's humble face. His casual posture. The effortlessness of their camaraderie. "Do I look good?"

Shayne half chuckles. "What do you mean?"

"No homo or anything. Just look at me. Don't think about it. Do I look good?" Drew smiles, outstretching his arms, flaunting his form. "Do I look hot?"

"Yeah dude," Shayne insists as humbly as he can. "I've seen a lot of guys. You look better than most of them."

Drew looks down at his body. Custom suit fragrantly fitted to his body. Arms not nearly as big as they could be. Shoulders too sharp. Pecs round mountains compared to Shayne's square hills. What did he expect? Shayne was never gonna say different. "Thanks," Drew mumbles. "See you on Monday, huh?"

"Sure, dude. Take it easy."

"Course." Drew holds the door for Shayne. Closes. Locks. Grabs a pinch from the sugar bowl. Rubs it across his gums. Shayne doesn't get high off his own supply, all natural to Drew's fake artificial posing, much like Theo's natural ability to do all he does without Scotch or coke or advisers or a conference room to trash or his own doubt punching him in the brain and gut and cock and balls and thighs and face that ugly fucking face and all the rest and Drew does a line a big one to go with his big lunch and races around the office and wants to get into a fight and feel like a fucking man and why does he have to get into a fight to feel like a man what a pathetic thing to think what's wrong with him he's a good guy Drew fucking Lawrence where's Larry ain't there work to do okay let's go let's do it fuck yeah!

4:00 meeting on 2. 4:15 phone call in his office on 7. 4:45 meeting on 4. 5:15 meeting on 6. Up down up down the elevator like a bouncy house and Larry always knows what to say to make Drew feel like he can do it was great and good and all that effort is worth all those smiles and everyone likes his words don't sound right as he says them even though they can hear and understand up sit down stand up walk a bit of a headache in his legs still he has to walk a straight line again at 5:30 another bump at 5:31 for good measure he's fine thanks for asking Larry good guy Larry and he's great too Drew fucking Lawrence and his bright ideas that everyone actually hates why don't they say anything he doesn't feel good so how can everything be going right or wrong or right or left behind something where is he on the floor or ceiling oh fuck who's calling?

Drew picks up the phone lying next to him in the dark. How did he get home? He swipes to answer. "Hello?"

"You fall asleep?"

Drew looks around his bedroom. "I think so."

"It's not late, is it?"

Drew checks his bedside clock. "Just after eight."

"Status update. How's our baby doing?"

"I'm not sure. It seemed pretty... To be honest, it was a lot."

"Fridays tend to get like that."

"This whole week's been a lot."

"You have no idea. You got the easy shit, bro."

Drew hesitates. "You're telling me it gets worse?"

"Ass-kissing investors, CFO reports. Set disasters. Oh boy are they a doozy."

Drew licks his dry lips. "Theo?

"Yeah buddy?"

"You're almost done over there, right?"

Silence on the line. "What's going on?"

"Nothing."

"What's wrong?"

"Nothing."

"Tell me."

"Nothing! It's just…" Drew sighs, adjusting his shoulders off the pillow. "I keep thinking my notes are shit and no one's telling me 'no,' and—"

"Aren't you being a bit dramatic?"

"Stop saying that. I know what's good. None of it was."

"I just went through the transcripts. I think you're doing fine. Matter of fact, you're phenomenal."

Drew sits up. "What transcripts? What are you talking about?"

"Larry sent them over. I just finished reading them."

"Why the fuck did he do that?!"

"Calm down. God, you're so sensitive tonight."

"He's MY assistant, Theo! I never agreed to that!"

"We talked about it before I left."

"And I said no!"

"No, you didn't."

Drew's heart races. "I know I did. I know I said no because..." He huffs. "I know I definitely said no."

"You definitely said yes."

Drew covers his eyes with a hand, his face contorted and ready to whimper.

"You feeling okay?" Theo asks.

"I don't know."

"You've always had a bad memory."

"No, I don't. I have a fantastic memory, actually."

"Then why don't you...?" Theo sighs. "That's not why I called. I'm congratulating you."

"For what?"

"For your first week as CEO, stupid! I'm so fucking proud of you! I had my doubts, let's be honest, but it seems like you're handling it just fine. I guess I was wrong."

Drew's face goes numb, not in the good way. "You think so?"

"Don't you?"

Drew's body trembles. Probably cause he's starving. "Of course," he lies.

"Think you can handle five more weeks?"

Ouch. Drew forces a smile, just in case Theo can see him. "Yeah. Sure."

"You going out tonight?"

"Maybe. I dunno."

"I heard they got new meat down at Sweet Vermouths. That sounds like fun, huh?"

"Yeah. Sure."

"Good. Get fucked up. Have a good time."

"Always do."

Theo chuckles. "Don't I know it. Talk to you Monday, bro." He hangs up.

Drew slowly lowers his hand, thinking back. He said no, right? He definitely said no. He's 85% sure he said no.

Drew cooks himself a perfect filet mignon with a Chianti reduction infused with pure unflavored whey protein powder. Thorough shower. He slips on his nightlife best. Dark gray Armani jacket, the one with the durable performance fabric and flattering stretch. Matching pants. White dress shirt. Splash of cologne. Rolex. Snuffbox of the good shit. Wallet filled to the brim with hundreds. He nurses a neat Domergue throughout, his erection hardening in anticipation of the night to come. His reflection helps too. Perfectly buzzed yet fit enough to drive, Drew takes the elevator to the garage, hops into his Jeep Wrangler and blows out of Marina Del Rey like a bat out of hell.

On the border of West Hollywood and Beverley Hills is a sleazy haunt by the name of Sweet Vermouths. It used to be a classy dance hall until the night its founder and most of the dancers got slaughtered, but after a delicate rebranding and a hefty cleaning bill, the WeHo staple was alive once more as the gayest den since Sodom, a sensual mix of club tables, speakeasy drinks, neon signs, dark blue lights, pulsating EDM, go-go boys on podiums, and enough streetwise among the new management not to ask questions, not be shocked, not to judge, and to tell no one what they see around the corner. It's only open on Fridays but doesn't close till 6.

Drew Lawrence parks his red Wrangler out front. The line of rowdy boys of generational wealth revert to schoolgirls at the sight of him. Whispers of his name drift across all auditory channels when he doesn't look, twice as loud when he does. The doorman greets him with a large smile. Drew claps his shoulder and palms a Benjamin.

Lou the bartender, a charming black hetero with more hair on his cheeks than his head, looks past the customers and prioritizes his favorite tipper. The spurned customers don't care. They already have the best dinner party story of their lives. "How are you, my man?"

"Long week," Drew tells Lou with playful seriousness. "A little birdie told me you got a new one."

Lou smirks. "Your birdie's got quite the nose."

"You have no idea."

Lou grabs a rocks glass. Opens the special mini-fridge marked "Lawrence." Pulls out an ice mold. Pops out a single ice ball clear as water. Kicks open a small step ladder. Climbs onto the bar counter. Reaches *above* the top shelf for their best spirit, an ornate bottle of Domergue 15 just for Drew Lawrence. Lou pours a double shot over the clear ice ball. Stirs just a bit with a long-necked spoon. Hands the glass of perfection to the man himself. Drew hands back $500.

A go-go boy named Terry peers through the backstage curtain at Drew Lawrence making his way to his usual table. He grew up watching Drew Lawrence movies. He studied his Wikipedia page at film school. But he knows Drew Lawrence in a different way behind the black velvet curtain of Sweet Vermouths. At first Terry assumed JJ was whispering about a different Drew Lawrence, like how the Ray Charles singing *Three's Company*'s theme song was neither blind nor black. Then he hoped JJ was just lying, or at the very least exaggerating. But then he heard the same thing from Dirk and Aarin and Trenton and Rod and Shawn and all the others. Every single go-go boy at Sweet Vermouths has a Drew Lawrence story.

Terry steps away from the curtain. Sits on an amp box. Cold inevitability finally sinks in. He's assigned to stage 3. Drew Lawrence is sitting by stage 3. That's how all Drew Lawrence stories start.

Terry dances under his real name. He loves Chinese food and playing baseball with his roommates. He catches *SNL* every time it's on and proudly binges *Gilmore Girls* on DVD. He works out every day because he likes it, not because he has to. He's got an IQ of 145 and the imagination of a second grader. He graduated *summa cum laude* from his alma mater. Thanks to Sweet Vermouths he's only one year away from paying off his student loans. He adores his father more than anyone else in the world. Terry's more than a pretty face or a six pack or a good time. He's a go-go boy, not a stripper. He doesn't give lap dances. He doesn't drink on the job. He doesn't use ever. He doesn't stick dollar bills under his waistband. He doesn't fuck anyone. Such stalwart stances mean nothing to the managers, not when it comes to Drew Lawrence. It's a Sweet Vermouths go-go boy rite of passage. No matter how Terry feels or thinks about it, it's gonna happen. And if he really wants his screenplay to get made one day, he has to let it happen.

Drew leans back in his booth, perpetually smiling for the eyes on him, wherever they are. The strobe lights change their pattern. The DJ hollers over the speakers. The go-go boys walk out on stage. Color coordinated high tops, jockstraps and snapbacks. Nothing else. The young man on stage 3 is gorgeous. More hunky than muscled. Just enough blond hair on his athletic arms. No tattoos. No piercings. Clean shaven face. Fantastic abs. Toned ass, just enough to grab. Handsome jaw. A stunning face more impressive than his body. Skin shining with sweat. Healthy color to his cheeks. Beautiful lips with a hint of spittle. Good smile. Great teeth. Clean blue eyes. His color scheme of light gray and cardinal red reminds Drew of the Los Angeles Angels.

Terry avoids eye contact with Drew Lawrence for as long as he can. He flips his hat around to make the bill face forward.

Drew moves closer to the stage. "Why'd you do that?" he asks.

Terry keeps on dancing with a coy smile. "Do what?"

"Flip your hat around?"

"I like it this way."

Drew's eyes never leave Terry's. "Do you know who I am?"

"Of course."

"Who am I?"

Terry hesitates, his body never missing a beat of the music. "Drew Lawrence."

Drew smiles. "Call me Drew."

"Okay."

Drew stands silently. Terry's not saying any more. "What do you want me to call you?" he asks finally.

"Terry."

"Is that your real name?"

"I'm not a stripper." Terry can't believe he just said that. It just came out. His heart pounds as he looks at Drew. Maybe he didn't hear him.

Drew absolutely heard him. He smirks, a genuine one this time. "I'm gonna fucking tear you apart."

Terry goes numb. He hates that Drew said that. He hates how he hasn't stopped dancing once during the entire conversation. He hates his managers for putting him in that situation. He hates that he can't step off that stage without getting fired. He hates Drew getting everything he wants so easily. More than anything he hates that savage line, so unapologetically degrading, turning him on so much. "I know," Terry replies, his erection poking his jock.

"Do you want me to?" Drew asks, hoping so hard for a yes.

Terry hesitates. "Yes." He's not even lying.

"Are you sure?" Drew asks. He doesn't normally ask twice. This week more than ever he needs to be sure. 100% sure.

Terry looks straight into Drew's eyes. Lifts his hat. Fluffs his hair a bit. Puts the cap on backwards. "Yes."

Drew grins. Hot blood coursing through his veins. Muscles tightening. It's the first time he's felt like a real man all week.

JACOB

Snow (Hey Oh)

INT. WHITMAN UNIVERSITY - LB 710 - WATER CLOSET - NIGHT

Harsh florescent lights click on, BUZZING softly. Nich and Jacob squeeze in, the party still going behind them.

JACOB
Why are we--?

NICH
Close the door.

JACOB
I'm not sucking you off.

NICH
I know. Just close the door.

Jacob reluctantly shuts the door. Nich rolls a hand around his pocket.

NICH (CONT'D)
Got a surprise for you.

Jacob sips his cup of pure vodka. Nich pulls a TWO-GRAM BAGGIE OF COCAINE from his pocket.

NICH (CONT'D)
Welcome home, dude.

Jacob holds it up. His face goes blank.

NICH (CONT'D)
Didn't want TJ or Rian hogging it all. That there's just for us.

Jacob hands the baggie back.

JACOB
No. I-I don't want...

NICH
What? Why not?

Jacob looks at the cup in his hand. Places it on the toilet's tank.

NICH (CONT'D)
C'mon, dude. Just a couple lines.

JACOB
(rubbing his eyes)
No, man. I'm sorry.

NICH
I don't wanna do it alone!

JACOB
You're gonna have to.

Nich exhales, confused.

NICH
You said you did it before.

JACOB
I did.

NICH
You liked it, didn't you?

Jacob takes a deep breath.

JACOB
Last time was with Christopher.

NICH
Who?

JACOB
I told you about Christopher.
(pause)
Remember? The guy in Italy? The guy? The older American guy?

NICH
Christopher?

JACOB
Yeah, remember?

Nich gasps sharply.

NICH
Holy fuck, dude! Oh my God, I am SO sorry!

JACOB
It's okay.

NICH
I complete forgot about the... Oh, fuck dude! No wonder!

JACOB
It's fine. Really.

NICH
(scooching to the door)
Don't worry about it. I'll just give to Trevor.

JACOB
Wait.

NICH
He won't mind. He loves this shit.

JACOB
Don't. Just wait.

Nich looks at Jacob, confused.

JACOB (CONT'D)
Did you get that just for me?

NICH
Yeah.

Jacob hesitates.

JACOB
Why?

NICH
You know, I just...
(bashful shrug)
I just, just... You're just such a pal, man. And I'm not very great at being... I'm a bit much, you know, and...
(scoffs)
God, I don't know what I'm saying.

Jacob softens.

NICH (CONT'D)
I just thought... Here's something we could do together. And it's something you actually like, you know? It's not too much for you.

JACOB
It's not really a problem.

NICH
I know, but... I don't wanna guilt you or anything.

Jacob doesn't talk.

NICH (CONT'D)
Hey, I'd feel the same way about it if that happened to me. That just sucks the fun out of it.

JACOB
Something like that.

NICH
Okay then.

Nich turns the doorknob.

JACOB
Wait.

NICH
What?!

JACOB
Close the door.

Nich shuts the door.

NICH
What?

Jacob rubs his jaw.

JACOB
What the hell.

NICH
Really?

Jacob nods.

NICH (CONT'D)
You sure? It's no big deal if you're not sure.

JACOB
I'm sure.

NICH
Hell yeah, man!

Nich bear-hugs Jacob.

NICH (CONT'D)
Let's fucking GOOOO!

Jacob chuckles, fighting Nich off.

JACOB
C'mon. Everyone's gonna think I'm blowing you.

NICH
"Not that there's anything wrong with it!"

Jacob re-locks the bathroom door. Nich puts down the toilet lid. Opens the baggie.

JACOB
Where're you gonna put it?

NICH
Seat's clean.

Nich dumps the baggie out. Jacob pulls out his wallet and hands Nich a credit card.

JACOB
It's not mixed with anything bad, right?

Nich cuts four lines. Jacob pulls out a dollar bill from his wallet and rolls it up tight.

NICH
Look who knows what he's doing.

JACOB
Movies.

Nich steps aside, gesturing to the lines.

NICH
Ladies first.

JACOB
Bitch, you're the one that put the seat down.

NICH
I realize that.

JACOB
AND you have pink hair!

NICH
Fine, okay, SLUTS first.

JACOB
Thank you! Ugh! Finally, a moniker I've earned.

NICH
And don't take it all. Save some for me, ho.

Jacob glares at Nich.

NICH (CONT'D)
(hands up, surrendering)
I'm sorry! MISTER Ho!

JACOB
(angry finger)
HEY! That's DOCTOR Ho to you!

NICH
I'm very sorry, Doctor Ho. It won't happen again.

JACOB
It better not!
(trying not to laugh)
I DID NOT FUCK MY WAY THROUGH FOUR YEARS OF MEDICAL SCHOOL FOR NOTHING!

Nich laughs his ass off.

Jacob gets down on his knees, face to face with the cocaine.

JACOB (CONT'D)
And I got all that student debt, and...

Jacob's stomach growls.

JACOB (CONT'D)
I'm getting hungry. Must be all this talk of cock, and...

Jacob stares at the white powder. He's not laughing anymore.

JACOB (CONT'D)
I'm really doing this, aren't I?

A KNOCK on the door.

NICH
Just a minute!
(hushed)
Come on!

Jacob puts a finger to his nostril, bends over and SNORTS a line.

MATCH CUT TO:

DREW

Mirror, Mirror

Drew snorts a big bump of the good shit and Terry snorts his second and Drew pins him against the dirty bathroom wall and lifts his big arms up and licks his neck and kisses him deep as Terry laughs this kind of chuckle and Drew pulls his hair back and spits on his face and wipes it around and kisses him hard and he kisses back wrapping his arms around Drew and his big arms and broad shoulders in that nice suit and Drew bends over and picks Terry's hat off the floor and puts it on Terry backwards and pushes his head down so Terry gets down on his knees and looks up at Drew and he smiles down and slaps Terry's cheeks and Terry laughs as he unzips and whips out Drew's cock and holds it in wonder and kisses it and starts sucking as Drew throws off his jacket and loosens his tie and rolls up his sleeves and moans thanks to Terry's experienced mouth so warm with the tongue rolling around and sucking, no teeth, and deep, so deep until he gags and thick spit drools out his mouth and a bit of snot out his nose and some tears and Drew smacks Terry's hands away and grabs Terry's smart head and shoves in as deep as he could and Terry tries to hold on as Drew keeps pounding but Terry starts gagging but Drew fucks harder and Terry moans and gags and Drew pulls out and Terry gasps and coughs his face red head fuzzy and he's dizzy and suddenly he's up and Drew bends him over and kicks his right high top over to spread his stance and Terry's hands against the wall as Drew touches every inch of his body his coarse leathery hands going everywhere they want and his tongue and Terry's there in the public bathroom and some dudes come in and look at him and smile and it's Drew Lawrence and some whore some fucking bathroom slut a hot piece of ass Drew owns and could pimp out if he so pleases and they laugh and some cheer and Drew keeps licking and even high fives one as he sticks his Hollywood fingers inside Terry and spreads him open and stretches around and turns him inside out and gets his wet hole wetter and deep as he can and Drew wraps a big hairy arm across Terry's chest up at the neck and Terry holds on to his strong muscled arm as Drew taps his door little pig little pig let me in and he does and he's so loose how is he so loose already and wow Drew's in there he's inside Terry raw and he fucks Terry raw like the little piggie he is and Drew grunts and whispers fucked up things in Terry's ear and Terry moans intelligibly so happy and his cock is dripping through his jockstrap as Drew pounds him and Terry sees stars and he's moaning for more and Drew gives him more and holy shit it's so much more but Terry loves it he loves it so fucking much and he needs it and Drew holds his hips and pounds so hard and can't stop and Drew's sweating down his chest and he can feel every muscle in his body getting tight and he feels strong and badass and hot and powerful so powerful and he wraps his fingers around Terry's soft and smooth and warm neck and squeezes and the veins on Terry's neck pop and his eyes roll back as he bucks harder against Drew and moans something else speaking in tongues and Drew squeezes just a bit harder and fucks the life out of Terry and Terry drools all over the floor and Drew can't hear the cheers behind him or feeling the pats on the back he just feels Terry and Terry feels only Drew fucking Lawrence and doesn't remember a thing and doesn't hate anything and doesn't love his roommates or his dad or knowledge or his degree or his stories and his IQ's no more than a pile of mush as Drew wrings it out of Terry he squeezes Terry so much and Terry loves it and he doesn't want anything except Drew's cock just more cock nothing except his cock and cum and Drew shooting a big fat load into him and squash him like the puny bitch he is with snot running down his face and he's crying with a big smile and drool seeping out of multiple parts and precum trickling out like a faucet and sweat coming out of every pore and Drew takes off his shirt leaving just a loose tie a silk noose and a Rolex too and Terry's sweat is all over him and his lip tight with gritted teeth and coke under his nose and wet hair as he grunts like an animal and readjusts his grip on Terry's neck and finally lets go and Terry gasps hard but Drew keeps on fucking him and calling him a whore and a slut and a dirty boy and nothing and Terry speaks in tongues and he can't see anything when Drew throws him on the ground and Terry's wet cheek picks up grime and there's a lot of shoes going to and fro at the urinals and the stalls and washing their hands and standing by to watch Terry's ass in the air getting fucked by a big bulging producer man and his knees hurt and Drew's dick hits that spot again over and over and over and over and Terry's eyes roll back again and he can't take it anymore even though he wants it and keeps on wanting it and he can't for much longer but it doesn't stop and Terry doesn't want it to stop because he loves it and Drew keeps pounding again and puts his foot on Terry's face that sweaty sock pressing and squishing on his cheek and dripping down and pressing Terry into the tile into the floor and the grime and he moans and laughs at once and fucking barks as Drew spits at his face and lies on top of him Drew's whole body weighing down on him and he can't smell anything but sex and sweat and musk and Drew wraps his sweaty arms around Terry's chest and fucks him on the floor just pounding away and Terry can see stars again and Drew's growling and biting his neck and spitting into his mouth and kissing him without slowing down his hips and Terry can't breathe so Drew breathes into him and Terry's filled with Drew all the way from both ends and he can't see light just shadows and distorted voices and cheers and feet as Drew wrings Terry some more and tears fall down and more drool and the more Drew squeezes the more comes out and Terry shoots his load into his jock and his hole twitches and Drew notices and it's so hot and he doesn't stop fucking Terry and bucks his hips and flattens his palms on the floor those big beefy arms of his and does push-ups down and up and down and up and slamming into Terry every time thrusting his cock in every time and his hole's not even tight anymore not even close as Drew keeps pounding his push-ups and he makes it to sixty and laughs hard and kisses Terry all over with a smile as he keeps pounding away and Terry's moaning and yelping and begging over and over just begging like a bitch and Drew asks what he wants and Terry wants his load he wants his fucking load inside him so deep inside he wants to taste it in his drool and he tells Drew all this but it comes out like gibberish and Drew feels it coming finally and he groans and yells as his guttural voice reverbs off the walls just as he shoots a ton into Terry and his muscles seize and he finally unclutches his arms and collapses onto Terry and rolls off and some dude helps Drew up and all the other guys are applauding and no one has cell phones or cameras thank God Drew's glad and helps Terry up and kisses him and Terry holds Drew tight and thanks him and Drew gives him a thousand and smacks his ass and sends him off and Terry slides pooled spunk out of his jock pouch his strap complete soaked through and he washes his hands and stumbles out to tell the boys all about it and Lou gets him a beer on the house and he's still high and not in his body but he's happy he's so fucking happy.

Drew slides his underwear back on. Wipes his face with a paper towel. Feels like a million bucks. Washes his hands. Looks up.

Drew thinks he's looking at a goblin at first. Ghoulish black circles around the eyes. Big red pimples prime to burst peppering the cheeks. Leathery skin. Every pore visible with startling detail. Freaky wrinkles around the mouth. Barely any hair left on the head. No fat left on the gaunt face. Nostrils glowing red. The bathroom's fluorescent lighting makes everything look wrong. Yellow-green tiles. Dirty once-white porcelain. A funky realm both septic and antiseptic at once. And Drew feels the same inside his body. He wants to vomit at how he looks. How he's always looked. He wants to cry. So so much he wants to cry. What happened? What the fuck is wrong with him? What did he just do? Why isn't he crying? He's sad. His lip's trembling. Where's the rest? His eyes so red they're practically bleeding. That's what scares him the most, those red eyes. So dry. Everything's dry. Barren tear ducts. Veins filled with sand. He feels old and dusty and stagnant with cracks along his lips and a bloody nose and dust in his throat, the sand wrapping around him as he sinks down down down, clutching around him down down down, too parched to cry out, no one around to pull him out of the quicksand he knows he's sinking into that everyone says it isn't real, just in his head.

In the absence of crying, Drew lowers his head and sputters hot exhaust into the sink.

WHALE

The Great Disappointment

Whale stumbles out of The Factory. It's late. The sun's gone. He can still smell the exhaust from the other interns' rides. He looks around for his. A blue Prius drives down the drive, its brights flashing. Whale holds up a hand, hailing the driver. It slows to a park. "Hey buddy!" Darryl cries out the window, a smile on his face. "God, what are the chances, huh?"

Whale looks up at the stars with a lamenting frown. He opens the backseat door and hops in.

Darryl drives onto the 2. "I saw the notification and I said, 'Hey isn't that where I dropped that guy off this morning?' and sure enough!" He smirks at Whale in the rearview. "So? How was your first day?"

Whale stares at the window. He's not gonna cry. Not here. Not in front of him.

```
                    WHALE
        Fine.
```

"Just fine, eh?" Darryl teases. "I get it. Trying to keep humble now. I mean, don't mind me. I'm just a Ridr driver." He chuckles. "So, The Professor. Is he taller than he looks in the photos? Because he sure looks like a shrimp."

Whale doesn't say anything. No tears. Not until he gets home. He can hold on till then.

"Where's all that big talk from this morning?" Darryl asks. "You were all excited. Long day?"

```
                    WHALE
        You could say that.
```

Darryl looks at the rearview mirror. "So did you decide if you're the next—?" His smile fades. Whale's face is contorted, wet eyes shining from the passing streetlights, lips moving with intentionally stifled breath. Darryl faces forward, his heart heavy. He says nothing else.

Whale gets out of the Ridr. Too tired to rate or tip. Later. He opens the door. The whole house reeks. Alex is watching *The Wolf of Wall Street* again, buried in the couch under a cloud of pot smog. "Hey dude," Alex rasps. "How was it?"

Whale's face is ready to melt. He just wants to close off everything and fade away into the night. He'll settle for his room. He walks past Alex.

"Dude!" Alex cries, standing up. "What the fuck?"

```
                    WHALE
        What?
```

Alex shrugs angrily. "The almond milk?!"

Whale closes his eyes.

```
                    WHALE
        I'm sorry. I forgot.
```

"You had one fucking job!"

```
                    WHALE
        I had an awful day. I didn't stop and get milk. Big
        deal. Get off my back about it.
```

"Okay. That's fine. Maybe I wanted cereal in the morning."

```
                    WHALE
      You could've gotten it yourself.
```

"You the one that offered, jackass! How about you fucking text me the next time you change your mind?"

```
                    WHALE
      They took our phones.
```

"Then you should've gone."

```
                    WHALE
      I FUCKING FORGOT! SHUT UP ABOUT IT!
```

Alex stares blankly. Whale's body trembles with fury.

```
                    WHALE (CONT'D)
      I'm so glad your whole world revolves around whether
      or not you have almond milk with your cereal! Life is
      just one fucking party for you, isn't it?! I spent
      years working my ass off for this thing, this was all
      I had, and now it's gone! I can't fix it! I'm gonna
      end up a pitiful wretch like you and there's nothing
      I can do about it!
```

Whale turns away. Storms into his room.

"Hey asshole!" Alex yells. "You shoulda told me were a fucking lunatic when you—"

Whale SLAMS the door, hurting his hand. He kicks a dresser. Unleashes a loud angry wave of tears. He collapses onto the floor, wailing loudly, snot dribbling into his mouth, throat going hoarse with every cry. The Professor's crapeating grin flashes across his mind. Whale smacks his head with both hands. He instantly regrets doing so, whimpering in pain. His head throbs. He can't look in the mirror. He looks up at his *Pulp Fiction* poster. The corner's off the wall again.

Whale smacks the corner down. It unpeels again. Whale presses it again. Again. Again. He rips the poster off the wall. Tears the effer in half. Shreds Uma to bits. Throws the pieces around the room. Falls on the bed. Smushes his face into the pillow. Cries into the soft foam. His growls vibrate across his whole face. He's burrowed in that dark little hole. Nothing to see. Nothing to hear. Only the anger and shame he brought with him. Slowly fading to nothing. Passes out.

JACOB

Twilight Zone

INT. WHITMAN UNIVERSITY - LB 710 - JACOB'S ROOM - DAY

Jacob jolts awake on the floor, head resting on a pile of dirty clothes. He looks around. Sun is angled through the window. He gasps. Looks at his alarm clock.

"1:35 PM"

Jacob jumps up. Instantly stumbles over, clutching his stomach, weak everywhere. He hunches over his bunk bed. Face down. Deep breaths. He notices his bedroom door is closed. And everything's quiet.

CUT TO:

IN THE HALLWAY

Jacob pokes his head out. Looks both ways. No red Solo residue. No trash anywhere. The other bedroom doors are closed.

JACOB

Hello?

CUT TO:

INT. FILM IMMERSION - DAY

Jacob wanders out of Suite 710, too intimidated by the eerie silence to fruitlessly call out. The open floor plan common room, complete with a full kitchen and TV room enclosed in glass, large stretches of empty carpet in between, looks far too big without a hundred students roaming around.

Jacob stops and stares, a lonesome frown growing. He turns around slowly. Inches back toward Suite 710.

DISSOLVE TO:

INT. SUITE 710 - BATHROOM MIRROR - DAY

Jacob studies his bloodshot eyes in the mirror, glasses off. A dial tone rings on his iPhone's speakerphone.

RIAN (V.O.)

Hey! You just wake up?

JACOB

(bitter)

Yeah.

RIAN (V.O.)

Damn. Good for you.

JACOB

No, not good for me! What happened to us going to South Street, huh? We were supposed to go.

RIAN (V.O.)

I know, but you got so fucked up. We had to go without you.

Jacob closes his eyes.

RIAN (V.O.)

Do you remember anything?

JACOB
When did I pass out?

RIAN (V.O.)
Around 3:30, I think.

Jacob looks into the water closet, its toilet scrubbed clean.

RIAN (V.O.)
It was fun, though. I was gonna order pancakes for you to-go but then I thought they'd be too cold or soggy by the time you got up.

JACOB
Why didn't you wake me?

Silence on the line.

JACOB (CONT'D)
You promised. To my face, you promised.

RIAN (V.O.)
You had such a rough day, man. I thought you needed the sleep. I-I'm sorry.

Jacob sighs. Lowers his head.

JACOB
Did you guys get off alright at least? I know Carter's a bit strict when it comes to the insp--

RIAN (V.O.)
My mom just pulled up. I gotta go.

JACOB
Oh, okay. Tell her I said hi.

RIAN (V.O.)
Sure. Text me later, alright?

JACOB
Alright. Bye-bye.

RIAN (V.O.)
Bye dude.

Jacob ends the call. Looks at his cheeks in the mirror. Tentatively lifts his upper lip. Gunk all over his teeth, inflamed gums, ugly yellow teeth. His lip curls, tears coming on. Puffy eyes ready to cry. His face suddenly goes blank. He jolts into the bathroom. Flips up the toilet lid. Drops to his knees. Sticks his head into the bowl. RETCHES. No vomit, just a lot of noise. Some esophageal clicking. Persistent taste of bile. Jacob takes slow, comforting breaths.

JACOB
C'mon, goddammit.

Jacob sticks his head dangerously deep into the bowl, warm breath floating around him, the waterline shuddering. Makes eye contact with the reflection in the toilet water, afternoon light shining behind his shadowed head. He readjusts his knees. Closes his eyes.

JACOB (CONT'D)
Please.

Jacob RETCHES again. Nothing. He stays where he is, his head in the toilet, and waits.

SLOW FADE TO BLACK.

END OF PART ONE

PART TWO

My Name is for My Friends

WHALE

Apocrypha

Whale sits through Sunday Mass with nothing on his mind except the internship. Otherwise he's just a mannequin, a cold plastic hollow vessel kneeling on cue, standing on cue, saying all the appropriate words. Not the words he'd been taught in Catholic school, of course. Pope Benedict gone and changed the translation six years ago, single-handedly forcing every single Catholic in the English-speaking world to relearn the lines from scratch. Didn't matter how much practice they had, how many years of dedication, how quick their secondhand instinct was, because it was all made worthless overnight. If anyone slipped up, if someone said "and also with you" instead of "and with your spirit," they suddenly looked like fools. Stupid, stupid fools.

If someone bothered to ask Whale how his internship was going, he honestly wouldn't know how to answer. He's been there six hours a day, five days a week, for almost a month already and nothing's happened. It's like he's getting paid to sit in a computer lab with no goals, no tasks, no lectures, no textbooks, absolutely no feedback. He knows he's missing something. Bumps is there before he arrives and after he leaves. Cashew frequently skips his lunch break to maintain his flow. Worst of all was Peabrain. He could type faster than Whale assumed was humanly possible, a constant clacking that never stopped, a metronome on its maximum settling with just as mechanical a pace. It didn't matter which computer Whale took, Peabrain's finger-punches kept distracting him, those loud spine-tingling shots relentlessly echoing across his brain. Whale couldn't read a single page without stopping. He wanted so much to log onto YouTube and play some music, some PSB to keep him in a familiar cerebral headspace, but he wasn't sure if that was allowed. And he daren't ask The Professor. Oftentimes Whale looked up at that cube, that sometimes-frosted sometimes-transparent Bond lair, and spent entire hours hating that awful man. Once Whale looked up and saw The Professor looking back at him. He might've been smirking too.

Every so often The Professor descended, his footsteps sending icy jitters down their spines simultaneously. Never speaking. Never looking over screens or printouts. Just reminding them he was there. What a douchebag, so cocky in that frat boy grown up kinda way, the type of dude that could hop out of bed at five in the morning and do pushups on the bedroom floor. He expects to get everything he wants because he always has and realistically always will. What's so effed up is all that immature DILFy rowdiness actually turning Whale on. The more he sees The Professor and his tight chest and big selfish hands, the more he fantasizes his boss dominating him in that cube and fucking him like he's nothing. It makes him sick, but it keeps happening the more he sees him and it's only getting worse.

Whale's just about to finish a predictable, well-intentioned afterlife comedy-drama titled *What the Hell* when The Secretary gently taps her flawless nails on his shoulder. "Whale? It is Whale, right?"

```
                    WHALE
        Yeah.
```

"The Professor wants to speak to you in his office."

Bumps, sitting just a few computers down, looks over. Peabrain hasn't stopped typing, practically white noise at this point.

```
                    WHALE
        Right now?
```

"Yes, right now," The Secretary says.

Whale saves his Word doc and quickly log off the computer. Follows The Secretary to the staircase. He looks up the transparent spine, his stomach turning in knots.

"Go on," The Secretary mutters, gesturing. "He's waiting for you."

```
                WHALE
Just give me a moment. I'm afraid of heights.
```

The Secretary rolls her eyes. "Just don't look down."

```
                WHALE
I know that!
```

The Secretary struts off with appalling disinterest. Whale watches her go, instantly sorry for snapping like that, before starting his ascent. He's so focused on not looking up or down, just staring blankly ahead, all his brainpower triple-checking the stability of that strange staircase, that he's not thinking about why he's been summoned. But like a hangover following a night of vodka, it all hits him at once when he reaches the top. The Professor is gonna have it out with him. His feature coverage, all forty-four so far including *What the Hell*, was everything The Professor didn't want. Or the overall quantity of output was drastically small. Or maybe he did nothing wrong, which is why this is his first time in the inner sanctum? Maybe it's just a check-up? Or perhaps...?

Whale opens the black wooden door, furrowing his brow at the foreign sound of laughter. The Professor's effing laughing at a video on his phone. Not a sinister Jeff Bezos laugh or a *Jackass* kick-in-the-balls one either. A genuinely wholesome *America's Funniest Home Videos* laugh.

"Whale," The Professor says in between deep-breathed chuckles, "Whale, come look at this."

Whale tentatively approaches the desk, realizing mid-stride that the glass cube was transparent, clear as Saran Wrap, nothing between his feet and the ground but thirty feet of open air. His whole body shakes.

The Professor turns his phone to Whale, revealing a video of a laughing ten-year-old boy jumping on a bed with a gorgeous blonde woman. "It's my son Felipe. He's in Sacramento with his mother visiting her family. They made this for me."

Whale laughs. Felipe's innocent cackles are contagious.

```
                WHALE
That's your wife?
```

"Yes. Sophie."

```
                WHALE
She's beautiful.
```

"Thank you. Thank you." The Professor looks at the video one last time and laughs. Whale watches his face as he does it. Brevity is so strange on The Professor. Strange to Whale, at least. Maybe there's someone in there after all.

```
                WHALE
What was it you needed me for, Professor?
```

The Professor pockets his phone with a warm sigh. "Ah, yes. Of course." He points to his desktop, looking at Whale with his usual business face. "I've been looking over the updates you just sent me. Why isn't there anything on Locarno?"

Whale's lungs evaporate.

```
                WHALE
I didn't know you wanted that.
```

"I told you Day One."

```
                    WHALE
        You didn't mention it again, so I just assumed--
```

"You didn't need reminding about writing coverage. That's all you seem to be able to do. I don't need readers. Any idiot can read. PEABRAIN can read!"

Whale nods, avoiding eye contact with The Professor while also trying not to look down.

```
                    WHALE
        I'll get started on Locarno right now, I promise.
```

"Locarno is over! It ended last week! Why do you think I'm asking you about it?!"

```
                    WHALE
        I didn't know.
```

"What, did you think it was all year long?!"

```
                    WHALE
        Of course I knew it was gonna end. I didn't know it
        already did.
```

"Well, you should've!" The Professor cries. "How do you expect to make it in this industry if you don't know the fucking basics!"

```
                    WHALE
        I'm sorry, I just--
```

"What?!"

Whale swallows.

```
                    WHALE
        I'll do better.
```

"You have to." The Professor scowls at Whale one last time before returning to his computer.

Whale doesn't move.

The Professor looks up. "What is it now?"

```
                    WHALE
        What did you think of the coverage I sent you?
```

The Professor stares. "What?"

```
                    WHALE
        Is that what you wanted?
```

"I wanted coverage."

```
                    WHALE
        I meant to say, is that--
```

"Is it coverage? That's what you're asking?"

```
                    WHALE
        No, I--
```

"How the FUCK did you graduate *magna cum laude*?!" The Professor shouts, shaking the cube. "You fucking retard! What were you, the pity honoree?!"

```
                    WHALE
        I just want to know if I'm doing it right.
```

"Oh, I see. You want feedback."

```
                    WHALE
        Yes.
```

The Professor shrugs exaggeratedly. "You don't know?"

```
                              WHALE
          Know what?
```

"Am I speaking Dutch or something?!"

```
                              WHALE
          What am I supposed to know?! Tell me! Please!
```

"I'm supposed to tell you—?!"

```
                              WHALE
          What's wrong?!
```

"You should know!" The Professor cries, his throat straining. "If there is anything wrong with your work, you should know it and fix it BEFORE you send it to me!"

```
                              WHALE
          There's nothing wrong--
```

"I'm not an editor. I don't have time to hold your hand through a rough draft."

```
                              WHALE
          They're not rough drafts! I just want to know if it's
          what you want.
```

The Professor scoffs, a bitter grin on his face. "I can't believe it."

```
                              WHALE
                         (panicked)
          No, no, let me rephrase--
```

"I don't know how many fucking participation trophies you got as a kid, but in the real world no one owes you anything! Life does not give you feedback. You either know what you're doing or you don't."

Whale hesitates.

```
                              WHALE
          For the record, my generation never asked for
          participation trophies.
```

The Professor leans back in his chair in disbelief. "Holy shit!"

```
                              WHALE
          You're the generation that gave them to us. I only
          got one and I knew it didn't mean anything. I never
          expected--
```

"Jesus fucking Christ, you don't shut up, do you?"

```
                              WHALE
          This is an internship! You're supposed to tell us
          what to do!
```

Whale maintains eye contact with The Professor. The silence is scarier than the height.

The Professor sighs, soft and slow. "I'll be honest, Whale. When I read your screenplay, I literally said to myself, 'Wow! Finally! Here's someone who actually knows their shit.'" The Professor shakes his head. "Boy oh boy, was I fucking wrong."

Whale wants to cry so bad right now.

"I really should get my head examined," The Professor mercilessly continues. "No, actually I'll just switch to a simple application next year. No portfolio, just a resume and cover letter and all that bullshit. Because of you. That'll be your contribution here."

Whale looks away, feet frozen in place, his lip trembling so hard it hurts his jaw.

"Get out," The Professor orders. "I got a lot of shit to do, even if you don't." He clicks his mouse, his attention back on his computer.

Whale takes a deep breath.

WHALE
Sir?

The Professor looks at Whale. Whale clears his throat, trying his hardest to sound calm and professional.

WHALE (CONT'D)
I really never do this, but one of the things I have a problem with is that I have a hard time--

"No, no, I know where you're going with this! Shut up!" The Professor shrugs with desperate curiosity. "What is it with your generation and the mental health shit? Is it a label thing? A horoscope? You mommy dropped you as a baby, or maybe she gave you one too many vaccines, cool. Get over yourself." He points to the black wooden door. "And get the fuck out while you're at it. I've told you three times now."

WHALE
You only said it twice.

"You're not helping your case."

Whale timidly makes his way toward the staircase. Looks back.

WHALE
Can I play music while I work?

The Professor furrows his brow. "On what?"

WHALE
My computer.

"Get the fuck out of here!"

WHALE
Is it allowed, yes or no?!

"Try it," The Professor says calmly. "See what happens."

Whale stops talking. His knees buckle as he descends the stairs. By the time he reaches the ground he's too shaken to work. Too tired to cry.

DREW

The Cone of Silence

No matter how many six-inch hot subs Drew shoves down his throat, his chest still hurts with every thump. If Larry wasn't eating with him, he'd reach under his shirt and press three callused fingers against his hairy chest, as if that would do anything. Such a dramatic gesture is ultimately fruitless. He knows it's not a heart attack. It happened the other day and a few times more last week, ever since Shayne added Stan to his regimen. Left ass cheek gets the Stan, right cheek gets the Tren. Shayne swore stacking wouldn't kill him, right? Ripped blond son of a bitch. Three weeks of oily skin. Borderline heart attacks. His organs vibrating just beneath his skin. Maybe Shayne isn't the qualified medical professional he thinks he is.

Drew snorts a bump of the good shit to numb the Gettysburg reenactment rummaging around his guts. Washes it down with some Domergue. Yummy. What a good lunch.

Desperate to punch or fuck something or else he'd explode, Drew settles for a quick restroom handicap stall wank and a few dozen pushups on the floor of his office. Those curious glances of his staff passing by the window get Drew hard again, but he bought himself some time with that handicap stall wank. What a good phrase, handicap stall wank. Handicap stall wank. Handicap stall wank. Handicapstallwank. Handicapstallwankhandicapstallwankhandi—

"They're ready for you, Mr. Lawrence," Larry tells him, holding the door open.

Drew sits up at his desk. How long has he been sitting? What time is it? "Yes, of course." Drew stands, smoothing out his pant legs. "It's the, uh... uh..."

Larry doesn't say anything. Watches a grown man strain.

Drew moves his hand around. "The, uh... the... the... the... uh, the..." He snaps his fingers.

"The *Glory* dail—"

"The *Glory* dailies, Larry! Go fuck yourself with that fucking autocorrect! Goddammit! I know what I'm fucking doing, Larry! You asshole!" Drew storms past Larry out the door. Suddenly stops. Looks around the hall. Turns around.

Larry gently points in the other direction.

Drew huffs. Marches past Larry toward the screening room. Larry walks alongside. Drew avoids eye contact. "It's not—"

"You don't have to say anything, Mr. Lawrence."

"I just..."

"I know." Larry pats Drew's broad shoulder. "Don't worry."

Drew smiles ever so slightly. His muscles relax.

Drew gives distracted handshakes to *Glory*'s chief production team as Larry re-introduces them. Producer Damon Muller. Director Griffin Thirlwall. DP Hildegard Hiekkaharju. 1st AD Janet Gower. 2nd AD Sammie Daguerre. PAs Harold Drayton and Nolan Kantor. Drew sits in the front, the best seat in the house. He hasn't felt this excited to see a film in the last ten years. *Glory* was a pet project of sorts, a spec he pulled from the slush pile with the sole intention of turning it into the next *Lawrence of Arabia.*

Ten minutes in, raw footage playing before his eyes, Drew's smile is long gone. He looks behind him. The crew don't seem fazed at all. Drew returns to the farce playing out before him, that colorful cast of characters in silly 80s music video costumes quipping stale banter in front of a green screen. "What's going on?" he whispers to Larry. "I thought we were watching *Glory*."

Larry snaps out of his trance. "What do you mean?"

"You said we were watching *Glory.*"

Larry side-eyes the screen briefly. "This is *Glory.*"

Drew shakes his head. The wooden protagonist. The awful attempt at humor. The lame blocking. "No, it can't be. They're playing the wrong movie."

"Mr. Lawrence."

"This is cookie-cutter Marvel shit. Where's the *Blade Runner*? Where's the *Mad Max*?"

"They followed all your notes."

"This is NOT *Glory*!" Drew says a bit too loudly. He whips his head around. The crew definitely heard him. Shit.

"Mr. Lawrence," Larry whispers deliberately. "This is *Glory.*"

Drew shakes his head, sitting back, his hand holding his chin up. Larry's right. Audience surrogate protagonist. Morally ambiguous hero sidelined "to make him more mysterious." "Memorable" costumes. Enhanced colors. Light and inoffensive humor. "Uncomplicated" staging. More exposition. Adorable animal companion added for the merch. Quotable catchphrases. And they're fighting giant elephants, just like he wanted. They honored every point on Drew's wishlist. That wasn't the problem. Drew was the problem. Still drunk from lunch. Still hungover from last night. Hopped up on the good shit and the cheap shit and the Tren and Stan are fighting each other making his acne worse and he can't do sixty pushups anymore he can't even do fifty and he couldn't even cum in Dallas the new meat at Sweet Vermouths last week and Theo keeps calling and complimenting him and Drew pops to the bathroom to sneak a line and can't sit still anymore and screams "TURN IT OFF" and grabs a beautiful white and gold vase on the pedestal next to the screen and throws it at *Glory's* face and it rips a gash with porcelain bits flying out the *Glory* hole and "WHAT THE FUCK IS WRONG WITH YOU PEOPLE?! WHAT IS THIS SHIT?! LOOK AT IT! IT'S FUCKING AWFUL!"

Larry stands up. "Mr. Lawrence, you really shouldn't—"

"SHUT THE FUCK UP, LARRY!" Drew hollers, the beast unleashed. He grimaces at the terrified crew glued to their seats. Veins pulsing fast. Skin hot to the touch. "YOU KNOW IT SUCKS, DON'T YOU?!" he hollers, natural bass shaking the furniture. "YOU'RE NOT STUPID! LOOK AT THAT! *NONE OF YOU* THOUGHT THIS WAS A BAD IDEA?! SHUT IT DOWN! SHUT THE WHOLE FUCKING THING DOWN!" Drew kicks a chair, busting the bottom off its hinge. "PLEASE, *PLEASE* TELL ME WHEN I'M WRONG! HELP ME OUT, PEOPLE! CORRECT MY SHITTY IDEAS! THAT'S OKAY! BUT YOU HAVE TO TELL ME!" Drew repeatedly slaps the side of his head. "*I NEED TO HEAR IT!*" he roars, drawing his words out.

Larry closes his eyes, mouth contorted, deeply ashamed.

The *Glory* crew keep their heads down, staring at the seats in front of them.

Drew stands there. Gorilla arms hanging down. Nails digging into his palms. Panting like a madman. His shoulders slump. His head hurts. It's throbbing. "I'm sorry," he whimpers. "I thought..." He sighs. Wanders out of the screening room.

Larry stands slowly. "Wait here," he tells the crew. He whips out his cell. Checks the time. Steps out.

Harold finally lets go of his armrests. "What do we do now?" he meekly asks.

"We wait," Janet says. She's more inconvenienced than perturbed. "He's probably gonna make us sign something."

Harold looks at the others, frowns of disappointment on their faces. "I meant about *Glory.* What are we—?"

"Nothing," Damon mutters. "We did everything he asked."

"But—?"

"What's with all the questions?" Janet snaps.

"Nothing, I just..." Harold looks at the hole in the screen, all those porcelain shards on the floor. "Shouldn't we tell him what we think of his notes?"

"Go ahead," Griffin murmurs. "Get yourself fired."

"But if that's what he wants—?"

"When he calms down, he'll forget he ever said it," Janet murmurs.

Harold hesitates. "Has he always been like this?"

Janet looks away. None of the others say anything either.

Harold sits back, bumping his brows. "Guess that's a no."

"He wrote *Atomic* for Christ's sake," Janet blurts. "You ever see that?"

"Once."

"I saw it twenty times when it came out. It changed my life." Janet stares at Harold. "He was *twenty-five*."

Harold frowns.

Janet flicks a porcelain shard off her knee. "You don't tell Drew Lawrence how to do his job."

JACOB

Dancing with Myself

INT. WHITMAN UNIVERSITY - LB 415 - DAY

Jacob pushes the vacuum with enthusiastic gusto, its engine WHIRRING. Blank face. Mind somewhere else. "Shine On You Crazy Diamond, Pts. 6-9" by Pink Floyd blasting through his headphones.

He reaches the final bedroom and stops. Looks around the empty suite, checking for missed spots. All done. He shuts off the vacuum. Removes his headphones. Wraps them up. Pockets them. The silence is startling, like he's surrounded by emptiness.

CUT TO:

INT. 4TH FLOOR COMMON ROOM - DAY

Jacob eagerly trails Carter (handsome as always in a tight baseball tee) as he inspects the open floor plan, checking off a list.

CARTER
And the bathrooms?

JACOB
Did them first. Not much to vacuum in there. Didn't think that would be a problem.

CARTER
You wiped down the toilets too?

JACOB
Outside, inside, all around, crevice behind the seat. I can tell which suites were for the boys. Such a difference.

Carter laughs.

CARTER
That's funny.

Carter studies the glass surrounding the TV room.

JACOB
Let me know if I missed any spots.

CARTER
No, you're good dude. Holy shit.

JACOB
Thanks.

Carter checks a box on the form.

CARTER
Glad I asked you. You're way ahead of schedule.

JACOB
That's not a bad thing, right? Like am I gonna have to do it all over again in August?

CARTER
No, you'll be fine. All the summer students this year are off-campus so you'll be good as long as you clean up after yourself.

JACOB
What about your room?

Carter lets out a self-deprecating chuckle.

CARTER
I'll take care of that myself, thanks.

CUT TO:

INT. 7TH FLOOR RA OFFICE - DAY

Carter plops behind his desk, signing off on a form. Jacob stands close by.

CARTER
Any plans for the weekend?

JACOB
I just got 11/22/63 by Stephen King. Thinking of going out to Public Gardens and just plowing through it.

CARTER
Supposed to be a great day tomorrow.

JACOB
That's the idea.

Carter rips off a receipt, pausing to think.

CARTER
Isn't Pride on Sunday?

JACOB
Yeah.

CARTER
You must be looking forward to that.

JACOB
Not really.

CARTER
I thought you went every year.

JACOB
I went last year in Philly, but I don't know anything about what it's like up here. I only just turned 21. I've never been in an American bar before.

CARTER
Just Google "gay bars."

JACOB
Yeah, but just because it's a gar bar doesn't mean it's worth a damn.

CARTER
That's why there's reviews.

JACOB
Nah, I need a local's opinion, but...
(waving his hands)
I dunno. I'll think about it.

CARTER
Whatever you want, dude.

CUT TO:

INT. SUITE 710 - JACOB'S ROOM - DAY

Jacob very slowly opens his eyes. Takes a deep breath, almost disappointed. He scoots up, leans over the edge of his mattress, and pulls up his alarm clock underneath.

"12:05 PM"

Jacob puts it back with a groan. Lays back in bed, frowning with regret.

CUT TO:

BY THE BATHROOM MIRROR

Jacob fills his red canteen with sink water, avoiding eye contact with his reflection.

CUT TO:

BACK IN JACOB'S ROOM

Jacob pops the Thursday compartment on his 7-Day plastic pill strip. Places the round white pill on his tongue. Washes it down with water. Places the oval red pill next. Washes it down. Chugs more for good measure.

CUT TO:

EXT. LITTLE BUILDING - DAY

Jacob steps out onto the shaded Boston street, 11/22/63 in his hand. He heads to the building next door, THE BIG BUILDING, taps his Whitman University student ID on the scanner, and walks inside.

CUT TO:

INT. BIG BUILDING - DINING HALL - DAY

Jacob sits down with a chicken Caesar salad wrap, a side of Mac and Cheese, and a bottle of water. The rest of the dining hall (The "DH" as the kids call it) is empty. Very freaky. Quite Chernobyl.

Jacob picks up the wrap and takes a massive bite. Chews. Swallows. Deepthroats the rest of the wrap. Chews a bit more and forces it down. Cracks open the bottle of water, puts it to his lips, and glugs the entire bottle in thirty seconds, his throat gulping along, no break. Finishes. Immediately CRUSHES the plastic bottle. BURPS. Whisks the Mac and Cheese into his mouth with a plastic fork. Scrapes the last. All done.

He takes a deep breath. Stares at the garbage on his tray. Looks down at his fatty belly.

CUT TO:

EXT. PUBLIC GARDEN - DAY

The lake shimmers in the sunlight, willow trees and colorful flowers all around.

Jacob takes it all in, his back against a tree, ass in the dirt. He cracks open 11/22/63. Flips past the epigraph and all that introductory bullshit. Stares at the first page.

"Chapter 1"

Jacob looks up, thinking of something. He half-closes the book, his finger holding his place, and he stays like that, zoning out, eyes perusing the beautiful landscape. He bites the nails on his other hand.

CUT TO:

INT. WHITMAN UNIVERSITY - LB 710 - JACOB'S ROOM - DAY

Jacob cracks open his black Rhino chest, lifting the lid to reveal a HORDE OF BLU-RAY CASES perfectly organized to fit. He scans the titles briskly. Lifts a dozen or so to reveal two more tiers underneath. He scans them too, frowning.

JUMP CUT TO:

MINUTES LATER

Jacob leans back in his chair. Grabs a Dr. Pepper from the mini-fridge. Snaps its neck. Chugs the first third in one go. Returns his attention to the computer monitor on his desk, his laptop plugged in.

Lawrence of Arabia plays before him, its legendary cinematography filling every inch of the monitor, beautifully restored in 1080p from a 4K scan for its 50th Anniversary release.

Jacob slurps more of his soda, unimpressed. Maurice Jarre's score plays the same notes it did last time. Peter O'Toole says the same lines he did last time, the same way he did last time. All those classic scenes to come just as far into the runtime as they were last time.

Jacob sighs. Impulsively ejects the disc from his laptop.

CUT TO:

INT. SUITE 710 - LIVING ROOM - DUSK

Jacob lays on the couch sideways, scrolling through Vine at low volume. He sighs. Turns off his phone with a frown. Takes off his glasses. Rolls over. Fetal position.

CUT TO:

INT. SUITE 710 - JACOB'S ROOM - NIGHT

Jacob lies on his bed belly-down, legs in the air, and watches porn on his laptop.

INSERT - MOODY BACKROOM THREEWAY

A handsome WALL STREET DADDY (40) in a suit roams a dark backroom, a dozen shirtless horny guys watching him. Two hunks in particular, a BLOND (30) and a BLACK-HAIRED (28), are all over the Daddy, muscles shining with sweat. The Daddy, though outnumbered, is the one in control. He seduces the Black-Haired one especially, little by little until he's fucking him in front of the crowd.

BACK ON JACOB

Jacob studies the actors' bodies. The atmosphere. The mood lighting. The cinematography. The way the music is edited in. The director's choice of pacing. The way the different angles are more erotic than a simple tripod one-take. Jacob closes the video, bored. Opens a new one.

INSERT - FAUX COLLEGE GANGBANG

A backwards-cap wearing JOCK MUSCLE BOTTOM (27) with massive arms and a flawless ass gets double-teamed by HORNY COLLEGE BOYS (30s). The bottom eagerly takes it from both ends.

BACK ON JACOB

Jacob watches, a deep envy brewing inside him.

CUT TO:

INT. BIG BUILDING - CONVENIENCE STORE - NIGHT

Jacob places A PINT OF BEN & JERRY'S on the counter. Throws on a KING SIZE BAGGIE OF PEANUT M&M'S.

CUT TO:

INT. LITTLE BUILDING - SUITE 710 - JACOB'S ROOM - NIGHT

Jacob rips open the M&M's. Slides a couple directly into his mouth. He's watching The Graduate, already in progress:

INSERT - THE GRADUATE

It's the famous final scene. BENJAMIN BRADDOCK made it to the church in time only to find ELAINE ROBINSON kissing her groom CARL SMITH.

BENJAMIN

Oh, Jesus God. No.

Benjamin slams his hands on the glass repeatedly.

BENJAMIN (CONT'D)
E-LAINE! E-LAINE! E-LAINE! E-LAINE!

The congregation looks up in shock at Benjamin ratting the glass with tiny fists. MRS. ROBINSON watches with a devilish grin, her pissed soon-to-be-ex-husband MR. ROBINSON sitting next to her.

MR. ROBINSON
I'll take of him.

MRS. ROBINSON
(stopping him; menacing)
He's too late.

Benjamin keeps slamming his hands on the glass.

BENJAMIN
E-LAINE! E-LAINE! E-LAINE! E-LAINE!

Elaine, her eyes wide with shock, walks down the aisle toward Benjamin. She looks at her mother's stern stuttering. Her father's. Her groom's angry face. She looks up at Benjamin.

ELAINE
(screams)
BEEEENNNNN!

Benjamin widens his eyes. Bolts down the stairs. Mr. Robinson's waiting for him, fists up.

MR. ROBINSON
You crazy punk!

Mr. Robinson lunges for him. Benjamin hops over the railing, punches Mr. Robinson, hits him with the back of his elbow, knocks Carl and several other guests like dominos.

Elaine sneaks through in time. Mrs. Robinson grabs her arm, spinning her around, desperate.

MRS. ROBINSON
Elaine! It's too late!

ELAINE
NOT FOR ME!

Mrs. Robinson SMACKS the shit out of Elaine. Twice.

BACK ON JACOB

Jacob snorts, mouth full of M&M's.

JACOB
Same.

He crumples the M&M's wrapper. Tosses it into the empty Ben & Jerry's pint.

CUT TO:

IN THE SHOWER

Jacob rises Prell out of his hair, zoning out. Blurry streams of hot water run off his hair, loud SPLATTERING onto the drain, soapy water spinning around and out.

CUT TO:

IN THE HALLWAY

Jacob steps out of the bathroom, dripping wet and naked. Puts on his glasses. Waddles to the front door. Opens it.

CUT TO:

INT. FILM IMMERSION - CONTINUOUS

Jacob passes suite after suite, a trail of wet footprints behind him, directly toward a door marked 717. He stops outside. KNOCKS three times.

CUT TO:

INSIDE SUITE 717

Carter lifts his head, confused. He's wearing a white tank top and boxers. He stands, walks to the door and opens it. A nude Jacob smiles casually.

JACOB
Hey.

CARTER
Hey dude. What's up?

Jacob steps into Carter's room, his dick already hard.

JACOB
I just thought... what the hell, you know?

They simply look at each other, Carter silently processing Jacob's naked body.

JACOB (CONT'D)
Sorry about the flab.

CARTER
Don't be.

JACOB
You're just so... you know.

CARTER
I know.

Carter steps closer to Jacob, his breath fogging Jacob's glasses.

CARTER (CONT'D)
What took you so long?

JACOB
I don't fucking know.

They kiss passionately, Carter's big hairy arms wrapping around Jacob, squeezing him tight. Jacob caresses Carter's face, his hair, his shoulders, touching everything he can. He moans, overwhelmed all over.

SMASH BACK TO:

INSIDE THE SHOWER

Jacob climaxes into the drain, his body tensing, left arm supporting himself against the shower wall. His breath slows, brain returning to normal. Pure pathetic shame creeps in. He suddenly remembers where he is. Who he is. Everything he ain't.

Jacob sinks to the floor of the shower and sits.

Just sits.

SLOW FADE TO BLACK.

INT. SUITE 710 - JACOB'S ROOM - DAY

Jacob POPS open the Friday compartment on his pill strip.

JUMP CUT TO:

A COUPLE HOURS LATER

Jacob types away on his laptop, adding to his new screenplay. Side 3 of Led Zeppelin's Physical Graffiti plays on the turntable. Jacob stops to stretch. Glances out the window.

A HANDSOME MAN (mid-20s) talks to his HOT FRIEND (mid-20s) outside the Boylston T stop across the street. Tight clothes over fit physiques, the Hot Friend in a baseball cap, the Handsome Man with styled brown hair.

Jacob wipes his glasses. Scoots toward the window for a closer look. The men have a decent berth between them, a sign of mutual heterosexuality, maintaining eye contact with full-body ease. Jacob's focus volleys between their mute lips, the way HAL does in <u>2001: A Space Odyssey</u>. He wonders what they're talking about. He's jealous again. Not of their bodies, of something else. Something he can't quite place.

A THIRD DUDE (mid-20s) races across the street to join them. He fistbumps the Handsome Man, the Hot Friend, smiles all around. They head into the T station together, just in time no doubt to catch the next Green Line to who-knows-where.

Jacob's lips purse. He SLAMS his laptop shut.

CUT TO:

INT. SUITE 717 - DAY

KNOCK-KNOCK-KNOCK. Carter lifts his head, confused. He's wearing a white tank top and boxers. He stands, walks to the door and opens it, revealing a fully clothed Jacob.

JACOB
Hey.

CARTER
Hey dude. What's up?

JACOB
What do you use in your hair?

CUT TO:

INT. FENWAY TARGET - DAY

Jacob stops in the men's styling aisle. Double-checks the picture on his phone. Compares it to the dozens of products on the shelf. Finds a match: American Crew Molding Clay. He picks up a couple jars and heads for checkout.

CUT TO:

INT. GREEN LINE TRAIN - DAY

Jacob sits on the T, the car wobbling. Googles "Likes Boys T-Shirt." Clicks the Shopping tab. Finds a white shirt with "LIKES BOYS" in big, thick black letters on Get-A-Tee.com for $29.99. Jacob selects XL. Adds it to the cart. Scrolls down to the shipping options:

"Standard Shipping: Free (Friday, June 17)"

"Expedited Shipping: $4.99 (Monday, June 13)"

"One-Day Delivery: $32.99 (Saturday, June 11)"

Jacob hesitates. He taps One-Day Delivery and checks out before he could change his mind.

CUT TO:

INT. WHITMAN UNIVERSITY - SUITE 710 - JACOB'S ROOM - DAY

Jacob POPS open the Saturday compartment on his 7-Day plastic pill strip.

CUT TO:

IN FRONT OF THE BATHROOM MIRROR

Jacob picks up a jar of molding clay. Unscrews the lid. Picks up a wad with his fingers. Smears it across his damp hair. Stops to look. Cringes. He flicks it around some more, making it worse.

He looks at you through the mirror.

JACOB
(breaking fourth wall)
Probably should've dried it first.

CUT TO:

IN THE SHOWER

Jacob runs hot water over his head, scrubbing the gunk out of his hair.

CUT TO:

BACK TO THE BATHROOM MIRROR

Jacob's hair dry this time, he runs a smaller amount of molding clay just up the front. Flicks it. He frowns at the aggressively sharp spike. Makes disappointed eye contact with you.

CUT TO:

INSIDE JACOB'S ROOM

Jacob watches a YouTube tutorial titled "How to Give Yourself a Fauxhawk," his hair still frozen at a 90-degree angle.

CUT TO:

IN THE SHOWER

Jacob shampoos again.

CUT TO:

BACK TO THE BATHROOM MIRROR

Jacob eases the molding clay into dry hair. Flicks it about, light and gentle. Steps back. Stares at himself in the mirror.

JACOB
Holy shit.

Jacob grins, exposing his gunky teeth. Instantly frowns. Looks down at his electric toothbrush, bone dry for almost a year.

JUMP CUT TO:

SECONDS LATER

Jacob scrubs furiously, bloody toothpaste lather dribbling out of his mouth.

CUT TO:

INSIDE JACOB'S ROOM

Jacob scrolls through the Reddit comments to his question on r/askgaybros: "What are the best gay bars in Boston?" Where are the non-sarcastic responses?

His iPhone dings. Jacob taps the email app.

"PACKAGE NOTIFICATION"

He jumps to his feet.

CUT TO:

INT. LITTLE BUILDING - MAIL ROOM - DAY

Jacob hands the MAIL MAN (60s) his Student ID. The Mail Man struggles to read the surname.

MAIL MAN
An-drezz-juh?

JACOB
Andrezj.

The Mail Man looks at the ID again, confused.

MAIL MAN
Like Andre the Giant?

JACOB
Like Andre the Giant.

The Mail Man hands the ID back.

MAIL MAN
Sorry.

JACOB
Tell me about it.

CUT TO:

IN THE ELEVATOR

Jacob rips open the package, revealing A WHITE T-SHIRT WITH BIG BLACK LETTERS:

"LIKES BOYS"

Jacob beams. No misprints, no errors, the right size. He hugs the shirt as tight as he can.

CUT TO:

INT. SUITE 710 - JACOB'S ROOM - NIGHT

Jacob hangs the shirt in his closet. Caresses the fabric one last time before closing the door.

He grabs his clock. Sets the alarm for 8:00 AM. Strips his clothes. Removes his glasses. Slides under the covers. Smiles. Flicks off the light.

JUMP CUT TO:

THE NEXT DAY

The alarm beeps. Jacob slams the clock. Slides out of bed. Puts his glasses on. Pops open the Sunday compartment of his pill strip.

CUT TO:

IN FRONT OF THE BATHROOM MIRROR

Jacob glides the molding clay into his hair. He compares his reflection with a candid photo he secretly took of Carter Jackson and his frat brothers eating in the dining hall. Jacob looks back at the mirror. He really did it.

JACOB
Eureka.

Jacob spritzes Unpredictable Pour Homme on his neck and wrists.

CUT TO:

INT. FILM IMMERSION - DAY

Jacob steps out of Suite 710 in his "LIKES BOYS" shirt. He stops at the sound of television down the hall.

CUT TO:

INSIDE THE TV ROOM

Carter sits in a chair, distraught, his eyes glued to CNN. Jacob knocks on the glass door and pushes in.

JACOB
What did Trump say this time?

CARTER
They're still talking about Orlando.

Jacob freezes.

JACOB
What happened in Orlando?

Carter turns up the volume.

REPORTER (V.O.)
Forty-nine dead, fifty-three wounded. The motive of the gunman is yet unclear.

JACOB
Where did it happen?

CARTER
A gay club. Pulse.

Jacob stares at the screen. They're showing pictures of the deceased, their names being read one at a time. So many young guys. And they all looked so happy.

Jacob can't speak.

CARTER (CONT'D)
It's the deadliest mass-shooting in American history.

JACOB
Really?

CARTER
That's what they said.

Jacob keeps watching, a great unease overwhelming him.

REPORTER (V.O.)
President Obama released a statement, calling the shooting an "act of hate" and an "act of terror." Senator Clinton tweeted: "Woke up to hear the devastating news from FL. As we wait for more information, my thoughts are with those affected by this horrific act." Republican presidential nominee Donald Trump tweeted his reaction: "Horrific incident in FL. Praying for all the victims & their families. When will this stop? When will we get tough, smart & vigilant?"

CARTER
Fucking asshole.

Jacob swallows awkwardly.

JACOB
I better get going. The parade starts in an hour.

Carter squints in weary disbelief.

CARTER
You're still going?

Jacob hesitates.

JACOB
I dunno.

CARTER
I don't think I can get any work done today. Why don't you stay in? We can watch something.

Jacob stares at Carter sitting there, muscled arm flung behind him, waiting on his response.

JACOB
I think I've been cooped in here long enough.

Carter nods.

CARTER
Just be careful, alright?

JACOB
Nothing's gonna happen.

Carter sighs, unsure. Jacob briefly glances at the screen.

JACOB (CONT'D)
I'm not letting the terrorist win.

Jacob reluctantly leaves the TV room, heading for the elevator.

WHALE

Catechism

Whale enters the confessional and kneels. The Priest motions the sign of the cross. "In the name of the Father, the Son, and the Holy Spirit, Amen."

```
                    WHALE
      Amen.
```

Whale hesitates.

```
                    WHALE (CONT'D)
      I'm sorry, Father. I don't do confession often. I
      don't really remember what I'm supposed to say next.
```

"There should be a card right next to the grate.

Whale strains to see in the dark.

```
                    WHALE
      Ah, there it is.
              (reading)
      "Bless me, Father, for I have sinned. It's been..."
```

Whale pauses to calculate.

```
                    WHALE (CONT'D)
      "...nine months since my last confession."
```

"Tell me your sins."

```
                    WHALE
      I am in this internship with a really famous producer
      and he's an awful person. He insults me at work. He
      calls me stupid using, you know, other words. He
      doesn't teach me be a better worker in my field. I
      think he's trying to toughen me up, you know? To weed
      out the weaklings. I don't want to lose my chance at
      the job, but today he really let me have it and I'm
      starting to realize that I'm not gonna get the job
      unless I become the kind of person he wants me to be.
```

"Do you have anything to confess?" the Priest blurts. His impatience gives Whale pause.

```
                    WHALE
      No, I don't want to. That's why I'm here.
```

The Priest sighs. "Normally I have this conversation in my office. This is the only time we hold confessions all week."

```
                    WHALE
      I'm sorry. I don't wanna hold you up and keep
      everyone waiting. I just... I need help.
```

"In that case..." The Priest shifts in his seat, his frock rustling. "We are God's imperfect creatures. We all sin. It's in our nature. That is why the truly devout, our monks and our nuns, isolate themselves from the world in celibacy, silence, lifelong dedication to the Lord. The rest of us cannot avoid sinning. It's all around us. God knows this. All He wants for us to resist its control."

```
                    WHALE
      I refuse to believe that.
```

"You do?"

```
                    WHALE
      We're not supposed to break God's commandments. There
      has to be a way for normal people to be good without
      being a monk or a nun, right?
```

"Do you know what sin is?"

```
                    WHALE
      Of course.
```

"And do you consider the Bible to be an accurate compilation of what constitutes a sin?" Whale hesitates.

```
                    WHALE
      No.
```

"Why not?"

```
                    WHALE
      Because the Bible says being gay is wrong. I'm not
      ashamed of it. I'll never confess for that.
```

"But the Bible doesn't say being gay is wrong. They didn't know about sexual orientation in ancient times. They simply equated men copulating with other men as they would masturbation, self-mutilation, rape. All you need to do is to walk through West Hollywood to know being gay is really about love."

```
                    WHALE
      During the day, at least.
               (pause)
      I don't think you're answering my question.
```

"The Bible is the Word of Lord. The God that cast Adam and Eve out of Eden and unleashed the Flood and sent the plagues unto Pharaoh is a vengeful God, a merciless God. And the God that sent us His son, the one telling us to love one another as they love themselves, to honor our parents and our maker, to respect the world around us, not to covet what we don't have, to forgive even our worst enemy, that's the same God. Did something change? Were both sides there all along? We have no answers for such questions. All we have is what we see around us every day."

```
                    WHALE
      What are you saying? That the Bible doesn't matter?
```

"Of course it matters," The Priest replies. "But when you take into account the world as it is today, with all we know about the universe, medicine, science, the Bible is losing its relevance. Modernity has tested the strength of God's rules. It used to be that missing Sunday Mass was a serious sin, but that was made for a time when people didn't work on Sunday had no excuse otherwise. On the other hand, we charge interest on loans and pay disproportionate taxes. Divorce, abortion, masturbation, pornography, and drug abuse are all approaching normalcy. Our own priests have fallen into complacency and abuse. And there is even talk about the future of the Vatican's negative stance toward same-sex marriage. Society is modifying Christianity when it always used to be the other way around." The Priest pauses to gather his thoughts. "The fact that the values of our world are drifting away from God's written teachings means one of two things is happening. The first is that Satan is winning and God's power is weakening among men, which is why the men and women that spew hate, encourage division, and live a greedy, selfish life on the backs of others are being rewarded. The second is that God hasn't lost control at all, that this shift is merely a test, a way for us to understand what God wants without being told. That's what faith is. That's why we call it the mystery of faith. True faith is believing without answers, acting without guidance except what we ourselves know to be right. Is a man shooting heroin a sinner if he is ashamed, if he's simply a good man brought down by others to a dark place? He is committing a sin, sure, and it used to be that he wouldn't be considered worthy of God's love, but now we know there's more to the story than that."

Whale ponders the Priest's words.

```
                WHALE
Do you really believe it's the second one?
```

The Priest hesitates. "Let's just say, I'd rather not believe the first." He discreetly looks at his watch. "Did I answer your question?"

Whale leaves the booth. Standing outside is a man with a cross frown. He huffs at Whale as he enters the confessional. Taking his place outside the booth is an equally impatient woman, possibly a waitress, and behind her is a young man in a suit, and an old man with a walker, and a man with bad teeth in a stained T-shirt, and another man, and another woman, more, more, more as Whale goes down the line, the parade of rush hour sinners stretching outside and around the corner.

DREW

Made in America

Larry Lin sits on a loveseat outside the screening room, phone clutched with both hands. Mr. Lawrence isn't okay. His boss of seventeen years has been spiraling out of control for four months now. If Larry doesn't make the call, he's only gonna end up hurting someone. He's already hurt himself. Mr. Lawrence might hate him at first, but it's for his own good. He'll understand that eventually. He always does.

Larry slides open his phone. Calls Alan Lovelace.

"Hello?" a scratchy voice answers.

"Did I wake you?"

"Yeah."

"Oh God, I'm sorry. I didn't think you'd be—"

"It's okay. It's only me wanting to sleep in for once in my goddamn life." Alan chuckles.

Larry forces out a chuckle too. "Yeah, I'm sorry."

"What is it, Lar?"

"There's a bit of a problem here."

Sheets rustle over the line. "What kind of problem?"

Larry hesitates. "Drew had a bit of a meltdown just now."

"How bad?"

"Public."

Alan sighs. "I see."

"Just the crew on *Glory*. I have them contained. I'll make 'em sign NDAs soon as I'm done with you."

"I take it you want me to tell Theo?"

"Don't go into too many details, just..." Larry slams his eyes shut. Sneezes.

6,000 miles away, a semi-naked Alan Lovelace says, "Bless you." He's in his forties. Tall. Thin. Gaunt face. Large bags under his eyes. Premature gray hair.

"Thanks."

Alan grabs the yellow pad next to his King bed and clicks a pen. "Start at the beginning." He jots everything down. Where it happened. The names of everyone there. Everything that broke. "Could've been worse," Alan insists. "You should see the rooms."

Silence on the line. "Have you?"

"After? No. Just stories, you know? Carlos."

"I'm afraid to look."

"Don't. We're not supposed to."

"Alan?"

"Yeah?"

"Is it true, um..." Larry hesitates. "The cleanup guys. Does Mr. Landreth really—?"

"Deport them? Yeah. All the time."

Larry's breath fuzzes the line. "That's fucking depressing."

"Yeah? Guess who has to make the call."

Larry stops talking. So does Alan. They just sit there, their minds thinking the same thing.

"Just break it easy to Mr. Landreth," Larry says. "I don't want Mr. Lawrence's trial to end early because I snitched."

"I'll wait till breakfast to tell him. Four hours or so. Call me if you change your mind, okay?"

"Okay. Try to get some sleep."

"Hardly. Ciao."

"Seeya." Larry hangs up first.

Alan locks his phone. Looks down at the pad. Rereads it. "Yikes," he whispers. He looks around his hotel room, lit only by the yellow lamplight. He gets up. Slides open the blackout curtains to reveal more black outside. No sun for hours. Just cold skyscrapers. Alan frowns. For three weeks now they've been lying around the Four Seasons Beijing, pretending to be 100 miles away at Liu Míng's UniTopia Pictures in the middle of a six-week contract dispute. He doesn't wanna know why Theo's lying to Drew. It's not his business. He gets paid six figures not to ask questions. The only thing he wants is a good night's sleep. Just one.

Four hours later. No callback from Larry. Alan grabs the bedside phone and dials 321. The phone rings and rings. Eight dial tones. Alan hangs up. Grabs his cell.

The lobby cafeteria is full of Western businessmen and their Chinese associates standing in the breakfast burrito line. Finally stepping up to claim his prize, his tummy rumbling from the smell alone, is Theodore Landreth, forty years old, a man that wears expensive suits, drives incredibly vain sports cars, trains himself to have a subtle vaguely European accent, and invests thousands of dollars into a convincing toupee collection so he'd appear so dashing, so intimidating, that everyone in Hollywood and China would forget he was shorter than a Girl Scout.

Theo carries his breakfast burrito tray through the open-air garden dining area and sits across from Liu Míng himself. Late thirties. Permanent scowl. Alarmingly square head. The dude's a walking Thwomp.

"Took you long enough," Míng murmurs. "I already finished."

"Shut up." Theo grabs his burrito with two hands, tongue salivating for some eggies, just as his cell phone rings. Theo throws the burrito down with a scowl. "Goddammit," he mutters, swiping. "What is it, Alan? I'm busy." He listens, his bitterness vanishing. "I see."

Míng looks at Theo. Something's definitely wrong.

"Who called you?" Theo accidentally makes eye contact with Míng. Looks away. "That bad, huh?" He scratches above his eyebrow. "Thanks. No, it's better you did. Thank you." Theo hangs up. "Fuck you, Alan. My breakfast is cold now."

"What happened?" Míng asks.

Theo picks up the burrito and takes a lukewarm bite. "Why aren't there microwaves? They have them everywhere in the States."

"That's not classy."

"I thought you guys don't believe in classes."

Míng doesn't laugh. Not even a smile. "What did Drew do?"

"Can't I eat my breakfast first?"

"Just tell me."

Theo throws the burrito down again. "He had a bit of a meltdown in the screening room. That's all."

"Public?"

"Yes." Theo hesitates. "And he broke the vase you gave me."

Míng stares, his blood boiling. "The one my grandmother carved for you in the Nanjing mountains."

"Oh my God, please don't make this a thing."

"Theo, that porcelain was inlaid with real ivory! Do you have any idea how many elephants she killed to make that?! What a pain in the ass it was to get it through customs?!"

"I get it."

Míng shakes his head. "You put a priceless vase that could've been on display in the Louvre in your cinema room?"

"The best one. For the biggest projects."

"In your *cinema room*."

Theo puts his hands together with a genuine smile. "Míng, your grandma's vase was the greatest birthday gift I ever received. Unbelievably gorgeous. Beautiful. I put it in a room I visit frequently because that's just how much I love looking at it." Theo holds up a hand. "*Loved.*"

Míng sighs harshly. "This just keeps getting worse and worse."

"Don't worry. I've got everything's under control."

"No." Míng shakes his head. "I've had enough. End it today."

"I can't."

"Why not?"

"Because I told Drew he'd be man of the house six weeks. Now stop pestering me."

Míng glares. "He broke my grandmother's vase."

"Again with the vase."

"He had a violent meltdown in front of producers. He's ruining projects. He's not making the right decisions fast enough. Problems are festering that he's ignoring. Every day you leave him in charge is costing you money, money you're gonna need when something drastic happens, and something drastic *always* happens."

"You're not our boss anymore," Theo retorts. "You run your business your way and I'll run mine."

"I'm not allowed to, remember?"

"He's too fucking smart. We can't leave any crumbs."

"I can't even go on my computer and manage my company during the fucking *busy season*?"

"We're supposed to be in a contract dispute."

"They don't have contract disputes in March?"

"If I let him run the place in a slow month, he might actually get the hang of it."

"I'm not staying here another three weeks because of a fucking pinkie promise."

"You didn't have a problem agreeing to it when you needed my signature."

Míng hesitates. "You never put it in writing."

Theo points a challenging finger. "I have the right to void the whole thing at my discretion. *That's* in writing. So if you want to leave now, I won't stop you, but don't expect the deal to go through."

Míng glares off. "You know what most people do to avoid promoting someone they don't want to promote? They say no."

"You and I both know how damaging that 'no' can be."

Míng lowers his eyes. "That's different," he murmurs.

"I don't think so."

"Fathers and sons have a completely different set of expectations. Drew is not your son. He's not your family. He's a friend at best. Friends can be replaced. Employees can be replaced. You can't replace blood."

"I'm not replacing Drew," Theo states. "I've invested almost twenty years into that man. I taught him everything he knows about the business. He's an extension of myself at this point. The reason Not That Nutty's still here, the reason it works — so well in fact that *you* came to *me* with a ten year co-production deal — is because I'm number 1 and Drew's number 2. When we were both number 1, it was a shitshow. But Drew is the best worker bee anyone could ever ask for. He might be an overly complicated computer program you need to take a fucking class to understand, but I took that class. I know how to program him. It's a pain in the ass but he can do your job better than you ever could. He just has a bit of ego problem. If he doesn't like where he's at, he tries to change, and because he can't go down, he can only go up." Theo shrugs. "I'm just showing Drew how lucky he has it having a best friend as a boss. He'll realize I'm right, that he's better off staying Head of Production, and everything will be exactly the way it was before, but the only way that's ever gonna happen is if it's his idea. If I end the trial run now with three weeks left on the books, he'll blame me for depriving him a chance to redeem himself and this will only repeat itself and THAT'S when it gets expensive."

Míng stares blankly.

Theo nods. "Now please let me eat my cold-ass burrito." He peels the tortilla off the plate and takes a big bite.

Míng watches him eat with alarming focus.

Theo blinks. Swallows. "What?"

"Did I ever tell you about a man I met about..." Míng bobs his head. "Mmm... sixteen, seventeen years ago? I dined with him in Los Angeles. Now *that* was a man. Strong. Level-headed. Didn't give too shits about what needed to be done. You see, he wasn't burdened by conventional morality and maudlin sentimentality."

Theo sits back, his head bowed, uneasy.

"You know why I chose that man to run my Hollywood satellite?" Míng asks softly, his cruel undertones hitting Theo where it hurts. "Because *that man* was the greatest fucking producer I ever met."

Theo looks up, trying with all his might to appear unfazed. "Míng…"

"What the FUCK happened to you, Theo?"

"Nothing's happened to me."

"Not from where I'm sitting." Míng scoffs, leaning back, resting his arm on the top of his metal chair. "You know what I think? I think you let Drew change *you*. You taught him the business while he taught you how to be a pussy."

Theo lets out a despaired sigh. "I can't—"

"He's just an employee, Theo. An employee that's bleeding your company dry with his flaunting and unprofessional candor."

"I have a responsibility—"

"You have a responsibility to your company. To your investors. To your partners. What good is a ten-year co-production deal if you're not even gonna be around in ten years? This affects me now, my interests, and I say Drew Lawrence is a loose cannon. We cannot give Oscar Blitz any material he could use against us. That'll be the end of everything."

"I know. You're right. Just—"

"No Head of Production should be this high maintenance," Míng says, jabbing the table with a pale index finger. "Maybe he was great once, but he sure isn't anymore. You better off get rid of him and make Larry your Head of Production."

"Larry?"

"Doesn't even have to be Larry. Anyone's better than Drew at this point. Just get rid of him." Míng grabs his glass of water. "If you don't, I will."

Theo chuckles. "You're gonna fire *my* Head of Production?"

"Who said anything about firing?" Míng drinks the entire glass in one go.

Theo furrows his brow, his blood tingling. "Then what are you talking about?"

"Oh please." Míng places the empty glass on the table. "You know what I'm talking about. Just say the word and I'll call my guy in LA. He'll do the rest."

Theo can't breathe. "I'm good, thanks."

Míng furrows his brow a bit. "Out of curiosity, what exactly do you have a problem with? It'll never come back to you. I would know."

"Oh, you would?"

"You don't believe me?"

Theo looks down at his breakfast burrito. "No, I do, I just..." He pauses. "I dunno, I just don't see the point."

"What are you afraid of?"

"I'm not afraid of anything. I just don't do that."

"Neither did I, until I did. It's the only secure option, Theo. No hassle. No stress. Barely any money."

Theo's lips flutter. "I mean..."

"The only reason I can see you being against it is because you're afraid of some God."

"You know I don't believe in that."

"Then what's the problem? If you don't believe in God and there's no legal consequences, why the hell wouldn't you?"

Theo runs a tongue along across his teeth. "Because I'm an American. We don't kill our enemies anymore. We gaslight the shit out of them. It's more economical that way. We might not have invented the movies, but we sure as hell invented that. *With* a movie no less. What's more American than that?"

Míng stares with cold eyes. "He sure does a lot of coke though."

"Yeah, so what?"

Míng nods, casually looking off. "And he drinks a lot."

"Yeah."

"And he's on steroids now."

Theo hesitates. "I never told you that."

"And he fucks a lot. And works out a lot. That's quite a lot for a man his age. I supposed he can have heart attack in, oh..." Míng shrugs with a smile. "Twenty minutes."

Theo stares for a long time. "That'd be quite the coincidence, considering we're talking about it right now."

"He doesn't have a family."

"Yes he does."

"Not like mine though."

Theo shakes his head. "No one on Earth has a family like yours."

Míng smirks. "Let's just say it happens. Would *anyone* miss him? A man that fucks and takes and burns everything he touches? You can't mourn a man like that."

"I could," Theo says, scratching the back of his head.

"But would you avenge him?"

"I thought you said it was a heart attack."

Míng hesitates. "Something else then." He pauses. "Hypothetically."

"Oh, *hypothetically*!" Theo says with delight. "Well then yes, of course I would."

Míng wipes his mouth with a napkin. "If you were still the Old Theo, I'd be shitting my pants right now." He stands up. "But you're not."

Theo forces a chuckle. "I'm serious. I'll do it."

Míng squints. "Sure, Jan." He walks away.

Theo jumps up. Races after him. "Where do you think you're going?"

"I'm going back to my room. I gotta make a long-distance phone call."

Theo grabs Míng's left arm with both hands. "Wait! C'mon!"

Míng instantly whips his arm away. "You know what I want." He turns. Quickly spins back. "And for the record, the co-production deal was mutual! I never crawled to you! How dare you imply otherwise!" Míng storms into the lobby, leaving Theo a shivering, pathetic mess.

6,000 miles away, Drew Lawrence speeds down the I-10, weaving in between cars with his intimidating red Jeep Wrangler, convertible top down, warm afternoon wind punching him in the face. Other cars honk in anger at the speed demon cutting them off, that asshole with the JEEPGUY license plate.

Drew veers off and catches Route 1 at Santa Monica just as his cell phone rings. He accepts the call with his steering wheel. "Drew Lawrence," he shouts over the wind.

"What the FUCK is going on over there?!" Theo yells through the Jeep's speakers.

Drew's heart skips a beat. "I don't know what you're talking about."

"Trashing the screening room?! Screaming at the producers?! Breaking my ivory vase?!

Drew opens his mouth, too stunned to formulate words.

"What, you didn't think I'd find out about that?!" Theo asks.

"How did you—?"

"We talked about this! If you wanna vent, use one of the conference rooms! ALONE!"

Drew slows behind standstill traffic. "Larry told you?"

"You better fucking hope it was Larry! What the fuck is wrong with you?!"

"I-I'm sorry, I just—!"

"It's over, Drew. You failed. I'm heading home. Seeya Monday."

"Wait!" Drew hollers, his blood running cold. "No! No! No! No! No! That's not fair!"

"Fair? You wanna know what's not fair? The fact that I have to come back in the middle of negotiations because you couldn't do a single fucking thing right!"

"I can still do this!" Drew cries at the top of his lungs.

"No, you can't! Do you have any idea how embarrassed I am? I had to apologize to Míng for you breaking his grandmother's vase! She carved it in the fucking Nanjing mountains! She actually killed elephants for that ivory! I loved that fucking vase! You fucking destroyed it!"

"Theo, wait!"

"If this deal doesn't go through, I'm holding you personally fucking responsible!"

"Just give me another chance!"

"Why should I?! Do you have any concept as to how close you got to fucking everything up for us?! If Oscar ever got his hands on this, it's over! You hear me?! OVER!"

"They're not gonna talk! They signed NDAs!"

"SO DID SNOWDEN, ASSHOLE!" Theo hollers. "I don't care about the drugs. I don't care about the booze, or the boys. You do you. Get things done your way. But you cannot, CANNOT, give anyone a reason to run to Oscar Blitz! I thought I could trust you with that kind of responsibility."

"You can!"

"CLEARLY I CAN'T!"

"SHUT UP!" Drew shouts, a blood-curdling scream. "I SAID I CAN DO IT! I CAN FUCKING DO IT! JUST TRUST ME, OKAY?!" Drew slams on his horn at the traffic jam. "FUCKING MOVE IT!"

"Fuck you, pal!" someone yells back.

Drew slams the gas and gets on the shoulder, shifting the gearshift into third. He speeds down the 1. "I swear to God, buddy, I can fucking do it!" he begs, his voice pathetically wavering. "It was just one time. I've learned from it. I'm just a bit dysfunctional right now, okay? I'm just really sick right now from the... from the... you know the-the stuff, the stuff Shayne gives me, you know, and it's fucking me up, and I'm hot and cold and I'm just pissed off all the time, and I can't even go five minutes without wanting to blow my goddammed brains out!"

Theo freezes at the raw anger in Drew's voice. "This is what you wanted, isn't it?"

"FUCK YOU!" Drew screams. He slams on the breaks, smacking the gearshift into neutral. He re-shifts back into second and cuts across two lanes just in time for the Marina del Rey exit.

"I WANT TO DO IT! I CAN DO IT! JUST TRUST ME, OKAY?! PLEASE! JUST LET ME FINISH THE TRIAL! I'LL PROVE IT TO YOU!"

Theo closes his eyes. Rubs his temple. "Drew, I can't."

"COME ON! TWO-THIRDS, REMEMBER?! IT'S ONLY BEEN HALF! JUST GIVE ME ANOTHER WEEK! I'LL MAKE IT UP! I *PROMISE!*

Theo swallows, his mouth dry. He lowers his head. "Drew..."

"Please, buddy, come on, I... I need this. I promise it'll never happen again."

Theo takes a deep breath. Shakes his head. "I can't take that chance."

Drew slams his eyes shut. Slams his head back against the headrest. And again. Over and over, growling angrily.

Theo can hear the thumping leather and guttural pain emanating from Drew. He moves the phone away from his ear. Stares at a spot on the ground. Focuses on it. Tunes out Drew as much as he can. The thumps slow. The wailing settles down, Theo gently places the phone back to his ear. "You finished?

Drew just sits there, back flush against the seat, cars rushing by, desperately calming himself down.

"See, that's what I'm talking about," Theo says calmly. "Even if I was gonna give you another chance before, why the hell would I now? A grown man having a tantrum on the side of the road like a fucking child."

Drew is too exhausted to say any more.

Theo licks his lips. Moves to hang up. Puts it back to his ear. "Drew?"

"Yeah."

Theo rubs his temple. "I'm sorry for putting you in this position."

Drew swallows. "I thought I..."

"I know you did, buddy. I know. You just can't do everything."

"I know."

"I didn't mean to be so mean about it. I was just so convinced you could, you know? I'm just so disappointed."

Drew closes his eyes. "Me too."

"Maybe it's for the best it happened like this. I don't want to force you to do anything you can't, and now you know you can't." Theo pauses. "Right?"

Drew's lips flutter. "I'm so sorry."

"Don't sweat it, bro. I'll be back in the office Monday, and everything will be back to the way it was."

Drew opens his eyes a bit. "I don't want go back to the way it was."

Theo hesitates. "But you're so good at it."

"I was just working hard to show you I could be CEO again. That's the only reason."

Theo frowns. "I don't want to lose you, man. You're too valuable."

Drew sighs. "Thanks."

"I'll see you Monday, alright?"

"Yeah."

"Bye." Theo hangs up. Scrolls through his phone, his fingers twitching as he looks for Míng's number. He finds it. Hesitates touching it. Scrolls back up. Taps Alan's number instead. "Alan! Call Míng immediately and tell him he can go home! NOW!" Theo hangs up. Slouches in his chair. Painfully replays Drew's reaction.

Theo inches down the hall to Room 321. Taps the sensor. Opens the door. He's about to gather his things in the sitting area when he hears metallic jangling coming from inside his bedroom. Muffled cries. Theo huffs with a groan. Can this day get any worse?

Theo opens his bedroom door to reveal a naked woman, very thin, very pale, spread-eagled on the bed, ass-up, blindfolded, wrists and ankles locked onto spreader bars. "Please!" she cries with a pitiable whimper. "Let me go! I just wanna go home!"

Theo stands at the threshold, taking in the sight with a sharp erection pressing against his metal fly.

"God, please!" the woman sobs, straining against her restraints. "Don't—

"Peanut brittle, Suyin."

Suyin instantly stops sobbing. "Why? What's wrong?"

"Drew's having a nervous breakdown. I have to leave tonight."

"Aww, Drewie?" Suyin coos. "Poor guy."

Theo sits on the bed beside the bound and spreadeagled Suyin. "I'm sorry we have to cut this short."

"Guess I waxed and starved myself for nothing, huh?"

"I'm still paying you for the full day."

"I sure hope so." Suyin rattles her restraints. "Can you let me out of here now?"

"Yeah," Theo mumbles. He pulls out the tiny steel key. Slides it into the lock on her left wrist. Stops. "Suyin?" he asks, pulling the key out.

Suyin rattles again. Everything's still locked. "Yeah?"

Theo sits, facing forward again. "You and I've known each other for a while now, right?"

"Yeah."

"Don't tell anyone this."

"Who am I gonna tell?"

Theo hesitates. "Míng was gonna assassinate Drew."

Suyin frowns a bit. "All the way out here? How?"

"He knows a guy, apparently." Theo shakes his head. "I almost lost him."

"Are you..." Suyin swallows nervously. "I mean, you don't seem pretty fazed. Does he do this a lot?"

"I'm not shocked, really. I've heard stories. Rumors, you know, but..." Theo purses his lips. "I just never thought I'd be on the receiving end of it."

"I thought you said Drew was."

"I threatened to retaliate. If he's willing to kill Drew over a broken vase and an extra three weeks in the Four Seasons, why wouldn't he go after me for standing up to him? He clearly doesn't trust me anymore." Theo looks down at his hands. "I'm getting worried, Suyin. Míng and I just signed a co-production deal. If my business starts suffering, it's gonna drag UniTopia down with it. One day Míng might just see me more valuable dead than alive."

"I know you like Drew, but..." Suyin shrugs, her chains jangling. "Sounds like you're better off without him, honestly."

Theo frowns. "I've never been without him before. I don't have anyone else. No friends. Míng has a family. I don't even have that. Nothing to scream about at least." He pauses. "Drew's all I have. And now I'm scared and I can't even talk to him about it. I can't tell him the real reason I went out here because he'll never forgive me. I can't tell him about Míng because Míng might just find out. I really shouldn't even be telling you."

Suyin takes a deep breath. "What happened to Drew? Is he okay?"

"He'll make it through. He's a tough guy."

"Do you have any idea what caused the breakdown?"

"Me."

"You can't blame yourself."

"This time I can. It was all me. I orchestrated it."

Suyin hesitates. "What do you mean you orchestrated it?"

"Ever since he got back from Boston last summer he's been wanting to be equal partner. When I ran out of excuses he'd buy, I said the next time I was out of the country, I'd let him take over as a sort of trial run. If he thought he was ready, I'd make him co-CEO. I was never gonna give him veto power. No way. We work so much better as a team." Theo pauses. "But I know Drew by heart, so I decided to make it so that he'd never want to be CEO of anything anywhere ever again."

Suyin rattles her restraints.

"Just a moment," Theo says. "I started with the coke. He was already hooked on it, it would've been so much harder if he wasn't, but he only used on weekends, so I started encouraging him about four months ago to start using at work. Little comments. How cool he'd look having a sugar bowl of coke on his desk. He's super insecure. Any mention of the word 'badass' he does it. Then I moved on to the Scotch. I told how fucking fantastic it feels to drink Domergue while on coke. That's the only push he needed. He did the rest himself. But that's not enough, you know. I needed to introduce something he didn't understand, something foreign to really fuck up his instincts, so I decided to get him hooked on steroids. I doubled down on his body dysmorphia by implying he was losing muscle strength now that he's forty and I offered to get him a personal trainer. He said sure and I introduced him to this a guy I know, Shayne. Now Shayne is a fucking wizard. He knows just how to play gym bros and get 'em all stacking within a month. And he gets paid per brand, so he gives them as much he can without actually killing them. I love him. Great guy. But that wasn't gonna be enough for Drew, especially if he was just sitting behind his desk all day. I needed to get him on a cycle that would only get faster without me being there to speed it up, so I came up with the idea of having him trash a conference room up every time he felt it, which I figured would only make him wanna use more throughout the day. Ooh, I even got a special team of wetbacks to clean up after him. They don't understand a word of English, so as long as I kept deporting them, they'll never be a problem for me. And at that point I was starting to think it was enough, but... ehh, I didn't want to take the chance of him powering through that. This was a very expensive charade. It had to work on the first try or else what was the point. So I started playing on his paranoia, right, and that was hard at first, but I eventually got him to believe that anytime his assistant Larry or any of the other producers, Simmons, Johnson, our receptionist Doris, that they always lied to me 24/7, and that they would start lying to him when he became Acting CEO. The idea was to put pressure on him to get it right on his own because, without me, he'd never get honest feedback. And of course I'd shower him with compliments, saying I read transcripts Larry sent me or whatever, you know, but he's smart, Drew. Very smart. Every once in a while he'd figures out how much I lie to him, so then I lie about the lying and blame the bad memory he doesn't have. And I'd call him out for doing all that coke at work, and he's so sensitive when he's criticized, lot of overreacting, so I always make sure to point it out when it happens so he'd snort a few to feel better." Theo bobs his head. "And so, when I determined he had achieved a perpetual and self-sustaining state of dependence, *that's* when I told him, out of the blue, that I had to go out of the country for six weeks smack-dab in the middle of our busy season to sign a ten year co-production deal with our old boss Liu Míng, which is actually true, except it wasn't gonna take six weeks. It only took two hours. Drew doesn't touch the contracts. I don't let him. He doesn't know. He bought it." Theo furrows his brow. Looks at Suyin. "Are you still breathing?"

"Yeah."

"Oh." Theo blinks. "Well? What did you think?"

Suyin opens her mouth. Closes it. "I'm sorry, were you bragging?"

"*Bragging*? What?"

"Or were you asking if I think you overdid it?"

Theo scrunches his face. "What are you talking about?"

"What are you asking me?"

"Now that Míng made me end the trial early, you can see my problem, right?"

Suyin hesitates. "You just gave Drew a thousand reasons to quit?"

"No, he's gonna hate me for not giving him a chance! God, what are you, stupid?" Theo scoffs.

Suyin eyerolls under her blindfold.

Theo frowns, thinking back. "I don't know, maybe I did go too far." He pauses. "I could've killed him myself. That would've been awful. He just looks so tough, you know? I keep forgetting it's all show."

"Don't think of it like that. Just think of it like... you're coming back to help your friend that's in trouble. That's all it is. It's mercy."

Theo smiles, suddenly encouraged. "Mercy. Yeah. You're right. What's Míng talking about? I can't get rid of Drew. He's my buddy. There's nothing wrong with keeping my buddy with me all the time."

"Unless he doesn't want that, of course."

"What? What do you mean?"

Suyin hesitates. "What do you think I mean? What if Drew wants to do something else?"

"Then I change his mind. It's not that hard."

Suyin purses her lips. "I see."

"No you don't, bitch. You blindfolded." Theo laughs heartily. "Oh, I'm sorry, *brindforded*!" He laughs harder, making himself cry.

"Please untie me."

"Calm down, ho. I paid for the whole day." Theo smacks her ass.

JACOB

Spirited Away

EXT. TREMONT STREET - DAY

Rainbow confetti flutters down from the gorgeous blue sky, loud CROWD NOISE all around, landing on a parade float. A pair of big black boots stomp on it, worn by a GO-GO BOY (26) in black cutoff shorts and nothing else gyrating his hips with a flirty smile, his six-pack covered in sweat and glitter. Seven other GO-GO BOYS (20s-30s) to his left and right dance in perfect unison for the amusement of the tank top/bandana wearing CROWD surrounding the float.

Jacob stands on the sidelines, a huge grin on his face. Dazzled by the colors. By the pop music. The unified camaraderie. The sheer volume of hot guys and shiny confetti.

CUT TO:

EXT. CITY HALL - ON STAGE - DAY

A DRAG QUEEN slays it to an overplayed Beyoncé anthem in front of a CAMPY AUDIENCE.

CUT TO:

OVER BY SPONSOR ROW

Rows and rows of tents surround the stage. There is a long line by the entrance, hundreds of people waiting to pay the $30 fee.

Jacob strolls past the tents one-by-one with a mixed expression. Cheap corporate swag. Progressive activists handing out pamphlets for causes that have nothing to do with LGBT issues. Shameless advertising for HRC and HRC (Human Rights Campaign and Hillary Rodham Clinton respectively). Everything's very safe, very sanitized, and quite square.

CUT TO:

AT A FOUNTAIN

Jacob sits on the edge, calmly enjoying the acoustic lesbian on stage. HUGO (41) walks by, an attractive Syrian American with short hair and a great body. Jacob looks at him from afar.

Hugo makes eye contact with Jacob. Smiles.

JUMP CUT TO:

MINUTES LATER

Jacob and Hugo sit next to each other on the fountain's rim.

JACOB
This is a lot like the one in Philly.

HUGO
I've never been.

JACOB
It's really nice.

HUGO
You ever been to New York Pride?

JACOB
Not yet.

HUGO
It's great. All the straights leave town. It's like the whole city is gay.

JACOB
That's kinda weird.

HUGO
Tell me about it.

Two campy daddies approach Hugo, TAYLOR (42) and BRENT (40).

BRENT
(to Hugo)
There you are!

HUGO
Ready to go?

BRENT
Yeah, let's go.

Hugo stands.

HUGO
Brent, Taylor, this is Jacob.

JACOB
(waving)
Hi.

TAYLOR
Hi Jacob.

JACOB
Where you guys headed?

TAYLOR
Boxer.

JACOB
What's that?

HUGO
Jacob just turned 21.

BRENT
Oh my God, you're such a baby!

JACOB
Thanks.

TAYLOR
God, I'd kill to be 21 again.

BRENT
Enjoy it while you can. It'll be gone soon.

JACOB
If only.

HUGO
(kissing Jacob's cheek)
Let us go, sweetie.

JACOB
Is it okay if I follow you guys to Boxer?

Hugo looks at Brent and Taylor. Everyone's ambivalent.

CUT TO:

EXT. TREMONT STREET - DAY

Hugo, Brent and Taylor walk in a row, gabbing. Jacob awkwardly follows along.

HUGO
Can you believe they charge a cover at Heather's now?

TAYLOR
That's a shame. I know one of the bartenders there. Wanted to catch up.

HUGO
Who?

TAYLOR
Remember the old queen we bumped into in P-Town, what was it... five years ago?

BRENT
The blond?

TAYLOR
NO! Not him! Yuck.

HUGO
Oh, the one with the long hair?

TAYLOR
Yes!

BRENT
Wow, I forgot all about him. He works at Heather's?

TAYLOR
Part-time. He moved to Springfield with his boyfriend. I think they're still together.

HUGO
The gardener, right?

BRENT
I thought he said he was an author.

HUGO
No, he was definitely gardener. Remember, we joked about him looking like Willie Nelson in twenty years?

BRENT
Oh, you're right.

JACOB
How'd you guys meet each other?

HUGO
I used to work with Taylor and we met Brent through some mutual friends.

JACOB
What did you and Taylor--

HUGO
God, whatever happened to Betty and Tilly?

TAYLOR
They broke up.

HUGO
NO!

TAYLOR
I told you!

HUGO
Shut the fuck up! No you didn't!

BRENT
They didn't break up!

TAYLOR
Yes they did! Tilly's in Montreal now and Betty's living with her brother in SoHo.

BRENT
They're BOTH in SoHo! I just saw them at Scottie's birthday party last year.

JACOB
What are they, lesbians?

HUGO
(laughing)
No, honey, we just call them that.

BRENT
Scottie gained weight.

HUGO
Ah, that's a shame.

Jacob slows his pace, awkwardly retreating behind the threesome.

TAYLOR
He's not still mad at me, is he?

BRENT
Why would he be mad at you?

CUT TO:

INT. BOXER - DAY

A gay sports bar. Busy but tame. Everyone over the age of 40. Every TV tuned in to the Sox game. Taylor, Brent, Hugo and Jacob sit at a table. A cute blond WAITER (30) walks up.

WAITER
What can I get you guys?

TAYLOR
Four Coors on tap.

JACOB
Not for me. A screwdriver, please. Ultimo if you have it.

WAITER
(jotting)
Three Cools draft, Ultimo screwdriver.

JACOB
Separate check for me.

TAYLOR
No, I'll get it.

JACOB
Aw, thanks.

The Waiter nods and dashes away. Jacob turns to Taylor. He's watching the Sox game. Hugo and Brent too. Jacob looks aimlessly around the bar. Lets out a bored sigh.

The Waiter returns and hands out their drinks. Jacob sips his screwdriver.

JACOB
I think I'm just gonna stay for this drink, if that's okay.

TAYLOR
(shrugging)
Do your thing, honey.

JACOB
What's that bar we passed down the street? The one with all those people outside?

BRENT
Lumber's.

JACOB
How is it?

TAYLOR
Used to be the best until a couple years ago.

JACOB
What happened a couple years ago?

TAYLOR
The straights took over.

BRENT
God, you shoulda seen it in 90s.
(exhaling nostalgically)
Those really were the days.

Jacob frowns. He only just got here.

JACOB
So it's not gay anymore?

TAYLOR
No, it's still gay, but... You'll see.
(pause)
Check it out. You'll like it.

Jacob shrugs.

JACOB
Why not.

SMASH CUT TO:

INT. LUMBER'S - MAIN BAR - DAY

Everyone's squeezed in like sardines. All the TVs play music videos from the 2000s. Lots of women too, college allies with their gay besties motivated by fascination and all the likes they're gonna get on Insta.

Jacob crawls his way to the counter. The sole BARTENDER (30), practically a Calvin Klein model and possibly straight, struggles to keep up with orders.

Jacob waits patiently, frowning a bit.

CUT TO:

EXT. LUMBER'S - STANDING ZONE - DAY

Jacob sips on a puny plastic cup screwdriver in the outside standing zone. He casually looks around. Notices a CUTE NERD (21) in black glasses and red flannel from across the room. Bit of a belly. Messy brown hair.

Jacob smiles. Waves sweetly.

The Cute Nerd grins bashfully. Walks over to Jacob.

CUTE NERD
What's your name?

JACOB
Jacob.

CUTE NERD
Austin.

They shake hands.

JACOB
I just want to get this out of the way, you're fucking adorable.

AUSTIN
Thanks. You're really cute too.

Austin points to Jacob's shirt.

AUSTIN (CONT'D)
Heard you like boys.

JACOB
My reputation proceeds me.

They laugh.

CUT TO:

INT. LUMBER'S - MAIN BAR - DAY

Austin and Jacob sip their second rounds at a high-top.

JACOB
I don't get the appeal, honestly.

AUSTIN
Really?

JACOB
Yeah, I was expecting it to be...

AUSTIN
Funnier?

JACOB
Good.

Austin furrows his brow.

AUSTIN
I see.

JACOB
It's just too boring. And I love slow-burn movies. Some of my favorite movies are three hours long or more. Godfather Part II, Lawrence of Arabia, Lord of the Rings: Return of the King. But Totoro's only seventy minutes long and he doesn't show up for thirty of it.

AUSTIN
Neither did the shark in Jaws.

JACOB
You didn't SEE the shark, but he was there from the very beginning. Very different point.

AUSTIN
What animes DO you like?

Jacob hesitates.

JACOB
You know, that's a funny question.

AUSTIN
It is?

JACOB
I'm really more of a casual fan. Most of the animes out there are long and rambling with no rush to actually end. Naruto and One Piece are, what, a thousand episodes each and counting?

AUSTIN
It's about the journey, not the destination.

JACOB
But the ending's the most important part. Good or bad, you need an ending. It's the culmination of every single moment and character and plot twist and... Without a destination, the journey is meaningless.

AUSTIN
So when you watch <u>Lawrence of Arabia</u>, with all those ups and downs, all you're doing is waiting for it to end?

JACOB
They wouldn't be "ups and downs" without that ending.

AUSTIN
What would they be then?

JACOB
A waste of my time.

Austin stirs his drink, nodding.

JACOB
I didn't really answer your question, did I?

AUSTIN
(chuckling)
No, you didn't.

JACOB
<u>Death Note</u> and <u>Fullmetal Alchemist</u>.

AUSTIN
Okay.

JACOB
But only the manga.

Austin furrows his brow.

AUSTIN
Really?

JACOB
I've always loved graphic novels. They're the only books I can read nowadays with my limited attention span. You ever read <u>Watchmen</u>?

AUSTIN
No, but I've heard of it.

JACOB
Honestly, it's the only superhero anything I can stand. Because it has an ending. When people die, they stay dead. All their choices have consequences. And it isn't about punching or treasure hunting or fantasy deus ex machinas, all that "power of friendship" bullshit, it's about America and corruption and how the world would actually react to the existence of a Superman. Sorry, I'm getting too far from the point again. <u>Death Note</u>. <u>Death Note</u> is a fucking masterpiece. That ENDING!
(pleasured exhale)
Ryuk writing Light's name in the Death Note, Light realizing he's gonna die of heart attack in forty seconds and there's nothing he can do to stop it, realizing there's no afterlife, nothing after death, just black, and it's all gonna be gone in forty seconds, and he just starts crying and begging and pleading, "I don't wanna die! I don't wanna die!" It's disgusting. It makes me sick, and it's so sad and pathetic and dark and real, and then they turned it into an anime and fucking ruined it.

AUSTIN
I didn't know that wasn't the original ending.

JACOB
It would be the only thing they changed.
(laughs)
I mean come on, Light running away, laying on the steps, dying all calm, all that shining sparkly

light, the ghost of L floating over him, it's just so...

Jacob waves his hand, struggling to find the word.

JACOB (CONT'D)
Hollywood.

Austin's brown eyes sweetly stare. Jacob chuckles.

JACOB (CONT'D)
Sorry, I'm talking too much.

AUSTIN
No, I love hearing you go. It's electrifying.

Jacob smiles with copious flattery.

JACOB
(singing)
"You better shape up..."

AUSTIN
What?

JACOB
Grease.

AUSTIN
I hate musicals.

Jacob is taken aback.

JACOB
Of course you do.

A pale, toned PARTY ANIMAL (22) in a mesh crop top covered in glitter walks by with a martini. He suddenly stops at their high top.

PARTY ANIMAL
(to Austin)
There you are. I couldn't find you.

AUSTIN
I've been here.

The Party Animal looks at Jacob, his slender body stiffening with confusion.

PARTY ANIMAL
Hello.

AUSTIN
Douggie, this is Jacob.

Douggie looks at Austin knowingly.

DOUGGIE
Good thing I found you.

AUSTIN
We were talking about anime.

DOUGGIE
You found someone you could talk about it with.

Jacob furrows his brow.

DOUGGIE
(to Jacob)
Inside joke.

JACOB
If you two wanna be alone, I could--

DOUGGIE
No, it's fine.
(to Austin)
Do you need to close your tab, or--?

AUSTIN
No, we're good.

JACOB
Where you guys going next?

DOUGGIE
Machine. Wanna come?

Jacob smirks, checking with Austin.

JACOB
Sure. Sounds like fun.

DOUGGIE
I'll be outside.

Douggie struts away.

JACOB
Don't think Douggie likes me.

AUSTIN
He's a bit wasted right now. He's a great guy.

JACOB
You two aren't...?

Austin laughs abruptly.

AUSTIN
Fuck no! Douggie's just a friend.

Austin puts his arm around Jacob's shoulder. They kiss.

AUSTIN (CONT'D)
God, you're so hot.

JACOB
Thanks. You too.

Austin kisses Jacob again and opens the door. Jacob follows out. The door closes.

MATCH CUT TO:

INT. MACHINE - MEN'S ROOM - NIGHT

Jacob pushes the door in, pulsating HOUSE MUSIC flowing behind him.

Jacob walks over to the sink. As he washes his hands, he catches a glimpse of his reflection. Maybe it's the lighting or just the alcohol, but he likes what he sees. He's actually attractive after all.

CUT TO:

OUTSIDE THE MEN'S ROOM

Austin waits, sipping on a beer. The dim nightclub, lit only with neon spotlights, is packed with MEN both young and old, the MUSIC incredibly loud and intoxicating.

Jacob walks out of the bathroom. Smiles at Austin.

AUSTIN
Having a good day?

JACOB
I am.
(looking around)
Surprised how many people are here considering what happened in Orlando.

AUSTIN
Isn't it awful?

JACOB
It's so sad I don't even want to think about it.

AUSTIN
There's the answer.

Jacob nods.

AUSTIN (CONT'D)
On the other hand, you get the ones too sad to even think, like my... other friend. He didn't even want to get out of bed this morning.

JACOB
I don't get that, you know? It happened. I know it's hard for me to say, but it did. Why should we let it ruin our day?

AUSTIN
That's what I told him. I don't even think he's that upset about it happening. He just feels it's his duty to stay depressed. As if we're all celebrating.
(pause)
He can be such a fucking jackass sometimes.

Jacob notices Austin's pained expression.

JACOB
You okay?

Austin forces a smile under glossy eyes.

AUSTIN
Yeah, I'm fine.

Jacob caresses Austin's face. Goes in for a kiss. They make out, Austin building in passion, their erections grazing each other.

Jacob pulls away, rolling his tongue around his mouth.

JACOB
What is that?

AUSTIN
My beer?

JACOB
I think so.

Austin holds up the bottle.

AUSTIN
Want some?

Jacob stares at the bottle.

JACOB
I don't think I like beer.

AUSTIN
Just try it. It's a wheat beer.

JACOB
A wheat beer?

AUSTIN
Try it.

Jacob takes a small sip. Hands the bottle back.

JACOB
It's good.

AUSTIN
I'll buy you one.

JACOB
Nah, there's no need.

AUSTIN
No, it's nothing. I prefer drinking out of the bottle. It's quite phallic.
(seductive)
You looked really good doing it too.

Jacob flushes, his erection twinging.

JACOB
I'll pass.

AUSTIN
You sure?

JACOB
Don't wanna ruin anything by mixing.

Austin smirks. Kisses Jacob again.

CUT TO:

ON THE DANCE FLOOR

Austin and Jacob dance, arms around each other, surrounded by hot horny men, Jacob's styled hair deflating with sweat, lips red from kissing, eyes closed, body moving in unison with Austin's.

Douggie watches Austin and Jacob from across the floor, a worried look on his face.

CUT TO:

BY THE BAR

Jacob hunches over the counter, waiting for the bartender to make his screwdriver and open Austin's next beer. He smiles to himself. Scans the room to look for Austin. Spots him sitting outside the bathroom door talking to Douggie. Actually Douggie's the one doing the talking. Lecturing, by the looks of it. Austin's head is down, eyes intense, a bit of a frown.

Jacob's smile flutters away, a cold unease growing in his chest.

CUT TO:

OUTSIDE THE MEN'S ROOM

Jacob walks up to Douggie with a screwdriver and wheat beer bottle in his hands.

JACOB
Austin in there?

DOUGGIE
Yeah. He just wants to get out of here.

JACOB
Oh. Where to?

Douggie looks off.

DOUGGIE
Don't take this the wrong way, but I don't think you should come with us.

JACOB
Why not?

Douggie hesitates. Jacob frowns, finally realizing.

JACOB (CONT'D)
He's got a boyfriend, doesn't he?

Douggie looks at his feet.

DOUGGIE
I know it's not you. You're a really nice guy. He just doesn't know what he wants right now.

JACOB
How serious are they?

DOUGGIE
They live together.

Jacob exhales with a hint of hurt.

JACOB (CONT'D)
It's fine. I completely understand.

DOUGGIE
You sure?

Jacob chuckles, halfhearted but sincere.

JACOB
It sucks he didn't tell me.
(pause)
But I'll be okay.

Douggie pats Jacob's shoulder.

DOUGGIE
Happy Pride, sweetie.

He kisses Jacob's cheek, then the other.

JACOB
Happy Pride.

Douggie smiles with gratitude. Pushes into the bathroom.

Jacob's lips smash together in a scowl. He places Austin's beer bottle on the wall shelf.

CUT TO:

IN A CORNER

Jacob sits on a sofa, bored. A PRETTY WOMAN (22) plops next to him, eyes glued to her Android.

JACOB
You want me to move?

The Pretty Woman smiles politely.

PRETTY WOMAN
It's okay. I won't be long.

Jacob huffs.

JACOB
(whispers to himself)
"Everyone comes and goes so quickly here."

PRETTY WOMAN
Hm?

JACOB
Nothing.

The Pretty Woman pockets her phone.

PRETTY WOMAN
I heard you. What did you mean?

Jacob shrugs halfheartedly.

JACOB
I've spent the whole day hitchhiking, bar to bar. It's kinda fun actually. Like I'm on an adventure. But really it's made me realize how aimless I am.
(pause)
Kinda sad when you think about it.

PRETTY WOMAN
I don't think spontaneity is sad. I'd kill for a day to do whatever I wanted, no plans or people to depend on. Look at me. I'm a straight girl in a gay bar waiting for a flaky bitch.
(chuckles)
I sure don't wanna.

JACOB
What's wrong with gay bars?

PRETTY WOMAN
Nothing's wrong with them. They're just not my thing.

JACOB
That's how I feel about straight bars. There's something alien planet about them. I can't really explain it.

PRETTY WOMAN
They make you feel gay.

Jacob smiles.

JACOB
Yeah.

PRETTY WOMAN
This makes me feel straight. I empathize with you guys a ton. This fucking sucks.

Jacob laughs.

JACOB
Maybe that's why I love gay bars so much. There's familiarity everywhere, even among the variations.

The Pretty Woman checks her phone again.

PRETTY WOMAN
Goddammit.

JACOB
Who are you waiting for? Gay friend?

PRETTY WOMAN
Bi boyfriend.

Jacob raises his brow.

JACOB
That's a new one.

PRETTY WOMAN
I throw him a bone every once in a while.

JACOB
I won't ask what that means.

PRETTY WOMAN
Neither do I. That's part of the deal.

Jacob chuckles. Holds his hand out.

JACOB
I'm Jacob.

PRETTY WOMAN
(shaking Jacob's hand)
Sandy.

Jacob furrows his brow.

JACOB
Sandy?

SANDY
Yeah.

Jacob lets go of Sandy's hand.

JACOB
Your name's actually Sandy?

SANDY
Yeah. Why?

JACOB
You ever see Grease?

SANDY
I fucking hate it.

JACOB
Because of your name?

SANDY
No. I hate all movie-musicals in general.

Jacob clicks his tongue, looking away.

SANDY (CONT'D)
What now?

JACOB
I can't believe movie-musicals are such an acquired taste.

SANDY
You're a theatre kid, aren't you?

Jacob nods.

JACOB
In high school, yeah. Every summer I sat at home, eating Oreos by the sleeve, and watch Sound of Music, Producers, Grease, Wizard of Oz, and Singin' in the Rain over and over again, just those five.

SANDY
You never got sick of them?

JACOB
Never. By the time I got to the last one I'd crave the start of the cycle again.

SANDY
Familiarity everywhere, even among the variations.

JACOB
Exactly.

Jacob goes silent. Sandy double-checks her phone.

SANDY
What's your story? Why're you couching it?

JACOB
I'm just...

Jacob looks at Sandy. She's curious.

JACOB (CONT'D)
A guy tried to cheat on his boyfriend with me.

SANDY
Hot.

JACOB
Not hot. He wasn't gonna tell me. Or his boyfriend.
(pause)
Right when I was just starting to like him.

SANDY
Sorry it didn't work out.

JACOB
Thanks.
(looks down)
I think it's my shirt.

SANDY
Yeah, it's pretty swinger-y.

JACOB
Not even subtle, is it?

SANDY
It's literally a label.

JACOB
But it's self-imposed, so it's fine, right?

Jacob chuckles a bit. Goes silent.

JACOB (CONT'D)
This wasn't what I wanted.

SANDY
Why'd you wear it then?

JACOB
Oh no, I picked this specific shirt. Just not for that reason.

SANDY
Why then?

JACOB
You ever see <u>Glee</u>?

SANDY
No.

JACOB
For the Lady Gaga episode, when they perform "Born This Way," everyone wears a shirt with what they're most insecure about. Kurt the gay kid wore this exact shirt.

SANDY
So it's an obscure pop culture reference?

Jacob looks off, smiling a bit.

JACOB
Two years ago I never could've worn this shirt in public, or in private. Now I can.

Sandy smiles.

SANDY
That's actually really cool.

JACOB
It makes me look desperate.

SANDY
No, that really makes a difference.

JACOB
Really?

SANDY
Yeah. Most people are simple-minded. They see something and automatically assume it's base or unholy, but really it's a culmination of a big journey they don't even know about.

Jacob takes a deep breath.

JACOB
I dunno. Maybe I should just go home.

SANDY
What time is it?

JACOB
8:00 I think.

SANDY
It's too early.

JACOB
I know. And it's not like I have anything better to do.
(pause)
Funny thing is, you think my day's been all spontaneous but it's actually the first time I've had real structure in a very long time. Who knows when the next time will be, if there'll even be a next time?

Sandy shrugs.

SANDY
Well, if today really is such an unusually structured day for you, why end it now? Maybe you'll find another hot guy to hitchhike to a better bar, one you like better than this one. Or maybe you'll find the one guy who looks at that shirt and only sees what it really means.

JACOB
I dunno.

SANDY
Or just find a guy to fuck your brains out. Just find something. End it on a high note. Make the journey worth it. Otherwise it's just a waste of your time.

Jacob stares at Sandy.

JACOB
Were you at Lumber's earlier?

SANDY
What's Lumber's?

Jacob keeps staring at Sandy. Sandy smirks.

SANDY (CONT'D)
What?

Jacob licks his lips.

JACOB
Nothing.

He stands.

SANDY
Pick a big black one.

She winks. Jacob chuckles.

JACOB
I'd be happy with anyone, honestly.

SANDY
Good luck, Jacob.

JACOB
Thanks.

Jacob walks toward the bar, reinvigorated. Looks back at the sofa. It's empty. Sandy's gone.

Jacob furrows his brow. He scans the club. The bathroom. The door. Nothing. No women in sight. Jacob's weirded out.

JACOB (CONT'D)
"Everyone comes and goes so quickly here."

CUT TO:

ON THE DANCE FLOOR

Jacob winds through the strobe-lit dance floor, looking at the lustful DANCERS with surreal wonder, like a tourist in a dreamworld. Standing in the middle of the dance floor are two MEN violently making out. Jacob stares at the men as if they were a piece of art in a museum. Keeps walking.

Jacob moves his body to the music, slowly at first, settling into the vibe of the crowd. He moves his arms, his hips, his legs, his mind switched off. He's actually a really good dancer, full of energy and rhythm. He feels an unfamiliar sensation, a fantastically cathartic sense of peace.

A shirtless BUFF MAN (30) in a backwards baseball cap watches Jacob dance from afar. They lock eyes. Jacob approaches the Buff Man. Brings him in for a kiss, their tongues forcing themselves into each other's mouths. The Buff Man wraps his strong arms around Jacob, stroking his back, squeezing his ass over his shorts.

A BLOND BYSTANDER watches Jacob and the Buff Man make out, impressed, turned on. Jacob looks back, his mouth still locked with the Buff Man's, and winks.

WHALE
Sodom

Whale can hear "Gloria" from the front yard. What a shock. Alex is watching *The Wolf of Wall Street* again.

"Hey dude," Alex says. "I'm finishing off the tequila. Want some?" Whale trudges through the messy living room.

```
                    WHALE
        No thanks. I'm working out.
```

"Suit yourself." Alex sips his glass, eyes glued on Leo and his hedonistic exploits. "You're late today."

```
                    WHALE
        I went to confession.
```

Alex chuckles. Whale knows the movie by heart now. It wasn't a funny scene. He's just joshing, of course, but Whale didn't like it. It was mean.

Whale changes into a muscle tank and gym shorts. Stands below his over-the-door pull-up bar. He raises his arms, gripping the foam handles, his pits exposed. On a hunch he looks toward the couch. Alex's gaze lingers a bit before returning to the movie. Whale hesitates for a moment before re-tightening his grip and lifting his legs off the ground, pulling his body up with ease.

Three sets of pull ups, two sets of bicep curls, and three sets of push-ups later, Whale makes his way to the kitchen sink. Rinses out his shaker bottle. He can sense Alex walking toward him in his peripheral.

"Thanks for that," Alex whispers.

```
                    WHALE
        For what?
```

"You know what."

Whale pours tap water into the shaker bottle. Methodically tosses in the plastic spiky ball. Adds one scoop of unflavored whey protein powder.

```
                    WHALE
        You really have a problem.
```

"Oh, I do?"

Whale points to the TV, *The Wolf of Wall Street* still playing.

```
                    WHALE
        This is starting to piss me off.
```

"Says the guy blasting Pet Shop Boys 24/7."

Whale shakes the bottle, the spiky ball rattling back and forth in soft revolutions. Alex stands closer to Whale's back, a sly smile on his face. He touches the back of Whale's neck. Drags his finger down the length of his muscle tank. He stares at Whale's right shoulder as he shakes the bottle, bent just enough to flex his triceps, biceps, and deltoids. "You really love putting on a show, don't you?" Alex says, wrapping his left arm around Whale's waist, palm flat across his tight abdomen.

WHALE
I can't close the door when I do push-ups.

"Would you really want to?"

WHALE
I would, actually.

"Why?"

WHALE
I do more that way.

Whale pops the top of his shaker, tilts his head back and downs the mixture. Alex wraps his other arm across Whale's collarbone as he gulps and kisses the right side of Whale's neck, rolling his tongue around, nibbling slightly, bumping his erection against Whale's ass. Whale's fully erect himself.

Whale tosses the shaker bottle into the sink. Turns his head. Makes out with Alex, their eyes closed. They both stink, Whale's cologne diluted with sweat, Alex's stale bathrobe musk with notes of pot, but they take in as much as they can with their noses. Alex pulls away first, Whale gasping for more. "You know, I really find this whole tenant-landlord thing really fucking hot." Alex slides a hand down Whale's shorts and squeezes his buttcheeks.

WHALE
I'm still paying rent.

"Even still..." Alex sticks a finger between Whale's buttcheeks. Caresses his hole. "I think you've earned yourself a discount."

WHALE
That's not what this is.

"I know it's not. I remember." Alex sticks his nose down the collar of Whale's shirt. Breathes in. "It's just sex." He rubs Whale's hole a little harder. Whale inhales sharply. "Yeah, I know what you like," Alex murmurs. He gets down on his knees, pulls Whale's shorts down, and sticks his face into Whale's ass. Whale bends over the kitchen sink, moaning softly as Alex rims him. "God, I missed this," Alex mumbles.

Whale forces his eyes open.

WHALE
Alex?

"Yeah?" Alex whispers, his pace still the same.

WHALE
Can we...?

Whale interrupts himself with an exhale of pleasure.

"What was that?" Alex says with a chuckle. "Couldn't hear you."

Whale struggles to focus. He leans forward, his butt running away from Alex's tongue.

WHALE
Alex.

"What?" Alex whines, getting back to his feet. Whale turns around.

WHALE
I just wanna talk a moment.

"Okay. What?"

WHALE
I've been thinking, and...

Alex props his hands on the rim of the sink, one of each side of Whale, trapping him in. "Yeah?"

```
                    WHALE
      I don't wanna be just f-buddies anymore.
```

Alex's flirty facade fades. "You're not catching feelings, are you?"

Whale laughs.

```
                    WHALE
      No.
```

Alex smirks, stepping closer to Whale. "I don't believe you."

```
                    WHALE
      I'm not. Believe me, you're not my type.
```

"Oh right," Alex teases, wrapping his arms around Whale's waist. "I'm a pitiful wretch whose whole life revolves around whether or not I have almond milk in my cereal, I remember."

```
                    WHALE
      I said I was sorry.
```

"In more ways than one."

```
                    WHALE
      Alex.
```

"Chill bro, I'm just fucking with you," Alex whispers, his hands roaming down Whale's ass. "Before I fuck you." Alex kisses Whale. Whale relents for a moment before pushing away again.

```
                    WHALE
      I'm serious. I've already done the casual sex thing
      to death. I want something more now.
```

"I don't do boyfriends."

```
                    WHALE
      That's fine.
```

"Then what do you want? 'Hi honey, how was work?'"

```
                    WHALE
      Well, yeah. Kinda.
```

"Fine. How was work?"

```
                    WHALE
      Awful.
```

"What else is new?"

```
                    WHALE
      The Professor called me into his office today. I
      missed a big assignment and he really ripped into me.
```

"That's too bad."

```
                    WHALE
      And the problem is I agree with him 100% but there's
      no way I can prove that to him. It's such a vague
      atmosphere over there. Even though I'm conscious of
      it, I can't get over it. I just keep picking up where
      I left off.
```

"I don't like this," Alex says, kissing Whale. "It's hotter if we don't get personal."

```
                    WHALE
      For how long?
```

"As long as it takes." Alex moves in for another kiss. Whale backs away.

```
                    WHALE
        Not for me. Not anymore.
```

Alex half-frowns. "I can't give you anything else. I don't want to. You wouldn't want me to either. Not really."

```
                    WHALE
        I know.
```

"Let me cheer you up," Alex says, his horny glaze returning. "That's why we're doing this, right? Nothing's broke. Not with me. Certainly not with you."

Whale wraps his big arms around Alex.

```
                    WHALE
        I'll compromise then.
```

"How?"

```
                    WHALE
        It can stay just sex but only with each other.
```

Alex chuckles. "For how long?"

```
                    WHALE
        Until we don't.
```

"But you're so fucking hot, bro! Why can't we both be open? I'm sure there's plenty of other dudes you'd rather be with."

```
                    WHALE
        I'm not shopping around.
```

"That's fine, you do you. But let's be honest, monogamy doesn't work."

```
                    WHALE
        It's still what I want.
```

Alex hangs his hands off Whale's arms. "Look, the reason I dropped out of Yale wasn't because I couldn't do it. I earned my way in fair and square. I was gonna be a fucking lawyer. But you know what happened? I was sitting in Branford courtyard and realized I was doing exactly what my father did, who did exactly what his father did. I wasn't living my life. I was just reliving theirs. I mean, think about it bro, the Boomers had to get married. They had to stay monogamous. They had to have kids. That's what their society was designed around. We don't have to do anything the way our parents did, especially guys like us. If we wanna go our entire lives alone, great. If we wanna be lifelong bachelors or junkies, whatever. There's no borders, no binaries, no constructs anymore. No one cares anymore. We can fuck each other and a bunch of other guys and nothing bad will happen. Honestly, you should be flattered that I'm fucking you because I chose you over someone else."

```
                    WHALE
        That's monogamy.
```

"No, it's not. I have thousands of options and nothing stopping me from having them but right now I want you. Not because I have to. Not because society would say I'm bad. Because I want to. Because you give the best head. And you take my cock like a champ. And I wanna lick every inch of your body, inside and out. And you can lick me everywhere too, just like you do so goddamn well. But I'll get tired of using your body, you'll get tired of using mine, and we'll find better ones somewhere else."

```
                    WHALE
I know we're naturally programmed to think there's
something better somewhere else, but that's just a
myth. Trust me, I know. It's not even a matter of
grass being greener. There might not even be grass!
```

Alex raises a jolly finger. "Yes! Grass! Absolutely!" He opens a side drawer. Pulls out pot and papers. Whale watches Alex roll a joint like it was nothing.

"You're wrong, by the way," Alex murmurs, the joint in his mouth. "There's always something better somewhere else." He lights the blunt with a kitchen lighter. "Thinking there's something you can do to keep it that way forever, that's the myth." He inhales. Holds it in. Blows it into Whale's mouth, ending it with a kiss. They make out. Minds blank. Clothes flying away. Bodies falling to the floor.

It's almost dark by the time Alex and Whale finish. They hold each other on the linoleum floor, Alex's smelly bathrobe covering their bodies. Whale sighs and stands up. "What's up?" Alex croaks.

```
                    WHALE
I'm going out.
```

"Cool." Alex marvels Whale's body shining in the moonlight. "Any particular reason?"

```
                    WHALE
I wanna walk around. Alone.
```

Alex shrugs. "You do you, bro."

Whale slips on a pair of shorts and a flattering polo in his room. Looks over at his mirror. Stares at his reflection. He said he wouldn't call. It's not an option. It can't be. That was the plan. Whale pulls out his iPhone. Goes to his favorites list. That's right, Whale deleted it already. Because it wasn't an option. But everything's changed since then. Too much was different. He needed something from before, something to go his way. It'd be worth it just to hear his voice again.

Whale opens Messages. Nothing. Darn his past self. Why'd he have to be so thorough? Then he remembers the one remnant he didn't kill, the one he intentionally left alive. Flips back to the phone app. Taps Missed Calls. Scrolls down, scouring the list for a number starting with 856. He finds only one.

(856) 150-6869

Is that him? Has to be. He doesn't know anyone else from New Jersey. Whale taps the number and puts the phone to his ear. The dial tone rings once.

Twice.

Thrice.

Four times.

Five.

Six.

"The number you are trying to reach...."

Whale hangs up. Locks his phone. Heads outside.

DREW

Citation Needed

Drew Lawrence lays on his bed in the dark, his mind still buzzing from that apocalyptic phone call with Theo. Underneath the static grows a thin, dangerously comfortable bubble of relief, a cushion he's felt many times but always denied. This is it. Nothing more to attain. All he'll ever have is what he has right now. Just the same or less.

It's Friday. Sweet Vermouths opens in two hours. He better just leave well enough alone.

Something's buzzing on the bed. Drew bends his head up. His cell's not ringing. Oh wait. Drew looks over at the alarm clock. It's his other iPhone, his private line. He hasn't touched it in weeks. Who could be calling at this hour? He reaches up. Grabs his personal cell. Recognizes the caller ID.

+1 (610) 295-5077
Philadelphia, PA

"Nope." Drew tosses the personal cell on the bed. Lets it ring itself to voicemail. He stares up at the ceiling, the vibrating iPhone still shaking the sheets. He suddenly gets worried. It's been over a year. Maybe he should answer it. The buzzing stops. Drew looks up at the blank screen resting beside him. No second call. He waits again. No voicemail either it seems. Should he call back? Nah. He's not in the mood to initiate such a heavy overdue conversation. No voicemail. It couldn't have been that important.

Dinner. Shower. Drew stands before his closet, flicking through his many suits. He catches a glimpse of his naked physique in the mirror, half illuminated by the bathroom light. That ghoulish reflection in Sweet Vermouths' bathroom mirror is still on his mind. Has been for weeks. Drew can't go back to that. Never ever again.

Drew pushes aside the suits. Fingers through his rarely worn plainclothes. Polos. Tank tops. Casual button-ups. Graphic tees. Boots. Sneakers. High-tops. Cord bracelets. Necklaces. Hats... Drew stops on the hats. Pulls out a weathered red cap with a prominent white Nike swoosh on the front. Drew steps back into the light for a better look. All that wear. Those little details.

Drew dons the red Nike cap. Slides on a pair of blue jeans. Slips an orange polo over his head. As soon as the cotton touches his shoulders he knows it's not gonna fit. He can't even lower his arms. Drew immediately tosses it on the floor. Checks his arms in the mirror. All his suits are custom for a reason. He's just gotta bite the bullet and settle for sleeveless. Not a muscle shirt or circuit party tank. Something classy. Drew pulls out a red flannel button-up. Grabs scissors from the kitchen drawer. Snips off the plaid sleeves. Buttons it on before the mirror. Adjusts the collar. Hot but humble. Perfect. He slips on dark brown Timberlands. Pockets his work cell. Thinks about Theo. Changes his mind. Tosses it back on the bed. Pockets his personal cell. Heads out. He makes it halfway to Sweet Vermouths before realizing he forgot to snort a line or sip a Domergue for the road. He didn't even think of it.

Drew parks his red stallion outside Sweet Vermouths. A line's already forming outside the closed doors. Drew locks his Jeep. Leans against the driver-side door. Studies the sign above Sweet Vermouths' entrance, that martini glass with the neon olive curlicue. How phony. A few in the queue glance at the red-clad muscle man leaning against the red Jeep but that's about it. A conflicted frown forms on Drew's face. What the hell did he expect Clark Kenting it? Someone to shout, "Superman?" "Kal-El?" He's applying without a resume, like everyone else. He already hates it.

Drew crosses his arms, his forearms bursting. He glances around. A few pedestrians nod politely as they pass him. That's something, right? A young man in a Superman T-Shirt slows to give Drew the ol' up-and-down. Drew can't believe it. How serendipitous.

"Nice frame," the Young Man says with a light register. "Of the car."

Drew looks at his Wrangler. "It's not a car, it's a Jeep."

"Oh, you're one of those people."

"What people?"

The Young Man circles to the back of the Wrangler. Chuckles at the license plate. "Knew it."

"I'm not really a Jeephead."

"Says the guy who can't call his Jeep a car."

A chill races through Drew's body. He said it the same way too.

The Young Man leans beside Drew. Crosses his arms. "So what are we looking at?" he asks, jutting his chin at Sweet Vermouths.

Drew faces forward. "Apparently if you look at it the right angle, for a split second it turns into a Red Lobster."

"Bout time."

"Don't get too excited. It's more like a taco truck Red Lobster."

The Young Man hums. "You've seen it?"

"Loads of times."

"Loads." The Young Man looks down at Drew's crotch. "Good. I'm pretty freaking hungry."

Drew smirks. Turns his head.

The Young Man's already looking. Before Drew could ask, the Young Man holds out his hand. "Jimmy. Jimmy Lyons."

Drew takes Jimmy's hand with a nod, hesitating. "Brian."

"You forget for a second?"

"I dunno, I just..." Drew shrugs with a smile.

Jimmy smiles back. "Brian, huh? Like Brian Griffin?"

"Yup."

Jimmy studies Drew's triceps. "I can see it."

Drew knows the next line. "You're calling me a baby?"

Jimmy cocks his head back. "Oh, come on!"

"What?"

"You've never seen *Family Guy*?"

"I've never seen *Family Guy*," Drew lies.

"I don't believe you."

"Brian's not the baby?"

"That's Stewie. Brian's the dog."

Just hearing that name again gives Drew pause. "You're calling me a dog?"

"I'm not saying you take it like one," Jimmy says. "You do look quite alpha though."

Drew's cock twinges. "Maybe I am."

Jimmy scoffs. "You could be a bit more subtle about it. How old are you anyway?"

The directness makes Drew laugh. "How old, um..." He clears his throat. "How old do you think I am?"

"Forties."

Drew raises his brows. "Fort*ies*?!"

"I'm right, aren't I?"

Drew scratches his head through his hat. "I just turned forty."

"Ok." Jimmy shrugs. "Who cares? You're forty."

Drew looks at Jimmy's features. Short dirty blond fauxhawk. Decent jaw. Yellowish teeth. Big pink lips. Very pale blue in his eyes, almost gray. Not perfect. No one was. "Wanna go in?" Drew asks.

Jimmy hesitates. "Together?"

"Unless you were looking to meet someone else."

"Maybe."

Drew nods. "Okay."

Jimmy blows his lips. "You give up easy, don't you?"

"I'm playing coy."

"Sure you are."

Drew and Jimmy look at each other in comfortable silence. "You wanna?" Drew murmurs.

Jimmy takes a deep breath. "I suppose. I don't have my ID on me though."

"Why not?"

"Left it in the car."

Drew scoffs. "Sure you did."

"I did!" Jimmy insists with a laugh. "Really!"

Drew smirks skeptically. "Don't worry. I know the door guy."

"You know the door guy? What are you, some Hollywood big shot?"

Drew softens. Jimmy's looking back with a playful gleam. He doesn't know. He really doesn't know. "Friend of a friend," Drew answers. "He's cool."

Jimmy nods. "You lead, Brian."

Drew takes a step toward Sweet Vermouths. Halts. Looks up at the sign. "On second thought..." Drew faces Jimmy. "Let's go somewhere else."

Jimmy looks at the club with a frown. "Really?"

"There's a pub down the street. We can talk there."

"Whatever."

"It's really a restaurant with a bar. They won't card you there."

Jimmy smirks. "I told you, I left it in the car."

"Please," Drew says, waving his hand a tiny bit. "Don't bullshit a bullshitter."

All levity drains from Jimmy's face. A bit of guilt drips in.

Drew quickly wraps an around Jimmy's shoulder. "Don't worry. I'm only teasing."

Jimmy tentatively smiles. He wraps an arm around Drew's lower back. Fondles Drew's butt as they walk side by side down the street.

JACOB

Carol

INT. THE BLACK BEAR - GROUND FLOOR BAR - NIGHT

DOZENS OF MEN fill the dimly lit leather bar, nursing either Drambuie on the rocks or massive handles of draft beer for $25, nothing in between. Half of the TVs play still image slideshows of gay porn, the other half play live coverage of the 70th Annual Tony Awards. OLD BEARS shoot pool in the corner. It's after 10:00 but Pride ain't over yet.

The steel door opens. Four men walk in: Jacob, the Buff Man, and the Buff Man's buddies OZZIE (34) and HARRIET (32), real names unknown.

JACOB

Now we're talking!

BUFF MAN

Is this like that place in Florence you were talking about?

JACOB

It's very, very similar. Though I doubt there's actual hardcore sex going on downstairs.

BUFF MAN

You'd be surprised.

JACOB

Restroom! I'll be back.

BUFF MAN

Want me to come along?

Jacob chuckles.

JACOB

Maybe later.

Jacob scampers away.

Ozzie and Harriet glare at the Buff Man.

HARRIET

What the fuck, Mark? You're getting married on Friday!

MARK

I know, but...

OZZIE

No buts about it, mister. Let's go.

Mark crosses his arms, conflicted. He looks toward the restroom.

MARK

Can't I just...?

Ozzie grabs Mark by the arm and drags him outside. Harriet follows.

Jacob wanders back, looking around.

JACOB

Guys?

CUT TO:

BY THE POOL TABLE

Jacob watches the old bears play. Scans the men sitting at the counter. A Cute Boy catches his eye.

Jacob finishes his drink. Adjusts his T-Shirt. Wanders toward the bar. Takes three steps and halts with recognition.

The Cute Boy is Austin. Sunken face, too trashed to comprehend everything. Douggie's standing next to him, seconds away from turning around and seeing Jacob.

Jacob slinks away. Rounds a corner and races downstairs.

CUT TO:

BASEMENT BAR

The basement is packed with a mass of OLDER MEN talking, the majority of them shirtless or strapped in leather harnesses. The naughty red light bulbs create a dim erotic miasma that clashes with the sterile white light pouring down the stairs.

All eyes are on Jacob coming down the stairs, the new meat. One by one they look away. Could be his weight, or the tacky shirt, or his glasses, or messy hair, anything really. Before Jacob could process the attention, it was gone.

Jacob wanders through the crowd, eying the cute men around him. The uninterested ones look away instantly. The ones looking back he doesn't really care for.

Turning around, Jacob spots a RED NIKE BASEBALL CAP shining in the clean light of the stairway, an older man appearing to be in his late thirties or early forties in fantastic shape. Big arms and pecs stretching his orange polo shirt. Decent ass in his blue jeans. A nice layer of dark brown scruff on his fantastic jawline, his mustache slightly longer than his beard.

Jacob approaches Red Baseball Cap slowly, staring directly into his eyes.

Red Baseball Cap makes eye contact. Casually looks off.

Jacob passes Red Baseball Cap and starts up the stairs. Stops and turns around. Red Baseball Cap isn't looking back. Jacob sighs. Keeps walking upstairs.

CUT TO:

GROUND FLOOR BAR

Jacob scans the faces at the counter. No sign of Austin or Douggie.

CUT TO:

SECOND FLOOR BAR

The second floor is much trendier than the other two. The Tony Awards blast at full volume. Jacob watches from the counter, sipping on a screwdriver.

INSERT - THE 70TH ANNUAL TONY AWARDS

BARBRA STREISAND (74) opens the envelope for Best Musical.

BARBRA STREISAND

And the Tony goes to...

(pause)

Hamilton!

The cast of Hamilton jumps for joy on stage.

BACK ON JACOB

Jacob sighs, not really giving a shit.

CUT TO:

BASEMENT BAR

Jacob leans against the wall, his drink long finished. Twenty-one years of waiting and for what? This? More social bullshit?

A HEAVY MAN (40s) sits by himself at the counter with a passive frown. He's not particularly attractive, obviously lonely but with a sturdy posture of acceptance.

Jacob watches the Heavy Man with a heavier heart. That's gonna be him in twenty years, isn't it?

The Heavy Man notices Jacob looking at him. Smiles.

Jacob smiles back. Places his empty cocktail glass on a nearby shelf. Sits next to the Heavy Man at the counter.

JACOB
Hey.

HEAVY MAN
(bashful)
Hey.

JACOB
Happy Pride.

HEAVY MAN
Happy Pride.

JACOB
What's your name?

HEAVY MAN
Ken.

JACOB
Hi Ken. I'm Jacob.

KEN
You're very beautiful.

JACOB
You too.

Jacob slowly leans in. Kisses Ken on the lips. Ken kisses back. Jacob gently pulls away.

JACOB (CONT'D)
I'm sorry. Was that okay?

KEN
Yeah.

JACOB
I should've asked.

KEN
No, it's fine.

Jacob takes a deep breath.

JACOB
I'm gonna go.

KEN
You don't wanna stay?

JACOB
I'm just gonna look around some more, if that's okay.

Ken nods, a bit disappointed.

KEN
Do what you want.

Jacob hesitates.

JACOB

I'm sorry.

KEN

No. Thank you.

Jacob smiles.

JACOB

You're welcome.

Jacob wraps his arm around Ken, squeezing a half-hug. He stands up and wanders toward the stairway. Ken watches him go with mixed emotions.

Jacob climbs the first step.

RED BASEBALL CAP (O.S.)

Excuse me?

Jacob turns around. Recognizes Red Baseball Cap smiling back at him.

RED BASEBALL CAP

What does your shirt say?

Jacob looks down at his chest. The font is massive and the words themselves are short and simple. Jacob holds out the bottom of his shirt with a knowing smirk.

RED BASEBALL CAP (CONT'D)

"Likes Boys."

JACOB

You like it?

RED BASEBALL CAP

Yeah. I got one just like it at home. It says "I Know What Boys Like."

Jacob nods.

RED BASEBALL CAP (CONT'D)

You know the song? The Waitresses?

JACOB

I only know it from <u>Family Guy</u>.

RED BASEBALL CAP

How does it go?

JACOB

"I know what boys like, boys like, boys like me."

Red Baseball Cap smiles, very wholesome.

RED BASEBALL CAP

Very good.

JACOB

Thank you.

RED BASEBALL CAP

You're not heading out, are you?

JACOB

Thinking about it. Haven't decided yet.

RED BASEBALL CAP

What's your name?

Jacob descends. He and Red Baseball Cap are the same height.

JACOB

Jacob. You?

RED BASEBALL CAP

Stewie.

JACOB
Like Stewie Griffin. There you go.

STEWIE
Yeah.

JACOB
I don't think I've ever met a grown man named Stewie. It's short for Stewart?

STEWIE
Yeah. I don't like it.

JACOB
Me neither. It's way too close to Stuart Little.

STEWIE
That's the mouse, right?

Jacob hesitates. Chuckles awkwardly.

JACOB
He's actually not a mouse.

STEWIE
What do you mean he's not a mouse?

JACOB
In the movie he's a mouse, but in the book he's a little boy that looks like a mouse. It's a birth defect or something.

Stewie scrunches his face.

STEWIE
WHAT?!

JACOB
It's true. Look it up.

Stewie laughs in disbelief.

STEWIE
I'd much rather be a little white dog than that.

JACOB
What?

STEWIE
Stewie's the dog, right?

Jacob gapes.

JACOB
You've never seen it!

STEWIE
(laughing)
He's not the dog?!

JACOB
That's Brian. Stewie's the baby.

STEWIE
The ugly baby?

JACOB
The hyper-intelligent, ambiguously gay baby.

STEWIE
I always thought Stewie was the dog.

JACOB
I can't believe you've never seen Family Guy!

STEWIE
Why not?

JACOB
Everyone's seen <u>Family Guy</u>.

STEWIE
Who's everyone?

JACOB
Huh?

STEWIE
Who's everyone?

Jacob stares at Stewie.

JACOB
How old are you?

Stewie hesitates.

STEWIE
How old do you think I am?

Jacob steps back and gives Stewie a once-over.

JACOB
Thirties.

Stewie suppresses a grin, flashing his eyebrows up.

JACOB (CONT'D)
Did I get it?

Stewie scratches his nose.

STEWIE
Thirty-nine.

JACOB
Oh, just about. What do I win?

Stewie smiles. Jacob smiles back.

CUT TO:

SECOND FLOOR BAR

Jacob and Stewie sit at the quiet counter. Jacob finishes his screwdriver.

JACOB
"Andre," A-N-D-R-E-Z-J.

STEWIE
Ouch.

JACOB
No one says it right, no one spells it right. I despise it with a passion.

STEWIE
What is it, Polish?

JACOB
I wish it was Polish. At least I'd be something. What about you?

STEWIE
Hanz.

JACOB
Like Hans Gruber.

STEWIE
But with a Z. People get that wrong a lot.

JACOB
Think mine's worse.

STEWIE
I have to agree with that.

A BARTENDER (40) approaches Jacob.

BARTENDER
Another screwdriver, baby?

JACOB
A shot of Ultimo, I think.

STEWIE
Make it two.

JACOB
I'll get them.

STEWIE
No need.

JACOB
No, I want to.

STEWIE
(smiling)
Okay. Thank you.

Jacob pulls out cash and puts it on the counter. The Bartender drops off two shots. Jacob raises his.

JACOB
To high maintenance surnames.

STEWIE
High maintenance surnames.

They down their shots. Stewie cringes. Jacob doesn't even flinch.

STEWIE (CONT'D)
How'd you do that?

JACOB
No gag reflex.

Jacob winks. Stewie coughs.

STEWIE
You go to school in Boston?

JACOB
Whitman, just across the street from Boston Common.

STEWIE
That's the park, right?

Jacob hesitates.

JACOB
Yeah.

STEWIE
What's your major?

JACOB
Screenwriting.

Stewie stares.

STEWIE
Screenwriting?

JACOB
Technically it's Video and Media Production with a concentration in Writing for Film and Television.
(pause)
I've also got a minor in Literature if that means anything.

STEWIE
That's really cool.

JACOB
What about you? What brings you to Boston?

STEWIE
What do you mean?

JACOB
You're obviously haven't been here long. I've only been here three years but even I know Boston Common's a park.

Stewie laughs.

STEWIE
I see.

JACOB
Well?

STEWIE
Work. I run my own business.

JACOB
Really? What your business?

STEWIE
Smalltown Trainers.

Jacob nods.

JACOB
Smalltown Trainers.

STEWIE
I provide in-home personal training for people with intellectual and developmental disabilities.

Jacob stares at Stewie.

JACOB
No, you don't.

Stewie furrows his brow a bit.

STEWIE
Yeah, I do.

JACOB
Really?

STEWIE
Yeah.

JACOB
You're not just saying that because I'm a fat guy with autism?

Stewie hesitates.

STEWIE
You have autism?

Jacob laughs.

JACOB
Oh wow.

STEWIE
That's not what I meant.

JACOB
No, I know I'm fat. I can take it. I'm a big boy.

Jacob chuckles.

JACOB (CONT'D)
But yes, I am autistic. Technically I was diagnosed with Asperger's, but everyone's calling it "The Spectrum" now, so... Who the fuck knows anymore.

STEWIE
I never wouldn't thought.

JACOB
Bullshit.

STEWIE
I can see it now, but I never would have if you hadn't said anything.

JACOB
Glad to hear that, at least.

STEWIE
And you're NOT fat.

Jacob shakes his belly.

JACOB
You sure about that?

STEWIE
I don't care about that.

JACOB
Really?

STEWIE
I only like guys from the neck up.

Jacob looks into Stewie's eyes.

JACOB
If you like me so much, why'd you snub me earlier?

STEWIE
When did I do that?

JACOB
I was walking right past you and you looked away.

STEWIE
I was being coy.

JACOB
I thought you weren't interested.

STEWIE
Why wouldn't I be? You're the hottest guy here.

Jacob bites his lip, cocky.

JACOB
So, Stewie Hanz.

STEWIE
Yes, Jacob Andrezj?

JACOB
I've got two questions for you.

STEWIE
Okay.

JACOB
You've got to be completely honest.

Stewie hesitates.

STEWIE
Alright.

JACOB
Do you have a boyfriend?

STEWIE
No.

Jacob pauses.

JACOB
You're not married or have kids or live with somebody or anything?

STEWIE
No. Not at all.

Jacob stares at Stewie. Eyes him up and down.

JACOB
Good.

Stewie stares back, his breath quickening.

STEWIE
What's the second question?

CUT TO:

IN THE BATHROOM

Stewie and Jacob make out furiously, arms wrapped around each other.

STEWIE
I never do this!

JACOB
Me neither!

Jacob slams Stewie against the wall. Pulls down his pants. Drops to his knees.

JUMP CUT TO:

LATER

Jacob gargles and spits tap water into the sink. Stewie watches Jacob wash his hands. Jacob looks up at Stewie's reflection.

JACOB
I love your hat. Red's my favorite color.

STEWIE
Really?

JACOB
Yeah. You should see the leather jacket I just got in Florence.

STEWIE
You should see my Jeep.

Jacob freezes.

JACOB
What.

CUT TO:

EXT. THE BLACK BEAR - NIGHT

Parked on the street is a scarlet red 2-door 1998 Jeep Wrangler with the top down. Jacob walks around it, eyes wide. Stewie watches from the curb.

JACOB
It's beautiful.

STEWIE
I had a feeling you'd like it.

Jacob reads the license plate:

"JEEPGUY"

JACOB
You really into cars or something?

STEWIE
It's a Jeep, not a car. And no, not really.

JACOB
Says the guy who can't call his Jeep a car.

STEWIE
I pride myself at not having just a car. They're all the same nowadays.

JACOB
Not Ferraris.

STEWIE
I could never get a sports car. A-holes drive sports cars.

JACOB
And you don't want to be confused with an asshole when you're on the road?

STEWIE
I think sports car drivers become a-holes. I don't want to become an a-hole.

JACOB
But you can't have something basic?

STEWIE
Never.

Jacob looks inside the car. Notices the manual shift.

JACOB
I read somewhere that 75% of all cars in America are either silver, black, or white.

STEWIE
I'm not surprised. Too many people want to be exactly like everyone else.

JACOB
Isn't it awful?

Stewie pulls out his keys.

STEWIE
Where do you live? I'll drive you home.

JACOB
You don't have to.

STEWIE
You just gave me the best blowjob I've ever had. It's the least I can do.

JACOB
Bullshit.

STEWIE
It's true. Honestly.

Jacob laughs.

JACOB
I'll take it anyway.

Stewie gets in. Reaches over to manually unlock the passenger door. Jacob hops in.

STEWIE
Where to?

JACOB
I still live on campus, actually.

STEWIE
I thought you said you were done till Labor Day.

JACOB
I'm doing a custodial program there. They're letting me stay for the summer as long as I clean the residence hall.

STEWIE
Okay. It's on Boylston, right?

JACOB
Just keep heading east and I'll let you know when.

Stewie starts the Jeep. The engine blazes to life. Stewie detaches the emergency break, shifts into first, and drives off.

CUT TO:

I/E. STEWIE'S JEEP - CONTINUOUS

Stewie shifts into second gear. The wind picks up, buffeting Jacob's hair.

STEWIE
Look at the mileage.

Jacob leans over to get a good look at the digital odometer:

"250463"

JACOB
Is that a lot?

Stewie laughs.

STEWIE
"Is that a lot?" The Jeeps they make nowadays can't even do that.

JACOB
I wouldn't know. I still don't have my license yet. How long have you had it?

STEWIE
Bought it new in '97. Drove it cross-country in '02.

JACOB
All by yourself?

STEWIE
Yeah. Brick, New Jersey all the way to San Diego. I saw the Grand Canyon, stopped in Palm Springs, Las Vegas...

JACOB
LA?

STEWIE
LA, yup.

Jacob smiles serenely.

JACOB
What's it like?

Stewie looks over at Jacob.

STEWIE
If there was a place I wished I could've stayed longer, it was LA.

JACOB
Whitman has a campus on Sunset Boulevard.

STEWIE
Really?

JACOB
Not a full-time campus. One of those one-semester-at-a-time programs.

STEWIE
I guess you're not going.

JACOB
Why do you say that?

STEWIE
You just got back from study abroad.

JACOB
LA's different. Half the credits go to an actual Hollywood internship.

STEWIE
Oh wow. That's cool.

JACOB
Deadline's this week. It's like a lottery thing.

STEWIE
You gonna do it?

JACOB
Nope.

Stewie hesitates.

STEWIE
It sounds like a great career move.

JACOB
That's what Mom says.

STEWIE
Okay.

JACOB
Which is why I'm not doing it.

Stewie furrows his brow.

JACOB (CONT'D)
It's a long story. Don't worry about it.

Jacob leans back, thinking.

JACOB (CONT'D)
God, you were only 25!

STEWIE
Huh?

JACOB
It must've been so cool, speeding down the highway with nothing but yourself, going wherever you wanted to go.
(pause)
What about your job?

STEWIE
I got laid off. That's why I did it.

JACOB
When did you start your business?

STEWIE
Right after the trip.

JACOB
Is that what you went to go to school for? Personal Training?

STEWIE
No. I double-majored in computer science and mathematics at Kean University.

Jacob goes silent.

JACOB
That must've been a rough adjustment.

STEWIE
Not really. I always wanted to go into my own business. Be my own boss. Set my own hours.

JACOB
Yeah, but it's not the field you wanted to be in.

STEWIE
It's what I want now. I like it. Got no complaints.

Jacob frowns a bit. How sad to settle like that.

JACOB
Can I put on some music?

STEWIE
Of course, Sexy.

Jacob flips through the Jeep's Sirius XM channels.

STEWIE (CONT'D)
You need a channel list?

JACOB
No, I'm good.

Jacob stops on "Layla" by Derek and the Dominoes, seconds away from it transitioning into the piano second half.

JACOB (CONT'D)
I love this one. It's like the <u>Death Proof</u> of songs.

Stewie furrows his brow at the obscure reference.

STEWIE
Yeah. It's good.

JACOB
I've been really getting into songs with multiple parts, like how this just becomes a completely different song halfway through. Meat Loaf does that a lot. Pink Floyd. "Abbey Road Medley." "Stairway to Heaven" to an extent, you know, with the crescendo. "Free Bird" too. That's probably my favorite song of all time right now, "Free Bird."

Stewie looks at Jacob, confused.

JACOB (CONT'D)
You know "Free Bird" by Lynyrd Skynyrd?

Stewie laughs from shock.

STEWIE
Of course.

JACOB
You don't like it?

STEWIE
I used to love it. I'm sick of it now.

JACOB
I only just found out about it. Can't get enough.

Jacob looks up at the night sky, all those little stars.

STEWIE
I can't believe a young guy like you likes all that older music.

JACOB
As opposed to what? The masterpieces coming out nowadays?

Jacob looks over at Stewie, the streetlamps fluttering across his face. It's quite majestic. Stewie looks back at Jacob, surprised to make eye contact. A grin fills his face.

STEWIE
(whispers)
So cute.

Jacob melts in his seat. Stewie pets Jacob's head sweetly. Jacob closes his eyes.

CUT TO:

EXT. LITTLE BUILDING - NIGHT

Stewie parks the Jeep outside the lobby.

STEWIE
This it?

JACOB
Yup.

Their eyes linger on each other.

JACOB (CONT'D)
Can I have your number?

STEWIE
Okay.

Jacob smiles. Hands over his iPhone.

JACOB
Go ahead and call yourself.

Stewie dials his cell number and hits call. Jacob hears a soft buzzing from Stewie's pocket. He takes the phone and hangs up.

JACOB (CONT'D)
Well then.

Stewie nods.

STEWIE
Good night, Jake.

JACOB
Jacob. I absolutely hate getting called Jake.

STEWIE
Okay.
(pause)
Night, Jacob.

JACOB
Night, Stewie.

Jacob leans in for a kiss. Stewie cocks his head back, looking around.

JACOB (CONT'D)
What? What's wrong?

STEWIE
What if someone sees us?

JACOB
Who cares? Just kiss me.

Stewie leans in and kisses Jacob sweetly. "We Can Work It Out" by The Beatles plays out of nowhere, startling them both.

STEWIE
What is that?

JACOB
Mom's calling me. I better take it or else she'll think I'm still pissed at her.

Jacob surprises Stewie with a peck on the lips. Answers the phone before Stewie could react.

JACOB (CONT'D)
(into phone)
Hey Mom.

Jacob unbuckles his seat belt. Opens the passenger door.

JACOB (CONT'D)
(into phone)
No, I'm sorry, I didn't hear it. I've been at Pride all day.

Jacob steps out of the Jeep. Shuts the door. Waves sweetly at Stewie. Stewie waves back.

JACOB (CONT'D)
(into phone)
I heard all about it.

Jacob pulls a Student ID from his wallet, shoulder-smushing his iPhone against his cheek.

JACOB (CONT'D)
(into phone)
Because I knew nothing was gonna happen. The odds of another one would've been astronomical.

He taps the security scanner. The entrance door CLICKS. Jacob struggles to pocket his wallet without dropping the phone.

JACOB (CONT'D)
(into phone)
C'mon, now you're just being paranoid.

Stewie hops out of the Jeep and rushes to the door. Pulls it open before it auto-locks.

JACOB (CONT'D)
(to Stewie)
Thank you!

STEWIE
It's no problem.

JACOB
Drive safe.

STEWIE
I will.

Jacob holds the door open with his back. Stewie returns to his Jeep.

JACOB
(into phone)
No, it's just a guy I met. He drove me home.

Jacob rolls his eyes at Stewie. Stewie chuckles.

JACOB (CONT'D)
(into phone)
Yes, I know. I know.
(pause)
He's not a psycho.
(pause)
Because he isn't. He's very sweet actually.
(pause)
Stewie. Stewie Hanz.

Jacob enters the Little Building, the door closing softly behind him.

Stewie watches Jacob through the lobby window bickering with his mom.

Waiting for the elevator, Jacob looks out the window. Smiles at Stewie. He waves. Stewie waves back. The elevator arrives. Jacob steps in, the doors close, and he's gone.

Stewie lets out a slow sigh, a warm smile lingering. Contemplative silence. He reluctantly disables the emergency break. Drives off.

CUT TO:

INT. LITTLE BUILDING - 5TH FLOOR COMMON ROOM - THE NEXT DAY

Jacob vacuums the carpet with a faint smile. His headphones blast "Layla."

"Kara Remembers" from Battlestar Galactica, his default ringtone, interrupts the music. Jacob grins at caller ID. Quickly answers it.

JACOB
I was just thinking about you.

STEWIE (V.O.)
Me too.

Jacob bites his lip, curling into a smile.

STEWIE (V.O.)
How are you?

JACOB
Doing okay. Sucking off at the moment.

STEWIE (V.O.)
Uh-huh.

JACOB
Crumbs, of course. Off the carpet. Some dust. With a vacuum.

STEWIE (V.O.)
Am I interrupting?

JACOB
I'm on autopilot when I do it. Glad to have the company.

STEWIE (V.O.)
Glad to be company.

Silence on the line.

STEWIE (V.O.)
Do you wanna meet up Sunday night?

Jacob struggles to suppress his joy.

JACOB
Yeah, sure. You wanna come over here? There's no one around. We could watch a movie too if you want.

STEWIE (V.O.)
What about dinner?

Jacob hesitates. His heart races.

JACOB
Yeah, sure. I can make pasta if you want.

STEWIE (V.O.)
You sure?

JACOB
I just did a semester in Florence. I've been dying to show off my new culinary skills.

STEWIE (V.O.)
Okay. I'm looking forward to it.

JACOB
Me too.

Silence on the line.

STEWIE (V.O.)
Well, I'll let you get back to it.

JACOB
I'll be done in about an hour. Wanna talk then?

STEWIE (V.O.)
Yeah, sure.

JACOB
Great. I'll call you.

STEWIE (V.O.)
Don't suck too much.

Jacob chuckles.

JACOB
I'll space it out, I promise. Talk to you later.

STEWIE (V.O.)
Later, sexy boy.

JACOB
Bye-bye.

Jacob hangs up. He grins hard, galloping in place, squealing a bit. He regains his composure and turns on the vacuum.

WHALE

Gomorrah

Whale gets off the Metro at Hollywood & Vine. The sun's gone, all the streets artificially illuminated, as phony a daylight as anything in La La Land. Whale wanders at a slow pace, a warm breeze passing through him. He's wearing a polo when everyone else is wearing a light jacket. He ponders the on-the-nose irony that he hasn't let California's climate change him deep inside and make him think the warm desert nights are cold the way everyone else blah-blah-blah and he hates himself for it. Such poetic bullcrap for such a hard business town.

Whale slows at the sight of a black man in an Adidas tracksuit handing a baggie of coke to the driver of a silver sedan. He looks around, scanning for cops or Karens walking their kids on leashes, someone who'd freak out at such a sight, but there's none around. The driver of the silver sedan hands the Dealer money and drives off. The Dealer pockets it fast and returns to his post. Whale stays where he is, debating whether or not to say anything. He just witnessed a drug deal. And as white as it was for him to think so, it was just like it was on *The Wire*.

The Dealer looks at Whale. "Hey man, what you want?"

WHALE
I'm okay, thanks.

Whale walks on. Stops. He looks back at the black man.

WHALE (CONT'D)
Can I ask you something?

"Shoot, dude."

Whale points to where the silver sedan used to be.

WHALE
You just...

"Sold some snow? Yeah."

Whale looks around for witnesses.

The Dealer's amused. He holds up a fist. "Brandon."

Whale tentatively fist-bumps back.

WHALE
Nice to meet you, Brendan.

"Brandon."

WHALE
Brandon, yeah.

Whale looks around again.

WHALE (CONT'D)
You really deal out in the open like this?

"Man, why you whisperin?" Brandon exclaims. "Ain't no cops around. Cops don't care about this shit."

WHALE
Hate to break it to you, but yeah they do.

"Nah. You know when they care? When some white bitch ODs. Or when some good-for-nothin Compton nigga shoots across the street and hits a baby or some shit. It hasta hit the news is all I'm sayin. That or one of them annual report with drug statistics tellin the pigs to cover their fat asses."

```
                    WHALE
        I could be an undercover cop.
```

Brandon blows his lips. "Please, you ain't no cop! You ain't even human." Whale frowns.

```
                    WHALE
        I know. I'm a whale.
```

"What? A whale?" Brandon flaps a dismissive hand. "Nah, man, I know you mean no harm. That's all I meant. You got muscles and shit, but I know you come in peace."

Whale nods imperceptibly. Turns to walk away.

"What accent is that?" Brandon asks.

```
                    WHALE
        I have an accent?
```

"Where you from?"

```
                    WHALE
        You ever been to Philly?
```

"Hell yeah, bro. My nigga Tom Hanks." Brandon laughs. "*Rocky* and shit."

```
                    WHALE
        Well I'm not actually from Philly. I was born nearby,
        30 minutes away. Phoenixville.
```

"Phoenixville? Sounds fire."

Whale laughs at Brandon's pun.

```
                    WHALE
        Yeah, I loved it there.
                  (pause)
        It's weird though. I never knew until I became an
        adult that Phoenixville has a really bad drug
        problem.
```

"Must've been in a real bougie neighborhood."

```
                    WHALE
        Not really. I think it's because I went to school in
        Rosemont, about 20 minutes outside Phoenixville. I
        only went there and back home.
```

Whale looks off, memories flying back.

```
                    WHALE (CONT'D)
        Except this one summer. Right after 11th grade I
        wanted to get out of the house more, but I didn't
        know how to drive, so I took my dad's bike and rode
        all around town. Anywhere I wanted. I went to the
        library and read manga all day. I'd bike over to
        Pertucci's for some orange-vanilla soft serve. Rode
        through the cemetery. Caught a flick at the Colonial
        Theatre. They filmed The Blob there. You ever see
        that?
```

"The what?"

```
                    WHALE
        The Blob with Steve McQueen.
```

Brandon's face lights up. "Steve McQueen?! Really?!"

WHALE
The white one.

Brandon instantly deflates. "Ah man! Fuck!"

WHALE
It's about this pink Jell-O from outer space that eats everything it touches. There's a scene where it gets into the movie theatre and all the teenyboppers run out into the street, screaming their heads off. That's it. That's Phoenixville.

"You went there?"

WHALE
Yeah.

"What's it called?"

WHALE
The Colonial Theatre.

Brandon scoffs. "It would be called that. Probably plays *Gone With the Wind* all the time, huh?" He laughs. Whale chuckles uncomfortably.

WHALE
It's a nice place.

"What'cha see there?" Brandon asks.

Whale hesitates.

WHALE
Gone With the Wind.

Brandon drops his smile.

WHALE (CONT'D)
Shaft was sold out.

Brandon punches Whale in the shoulder. "I'm just fucking with ya, man. What else did you do in Phoenixville?"

WHALE
Not much. Wanted to do more but Dad threw out the bike.

"The fuck he do that for?"

WHALE
There was too much stuff in the garage.

"He didn't even ask you?"

WHALE
It was his bike.
(pause)
Maybe it's good he did that, you know, because of all the drugs.

Brandon shakes his head. "Drugs ain't all that bad. Everyone does drugs."

Whale looks off, a somber frown on his face.

WHALE
(softly quoting)
"Who's everyone?"

"Everyone, man!" Brandon exclaims. "Just cause you do drugs don't make you no junkie. You know who does drugs? Politicians. Producers. Waitresses. Taxi drivers. Housewives. The pigs. Yuppie college bitches. Don't matter where you are, how much you got, how much you make. Life's hard, man. Everyone needs something."

```
                    WHALE
     Not me.
```

"Oh really?" Brandon asks. "Then why'd you come out here, man?"

Whale doesn't respond.

"Everyone who wasn't born here, the ones that actually went out of their way to come here, they all end up disappointed. I saw this video on YouTube, one of them courses on film history. The professor said there's only two types of stories about LA."

```
                    WHALE
     Boosters and Noirs.
```

Brandon grins. "You saw it too?!"

Whale chuckles.

```
                    WHALE
     No. When I was in college, I took a whole class on LA
     stories.
               (scoffs)
     How stupid that sounds now.
```

Whale looks at Brandon and sighs.

```
                    WHALE (CONT'D)
     I'll leave you be, Brendan.
```

"Brandon."

```
                    WHALE
     Nice meeting you.
```

Whale walks away. "Yo! College boy!" Brandon calls, pulling a baggie from his pocket. "Here, on the house." He tosses it at Whale. It bounces off Whale's sneakers and flops on the ground. Cocaine.

Whale picks it up. Hands it back to Brandon.

```
                    WHALE
     I don't want this.
```

"Nah, man. Keep it."

```
                    WHALE
     I'm not.
```

"What are you afraid of?" Brandon asks. "If anyone's getting arrested it's me. And what would they get me for? It's illegal to sell, illegal to make, illegal to move, but last I checked it ain't illegal to give away."

```
                    WHALE
     It's not good business.
```

"You're not 'business.' You made that clear." Brandon points to the baggie. "That is *advertising*, my man. You try it out, you like it, you come back to me, and I'll get some of the good shit." He raises a finger. "But then you gotta pay. It's the Sample Incentive Stratagem."

Whale raises his brows.

Brandon shrugs. "I take YouTube business courses too."

Whale studies the baggie of cocaine. Rolls it around his fingers. Looks back at Brandon.

"Come on," Brandon says encouragingly. "It'll take the edge off."

Whale takes a deep breath. Pockets the coke.

```
                    WHALE
        Okay.
```

"That a boy!" Brandon says, slapping Whale's arm. "I'll be here."

Whale nods politely and walks on. Turns the corner toward Sunset Boulevard. Soon as he's out of visual range of Brandon, he removes the baggie from of his pocket and tosses it into the first available trash can.

Whale walks five steps before slowing to a stop. Looks back at the trash can. Stares. Reluctantly wanders back, retrieves the baggie of coke, and walks on.

JACOB

Part of Your World

INT. WHITMAN UNIVERSITY - LB 710 - BATHROOM MIRROR - NIGHT

Jacob slides American Crew Molding Clay through his hair, singing and dancing along to Billy Joel's "Uptown Girl." He's wearing a tan Godfather graphic tee and blue jeans.

DOC BROWN (V.O.)
GREAT SCOTT!

Jacob looks at his phone. A text from Stewie.

"I'm outside, sexy!"

Jacob grins. He slides on his red leather jacket. Races out the door.

CUT TO:

EXT. BIG BUILDING - NIGHT

Stewie waits outside the doors in a lavender Calvin Klein polo, gray shorts, and the same red Nike baseball cap. He waddles back and forth on his heels, whistling ambiently.

JACOB (O.S.)
Wrong one.

Stewie whips his head. Jacob's waltzing over with a warm smile from the building next door.

STEWIE
I thought you said the little building.

JACOB
I did. That's the Big Building.
(points behind)
THAT's the Little Building. Whitman's absolutely obsessed with irony.

STEWIE
Not very subtle.

JACOB
I think that's the point. Like a comment on irony or something.

Stewie chuckles. Jacob rolls his eyes.

JACOB (CONT'D)
I know, believe me.

Jacob looks up at the Little Building, unsure.

JACOB (CONT'D)
We don't have to stay if you don't want.

STEWIE
It's okay. I wanna go in.

Stewie smiles. Jacob kisses him.

JACOB
I'm glad it's a date.

Stewie hugs Jacob. Jacob nestles his head on Stewie's shoulder, smiling, savoring. Stewie kisses Jacob's temple.

STEWIE
You smell great.

JACOB
Thanks. It's called "Unpredictable."

Stewie pauses.

STEWIE
That is a FANTASTIC name.

CUT TO:

INT. LITTLE BUILDING - LOBBY - NIGHT

A portly SECURITY GUARD (40s) sits patiently behind the desk. Jacob holds the door open for Stewie.

JACOB
I can't believe it's only been a week.

STEWIE
I know, I was just thinking that.

SECURITY GUARD
Your IDs, gentlemen.

STEWIE
Excuse me?

JACOB
He needs to scan your driver's license to let you into the building.

Stewie hesitates.

STEWIE
Oh. Right.

Stewie pulls out his wallet. Jacob taps his student ID on a scanner, the red LED turning green.

Stewie discreetly hands his driver's license to the Security Guard. He scans it and hands it back.

SECURITY GUARD
Good to go.

Stewie takes the driver's license face-down and instantly pockets it. Jacob catches this.

JACOB
Are you hiding your license from me?

Stewie looks at Jacob.

STEWIE
What?

JACOB
You are, aren't you?

STEWIE
No. It's a really bad picture of me. My hair looks awful.

Jacob purses his lips.

JACOB
I know what you mean.

Stewie relaxes as Jacob pushes the elevator button.

JACOB (CONT'D)
My sister and I can't stand getting our picture taken. Must be an Asperger's thing.

STEWIE
Melanie?

JACOB
Karen.

STEWIE
Your twin?

JACOB
No. Melanie's the neurotypical twin, Karen's three years older and autistic.

STEWIE
Got it.
(pause)
I'm just so used to my twin being exactly like me.

Jacob chuckles.

JACOB
Melanie's half my height, loves hip-hop and country and nothing else, and she got a full ride scholarship to Eastern by playing softball. If we didn't have share a birthday and a bathroom, you'd never know we were twins.

Stewie nods. The elevator still hasn't arrived.

STEWIE
Which one of you is older?

JACOB
Me, six minutes. You?

STEWIE
Me, three minutes.

JACOB
Hell yeah, another one.

Jacob and Stewie high five, chuckling. They keep waiting, their glee fading off.

STEWIE
You shared a bathroom with your sister?

JACOB
Don't get me started on that.

DING! The elevator doors open.

CUT TO:

INSIDE THE ELEVATOR

Jacob and Stewie calmly stand next to each other.

JACOB
I've never really noticed how slow this is.

STEWIE
What'd you get your father for Father's Day?

JACOB
Nothing. What about you?

STEWIE
My father passed away seven years ago.

JACOB
Oh, I'm sorry. He couldn't have been that old.

Stewie shakes his head.

JACOB (CONT'D)
What was it, if you don't mind me asking?

STEWIE
Stage IV lung cancer. He only made it three weeks after his diagnosis.

JACOB
Fuck. God, that's awful.

Stewie frowns, the wound still sore.

STEWIE
Twenty-three days actually.

Jacob gives Stewie a big hug.

JACOB
I'm sorry.

STEWIE
Thank you.

Stewie kisses Jacob's head.

STEWIE (CONT'D)
You're such a sweetie.

Jacob smiles faintly.

JACOB
Does your mom know about me?

Stewie looks at Jacob, confounded.

STEWIE
No.

JACOB
She's not homophobic or anything is she?

STEWIE
No. I just didn't tell her.

JACOB
Why not?

Stewie hesitates.

STEWIE
She'd think you're too young.

JACOB
Uh-huh.

Awkward silence.

STEWIE
You already told your mom I was thirty-nine, I take it.

Jacob looks at Stewie, a bit ashamed.

JACOB
I tell her everything.
(pause)
How'd you think I figured out it was a date?

Stewie nods subtly. Goes silent for a moment.

STEWIE
How'd she take it?

JACOB
You being eighteen years older than me?

STEWIE
Yeah.

Jacob hesitates.

JACOB
Doesn't matter what she thinks.

CUT TO:

INT. FILM IMMERSION - NIGHT

Stewie and Jacob wander through the quiet and empty open floor plan.

STEWIE
This is really freaky.

JACOB
I know. Reminds me of those closed down Toys "R" Us's. All that vacant warehouse space. Everything all disproportionate.

STEWIE
Where are the chairs?

JACOB
There's a few in the kitchen and in the TV room over there, but we mostly sit on the floor. Very bohemian.

STEWIE
You have to clean everything by yourself?

JACOB
Just LB.

STEWIE
LB?

JACOB
Little Building. Sorry, college uses a lot of acronyms.

STEWIE
Like what?

JACOB
DH is a big one. Dining Hall, first floor of the Big Building.

STEWIE
That's another residence hall?

JACOB
Yeah. Little Building, Big Building, Paramount Way over on Washington, and down Boylston by the Edgar Allen Poe statue is The Weird One.

STEWIE
The Weird One?

JACOB
Smaller than the Little Building, bigger than the Big Building, and closer than Paramount Way with a triangle top: The Weird One.

STEWIE
Why don't they just call it the Weird Building?

JACOB
Because it's a comment on the superficial lack of unity in a postmodern world.

STEWIE
In other words, they forgot.

JACOB
Exactly.

Stewie approaches the glass TV room.

STEWIE
This is cool.

JACOB
Someone's always using it for something. Movie nights. Comedy Central.
(scoffs)
CNN.

STEWIE
I'm sure.

JACOB
This floor's a learning community too.

STEWIE
What does that mean?

JACOB
Most of the floors at Whitman are just normal, you know, scenarios. This is one of the themed floors.

STEWIE
Co-ed?

JACOB
The suites are gendered but the floors themselves are all mixed. Each residence hall has two learning communities. The Big Building has one for WLP majors... Writing, Literature, and Publishing. The Weird One has a quiet floor for the sensory sensitive, like the last car on an Amtrak.

STEWIE
I see.

JACOB
The two in LB are Eco-Friendly on 14 and this one, Film Immersion. 100% film majors.

STEWIE
Are there a lot of other majors?

JACOB
Oh my God yeah. Communications. Marketing. Poly-Sci. Lot of left-brain bullshit.
(smirks)
No offense.

Stewie shrugs, amused.

JACOB (CONT'D)
How does this compare to Kean's dorms?

STEWIE
I wouldn't know, I never lived on campus. And I always had Ron around, so I never needed to socialize. He's always been my best friend.

JACOB
What was his major?

STEWIE
Computer Science and Mathematics.

JACOB
Did you guys dress alike too?

Stewie laughs.

STEWIE
Not identically, but...
(pause)
Honestly, we really have the exact same taste in everything. Clothes. Music. Friends. The way we talk. Our mannerisms. Until our mid-twenties, that is.

JACOB
What happened then?

STEWIE
I found boys, he found girls. Ever since then we've become opposites, but only since then.

JACOB
The ultimate twin study.

STEWIE
Absolutely.

JACOB
Where's he now?

STEWIE
In Maryland with his wife. Working for the government. Drinking beer. Playing golf. Poker nights with the other straight couples.

JACOB
You still see him, don't you?

STEWIE
When I was still in Jersey I saw him all the time. But now, forget it.

Jacob takes Stewie's hand.

JACOB
C'mon. I wanna show you my suite.

STEWIE
Your sweet what?

Jacob snickers. Leads Stewie off.

CUT TO:

INT. SUITE 710 - NIGHT

Jacob unlocks the door and holds it open for Stewie.

JACOB
Not bad, huh?

STEWIE
It's big.

Jacob points toward the bedroom doors.

JACOB
First on the left's mine. The others were my suitemates'.

STEWIE
All singles?

JACOB
Yeah. Juniors and Seniors don't normally stay on campus. When they do, they usually get the single rooms. I got mine with my disability accommodations.

STEWIE
You never had to share a room with someone?

JACOB
Freshman Year I had a roommate. I started requesting sophomore year and I've been in a single room on Film Immersion ever since.

STEWIE
And your suitemates, they were assigned?

JACOB
No, I met them in Anime Club Sophomore Year and requested them as my suitemates. It's great because Film Immersion is a first-come first-serve thing, and thanks to me they all get to stay here too.

STEWIE
You use your autism to jump the waitlist?

JACOB
If you got it, use it, right?

STEWIE
Do you really NEED a single room on this floor?

Jacob hesitates.

JACOB
I want to be on this floor.
(pause)
The single room thing is an actual necessity though. I need a place to unwind and... It's a thing, um... Asperger's people have, like... It's a sensory overload thing and I need a place to, you know, get away from all that, just to reset. I had the single room in Florence too. Thanks accommodations.

Stewie nods slowly.

JACOB (CONT'D)
They have single rooms out there in the hall that aren't in a suite, but Mom thinks it's better for me to be in a suite to prevent isolation and keep me social.

STEWIE
Okay.

Stewie wanders to the end of the hall, inspecting.

STEWIE (CONT'D)
I guess one of the perks of being a custodian is you don't have to move out.

JACOB
No. I still do.

STEWIE
Why?

JACOB
They reassign the rooms from scratch every year. Makes it easier. Besides, there's a suite on the other end of the floor reserved just for Seniors living on campus. It has a view of the park and everything. Best seat in the house.

STEWIE
I guess you can just go in and spend a night there if you wanted to.

JACOB
No, Carter has all the keys.

STEWIE
Who's Carter?

JACOB
The RA. He's here with me, down the hall.
(pause)
I sorta have a crush on him.

Stewie raises his brows.

STEWIE
Is he hot?

JACOB
Gorgeous. Of course he's straight.

STEWIE
What does he look like?

Jacob pulls out his phone.

JACOB
I took a few pictures of him.

Jacob shows Stewie his phone.

JACOB (CONT'D)
Sometimes I see him in the library or in the DH or watching TV, chatting with his frat bros and I just... can't help myself. He's just so fucking hot. And I can't really jerk off to just my imagination.

Stewie looks at Jacob, a bit disturbed.

JACOB (CONT'D)
That's him right there. That was, uh, last November I think.

Stewie swipes through the photos.

STEWIE
How does he not catch you taking these?

JACOB
Lots of practice.

Jacob looks up at Stewie.

JACOB (CONT'D)
Well? What do you think?

Stewie shrugs.

STEWIE
He's okay.

JACOB
Just okay?

STEWIE
He's not my type.

Jacob sighs. Takes his phone back.

STEWIE (CONT'D)
(light laugh)
What?

JACOB
I don't know.
(pause)
What IS your type?

Stewie rubs the back of his head.

STEWIE
That is, uh...

JACOB
It's okay if you don't know.

STEWIE
Oh, I know. It's just become a running joke between me and my friends that I only want Mr. Perfect.

JACOB
Who's Mr. Perfect?

STEWIE
Mr. Perfect doesn't exist. Nobody's perfect. Mr. PREFERENCE on the other hand, well... He's just a nice, fun, cute boy who doesn't smoke or do drugs. No tattoos. Not too obese or muscled. White.

JACOB
White? Why?

STEWIE
I'm only attracted to white guys.

Jacob hesitates.

JACOB
Okay.

STEWIE
And no redheads or black-haired guys, just blond or brown hair. Not too long or buzzed off, just enough bangs to cover the forehead. And not a slut or someone who sleeps around a lot. Just a spontaneous, sweet guy that likes to have a good time. But he can't have a beard. He has to be clean shaven, and not covered in body hair either. And he doesn't have to like the Mets, but he absolutely CANNOT like the Yankees.

JACOB
That's really a dealbreaker for you?

Stewie stares at Jacob with utmost seriousness.

STEWIE
Of course.

JACOB
Is that it?

STEWIE
Just one more, no piercings.
(pause)
And he can't be too queeny or flamboyant. Just a fun, masculine, clean-cut boy next door with all of his teeth and bangs covering his forehead.

Jacob stares, struggling to process.

JACOB
My hair doesn't cover my forehead.

Stewie looks at Jacob's hair.

STEWIE
(puzzled)
I know.

CUT TO:

INSIDE JACOB'S ROOM

Jacob unlocks the black Rhino chest and lifts the lid, revealing his massive Blu-Ray collection.

STEWIE
Woah.

JACOB
I know. Only took three years to accumulate.

STEWIE
How many are in here?

JACOB
Around three hundred, I think. I call it my Dark Chest of Wonders.

STEWIE
Your what?

JACOB
It's a song by Nightwish. They're Finnish Evanescence except a little bit harder.

Jacob points to the crates of LPs next to the desk.

JACOB (CONT'D)
Speaking of, there's my record collection.

STEWIE
You actually have records?

JACOB
Everyone has records, you kidding me?

Stewie flips through the LPs.

STEWIE
Alphabetized.

JACOB
Of course.
(pause)
That's actually a big problem with having a fucking pirate's chest of Blu-Rays. There's so many types of cases and different sizes, there's no way I can realistically organize them. I'm the only one who'd know where everything is.

STEWIE
You must be popular on this floor with a collection like this.

Jacob frowns.

JACOB
I certainly thought I'd be.

CUT TO:

IN THE HALLWAY

Stewie carries Jacob's laptop and charger. Jacob closes his bedroom door, a Blu-Ray case and HDMI cord in his hand.

STEWIE
Your other suitemates screenwriters too?

JACOB
Directors.
(pause)
Actually Nich is a Cinematography major.

STEWIE
"Niche"?

JACOB
Short for Nicholas.

STEWIE
Is that another commentary on subtlety or something?

Jacob laughs.

JACOB
No, just a coincidence.

CUT TO:

INT. FILM IMMERSION - NIGHT

Jacob leads the way to the TV room. Stewie follows, his hands full.

JACOB
TJ comes from a lot of money. The idea is that he bankrolls the four of us to stay in LA after graduation until we make enough to be self-sufficient. I'll write everything, of course.

STEWIE
You guys any good?

JACOB
I think so. We get along great. That helps a ton.

STEWIE

No, I mean do you guys think you're ready to be taken seriously out there? Or are you more in the "hone your craft" phase?

JACOB

Oh, we're ready. I'm writing my fifth feature now. Everyone else has at least three shorts shot and finished a piece.

STEWIE

Is that enough?

Jacob stops walking. Turns to face Stewie.

JACOB

When I was studying abroad, one of classes was the Cultural History of Florence. We learned all about the Medici Family. They had bank. Literally, they owned banks for hundreds of years. They're the ones that single-handedly paid for the Renaissance. The Duomo, the David, Giotto's Bell Tower, the Mona Lisa, that was all them financing great art from great masters. The Renaissance wasn't just about the talent. It was really about the money it took to pay for the best materials, to afford the creative freedom Michelangelo and Da Vinci had. That's what art really is, a very expensive, very personal investment with no return. You can have art without a budget, of course, but you always end up getting what you pay for.

STEWIE

Who pays for art in Hollywood?

JACOB

The Weinsteins. A24. No one else really. Recently big studios are using their record-breaking profits from mega-franchises like Marvel and <u>Star Wars</u> to finance more artsy auteur films in the Oscar circuit. That's why this decade's had the best movies. More money available to throw away on art.

STEWIE

That's what you guys wanna make? Artsy films?

JACOB

Blockbusters nowadays are just necessary evils. Like the actual banks Lorenzo di Medici made his fortune from. Art has never been more "in." There's a New Hollywood Renaissance happening out there. We just gotta make it fast before it ends.

CUT TO:

INSIDE THE TV ROOM

Jacob plugs his laptop into TV via HDMI. Stewie waits on the couch.

STEWIE

You don't eat popcorn or anything?

JACOB

No.

STEWIE

Me neither.

Stewie looks at the empty Blu-Ray case.

STEWIE (CONT'D)

<u>Vertigo</u>, huh?

Jacob puts the disc into his laptop's Blu-Ray drive.

JACOB

1958, Jimmy Stewart and Kim Novak.

STEWIE
I've never even heard of it.

Jacob joins Stewie on the couch.

JACOB
It's a Hitchcock. Two years before Psycho.

STEWIE
Oh, I love Psycho.

JACOB
Don't get your hopes up. This ain't Psycho.

STEWIE
What is it?

Jacob thinks.

JACOB
You'll like it. It's about a guy with a shit ton of preferences.

STEWIE
Is he picky about hair?

Jacob laughs.

JACOB
Yes.

Jacob curls up next to Stewie. Stewie looks up at the bright florescent lights throughout the common room.

STEWIE
Can you do something about the lights?

JACOB
No. They're always on.

STEWIE
All night?

JACOB
Yup.

STEWIE
That's incredibly wasteful.

JACOB
Tuition's $50,000 a year. They gotta spend it on something.

STEWIE
Yeah. Actual janitors.

JACOB
Shhh! It's starting.

Stewie kisses Jacob's forehead. Jacob smiles, his eyes glued to the screen.

DREW

Where Everybody Knows Your Name

Drew and Jimmy sit in a booth inside Marcus MacDonald's, a handsome Irish pub with great mood lighting. A blond server in tight green plaid walks over. "Name's Tyler." He smiles at them both. "What'cha guys drinking tonight?"

Drew glances at Jimmy. "Well?"

Jimmy looks down nervously. "You pick."

"I'll give you guys a moment," Tyler says, stepping away a bit.

"No, we know." Drew interrupts. He looks at Jimmy. "You ever have Guinness?"

Jimmy hesitates. "Yeah. Of course. I love Guinness."

Drew smirks. What a liar. "Two Guinnesses," he tells Tyler. "One for each of us. Room temp if you got it." Drew looks to Jimmy. "That's how they drink it out there."

Jimmy nods, impressed.

Tyler jots the simple order on the pad. Looks at Jimmy. Smirks subtly.

Jimmy's cheeks flush.

Tyler holds his gaze on Jimmy for a bit. "Be right back, guys." He wanders toward the bar.

Drew furrows his brow. Holds hands up. "Right in front of me?"

Jimmy flashes a braggart's grin. "He probably just assumed you're my dad."

Drew instantly deflates. "Whatever."

"What are you, jealous?"

"Please."

"You are, aren't you!"

"I could get him if I wanted him."

"Oh really?"

Drew stares knowingly. "*Believe me.*" He takes a deep breath. "So. Jimmy."

"Brian."

Drew almost furrows his brow. Thank God he didn't. "How's life? You have a good week?"

Jimmy bursts out a chuckle. "You don't get out much, do you? 'You have a good week?'"

"Yeah, that was, uh..."

"Don't waste my time on preemptive reciprocation. Tell me."

Drew moves his hands indecisively. "I don't want to..."

"It's my idea. What's on your mind?"

Drew exhales slowly through his nose. "It's so stupid, honestly."

"I'm sure it is!" Jimmy exclaims. "A lot of life is stupid when you overanalyze it. Whatever it is ain't stupid to you, is it?"

Drew leans back, right arm stretched across the booth. "I'm in a bit of crisis at the moment."

"Okay."

"I just feel like..." Drew scratches his chin. "Like there are days when I feel like the master of the universe, limited only by my inability to believe it to be true." He goes quiet. "And other days I feel like an elephant."

"An elephant?"

"Big nose. Always charging. Lumbering around. Knocking over things. Getting whipped by a ringmaster. Performing tricks against my will for peanuts. Obsessed with nut."

Jimmy bumps his brows with a growl.

Drew smiles. It fades fast. "Not being able to forget, even if I wanted to. Always feeling ignored by everyone else in the room. Afraid of mice." He pauses, withdrawing inward. "Can't jump."

Jimmy furrows his brow. "Jump?"

Drew blinks back. "Sorry. Inside joke."

Jimmy looks around. "Inside joke with who?"

Drew smiles enigmatically. "With *whom*."

"Huh?"

"Inside joke with *whom*."

Jimmy chuckles. "Hey, I don't know about all that. You're sweet. And I like big noses."

"Thanks." Drew looks around the pub, sighing wistfully. "I always feel like myself in places like this."

"Why's that?"

Drew runs a tongue across his teeth. "I dunno." He pats his right hand on the cushion. Taps off-beat on his thigh.

Jimmy thinks of something to say. Leans in. "This uh... ringmaster you mentioned. Is he your boyfriend?"

"I wish." Drew suddenly drops his smile. "Oh, no, no not with Th... not with him. I mean in general."

Jimmy nods. "Who is he then?"

"My business partner."

"You in the industry?"

"No," Drew instantly lies. "I run a speakeasy in Los Feliz. Knock Twice. You ever been?"

"Are you serious?!" Jimmy scoffs with disbelief. "Dude, I work at Harry 79 right next door!"

Drew stares. "You work there?"

"I'm a server! That's so weird!"

Drew shifts in his seat. "Yeah, that's uh..." Clears his throat. "Quite the coincidence."

"You run it with PT Barnum? The speakeasy?"

"Only technically. We used to run it together, just the two of us, back in the day. Then we started losing money and had to restructure everything. Changed its name. It's more corporate now. Ever since then I've been more like the GM and he's the owner." Drew exhales roughly. "And for good reason, apparently."

"I don't see what the big deal is. What could go wrong at a bar?"

Drew looks into Jimmy's clean eyes. "You'd be surprised." He rubs his biceps, softening. "Tell you the truth, he's my only friend. Isn't that so pathetic? Forty years old and I only got one friend?"

"That's not as uncommon as you think. There's a lot of people in the world. What are we up to now, eight billion?"

"*Way* more than that."

"Even still, that's eight billion years of human existence happening simultaneously every year."

Drew cocks his head back. "Holy fuck."

"Makes everything smaller, doesn't it?" Jimmy looks around. "Think about how many people you meet on a yearly basis. Not that many, right?"

Drew shrugs.

"So imagine what it would be like if you didn't run a bar," Jimmy says. "Or lived in a shittier country. Or had a worse upbringing growing up. I'm sure there's at least ten million that go their entire lives without touching another living soul."

"You mean metaphorically?"

"And literally. Ugly people. Frightened people. Men in general really. That's why I came to LA. I don't wanna be found dead in my house three weeks later because of the smell. I'm gonna be somebody or die trying."

Drew nods. "What about your family?"

"If I can still call them that?" Jimmy scoffs. "They're 30 miles out of Seattle."

Tyler returns with a pair of dark bottles. "Two room temp Guinnesses."

Drew hands over the corporate card Theo hates him using. "Go ahead and run it."

"Sure thing, boss." Tyler walks away.

Jimmy raises his brows. "How about that?"

Drew grins. "Yeah, that was really hot." They raise their bottles for a toast. They drink.

Jimmy instant gags on his. Forces it down. "Oh."

Drew smirks knowingly. "Thought you said you had it before."

Jimmy puts his bottle on the table. Moves it away. "Must not be a beer guy I guess."

Drew takes a big sip of his. "So what's the big end goal for you, Jimmy Lyons?"

"Screenwriting."

Drew's stomach turns like a rotisserie chicken. "Screenwriting?"

"I'm taking online classes at UCLA. It's not great, but I don't have much of a choice. I need my job. It'll take a couple years longer to get my diploma though. That's what really bites."

Tyler returns with the receipts. Hands it to Drew. "Here you go, sir."

Drew takes the bill, instantly pocketing his credit card before Jimmy could see his real name. "Thank you."

"Top's for you." Tyler hands Drew a pen. "Bottoms for me."

Drew stares at Tyler, his face turning into putty.

Tyler winks. Nods at Jimmy. Walks away.

"I think I just came," Jimmy declares.

"Was he saying what I think he was saying?" Drew asks.

Jimmy bounces in his seat. "Ooh! Ooh! Can we keep him? Please? Please?"

Drew chuckles. Puts his pen to the top receipt. "What's your genre?"

"Don't really have one. I just like movies that matter, you know?"

Drew suddenly stops signing, a chill running down his spine.

Jimmy doesn't notice. "And I know I have limited life experience, but I see things. Patterns. I'm so far removed from everything going on around me that I actually think I'm better off to write about it, you know? Not bogged down by stress or debt or bad relationships like everyone else my age. Movies are my life, you know? Everyone loves them. And there's so many stories you can tell on film. So many ways you can sculpt a series of pictures and audio to make you feel like you're in another place. Another body. Another life. I've learned so much about the world from watching movies. Not necessarily one movie at a time. I always cross-reference them. Two of my favorite movies from 2015 are *Carol* and *Brooklyn*. You ever hear of them?"

Drew smiles. "No," he lies.

"They're both about women in New York City in 1952. In the same Oscar year! How does that happen?" Jimmy nods. "Always thought that was cool. Anyway, *Brooklyn*'s about an Irish immigrant finding a new life in, you guessed it—"

"Queens."

"Funny. And *Carol*'s about two women. One's rich and married and the other's young and carefree. They meet by chance and fall in love. And remember, that's in a time when you can't be gay. And it's directed by a gay man, so it's not all about tits and pussy and..." Jimmy gags. "You know. It's really about emotion. So you got two movies from 2015 depicting New York in 1952, but in *Brooklyn* it's a haven. A beautiful land of opportunity for immigrants. A chance at a new life. In *Carol* it's a prison. All those barriers and classes. Rigid rules keeping two soulmates apart. Trapping them in old ways. Cold. Relentless." Jimmy shakes his head. "It's just so cool thinking of life like that, you know? Everyone around you has a story. Even if it doesn't mesh with yours, it's still valid. If everyone can just get past all that surface level bullshit and their own bias, they'll find something in there they can understand and relate to. That's why we have movies. That's what they do." Jimmy beams proudly. "And that's why I wanna make them."

Drew stares at Jimmy with profound wonder.

Jimmy tries not to laugh at Drew's expression. "What?"

"You remind me of someone I used to know."

Jimmy flashes his brows up. "A boyfriend?"

"I haven't seen him in a long time." Drew sighs. "I still think about him though. A lot, actually. Recently."

"You miss him?"

Drew nods with cold eyes. "I really do."

Jimmy smiles sympathetically. "Tell me about him."

"He was really mature for his age," Drew whispers. "Very smart. Sweet. Always made an effort with everything. A bit fat, but he was never really bothered by it. More than anything, he knew *exactly* who he was. What he could do. What he couldn't. The difference between right and wrong. He didn't want to hurt anyone or stomp on anyone's toes. To him, a perfect world was just..." Drew shrugs. "Peaceful coexistence."

Jimmy senses vulnerability in Drew's face. "Who was he? What's his name?"

"Jacob." Drew smiles warmly. "Jacob Andrezj."

"Wait." Jimmy sits up. "Not with a Z and a J at the end?"

Drew goes numb. "Yeah. How did you know?"

Jimmy scoffs, a massive grin on his face. "*The Surgery*! Dude, I fucking LOVE *The Surgery*! You have no idea. I'm like the only person who seems to even know about it. It's what made me want to be a screenwriter in the first place."

Drew nods. "It's good."

"Good? It's PERFECT! It should've won Live Action Short Film. It was fucking robbed, I'm telling ya."

"That's debatable."

"And the guy that directed it, Ree-an something? Hoffman? Ree-an Hoffman?"

"Rian Hoffman."

"Oh." Jimmy chuckles. "God, I've been pronouncing it 'Ree-an' all this time."

"He gets that a lot, I'm sure."

"He put so much emotion in everything, even the B-roll. There's like a whole other story going on from just the performances."

Drew half-frowns. "A bit low budget, don't you think?"

"And that's a bad thing? Money doesn't guarantee quality. In fact you stop adding immersive value and start detracting personality. Look at Drew Lawrence's movies for example. God, you ever see one of those?"

Drew stares. "I dunno."

"You would know, believe me." Jimmy laughs. "They suck ass."

Drew frowns. "I'm sure they don't suck—"

"You know what it is?" Jimmy leans back, thinking. "What's that movie he put out eight years ago? *The Adventures of Franklin and Ashley*?"

"Oh yeah. I've seen that."

"It was good, I admit." Jimmy pauses. "Which is why Not That Nutty's been rehashing *Franklin and Ashley* ever since."

Drew pauses. "I don't think that's—"

"A married couple makes a bet to see who could cheat on each other first, shenanigans ensue, then it's revealed to be a commentary on modern love with a satirical dig on the two-party system."

"And that's hysterical."

"So it's pretty much... admittedly silly premise... second act break twist adds surprise depth... on-the-nose metaphor of whatever's going on the headlines." Jimmy shrugs. "Every single Not That Nutty movie uses that formula. *Cameron's Run. Glitterbomb. The Great Train Mystery. Two Cows and a Chicken. Top of the Morning. Labor Day. A Pinch of Salt.* It keeps going from there. It's like he took the one thing he actually did right and milked the shit out of it. Am I wrong?"

Drew blinks. "I'm not really sure."

"And what the fuck is up with all the elephants?!"

"Elephants?"

"Haven't you noticed that every single Drew Lawrence movie has an elephant shoehorned into the third act? They're fighting an elephant. They're dreaming of elephants. There's an elephant painting. An elephant statue. It's stupid."

Drew hesitates. "I-I think it's supposed to be a metaphor on the elephant in the room."

Jimmy stares blankly. "Yeah. Everyone knows that. That's why it's stupid. He really thinks we can't get it?"

"I mean, hey, at least he's putting out original content. He's not recycling old IPs."

"You ever hear of *Black Mirror*?"

Drew widens his eyes. "Have *I* heard of *Black Mirror*?!"

"It's an old show, just checking." Jimmy sighs. "Drew Lawrence movies are like bad *Black Mirror* episodes. They think they're so smart and witty but they just take whatever flash-in-the-pan topic people are angrily tweeting about, swap humans for aliens, politics for sex, flip the genders or races, throw in an elephant at the end, copy the aesthetic of whatever box office hit just came out, fuck up the execution, and release it five years too late. That's it. And the worst part is people eat that up! They fall for it every time! Drew Lawrence and Theo... what's-his-name are shysters. They've found a way to make billions selling shit. And not even new shit!"

Drew scratches his eyebrow. "When you actually stop and think about the sheer amount of work that goes into each one, there's just no feasible way to finish fast enough to—"

"Doesn't matter. They're not adding anything. They're all just a waste of time."

Drew takes a deep breath. "You know what?" He bits his lower lip. "I think I have to agree with you on that."

Jimmy smirks. "Good." He frowns at his slightly empty Guinness bottle. "Whatever happened to Jacob Andrezj? He hasn't made anything since *The Surgery*."

"I'm sure he's around." Drew stares at Jimmy. "Matter of fact, he—"

"I'm sorry to interrupt," says a black bartender with an alarmingly wide smile and a glass of Domergue 15 on the rocks. "I'm Durrell. I recognized you from behind the bar and just wanted to send this over."

Drew glares at the glass. "I didn't order this."

"It's on the house, of course." Durrell places the glass in front of Drew. "I just wanted to thank you for stopping by. I know you have plenty of other options."

Jimmy looks at Drew, perplexed.

"I hope I got it right," Durrell adds eagerly. "My cousin works at Sweet Vermouths. He told me just how you like it."

Drew nods with a polite smile. "Lou's your cousin?"

"Yes sir. He always speaks very highly of you."

"I'm sure he does," Drew makes awkward eye contact with Durrell. Tenderly lifts the glass. Ice chunks, not even a mold. He can already tell by the smell that's it way too watered down. He sips. Tries not to gag. "It's good," Drew lies with a grateful nod.

"Thank you, sir." Durrell nods at Jimmy. "Have a good night."

Jimmy scoffs, weirded out. "You too."

Durrell wanders off. Drew puts the glass far, *far* away from him. "What were we, um...?" He matches eyes with Jimmy.

Jimmy grins back. "You're somebody, aren't you?"

Drew hesitates. "Aren't we all?"

Jimmy shakes his head. "You're somebody."

Drew's eyes sag. The jig is up.

JACOB

Adaptation.

INT. FILM IMMERSION - TV ROOM - NIGHT

Stewie cocks his head back.

STEWIE
That's it?!

JACOB
Yup. That's how it ends.

Jacob gets up. Shuts off the laptop. Rejoins Stewie on the couch.

JACOB (CONT'D)
Well? What did you think?

Stewie grins at Jacob's childlike earnestness.

STEWIE
It's not as good as Psycho.

JACOB
It's not trying to be Psycho.

STEWIE
What was all that stuff at the end? It turns into a completely different movie.

JACOB
I know. It's the "Layla" of movies.
(chuckles)
In more ways than one.

STEWIE
What was the point of Judy writing the letter if she was just gonna throw it away?

JACOB
We had to find out the twist somehow.

STEWIE
It would've been so much cooler if we didn't know Judy was Madeline until the end.

JACOB
By knowing the twist before Scottie starts changing her, we understand Judy's point of view throughout. Think about it. She loves Scottie but he's only in love with a fictional version of her. But she would rather stay and let him change her back into Madeline because at least he'd love her. It's quite sympathetic considering it's 1958.

Jacob starts biting his nails.

JACOB (CONT'D)
The whole thing's kinda Gatsbyesque too.

Stewie is taken aback by Jacob's chomping and tearing. He downplays his revulsion.

STEWIE
The Great Gatsby?

JACOB
You ever read it?

STEWIE
No.

JACOB
It's sad. Gatsby has everything. Lots of money. Lots of power. Lots of friends. Big parties. A mansion. Fancy cars. But he can't turn back time. Reclaim everything he lost. Undo his mistakes. Just like Scottie with Judy at the end there, literally reliving the past, forcing her to climb that tower. Even the green light in Judy's apartment is a Gatsby reference.

STEWIE
It is?

JACOB
Fitzgerald loves symbols. It's also a commentary on his generation, what he really thought of them, those vain greedy degenerates of the Roaring Twenties.

STEWIE
And that's what Hitchcock did with Vertigo?

JACOB
Not the generation part per se, but it is secretly autobiographical.

STEWIE
How so?

JACOB
Think about it. Scottie meets Madeline and she's married to someone else. Wealthy, beautiful but also really sad. He wants to protect her. But he fails. He couldn't save her. So when he meets a shopgirl named Judy that looks a bit like her, and he tries to help her too. But then he buys her expensive clothes, shoes, jewelry--

STEWIE
--Blonde hair.

JACOB
Exactly. And at the end, when he reenacts the events of Madeline's "suicide," he's literally directing Judy, creating almost an alternate reality where he overcame his fear of heights and made it to the top in time. Really makes you wonder if something happened to him, Hitchcock. Is that why he's so obsessed with blondes in the first place? People didn't understand Vertigo at first because they didn't make that connection, but now it's one of his most acclaimed films. It's a portal into his mind.

Jacob rubs his temple with a single finger, looking off.

JACOB (CONT'D)
So many people go their entire lives without being seen. The things they do, the little ancillary things, unwitnessed. Their true feelings unheard, unacknowledged. That's all we really want, isn't it? The reason we become writers, actors, artists, businessmen, politicians. We want love, sure. Respect. Some settle for being feared, even loathed. But to live your entire life, your one stretch of time on this Earth, with no one even noticing?
(pause)
That's the worst thing in the world.

Stewie nods solemnly.

STEWIE
(points to TV)
There's absolutely no way I'd be able to figure that out unless you told me.

JACOB
I've seen it a lot.

STEWIE
How many times?

JACOB
Not as much as some of the others I own. I only just watched it last year, so... six times now? But watching it with you is like I'm unconsciously seeing it for the first time again.
(pause)
I've never experienced this before.

STEWIE
You re-watch a lot of movies?

JACOB
It's how you get all the details, how and why point A gets to point B. No one wants the same old thing. You have to see too many movies in order to know what HASN'T been done before. What no one expects you to do.

CUT TO:

IN THE KITCHEN

Jacob stirs a pot of tomato sauce on the stove, a second pot of boiling water next to it. Stewie sits at the large table, a propped arm holding up his chin.

JACOB
Who We Are was my first. A movie buff with Asperger's named Josh meets a developmental psych major named Kevin in a club. Kevin sees Josh at his most autistic and loves him anyway, and Josh learns to become more optimistic once their relationship becomes long-distance. I've never been in a relationship, so I was really going off on what I'd seen in movies.

Jacob dumbs a box of penne into the boiling water.

STEWIE
I assume this was after you came out?

JACOB
Oh yeah. I never would've been able to write anything gay while I was still in the closet.

STEWIE
You probably knew just as much about girls than you did about other guys.

Jacob sets the timer.

JACOB
I wanted Josh to be a gay Asperger's guy. Bad enough we have such shitty representation as it is.

STEWIE
You got Rain Man.

Jacob adds spices to the tomato sauce.

JACOB
Rain Man's not autistic, he's a savant. I can't count matchsticks. I'm not good at math. I'm not anti-social either, I actually prefer being around people. And I'm quite capable of having multiple obsessions, none of them involving trains or bugs.

STEWIE
What does that mean?

JACOB
Every autistic kid on TV is obsessed with either trains or bugs. And that's another thing, why are they all kids? We don't grow out of it. We're out here, we exist, but we're not in the movies. You know why? Because there aren't any autistic screenwriters telling autistic stories.

Jacob stirs the tomato sauce.

JACOB (CONT'D)
I wanted to write a romance because I always liked the story of how my parents met.

STEWIE
How did they meet?

JACOB
My mom was in some bar in New Hope, PA. My dad's sitting next to her. She leans over and asks him for the time. He says something like, "The clock's over there," or something. Just blows her off. My mom rolls her eyes and makes some comment about how she has to get back to auditing. My dad looks up and says, "You audit? So do I." There you go. The rest was history.

STEWIE
Wow.

JACOB
So cinematic, right? I obsessed over that growing up. Doesn't matter where or when, it can happen from anyone, even the asshole sitting next to you.

Jacob's smile loses strength.

JACOB (CONT'D)
The divorce kinda changed that though. Now it's a red flag she should've avoided to save herself a nightmare.

STEWIE
Divorce is rough.

Jacob nods a bit, staring off.

JACOB
There's nothing worse than knowing you're only here because of two people who were never meant to be together.

Stewie frowns. Jacob takes a deep breath. Returns to the stove.

JACOB (CONT'D)
My second was a rom-com called Daddy.

STEWIE
Daddy?!

JACOB
Eddie comes out to his parents, Patricia and Walter, but just as he does, his dad reveals HE'S gay and has been cheating on Mom with men for years and wants a divorce. Walter completely stole Eddie's thunder, and now Eddie can't express himself without his mom bringing it all up again. And his dad has no regrets whatsoever, finally free from that awful marriage. Two years later, Walter's getting remarried to a guy he met while he was in France. Eddie goes to meet the fiancé for the first time when he sees a cute young guy named Peter across the bar. And they flirt and

offer to see each other... but then Walter shows up introduces Peter as his fiancé.

STEWIE
How old is Walter?

JACOB
Walter's in his early fifties and Peter's in his low twenties.

STEWIE
A thirty-year age gap, huh?

JACOB
Yup. So there's Eddie having an affair with his twenty-something future stepdad, and then his drug addicted vengeful mother finds out and tries to sabotage the wedding. Ultimately Walter finds out about Peter and Eddie and calls off the wedding. Patricia's thrilled and accidentally ODs. When she comes to, she realizes she put Eddie through hell for making the divorce so tied to his sexuality. Eddie and Peter go find Walter and Walter finally apologizes for doing what he did to Eddie, being on the receiving end of what he did to Patricia. And finally, Walter and Patricia make up. They realize their marriage wasn't so bad after all and all four go to a Pride parade together.

Stewie smiles.

STEWIE
That's really sweet.

The timer beeps. Jacob grabs a colander and dumps the pasta.

JACOB
Number three's Through the Red Door. I only finished it a few months ago during my spring break in Sicily.

STEWIE
Sicily, huh?

JACOB
Yeah. I was in Taormina in this Airbnb that had a roof with a 360° view. It was amazing. Out of season, so the whole place was a ghost town. It was nice. I never lived alone before. I don't like it now, but it was nice in a bite-sized way.

STEWIE
What's Through the Red Door about?

JACOB
It's a pastiche combining The Godfather, The Great Gatsby, Back to the Future, and Carol in one movie.

STEWIE
(chuckling)
Okay.

JACOB
2003. A closeted gay guy named Mitch is tasked by his legless great-grandfather Jack to go back in time to the Roaring Twenties and stop a gangster named Billy Black from pushing Jack in front of a car and ruining Jack's career as an Olympic runner. In order for Mitch to get to Billy Black he has to befriend Billy's number two man, Tommy DeWinkle, and Mitch does this by reading Tommy's diary that got published after Tommy killed himself right after the stock market crash. Mitch goes back in time to 1928, finds Tommy, they start becoming close friends, and then Tommy reveals he's gay and in love with Mitch. Ultimately Mitch and Tommy stop Billy in time, Jack

is saved, and Mitch and Tommy go back to the future together.

STEWIE

Cool.

Jacob throws the penne into the sauce. Stirs it in.

JACOB

I wrote it because I wanted more gay representation before World War II. And I think it's cool that Mitch only comes out when he meets Tommy. Like they're both in the same situation despite being eighty years apart... but they find each other and save each other's lives.

STEWIE

That's so sweet.

JACOB

I did this thing I'm really proud of, during the climax. Billy Black catches Mitch and Tommy in bed together, and Tommy runs off to get away from Mitch, and Mitch stops him at the station and tells him he's from the future. To prove it Mitch reads from his copy of Tommy's diary. Then he gives Tommy the book and tells him to go to the last page.

STEWIE

Oh. Wow.

JACOB

I know! Isn't that so cool?! I can't believe I actually wrote that. A little existential surprise hidden in a gay sci-fi/gangster mashup. Really spices up the sauce.

Jacob adds more spices into the sauce.

JACOB (CONT'D)

My fourth one's not that great though. I wrote it right after I got back to Florence.

STEWIE

What's it called?

JACOB

<u>Murder in Milan</u>.

STEWIE

Sounds like a horror movie.

JACOB

I was trying to be clever with it. It's split into chapters like <u>Kill Bill</u>, it has eight main characters like <u>The Hateful Eight</u>, the most important one getting killed in the first scene and we learn everything about him through flashbacks like <u>Citizen Kane</u>. I wanted to have a realistic murder mystery you couldn't predict, but it just ended up a self-indulgent mess.

STEWIE

What's it about?

JACOB

A group of Americans are studying abroad in Italy and they have this one roommate, Wes. They don't like him very much. He's awkward, unfiltered, too sexual at times. They actually try to kick him out. But when Wes ends up dead with suspicious circumstances, they investigate who he was and realize how wrong their first impressions were.

Jacob serves the pasta and hands a bowl to Stewie.

JACOB (CONT'D)
Wine okay?

STEWIE
Sure.

Jacob pours two glasses of Chianti. They eat.

STEWIE (CONT'D)
This is delicious.

JACOB
Thank you.

Jacob sips his wine.

JACOB (CONT'D)
I based Wes' roommates on my roommates in Florence. I was so involved with getting their personalities accurate that I kept calling them by their aliases. It was so embarrassing.

STEWIE
The one you're working on now, that's number five?

JACOB
Yeah.
(hesitates)
Technically it's number six.

STEWIE
Why technically?

JACOB
Right after Murder in Milan I started a new one called A Night With Myself. It ended up being forty pages. That's too long for a short and too short for a feature, so I don't know what it is.

STEWIE
What's that about?

JACOB
A college Senior named Michael crosses paths with a strange guy named Mikey at a bar. Turns out Mikey is Michael twenty years in the future, and he's time-traveled back to 2016 to spend a night with his younger self. As the night goes on, we start finding out more about Mikey's life in the future and how hard life's been to him and the real reason he went back in time...

STEWIE
That's really cool! That might be my favorite of the bunch.

Jacob stares off.

STEWIE (CONT'D)
You okay?

JACOB
Yeah. Why?

STEWIE
I dunno. You look kinda intense.

Jacob resumes eating.

JACOB
I based it off of something that happened to me in Florence.

STEWIE
You met an older version of yourself in a bar?

Jacob hesitates.

JACOB
We had so much in common, I actually joked around that he was.

Stewie realizes the seriousness of Jacob's tone.

STEWIE
What was his name?

JACOB
Christopher. He was older too. Forties, I think.

STEWIE
Did you put everything in the movie? Short, whatever?

JACOB
No.

Jacob looks at Stewie.

JACOB (CONT'D)
It's not that long. You wanna read it after this?

STEWIE
Absolutely.

Jacob smiles.

JACOB
You ever read a screenplay before?

STEWIE
No.

JACOB
It's not that hard. I'll help you out.

STEWIE
Oh, I almost forgot.

Stewie pulls out a CD from his pocket and places it on the table:

"Pet Shop Boys: <u>Discography: The Complete Singles Collection</u>."

STEWIE (CONT'D)
I was thinking about music you might like. I've got a collection of my own, though I think CDs are a lot more obsolete than records these days.

JACOB
"Pet Shop Boys?" Never heard of 'em.

STEWIE
They're a British duo from the 80s.

JACOB
I hate 80s music.

STEWIE
Try it out.

Jacob scrunches his face, whining indecisively.

JACOB
I really don't like the 80s.

STEWIE
I lived through the 80s. It was great.

JACOB
Yeah, but you were a kid. Everyone loves their childhood. Doesn't mean the 80s were that good. I lived through the 2000s and that certainly wasn't a great time for music.

STEWIE
Just listen to them.

JACOB
I don't even know them.

STEWIE
And that means they're bad?

JACOB
I know a lot about music. If I've never heard of them, that's not a good thing.

STEWIE
You never heard of "West End Girls?"

JACOB
No.

STEWIE
"Opportunities?"

JACOB
No.

STEWIE
You have to have heard "It's a Sin."

JACOB
No, I haven't. None of them were hits.

STEWIE
Yes, they were!

JACOB
Not big ones.

STEWIE
"West End Girls" went to Number 1.

JACOB
Then why haven't I heard of it?

STEWIE
I don't know! Just listen to them. You'll like it.

Jacob looks at the CD cover.

JACOB
Do they sound like they're from the 80s?

STEWIE
Yes.

JACOB
Then I won't like it. I know what I like and I don't like 80s music for a reason.

STEWIE
Don't knock an entire decade without hearing it.

JACOB
I've heard the 80s. They're fucking everywhere. Everyone my age loves the 80s. It's in all the movies and TV shows now. I can't stand it. No one cared about the 70s or the 60s but all of a sudden the 80s is the greatest decade ever? C'mon.

STEWIE
All I'm asking is for you to listen to a few songs. You showed me a movie I never saw before. It's only fair.

Jacob takes a deep breath. Reluctantly opens his laptop.

JACOB
Fine.

Jacob pops in the CD.

JACOB (CONT'D)
Which one first?

STEWIE
"It's a Sin."

Jacob double-clicks Track 5. Electronic drums rumble before being replaced by synth-strings and a strange voice over choral singing. Thunder cracks and the beat kicks in, catchy synth keyboard over a drum loop. Neil Tennant sings in falsetto.

Jacob listens to the lyrics with a perplexed brow.

JACOB
Sounds kinda gay.

STEWIE
They are.

JACOB
Gay?

STEWIE
Neil is, the singer. The other guy Chris may or may not be. I think he is.

Jacob listens a bit more.

JACOB
They're very theatrical.

STEWIE
I know. That's their thing.

Jacob bobs his head unconsciously.

JACOB
I can't believe there were gay guys singing about being gay in the 80s.

They listen to the flamboyant finale. The song ends.

JACOB (CONT'D)
That was, uh...

STEWIE
Well?

Jacob looks at Stewie, embarrassed.

JACOB
Yeah.

STEWIE
Yeah what?

Jacob grins.

JACOB
That was really fucking good.

STEWIE
See? I told you.

JACOB
Which one should I play next?

CUT TO:

INT. SUITE 710 - JACOB'S ROOM - NIGHT

Jacob double clicks on "A Night With Myself.fdx" on his laptop.

JACOB
Ready when you are.

Stewie pulls out his phone.

STEWIE
Just a minute. I gotta call my mother.

JACOB
What's wrong?

STEWIE
Nothing. I call her every night.

JACOB
Every night? Really?

STEWIE
Yeah.

JACOB
What do you talk about?

STEWIE
Everything that happened to me that day.

JACOB
And she actually wants to hear it?

STEWIE
Of course.

Jacob smiles.

JACOB
Where's she now?

STEWIE
Living with my sister and her family.

JACOB
You never mentioned a sister.

STEWIE
I have two. Abby and Christine.

JACOB
Which one's your mom living with?

STEWIE
Abby, her husband Mark, and their three kids.

JACOB
Is Abby older or younger?

STEWIE
Fifteen years younger.

JACOB
Fifteen years?

STEWIE
Yeah.

JACOB
What's the story behind that?

STEWIE
Just a sec. I gotta call Mom.

JACOB
Call her a what?

Stewie laughs on his way out. Jacob stands by the open door, eavesdropping on Stewie in the living room.

STEWIE (O.S.)
Hello.
(pause)
I'm okay. What about you? You excited about Florida?

Jacob returns to his chair.

STEWIE (O.S.) (CONT'D)
It's gonna be so warm down there.

Jacob pulls out his phone. Stares at his contacts, his mom's number at the top of his Favorites list.

STEWIE (O.S.) (CONT'D)
Not much. I'm just hanging with a friend of mine.

Jacob taps his mom's number. The dial tone rings.

HELENA (V.O.)
Hello?

JACOB
Hey Mom. How's it going?

HELENA (V.O.)
I'm good. Just tired. What's up?

JACOB
Just wanted to see how you were doing.

HELENA (V.O.)
I'm getting ready for bed.

JACOB
Oh. Okay.
(pause)
Should I call later?

HELENA (V.O.)
No, it's okay. I just can't talk long.

JACOB
I'm sorry. I didn't think.

HELENA (V.O.)
If you ever had a full-time job, you'd know not to call this late on a worknight.

JACOB
I'm trying, alright?!

HELENA (V.O.)
I'm just teasing.

JACOB
I don't find it funny.

HELENA (V.O.)
Well, clearly this isn't a good time for us to talk.

JACOB
Okay. Sorry. Goodnight.

HELENA (V.O.)
Night.

Jacob pockets his phone, sighing angrily.

JACOB
(breaking fourth wall)
She complains I don't call her and then she pulls this shit. But the moment I call her out on it, she accuses me of calling her a bad mother.

STEWIE (O.S.)
Who are you talking to?

Jacob looks over at Stewie standing at the threshold.

JACOB
I was talking?

STEWIE
I heard you whispering under your breath.

Jacob shifts in his seat.

JACOB
I do that sometimes. It's an Asperger's thing. I retreat within myself, kinda like a recharge.

STEWIE
And you talk to yourself?

JACOB
Well, it's kinda like I...

Jacob scoffs, embarrassed.

JACOB (CONT'D)
It's really stupid. I...
(hesitates)
I talk to the camera.

Stewie furrows his brow.

STEWIE
Like Ferris Bueller?

JACOB
Like I said, it's really stupid.

STEWIE
I don't think so. I think a lot of writers talk to themselves.

JACOB
What about actors-turned-writers?

STEWIE
That explains it then.

JACOB
Pick something for us to listen to.

Stewie flips through the LP collection.

STEWIE (CONT'D)
How am I gonna read it?

JACOB
We'll act it out. I'll do the action lines.

STEWIE
The what?

JACOB
Oh that's right, you've never read one.

Stewie puts a record on the player and puts the needle on. The hard guitar and theatrical piano of Meat Loaf's "Bat Out of Hell" crackles through the cheap speakers. Jacob stares, freaked out.

STEWIE
What's wrong?

JACOB
Nothing. I just... I've got a bad memory associated with this song.

STEWIE
I can change it.

JACOB
No, it's fine. I need to replace it with something good.

Jacob looks at the open file of <u>A Night With Myself</u>. His blood chills. Both at once. What are the odds of that?

JACOB (CONT'D)
You know what, I don't think we should read this after all.

STEWIE
Why not?

JACOB
It's not that good. I kinda wanna workshop my new one actually, if you don't mind.

Stewie shrugs.

STEWIE
Sure. Whatever you want.

JACOB
Great.

Jacob instantly closes <u>A Night With Myself</u>.

JACOB (CONT'D)
I spent the last two summers at my mom's house in Conshohocken. She didn't like me not having a job, so I got a job at Beef 'n' Fries.

STEWIE
How was it?

JACOB
Absolutely awful. $7.25 an hour doing the absolutely most mundane tasks you can think of. It ruins your brain. When I was there, there was this guy working there with me, his name was Rob, and he was the absolute worst worker there. One of those pretty boys too, you know? The kind that would make it big on Vine.

STEWIE
What's Vine?

JACOB
And he was so full of himself too. He smoked pot all the time. Never wanted to work weekends because he had all these hip-hop concerts to go to. Partied every night. Always late for work. Always on his cell phone. He pissed off customers because he kept forgetting food and always serving it to them cold. I even saw him snorting coke in the parking lot once.

STEWIE
He didn't get fired?

JACOB
The manager and Rob's dad were friends growing up.

STEWIE
You should've said something.

JACOB
I wanted to. Why should he get to do whatever he wanted while I had to follow all the rules? It's not fair, but what was I gonna do? It was only Beef 'n' Fries.

STEWIE
Doesn't matter.

JACOB
But then I started thinking: Why was Rob like that? I don't think people are born bad. And they're not made bad either, not deliberately. Anytime you hear about an "evil" person is really just a human being in a bad place. Rob did what he did because his family spoiled the shit out of him. His daddy was always there to bail him out. As far as Rob knew, he wasn't

doing anything wrong. And all of us working there, staying silent and getting pissed at him on the sidelines, we weren't helping either. Rob just kept getting worse. It's the lack of consequences that made him the thing he was. That's what Drive-Thru's ultimately about.

Jacob opens "Drive-Thru.fdx"

JACOB (CONT'D)
The year is 2026.

STEWIE
2026?

JACOB
It's not futuristic or anything, just ten years from now.

STEWIE
You're not gonna include anything like flying cars or--

JACOB
You wanna hear it or not?

STEWIE
Go ahead.

JACOB
The year is 2026. Ten years earlier, in the summer of 2016, eighteen-year-old Bobby Sanford beats the shit out of a customer in a fast food restaurant in Conshohocken, Pennsylvania. An amateur video of the assault goes viral.

STEWIE
Don't spoil anything.

JACOB
It all happens on the first page. The media goes wild for that video. It makes it on The View. There's a formal investigation into the management. Pretty much that one incident brings down the entire company in ten years.

STEWIE
Yikes.

JACOB
On the ten-year anniversary of the incident, a documentary filmmaker interviews the former crew members and Bobby Sanford himself, to find out why Bobby did what he did, only to discover the story is a lot less black and white than originally assumed. It intercuts the three months leading up to the incident in 2016.

Jacob turns the computer toward Stewie.

JACOB (CONT'D)
You ready?

STEWIE
I don't... What am I looking at?

Jacob points to the first line.

JACOB
That's the Scene Heading. INT means interior, EXT means exterior. That's the location, then if it's during the day or at night. Everything else is self-explanatory.

STEWIE
What does "V.O." mean?

JACOB
Voiceover.

STEWIE
What does "O.S." mean?

JACOB
Off-screen.

STEWIE
What's the difference?

JACOB
Voiceover is to be dubbed in later. Off-screen means they're there, just off-camera.

STEWIE
That's a bit confusing.

JACOB
You get used to it.

Stewie smiles at Jacob.

STEWIE
Ready?

JACOB
Yup.

Stewie clears his throat.

STEWIE
(reads)
"Fade in..."

WHALE

Virgil and Dante

Whale sits at the counter of Brique, a French piano bar on the corner of Sunset and Argyle, rubbing the little baggie of cocaine between his thumb and index finger like a rabbit's foot. A white rabbit's foot. Jefferson Airplane wafts through his brain. Then Jackson Browne's "Cocaine" from *Running on Empty*. Whale senses the Bartender coming and quickly pockets the baggie. Pulls out his iPhone. No missed calls. He taps that 856 number. Puts it to his ear. The dial tone rings thrice. Voicemail. Whale hangs up before the beep. Just after midnight on the East Coast. He's probably on the phone with his mom. Whale calls a second time, toes tapping on the stool's footrest, his heart pounding in anticip—

Voicemail again, this time after two. Whale hangs up again, instantly regretting not leaving a message this time. Maybe it's for the best. He saw it ring twice. He knows who it is. He'll call back when he's done. Whale pockets the phone.

The Bartender approaches, a pale man with a sharp nose. "What'll it be?"

```
                    WHALE
    Ultimo screwdriver, please.
```

"ID?"

Whale pulls out his wallet. Slides out his Pennsylvania Driver's License. Holds it out between two fingers.

```
                    WHALE
    My Cali's in the mail.
```

The Bartender nods with the read receipt of smiles. He studies the DOB and picture.

```
                    WHALE (CONT'D)
    On second thought...
```

The Bartender looks up. Whale ponders some more.

```
                    WHALE (CONT'D)
    Courvoisier sidecar. No sugar rim.
```

The Bartender's brows bump up. "Yes sir."

Whale slides the ID back into his wallet, his wallet back into his shorts. He looks around the place. Calm pianist playing an obscure showtune. Surprisingly dead for a Friday night in August. Only a couple other patrons on the opposite side of the rectangular counter and a few at the high tops by the window, eyes glued to their phones. The hard rattle of ice turns Whale's head toward the Bartender but he stops at the sight of the man that just walked in. The man in the fedora. The purple fedora with an extra-wide sombrero rim. He gets weirder the more Whale looks at him. Light purple scarf loosely wrapped around his neck, a psychedelic pattern devoid of rhyme or reason. Green plaid trenchcoat with no buttons or closures, hanging wide open. Silk long sleeve shirt with a pattern mixing tiny cheetah spots with bright pink paisley. Slim fit leather pants the color of yellow mustard. Brown topsiders over gray socks. Whale can barely see a face underneath that mauve sombredora, but he has a feeling the Weird Man could see him fine enough.

The Weird Man sits two stools down from Whale. Removes his gigantic hat to reveal a bald man with a shockingly ordinary face and plasticky skin. Whale can't tell if he's thirty or seventy. The Weird Man tosses the purple hat onto the counter, its rim's diameter longer than the bar itself. Disturbed air flies across Whale's hairy forearms. The Weird Man snaps his fingers, his many rings clinking against each other. "Hey barkeep!" he shouts in a shaky feminine vibrato ala Paul Lynde.

The Bartender pours Whale's sidecar into a coupe glass. "Just a second, sir."

"LA Manhattan, on the rocks. Make it snappy." The Weird Man looks over at Whale. Smiles.

The Bartender defiantly delivers Whale's drink with deft deliberation. He pauses to sigh before returning to the Weird Man. "What would you like?"

The Weird Man squints. "You heard me."

The Bartender frowns bitterly before walking to the opposite side of the rectangle.

The Weird Man turns to Whale. "Holy fuck, that was badass!" he says with flamboyant glee. "What do you think?" He gestures to his costume. "'Good, Bad & Ugly.' That's the theme."

Whale can't help but chuckle.

```
                    WHALE
      Don't think you're getting that drink.
```

"Of course I am. I'm a regular here. They might roll their eyes and shake their heads, but they cave. They always do." The Weird Man hops one stool closer to Whale. "Haven't seen you here before. What'cha drinking?"

```
                    WHALE
      Sidecar.
```

"Ooh!"

```
                    WHALE
      Courvoisier and Cointreau with a splash of lemon
      juice.
```

The Weird Man hums. "Fancy man."

```
                    WHALE
      Not quite.
```

"I'll be the judge of that." The Weird Man laughs. "Always am."

The Bartender reluctantly returns to the Weird Man. "Excuse me?"

The Weird Man looks up. "And he's empty handed."

"I'm sorry, sir. I'm not quite sure what it was you wanted."

"An LA Manhattan."

The Bartender hesitates. "Of course," he says with a small smile. Returns to the other side of the bar.

Whale leans toward the Weird Man.

```
                    WHALE
      What is an LA Manhattan?
```

The Weird Man looks Whale straight in the eye. "I have absolutely no idea."

```
                    WHALE
      You don't know what's in it?
```

"No clue."

```
                    WHALE
      Where'd you hear about it?
```

"I didn't. I made it up."

Whale stares.

WHALE
What do you mean? What did you just order?

"I don't know," the Weird Man says in a strange panic. "You think he's gonna come back with something?"

WHALE
I don't know.

"I sure hope not," the Weird Man mutters. "But it sounds real, right? LA Manhattan? I kinda like it."

Whale looks around for witnesses.

The Weird Man slaps Whale's shoulder. Points at one of the hightops. "See those guys? The couple? They're talking about me."

Whale looks at the hightop in question. A man and woman close together, eyes locked, soft whispers between them.

WHALE
You can hear them from here?

"No."

WHALE
Then how do you know they're talking about you?

The Weird Man laughs. "Because they always do!"

WHALE
Whatever.

Whale lifts his coupe glass just as the Weird Man holds out his hand. "Oscar."

WHALE
I know who you are, Mr. Blitz.

"That doesn't mean we've been introduced, now does it?"

Whale puts down the glass. Before he can shake Oscar's hand, Oscar slaps Whale on the shoulder again. "And cut it out with that Mister shit! I'm not 'Mister Blitz!' The only mister I am is a mystery!" Oscar laughs abruptly and shakes Whale's hand. "Come come, dear boy. Have a sense of humor. You know my name, so what's yours?"

Whale slides his hand away from Oscar's desperate grip.

WHALE
Jacob.

"Ah, Jake. Jakey-boy."

WHALE
That's not my name.

"Neither is mine." Oscar winks.

WHALE
No, I mean 'Jake.' My name is Jacob.

"Isn't Jake short for Jacob?"

WHALE
Not to me.

Oscar smiles slyly. "You really hate being called Jake, huh?"

WHALE
Yeah, I really do.

Oscar nods. "Okay then." He pauses. "Jake."

```
                    WHALE
        You're just an a-hole now.
```

"Hey, if you really didn't want me to piss you off, you shouldn't have told me how."

```
                    WHALE
        I didn't think you actually would.
```

"And that was a mistake." Oscar claps his hands loudly. "Barkeep! Come come, I'm fucking thirsty here!"

```
                    WHALE
        They're gonna throw you out.
```

"THEY WOULDN'T DARE!" Oscar shouts with a laugh.

Whale scratches an eyebrow, totally embarrassed.

```
                    WHALE
        Call me Jake. Whatever. It's not like it's an insult,
        you know. It's just my name.
```

Oscar bobs his head. "What's in a name, huh?"

Whale shrugs, nodding a bit.

"You know why I chose Oscar Blitz?" Oscar asks.

```
                    WHALE
        I have a feeling you're gonna tell me.
```

Oscar raises a finger. "O, as in 'Oh my God, it's Oscar Blitz!'" Second finger. "S, as in 'Some day we're having... Oh fuck, it's Oscar Blitz!" Third. "C, as in 'Can you believe Oscar Blitz found out about you and me?'" Fourth. "A, as in 'And I would've gotten away with it too if it weren't for you meddling kids and Oscar Blitz!'"

Whale rubs his faces with both hands.

Oscar opens his entire right hand. "R, as in 'RUN! *Señior* Blitz is coming!'" he says in a racist Mexican accent. Finger number six. "B, as in '*Blödsinn! Es gibt keine Möglichkeit, dass* Oscar Blitz *das herausfinden kann!*'"

Whale lets out a bumpy chuckle.

Oscar raises another finger, seven. "L, as in..." He goes quiet. Points a hesitant finger off. "Look, there's Oscar Blitz." He pauses. "FUCKER!" He holds up finger number eight. "I, as in 'Interesting, Oscar Blitz is,'" he says in a scarily accurate Yoda impression. "'Ehhher.'"

Whale checks for witnesses again.

Oscar raises a ninth finger. "T, as in 'Terrible, what happened to Billy. But that's what you get for having a secret worthy of Oscar Blitz!" He finally gets to the final finger, his left thumb. "'And Z, as in 'Zounds! Oscar Blitz strikes again!'" Oscar silently stares at Whale, searching his face for a reaction.

Whale's mouth lowers a bit. He clears his throat. Leans in a bit.

```
                    WHALE
               (whispers)
        I only let you go on to hear what Z was gonna be and
        that was so underwhelming.
```

"Zounds," Oscar repeats, unsure. "Zounds is... something."

```
                    WHALE
        Yeah, I just want the last two minutes of my life
        back.
```

The Bartender tenderly approaches Oscar, empty-handed again. "Umm, sir?"

Oscar looks at the Bartender with accusing eyes.

"I'm sorry, sir," the Bartender tells him. "I don't quite know what goes into an LA Manha—"

"Get me a whisky," Oscar interrupts. "Scotch. What's good here?"

The Bartender blinks rapidly, both relieved and terrified. "Which brand would you prefer?"

"Which brand?" Oscar looks at Whale. "Which brand?"

Whale looks between Oscar and the Bartender.

WHALE
Domergue?

Oscar nods with gusto. "Domergue." He faces the Bartender. "Glass of Domergue, on the rocks. And none of that Red Label shit. Single malt. Pre-war."

The Bartender half-turns to go. Stops. "Pre-war?"

"Before the war."

The Bartender hesitates. "Which war?"

"Surprise me."

The Bartender sighs helplessly and retreats again.

WHALE
You are a lot more... eclectic than you are on your show.

"Eclectic!" Oscar marvels. "I love that!"

Whale shrugs, sipping his drink.

"First rule of LA, never let your true self be known. Gotta keep 'em guessing." Oscar looks Whale up-and-down. "How long have you been here? A month?"

WHALE
Is it so easy to tell?

"You're too self-aware. It's way obvious. I can smell it from Ventura."

WHALE
What does that even mean?

"You'll see." Oscar adjusts his pants, pinching the sulfur leather down his hipline. "Come come, my boy. Focus not on mine jape but on the content of my words."

WHALE
I can't take you seriously when you're wearing that crap.

"That's why I'm still here. The moment the marks take me seriously, I stop winning." Oscar pats the counter patiently. "But you already know what I do, and I don't know what you do. What do you do?"

WHALE
I'm an intern.

"With whom?"

Whale opens his mouth to answer.

"Let me guess," Oscar interrupts. "The Professor."

Whale hesitates.

WHALE
How did you know?

Oscar grins. Claps triumphantly. "By Jove, I still got it! It's your fixation on names, Jakey-boy. If it were your nose or the size of your tits, it'd be Gary Glenn or Harvey Weinstein."

WHALE
You know about the nicknames?

"Oh yeah. I've been trying to take down that asshole for years." Oscar smirks. "Anything to report?"

```
                    WHALE
      Not to you.
```

"Oh, you're one of the good ones?" Oscar asks skeptically.

```
                    WHALE
      Huh?
```

"He never has good ones anymore. He likes it that way. Sadistic fuck."

```
                    WHALE
      What are you talking about?
```

"You'll know what I mean sure enough, if you don't already." Oscar cranes his head for the Bartender. "Asshole." He looks back at Whale. "What's yours?"

```
                    WHALE
      My a-hole?
```

"Your nickname. What hath the Almighty christened thou with?"

```
                    WHALE
      "Whale."
```

Oscar furrows his brow. "'Whale?'"

```
                    WHALE
      Yup.
```

Oscar looks at Whale's chest and shoulders. "He must be having an off year. You're not even fat."

```
                    WHALE
               (quoting)
      "No. I'm different."
```

"What?"
Whale smirks

```
                    WHALE
      Inside joke.
```

Oscar shrugs. "If your name was Jonah, I'd see it, but..."

```
                    WHALE
      I used to be.
```

"What? Named Jonah?"

```
                    WHALE
      Fat.
```

"How bad we talking?"

```
                    WHALE
      My all-time high was 245.
```

Oscar nods cordially. "Congratulations. What are you now, 180? 190?"

```
                    WHALE
               (furrows brow)
      185.
```

"Perfect! That explains it."

```
                    WHALE
Maybe you should be a weight guesser, you know, when
the whole Perez Hilton shtick runs its course.
```

Oscar shifts his body away, stunned by the shift in Whale's tone. "I'm a watchdog journalist."

```
                    WHALE
I'm sure TMZ thinks they are too. On paper, of
course. Tax purposes.
```

"Ha ha ha!" Oscar verbalizes. "You know why he uses nicknames, Blubber Boy? Because of me. Because he knows if one of you guys run to me, you'll never be able to prove beyond a shadow of a doubt that your nickname actually refers to you."

```
                    WHALE
You have no idea what you're talking about.
```

"Just because I haven't been able to prove anything doesn't mean I don't know what goes on in there. I've seen it many times. Other Factories. Other Professors. They're everywhere, hundreds of them in this town, running amok, doing whatever they please, thinking they're getting away with it. But the only thing that can stop them is me and they fucking know it."

Whale glares at Oscar.

```
                    WHALE
You're not the center of the universe, you're not a
journalist, those people were not talking about you,
you're not cool for being a jerk to that bartender,
and you know nothing about me or what's going on with
my job. I'm complicated. Everyone's complicated. No
one knows the whole story about anything. The ones
who think they do, the ones who say they have all the
answers, never do.
            (pause)
And if you call me Blubber Boy one more fucking time,
I will smash this coupe glass in your face.
```

Oscar looks at the coupe glass. Back at Whale. "Blubber Boy was harsh. I'm sorry."

Whale nods, his blood pressure spiking.

Oscar faces forward with a wistful sigh. "Do you want a job, Jacob?"

Whale stares back.

```
                    WHALE
What?
```

"If you don't have any qualms about photography that is. My studio is just down the block. We can pop over there and get all the paperwork taken care of. You can start on Monday. Unless you wanna do one of those 'Fuck you' walkouts at The Factory. I always find them immensely satisfying. We'll be able to protect you from any repercussions."

```
                    WHALE
You serious?
```

"I am 100% serious. My own personal feelings about The Professor aside, his type, the drill-sergeant-to-interns type, has no relevance in modern society. He's trying to beat you into becoming just like everyone else. Look at me. Look what I'm fucking wearing. Tell me I spend my days trying to be like everyone else."

```
                    WHALE
I've only been there a month.
```

"And how's it going?" Oscar asks knowingly. "You really think a job's waiting for you at the end of the rainbow?"

```
                              WHALE
            I don't want to be a paparazzi.
```

"Paparazzo. Paparazzi's plural. And that's not what it is. It's a chance for you to do what you want, not what you're told."

```
                              WHALE
            Do you get their consent when you publish those
            photos?
```

"If they gave a shit about consent, I wouldn't have to."

```
                              WHALE
            You make a living taking down career professionals,
            do you not?
```

"Toxic men in power do not get my sympathy, especially when there is no one else in this goddamn town with the nerve or the resources to stop them."

```
                              WHALE
            I don't care. It's wrong.
```

"According to who?"

```
                              WHALE
            I'm not one for following agendas, especially
            political ones, but I believe in the Golden Rule
            above all else.
```

Oscar rolls his eyes.

```
                              WHALE (CONT'D)
            And you can call me naive all you want, I'll still
            believe it. I wouldn't want all my years of hard work
            mercilessly destroyed because of one lapse in
            judgment. There are more than two sides to a story
            and I'm sick to death of nuance being thrown out
            every day like it's an effing wet rag.
```

"I understand a lot more than you give me credit for," Oscar murmurs. "I've been doing the show for twenty years. You know why it's still on? Why I still have an audience? Why my word and my name have weight, even nowadays? Because I don't make shit up. I don't even exaggerate or distort anything. It'd certainly make my job easier. A hell of a lot easier. Save me a lot of time and money. But I think it's wrong. I'm not just talking morally. Professionally, it's utterly disgraceful."

```
                              WHALE
            No one cares about facts anymore.
```

"Fantasy gets more clicks, that's true. But even in the Digital Age, maybe *because* we're in the Digital Age, we crave truth above all else. It's just a lot harder to believe the truth when it's right in our face. Photos and witness testimony don't mean shit anymore. You know what does? Uninterrupted videos. Clear voices on tape. That's all I use. That's all anyone believes nowadays. And I don't waste my time on silly things like drunken DUI rants or hooker rendezvous. I only care about the shit that really matters. Every man I've taken down, every single one of them had it coming."

Whale takes a deep breath.

```
                              WHALE
            It doesn't matter if they deserve it or not. It's
            still wrong.
```

Oscar stares at Whale with a strange mix of annoyance and pride.

The Bartender finally emerges with a glass of Scotch. "I'm sorry about the delay. We had a hard time finding the Domergues."

Oscar snatches the glass with both hands. "Don't go anywhere!" He swirls Scotch around the tumbler. Takes a long whiff. Sips. Immediately spits it out. "What the FUCK was that?!"

The Bartender stammers. "I'm so sorry, uh..."

"How old is this?"

"Ten years."

Oscar raises his brows. "Ten years?! How the fuck is 2007 pre-war?! What did you pick, the War on Christmas?!"

"Arab Spring."

"The Arab Spring wasn't a war! It was a series of anti-government armed rebellions!" Oscar slides the tumbler across the counter, a bit of Scotch hitting his fingers. "I want to speak to the manager! Tell him Oscar Blitz is very pissed off!"

The Bartender, too exhausted to retort, picks up the tumbler and wanders off.

Oscar licks his fingers. "Too bad. That was really good." He notices Whale's empty glass. "Just one tonight, huh?"

WHALE
You keep scaring him away.

Oscar wipes a spot on the counter with a bev-nap. "I'm not gay, by the way."

Whale blinks.

WHALE
Alright.

"Just wanted to make it clear."

WHALE
Fine by me.

"Good." Oscar wipes the corners of his mouth. "It's just really important to me that you *believe* I'm not gay."

Whale smirks.

WHALE
You know, you keep SAYING you're not gay--

"I'm not."

WHALE
I know, I hear you, I hear you.

Whale gestures with his hands, trying to phrase it right.

WHALE (CONT'D)
But the guys who really go out of their way to say that they're not gay... are the ones that end up being gay.

"Cool. I'm not gay though."

WHALE
Right.

"I didn't sit next to you because I'm gay. I didn't offer you the job because I'm gay. I sat next to you because you looked normal and kinda chill about it, and I offered you the job because you kinda, sorta impressed me."

WHALE
Which is fine. But you can still do all that and be gay, you know.

"I can't make myself be gay."

```
                    WHALE
      No one's making you be gay.
```

Oscar squints. "I kinda feel like you'd be happier if I was gay."

```
                    WHALE
      I didn't say that.
```

"I just got this feeling..."

```
                    WHALE
      All I'm saying is, if you're really not gay, why
      bring it up at all?
```

"What do you mean 'if I'm really not gay?' I'm not gay."

```
                    WHALE
      But I never asked if you were!
```

"Which is why I had to clarify that I wasn't. If I didn't say anything, you would've assumed I was gay."

```
                    WHALE
      If you didn't say anything. Now I'm not so sure.
```

"Would it matter if I was gay?"

```
                    WHALE
      It doesn't matter one way or another, which why it's
      so weird you went so out of your way to say you
      weren't gay!
```

"How is it weird if I'm not?"

Whale groans, both palms rubbing his eyelids.

```
                    WHALE
      I just wanna go home.
```

"Just a second," Oscar whispers, patting Whale's arm. "Watch this."

```
                    WHALE
      I really don't wanna--
```

Oscar shushes.

The Manager, a short French Man with a large black mustache, floats toward Oscar with a big grin on his face. The cross-faced Bartender follows with a loosely held bottle of Scotch. "I deeply apologize, Mousier Blitz!" the Manager croons in a thick accent. "Please forgive Aiden. He tries, but he's still new."

"I've been here three years." Aiden retorts.

The Manager hisses French curses at Aiden. Gives Oscar a desperate smile. "I've had Aiden retrieve a bottle of Domergue 15 from our private collection. I deeply, deeply apologize for his errors." Aiden side-eyes the Manager as he holds out the bottle.

Oscar inspects the label. "Very nice, thank you, but I'm afraid I can't afford the whole bottle."

"Don't worry, Mousier Blitz, it is on the house."

Oscar puts a hand to his chest, moved almost to tears. "Mousier Goutier! I cannot accept that."

Mousier Goutier hesitates. "In that case—"

"Eh, what the hell." Oscar snatches the bottle. Unwraps the foil top. "Two glasses, Aiden."

Mousier Goutier shuffles away. Aiden avoids eye contact as he places two tumblers on the counter and squeezes in two ice balls.

Whale stares at the bottle, bile brewing.

```
                    WHALE
     What do you need two glasses for?
```

Oscar uncorks the bottle and sniffs. "You're sharing, silly. You see? There is method to my madness."

```
                    WHALE
     I'm not sharing anything with you.
```

Oscar looks at Whale, his smile fading. "I went through a lot of trouble to get this for us."

```
                    WHALE
               (standing)
     Then I hope it was worth it.
```

"Where are you going?" Oscar quickly recorks the bottle. Holds it out. "Take the bottle, at least."

```
                    WHALE
     No.
```

"You're not gonna take the job. The least you can do is take a free bottle of good Scotch."

```
                    WHALE
     You scammed these people. I refuse to profit from
     that.
```

Oscar stands. "Jacob, wait."

```
                    WHALE
     What?
```

Oscar pulls out his wallet. Hands out a business card. "If you see something, say something."

```
                    WHALE
     I don't want it.
```

"OHMYGOD, YOU'RE SO COOL! Take it anyway." Oscar holds the card out more. Whale takes it with a frown. Reads the phone number and address.

```
                    WHALE
     Your studio really is down the block.
```

"I told you, I'm not a liar."

```
                    WHALE
     But you are a crook.
```

"Don't hate the player, hate the game. I'm just the one with all the cheat codes."

Whale pockets the card, sliding it between the cocaine baggie and his thigh.

```
                    WHALE
     Emphasis on cheat.
```

"It's the only way to win a broken game." Oscar returns to his stool. "And don't worry, the job's still on the table."

```
                    WHALE
     I will never call you.
```

"Wouldn't be so sure if I were you." Oscar uncorks the Scotch. Pours himself a glass. "You might be the first person I've ever offered a job to, but I've given that card to quite a lot of LA neophytes. They all call. It's just a question of time." Oscar raises his tumbler of Domergue. "Welcome to Hollywood, Blubber Boy. Hope the high ground's worth it."

Whale doesn't move. He just stands there, halfway between the counter and the door, his heart racing.

Oscar winks and sips his Domergue.

DREW

Eat Your Wheaties

Drew unlocks his condo door. Holds it open for Jimmy. His personal cell buzzes against his hip. He discreetly unearths his phone to check the caller ID.

(610) 295-5077
Philadelphia, PA

Drew double taps the power button. "You want something to drink?" he asks, locking the condo door.

"What do you have?" Jimmy murmurs, running his fingers along Drew's black leather sofa.

Drew makes his way to the kitchen. Opens the stainless-steel fridge. "I only got IPAs."

"Nothing stronger?"

"They're pretty freaking strong."

"Stronger than beer, I mean." Jimmy plops on the sofa, feeling the leather with both arms outstretched.

Drew's cell rings again. He slams the fridge door. Quick draws it.

(610) 295-5077
Philadelphia, PA

"C'mon, I got company." Drew sends it to voicemail. Holds the power button down. Shuts the phone off.

Jimmy turns his head behind him. "Everything okay, Drewie?"

"Don't!" Drew quickly calms himself. Reopens the fridge door. "Sorry, just... Don't call me that."

"What am I supposed to call you?" Jimmy scoffs. "I can't call you *Brian*."

Drew withdraws two bottles of beer. Makes his way back to the living room. "Drew is fine."

"Is it short for Andrew?"

"Just Drew."

Jimmy grins. "Drew fucking Lawrence! This is so surreal!"

"Yeah, that wears off." Drew holds out one of the beers.

"I told you I didn't want beer," Jimmy says, looking up.

"Beer's all you get."

"Why?"

Drew stares. "You know why."

Jimmy takes the bottle with a half-hearted frown. "I didn't mean what I said before. I just assumed you hated Drew Lawrence movies. I've always liked them. I love everything you put out."

Drew plops down beside Jimmy. Twists open his IPA. Throws the cap across the room. "Wanna watch something?"

Jimmy places his unopened bottle on Drew's wooden coffee table. "Wanna watch *Atomic*?"

"Nope." Drew takes a big swig of his beer.

"You don't like watching your own movies, huh?"

Drew frowns at Jimmy's IPA. Grabs a coaster. Places it under the frosted bottle. "Just think of something else."

Jimmy studies Drew's slouched posture. His lonesome face. The way he's guzzling IPAs like water. "Was it something I said?"

Drew finishes his IPA already. "Don't know what you mean."

"You were all fine and fun before, but now you're just... I don't know."

Drew shrugs. "Don't meet your heroes."

"You're not my hero."

Drew looks at Jimmy. Laughs harshly. "That's right. I forgot."

"You're not a bottom, are you?" Jimmy randomly asks.

"No, I'm not."

"Thank God!" Jimmy says with a chuckle.

"Don't get your hopes up, kid." Drew grabs Jimmy's open IPA. "I'm not fucking you." He swigs.

Jimmy frowns. "I'm not a fucking kid."

"It's a compliment. Enjoy it while you can."

"I'm so sick of that 'enjoy your youth' bullshit! I'm just as much of a man as everyone else!" Jimmy slouches, the real Italian leather squeaking. "We live in a society that worships youth and being young as the ultimate ideal while also openly discriminating against young people. I don't get it."

"Neither do I."

"Was it like this when you were my age?"

Drew nods, finishing his second beer. "Absolutely."

Jimmy looks at the end table behind the sofa. Notices a crystal bowl. He stands up excitedly. "Shit, is that what I think it is?"

Drew turns his head. Jimmy's heading for the cocaine. "That's not for you!" he cries, jumping to his feet.

Jimmy opens the lid. "Oh my God!"

"Give me that." Drew snatches the lid out of Jimmy's hand.

"Let's do a line together!"

"No."

"C'mon, I'll be just like a real Hollywood producer!"

"Jimmy!" Drew scolds. "It's not cool. Don't even start. Believe me."

Jimmy stares at the picture frame next to the coke bowl. "Is this you?" He picks it up for a closer look. Drew is standing by himself, half-leaning against the wall of a neon lit bar, a warm smile on his face. He's wearing the same red baseball cap, a polo shirt over blue jeans. His muscles are noticeably smaller than they are now. "You're really handsome in this."

Drew studies the photo over Jimmy's shoulder, a soft frown growing. "That was last summer. I was representing Not That Nutty at the Boston Film Festival. I stuck around for Pride. That was taken at the Black Bear. They were taking photos for their website or something. I liked how I looked so I kept it."

"That's kinda small beer. Aren't you guys usually at Cannes or Venice?"

"I wanted to go. I always liked Boston." Drew's eyes unfocus, an ancient wound resurfacing. "And I was looking for someone."

Jimmy looks to Drew for elaboration.

Drew doesn't notice. His mind's somewhere else. Somewhere painful.

"Did you find him?" Jimmy asks.

Drew blinks back to reality. "What?"

"The guy you were looking for?"

Drew lets out a cold breath. "For a moment I thought I did, but..." He dons a self-conscious smile. "Nope. Just some guy that looked like him." Drew takes the frame from Jimmy. Puts it back where it belongs. "I tried."

Jimmy watches Drew walk back into the kitchen, too shook to move.

Drew grabs another IPA from the fridge. Twists it off. Guzzles half in one go. He notices Jimmy's expression, that hard pitying frown. "What do you want me to say? I wanted this more. I've got the greatest job. I don't have to do shit and I get paid a crap ton of money. My best friend's my boss. Do you have any idea how much I get away with because of that? I can do anything I fucking want!" He laughs, clearly drunk.

Jimmy doesn't say anything.

Drew sighs, replacing his smile with a bitter scowl. "I'm surrounded by kids jerking off to only good thing I ever made when I was twenty-five. That's a lot of pressure, you know? Pretending I still got it. It's like a constant buzzing in my head." Drew pauses. "And it just makes me so fucking mad. Why can't I just be fucking happy, you know? Happy to finally have everything I worked my ass off to get? Like you said, I'm somebody! I have fucking notoriety! I'll never have to worry about money ever again! I can just go the rest of my life coasting and floating, so why do I keep feeling like such a fucking failure?! Look at me! I'm fucking jacked, but then I look in the mirror and I hate that I'm not MORE jacked!" Drew's face contorts. "What the fuck?" he whines. "I'm fucking killing myself, and for WHAT?!" Drew holds out his strong arms. Lets them fall to his sides. "For what?"

Jimmy walks up to Drew with puppy dog eyes. Puts his arms around him. Rests his head against his breast. Squeezes as tight as he can.

They stay like that, standing in Drew's kitchen, holding each other.

Jimmy takes Drew's face with soft hands. Kisses him on the cheek.

Drew smiles sweetly.

Jimmy nods with a smile of his own.

Drew puts an arm around Jimmy's shoulder. Leads him into the living room. "I'm sorry."

"It's fine." Jimmy sits beside Drew on the couch. "Somehow I knew under all those muscles and those ridiculously expensive suits was a person."

Drew nods.

"That's why you didn't want to tell me, isn't it?" Jimmy asks. "The moment they find out, that person's gone."

Drew nods again. "It sure was nice while it lasted."

"When was the last time you...?"

Drew scoffs. "Too long."

Jimmy caresses Drew's face. "It's not too late, you know."

Drew looks into Jimmy's eyes. "This is all I know now."

"I refuse to believe that."

Drew squints. "I can't tell if you're really stupid or... wise."

Jimmy chuckles. "I'm not stupid."

"Stupid people don't know they're stupid."

"I'm not stupid."

Drew looks over at the cocaine bowl. He looks back at Jimmy. "You're still a bit untrained."

Jimmy blinks. "Isn't the same as stupid?"

"You ever read King Arthur?"

"I might've. I don't really remember."

Drew smiles warmly. "Arthur was destined to do great things. But he was just a boy. And he thought he was just a normal boy, but he wasn't. He was descended from Kings. So many men wanted to pull that sword from the stone and claim the throne for themselves, but it was Arthur who did it. But he wasn't ready yet. He needed Merlin's help to understand his destiny. His lineage. What he was capable of. That the world was messy and filled with people, bad people. Arthur and his men, the Knights of the Round table, needed to be the source of honor and respect and duty, all the values England lacked at the time. King Arthur would've been nothing without Merlin. Even he needed a role model. Someone to help him remember the big picture."

Jimmy smiles.

Drew softens. "You're so intelligent, Jimmy. I can already tell. You can accept a difference of opinion. You seek answers in people. You will be a great man one day. But you still need a role model. Because life... it's so much stranger than you think is. The world is full of people who have to choose between what is right and what is easy." Drew's breath wavers. "And one day, if you're lucky, you'll know all on your own."

"That's beautiful," Jimmy whispers.

Drew nods. "That's what I need to do. Something has to come out of all this. All these years... They need to help someone if not me."

Jimmy hesitates. "What are you saying?"

"You have a screenplay, don't you? I'm sure you do. Everyone does in this town."

Jimmy gasps. "You serious?"

"I never had a role model out here. One looking out for my interests, at least. You could do everything I did in half the time. You just need my help." Drew smiles. "Maybe that's who I'm meant to be. The guy that walked so Jimmy Lyons could run."

Jimmy starts tearing up. "I can't believe what I'm hearing."

Drew's eyes unfocus. "That's what I want to be known for. That's what I can do. Then it'll all be worth it."

Jimmy kisses Drew on the lips. Instantly pulls away, embarrassed. "I'm sorry, I didn't mean to—"

Drew kisses Jimmy back. Deep. Passionate. They stop for air, panting into each other. Drew looks into Jimmy's eyes. "Do you wanna—?"

"Fuck yes." Jimmy pushes his tongue into Drew's mouth. They hold each other tight, warm breath intermingling, their speed and intensity increasing with every kiss, every graze, every squeeze. Drew lifts him up, Jimmy's lips still glued to his, and carries him into the bedroom.

JACOB

Before Sunrise

INT. WHITMAN UNIVERSITY - LB 710 - JACOB'S ROOM - NIGHT

Jacob and Stewie lay naked with sheets up to their waists.

JACOB
Can I ask you something?

STEWIE
Of course.

JACOB
Do you think there's something wrong with me?

STEWIE
It can happen to anyone. You're too young for something to be wrong.

JACOB
Not that. I know I'm good there.
(pause)
I meant... From your limited exposure of me, when you look at me or when I talk...

Jacob hesitates. Looks Stewie in the eye.

JACOB (CONT'D)
Do you see someone... broken?

STEWIE
No.

JACOB
Not at all?

STEWIE
Not even a little.

Jacob smiles sweetly.

JACOB
It's not just me then.

STEWIE
What do you mean?

JACOB
I've been so comfortable around you. I don't feel like I have to hold back anything, you know? I can just say whatever comes in my mind. Filtering myself is so exhausting, like holding ten pound weights over my head all the time.

STEWIE
I felt the same way when I finally came out. Being able to talk about guys like that was such a relief.

JACOB
Oh my God, same! I think I went too vulgar at first. I was just so thrilled I could finally locker-room talk, I didn't realize straight dudes don't like hearing that about other guys. Even allies have their limits.

Stewie caresses Jacob's cheek with a soft finger.

JACOB (CONT'D)
The only other time I felt like this was when I was over in Italy. I really knew what myself felt like. And now that I'm back, I don't want to lift those ten-pound weights anymore.

Jacob stops to think.

JACOB (CONT'D)
Grades 6-12 I went to this place called Eagle Ridge Preparatory School. It's just for kids with learning disabilities. ADD, ADHD, Asperger's, Bipolar. Everyone was just like me. It was small too. Like a small town. Like Hogwarts, you know? A home away from home. Sometimes even more of a home than home.

STEWIE
I don't know what that is.

JACOB
Which part?

STEWIE
Hog... Hog... what?

JACOB
Hogwarts.

STEWIE
What is that?

Jacob laughs.

JACOB
You really live under a rock, don't you?

STEWIE
What, is it a movie?

JACOB
It's the school from Harry Potter!

STEWIE
Oh.

JACOB
(mocking)
"Is it a movie?"

Stewie laughs hysterically.

STEWIE
I didn't know!

Jacob shakes his head.

JACOB
It was a little utopia in a way. I wouldn't be up here if they didn't help me feel like a normal person. But then I started feeling alien again, surrounded by normal people. Neurotypical people, I mean. But I was around people who weren't like my family. Doing different things. Believing different things. I was actually around gay people too.

Jacob frowns.

JACOB (CONT'D)
But every few months I'd fly down to Conshy and tried to re-acclimate to my family, or at least the people who used to be my family. It was like I was back on stage, you know? Trying to remember all those lines, not to say the wrong thing, always staying in character. It's so obvious to me now.

Jacob takes a deep breath, his eyes unfocused.

JACOB (CONT'D)
I didn't think I could be like I was in Florence again, but I did. And I did it on the first try. If that's not a confidence booster, I don't know what is.

Stewie studies Jacob's face. Pets his hair.

STEWIE
You haven't been beaten up by the bars yet. All that rejection, loneliness, getting hurt. Your friends suddenly getting old, mellowing out and moving away. You get so used to looking for what you want and you can't change.

Stewie sighs.

STEWIE (CONT'D)
I wasn't even gonna go out because of what happened in Orlando. That's my worst nightmare. That and getting HIV.

JACOB
Good thing you missed all that, huh? That would've been awful to live through.

Stewie hesitates.

STEWIE
But I went out anyway.
(pause)
And you waltzed in, just like that.

JACOB
And you almost lost me.

STEWIE
I was trying not to be as obvious as you were.

JACOB
I wasn't being obvious.

STEWIE
Oh yes you were! I could tell as soon as I saw you that you were on the hunt. You were actually kinda aggressive.

Jacob sighs, deflating.

JACOB
Goddammit.

Stewie flinches subtly.

STEWIE
What?

JACOB
I hate hearing that.

STEWIE
There's nothing wrong with it.

JACOB
I just felt so cool and flirty in the moment. God, I must've looked so stupid.

STEWIE
No, you didn't. When you came down again, I followed you.

JACOB
What? When?

STEWIE
You didn't see me sitting next to you at the counter?

Jacob hesitates.

JACOB
No.

STEWIE
I was right next to you when you were making out with that troll.

JACOB
Don't be mean.

STEWIE
And believe me, when I saw that I said to myself, "Forget him."

JACOB
He was sitting by himself. I felt bad for the guy. I wanted to make him feel better. That's all.

STEWIE
I didn't know what it was.

JACOB
You wouldn't have done the same?

STEWIE
I don't just kiss people.

Jacob frowns.

JACOB
I'm sorry.

Stewie caresses Jacob's shoulders.

STEWIE
It's in the past.

JACOB
I could've really fucked it up, huh?

STEWIE
That's not what I'm saying at all.
(smiles)
I saw you walk away and realized what was going on and didn't wanna miss my chance again. I'm so glad I didn't.

Jacob smiles.

JACOB
What a line, huh? "What does your shirt say?"

STEWIE
I really didn't know what it said.

Jacob chuckles in disbelief.

STEWIE (CONT'D)
I couldn't see down there! The lighting was terrible!

JACOB
And here I was so proud of myself that I picked up on something unsaid only to find out it wasn't even unsaid in the first place.
(pause)
Wait.

They laugh.

STEWIE
You have no idea how much I needed this. Just lying around. Talking. Watching a movie. Reading a movie. Listening to music.

JACOB
I know. This was so much fun.

STEWIE
I haven't stopped thinking about you all week. I can't even remember the last time that happened.

JACOB
It's never happened to me before. It's really nice.

STEWIE
You're just so much fun. You're kind. Super smart. I couldn't even leave my parents' house when I was in college. You went halfway around the world. That's just crazy. You're so mature for someone your age.

JACOB
"For your age." I hate that.

STEWIE
I actually forget you're only twenty-one.

JACOB
That's not as young as people think it is.

STEWIE
Yes it is.

JACOB
You were twenty-one once. Don't you remember having a brain and feeling like an adult?

STEWIE
I remember THINKING I had a brain and felt like an adult.

JACOB
But I actually know what I sound like and how I come off as and I actually go out of my way to learn and improve.

STEWIE
That's already better than most adults.

JACOB
Really?

STEWIE
You have no idea how rare it is for someone to actually admit they're wrong.

Jacob looks into Stewie's eyes and smiles. Stewie smiles back. They hug, squeezing nice and tight, rocking back and forth.

SLOW FADE TO BLACK.

THE NEXT MORNING

Jacob opens his eyes. Sun's only just rising. Stewie sits on the edge of the bed in his underwear, looking off, frowning.

JACOB
You get any sleep?

Stewie shrugs.

STEWIE
Not really.

JACOB
What's wrong?

Stewie sighs. Rubs the back of his neck.

STEWIE
I haven't been entirely honest with you.

Jacob tenses up.

JACOB
You're married.

STEWIE
No.

JACOB
You're with someone though.

STEWIE
Please just listen.

JACOB
Okay.

Stewie faces Jacob, struggling to maintain eye contact.

STEWIE
I've been up all night trying to... figure out how to tell you.

JACOB
Just tell me.

STEWIE
I should have told you before. I couldn't find the right moment.

JACOB
You're scaring me.

STEWIE
I'll just say it.

Stewie stares at Jacob.

STEWIE (CONT'D)
I'm not thirty-nine.

Jacob immediately scans Stewie's face for signs.

JACOB
Are you in your forties?

Stewie doesn't respond. He looks away slightly.

JACOB (CONT'D)
(whispers)
Please tell me you're not in your fifties.

STEWIE
I'm fifty-two.

Jacob's face doesn't budge. Thoughts and questions going round his mind in different directions, body tingling and tightening in the wrong places, cold stillness overwhelming him.

JACOB
Fifty-two?

Stewie nods solemnly. Jacob slides out of the bed. Slips into a pair of pants.

STEWIE
Say something.

JACOB
Why would you lie to me about that?

STEWIE
I wasn't lying.

JACOB
Oh really?

STEWIE
I wasn't trying to lie to you. You asked me how old I was and I said "How old do you think I am?" You said

"Thirties," so I said the highest number in the thirties.

JACOB
You should've told me the truth.

STEWIE
You said "Thirties!"

JACOB
Don't blame this on me. You knew you were lying.

STEWIE
I need you to understand. When someone asks me how old they are, they don't want the truth. They want me to be young. I thought it wasn't going to be anything more than a hookup. I just wanted to meet your expectations.

JACOB
I wasn't EXPECTING you to be thirty. I genuinely thought you were in your thirties.

STEWIE
Don't I look great for someone my age?

JACOB
Don't change the subject.

STEWIE
I'm not! This is literally the subject!

JACOB
You lied to me. You had an entire week to tell me.

STEWIE
I wanted to tell you in person.

JACOB
I already told my friends you were thirty-nine! I already told my fucking Mom!

Jacob covers his face. Stewie shifts.

STEWIE
I realize that. But you have to understand something.

JACOB
There's nothing more to understand.

Stewie hesitates.

STEWIE
I think I felt something for you last night. I want to start something with you, and that means full disclosure at the start.

JACOB
This isn't the start anymore.

STEWIE
In the grandest possible scheme of things, it really is.

Jacob sighs.

STEWIE (CONT'D)
I'm still the same man I was last night. If you really think about it, what's changed?

Jacob looks at Stewie. Reanalyzes his face.

STEWIE (CONT'D)
I don't care if you're twenty-one, thirty-one, forty-one, or fifty-one. You're a great person, Jacob. I really, really like you. I don't want this to...

Stewie's breath shakes.

STEWIE (CONT'D)
I'm not a liar. I really, really want you to believe me on that.

Jacob looks at the floor. Sits up.

JACOB
There's something I've kept from you too.

STEWIE
There is?

Jacob crosses his arms. Takes a deep breath.

JACOB
I'm sixteen.

STEWIE
WHAT?!

Jacob cackles.

JACOB
Oh my God, you actually fell for that?!

Stewie furrows his brow.

STEWIE
Yeah, why...? You have a college ID!

Jacob shakes his head, amused. Looks at Stewie.

JACOB
Guess that makes us even.

Stewie smiles warmly, a huge weight off his shoulders.

CUT TO:

EXT. LITTLE BUILDING - DAY

Jacob walks Stewie out.

JACOB
The DH opens in an hour if you wanna stick around.

STEWIE
I'm interviewing a new trainer at 1. I really need to get some sleep before then.

Jacob nods.

JACOB
I think I overreacted a bit up there.

STEWIE
I don't blame you.

JACOB
It's unlike me.

STEWIE
I know it is.

Jacob smiles. Stewie looks up and down Boylston Street.

STEWIE (CONT'D)
I really need to get gas. Where's the cheapest station around here?

JACOB
I have no idea.

STEWIE
Oh, that's right. You don't have a license.

JACOB
I have a permit if that makes me slightly less pathetic.

STEWIE
You're not pathetic. You're wonderful.

Jacob lowers his eyes.

JACOB
Drive safe, okay?

STEWIE
Of course.

Stewie hugs Jacob nice and tight. He looks around before kissing Jacob on the lips. He caresses Jacob's cheek with his thumb. Turns and walks toward the parking garage.

JACOB
Stewie.

Stewie stops and turns. Jacob takes a deep breath, unsure of himself.

JACOB (CONT'D)
You work from home, right? You set your own hours?

STEWIE
Yeah.

JACOB
How busy are you this week?

Stewie stops to think. He shrugs.

STEWIE
I'm still in a bit of a transition with the move. Why?

JACOB
You free tomorrow night?

Stewie hesitates.

STEWIE
As a date?

JACOB
Yeah. As a date.

Stewie smiles warmly.

CUT TO:

INT. LITTLE BUILDING - SUITE 710 - JACOB'S ROOM - DAY

Jacob closes the door. Disheveled sheets. Bat Out of Hell resting on top of his turntable. Vertigo's Blu-Ray case on top of his laptop.

Jacob pulls his chair out. Clears the top of the laptop. Flips open the lid. Logs onto Facebook. On his profile page, in between public posts ranking movies and ranting about film-related talking points, are private posts only Jacob can see: diary entries, long-winded ones. Some describing his sexual encounters with all the vulgar details. Some angrily venting about his mom. Others lamenting his life with equal parts anxiety and depression.

Jacob starts a new post. Switches the privacy setting to Only Me. Starts typing.

JACOB (V.O.)
"Stewie Hanz is 52."

Jacob pauses, tapping his finger in contemplation. Resumes typing.

JACOB (V.O.)
"My reaction was anally about the literal number. 39

made him eighteen years older than me. 52 makes him thirty-one years older, which admittedly sounds bad. But he was already older in that vague hypothetical sort of way, and I accepted the reality of dating an older man two days ago. Does an extra thirteen years really change the facts? He's still younger than both my parents. And he certainly doesn't act like a 52-year-old."

Jacob smirks.

JACOB (V.O.)
"Ironic. When I told my mom about Stewie on Friday, I insisted he didn't act like a 39-year-old. Guess I was right about that, huh?"

Jacob pauses. Thinks some more. Resumes.

JACOB (V.O.)
"My next wave of reaction is about the future. It's still very early to declare, I know, but the age revelation changes things a bit. When I told Mom about Stewie being 39, she said, 'You know there's no way it's gonna last.' Part of me got hurt when she said that so matter-of-factly, her only source of info merely a serious of stats fit for a Tinder profile she could easily swipe away. But she wasn't there last night. Thank God she wasn't. If she had been, if her self-fulfilling prophecy really had loomed large over our mutual merriment, I wouldn't feel what I feel now, which is that last night was one of the greatest nights of my life. I hope I'm not merely projecting. It was not only my first date with Stewie but also my first first date ever."

Jacob hesitates. Slowly resumes.

JACOB (V.O.)
"But I've never felt so complete, so happy, so respected as I have been in the presence of Stewart Hanz Jr. And as for the stated reasons behind his white lie? I don't have to overthink it, I simply don't care. The only care I bring to the table is the standard amount socially expected in the event of ANY lie, white or worse. But the awful truth is that Stewie was right. If I knew he was 52 at the start I probably wouldn't have asked for his number. I probably still would've blown him, even though he's now the oldest man I've ever fucked by at least five years. But I never would've given it a chance. It doesn't excuse his dishonesty of course, I gotta stay on the lookout for that, but I really believe he was in too deep. He chose his moment well. If I were in his shoes, I probably would've done the same thing."

Jacob takes a deep breath. Rereads his post so far. Resumes typing.

JACOB (V.O.)
"I do admit, even if Stewie does pass for a much younger man, the age gap is still obvious in my mind. I find myself actively forcing myself not to think about it. But I can't think of single thing about him that doesn't mesh with me. I usually don't mesh with anyone. That's all we have to go on, isn't it? Our feelings? Trust in ourselves? In people?"

Jacob rereads one last time. Satisfied, he clicks Post. Closes the browser. Just as Jacob's about to close his laptop, he suddenly remembers something. He taps his CD drive. CLICK. Just as he thought: Stewie's Pet Shop Boys CD.

Jacob pops the disc back in. Double-clicks Track 5, "It's a Sin." The song plays, Jacob bobbing his head with a smile.

MATCH CUT TO:

WHALE

Before Sunset

Whale sits on his bed with hunched shoulders, "It's a Sin" playing via Greatest Hits CD. He can still hear Alex and his buddies Carson and Bryce drunkenly laughing and shouting over each other in the living room. Sure sounds like a lot of fun out there.

Brandon's sample baggie of cocaine and Oscar Blitz's business card rest on the bed beside him. Whale looks over his souvenirs, the chorus of "It's a Sin" ringing truer than ever. His mind floats back to that Priest, how unsure the man was with the world. Nothing was sacred anymore, if it ever was. Maybe Whale's just being a prude again, the way he was when he first arrived at Whitman. Or maybe he was better off following his instincts, going with his gut. It was all a test, right? That's what the Priest said? That it was all a test?

Whale turns off the song, his heart heaving in his chest. Has it only been a year since Stewie first played him that song? Or was it one year already? Whale didn't know if time was speeding up or slowing down, only that it was off. It wasn't like that in Italy. He's a different man now. Not just the weight loss and the workouts. Not just the LASIK and the hygiene overhaul. He's a *better* man now. Maybe that's why he feels off. No one can see him be good out here. The few who have mock him for it. But was that the reason he returned to God in the first place? For others' approval? For Stewie's?

Whale pulls out his phone and calls the 856 number again. It's probably too late, even for him, but Whale's gonna leave a voicemail this time if only to explain the missed calls.

Dial tone rings once. "The number you are trying to reach... EIGHT, FIVE, SIX, ONE, FIVE, ZERO, SIX, EIGHT, SIX, NINE... is not available. At the tone, please record your message. When you are finished you may hang up, or press 1 for more options." BEEP!

```
                    WHALE
Hey. Hope you're doing okay. Sorry about all the
calls earlier. I just felt, you know... homesick, I
guess. Just a little, you know.
```

Whale takes a breath.

```
                    WHALE (CONT'D)
The internship's a bit... well... It's not perfect,
but I'm trying, you know. Playing it by ear at the
moment. I'm probably not getting the job. Which
sucks. I'm still hopeful though. Maybe it'll end up
like Whiplash, you know? I'll get that smile? Maybe
not. I dunno.
```

Whale puffs his cheeks.

```
                    WHALE (CONT'D)
And Alex turned out to be a massive pothead. Just my
luck, huh? He's fun and all, but... I dunno. I can't
really talk to him like I could...
```

Whale stops himself.

```
                    WHALE (CONT'D)
Anyway. Hope it's all okay out there.
          (pause)
Give me a call, alright?
```

Whale tightens his lips.

```
                    WHALE (CONT'D)
        I really need to hear your voice.
```

Whale lets out an exasperated sigh. Presses 1. "To start over your recording, press 1. To delete the voicemail you've just recorded, press 2. To repeat these options, stay on the line or press 9." Whale lets the voice repeat the options list a couple times, thinking over what was so wrong with the first time. He presses 1. BEEP!

```
                    WHALE (CONT'D)
        Hey Stewie! It's Jacob. How's it been? Just wanted to
        call and tell you how LA's going. In short, fabulous.
        My internship is going super well. I think I have a
        really good shot, you know? I'm not just saying that.
        In other news, Alex is really cool. We hang out a
        bunch. Gone out a few times. He's pretty chill about
        everything. I feel like I can really talk with him.
```

Whale closes his eyes.

```
                    WHALE (CONT'D)
        Oh, almost forgot. I got a job offer today. You ever
        hear of Oscar Blitz? He's a pretty big journalist.
        Google him. He has a big TV show, one of those
        watchdog interview ones. Anyway, I just happened to
        sit next to him in a bar an hour ago and we started
        talking and he offered me a job right there. A
        writing job too. Probably reporting more than
        fiction. But nowadays what's the difference?
                  (laughs)
        Anywho... I'm not really thinking about leaving the
        internship with The Professor, but it's good I have
        options, huh?
                  (pause)
        It's really working out. It's actually really working
        out. Call me when you can. I'll tell you all about
        it.
```

Whale's heart pounds in his chest.

```
                    WHALE (CONT'D)
        I really should go. It's getting late out here. I'll
        talk to you soon.
```

Whale quickly hangs up. His lip quivers, tears forming in his eyes. He shakes his head. Covers his face with his hands. Screams into them. Smacks himself in the head. Alex and his friends can't hear, thank God. The last thing he needed was more embarrassment.

Whale looks at his pillow. Not that again. It was awful enough the last time he had a meltdown. It didn't make him feel better. It just made him feel alone. What he wanted was to stop stressing. To stop having a meltdown.

Whale picks up the baggie, dumps the coke onto his desk. Cuts two lines with Oscar's business card. Rolls up a dollar. Snorts. He says fuck it and snorts the rest of the baggie. Stands up. Checks himself in the mirror. Smiles. Walks out to join Alex's party.

DREW

Before Midnight

Drew smacks Jimmy's side with the back of his hand. Jimmy jolts awake, his hair disheveled. "Oh. Morning."

Drew sits on the bed. Slides into a pair of gym shorts.

Jimmy looks around, squinting in the morning light. "What time is it?"

"Seven," Drew mumbles with a no-nonsense frown. "Get your things and go."

Jimmy blinks, trying to process. "What?"

Drew puts his sneakers on one at a time. "Don't make this a thing, alight?"

Jimmy slides closer to Drew. "What's wrong?"

Drew stands. Doesn't look at Jimmy, not even his reflection.

Jimmy doesn't budge, a sullen expression dawning. "I don't understand."

"Spare me. I'm not your first." Drew crosses his arms.

Jimmy frowns. Wraps himself back in the sheets. "Did I do something wrong?"

Drew spins around. "GET OUT!" he hollers, veins popping along his neck. "GET THE FUCK OUT OF MY HOUSE!"

Jimmy bolts out of bed. Fumbles his jean on.

Drew clears his coarse throat. "Fucking asshole. Getting me all worked up." He hocks. Spits into his toilet.

Jimmy flips sheets around. "Where's my belt?"

"Hurry up."

Jimmy gets on his knees. Looks under the bed.

"Hurry the fuck up!" Drew shouts.

"I need my fucking belt, alright?!" Jimmy snaps. "Then I'll go!"

Drew slips on an undershirt. "I got a lot of shit to do, even if you don't."

Jimmy finds his belt. Stands. Glares at Drew. Slides his belt through the loops.

Drew sits back down on the bed. Bends down to tie his laces. Nylon rubbing nylon. Steel clicking steel. Angry breaths.

Jimmy puts on his Superman shirt. "Guess all that role model shit was just a way to get in my pants?"

Drew stops tying his shoes. He stays hunched over, eyes staring at the floor. "I'm no role model," he whispers.

Jimmy waits for Drew to look back and apologize. Drew refuses to move until Jimmy leaves.

Jimmy nods to no one. Reluctantly steps toward the door. Looks back at Drew one last time. Drew turns his head away just in time. Jimmy sighs. Makes himself walk into the living room.

Drew keeps his breath quiet to listen to Jimmy in the other room. Opening the fridge. Running the sink. A bit of leather squeaking. A couple minutes of silence. A pair of footsteps stomping across the floor. The door opening. SLAM! Real silence this time.

Drew takes a deep breath. Plops on the floor. Assumes the position. Starts pushing up.

Shower. Scrambled eggs. Drew shoots a fresh load into the kitchen sink. Turns on the jet faucet. Ushers the sticky white lump down the garbage disposal. Imagines its journey into sewer on its way to Long Beach, destined to float out on black water or simply dissolve into the sand. The immediate post-orgasm shame lingers way too long for Drew's liking. Feels too much like poetic justice. He pops open his coke tin. Lifts the crystal bowl. Dumps the last of good shit into the tin. Snaps it shut. Slides it into his jacket pocket. Larry's gotta get him more.

Shit, he hasn't told Larry about Theo coming back early. They've got so much work to do now.

Drew grabs the iPhone off the kitchen counter. Taps the power button. Nothing. Oh right, it's his personal cell. He turned it off. Drew holds down the power button. The Apple logo appears, then his lock screen. BUZZ! BUZZ!

Missed Call | 3:03 AM
(610) 295-5077

BUZZ! BUZZ!

Voicemail | 3:03 AM
(610) 295-5077

Drew stares at the voicemail notification, instantly scared. He swipes. Types in his passcode. Navigates to the voicemail list. Hits play. Puts it to his ear.

Five seconds of the room tone. A woman scoffs. "You asshole." Silence. The message ends.

Drew furrows his brow. Looks at the phone number. The fuck he do this time? He's got his own life. If his sister didn't like it, she could shove it up her bleached doctorate ass. Or maybe she should've left a voicemail the first three times and not work herself up all night. Drew pockets the personal cell to call her back some other time. Better not let it linger. He grabs his work cell too and heads out the door.

Drew's barreling down the I-10, halfway to work, when his Jeep's low battery light turns on. Drew huffs. Pulls off at the next exit. Stops at the closest charging station. Gets out. Flips the charger lid. Plugs the prongs into his Jeep's electric engine. Gets back in. As he waits for his Jeep to charge, his mind wanders back to that morning. A twinge of regret grows. Maybe he was too harsh on Jimmy.

A bald guy knocks on Drew's window. Drew rolls it down. "Yes?" he asks.

"I'm sorry, are you Drew Lawrence?"

"Yes, I am."

"I knew it! I knew it!" The Bald Guy laughs. "How're you doing? Making them big bucks?"

Drew sneaks a peak at the progress bar on his generator's OLED screen. "Yup."

The Bald Guy stands back to get a good look at the Jeep. "I can see that." He looks inside. Notices Drew's gearshift. "Oh wow, it's one of those manual electrics I've heard about! You must be *rolling*!"

Drew rubs the leather steering wheel with pride. "It was gift from my boss. My fortieth birthday present."

"I didn't think Jeep made electric Wranglers yet."

"They don't."

The Bald Guy laughs. "That's some friend you got there."

"Yeah." Drew rubs his temple, looking off with a halfhearted frown. "He really is."

"How does it handle? Being a manual, I mean."

"Fine."

"Better than the real thing, huh?"

Drew smiles. "It doesn't stall if I fuck up the downshift. I can slam it into neutral and not worry about long-term damage. Three times the range. Green. Exhaust-free. Unbelievable speakers. It really is better in every way." Drew shakes his head. "But it's nothing like the real thing."

The Bald Guy furrows his brow.

Drew forces a chuckle. "Don't mind me. Big day ahead."

"Don't let me keep you then."

Drew waves politely. Rolls his window all the way up.

Drew exits onto La Cienega Boulevard. Fuck, he still hasn't called Larry. He plugs in his work cell. Taps Larry's number on the Jeep's touchscreen.

"Mr. Lawrence?" Larry answers uneasily.

"Don't worry, I know what day it is. I'm sure you're busy with plans or whatever, but Theo and Alan are coming back on Monday. I need you in. We're working all weekend."

Larry hesitates. "Mr. Lawrence, I..."

"Theo told me you snitched. It's okay. I forgive you. We just gotta get the docket cleared as soon as possible. Call everyone who's had a meeting scheduled and get them in either today or tomorrow. I don't want Theo touching any of it, understand? I wanna hold onto this while I still can."

Larry hesitates again. "You're on your way now?"

"I meant to call you back at the condo but I kept forgetting." Drew chuckles. "Maybe it's a good thing I won't be CEO after all, huh?"

Silence.

"Larry, what's with you?" Drew asks. "You're acting strange."

"Didn't your sister tell you?"

"That I'm an asshole? Yeah, she did." Drew pauses. "Hey, how'd you know about that? Did she call you to get my number or something?"

"That's all she said?"

"Yeah. 'You asshole.' Click. End of message." Drew furrows his brow. "Wait, what do you mean 'all she said?' Did she tell you something else?"

Silence on the line.

"Larry?"

"Um..." Larry pauses. "She called me last night around quarter to three. She said you hadn't been answering your personal cell."

"She kept calling at the worst times. So what?"

"Drew, your mom was the one trying to call you."

Drew blinks. "My mom?"

"I really don't know why your sister didn't tell you, but… Drew, your mom died last night."

Drew's face turns to stone. He keeps driving, his unblinking eyes frozen in place.

"I'm so sorry I had to be the one to tell you, Mr. Lawrence."

Drew licks his dry mouth. "You're saying *Mom* was the one trying calling me?"

"They were about to put her under for emergency surgery yesterday and, well... she never woke up."

Drew's heart races. "But w-why did...? Did the cancer come back?"

"That's what your sister told me."

Drew doesn't say anything.

"Mr. Lawrence?" Larry asks.

"I'm five minutes away, Larry. I'm just gonna start without you."

"You really don't have to come in today, Mr. Lawrence. Everyone would under—"

"Try to be in by noon." Drew hangs up. Turns at an intersection. He can feel his face tingling, like it's about to fall off. Thank God he wasn't high when he called Larry. The last thing he needed was another drug-induced anxiety spiral.

Drew pulls over on the side of the street. Puts JEEPGUY 2: Electric Boogaloo in park. Faces forward. Stares at the dashboard lights. He doesn't move for twenty minutes. Too unmotivated to get out of the Jeep. To keep driving. To do anything. The silence hurts. Everything hurts.

Like a zombie, Drew pulls his personal cell from his pocket. Taps his way to his Blocked Contacts list. Flicks all the way down to the bottom. Stops on a familiar looking number:

(856) 150-6869

Drew unblocks the number. Calls it. Puts the phone to his ear, his heart pounding.

One.

Two.

Three.

Four.

Five.

Six.

"The number you are trying to reach... EIGHT, FIVE, SIX, ONE, FIVE, ZERO, SIX, EIGHT, SIX, NINE... is not available. At the tone, please record your message. When you are finished you may hang up, or press 1 for more options."

BEEP!

Drew hesitates. "Hey." He clears his throat. "I know it's been a while since the last time I called. This might not even be your number anymore. Hell, I don't even know if you're still—" Drew stops himself. He can't even say it. "I only just found out my mom died last night. She was about to go under and... I don't know, I guess she kept trying to call me from Melanie's phone. Or maybe it was her phone. I don't know. I was too busy doing… I don't even know what. Nothing important." Drew pauses. "And I just realized I don't have anyone I can talk to that will understand. She's not just my mom, you know. She's way more than that. You know. You know what that's..." Drew's voice catches. "Uh…" He laughs. "I blocked your number, so if you've been trying to call all this time, don't think I didn't want you, I just…" Drew shrugs. "I guess I just didn't know what to say." He pauses, thinking back. "I quoted you last night. That King Arthur speech you gave me in P-Town. Merlin and all that." He nods to no one. "I was wearing your red cap too." Drew looks at the passenger seat beside him, imagining Stewie smiling back at him. How beautiful he looks. Drew's about to cry from that alone. "I just wanted to tell you that I love you." He closes his eyes. "I miss you. I miss you so fucking much." Drew opens his eyes. Instantly presses 1.

"To start over your recording, press 1. To delete the voicemail you've just recorded, press 2. To repeat these options—"

Drew presses 2.

"Your message has been—"

Drew hangs up. Tosses the phone onto the passenger seat. Shifts back into first. Drives off, barreling down La Cienega, gas pedal to the floor, crying out. His big arms start shaking as he's suddenly overwhelmed by raw emotion, ancient wounds popping open one by one. He slams on the breaks. Cracks open his coke tin. Grabs the tiny straw, desperate to numb the pain. Stares at the coke. So white and fluffy. The smell alone makes his throat twinge. That metallic aftertaste he loves so much.

Drew looks at himself in the rearview mirror. The lighting's better than it was in Sweet Vermouths but the goblin's still there. Ghoulish black circles. Bloodshot eyes wide with horror. Is he really gonna spend the rest of his life hating himself, wishing he never came to Hollywood in the first place? Who's he kidding, he'll never change. Life's too short. He needs to stop wasting time and start loving the freak staring back at him. It's more fun that way. A hell of a lot more fun.

But what if Jimmy's right? What if it really isn't too late? He can still be happy again. He can still have dignity again. He can still be Jacob Andrezj again.

Drew tosses the straw back in the tin. Snaps it shut. Unbuckles his seatbelt. Hops out. The warm air feels strange after all that time sitting in A/C, his pores wide open. He rounds the Jeep from behind. Stands over a sewer grate. Crouches down. Drops the coke tin into the sewer. He can hear its flat face smacking hard against the current like Javert.

Drew smiles. Hoists himself back to his feet. Climbs back in. Speeds down the boulevard. Wind buffeting his face. Hair flying around. He feels strong again. He hasn't felt this strong in years.

END OF PART TWO

PART THREE

Alas, You Resemble Your Father

WHALE

Sabbath

Alex, Carson and Bryce are all over him. Laughing. Fondling. Kissing. Smacking. Entering. All the attention Whale needs, even when it overwhelms him. Coke blasting through his veins. Left-over vodka. Shitty Chinese takeout. Poppers too. At some point the dream starts, Whale walking in a black void, shoes clip-clopping, echoing all around him. A pair of headlights behind him. A loud screech clawing toward him, like a subway, but then it's not a pair of headlights. Just one. And it falls on its side, still barreling toward him. Whale knows it's just a dream and tries to escape or at least save the man but it's no use. Maybe he can jump the bike before it hits him. Or maybe Stewie can fly in and save him like Lois Lane. But he's stuck. Attached to the floor. A floor in a black void? He has to just take it. But just as he's about to, Whale wakes up.

Looks around, confused. His bed, sheets all amok, but no one else. A warm space next to him. Bryce? Hell, maybe Alex. His hole's spread, prostate still sore. Whale looks up. Blinds closed. No, they were open, it was just pitch black outside. Saturday evening. He couldn't have had much sleep. Must've been the alcohol finally leaving his system, his liver snapping him back like an egg timer. His legs are sore as he gets up. Waddles to the living room.

Fog throughout. Warm weed. Alex and Carson on the couch smoking a bowl, making out. Bryce on his knees blowing them one at a time. Soft wet slurps. Whale watches from afar. He's jealous, sure, but too exhausted to start shit. He pisses in the toilet, his urethra stinging, piss barreling through the dried cum like that subway/motorcycle in his dream. He dwells on that freaky scene for the next few hours. Replays the dream. Changes small details just because he can, a quest for variety instead of the same old hat. None quite matches the shock of the first one.

"Kara Remembers" wakes Whale up. At first he's thrilled in his half-asleep delirium. Alex finally broke from his *Wolf of Wall Street* purgatory and replaced it with *Battlestar Galactica*, probably a Blu-Ray from Whale's massive CD case, his once great Dark Chest of Wonders now condensed into a portable Rolodex Whale calls Xanadu. But the music isn't coming from the living room. Whale's phone is ringing. He grabs it and looks at the caller ID.

(856) 150-6869
Cherry Hill, NJ

Stewie. He's calling him back. He's actually calling him back. But Whale's throat is too dry. He's still hungover. He's had a non-consecutive fourway with his affluent pothead roommate and his slutty yuppie buddies, under the influence of coke, poppers, and maybe more. Plus he got to the phone too late. Plenty of reasons not to slide his thumb. The music stops. The number vanishes. A polite notification appears on the lockscreen.

Missed Call | 7:12 AM
(856) 150-6869

Whale stares, waiting for something new. BUZZ! BUZZ!

Voicemail | 7:13 AM
(856) 150-6869

Not a long message. Maybe just a "Hey, saw you called, call me back, CLICK." Or a "Glad to hear you're alright, Baby Boy. We agreed not to be long distance so I'm gonna say goodbye now. Take care. Have a nice life. Sayonara." Or even a "Wow, that's unbelievable! Call me back and tell me all about it, Sexy!" But a day and a half later? That's not like Stewie. Maybe it *wasn't* Stewie. Maybe that number in his Missed Calls list was just some Indian spammer spoofing a Jersey number, claiming his name was something Western like "Dennis" despite an obvious New Delhi accent.

Whale stares up at the ceiling. He's really put himself into a Schrödinger's cat scenario, hasn't he? The moment he hits play on the voicemail, the moment Stewie sighs or hesitates or barrels out of the gate with praise or confusion or disinterest or hate, it all becomes real, the reality of Stewie without him. The damage done. The relief. The pain. The resentment. The consequences of Whale's blatant lie, a narrative he'd have to perpetuate to cover up his shame. The burden such pointless stress would bring on Whale's already overfilled life. How long will he have to keep up the charade? To what end? Look all that's happened because Whale made that first call. He's like a junkie. All that crap he did, the coke, the poppers, the booze, the pot, all that cock, all to fill the void, just him killing time. He's in damage control at work. He doesn't have time for this S-H-I-T.

Whale goes to his voicemail list. Deletes the new voicemail, unplayed, unheard. Goes to Missed Calls. Taps the info button next to that 856 number. Scrolls to the bottom. Taps Block This Caller. A disclaimer pops up. He taps Block Contact.

There. Now he didn't fail. He can believe what he wants to believe. Maybe it was Stewie, maybe it wasn't. Maybe he heard Whale's lie of a voicemail, maybe he didn't. Whale doesn't know. Now he won't have to. Because it's over. The cord finally cut. Connection severed. All remaining appeals exhausted. Escape pod self-sabotaged. Stewie Hanz isn't an option anymore. Just LA. As hard as that was on Whale's heart, he's also relieved.

Whale lifts his head. His door's ajar.

```
                         WHALE
        Hello?
```

No sounds from the kitchen.

```
                         WHALE (CONT'D)
        Alex? Bryce? Anyone here?
```

More silence. They must've gone to Roscoe's. Alex really loves Roscoe's. Whale looks at the clock. He really should get up now if he wants to make it to church on time.

Whale rolls over with a soft sigh. Closes his eyes. The silence of the house lulls him back to sleep.

JACOB

Those Summer Nights

INT. WHITMAN UNIVERSITY - LITTLE BUILDING - LAUNDRY ROOM - NIGHT

Jacob folds clothes out of the dryer, talking to Rian through his mic'd headphones.

RIAN (V.O.)
HE'S FIFTY-TWO?!

JACOB
Born in 1964. Same year the Beatles came to America.

RIAN (V.O.)
You're actually dating a Boomer?

JACOB
He's not a Boomer.

RIAN (V.O.)
'46 to '64. He's a Boomer.

JACOB
He grew up with MTV and his parents are Silent Gen. That makes him old Gen X.

RIAN (V.O.)
No, that makes you in denial.

CUT TO:

INT. STEWIE'S BOSTON APARTMENT - SAME

Stewie cooks himself dinner over the stove in his already furnished brownstone apartment. He talks to his mother CATHERINE (72) on speakerphone.

CATHERINE (V.O.)
How long has this been going on?

STEWIE
It'll be one month this Tuesday.

CATHERINE (V.O.)
I can't believe you, Stewie.

STEWIE
He's not a typical 21-year-old, Ma.

CATHERINE (V.O.)
He was a baby when you were in your thirties!

STEWIE
I don't think about that.

CATHERINE (V.O.)
No crap!

CUT TO:

SPLIT SCREEN - JACOB AND STEWIE'S PHONE CONVERSATIONS

RIAN (V.O.)
When's Stewie's birthday?

JACOB
February 24.

CATHERINE (V.O.)
What month was he born?

STEWIE
Ma!

RIAN (V.O.)
If it was late '64, I could see, maybe.

STEWIE
I don't think about that!

RIAN (V.O.)
But February's too early. He's a Boomster.

CATHERINE (V.O.)
Stewie, what month?

JACOB
The whole year was a transition year.

STEWIE
March.

CATHERINE (V.O.)
March of '95?

JACOB
Second off, you're missing the coolest part.

STEWIE
Yeah.

RIAN (V.O.)
I must be.

STEWIE
Ma, what are you doing?

CATHERINE (V.O.)
I'm checking something. Just a second.

JACOB
His mom was pregnant with him and his brother when Kennedy was assassinated.

CATHERINE (V.O.)
Yup! His mom had him during the OJ trial.

JACOB
Isn't that fucking metal?!

STEWIE
(cringing slightly)
Yikes.

RIAN (V.O.)
He's a twin?

STEWIE
While we're on the subject, can you believe he's a twin too?

JACOB
I know! What are the odds?

CATHERINE (V.O.)
Identical or fraternal?

RIAN (V.O.)
Identical?

JACOB
Yeah.

STEWIE
Fraternal. A sister.

RIAN (V.O.)
Do they look alike?

JACOB
I haven't met him yet. Stewie swears they don't look alike anymore, but he just might be used to it.

STEWIE
And that's not all, Ma.

JACOB
But wait, there's more!

STEWIE
You won't believe how much we have in common. He's got two sisters.

JACOB
We both have two sisters.

STEWIE
He loves his mom.

JACOB
We both have Mommie Dearests.

STEWIE
He's from outside Philly.

JACOB
He's lived in Jersey his whole life.

STEWIE
His mom lives only forty-five minutes from the Marlton condo.

JACOB
Before he moved up here he was living outside Cherry Hill for the past fourteen years. That's only forty-five minutes from Conshy!

STEWIE
He loves music.

JACOB
We have the exact same taste in music.

STEWIE
Old stuff. Beatles.

JACOB
Pink Floyd.

STEWIE
Led Zeppelin.

JACOB
Billy Joel.

STEWIE
Elton.

JACOB
ABBA.

STEWIE
Queen.

JACOB
Eagles.

STEWIE
He actually has a record collection!

JACOB
You should see his CD collection. He's got everything.

STEWIE
Lots of psychedelic rock.

JACOB
Disco.

STEWIE
Prog.

JACOB
Alternative.

STEWIE
I turned him on to the Pet Shop Boys.

JACOB
He introduced me to this group from the 80s, the Pet Shop Boys. They're like exactly my taste.

STEWIE
He's eating them up like crazy!

JACOB
They're theatrical, they've got fantastic lyrics, lots of songs about being gay. They put me in such a fantastic headspace.

STEWIE
He plays their greatest hits on repeat.

JACOB
I haven't been this obsessed with an artist since I first discovered The Beatles.

STEWIE
He knows more about The Beatles than I do!

JACOB
We go back-and-forth talking music trivia for hours! And he's a night owl, just like me.

STEWIE
Oh yeah, Ma, he's a night owl.

JACOB
We're even the same height, six-foot-zero.

STEWIE
We're both six-zero.

RIAN (V.O.)
You're not six-zero.

CATHERINE (V.O.)
You're five-eleven and seven-eighths, sweetie.

STEWIE
I know! So is Jacob!

JACOB
We're the same real height, the same fake height, the same Zodiac sign.

STEWIE
We pretty much dress the same too.

JACOB
We think the same.

JACOB & STEWIE
We talk the same.

STEWIE
It's just unbelievable, Ma.

JACOB
It's crazy. And he hates the same mainstream shit I do.

STEWIE
And he can't stand all the same-old crap either.

CATHERINE (V.O.)
Like what?

RIAN (V.O.)
Which mainstream shit?

JACOB
You know, football.

STEWIE
The Super Bowl for example.

JACOB
The Tonight Show.

STEWIE
All those crappy late night shows.

JACOB
Drag queens.

STEWIE
Drag shows.

JACOB
Beyoncé.

STEWIE
"Bey Once."

JACOB
Country music.

STEWIE
Country and rap.

JACOB
Hip-hop.

STEWIE
And he calls me every night, right after you.

JACOB
I call him all the time. We text literally all day.

STEWIE
Even before our first date, we learned so much about each other just by texting.

RIAN (V.O.)
What have you guys done?

STEWIE
I took him to New York Pride.

JACOB
I've been showing him off to everyone! Oh my God, he's so fucking hot!

STEWIE
He had a lot of fun.

JACOB
I can't keep my hands off him!

STEWIE
He's so sweet, you know?

JACOB
He's a bit weird about PDA, though.

STEWIE
But he wants to hold my hand in public and all.

JACOB
That's his generation, you know? They had to be really careful about that.

CATHERINE (V.O.)
You better not hold his hand. Don't even take the chance of ending up like that boy.

JACOB
Matthew Shepherd, AIDS, you know.

STEWIE
Don't worry, I won't.

JACOB
I'm trying to coax him out of it, but he's pretty set in his ways.

STEWIE
I feel bad that I can't be more comfortable.

RIAN (V.O.)
That's not good.

CATHERINE (V.O.)
Do what YOU want.

JACOB
I don't wanna overthink it, you know?

STEWIE
I know. Still.

RIAN (V.O.)
What kind of movies does he like?

CATHERINE (V.O.)
You take him to a Mets Game yet?

JACOB
Actually...

STEWIE
I want to, but he didn't seem too interested in baseball.

JACOB
He doesn't watch movies.

CATHERINE (V.O.)
Why not?

RIAN (V.O.)
What do you mean?

JACOB
He doesn't go to the movies.

STEWIE
He doesn't know any players.

JACOB
He doesn't know any A-list actors. ANY.

STEWIE
He barely knows the teams.

RIAN (V.O.)
What movies has he seen?

JACOB
Dude, I'm telling you, he's barely seen any.

STEWIE
Just the Phillies, Yankees, and Mets.

JACOB
He hasn't seen E.T. He hasn't seen Back to the Future, Lord of the Rings, Indiana Jones, Harry Potter...

CATHERINE (V.O.)
Does he watch ANY sports?

STEWIE
None.

JACOB
Ghostbusters, Avatar, GoodFellas...

RIAN (V.O.)
The Godfather?

JACOB
He's seen The Godfather, thank God.

RIAN (V.O.)
What about Titanic?

JACOB
He wasn't going to because of the hype but he did and loved it.

RIAN (V.O.)
Well, he has to have seen Star Wars.

JACOB
He has not seen Star Wars.

RIAN (V.O.)
HE HASN'T SEEN STAR WARS?!

JACOB
Actually, that's not true. He says he might have seen "the first one" in the year 2000, but I don't think that counts cause he can't recall anything that happened in it.

RIAN (V.O.)
"Might have?"

JACOB
It was on HBO or something.

RIAN (V.O.)
Which first one? Episode I or A New Hope?

JACOB
He doesn't know.

RIAN (V.O.)
HE DOESN'T KNOW?!

JACOB
I asked him if it was one of the Prequels and he said, "Prequels of what?"

STEWIE
I can understand it though.

JACOB
TV too. He only watches The Honeymooners and 70s sitcoms he watched growing up. All in the Family, Three's Company, Happy Days, Laverne and Shirley, The Odd Couple.

STEWIE
We do watch an episode of TV together every night. He's got me on this show called "Breaking Bad." You ever hear of it?

RIAN (V.O.)
Where did you find this guy?

JACOB
Under a rock, apparently.

CATHERINE (V.O.)
Must not be that popular.

STEWIE
It's actually pretty good.

RIAN (V.O.)
How can YOU of all people be with someone who doesn't watch movies?

CATHERINE (V.O.)
What does he do when you watch baseball?

JACOB
I'm sure he feels the same way about me not liking the Mets.

STEWIE
He just stays in and watches movies.

RIAN (V.O.)
Big baseball guy, huh?

CATHERINE (V.O.)
Without you?

STEWIE
No, he watches a lot with me.

JACOB
It's like half of his personality.

STEWIE
It's his major, Ma. Movies are his life.

JACOB
And I feel bad not watching baseball with him.

STEWIE
And I know he wishes I could talk more about them.

JACOB
But you know I had such a bad little league experience. It's tough to like a sport I spent years hating.

STEWIE
And I used to go out to the movies all the time. Unless it was too hyped of course.

JACOB
And don't get me started on Melanie's travel team shit.

STEWIE
But then all that <u>Ocean's Eleven</u>, <u>Green Mile</u> crap... ugh, that was it for me.

JACOB
You'd hate it too if you were forced to go to West Virginia or South Carolina for an entire week. Lying around shitty hotels and ballparks for hours on end, listening to all the softball parents spewing bullshit shop-talk all the fucking time.

STEWIE
Jacob swears movies were still good around that time and I was just picking the wrong ones back then.

JACOB
I told Stewie all that and he asked if it was more of a Melanie-in-the-spotlight thing than a boredom thing.

STEWIE
He's probably right.

JACOB
I said no at first, but you know what? He's probably right.

STEWIE
I wish I had him back then, weeding out the crap.

JACOB
I wish I had him back then, you know? It would've been so much easier.

CATHERINE (V.O.)
He would've been four.

RIAN (V.O.)
Yeah, a fifteen-year-old hanging with a strange forty-six-year-old in a crappy hotel or seedy ballpark.

JACOB
Stop kinkshaming me.

STEWIE
You know what I mean.

RIAN (V.O.)
You don't call him Daddy, do you?

CATHERINE (V.O.)
You're old enough to be his father.

JACOB
That is... none of your business.

STEWIE
His father's sixty.

RIAN (V.O.)
That's a yes, isn't it?

STEWIE
And we really don't acknowledge it.

JACOB
Maybe.

STEWIE
You should see how we are together.

RIAN (V.O.)
What does he call you?

STEWIE
He's so mature.

JACOB
Baby Boy.

STEWIE
And crazy smart.

RIAN (V.O.)
"Baby Boy?"

JACOB
Baby Boy.

STEWIE
He's just so much fun!

RIAN (V.O.)
Why not "Baby"?

JACOB
Because Gus was Baby.

STEWIE
He's the complete opposite of Gus.

RIAN (V.O.)
Who's Gus?

CATHERINE (V.O.)
Did you tell him about Gus?

JACOB
His last boyfriend.

STEWIE
I tell him everything.

RIAN (V.O.)
How long were they together?

JACOB
Five years.

RIAN (V.O.)
What?

JACOB
He was with the guy for five years, they never moved in together, and Stewie's the one that ended it.

RIAN (V.O.)
How do you not move in with a guy after five years?

JACOB
I don't know.

CATHERINE (V.O.)
He's never been in a relationship before?

STEWIE
Never.

JACOB
He swears it's ancient history, but if it really is, why can't he call me Baby?

CATHERINE (V.O.)
That's a lot of pressure.

STEWIE
I don't think so.

RIAN (V.O.)
Why did they break up?

JACOB
They had a fight.

RIAN (V.O.)
That's it?

JACOB
They never fought apparently.

RIAN (V.O.)
I repeat, THAT'S IT?!

STEWIE
He's so easy to be around. I can just be myself.

RIAN (V.O.)
Is there something WRONG with Stewie?

JACOB
Not that I can tell.

STEWIE
There's literally nothing wrong with him, Ma. And you know how picky I am.

JACOB
He's perfect, honestly.

STEWIE
There's still hope for him to get into baseball.

JACOB
And the few differences we have aren't the end of the world. Even the movie thing.

STEWIE
At least he's not indoctrinated or anything.

JACOB
Think about it, he's a clean slate. I can get him to like the weird artsy shit I do.

STEWIE
It'd be harder to make him a Met fan if he once preferred the Phillies or the Yankees.

JACOB
It's not like he hates the Prequels on principle, you know? He'd be more receptive to watching them.

RIAN (V.O.)
THEN he'll hate them.

JACOB
I like them.

RIAN (V.O.)
You're the only one.

JACOB
Maybe I won't be for long.

STEWIE
Before I forget, he's been asking to meet you.

RIAN (V.O.)
You're really into this guy, aren't you?

CATHERINE (V.O.)
I don't want to.

JACOB
I really am.

STEWIE
Ma! Just give him a chance.

JACOB
He's exactly like me. Literally, he's just like me in every way.

STEWIE
He means a lot to me.

CATHERINE (V.O.)
You just met him.

STEWIE
I'm telling you, Ma. He's exactly the kind of guy I've been looking for all this time.

JACOB
I love him.

RIAN (V.O.)
Really?

JACOB
(beaming; moved)
Yeah. I really do.

STEWIE
Last night he told me he loved me.
(pause)
And you know what, Ma? I told him I loved him too.

JACOB
He told me he loved me last night.

RIAN (V.O.)
Holy shit! Fuck man, I'm so happy for you!

JACOB
I know. I can't believe it.

STEWIE
This is for real, Ma. We're already talking about our holiday plans.

CATHERINE (V.O.)
I still think it's too fast.

STEWIE
We see each other every day, Ma. It feels right. I want to fly down to Abby's for Thanksgiving.

CATHERINE (V.O.)
I don't know.

STEWIE
If you refuse to talk to him when we get there, we'll leave and you won't see us for the rest of the time we're in Florida.

CATHERINE (V.O.)
You're that serious?

STEWIE
I've never been more serious about anyone.

CATHERINE (V.O.)
(deep sigh)
Fine.

STEWIE
Thank you.

CATHERINE (V.O.)
Of course.

STEWIE
I'll let you go. I gotta get some work done before I head over to Jacob's.

JACOB
I really should get going, dude. I gotta shower and tidy up the place.

RIAN (V.O.)
Date night with Stewie?

JACOB
Yup.

CATHERINE (V.O.)
What's the plan?

STEWIE
Nothing crazy. Just dinner and a movie.

JACOB
We're gonna make martinis, watch Mulholland Drive, and FUCK.

WHALE

Blessed are the Meek

Peabrain's typing echoes through Whale's brain. Bumps clicks her mouse two seats down. Cashew's flipping through printouts on a table, a pen in his mouth. But Whale just stares at the desktop. This was supposed to be his week, Friday's scolding putting him back on track, the week he made up for missing Locarno, the week to make his comeback. And he hasn't done shit. Why? Because he's distracted? Because he has a disability? So does Peabrain. He's powering through it. Whale put all his eggs in one basket, the wrong basket, and now he's wasting the opportunity of a lifetime. There's no hope, is there? Either he toughens up and gets it done or fails like a wuss. What will he do then? Pay off his student loans as a server? Write more screenplays that never get made? It'll be just a cute little hobby, won't it? He'll end up like Uncle Bart, won't he? A broken-down alcoholic with atrophied legs in a smelly house watching TV and getting fat and lonely and gross. His mom tried so hard to make him good, to avoid her brother's fate, but it's coming, he can see it now, it's coming, and he'll wish he was better and smarter and more driven and less broken with all the 20/20 retrospect, all the answers he can't see right now cause he's too fucking stupid, too fucking retarded, a fucking autistic freak full of fucking debt from a fucking screenwriting degree, living with a loser he found on fucking Craigslist cause he's got no college friends left, no allies he could have stayed with and his mother tried to tell him an artsy career wasn't a wise idea and he should've been more practical and he should've used his time at Whitman fucking learning something instead of sitting on his ass and dreaming dreaming dreaming like a fucking fool.

All that barrels over in Whale's mind, and with the loudest clack yet, Peabrain smacking Enter with his right pinkie, the geysers unleash a flood of tears down Whale's smooth face. He immediately feels seen. Naked. And sure enough when he whips his head toward Bumps there she is looking back. And when he jumps up Cashew's looking at him too. But Peabrain hasn't moved at all, which Whale finds more insulting than anything. And Whale runs to the bathroom and locks the deadbolt and slides to the floor and weeps as loud as he can. He dials it back out of fear of the others hearing, perhaps that bitch Secretary or maybe even The Professor himself. Oh, that would be awful. That would kill him.

A knuckle softly knocks twice on the door.

```
                    BUMPS (O.S.)
        Whale? You in there?
```

Whale swallows.

```
                    WHALE
        Yeah. I'm okay. Just give me a minute.

                    BUMPS (O.S.)
        You wanna talk about it?
```

Whale grabs the handle to hoist himself to his feet. He pulls the door open just enough to see Bumps' sweet face.

```
                    WHALE
        I'm alr--
```

BUMPS
Oh my God, you're crying!

Whale wipes his face.

WHALE
Not really.

Whale forces a smile, his lip quivering hard. Bumps lets out a little whimper. Wraps her arms around Whale. Hugs him nice and tight. Whale hugs back, letting the tears roll out, sobbing into her shoulder.

BUMPS
Let it out. Let it out.

Bumps waddles into the bathroom, arms still around Whale. The moment the door closes, Whale unleashes waves and waves of grief, moaning and wailing into Bumps' nice suit. Snot pours out of his nose, his fingers stopping it in time.

BUMPS (CONT'D)
I'll get tissues.

WHALE
No, I got it.

Whale bunches six TP squares into a triple-ply cushion. Blows wet snot into the soft white paper. He doubles over his nostrils. Wipes his eyes with his fingers. He chuckles.

WHALE (CONT'D)
God, it's so nice not having glasses anymore. I don't have to take them off or move them up to cry.

Bumps takes a deep breath.

BUMPS
Wanna tell me what happened?

WHALE
It's just a lot of little things, you know. Building up. I wish it was something easy like... I dunno, The Professor yelling at me every day, or his Secretary farting in my face or--

Bumps laughs. That makes Whale laugh too.

WHALE (CONT'D)
I know, right?
(pause)
But it's not anyone's fault. I'm just coming to the realization that my dream job might not be for me after all. I like myself too much to force it, you know?

Whale frowns. Throws the TP squares in the trash.

WHALE (CONT'D)
I never used to like myself.

Bumps leans against the wall.

BUMPS
This place is weird. Not just The Factory, LA. California. Everything.

WHALE
You're not from LA?

BUMPS
Fuck no. Baltimore, baby.

Whale grins.

```
                    WHALE
Thank God. I keep feeling like the only East Coaster
in town.

                    BUMPS
When I first came here, I took a Ridr from the
airport. It was like ninety degrees out, and I sweat
easy... Sorry.

                    WHALE
It's fine.

                    BUMPS
Just making sure. I sweat easy, right, and the driver
had all the windows open, so I asked if it was okay
if she could turn on the A/C. She looked at me in the
mirror and told me, "By the way, I know you're not
from here, but you better not say it like that to
other people. It could come off as offensive."
```

Whale laughs nervously.

```
                    WHALE
What?!

                    BUMPS
So I asked her what I should've said. She said, "A
real LA native would've said 'It's hot in here' and
that would be a sign for me to turn the A/C on."
```

Whale chortles.

```
                    WHALE
That's so strange and yet it makes all the sense in
the world.

                    BUMPS
We really are on another planet.

                    WHALE
We're in Downton Abbey, more like.

                    BUMPS
I haven't seen it. Is that a bad thing?

                    WHALE
Not at all. It's a world I actually understand.

                    BUMPS
Where's home for you? Jersey?

                    WHALE
PA. Philly area.

                    BUMPS
I've been to your art museum.

                    WHALE
I've been to your aquarium.
```

Bumps nods.

```
                    BUMPS
Glad to hear it.
          (pause)
The other guys aren't from the good coast.

                    WHALE
I wouldn't know. I'm not very popular, it seems. It's
high school all over again.
          (smirks)
If only.
```

BUMPS
I had coffee with Ke-- Peabrain. He's from Arizona. I think Cashew's from Oregon or Washington, something Pacific Northwest based on his accent. I had a roommate from Portland, she sounds like him. He's a bit stand-offish, don't you think?

WHALE
Like I said, I wouldn't know.

BUMPS
I don't think he likes me very much. Hope he's not an incel or something.

WHALE
He seems too determined to be an incel. They're a very defeatist group.
(pause)
Of course it's weird for me to transition from that to this, but I think you should know that I'm gay.

BUMPS
Believe me, I wouldn't be standing here if you weren't.

WHALE
So if Cashew were crying, you wouldn't console him?

BUMPS
Of course I would. I just wouldn't... you know.

WHALE
Give him the wrong idea.

BUMPS
Exactly.

WHALE
I didn't insult you just now, did I?

Bumps chuckles softly.

WHALE (CONT'D)
God, what did I say now?

BUMPS
You're really sweet.

WHALE
Thank you. You too.

BUMPS
But I don't think you know how great it is that you're so sweet.

WHALE
Not recently, no.

Bumps and Whale stand in silence. She holds the door open.

BUMPS
I wanna show you something.

Whale follows Bumps out of the bathroom. She leads him down the hall, round the corner, and into a copy room, empty except for four state-of-the-art copiers.

WHALE
Didn't know we were allowed over here.

Bumps opens a side office door, revealing a small computer nook, completely enclosed except for a small glass window with Venetian blinds looking out at the copy machines.

```
                    BUMPS
      I figured you didn't know about this. You would've
      already been here.
```

Whale steps in, eyes wide with wonder, giving Bumps enough berth to step out.

```
                    BUMPS (CONT'D)
      My brother's autistic. I'm really good at spotting
      the signs.
```

Bumps points up at the insulation.

```
                    BUMPS (CONT'D)
      Not sure how soundproofed it is. But the door locks
      and the blinds fold in, so... Even if you do play
      music in here, The Professor wouldn't necessarily
      know it's you. It's not like you'd be bothering
      anyone or crossing paths with him too often.
```

Whale taps the spacebar on the keyboard. The login screen pops up.

```
                    WHALE
      How long have you known about this?

                    BUMPS
      I've been printing a lot. It's my thing. Kinda wish I
      found it sooner. Might've helped you a lot.
```

Whale's breath wavers. Bumps nods with understanding.

```
                    BUMPS (CONT'D)
      I'd still be smart about the volume, if I were you.

                    WHALE
      Don't worry about me--

                    BUMPS
      Trisha.
```

Whale stares at Bumps. She holds out her hand.

```
                    BUMPS (CONT'D)
      I won't tell if you won't.
```

Whale shakes her hand.

```
                    WHALE
      Jacob.

                    BUMPS
      Nice to meet you, Jacob.

                    WHALE
      Nice to meet you, Trisha.

                    BUMPS
      Want me to close it for you?

                    WHALE
      No thank you. I got it.
```

Whale's eyes fall on her tummy. It's significantly smaller than it was a month ago. Her face looks frailer too, come to think of it.

```
                    WHALE (CONT'D)
      How are you taking all this?
```

Bumps unconsciously covers her belly, shrugging.

```
                    BUMPS
      One day at a time, I guess.
```

Whale nods.

```
                    WHALE
      I like that. One day at a time.
```

Bumps steps away.

```
                    WHALE (CONT'D)
              (calling out)
      Oh, Tri--! Um, I mean...

                    BUMPS
      Yeah?
```

Whale grins.

```
                    WHALE
      Good luck.
```

Bumps smiles back.

```
                    BUMPS
      Same to you.
```

Whale watches her go, still in disbelief. He softly closes the door. Logs onto the computer. Puts a PSB playlist on shuffle. Gets to work.

DREW

Bad Memories

Drew points at the mini movie posters circling the top of Not That Nutty's second floor conference room. "How long have they been up there?"

The twenty producers at the table, including the one Drew just interrupted, look up at the filmography halo above them, lots of swivel chairs squeaking out of sync.

Larry clears his throat. "Mr. Lawrence..."

"Sorry." Drew sits back up. Looks at the pale-faced producer four seats down. "Please continue, Simmons."

"Do you want me to start over?" Simmons asks.

"No. Yeah. Wait..." Drew thinks about that. He's been sober for thirty-six hours now. It's finally starting to get to him. "Go just... Do what you think is best."

Simmons looks down at his report. "*Road Work.* A road-trip romance between a brooding, woodsy hitchhiker — I was thinking Joe Pepperino or someone similar — and a bartender in her mid-thirties that still hasn't gotten it all together. They hate each other's guts at first. She's whiny, he's insensitive, but when she picks him up to beat up his ex, he agrees if she drives him to his hometown. But here's the twist: they—"

"Oh my God, they're in chronological order too!" Drew interrupts again, his eyes back on the 6-by-9 prints. "I can't believe I hadn't noticed them before!"

Larry slides his chair over to Drew. "Mr. Lawrence."

"Shh-shh! I'm counting." Drew bobs his finger along, mouthing silently.

"Seventy-two, sir."

"Goddammit, Larry. I have to start over now."

"There's seventy-two."

"Humor me, will you?" Drew goes back to counting.

Larry awkwardly smiles at everyone. "Can we, um... count them later? We've got a lot to..."

"Hm?" Drew turns his head.

"We're a bit behind schedule at the moment, so maybe it's best if we—"

"They're just pitches, Larry. We still got a day."

"I know, sir. But we really need to get this done before lunchtime if you wanna finish everything before Mr. Landreth returns."

Drew nods repeatedly, skuttering back to the present. "You're right. Of course. Simmons?"

Simmons scoffs with disbelief.

"We'll circle back to you, Jim," Larry intercedes. "Johnson, how about you go?"

"Sorry about that, Simmons," Drew says.

"It's okay, Mr. Lawrence," Simmons says sympathetically. "I was the same when my mom passed."

Drew goes cold. He actually forgot. Just for a moment.

Larry nods to the redheaded woman sitting across from Simmons. "Johnson?"

Johnson pulls out her notes. "*Added Sugar*, a dystopian sci-fi set in the not-so-distant future. The U.S. government approves a food additive meant to prevent cancer that actually turns the American people into mindless combative robots. It's a commentary on social media and how algorithms end up programming us. For the lead I was thinking Joan..."

Drew loses focus. Looks back up at the mini-posters. Seventy-two, huh? He has to take Larry's word on that. He's always hated counting silently. But it doesn't take a math whiz to notice the difference between those first ten and the other sixty-two. They were called Not That Nut Pictures in those days, back when they were the LA satellite of Liu Míng's newly formed UniTopia Pictures. Drew was only twenty-five then. Fuck. What a baby. He really didn't know anything, but he certainly gave a darn good impression. That's what really mattered.

Atomic (2021). Right in the middle of COVID too. None of them knew what to do when it first hit. Drew was quite used to being out of the loop of how things worked, being as young as he was, but when the grown-ups didn't even know? That fucked him up more than he thought it would. And Theo was such an ass in those days. Who could blame him? Every week it was something new. Shut down. Reopen. Shut down again. Masks. Vaccines. Boosters. Tests. Tests. Tests. What bedlam. But it came out alright in the end, didn't it? The whole town flipped upside down when they didn't win Best Picture. Everyone wanted it just as much as they did. That's very hard to get, you know, an upset loss. Drew and Theo had no idea how rare that was. They just felt like failures. Especially Drew. He was the one up for Adapted Screenplay. Theo never cared that much about directing. Or so he said.

Onio (2023). Not only did Drew HAVE to write the screenplay, he HAD to direct it. Must've been the Oscar noms. Delusions of grandeur. Picture it: Drew's twenty-six-years-old, never directed a movie in his life, adapting a novella he wrote when he was eighteen in fucking Budapest. It's 101 degrees outside. A storm wipes out all their sets the first week. Half the cast is out of commission with either COVID or food poisoning. He's bossing around guys twice his age. Pulling his hair out. He almost dies a few times. He was so sure *Onio* was a gonna be a train-wreck. So fucking sure. And Theo was too busy filming *First Murder in Tequilatown* to help him out. Who would've thought Drew would be the one breaking box office records and getting another Adapted Screenplay nom while Theo's the one winning Razzies?

First Murder in Tequilatown (2023). Their first flop. Theo vowed never to write or direct again. He told Drew he never liked how *Tequilatown* turned out, but Drew could tell that wasn't true. The backlash hurt him, no matter how much he claimed otherwise.

You Should Come to California (2024). CJ Marrow, oh my God. What. An. ASS! He seemed so normal in the beginning too. Fresh out of film school. Six-foot-eight with jerry curls. No muscle on him. Drew set the budget at $3 million. Marrow jacked it up to $50 million and doubled the runtime, adding thematic flashbacks and plotless black and white sequences. The twerp thought he was the second coming of Tarkovsky. His Sundance interview was just as bad as Coppola's *Apocalypse Now* at Cannes. And when that fucker won the Independent Spirit Award for Directing, Jesus, Drew wanted to shoot himself in the face. He didn't even care that he lost Best Screenplay. Marrow changed so much. It wasn't even Drew's by then.

Xanca (2024). *Onio*'s sequel, the one everyone but Larry declared inferior to the original. Larry said Drew added so much depth that was never in *Onio*, that he really made himself a bigger world. Drew couldn't see it. Theo made way too many rewrites. It was HIS fucking project! Theo had no right to do that! *Xanca* could've been up there with *Empire* and *Godfather II* if not for that godawful ending. Larry likes the ending. Of course he does. He also thinks Adam Sandler counts as an auteur.

Then came *Late* (2025) and *Pacé* (2025), two stinkers. CJ Marrow out. Theo didn't wanna do shit. Drew was doing all the work at this point. He didn't have time to write, so he picked a couple specs from the slush pile and just ran with them. Actually, Drew liked *Pacé*. He actually got the hand of directing at that point. It got him back to the Oscars. For Best Picture no less. And it actually won Best Original Screenplay. (The only time Not That Nut ever won a Screenplay Oscar and it wasn't even Drew's.) He even got nominated for Best Director. He was only thirty. That doesn't happen often. Honestly, if it wasn't for *Havremoer* he'd still be directing to this day.

Havremoer (2025). The last of the *Onio* trilogy. Drew's *Waterworld.* He almost wanted to accept his Worst Director in person. There was just no good way to bury it. It was too... out there? Who knows anymore.

MACBETH (2026). The film that ruined Drew's directing career. Larry tried to warn him too. "Shakespeare's tough," he said. "There's no one to blame but the director." But Drew didn't listen, did he? He thought he was so clever making Macbeth gay. How overambitious and lazy at the same time. Drew still thinks about those reviews. Every so often. Late at night.

Mr. Yuli (2026). The last thing Drew ever wrote. Middling returns. Golden Globe nominated, but no one gave a shit. The logline? Gay *Miss Julie.* What a golden goose he'd become.

That's when Theo came to him with the idea to spin off from UniTopia into a separate entity, a way to make big budget co-productions without Míng getting a cut. Theo even offered to take over as sole CEO. Drew would still be considered a co-founder but all he'd have to be was Head of Production. Theo made it sound so nice too. A chance for Drew breathe. To step out of the limelight. Just the fun part of the business, he said. Because he knew Drew was so tired of carrying them alone. So worn. Drew bought it, didn't he? He signed where Theo told him to sign and watched their baby get turned into a carbon copy of UniTopia itself. Writer's rooms. Marketing departments. Paying other people to do the work for them. Drew never had to lift a finger again. That's where it all went wrong.

"Mr. Lawrence?" Larry asks, tapping Drew's shoulder.

Drew blinks, returning to the present. "I'm sorry. I was miles away."

"Anything to share?"

"It's okay. I was just a bit..." Drew looks back up at those mini-posters. Shakes his head. "It used to be fun, Larry," Drew laments. "Even after everything, you can't say it wasn't fun."

JACOB

The Odd Couple

```
INT. DUMPLING CAFE - DAY

Jacob rushes inside, passing table after table. Spots Stewie sitting
by himself.

                              JACOB
                        (bleating)
                AYY BEE!

Stewie looks up from the menu.

                              STEWIE
                        (bleating)
                AYY BEE!

Jacob sits down, out of breath.

                              JACOB
                Sorry. I just wanted to add one more thing and I lost
                track of time.

                              STEWIE
                Drive-Thru?

                              JACOB
                Yeah. Oh my God, it's unbelievable.

                              STEWIE
                Ready when you are.

                              JACOB
                Me too. I always get the same thing.

Jacob moves in to kiss. Stewie backs away instantly.

                              STEWIE
                Back off, Boogaloo!

                              JACOB
                Oh. Sorry. Forgot.

                              STEWIE
                You're really out of breath.

                              JACOB
                Am I? Oh. Just hate being late for you, Sexy.

                              STEWIE
                It's okay. I'm usually the one always late.

                              JACOB
                Ten to fifteen minutes isn't late, right?

                              STEWIE
                Sometimes I'd be an hour late.

Jacob furrows his brow.

                              JACOB
                How could you be an hour late?

                              STEWIE
                I just was. It'd happen so frequently that whenever
                my family would have a get-together at Abby's house,
```

they'd tell me an earlier arrival time so I'd actually show up on time for once.

JACOB
That's awful.

STEWIE
I didn't mind.

JACOB
How could you not mind?

Stewie shrugs, no-brainer.

STEWIE
They're my family.

JACOB
Forgive me, but I have a different level of tolerance when it comes to family members intentionally lying to me.

The WAITER (30) approaches the table with a pot of green tea.

WAITER
Hello, welcome to Dumpling Cafe.

STEWIE
What's your name?

WAITER
Lin.

STEWIE
(pointing at Jacob)
I've heard nothing but great things about this place from this guy, Lin. He says it's the best place in the entire city.

Stewie winks at Jacob.

JACOB
(to Lin)
I go to Whitman. I'm here, like, all the time.

LIN
I have a feeling your father is going to love--

JACOB
He's not my father.

STEWIE
I'm not his father.

LIN
Oh.
(pause)
I'm sorry.

The three of them stand in awkward silence. Lin places the teapot down and scampers away.

STEWIE
Hope you're not too hungry.

JACOB
Can't believe it! That's the third time someone assumed that!

STEWIE
You can't believe it? I can.

JACOB
Yeah but you're like the complete opposite of my father. It's an insult.

They raise their cups.

STEWIE
Happy one month anniversary, Baby Boy.

JACOB
Happy one month anniversary, Daddy.

They sip a tiny bit. Jacob winces.

JACOB (CONT'D)
Fuck!

STEWIE
Did you burn your tongue?

Jacob nods.

JACOB
Kiss it and make it better?

STEWIE
(comical)
NOOO!

Jacob casually flips through the menu. Stewie folds his hands, admiring Jacob.

STEWIE (CONT'D)
What's your dad like? You never talk about him.

JACOB
He just sat around all day. Watched TV. Played on his laptop.

STEWIE
Video games?

JACOB
Microsoft Pinball. Solitaire. Chess. He always had Diet Coke nearby.
(pause)
And I remember he had holes in sweater. And his socks. And he'd always have Seinfeld on for hours on end.

STEWIE
I never found Seinfeld funny.

JACOB
Well, you're crazy. Seinfeld's the best. We watched every episode. It's the only thing we ever really did together.

Jacob runs his finger along the rim of his teacup.

JACOB (CONT'D)
He never taught me how to shave or how to dress good or how to act cool. Then again he really didn't do any of that. His mustache was a joke.
(pause)
But still he's an enigma, my father. Even now.

STEWIE
I didn't really know my father until I got older. He really wasn't any of that either.

JACOB
Yeah, but your parents stayed together.

STEWIE
They almost got divorced.

JACOB
Almost isn't quite the same thing.
(pause)
They were married six years before they had us, and they were together five years before that. Anyone who

says it's not because of the kids is a fucking liar, especially if two of them have autism.

STEWIE
I see it all the time. Always one parent giving it their all and the other either shutting down or leaving.

Jacob nods solemnly.

JACOB
When I was diagnosed, Mom spent hours researching Asperger's online, reading tons of books, trying to know what to do, what not to do. A lot of what she learned was out of date, Asperger's being a new field and all, but she really really tried.
(pause)
Dad just sat there. Tuning us all out. Like he didn't sign up for that shit.

Jacob frowns at Stewie.

JACOB (CONT'D)
But he would've stayed. He would've hated it, but he never would've left if Mom hadn't asked for the divorce.

STEWIE
At least your dad's still alive. You can still talk to him.

Jacob deflates.

STEWIE (CONT'D)
(apologetic)
I didn't mean it like that. I'm just saying it's not too late to have a relationship with him.

JACOB
You don't think I've tried? I've only seen him once or twice a year since the divorce. And that's his idea, not mine.

Jacob exhales softly.

JACOB (CONT'D)
The way Mom talks about him now makes me wonder if they ever loved each other.

STEWIE
That's not good.

JACOB
No shit that's not good.
(pause)
I think she expected to be happier instead of single and lonely while Dad's off losing weight and actually giving a shit with his new girlfriends.

STEWIE
You think she regrets it?

JACOB
If she does, she'll never tell us. God forbid we get some fucking transparency out of her. Dad too. What's the deal with you people? Can't any of you tell anyone how you really feel?

STEWIE
I really love you.

Jacob smiles.

JACOB
God, you're one of the rare ones, aren't you?

Stewie grins with a bashful shrug.

JACOB (CONT'D)
I just wanna talk to him. About his life, anything. But he can't do that. He just doesn't. Neither does Mom. When she does, it's usually about other people, only the bad stuff. It's depressing. But Dad... He can't even open up. And he doesn't even... I just...

Jacob exhales softly. Shakes his head.

JACOB (CONT'D)
I want him to look at me and ask... something. I know that's just his generation. He'll always be weird about the gay stuff, but he's okay with it. He told me he was.
(pause)
BECAUSE I'm his son. That's the only reason, apparently. I know he just wanted me to... But it didn't -- doesn't make me feel better.

Jacob shrugs.

JACOB
So until then, it's just... Seinfeld. GoodFellas. Back to the Future. Indiana Jones. Pirates of the Caribbean. Just an echo chamber of pop culture references.

Jacob picks up his teacup.

JACOB (CONT'D)
And that's not a relationship.

Stewie stares. Reaches across the table and takes Jacob's hand. Jacob squeezes Stewie's hand.

Lin awkwardly returns. Stewie instantly lets go.

LIN
I'll give you a moment.

JACOB
No, we're ready. Two orders of the soup dumplings to start with.
(to Stewie)
You'll love 'em. It's what they're famous for. They're the titular dumplings.
(to Lin)
For the entrees I'll have two veggie springs rolls, a large order of orange chicken, a small veggie lo mein, and a BBQ beef skewer.

Lin races to jot all that down.

STEWIE
(whispers)
That's just for you?

JACOB
I'm paying.

STEWIE
That's a lot of food.

JACOB
I finish it faster than it'll take for you to order.

LIN
(to Stewie)
It's true. He does.

Jacob furrows his brow. Lin shrugs.

LIN (CONT'D)
(to Jacob)
I just remembered I had you last week.

STEWIE
So did I.

Another three-way awkward pause.

STEWIE (CONT'D)
I'll have the kung pao chicken.

JUMP CUT TO:

LATER

Jacob lifts the lid of one of the wicker baskets of soup dumplings. Steam rolls out.

STEWIE
Piping hot!

JACOB
Be very careful.

Jacob grabs a pair of tongs. Gently picks one up. Places it on his dumpling spoon.

JACOB (CONT'D)
Just take a little bite on the side...

Jacob pierces the dough with a gentle nibble.

JACOB (CONT'D)
...and slurp the broth.

Jacob sucks the soup out of the inside of the dumpling. Shoves the rest of the dumpling into his mouth.

Stewie looks at the second basket underneath the first one.

STEWIE
Maybe you should've only ordered one basket.

JACOB
I always solo one.

STEWIE
I don't think I want a whole one to myself.

JACOB
You're not that hungry?

STEWIE
No, I am. I just think it's all a lot of calories.

JACOB
I'm sure it is.

STEWIE
For you.

JACOB
I think I'm fine.

STEWIE
You didn't order any vegetables.

JACOB
Veggie lo mein.

STEWIE
...is not a vegetable.

JACOB
It's Chinese. What do you expect?

STEWIE
I really think you shouldn't be eating this much food.

JACOB
What food?

STEWIE
This--

The entire dumpling basket is empty.

STEWIE (CONT'D)
When did you eat them all?! They just got here!

JACOB
I was starving.

Stewie sighs.

STEWIE
It's not good for you to eat that fast.

JACOB
You said you don't care about my weight.

STEWIE
I don't find it unattractive. I still care about your health. Back when I was a personal trainer, I was also a nutritional counselor. That's a lot of sodium and carbs for one person.

Jacob frowns.

JACOB
I'm trying, alright?

STEWIE (CONT'D)
I know you are.
(pause)
If you need help working out, I've got a lot of equipment in my apartment. We can do it together.

JACOB
I tried the whole personal training thing. It doesn't work for me.

STEWIE
It'll be a lot easier if we--

JACOB
Can we change the subject?

Stewie hesitates.

JUMP CUT TO:

LATER

A BUSBOY clears the wicker baskets. Jacob refills their teacups.

JACOB
What ever happened to Black Lives Matter? They were everywhere, like, two years ago.

STEWIE
I'm sure they'll be back.

JACOB
When Ferguson happened, all the colleges in the area staged a walkout in protest. We ended up spending the rest of class talking about it while simultaneously justifying our non-participation.

STEWIE
You didn't walk out?

JACOB
Don't get me wrong, I completely sympathize with unarmed black men getting killed by the pigs. I just want to learn, alright? I'm not racist just because I want to stay in the class I'm paying for.

STEWIE
It's all really silly, you know? Like the other day, I was watching the Mets and every commercial had a black person in it.

Jacob stares.

JACOB
What's silly about black people being in commercials?

STEWIE
What's silly is all these big corporations pandering to African Americans.

JACOB
Representation isn't pandering.

STEWIE
Yes, but EVERY commercial? African Americans are 20% of this country. They should only be in 20% of commercials. That's actual representation.

Jacob hesitates.

JACOB
You know that's really racist, right?

STEWIE
What?! That's not racist!

JACOB
You really shouldn't be saying that.

STEWIE
It has nothing to do with them being black! It's the corporations using virtue signaling to get minorities to buy their products. It's so phony! How can you not see that?

JACOB
You're still going? They're just commercials.

Stewie frowns, genuinely hurt.

Jacob scratches his forehead.

JACOB (CONT'D)
Wait. I shouldn't have said that, I...

Jacob sighs.

JACOB (CONT'D)
I don't do that. I don't say things like that. It's something I was coached into feeling was appropriate. It's not appropriate. It's rude. It insults people's intelligence. I'm sorry.

Stewie nods.

STEWIE
(gentle)
I accept your apology.

JACOB
I really, really hate talking politics. One of the perks about going to Italy, I thought, was to be able to get away from all the election bullshit. Turns out everywhere I went, all these Italians I'd meet in bars would ask me, "Who you voting for? Hillary, Bernie or Trump?" over and over, every time.

(laughs from shock)
Why would they assume I'd ever vote for Donald Trump? I'm gay! Why the fuck would I ever be a Trump supporter?!

Stewie stares back, a guilty look on his face.

Jacob's smile slowly fades.

JACOB (CONT'D)
You mean you're...?

Stewie nods.

Jacob grabs a glass, thinking.

JACOB (CONT'D)
We don't have to talk about it.

He drinks his water.

JUMP CUT TO:

LATER

Stewie's half-done his entree. Jacob's already done with all his.

STEWIE
By then I had twenty trainers providing service to a hundred clients all over the state of New Jersey.

JACOB
And they all had disabilities?

STEWIE
Yes. Some with autism, some with muscular dystrophy, cerebral palsy. They would never be comfortable going to a gym.

JACOB
I know that feeling.

STEWIE
Exactly.

JACOB
So what happened?

STEWIE
The Department of Developmental Disabilities decided to switch to a Medicaid model, which means the federal government would be footing half the bill, but one of the things they don't cover through Medicaid is personal training.

JACOB
What does that mean?

STEWIE
That means I had to change what my business provided. The closest thing to personal training is habilitative physical therapy.

JACOB
Like rehab?

STEWIE
Not rehabilitation, HABILITATION. Maintaining daily function.

JACOB
And you can't just turn your trainers into physical therapists?

STEWIE
They would need a license in physical therapy and that takes six years to get.

JACOB
That seems so unfair to you.

Stewie shrugs.

STEWIE
I had the choice. I could've stayed in Jersey and transitioned. I was going to. Then I found out one of my clients was moving up here, a very expensive client that paid out of pocket, and I didn't want to lose them, so I thought about it, and I decided to relocate Smalltown Trainers up here.

JACOB
But what about all those clients down in Jersey?

STEWIE
They're still with us until the transition is complete. I worked remote anyway, so this isn't really that different. And Massachusetts hasn't adopted the Medicaid model yet, so I'll be able to keep growing Smalltown Trainers up here in the meantime.

Jacob nods, impressed.

JACOB
You really have it all figured out.

STEWIE
I'm telling you, Baby Boy, if you really want to make it big in this country, you need to start your own business.

JACOB
That world's just so unfamiliar to me.

STEWIE
It's just like your screenwriting. Make it your entire world. That's why I know you'll be very successful. You're very passionate about it.

Jacob beams.

JACOB
Before I forget again. I know this is super last minute, but Mom reminded me this morning that I have to see my psychiatrist in Reading on Friday.

STEWIE
PA?

JACOB
I know it's a long drive, but if it's not too much trouble, can I get a ride down?

Stewie bobs his head thinking.

STEWIE
There's some stuff in my condo I've been meaning to go back for. We can stay there Thursday night and drive back after your appointment.

JACOB
Thank you! I'm sorry I can't reciprocate any of the driving.

STEWIE
Why not? You've got a permit.

JACOB
Mom barely taught me anything. And I have absolutely no idea how to drive stick.

STEWIE
Manual's a bit of an adjustment, but maybe you should try. How else are you gonna get the practice?

JACOB
No, I'm good.

STEWIE
Why not?

JACOB
I'm good. Thanks.

Lin walks by with a fresh kettle of tea. Switches it out with the old one.

JACOB (CONT'D)
(refilling his cup)
This stuff is like crack.

STEWIE
I don't know about you, but it's going through me like water.

Jacob sips. Winces.

JACOB
God FUCKING dammit!

Stewie stops eating, pissed.

STEWIE
Can you not do that?

JACOB
I'm sorry! I just burned my fucking mouth again.

STEWIE
No, THAT.

JACOB
What?

Stewie sighs. Returns to his food.

JACOB (CONT'D)
What, now my cursing's a problem for you?

STEWIE
You don't hear me cursing.

JACOB
You say cunt all the time!

STEWIE
Cunt's not a curse.

JACOB
CUNT'S NOT A CURSE?!

STEWIE
Cunt's not a curse.

Jacob stares.

JACOB
If cunt's not a curse, what the hell IS a curse?

STEWIE
That.

JACOB
Hell?

STEWIE
H-E-L-L is a curse.

Jacob chuckles.

JACOB
Oh come on!

STEWIE
A-S-S is a curse, F is a curse, bleepstard is a curse--

JACOB
"Bleepstard"?!

STEWIE
S-H-I-T is a curse, D-A-M is a curse--

JACOB
It's D-A-M-N.

STEWIE
Yes. Sucking jerkoff--

JACOB
Is a curse.

STEWIE
--is NOT a curse.

JACOB
Oh God, that is so stupid!

STEWIE
No it's not.

JACOB
Who even says "sucking jerkoff?!"

STEWIE
My mother.

Jacob looks off.

JACOB
Now it all makes sense.

STEWIE
Penis isn't a curse, pussy isn't a curse, vagina isn't a curse, dick isn't a curse, cock isn't a curse--

JACOB
You can say cock, but you can't say damn or ass?

STEWIE
Cock's still a dirty word.

JACOB
Which is not the same thing as a curse.

STEWIE
Correct.

JACOB
And that's what cunt is?

STEWIE
Cock is worse than cunt.

JACOB
CUNT IS WORSE THAN ALL OF THEM!

STEWIE
No, you know what's the worst? J.F.C.

JACOB
What, "Jesus Fucking Christ?"

STEWIE
Don't say that. And... God effing bleep-it.

JACOB
Do you say, "Oh my God?"

STEWIE
"Oh my God" isn't taking the Lord's name in vain. Throwing in a bleep is.

Jacob silently registers Stewie's admittedly inconsistent logic.

JACOB
You're not religious, are you?

STEWIE
Yup.

Jacob hesitates.

JACOB
Just in practice, or do you really believe in God and all that?

STEWIE
Of course I believe in God.

Jacob raises his eyebrows.

JACOB
You actually go to church?

STEWIE
Every Sunday. Sometimes Saturday night.

JACOB
Why didn't I know about this?

STEWIE
You never asked.
(pause)
Wanna come to church with me on Sunday?

JACOB
Not really.

Stewie nods emotionlessly.

STEWIE
You don't believe in God?

JACOB
I do not.

STEWIE
Does it bother you that I do?

JACOB
I don't wanna start anything.

STEWIE
It's okay, Baby Boy. This isn't the first time I've had this conversation.

Jacob hesitates.

JACOB
I grew up Catholic.

STEWIE
Baptized and everything?

JACOB
Baptized, Communion, Confirmed, everything. All of us were in Catholic school too.

STEWIE
Why'd you stop believing?

JACOB
It just makes more sense. Wasn't the Greek Pantheon just as relevant at the time as Christianity is now? In a thousand years, Christianity will be the same way.

STEWIE
Replaced by what?

JACOB
Logic, ideally. We know too much about the world and science and people thanks to the Internet. A lot of "unanswerable" questions have been answered. Divinity just has no place in modern society.

STEWIE
There is a difference between faith and organized religion. There's a moral code to Catholicism.

JACOB
Yeah, kill the gays.

STEWIE
That's not Catholicism.

JACOB
Really? Ever heard of the Westboro Baptist Church?

STEWIE
Baptist. Not Catholic.

Jacob hesitates.

JACOB
What about those crooked televangelists?

STEWIE
Also not Catholic.

JACOB
What are they?

STEWIE
Protestant.

JACOB
And all those Bible Thumpers in the Red States?

STEWIE
Baptists, Protestants, Lutherans... No Catholics.

Jacob hesitates.

JACOB
The Pope's Catholic. Last I checked he still hates the gays.

STEWIE
Pope Francis doesn't.

JACOB
He's against gay marriage.

STEWIE
He's still a vast improvement over that homophobe Pope Bend-a-Dick.

JACOB
Thought you said dick was a curse word.

STEWIE
No, I said it was a dirty word. And he deserves it.

Jacob silently registers Stewie's point.

STEWIE (CONT'D)
When he became Pope, I actually left the Catholic Church for five years.

JACOB
Really?

STEWIE
I was with Gus at the time. I went to his church instead.

JACOB
Gus went to church too?

STEWIE
Presbyterian. It's exactly the same as the Catholic Church except they're a tad more liberal. They still use the old words before Bend-a-Dick changed them.

JACOB
That actually doesn't sound so bad.

STEWIE
When Bend-a-Dick resigned and Francis became Pope, I went back to being Catholic.

JACOB
What about Gus?

STEWIE
We had broken up by then.

Jacob nods.

JACOB
So you've forgiven them, the Catholics.

STEWIE
Jury's still out.

JACOB
Why do you still go then?

Stewie shrugs.

STEWIE
The way I see it, no one knows if there's a God or not. If there isn't, all I lose is an hour a week. If there is, at least I'm covered.

JACOB
I admit, I'm surprised how logical you are with all that.

Stewie smiles.

STEWIE
Why?

Jacob stares. He doesn't know how to answer that one.

CUT TO:

INT. WHITMAN UNIVERSITY - LB 710 - JACOB'S ROOM - NIGHT

Jacob opens the Dark Chest of Wonders. Rummages around. Pulls out the Blu-Ray case for <u>The Tree of Life</u>. Pops it into his laptop.

INSERT - <u>THE TREE OF LIFE</u>

The famous 20-minute Creation Sequence, a breathtaking visual tour of the cosmos and a dramatization of Earth's creation and the spark of life, culminating with the dinosaurs and their extinction via meteor. An angelic soprano sings throughout, her voice belting F-sharps so hard it cracks his laptop's cheap internal speakers.

BACK ON JACOB

Jacob bites his nails as he watches, picking up on things he never noticed before. He's always interpreted this sequence as a scientifically accurate creation myth debunking the Adam and Eve story, but there's something quite beautiful in the poetic reverence of the primordial earth, something emotional and meaningful amongst otherwise chaotic and dispassionate phenomena. Perhaps Terrance Malick intended it to be an origin of life scenario in which both the secular and non-secular are correct, i.e. God wielding science to forge the universe. Maybe that's how Stewie sees it too.

SMASH CUT TO:

WHALE
Earthquake

Whale's phone alarm blares, snapping him out of his work-induced trance. 12:30. He stops the alarm, turns off the music, and logs off the computer. On his walk back from the copy room his mind is still racing, all the little ways he could access more scripts, more sales, more niche film festivals to cover for The Professor to make up for missing Locarno over a month ago.

Whale pushes into the men's room. Steps up to the urinal. Evacuates. He stares at the textured salmon paintjob. Wonders what color the women's room is.

The door pushes in behind him. Cashew steps up to the other urinal, the shorter one, the trickle of urine being the only sound in the room. "Haven't been seeing much of you," he murmurs, side-eying in that explicitly heterosexual way.

```
                WHALE
I've been in the copy room. There's a side office
back there.
```

"I know," Cashew says with a smirk. "Saw Bumps take you back there."

Whale plops his cock back in his briefs. Flushes. Zips up on the way to the sink.

"Gotta hand it to her," Cashew says. "She's not stupid."

```
                WHALE
What do you mean?
```

"Divide and conqueror." Cashew zips up. Flushes. "It's a long con. My dad saw it all the time back home. Joseph, Oregon? He told me about a real estate mogul named Gordy Pfefferman. Everyone hated him, but he owned half the commercial real estate in town, so they really didn't have much say about it. Anyway, there was a clothing store next door to our place, a mom-and-pop sort of deal, Capperman's." Cashew cuts in front of Whale standing idly in front of the sink. Obliviously flips the faucet. "Dad said Capperman's was on top of a natural stream. They had to build the store around it because they weren't allowed to fuck with it. But the owners wanted to expand, and there was no way they could do that without pissing off the ecology people. So Pfefferman came to them and offered to buy the place and gave them a great deal on a big house outside the main center of town. The owners were so desperate to get away from the competition stealing their customers, so they took it. But Pfefferman knew that part of town wasn't nearly as popular as the main square. Sure enough, five years later Capperman's went under and Pfefferman bought it back for peanuts." Cashew grabs a towel.

```
                WHALE
She just wanted to help me out.
```

"That's what she wants you to think. The question is why. What's her angle?"

Whale looks up at Cashew's reflection.

```
                WHALE
She was just helping me out.
```

Cashew throws the paper towels into the trash. "You two vying for the same job and she's just helping you out?"

```
                WHALE
Yeah.
```

Whale washes his hands. Grabs a paper towel. Dries his hands.

"You fucking her?" Cashew asks.

```
                    WHALE
        No!
```

"But you wanna fuck her, right?"

Whale stares Cashew in the eye.

```
                    WHALE
        I'm gay.
```

Cashew's smile fades. "Oh. That's surprising."

```
                    WHALE
        Thank you. I actually take that as a compliment.
```

"No, it's surprising she'd go after you at all. It doesn't make any sense."

Whale stares, no longer amused.

```
                    WHALE
        I told you. She just wanted to help.
```

Whale pushes the bathroom door open with a flat palm. "No, wait!" Cashew says, stepping forward. "I'm sorry."

Whale stops. Looks back.

"I didn't mean to be so forward," Cashew explains, a bit bashful. He suddenly furrows his brow. Steps past Whale. Pushes the door open more. Looks both ways. Steps back, the door closing. "Sorry. Peabrain's always lurking about. Stuttering prick's silent as a mouse when he wants to be."

```
                    WHALE
        What do you want?
```

"You heading out for lunch?"

```
                    WHALE
        I was going to.
```

"Wanna go together?"

Whale studies Cashew's face. Eager. No sarcasm or mocking.

```
                    WHALE
        Why?
```

"We've been here three months and haven't said one word to each other."

```
                    WHALE
        I don't know what's stopping you. Bumps already
        reached out to me and Peabrain.
```

"I bet she did. Funny, she hasn't said shit to me."

```
                    WHALE
        She thinks you're an incel.
```

"Well I think she's a two-faced bitch. Guess we're even."

Whale sighs, looking elsewhere.

"Well?" Cashew asks. "You wanna go with me or what?"

```
                    WHALE
        What's your name?
```

"I'm not telling you!" Cashew exclaims with a laugh.

WHALE
I don't go to lunch with people unless I know their name.

"And what, I'm supposed to just *trust* you'll tell me your—?"

Whale takes one step out the door.

"Wait! Wait! Okay!" Cashew sighs uneasily. Mouths two syllables.

WHALE
What?

Cashew shushes harshly. Moves a bit closer. "Theo," he whispers.

WHALE
(whispers)
Theo?

Cashew nods, perturbed.

Whale hesitates. Holds out his hand.

WHALE
Jacob. Nice to meet you.

Cashew and Whale awkwardly shake hands.

The two of them get a window booth at Wally McGree's, the 24-hour diner on the next block. The waitress, an artificial redhead who probably started there as a dainty waitress twenty years ago before becoming the no-nonsense worker she is now, walks by with a pad and pencil. "What'll it be, boys?"

"Just a plain bagel, nothing on it," Cashew says.

The Waitress raises a brow. "You want it heated, honey?"

"Neither. Just plain, room temp, nothing on it."

The Waitress stares a bit.

"Unsliced," Cashew adds with a hint of spite.

"Yeah. Sure." The Waitress looks at Whale. "The usual, Jacob?"

WHALE
And a crock of chili.

"Big or small?"

WHALE
Big as can be.

The Waitress nods, smiling. "Something to drink?"

WHALE
Café Americano.

The Waitress puts the pencil in her ear. "Be back with that Americano."

"Cherry Coke," Cashew mumbles.

The Waitress stares back. Holds gaze. Walks away.

"Cunt," Cashew whispers.

WHALE
She's alright.

Cashew leans back. "How's it going in the Fortress of Solitude?"

WHALE
Haven't been called up to his office again. Guess that's good.
(pause)
I do feel I'm getting more of a hang of it all. Doesn't seem so incomprehensible anymore.

"There's only so much going on, you know? So many films being made."

```
                    WHALE
        The picture can only get so big.
```

"Exactly."

```
                    WHALE
        It's proving an education, that's for sure. And I've
        had worse jobs.
```

"Really? Worse than this?"

```
                    WHALE
        You obviously haven't worked at Beef 'n' Fries.
```

The Waitress brings Whale's Café Americano on an otherwise empty tray.

"Where's my Coke?" Cashew asks.

The Waitress stares. "Didn't hear you." She walks away.

Whale adds half a packet of raw sugar and stirs his Americano.

```
                    WHALE
        My submission was a feature I wrote called Drive-
        Thru. Very similar scenario.
```

"Mine's a short I wrote and directed," Cashew says. "*First Murder in Tequilatown*."

```
                    WHALE
        Is that a play on Margaritaville?
```

"Margaritaville and EPCOT. Not the theme park, the unfinished community Disney was building in the 60s, the Futurist corporate town utopia run by Walt Disney himself. They scrapped it after Walt died and turned it into the park, but it would've had its own government, residences, businesses, mass transportation. Completely artificial. Everything manicured just right. Tequilatown's the same way. Ranch homes. Giant fence keeping everyone out. Always five o'clock, all day, forever. A Boomer paradise. But one day, there's a murder. Why? Why would anyone want to kill someone in a perfect place? An amateur detective starts asking questions. How far up it goes."

```
                    WHALE
        That's pretty cool.
```

"Thank you." Cashew hesitates. "I can send you the link if you want."

```
                    WHALE
        Yeah. Sure.
```

Whale hands Cashew his phone. Cashew types in his cell number. Texts himself. Hands Whale back his phone. "It's on my laptop. I'll send the URL when I get home."

```
                    WHALE
        Can't wait.
```

Cashew grins more. "It's based it off my hometown. Joseph, Oregon."

```
                    WHALE
        Yeah, you said. It's actually called Joseph?
```

"Yeah. It's small too. Really small. Only like a thousand people. We're right next to Wallowa Lake. It's green everywhere. Mountains. Literally looks like *The Sound of Music*. We even call ourselves 'Oregon's Little Switzerland.'"

```
                    WHALE
        Sound of Music's Austria.
```

"Whatever! You know what I mean." Cashew pauses. "My family owns Landreth Motors. It's been there almost as long as Joseph itself. My great-grandfather Kerrigan Landreth opened it in 1921. Carried it through the Great Depression, and then car culture boomed in the 50s. Grandpa Martin took over in 1960 and almost ruined everything."

```
                    WHALE
      What did he do?
```

"Nothing. That's the problem. He didn't give a shit. No discipline. No ambition. Pissed off all the regulars. Refused to expand. Dad took over in '82 and single-handedly saved the family business. He added the mini-mart next door, Landreth Motor-Mart. That's what revived our public image. Turned Landreth Motors into the biggest small business in town."

```
                    WHALE
      Oh.
```

"Believe me, having Calvin Landreth as my dad was a big fucking deal. I was like a celebrity at school."

```
                    WHALE
      You guys were really that big, huh?
```

"Oh yeah!" Cashew insists excitedly. "Everyone in Northeast Oregon goes to Landreth Motors. My dad always behind the counter. He's also a really cool guy too. Everyone loves him."

```
                    WHALE
      Surprised you didn't want to stay in Joseph and take
      over.
```

Cashew's excitement melts away. "I did." He clears his throat. "I was a shelf-stocker in high school. That was fun. Then I asked him if he'd let me take over one day and he said no."

Whale hesitates.

```
                    WHALE
      Do you have, like, brothers or...?
```

"No," Cashew says meekly. "Just me and Dad."

Whale stares.

"I-I kinda get it though," Cashew adds. "He just wants me to do my own thing. Make my own life." He pauses. "He's a bit of a perfectionist. No wonder. His dad almost fucked it up, you know?"

Whale nods, unconvinced.

"I still love my dad," Cashew says, assured. "He's such an inspiration to me. And he's always been supportive of me pursing a film career."

```
                    WHALE
      That must be nice.
```

"What does your dad do?"

```
                    WHALE
      Finance.
```

"Finance! That's cool. You're very lucky."

```
                    WHALE
      Not if you don't care about money.
```

"You care about money."

```
                    WHALE
      Not as much as Dad. Maybe that's the problem.
              (pause)
      I just don't see money as the ultimate success.
```

"How do you define success?"

Whale hesitates. Sips his coffee.

```
                    WHALE
      Getting to be exactly what you wanna be.
```

Cashew nods slowly. "What do you wanna be?"

```
                    WHALE
      An auteur.
```

"The next, Scorsese? Tarantino?"

```
                    WHALE
      No next anything. I absolutely adore Tarantino, he
      influences a lot of my work, but I don't wanna be
      just another knockoff. I wanna be me. I want people
      to get excited when the next Jacob Andrezj movie
      comes out. I got my own thing, just like Kubrick and
      Fincher and Wes Anderson have their own thing. I want
      people to analyze my films and talk on and on about
      me the way they talk about them. Even if I don't have
      the balls to direct, I can still be a screenwriting
      auteur like Sorkin.
              (pause)
      What about you? What do you wanna be?
```

"Louis B. Mayer," Cashew says with pride.

Whale chuckles, surprised.

```
                    WHALE
      Mayer? Why not Harvey Weinstein or Steven Spielberg?
```

"Because the old Hollywood types, the Louis B. Mayers, the David O. Seltznicks, they ran Los Angeles. Everyone was scared of them, what they'd do. Hey, if I can't run Landreth Motors, I might as well turn Hollywood into my own personal Joseph, right?"

Whale smiles slightly.

"Of course that leads into its own array of problems," Cashew continues. "I could end up like The Professor. Stuck in the past. Stagnant. How can he adapt or be of any value to anyone if he only surrounds himself with Boomers? You can't learn anything in an echo chamber. We're only there for the tax credit. He obviously needs the money."

Whale looks out the diner window. Somehow hearing Cashew saying it out loud feels weird. Sacrilegious even.

Cashew sighs. "He just doesn't have the knack for it, you know? Neither did Grandpa Martin. Guess it doesn't matter if you're in Joseph, Oregon or Los Angeles, California. If you coast, you die. And I'm not going to die."

Whale nods ambivalently.

Cashew blinks. "I'm sorry. I talk too much."

```
                    WHALE
      No, it's fine. I listen too much.
              (pause)
      Honestly I find your ambition refreshing. Right now
      I'm living with a hedonistic loser and working for a
      man who inhibits all growth whatsoever.
```

The Waitress arrives with Whale's chili. Whale pulls a stainless steel spoon from his pocket, its head deep, handle hammered with little hexagons like a honeycomb.

Cashew furrows his brow. "You seriously brought your own spoon?"

Whale looks up, swallowing chili.

```
                         WHALE
          Yup.
```

"What are you, like a germophobe or something?"

```
                         WHALE
          If I was germophobe, I wouldn't keep it in my pocket.
```

Whale returns to the chili. Cashew studies the spoon itself. "It's kinda cool, I guess. Where'd you get it?"

```
                         WHALE
                   (mouth half-full)
          It fell from the sky.
```

"What do you mean 'it fell from the sky?'"

```
                         WHALE
          Just what I said. It fell from the sky.
```

Cashew stares. "Did you *see it* fall from the sky?"

```
                         WHALE
          No.
```

"Then how do you know?"

```
                         WHALE
          Because it wasn't there one day and the next day it
          was.
```

Cashew raises a brow. "Where was this?"

```
                         WHALE
          Boston.
```

"Boston?"

```
                         WHALE
          Mm-hmm.
```

"You don't sound like you're from Boston."

```
                         WHALE
          I went to film school there. I was living with my
          boyfriend at the time. He had a special spoon he
          always reused. I didn't have a spoon of my own. Then
          one day I went outside and there was a spoon right
          there in the snow.
                   (pause)
          I haven't used it since I came to LA. Thought I'd
          make an effort today.
```

Whale finishes his chili. Licks his spoon. Wipes it clean with a napkin. Pockets it. Cashew stares. "What are you saying? God sent you a spoon?"

```
                         WHALE
          Too crazy to be a coincidence, don't you think?
```

"You don't believe in God, do you?"

```
                         WHALE
          Yup.
```

Cashew hesitates. "Doesn't that contradict the whole gay thing?"

```
                         WHALE
          Nope.
```

Cashew shrugs. "So, what? Do you just not believe in science or whatnot?"

```
                    WHALE
        Of course I believe in science.
```

"Oh, how silly of me to assume a grown man that believes in a sky being throwing down spoons believes in science."

```
                    WHALE
        I used to be a really big atheist, you know.
```

"Somehow, I don't believe that."

```
                    WHALE
        I was raised Catholic, I went to Catholic school for
        a few years, I went atheist during high school, and I
        returned to Catholicism in the last year or so.
```

Cashew looks elsewhere. "I think anyone who believes in God is stupid."

```
                    WHALE
        You think I'm stupid?
```

"Absolutely," Cashew says without hesitation. "It's disappointing cause I thought you were so smart.

```
                    WHALE
        You have a right to an opinion, of course.
```

"It's not an opinion, it's a fucking fact. Science is not a subjective field."

```
                    WHALE
        I don't see the two as being mutually exclusive.
        God's just an extension of science.
```

"How the fuck is God an extension of science?"

```
                    WHALE
        Sunsets.
```

Cashew furrows his brow. "Sunsets?"

```
                    WHALE
        When the sun leaves the atmosphere, there's a
        thousand tiny little variables in temperature and
        pressure and UV ray refraction off air molecules and
        the angle of gravitational pull and our viewing angle
        in relation to it and the limitations of our naked
        eye and what it can and can't perceive.
                  (shrugs)
        So why are they beautiful?
```

"What?"

```
                    WHALE
        Why are sunsets beautiful?
```

"That's an incredibly subjective question."

```
                    WHALE
        A baby can tell the difference between beautiful and
        not beautiful. Considering how chaotic and random the
        billions and billions of light years of our universe
        is, the fact that anything nets a positive out there
        is shocking. On Mars, the sun is so far away that
        sunsets are quite insignificant. On Mercury or Venus,
        they're not just deadly for human beings to witness,
        they're downright terrifying. But on this planet, the
        fact that sunsets are a daily occurrence we can
        experience with the naked eye, so pleasant to our
        rods and cones as to inspire solace and peace and
        beauty, is statistically impossible. So either we
        live in a very specific environment curated by a
```

```
higher power... or it's LITERALLY an astronomical
coincidence.
```

Cashew rolls his eyes. "I don't wanna talk about this anymore."

```
                    WHALE
You asked.
```

"Jacob. It's just a fucking spoon."

The Waitress arrives and drops off Cashew's room-temp unsliced bagel and Whale's chicken salad wrap with sweet potato fries.

Cashew bites into his bagel, ripping it away like it's a grenade.

Whale eats big bites, his eyes down on his plate.

Cashew chews, his eyes on Whale. "You got anyone out here? Family?"

```
                    WHALE
Nope.
```

"Friends?"

```
                    WHALE
Not really.
```

Cashew examines his bagel. "You're really on your own, huh?"

```
                    WHALE
I guess we both are.
```

"I got my dad with me, metaphorically speaking. Lots of advice I've retained."

```
                    WHALE
So do I.
```

"From your dad?"

```
                    WHALE
No, forget about my dad.
```

"Who then?

Whale chews, thinking back.

```
                    WHALE
Stewie.
```

"Who's Stewie?" Cashew asks, biting another chunk.

```
                    WHALE
My ex.
               (pause)
You'd like him, he runs his own business.
```

"Really? How old is he?"

```
                    WHALE
Fifty-three.
```

Cashew widens his eyes. "Fifty-three?! Gross."

```
                    WHALE
He was actually really hot.
```

"How long were you guys together?"

```
                    WHALE
A little over a year. It was a mutual in the end. I
got the internship, he has his business, so--
```

"Enough chit-chat," Cashew interrupts, tossing his bagel back on the plate. "Let's get to it."

Whale stops chewing, confused.

Cashew chuckles. "What, you thought I asked you to lunch because I thought you were cute?"

```
                        WHALE
        Didn't realize you had an ulterior motive.
```

"I know you didn't. That's what I've been telling you. It takes one to know one."

Whale stares, uneasy.

Cashew clears his throat. "In short, the end times are coming. The internship. The Factory. What happens in the next seven days will single-handedly determine who gets the job."

```
                        WHALE
        What are you talking about? We've still got two
        months.
```

"Back in Joseph, my dad worked every day of the week. That's a lot of hours by myself. I watched a whole lot of movies, probably more than you even. We didn't have many theatres around, just a lot of old VHS tapes and DVDs. Old movies. Classic Hollywood fare. Very structured, very cheesy. Lots of hits and misses. Seeing so many in a row, you start getting the feel of whether or not you'll end up liking the movie about two-thirds in. For years I had no idea why two-thirds was the point of no return, but then I went to Willamette and found out it had a name. I bet you even know what it is."

```
                        WHALE
        The Snag?
```

"The Snag, very good. First act's all setup, of course. Second act builds stakes, develops the chaos, establishes the individual plots. But once it hits the Snag, there's nothing more to add. It's all deconstruction from there. Your opinion is already formed. That's why this week matters. After that, The Professor will already have his pick in mind."

```
                        WHALE
        If you're right.
```

"I'm right. And even though you were pretty behind in the beginning, it seems we're all on equal footing now. Except Peabrain."

```
                        WHALE
        Peabrain?
```

"He's done coverage on twenty-five features PLUS all five novels this week alone."

Whale stares.

```
                        WHALE
        I didn't know that.
```

"How could you have? You've been in the back room for the past month and a half. You see? Bumps ain't fucking around. She's probably planning a move of her own. You being back there's just one less variable for her to worry about. But Peabrain's on a whole other level." Cashew looks around the diner. Leans in. "I need your help knocking him down a peg or two. To buy us time. It'll give us an equal shot at that job."

Whale doesn't move.

Cashew checks behind him. "We just have to delete his files before he sends them to The Professor on Friday."

```
                        WHALE
        Oh God.
```

"He'll assume Peabrain did nothing for the week. He'd have to start all over. By the time he catches up, we'll be miles ahead of him. I think I know a way how to, but I can't do it by myself.

I'm certainly not going to Bumps with this, she being so buddy-buddy with that retard. That leaves you as my only option."

```
                    WHALE
      Why do you hate her so much? Because she's a woman?
```

"No!" Cashew whispers harshly. He looks around again. "But you have to admit, her being a woman gives her an unfair advantage. She can fuck her way to the top anytime she wants to."

```
                    WHALE
      You don't know her. She would never do something like
      that.
```

"Wouldn't you?"

Whale's face goes numb.

Cashew keeps staring. "In a hypothetical scenario, if The Professor was gay, wouldn't you?"

Whale furrows his brow.

```
                    WHALE
      I don't--?
```

"When it comes down to it, we all would. But we can't. She can and she knows it. I was so focused on Bumps. I didn't even see Peabrain coming up from behind."

```
                    WHALE
      I'm not doing it.
```

"Oh come on, why not?!" Cashew whines, suddenly defensive.

```
                    WHALE
      If the Professor ever found out--
```

"The Professor wants fighters, remember? He's waiting for us to do something like this."

```
                    WHALE
      But it's not fair! Peabrain put in all that work. He
      deserves the job more than we do!
```

"If he really deserved the job, he'd be able to stop us in time. At least we could say we tried."

```
                    WHALE
      It's cheating!
```

"How is any of this cheating? What rule in American business says you can't do this?"

```
                    WHALE
      Why can't we just work harder?
```

"Why not both?" Cashew cries. "I don't get why you're so upset about this. We're not fixing the race. We're just Blue Shelling him."

Whale gapes, appalled.

"It's to be expected when you're in first place, right?" Cashew continues. "I'm doing all the work anyway. It'll never come back to you. Besides, he can't exactly be—"

```
                    WHALE
      Do you have any idea how juvenile it is using a Mario
      Kart metaphor to justify demolishing a career
      accomplishment he deserves?!
```

"You're just gonna give up?! Just hand Peabrain the job?!

```
                    WHALE
      Consider what would happen if the position was
      reversed. If Peabrain was Blue Shelling you, wouldn't
      you retaliate with just as much justification?
```

"I don't care."

```
                    WHALE
      Listen to me! If you do this, I'm telling you, this
      will spiral out of control fast and NONE OF US will
      get the job!
```

Cashew shakes his head. "So you're just gonna do nothing? Just sit back on your laurels and fucking *pray* he picks you?"

```
                    WHALE
      No, I'm gonna work my ass off to try and catch up. I
      suggest you do the same.
```

"Why should we put ourselves through all that extra work for nothing if we don't have to?"

```
                    WHALE
      That's the job!
```

"None of this is the job! That's what's so fucked up about it! It's the audition! You can follow all the rules you want when you get the job, but until then, nothing's off-limits! Worst case scenario we do it and still lose. But it's the only way either of us can win now and I can't do it by myself!"

```
                    WHALE
      I don't want to win like that!
```

"This is not about you!" Cashew hisses. "Jesus, stop being so fucking selfish!"

Whale shakes his head.

```
                    WHALE
      Please, just...
```

"You know what? Fuck you, I'm outta here." Cashew quick-shimmies out of the booth.

```
                    WHALE
               (soft)
      Theo, please--
```

"You tell anyone about this, I'm taking you down with me." Cashew heads for the door.

```
                    WHALE
      Theo!
```

Cashew pushes out of the diner. Whale sighs. Holds his head up. Waits for the check.

DREW

Welcome Back

Drew scratches lint off his lapel with his fingernails. *Scrunch scrunch scrunch.* Looks up at the elevators. Number's going up. "That's them, right?" he asks Larry, standing to his right.

Larry checks his watch. "Yup."

Drew looks around the 7th Floor reception area, making a head count of the all the producers, secretaries, clerks, and interns standing alongside them in semi-circle formation. "Doris!" he calls. "Has anyone seen Doris?"

Larry scans the room, searching. "Someone check the ladies room."

"Hold your horses!" an old lady calls from behind the human blockade. She waddles through the surprise welcome committee with a big camera in her hands. "Couldn't find the fucking thing."

Drew shushes sharply. "Everyone! They're here!"

Doris rushes into position as the elevator stops at 7. The doors open just as Drew, Larry, and the entire 7th Floor erupt in a mass of applause, cheers, and celebratory merriment. Theo and Alan step out. Surprised. Flattered. Overwhelmed. Doris snaps a photo. FLASH!

Theo grins wide, happy to see Drew still alive. Drew beams back.

Larry and Alan share an uneasy bit of eye contact. Awkwardly look away.

Theo claps Drew's hand and shakes it. They pull each other in for a tight bro-hug. Doris snaps another photo. FLASH!

Drew and Theo relocate to Drew's office. Theo beelines to the bar. Flips over two rocks glasses. "Someone's thirsty," Drew says, closing the door.

"The bitch in First Class cut me off at two. First Class! The fuck has this country come to?"

"I'm sure she was just doing her—"

"Fuck off with that." Theo opens the mini-fridge. Scrapes out two ice molds. "$10,000 on one day's notice for those fucking seats. I really should report the cunt."

"You know what bullshit airline policy is."

"Then change the policy or lose an expensive fucking customer. That's all I'm saying." Theo drops the molds into the glasses. They bounce with sweet musical tones. He grabs an open bottle of Domergue 15.

"None for me, thanks," Drew says, sitting down.

Theo stares at him. Blinks. "You're not going sober on me, are you?"

"Maybe I am."

Theo puffs his lips. Pours himself a serving and a quadruple shot anyway.

"I said I didn't want any," Drew speaks up.

"Yeah you do." Theo sits across from Drew. Hands him his glass.

Drew stares at it. Thinks. Puts it down on his desk. "I want to talk to you about something."

"You ever think about our time in the trenches?" Theo asks randomly. He sips his Scotch.

Drew shrugs. "I guess. Why?"

"It's crazy, you know?" Theo leans back with a smile. "All those hours on those shitty computers. That pretentious cube."

Drew frowns. He looks over at his big glass of Domergue.

Theo swirls his Scotch to get a good scent going. "And look at him now."

Drew thinks back. "One of the worst things The Professor ever said to me..." He looks at his glass of Domergue, his tongue salivating. "He said when he read *Drive-Thru* that he knew that I knew what I was doing. But then he saw me, how I was, and he was so disappointed I wasn't the same..." Drew pauses, searching for the right word. "That I wasn't the expert he thought he was hiring."

Theo purses his lips.

Drew looks down at his folded hands. "I wonder what he'd say about me now."

"Who gives a fuck?" Theo drinks more.

"What did you guys talk about up there?"

"In his cube? Nothing. He just wanted the opportunity to roast my cashew of a penis."

"Honey roasted cashew penis?"

Theo chuckles. "In the private intimacy of his personal fucking cube. Kinda gay when you think about it. No offense."

Drew's eyes unfocus.

"Imagine if he was gay," Theo says. "Could've been you."

Drew looks at the Domergue again. Reaches over. Picks up the glass. Puts it to his lips. Glugs half the glass in one go. He coughs.

"I knew it," Theo teases, smirking.

Drew coughs some more. "Fuck."

Theo chuckles. Claps Drew's back. "You okay there, buddy?"

"Theo, I want to talk to you about—"

"I just want you to know that I completely understand." Theo stands up. Leans his butt against Drew's desk. "It sucks getting your hopes up for a job that you're not suited for."

Drew sits up, his head already dizzy. "That's what I wanted to talk to—"

"And honestly, if we weren't such good friends, it wouldn't hurt so much."

"I know, but—"

"I don't want the last few weeks to affect anything here." Theo motions between him and Drew. "This... This is real."

"I know," Drew says with a nod. "I took the weekend to think it over. I don't blame you. I was out of control there."

"But you know it's not just that," Theo insists. "Even if you didn't break the vase and have that meltdown, it was never gonna work out. You just aren't CEO material."

"I completely agree."

Theo stares, taken aback. "You do?"

Drew sips some more. "Oh yeah. I took the weekend to think about it and I think I would've hated it. I don't even want to try it again. That was awful."

Theo scratches his forehead. Lets out an accidental chuckle.

"Are you surprised?" Drew asks with a smile.

"I don't know. I just thought it was gonna be harder than this."

"What was gonna be harder?"

"I mean..." Theo chuckles. "So we're all good?"

"Yeah, of course buddy. Why wouldn't we be?"

Theo inhales happily. "It's just not your thing."

"Not even a little bit." Drew maintains his smile. "It's yours."

"That's why I do it so well."

"Which is what I want to talk to you about."

Theo freezes. "Huh?"

Drew takes a deep breath. "Since Mom died, I've been thinking a lot about the past. You. Me. The Professor. Frankie."

"Frankie?! You're not still hung up on him, are you?"

"And I realized..." Drew gestures to the office around him. "This isn't what I wanted. This is what *you* wanted, actually. I just kept going along with it."

"What are you talking about?" Theo asks, trying not to let his panic show.

"I don't want to be Head of Production anymore."

Theo furrows his brow. "But you just said you didn't—"

"I want to spin off into a Not That Nut of my own." Drew holds his gaze. "I think it's gonna work this time."

Theo holds his mouth open, struggling to formulate. "Drew, your mom just died. You've had a crazy-ass month. If you just settle down, everything will go back to normal soon."

"I'm serious, Theo." Drew puts the half-full glass on his desk. "I don't want to make derivative shit anymore. If I die tomorrow, all anyone will say about Drew Lawrence was that he made billions making heavy handed, pseudo-intellectual trash. I want to be remembered as an artist. I want people to think I could've made a Best Picture winner if I wanted to, that I always had it in me. And I'm not blaming you or anything, I understand, it was never a priority for you. It might not be how you measure wealth, but it is for me."

"But don't you remember what a disaster it was?" Theo asks. "How long it took doing everything ourselves? Constantly second guessing ourselves? The fun got sucked out every time we started over. We burned through everything we had."

"But we have money now, more money than we know what to do with. We know so much more than we used to. And we've got contacts now. Influence. What was it all for if not to make whatever we wanted one day?"

"For people to take us seriously!" Theo exclaims. "We'll never get kicked around like interns ever again!"

"But don't you want to make something great?"

"You're my Head of Production. I can't replace you."

"Larry's already doing most of the job anyway, and I can always make time to help out if you guys need me. I just want a chance to make something new, something stylish, something different. I wanna get into Cannes, Theo! I wanna make a Criterion film! I wanna win Best Picture! We never won Best Picture. I think I can now. Just let me put all my energy, all my passion into one project and I promise you I can do it."

"So you wanna stop making money?"

"No, that's not what I'm saying at all."

"Actually it is." Theo returns to the bar. Refills his glass. "We're not artists, Drew. We hire photographers for a living. That's it. We get paid to hire people to take pictures. Still pictures. And then we hire other people to move said pictures around into a specific order so it looks like it's telling a story, one of thirty possible stories with a bunch of specifics thrown on top to make it seem unique. And then we assign this specific sequence of pictures a word or a phase, and we stamp that word or phrase onto posters and blast a bunch of those pictures out of context on TV and the Internet months in advance, just enough for people to know it exists. And then we get a horde of stupid morons to actually pay, voluntarily, to sit in the dark for two-to-three hours and watch a really loud slideshow. And because we're playing that slideshow so fast, we're actually tricking those stupid morons into thinking the pictures are moving. And if we play that slideshow five times a day, every day, in every city in the world for three months max, we make *billions of dollars*."

"There's no reason we can't do both," Drew says. "It'll be a satellite of Nutty, just like Nut was with UniTopia. You're gonna be Míng this time."

"And that's a good thing?!" Theo snaps.

Drew blinks. "What?"

"You know what makes the Criterion Collection?" Theo asks, deliberately changing the subject. "Obscure box office failures. The only ones that even know about it are college film bros, literally the definition of inexperienced. They don't know shit about making movies or how the industry works, but they'll sit through a seven-hour black-and-white Hungarian film they need an article to decipher just so they can make themselves sound cool at a party. *That's* what the Criterion Collection is. Vegetables for Hollywood wannabes. Not even hot vegetables. Undressed, ice cold vegetables."

"Vegetables are good for you."

"Of course they are, but they taste like shit if you're not in the mood for them. 98% of people aren't in the mood for them because they're morons, obese morons that eat candy for breakfast, lunch, and dinner, and we oh-so-cleverly repackage that candy so they don't realize they've been eating the same chocolate bar for the past thirty years."

"People notice," Drew mumbles.

Theo grins wide, his lips smacking. "So *that's* what this is about! I leave you alone for a few weeks and you start reading the comments!"

Drew's face goes blank. "You knew about this?"

"I'm CEO. Of course I know about the drinking game and the elephant memes and the toilet paper with your face on it."

"The WHAT?"

"The Internet's the worst, you know that."

Drew scoffs. "You never thought to tell me the world thinks I'm trash?"

"Why would I ever do that? Look at you! Look what you've turned into! It's already ruined your day. How can you get any work done if you let all that bullshit in your head?"

"It's feedback."

"They don't know what they want!" Theo shouts. "WE know what they want! We've got scientists and marketing experts on our side telling us how to keep their eyes on screen for as long as possible. What more could you want, Drew? You got a whole building full of people that will do anything you want them to do."

"This is not who I am!" Drew snaps. "I'm sick of being surrounded by yes men and instant gratification! I want work! I want stress! I wanna build toward something that actually pays off!"

"But what if it doesn't?"

Drew shrugs. "That just makes it part of the thrill."

"Our output is shit, I agree, but that's not our fault. That's what's selling. Not That Nutty is guaranteed money, Drew. Guaranteed. It pays for everything. The booze. The blow. The suits. The girls. The guys. The cars. Your condo. My mansion. Do you not remember how fragile the art world is? One bad movie, one critical stinker, one 'misunderstood masterpiece,' and they're done with you. You can make perfect films for the rest of time and no one will ever wanna see them."

"You don't know that."

"I know Hollywood, Drew. They don't forget. Remember *Havremoer*?

"Remember *Tequilatown*?" Drew counters.

Theo scowls. Points. "That's unfair."

"Oh, so you can dish it but you can't take it?"

"You need to calm down."

"No, you need to stop letting your personal failures prevent you from ever taking a risk again."

"I take risks."

"Do you even FEEL like Louis B. Mayer right now? I might not be the Classic Hollywood aficionado you are, but I'm pretty sure Louis B. Mayer never needed China's help to become Louis B. Mayer!"

Theo's face hardens. "Míng saved our ass from bankruptcy, bankruptcy YOU almost put us in because of the same artistic shit you're suddenly so nostalgic for!"

"Stop putting the blame on me! I wasn't the only one fucking up back then! Nor the first!"

"You were all for the restructuring back then. Just as much as I was. If anyone's to blame for derailing your career, it's you."

Drew frowns.

Theo softens. Struggles to look Drew in the eye. "And to answer your question, yes, I do feel like Mayer now because..."

"Because of what?"

"Because of you." Theo sips more Scotch. "There, I said it."

Drew looks at Theo, surprised.

Theo shrugs. "You had Stewie," he says softly. "You know you can do it. That's easy for you, but I never had that. I never... You're the best I got, man." He sighs. "I feel strong when I'm around you. I feel smart. I feel..." He lets out a self-deprecating chuckle. "I feel tall."

Drew keeps staring, freaked out by Theo's sudden display of vulnerability.

Theo nods. "It's stupid." He sips more Scotch. "I just feel like we're a team, bro. You're my Irving Thalberg, man. You're unbelievable. You're so driven and nice, and you're always there for me, and I can talk to you about anything, and we have fun together and... You carry so much for me. You should've broken your back years ago carrying this place, honestly. MGM just wasn't the same when Thalberg died. And now look at it. Look what it's become. I don't want that for this place. This is my home, man. This is my Joseph. Without you... It's just not the same without you."

Drew sighs. "C'mon man. You know I'll always be there if you need my help."

"But what if that's not enough?" Theo asks, letting his panic show this time. "If you're off doing your own thing, burning through all that money, what if I can't make enough to keep up? That'll be the end of everything. We'll be like we were back at The Factory, at the bottom of the totem pole. I don't wanna go back to that. I like where I am now. I like who I am now. Why can't you like it too? There's nothing wrong with keeping things as-is."

Drew hesitates, his eyes lowering slightly. "I don't want my dream to cost you yours."

Theo nods. "Thank you."

"But I do think it's time I start going after mine."

Theo sighs. Finishes his Scotch. "Sleep on it."

"If I overthink it, I'll give up. I don't want to give this up."

"That's why you sleep on it. Most of the time it's something that passes."

"I can't keep putting it off. Just let me have this."

"Drew," Theo mumbles. "I just got off a twelve-hour flight. I'm exhausted. Can we talk about this another time?"

Drew reluctantly nods. "Fine."

Theo claps Drew's shoulder. Walks out of the office.

Drew sits behind his desk, processing everything that just happened. He remembers the half-drunk Domergue sitting on the desk and grimaces, a deep bitter shame overwhelming his lungs. He explicitly told Theo he didn't want one. But Theo poured it anyway, didn't he? And such a big portion. Almost like he went out of his way to get back at Drew for even suggesting such a thing.

Theo's never gonna help him. If Drew really wants to break the cycle, he's gonna have to do it himself.

JACOB

Lawrence of Arabia

```
EXT. BOYLSTON STREET - NIGHT

Jacob and Stewie stroll side by side.

                        STEWIE
        What's this place called again?

                        JACOB
        LA Burdick. It's all the way down in Copley.

                        STEWIE
        I can't believe we're getting hot chocolate in July.

                        JACOB
        Liquid chocolate. Very different.

They walk in peace. Smile at each other.

                        STEWIE
        You ready for our road trip tomorrow, Baby Boy?

                        JACOB
        I think so. It's gonna be so cool, seeing your condo.

                        STEWIE
        Why? You've seen my apartment up here.

                        JACOB
        It was already furnished like that when you got it.
        The Jersey condo was your entire world for the past
        fourteen years. A blank canvas with Daddy all over
        it. I like that.

                        STEWIE
                  (dirty)
        I bet you do.

Jacob growls playfully. Stewie growls back.

                        JACOB
        I picked up my textbooks today.

                        STEWIE
        What are you taking?

                        JACOB
        Narrative Ethics, Images--

                        STEWIE
        What's Narrative Ethics?

                        JACOB
        Exploring moral and ethical principles through
        movies.

                        STEWIE
        Oh, so what you normally do.

                        JACOB
        Easy A, am I right?
                  (pause)
        Images of the Disabled.
```

STEWIE
"Images of the Disabled?"

JACOB
Kinda like a disability rights class that focuses on how people with disabilities are represented in pop culture.

STEWIE
That actually sounds like fun.

JACOB
I know! This place IS fun! And they all fill requirements too.

STEWIE
What else?

JACOB
Feature Writing Workshop.

STEWIE
Surprised you're taking that.

JACOB
I've never actually taken a feature writing class before.

STEWIE
You wrote five feature films and never actually took a class on it?

JACOB
Six, actually. It's so stupid that every other VMA major gets to do their real major stuff by Sophomore Year, but Screenwriting majors have to wait until Senior Year to actually learn how to write a Feature. It's BS, honestly.

STEWIE
Any other classes?

JACOB
Just one more. Human Health and Disease.

STEWIE
That's cool.

JACOB
Not really. I needed to pick a science class. I thought it was gonna be all about historical plagues like the Black Death and Cholera but really it's just a science class about cell structures and cancer and pandemics. I'm going to be a screenwriter, why would I need extensive knowledge on transmission rates and herd immunity and how vaccines work?

STEWIE
You can always write a movie about disease.

JACOB
They already did. It's called Contagion. A chef in Hong Kong doesn't wash his hands the one time he touches Gwyneth Paltrow and starts a worldwide pandemic that kills millions of people.

STEWIE
That's dark.

JACOB
Not really. A bit unrealistic if you ask me.

STEWIE
How's your GPA?

JACOB
Still rocking a three-six.

STEWIE
That's good.

JACOB
I used to be a 4.0, even after the divorce, but then I discovered cock and it's been dropping ever since.

STEWIE
How come?

JACOB
I took a step back from class is all. Focused some more on my social life.

STEWIE
That's good.

JACOB
Overdue is what it is. Back at Eagle Ridge, school was my entire life. I actually hated summer vacation because all I wanted to do was go back to school. I'm still like that, actually. Or maybe I just hate Conshy that much.

STEWIE
I loved summer. All my cousins lived in the same town we did. We'd always run around, get into trouble. Everyone hated school.

JACOB
How could you hate school?

STEWIE
How could like it?

JACOB
Because it's the best. All the class sizes at Eagle Ridge were no more than five people each. And we all had our own laptop provided by the school. And instead of gym five days a week, we had gym three days a week and the other two were for Group.

STEWIE
Group?

JACOB
Group therapy. Just everyone in a room talking about their problems.

STEWIE
That's helpful.

JACOB
Very helpful for a teenager. But I'm telling you, I was a real star student at Eagle Ridge. National Honor's Society, Student Ambassador, Honors List every semester. I graduated top of my class.

STEWIE
Really?!

JACOB
Of sixteen.

STEWIE
Yeah, but still!

Jacob shrugs, flattered.

JACOB
I designed the yearbook. Cross-Country team. Soccer team. Vocal group. Poetry team. Of course my big claim to fame was theatre. Two productions a year,

one in the Fall, one in the Spring, every year for seven years.

STEWIE
You really memorized all those lines?

JACOB
It's not that hard when you do it enough.
(pause)
We had a big awards ceremony every year. In my seven years at Eagle Ridge, guess how many acting awards I got.

Stewie pauses, thinking.

STEWIE
Two.

JACOB
Five.

STEWIE
Wow!

JACOB
Most people don't get one award, let alone two of anything, and I got FIVE! The two years I didn't win, 9th and 12th, I totally get. Those weren't good years.

STEWIE
What did you win for?

JACOB
6th Grade was for a student-written play. I played a hyperactive menace on the Jerry Springer show. 7th grade was another student-written one, a parody of the Price is Right. Small beer, but still, a win is a win.

STEWIE
Yes it is.

JACOB
8th Grade. I was Bottom in <u>A Midsummer Nights' Dream</u>.

STEWIE
I'm sorry, BOTTOM?!

JACOB
It's Shakespeare. That's the guy's name.

STEWIE
What guy?

JACOB
The guy that gets turned into a donkey.

STEWIE
The guy literally gets turned into an ass and his name is Bottom?

JACOB
(laughing)
Yeah.

STEWIE
No wonder you won.

Stewie spanks Jacob.

JACOB
10th grade, I was Juror #10 in <u>12 Angry Men</u>. I was the one with the big monologue about how the guy must've done it because he's poor and all poor people are scum or something like that.

STEWIE
That was a school play?

JACOB
Even the students who hated being forced to watch us every year said it was shockingly good.
(pause)
11th Grade I was Horton in Seussical. That's the lead.

STEWIE
You sang?

JACOB
Yup.

STEWIE
I can't imagine ever doing that on stage in front of a group of people.

JACOB
I used to do choir in Catholic school.

STEWIE
You got a good voice?

JACOB
I don't think so.

STEWIE
Still, that's a good resume.

JACOB
I'm not done. Saved the best for last. For my Senior Project, I wrote a novella.

STEWIE
A novella?

JACOB
It's called Onio. I was always a Shakespeare tragedy fan so I wrote my own.

STEWIE
You should turn it into a movie.

JACOB
That's what Mom keeps saying. I don't think it's that good honestly.

STEWIE
What'd you get on it?

JACOB
A-.

STEWIE
That's great!

Jacob bobs his head, not too enthused.

JACOB
I always felt the 20-page Joseph Campbell Monomyth I wrote in 10th Grade Mythology was better.

STEWIE
What's a 20-page Joseph Campbell Monomyth?

JACOB
Something way too complicated to explain and way too simple to justify such a lengthy explanation.
(pause)
God, I miss Eagle Ridge.

STEWIE
I can't believe how much you've done already.

JACOB
What have I done?

STEWIE
Acclaimed actor, prolific writer. You're a prodigy!

JACOB
God, I hate that word.

STEWIE
You took Pre-Algebra in 7th Grade.

JACOB
6th Grade, and I got Bs.

STEWIE
So what?

JACOB
Shouldn't I only be called a prodigy if I've actually done something to deserve it?

STEWIE
You have, Baby Boy! How can you not see that?

JACOB
I'm afraid if I let it get to my head, I'll end up peaking early and live the rest of my life reliving the past.

STEWIE
You're putting way too much pressure on yourself. You've got your whole life ahead of you to figure it out.

JACOB
I'm not the one putting pressure on myself. Mom's the one making me feel guilty for not putting in more effort. God forbid I waste a single day.

STEWIE
I'm sure she just wants the best for you.

JACOB
No, what she wants is for me never to be satisfied with what I have, just like she did with Dad.

STEWIE
Don't be ridiculous.

CUT TO:

INT. LA BURDICK - NIGHT

Stewie and Jacob sit across from each other, sipping on big mugs of liquid chocolate.

JACOB
My greatest fear is ending up an alcoholic couch potato watching TV in the dark in a sweat-drenched tank top and a big fat gut. Collecting welfare. No consequences for staying in bed all day. Nothing to look forward to. Every day the same. That might be Mom's Republican hatred of government handouts talking, but I truly wish that never happens to me.
(pause)
I don't want to settle for a life sitting on my ass wishing I did more. I want my life to mean something, you know? To make an impact. I don't need to be the greatest or the most loved, I just want people to look at what I've done in my life and say, "Wow, even after all he went through, he still found a way to make it work."

STEWIE
I think you're on track with that.

JACOB
Really? Cause I don't.

STEWIE
Why not?

Jacob sighs.

JACOB
I have to constantly filter myself because of my autism. I get too overwhelmed by social interaction and have to actually remove myself to recharge. I'm easily distracted, which is not helpful. I need familiarity in order to function. I'm always stressing about what will go wrong with everything I say or do, and that puts me in an awful funk of predictive paralysis which prevents me from actually doing anything.

STEWIE
You're overthinking a lot.

JACOB
Yeah, that's the problem! That's what anxiety is, overthinking everything.

STEWIE
It's not like it actually affects you.

JACOB
What are you saying? I don't have autism?

STEWIE
I'm sure if you lived two hundred years ago, they'd just call you a weirdo.

JACOB
They didn't know what autism was.

STEWIE
If your mom didn't drill into your head that you had autism, you wouldn't be so insecure.

JACOB
I am not insecure. I'm just being cautious.

STEWIE
You're miles ahead of everyone else your age. You're actually following your passion. You're not sitting at home doing nothing.

JACOB
I agree, but if I get too carried away I'll end up doing things I'll regret. I don't wanna end up like my Uncle Bart, but I don't want the story of my life to be <u>Lawrence of Arabia</u> either.

STEWIE
What are you talking about?

JACOB
You ever see <u>Lawrence of Arabia</u>?

STEWIE
I've heard of it.

JACOB
You know what it's about?

STEWIE
No.

Jacob sighs.

JACOB
My point won't make sense if you haven't seen it.

STEWIE
Summarize it then.

JACOB
You sure?

STEWIE
How long will it take?

JACOB
Ten minutes.

STEWIE
How long's the movie?

JACOB
Four hours.

STEWIE
I'm sure. Do it.

Jacob smiles as warm as a fresh cup of liquid chocolate.

JACOB
God, I got me a man sipping liquid chocolate in July asking me to summarize one of my favorite movies of all time.

Stewie grins childishly.

JACOB (CONT'D)
Okay.
(clears throat)
It's set during World War I. I didn't know this, not many know it actually, but while everyone was over in France and Germany fighting in the trenches, there's a whole other campaign happening in Arabia, like how World War II had the Allies fighting the Nazis in Europe and the Japanese in the South Pacific. It starts in 1916. The Ottoman Empire's on its way out, and the British and French forces are aiding local Arab tribes to revolt against the Turks.

STEWIE
I'm so glad you're summarizing. This sounds like a really boring movie.

JACOB
That's just the prologue. Believe me, it's actually really exciting. So this guy, T.E. Lawrence, he...
(pause)
Actually the movie really starts with his death. It's 1935, the war's long over. Lawrence is riding his motorcycle down the English countryside when a dip in the road obstructs his view of two boys on bicycles. He serves to avoid them, crashes his motorcycle and dies. He's only in his forties. Everyone he's ever known is at his funeral. Most hate him as a person but love his accomplishments. Only two people have anything good to say about him. One of them, Col. Brighton, calls Lawrence the most extraordinary man he ever knew, even though he never really knew him well. Then the movie flashes back to 1916--

STEWIE
What about the other guy?

JACOB
What other guy?

STEWIE
The other guy that liked Lawrence?

JACOB
You asked for a summary here. The other guy's not important. Anyway, the movie flashes back to 1916.

Lawrence is just another British officer in Cairo and he's weird. Clumsy. Very smart, but flowery. Idealistic. Obsessed with literature and music. Not enough real experience to be a proper soldier. And he's not tough either. His boss doesn't like his insubordination, but he agrees to send Lawrence into Arabia to find Prince Faisal, the head of one of the more ambitious Arab tribes, the Hashemite Bedouins. It's a crap mission for anyone else, but Lawrence loves the assignment. He says it's gonna be fun.

(pause)

Once he gets there... It's so beautiful. The desert's actually beautiful, a clean slate for him to be anything he wants. He was never really loyal to England, just himself. And he wants to get the Arabs independent from Turkey because of the principle of independence, the idealism of it, the fact that he personally can give it to them. Make a civilization out of them. They're skeptical at first, the Arabs. They think he's really working to get the Turks out so the British and French can swoop in, but Lawrence insists he isn't. And he wasn't. His bosses were, but he doesn't know that yet.

(pause)

One of Lawrence's first contacts is Prince Faisal's strongest soldier, Sherif Ali. He kills Lawrence's Arab guide in cold blood simply because he's a Hazimi of the Beni Salem, another tribe, and only Hashemite Bedouins can drink from Ali's well. Lawrence chastises Ali for this emotional, savage logic. He says, "So long as the Arabs fight tribe against tribe, so long will they be a little people, a silly people. Greedy, barbarous and cruel, as YOU are!" And Ali is impressed by Lawrence's balls and offers to guide him to Faisal, but Lawrence refuses on principle. He doesn't associate with murderers.

(pause)

Lawrence ultimately finds Prince Faisal and wins him over with dreams of Arabia's glory days, how their nation used to be, and he promises to make it happen without British control.

STEWIE

Make Arabia Great Again.

JACOB

Exactly. And Prince Faisal is interested in Lawrence's no-English way of independence, but the only way they can do that without the assistance of the British Army is a miracle, so Lawrence decides to make one. One of the Turkish strongholds is in Aqaba, a city on the coast. It's impossible to hit by sea because they have massive cannons that'll knock anything out of the water, and Aqaba is practically impossible to hit from the landward side because doing so would require crossing the uncrossable Nefud Desert, including an especially uncrossable patch of the uncrossable desert they call the Sun's Anvil. Lawrence knows if he can lead a small army across the Nefud and win over a neutral tribe waiting on the other side, the Howeitat, then they could take Aqaba by surprise and win the city. Lawrence gets Sherif Ali and his men to start their journey across the Nefud. The Sun's Anvil is the worst part, and they can only cross it at night, but thanks to Sherif Ali's help they do.

(pause)

But something goes wrong. They realize one of Ali's men, Gasim, had fallen off his camel in the middle of the night right in the middle of the Sun's Anvil. Lawrence wants to turn around and save him, but Ali tells him no, that Gasim will be dead by midday. But

Lawrence insists he can save him anyway. A Priest tells him "It's too late. Gasim's time has come. It is written." Lawrence looks at the Priest and says, "Nothing is written!" He turns his camel around and races back into the Sun's Anvil to save Gasim. Ali and the others stand around waiting for Lawrence to return, and as the sun rises they wonder if they'll ever see him again. But a black dot appears on the horizon. It's Lawrence. He's got Gasim. Everyone cheers. Ali gives him water and a fresh bed, praising his bravery. Lawrence looks at Ali, his eyes dry and red, and he croaks: "Nothing is written."

STEWIE
Nothing is written.

JACOB
Great line. One of the best in movie history.
(pause)
They manage to get the Howeitat, the mercenary tribe, on their side. Its leader is Sherif Ali's rival, the brutal Auda abu Tayi.
(cheery)
Played by Anthony Quinn!

STEWIE
Oh!

JACOB
But the night before they can take Aqaba, one of Ali's men kills one of Auda's men. Auda wants revenge. Ali's already thrown in the towel on the whole mission. To keep both sides happy for the sake of mission, Lawrence volunteers to be the non-partisan executioner of the murderer. And guess who it ends up being.

Stewie shrugs.

JACOB (CONT'D)
Gasim. The man he saved. So he has to kill him. And doing so disturbs him to his core.

STEWIE
Yikes.

JACOB
The next day they successfully ambush Aqaba from the landward side. It's unbelievable. Lawrence is no longer that goofy clown. He's the wisest man in Arabia. But the power's already going to his head. He starts thinking himself like a god. Then a few bad things happen to him. After they take Aqaba, Lawrence takes his two servants across Mount Sinai to Cairo so he can report to his English bosses what he was able to do in the name of Arabia. But on the way he loses his compass. He wings it, but in doing so he accidentally leads one of his servants into quicksand. Lawrence can't save him. He can only watch as he sinks down and dies.

STEWIE
What year was this out?

JACOB
1962.

STEWIE
Seems pretty brutal for '62.

JACOB
It gets worse. When Lawrence gets to Cairo, the Brits are ecstatic. But Lawrence doesn't want to go back to Arabia. He's still disturbed by his execution of

Gasim. It wasn't the killing part that disturbed him. It was the fact that he enjoyed it.

STEWIE

Yikes.

JACOB

But his greedy imperialist bosses flatter his ego and convince Lawrence to go back into Arabia anyway.

(pause)

Later on, he's trying to get lightning to strike twice. He's cocky, and against Ali's advice -- who by the way has started to become a lot more moral thanks to the influence of our man Lawrence -- the two of them try to take down Deraa, a town roaming with Turks. It doesn't work and the Turks capture Lawrence. The Turkish Bey and his men flog him, beat him...

(pause)

And rape him.

STEWIE

Oh my God.

JACOB

They don't show anything, but...

(pause)

Lawrence is gay. Actually gay. And a sadomasochist. That's how he finds out. That's what his time in the desert makes him realize. Because there's nothing in the desert, only what he brings with him. That's how he learns what kind of man he really is. And he doesn't like it. He's getting flogged and raped, but he enjoys it? That scares the S-H-I-T out of him.

Stewie finishes his cup.

JACOB (CONT'D)

After the Turks let him go, Lawrence returns to Cairo a broken man. He tries to resign again but his bosses reveal that the British and French are taking over Arabia after all, that everything they told Lawrence wasn't true. So Lawrence decides to fight one last time, without the British. He's gonna run the Turks out of Damascus and make Arabia independent and self-sufficient no matter the cost. But he's lost his morals. He pays mercenaries to fight with them, men with no idealism or care for the principle for independence. They find a Turkish convoy, easy prey, and Lawrence spends a day massacring them. He didn't have to. Even Ali begged him to go round. Lawrence betrays the trust of his friends Ali and Auda, losing their respect, but he justifies everything as part of the greater good. One of his allies, Jackson Bentley, an American reporter who thinks Lawrence is a hero, is appalled by the monster he's become. And all those that once looked up to him, who exalted him, now think he's just rotten.

(pause)

But it works. The Arabs run the Turks out of Damascus before the Brits could even get there and Lawrence starts an independent Arab government, the very end he was striving toward from the beginning.

(pause)

But the tribes can't unify. Their values are too old. Their worldview still barbaric and stubborn. Lawrence tries and tries, but they refuse to compromise, to put their tribal history aside and work together as a civilization. They just can't. So after everything Lawrence did, after all he gave up, he couldn't make it work. His dream of independent Arabia never came true. The British take over. Prince Faisal thanks Lawrence for his service, but once Lawrence leaves

the room, Faisal admits to the British General that he's glad to be rid of him.
(pause)
The desert chewed Lawrence up and spat him back out. He goes home a loser. Hated by his friends. Humbled and shamed by his hubris. Lonelier than ever. And at the very end of the movie, he's a passenger in a military vehicle and a motorcycle whizzes by their Jeep, a ghoulish omen of the demise waiting for him down the road.

Stewie takes a deep breath.

JACOB (CONT'D)
Doing nothing is bad. But fighting hard and fast, changing yourself in the process, for something that was never gonna be worth it?

Jacob shakes his head.

JACOB (CONT'D)
To me, that's worse than death.

WHALE

Sin of Omission

Alex Avery gulps down a craft IPA, his head shaved, red beard down to his collarbone, unblinking eyes frozen on Leonardo DiCaprio blowing cocaine into a hooker's pale ass. If only Leo could voiceover his life.

The screen door slams. Whale rushes in. Plops next to Alex on the couch.

"How was your day, sweetie?" Alex mumbles incoherently.

Whale crosses his arms.

Alex, way too drunk and high to care, faces forward as Leo rattles off all the drugs he takes on a daily basis. He throws a glass of OJ into the bushes! What a badass!

Whale pouts. Looks over. Stares.

```
                    WHALE
This guy at the internship, Peabrain. He's miles
ahead of any of us. He's probably getting the job.
And this other guy, Cashew, told me he needs my help
deleting his files before he submits them. Can you
believe that? I could get fired. Even if I don't,
it's freaking heartless to screw Peabrain over like
that, and for what? For him being better at his job?
And Cashew had the nerve to scream at me in public
about it, like I'M the unreasonable one.
```

Alex wonders where Margot Robbie is and what's taking her so long.

```
                    WHALE (CONT'D)
He actually called me selfish. Can you believe that?
Me?! SELFISH?!
         (scoffs)
He's such an effing hypocrite too, going on and on
about The Professor being such a bad businessman.
Well, a-hole, if you know so much about him, why
don't you just earn the job fair and square? No,
cause that would actually require doing work!
```

Alex scratches his balls.

```
                    WHALE (CONT'D)
You know who else has an echo chamber, Cashew? You,
only listening to Millennials. No wonder he's such a
cynic. There is such a thing as optimism, okay? Stop
kidding yourself.
```

Alex stares at his nails. Sniffs them. Stares at them. Furrows his brow.

```
                    WHALE (CONT'D)
He definitely doesn't have any friends. I didn't have
many friends. Look how I turned out. He chose to be
like this. Last summer he was probably running around
Joseph, Oregon playing Pokémon Go! with all the other
lemmings. And what was I doing? Cleaning the dorms,
getting paid, and writing my fifth feature, that's
what I was doing. Being an effing adult. He's just so
emotionally and intellectually short-sighted. He
actually had the gall to call me stupid for believing
in God! What nerve! Oh, I'm sorry I believe there's
something more than myself, that my life actually
matters, that what I do actually has far-reaching
```

consequences! Give me a freaking break. I'd actually care what I was doing to Peabrain. Cashew wouldn't have any confidence in his abilities if he did that. That's what happens when you cheat your way up. And then where would he be, huh? You tell me that!

"You're fucking pathetic!" Alex groans.

Whale bursts out laughing.

WHALE
YOU'RE calling ME pathetic?!

"All I'm hearing from you is 'fuck the internship' this, 'fuck the internship' that, how shitty The Professor is. You know what, I am sick to death of you coming into my house and whining all over my sofa!"

WHALE
I'm not whin--!

"You keep going on and on about responsibility and ethics and making something out of yourself but you're all talk! You don't do shit! I might be a fucking waste of space but at least I don't to pretend to be something I'm not!"

Whale's blood chills.

Alex stands. "You don't like Nut Guy's plan? Don't do it! At least he's doing SOMETHING!" He gets up. Storms into his bedroom.

WHALE
Cashews aren't nuts, brainiac! They're legumes!

"AND YOU'RE A PUSSY!" Alex slams the door.

Whale scoffs, mouth hanging open, shocked speechless. He grabs the remote.

WHALE
Don't worry, I got it.

He turns off *The Wolf of Wall Street*. Sits in silence. Cold pathetic silence. Alex's words hurt. They hurt because they're true.

What did he think was gonna happen, choosing a battlefield as his entry-level gateway? Not actually having to fight? It's not like he'd be the one doing the deleting after all. But what about poor Peabrain?

When Whale was first writing *Drive-Thru*, after an all-nighter of pure stream-of-consciousness, he closed the file to get some sleep only to wake up and find all the progress from his eight-hour single-sitting gone from the master document, a Dropbox sync issue between the conflicting versions on his laptop and the mobile app. The pain. The grief. The hardened reality of having to start over, being forced to transcribe improvised perfection from sheer memory hours after the fact. Whale felt like the worst human being in the world. Would he really put another person through such overwhelming self-hatred? All those hours of hard work wasted?

But what about Whale's degree, that B.A. in Media Production: Writing for Film and Television? If he doesn't end up with a job in the film industry, wouldn't all those hours of hard work be wasted? Whale doesn't have any business experience, not even enough hours operating a boom mic or editing to stand out on a resume. He'd have to start out as a PA somewhere, like every other film school schmuck. He'd be lucky to even get a writing job after all that.

Whale remembers Oscar Blitz's business card resting beside his alarm clock, its bottom edge still white from Brendan's freebie coke. That's the real immoral job, manipulating an established audience to cancel powerful people, the court of public opinion blacklisting them for life, a crime far worse than any transgression they could've possibly committed to inspire such "justice." What Cashew's asking of him is nowhere near as cruel as that. And again, Whale wouldn't be the one doing the actual deleting. He can still make up the difference and earn his job fair and square. Cashew and Peabrain are in the game, not him. He's Switzerland.

Is Whale really considering it? He doesn't know Peabrain the way he knows Bumps. He could be just as gentle and harmless. Then again he could be a complete a-hole. Homophobic even, not that it would matter to Whale. Or maybe he's just as immoral as Cashew. Then he'd really deserve to be taken down a peg or two. He could be anything, Schrödinger's personality archetype. Certainly doesn't help that he hasn't talked since The Professor so publicly shamed him. But he talked to Bumps. Anyone can talk to Bumps, even Cashew if he ever gave it a chance. So what does that say about Peabrain? In the absence of a concrete answer, does Whale really want to know? It would be so much simpler at this point in time to know nothing more, wouldn't it? His future career is at stake.

But even if the playing field is successfully leveled, can Whale really win the job fair and square?

DREW

Carry the One

Cazden Montgomery, a middle-aged bookish type with a soft brown comb-over, types into his spreadsheet, his mind far away in the beautiful world of decimal points and write-offs, when he's suddenly smacked awake by coarse knuckles clanging on his metal door's threshold. "Hey!" Drew greets, flying in like a gangbuster. "Cazden, right?"

"Uh, yeah," Cazden mumbles.

"Great!" Drew closes the door. Locks it.

Cazden furrows his brow. "Um, sir?"

"Drew Lawrence, Head of Production," Drew says, sticking his hand in Cazden's face.

Cazden awkwardly shakes it. "I know who you are, Mr. Lawrence. We've already met."

"We have?"

"You keep introducing yourself to me at every office Christmas party for the last fifteen years."

"I do not recall."

"You're always plastered."

"That sounds about right."

"And when I tell you I'm the CFO you blow raspberries in my face and say, 'Fuck you, Mom.'"

Drew's lungs evaporate. "Yikes."

Cazden closes his spreadsheet. "What can I do for you, Mr. Lawrence?"

"Alright Cazden." Drew sits down. "Or do you prefer Caz or Cazzy?"

"Cazden's fine."

"Okay. Cazden, here's what we're gonna do. You're gonna get on the phone, you're gonna call the wife, and you're gonna tell her you're working late tonight. You're helping me with something. It's a big project."

"Which one?"

"I'm about to tell you."

"Which wife I mean."

Drew blinks. "Which *wife*?"

"I guess it doesn't matter which one. You didn't remember, did you?"

Drew looks off. Does not compute. "You have more than one wife?"

"Technically I'm not married to either of them," Cazden explains, a bit embarrassed. "They're married to each other. I'm just an add-on. Actually we started as a thruple, and now there's this new guy, Kent, and there's been a bit of a power dynamic between the four of us. Catty's full lesbian but Katie goes both ways, and I was supposed to be way for Katie to be sexually fulfilled, but… I guess Catty's been jealous of the attention Katie's been giving me, so she's been sleeping with Kent to get back at her, even though she hates it. But now Kent and I are fooling around, and… I know he sees me as just sex, but I really like him and I'm dealing with feelings I never expected to have with another man. But now Kent's going after Katie! I'm just devastated. That's not helping anyone. And all this drama around the house, frankly, is not a stable environment for our three dogs, them being rescues and all, and—"

"Cazden, Cazden," Drew interrupts. "As fascinating as your exotic personal life is to me, I don't think now's the right time. I think we really need to get started."

"On what?"

Drew puts his hands together, gathering his thoughts. "How much does it cost to run a studio?"

Cazden scoffs. "Is that all?"

"Not a big studio. Just another department inside Not That Nutty, the way Nut was for UniTopia. I think we should start with this place, just so I get a basic idea, and then we can move on to the hypotheticals."

Cazden laughs. "Mr. Lawrence, I appreciate your enthusiasm to understand how your own business works, but you have no idea just how complicated that question was you just asked."

"Well, we're paying you, so..." Drew shrugs. "Take as long as you like to explain it. I want to hear it."

"It's not a matter of how long it would take… though that would be quite substantial." Cazden shrugs with a smile. "Frankly, it's a pain in the ass. I'd like to avoid that if I can. And I *like* pain in my ass."

"Let me tell you a story." Drew hunches over, eyes down. Deep breath. He looks up. "I'm sure you've heard that my mom passed away Friday night."

Cazden nods. "Of course. I'm sorry for your loss."

"Thank you." Drew pauses. "Her funeral's today. It's still going on right now. I couldn't go because of Theo coming back and the transition, but... Even if I could go, I probably wouldn't have. I haven't seen my family in a very long time." Drew swallows, his face hardening. "Her name was Helena. Helena Andrezj. Helena *Kieslowski* actually. She never changed her name back after the divorce. We didn't want her to. That would make it too real." Drew pauses. "She grew up in South Jersey. Real deadbeat central. And she was the black sheep of her family. Not because she got knocked up as a teen or became an alcoholic. The rest of them did that. No, she was the black sheep because she actually had ambition. She was gonna get out of Jersey and make something of herself. Her father was an old crotchety Archie Bunker type. Very bigoted and old fashioned. His name was actually Adolph too, which is... funny, I guess? But with a -ph and not an -f, so... Anyway, he always went by Al. And in Al's world, women didn't work. They made babies. But Mom didn't want that, so she saved up all her money and went off to college, the first of her family to do so. She cut all ties with them after that. We rarely saw them growing up and Al died before I was born. Lung cancer, I think. She told me once the day he died was the worst day of her life. I couldn't understand why, but…" Drew looks off. "I guess I do now."

Cazden looks down.

Drew snaps back to present. "She went to Columbia. Got her CPA. And one day she sits next to some guy in some bar in New Hope. Turns out he's a CPA too. His name was Dennis. He loved disco. A wrestler in high school. Originally from the boonies of PA, in a little town called Lock Haven, all the way up past State College. The Andrezjs might've been simple, but that house had a lot of love. That's something she never had. And he wasn't complicated. He was gentle. Funny. Someone she can do things with. They fell in love. Got married. She worked for Comcast before they got big. Started getting CFO jobs. They moved down to North Carolina. Worked down there. Then a few years later they moved back up to PA to a former steel town named Phoenixville. It wasn't glamorous, but it was homey. Mom was thirty-two. Dad was thirty-five. They really didn't have time to waste so... they started making a family. My sister Karen. Three years later my twin sister Melanie and me. And Mom was so happy. Much to her surprise, she loved being a mom, and the two of them worked harder than ever to build a real life for us. They got a beach house in Sea Isle, right there on the shore. When I was six we moved to the better side of town, a big house in a new development. She picked out everything. The perfect home she always wanted." Drew pauses. "It didn't take them long to realize Karen had something. And then I had something. Dad always had trouble staying focused at work for long periods of time, so he ended up changing jobs often. Mom ended up having to take more demanding positions to support all of us. They had to sell the beach house to pay for me and Karen's LD private school. They really took the time with us there. I stayed all seven years and graduated top of my class. Karen though, she… She fell in with a bad crowd. Went all klepto. Compulsive lying. Always threatening to run away. Then something happened." Drew goes quiet for a little bit. "They couldn't deal with it on their own, so they did everything her therapist recommended, which included sending her away to a wilderness program in Vermont. Mom didn't even tell Karen she was going somewhere until she pulled up to the airport. She stopped the car, told Karen her bag was in the trunk, she was getting on a plane and wasn't gonna come back for three months. Karen cried her heart out." Drew rolls his lips. "I hated Mom for doing that to her. Tricking her like that. Forcing her out." He goes silent. "Until she told me that sending Karen away was the biggest regret of her life."

Cazden frowns.

Drew sighs. "It ended up being two years, not three months. After the Vermont program ended, Mom sent her to an equestrian girl's school in Utah."

"Equestrian?" Cazden asks.

"Everyone gets a horse. Karen was a horse girl." Drew nods. "When they first sent Karen away, that was the beginning of the end. All that pressure and stress. Medical bills. Psychologists. Psychiatrists. Paying for everything. She just couldn't take it anymore. Her marriage was broken. They were always fighting. So she waited until we all graduated high school and got into college and decided her job was done. She asked Dad for a divorce. They sold the Phoenixville house. Dad met a fun girl named Daphne, got remarried and lived happily ever after. Mom never found anyone." Drew pauses. "A couple years after the divorce, she found some dirt in her company's books and they fired her. Took her years to find another job. Then she got breast cancer. That burned the rest of her savings. You'd think surviving cancer would make her more appreciative of life, but no, she got so much worse. Brushing so close to death turned her bitter. Cynical. She sold the Conshy house and forced Karen to move out on her own, but Karen couldn't stop wasting her money on junk she only hoarded, so Mom and Dad kept having to bail her out. Before Mom knew it, she was living in Melanie's spare bedroom. Melanie always felt she was such burden. And then the cancer came back, and…" Drew pauses. "Her whole life she was deathly afraid of anesthesia. Every time she was convinced she'd never wake up." Drew shakes his head. "They rushed her under and she never woke up."

Cazden looks off, moved.

Drew tightens his lips. "She put up with so much bullshit. The bad hand she was born into. A 28-year marriage crumbling from the inside. The dream of that beautiful family she never had growing up fading away year after year. She wasn't happy because she gave everything to us instead. But we gave her nothing in return. Why would we? She taught us young it was okay to disown your family. To keep moving and never ask for help. That handouts were bad. You had to get shit done yourself. Jettison all you have to." Drew pauses. "And that all came back to haunt her."

Cazden takes a slow breath in. Lets it flow out.

"But one thing she never taught us was how much things cost." Drew swallows. "Life isn't just gonna reward me for sacrificing my happiness, Cazden. I've only got one shot at this. You better walk me through everything and take your sweet-ass time doing so, because this needs to work." Drew stares with blue resolute eyes. "I'm not fucking around anymore."

JACOB

(Wish I Could Fly Like) Superman

I/E. STEWIE'S JEEP - DAY

Stewie drives JEEPGUY down the New Jersey Turnpike, Jacob in the passenger seat, convertible top down. Pet Shop Boys' "Left to My Own Devices" blasts from the Jeep's CD player.

JACOB
You really okay with me playing these guys all the time?

STEWIE
Sure.

JACOB
You can tell me if you're not.

STEWIE
No, I'm getting back into them now.

JACOB
You like them better because of me?

STEWIE
No. I've being hearing these songs for the past thirty years. I just got sick of them.

JACOB
I love them all.

STEWIE
I don't.

Jacob sits up, looking over.

JACOB
Really?

Stewie gives a wobbly hand gesture.

STEWIE
Some of them.

Stewie smiles at Jacob.

STEWIE (CONT'D)
You excited to see my condo, Baby Boy?

JACOB
(pulling out his phone)
Of course, Sexy.

STEWIE
What'cha doing?

JACOB
Just curious about something.

Stewie drives in silence for a bit. Jacob scrolls through Wikipedia.

STEWIE
There's not much we have to load in the back, but I'm gonna need your help, so no bellyaching.

JACOB
Hey, the Pet Shops Boys released nine albums AFTER this Greatest Hits came out.

STEWIE
They must not be any good. These were the only songs you ever heard on the radio.

Jacob shrugs.

JACOB
They probably just mellowed out.

STEWIE
Happens to everyone.

CUT TO:

EXT. STEWIE'S MARLTON CONDO - DAY

Stewie closes the Jeep door. Jacob hops out, looking around them. Outside the complex are a series of suburban neighborhoods, a web of residences smushed into the corner formed by two perpendicular highways, Route 70 and Route 73.

JACOB
How far away are we from Marlton?

STEWIE
This IS Marlton.

Stewie races up the wooden steps. Jacob follows slowly.

JACOB
(mumbles)
God, I hate Jersey.

CUT TO:

INT. STEWIE'S CONDO - DAY

The floor has fake wood paneling. The only light comes in from a pair of sliding glass windows. A worn sofa runs along the windowsill, perpendicular (not parallel) to the TV mounted on the wall. Across the room from the sofa is the kitchenette. The only other rooms Jacob can see are a small bathroom and a bedroom.

STEWIE
I just gotta get a few things out of the closet.

JACOB
Can I look around?

STEWIE
Sure.

Stewie walks into the corner and opens a door. Jacob wanders through.

On the walls are ornate framed photos you'd see at your grandmother's house. The stove isn't gas, just electric coils that glow red when turned on. Jacob walks through the kitchenette, narrow enough for one person only, and slides open a wooden pantry door. There's some food on the shelf, mostly oatmeal and cereal boxes. In the same pantry is a top loading washer and dryer, both at least ten years old.

CUT TO:

BATHROOM

Jacob walks in. The tile is cheap laminate. The mirror is sliced into thirds, each portion a door to the medicine cabinet. The shower is one of those tub-showers. The curtain is old looking too.

CUT TO:

BEDROOM

The Queen bed is made properly, but the windows are blocked by walls of cardboard boxes and workout equipment. Jacob turns to leave. Stops.

On the wall, lined perfectly with Stewie's bed, is an illustration of Jesus kneeling in prayer. Jacob gets uncomfortable looking at it.

CUT TO:

MAIN ROOM

Jacob kneels on the sofa, looking out the windows at the parking lot below.

A TATTOOED WOMAN (40s), one of Stewie's neighbors, sits on her ground-floor porch smoking a cigarette. He can smell it from here.

Over by the Jeep, a BALD MAN (60s) with a cross expression waits for his dog to finish pooping. He flicks the leash, walking away without picking it up.

Crossing the parking lot is a TALL MAN (70s), wandering like a zombie to the communal mailbox. He collects his mail. Wanders back to the cave he came from.

Jacob watches it all, his heart breaking.

CUT TO:

EXT. STEWIE'S MARLTON CONDO - SUNSET

Jacob and Stewie carry boxes down the stairs, loading them into the Jeep.

CUT TO:

INT. STEWIE'S MARLTON CONDO - BEDROOM - NIGHT

Jacob lays on the bed in his underwear, glasses off. He looks up at the ceiling. No recess lights. He never realized it until it got dark.

Stewie walks in, brushing his teeth with a manual scrubber.

STEWIE
What time's the appointment?

JACOB
Noon.

STEWIE
We should really be out of here by ten, just to be safe.

JACOB
Fine.

Stewie returns to the bathroom. Water runs. He spits.

STEWIE (O.S.)
What's wrong, Sexy?

JACOB
Nothing.

STEWIE (O.S.)
What?

Jacob huffs. He hates repeating himself.

JACOB
Nothing!

Jacob frowns at the blurry picture of Jesus. Stewie returns.

STEWIE
All done.

JACOB
It really takes you twenty minutes to brush your teeth?

STEWIE
Yup.

Stewie climbs into bed, slipping under the covers. Looks up at Jacob.

STEWIE (CONT'D)
(soft bleating)
AYY BEE.

Jacob crosses his arms.

STEWIE (CONT'D)
(bleating louder)
AYY BEE!

JACOB
(soft bleating)
AYY BEE.

STEWIE
What's up?

Jacob hesitates.

JACOB
I'm just imagining you in this place. Isolated from the rest of your family. Working here alone, eating here alone, sleeping alone.

STEWIE
I never thought I'd be here that long. It was always supposed to be temporary, just until I could afford a house.

JACOB
Relocating to Mass must not have helped.

STEWIE
Actually The Diva got me that apartment for practically nothing.

JACOB
I'm sorry, WHO?

STEWIE
I never mentioned The Diva? His real name's Michael but we all call him "The Diva." He was my first gay friend. I've known him twenty-eight years. He's a real estate agent. He's the one who sold me this place too.

JACOB
You're still getting that house you always wanted?

STEWIE
Once the business dies down I'll start looking.

JACOB
Up there?

STEWIE
Most likely.

Jacob frowns. Looks around the bedroom.

JACOB
You must've been so lonely here.

STEWIE
You know, I really wasn't.

JACOB
How could you not be?

STEWIE
I just wasn't. I've got no complaints. I had everything I needed. Stayed up as long as I wanted to. Played whatever music I wanted. Ate whenever I wanted. Watched every Met game. It sucks that I can't open the windows without smelling cigarette smoke, but that's really it.

Stewie smiles.

STEWIE (CONT'D)
Having you here really makes it the perfect package.

JACOB
I can't imagine how hard it must've been for you to not find Mr. Preference until you were fifty-two.

STEWIE
Believe me.
(pause)
You know, it's really all about timing. Me and Ron lived with our parents until we were thirty-five, and even then the two of us lived together until we were forty. It's not like I could've brought guys back home.

JACOB
What about Gus?

STEWIE
Gus and I never lived together.

JACOB
I know. Why not?

STEWIE
He still lived with his ninety-year-old mom. I didn't want to invade.

JACOB
You could've lived with him here.

STEWIE
That's what he said.

JACOB
Why didn't you?

STEWIE
He loved me more than I loved him.

JACOB
Why?

STEWIE
I dunno. He was just boring.

Jacob slowly turns his head.

JACOB
Your definition for the perfect partner is literally Gay Richie Cunningham. You're asking for boring.

STEWIE
His idea of a concert is a night at the Kimmel Center.

JACOB
What's wrong with the Kimmel Center?

Stewie blinks.

STEWIE
You like classical?

JACOB

Of course. When I was growing up my favorite Disney movie was Fantasia. Mom and I are huge Andrea Bocelli nerds. All autistic people love classical. All mythology nerds love classical. All melodrama addicts love opera.

STEWIE

You've actually seen operas?

JACOB

Of course I've seen operas. I've seen ballets, I've seen musicals, I've seen plays.

STEWIE

But you know how to make that fun. He used to get pissed when I pronounced Chopin like "Choppin." I'd pretend to play the violin and he'd say I was doing it wrong. He'd refuse to listen to "Night on Disco Mountain" because they changed the original. You're night and day with him. Gus was nice but he's a stick-in-the-mud.

JACOB

Five years is a long time to stay with a stick-in-the-mud.

Stewie rests his head on Jacob's flabby breast.

STEWIE

I could've loved Gus if I wanted to. I just wasn't ready.

Jacob looks down at the handsome Daddy resting on him.

JACOB

But now you are?

Stewie smiles up at his Baby Boy.

STEWIE

Yup.

JACOB

Do you think I am?

STEWIE

I think so. You might be young, but you understand what it's like to be lonely.

Jacob smiles a bit. They kiss.

STEWIE (CONT'D)

So sexy.

Jacob chuckles. Pets Stewie's head. Thinks to himself.

JACOB

Daddy?

STEWIE

Yes, Baby Boy?

JACOB

Did you stay with Gus for five years because you were trying to turn him into Mr. Preference?

Stewie furrows his brow. Sits up.

STEWIE

That's ridiculous.

JACOB

I just find it hard to believe you were waiting years and years for ME.

STEWIE
It's true. You're my Baby Boy.

Jacob takes a deep breath.

JACOB
I just have this feeling that... if I don't let you change me into what you want me to be, you won't love me anyone.

STEWIE
How can you say that?

Jacob doesn't answer.

STEWIE (CONT'D)
I never wanted anyone to BECOME Mr. Preference. I wanted Mr. Preference as-is. That's why it took so long.

JACOB
What about my hair?

STEWIE
Your hair's fine.

JACOB
You didn't like it the night we met.

STEWIE
That wasn't you. That was you emulating Carter. But honestly, I didn't even care about that. I only saw the potential.

JACOB
Yeah, potential to change me!

STEWIE
Potential you were already the boy I've been looking for. I just knew, the way you recognize someone.

Jacob frowns.

STEWIE (CONT'D)
I admit, I've second-guessed myself. Like when I saw you kiss that troll at the Black Bear.

JACOB
Don't remind me.

STEWIE
No, I was the one in the wrong. I assumed you were some bar floozy hopping from man to man, but that's not who you are.

Jacob crosses his arms.

STEWIE (CONT'D)
It was a sign of your compassion.
(pause)
And when you called me a racist, that really hurt. For a moment there, I even thought--

JACOB
(panicked)
What? Thought what?

Stewie hesitates.

STEWIE
But that wasn't you either. You told me it wasn't. And that's just further proof of your maturity and self-awareness. All the parts of you that are really you I absolutely adore.

Stewie places a gentle hand on the side of Jacob's face.

STEWIE (CONT'D)
(slow and deliberate)
I don't want YOU to change.

Stewie kisses Jacob nice and slow. Rolls over to sleep. Jacob lets it linger. Turns off the lamp.

CUT TO BLACK.

INT. STEWIE'S MARLTON CONDO - BATHROOM - DAY

Jacob steps out of the shower. Wipes steam off the mirror with a towel. Grabs a pair of scissors. Manscapes his pubes into the sink.

Jacob looks at his reflection. Stares into his eyes.

JACOB (V.O.)
"I had an existential moment just now."

Jacob keeps staring, standing naked, warm steam rolling around the poorly vented bathroom.

JACOB (V.O.)
"I stared at myself in the mirror for a good long while. Up close."

Jacob looks down at the reflection of his body. Flabby belly. Dark purple stretch marks around his belly button and under his arms. Big round beauty mark just above his groin. Creases under his breasts.

JACOB (V.O.)
"I saw every mark, hair, pore, and shade on my face."

Jacob stares into his eyes, cold expression.

JACOB (V.O.)
"I am not attractive. My smile is imperfect and I have resting bitch face. I have dark circles around my eyes that my glasses deceptively cover. I have a scar on my cheek. I'm forty pounds overweight with no plans to drop it because laziness. I have stretch marks. I have a fatty face with odd dips on my cheek bones. I look like a skeleton."

Jacob sighs. Returns to his manscaping.

JACOB (V.O.)
"I only see the reverse half of my face. It looks more natural than my exterior. My true exterior. The one with my real androgynous voice and reverse visage. I will never know what most people see."

CUT TO:

MAIN ROOM

Stewie makes pancakes at the stove. Looks over at Jacob lying on the couch and reading something off his phone.

JACOB (V.O.)
"Yet, somehow, men find me attractive. I don't know how that's possible. How could someone find ME attractive. Is it a fat thing? Is it a hairless thing? Is it that I look like a bitch?"

Jacob stares up at his phone, reading a private Facebook post with a blank expression.

JACOB (V.O.)
"I went to my private mirror and stripped naked, looking at my curved and flabby body. This is what men find attractive. But none of it is real."

CUT TO:

EXT. STEWIE'S MARLTON CONDO - DAY

Jacob and Stewie hop into JEEPGUY. Jacob looks up at Stewie's condo window.

JACOB (V.O.)
"I found out over spring break that not one person knows the real me. I'm an enigma."

Stewie starts the Jeep. Shifts into first. Drives off.

JACOB (V.O.)
"I'm slutty and vulgar with a kinder side that is contradictory."

CUT TO:

I/E. STEWIE'S JEEP - DAY

Stewie drives down the Schuylkill Expressway past the exit to Conshohocken. Jacob turns his head as the sign passes.

JACOB (V.O.)
"My family thinks I'm either a slut or that I'm rude, but I'm both neither and both of these. Not one person knows the true me. And that makes me sad. My own family sees a side of me that I'm not. A fractured Jacob."

Jacob faces forward, deep in thought.

JACOB (V.O.)
"Half of me never left Boston, and half of me will never reach Boston. I'm fractured between two states without a home in between. I'm an odd shell."

Stewie pets the back of Jacob's head with a goofy smile. Jacob smiles back.

JACOB (V.O.)
"This past year taught me that family doesn't truly exist, not for me. I never thought my family was so imperfect until this weekend, when I only had my sad mother to completely love me, and even then it wasn't absolute."

CUT TO:

EXT. ARBY'S DRIVE-THRU - DAY

Stewie inches closer to the first window as Jacob scans a sheet of coupons.

JACOB (V.O.)
"To some this fractured view of the world is enough cause for suicide. But somehow I know that isn't the answer. But why? Who am I living for?"

CUT TO:

I/E. STEWIE'S JEEP - DAY

Stewie drives along PA backroads, a Beef n' Cheese in his hands. Jacob holds up an open container of au juis sauce for Stewie to dunk into.

JACOB (V.O.)
"If I hate the world, why bother living in it?"

CUT TO:

INT. HIGHWAY REST STOP - BATHROOM - DAY

Stewie and Jacob stand at adjacent urinals, peeing together.

JACOB (V.O.)
"The hard answer to this question is something we were raised to throw away."

JUMP CUT TO:

LATER

Jacob washes his hands. Looks at himself in the mirror, remembering.

JACOB (V.O.)
"The answer is me."

CUT TO:

INT. HIGHWAY REST STOP - MAIN COMPLEX - DAY

Stewie and Jacob chase each other through the mostly empty complex, laughing.

JACOB (V.O.)
"Not the me that I saw in the mirror. Not the half of me I brought back to my broken home. Not the slutty disgusting me I have back here."

CUT TO:

I/E. STEWIE'S JEEP - DAY

Stewie and Jacob (silently) sing along to the Pet Shop Boys.

JACOB (V.O.)
"Somewhere in my fucked up life is me, a pure definition of me, my Rosebud. I decided I need to tell someone me, all of me."

CUT TO:

EXT. DOCTOR'S OFFICE - DAY

Stewie parks his Jeep outside a door with "Dr. Beth Collins" on the door. Jacob and Stewie hop out.

JACOB (V.O.)
"But it has to be someone special. Someone who wouldn't be bored or tired of me. Someone who could be the voucher at my funeral and say who I really was. Who I am right now."

CUT TO:

INT. WAITING ROOM - DAY

Jacob flips through Entertainment Weekly beside Stewie. Shows him a two-page spread, (silently) explaining who those people are.

JACOB (V.O.)
"And that person isn't me right now."

A RECEPTIONIST comes in. Jacob hears his name. Stands up.

JACOB (V.O.)
"I need to know what I am and who I am, not in terms of labels, but a single label that covers me."

Jacob waves sweetly at Stewie.

JACOB (V.O.)
"The true me."

Stewie sweetly waves back.

JACOB (V.O.)
"The whole me."

CUT TO:

INT. DR. COLLINS' OFFICE - DAY

DR. BETH COLLINS (45), a bit heavy with Rachel Ray hair, sits at her desk as Jacob sits on a couch.

JACOB
(reading from his phone)
"I need my Rosebud. I need me." And I signed it,

"Jacob David Andrezj. The homosexual, Aspergers-afflicted, selfish, slutty, lazy, kind, emotionless, expressionless, untrusting, hurt, confused, conflicted, obsessed, and lonely... twin... enigma."

Jacob pockets his phone.

JACOB (CONT'D)

I know it's cringy at the end there. That's just how I write my private posts.

Dr. Collins takes a deep breath, registering everything.

JACOB (CONT'D)

I wrote that a year and a half ago, Dr. Collins. That could have easily been written today. That's a problem.

DR. COLLINS

We can always adjust the levels.

JACOB

No, I'm serious. I want to be completely off the meds.

DR. COLLINS

I think that's a mistake.

JACOB

I know you do. But I'm not happy. I'm not. I think I can finally speak up about it. Doing nothing isn't making it any better. It's just making me feel trapped in a comfort zone that isn't even making me comfortable anymore.

DR. COLLINS

Is Stewie the one putting you up to this?

JACOB

Stewie has no idea I'm doing this right now. But now that I have him, I feel like I'm not broken anymore. I've been taking anti-psychotics since I was ten years old. I didn't even understand what was going on at the time. Mom just told me to take a pill every morning and I did. It was never my idea.

(pause)

That being said, of course, I'm in a much better place now because of that. But there is something I don't think you or Mom understand about autism. If you don't tell me something, no matter how stupid it is, I genuinely won't get it on my own. For years I slept through First Period, completely out of it, like I had been drugged. Of course I never realized it was the Risperdal doing it. You'd think I would, but that's what I'm saying. I genuinely thought I was possibly narcoleptic. At the end of the year, I always sent an email to my teachers apologizing for my lack of sleep, begging them to understand and not to fail me because I kept coming to class exhausted. And you know what, it worked. I got As anyway. I sure as hell didn't deserve it. And it happens to this day. I can't go twenty minutes into my 8 AM classes. Who knows how much knowledge I'm missing. I have no trouble bullshitting my way out of it with my professors from the sheer amount of practice alone.

(pause)

If I hadn't fucked that guy last year, the special ed teacher, I probably wouldn't have realized on my own how much of my problems were because of my meds. The sleeping, the difficulty ejaculating, the weight retention.

Jacob opens his arms, showing his flabby belly.

JACOB (CONT'D)
Look at me! I lost forty pounds just from switching brands. I only ate pasta the entire time I was in Italy.

DR. COLLINS
I've noticed.

JACOB
What exactly was the endgame with the meds?

DR. COLLINS
What do you mean?

JACOB
If I didn't have problems cumming and asked to switch brands, if nothing had changed, how much longer was I gonna be on the Risperdal and Zoloft?

Dr. Collins hesitates. Looks down at her desk.

JACOB (CONT'D)
That's what I thought.

DR. COLLINS
Look, if it helps your anxiety and depression--

JACOB
I was ten! A lot's happened to me since then. I'm ready to finally join the real world.

DR. COLLINS
I can understand if you want to wean off the Lexapro, but you might want to reconsider getting off the Prozac.

JACOB
It was my idea to be on antidepressants in the first place. I was never diagnosed with depression. I was a thirteen-year-old boy experiencing hormones for the first time. But you didn't stop me, did you? You approved it anyway.

DR. COLLINS
I approved the Zoloft because you told your mother you were having suicidal thoughts.

Jacob sighs hard. Rubs his temple.

JACOB
So that...
(pause)
I didn't know "suicidal thoughts" wasn't the same as "thinking about suicide."

Jacob goes quiet. Folds his hands.

JACOB (CONT'D)
It was just something I said in the heat of the moment. Mom and I were fighting about something, and I stormed upstairs into my room...
(pause)
It was just a thought anyone would have when they're upset. I was never actually gonna do it.

DR. COLLINS
What was it?

Jacob hesitates.

JACOB
I imagined myself going down into the kitchen, grabbing a steak knife, and slashing my wrists open in front of her.

Dr. Collins frowns.

JACOB (CONT'D)
But that was the only time. And I was just angry and seething and... So then I got scared. I started crying and...

Jacob shifts his stance uncomfortably.

JACOB (CONT'D)
Don't... Don't judge me for what I'm about to say, okay? I'm not proud of this.
(pause)
When I went downstairs crying to my mom about the "suicidal thoughts" I just had...

Jacob shakes his head.

JACOB (CONT'D)
I was faking it. The thought was real, but I knew I was never going to do it.

DR. COLLINS
Why would you do that?

JACOB
Because I wanted to be on antidepressants. All those commercials where they take those pills and their monochrome world turns into a colorful one. I thought they were happy pills. I thought, "Why not? What's the harm with more happiness?"

Jacob tries not to cry.

JACOB (CONT'D)
I thought worst case scenario you'd say no because I didn't need it. And I'm not blaming you, but it's not like you tried talking me out of it the way you are now. I didn't know I was gonna get fat because of it. I didn't know it would actually generate REAL suicidal thoughts.

Jacob wipes his eyes.

JACOB (CONT'D)
I never needed antidepressants. And I don't think I need an anti-psychotic anymore either.
(pause)
I'm better now. It did its job.

Dr. Collins sits up.

DR. COLLINS
I can't stop you if this is what you want. All I can say is that, in my professional opinion, I am against the idea.

JACOB
Karen has Aspergers. But in HER doctor's professional opinion, she had ADHD. They gave her the right pills for the wrong thing for years. She told me once she could hear voices. And all those mood pills just fucked her up. Suddenly she's compulsively lying, stealing the car in another attempt to run away, screaming at my parents, checking herself into a psych ward one time. And the bad girls at Eagle Ridge didn't help. Taking her to parties. Getting her to shoplift. And the boys?
(pause)
I don't understand how anyone could that to do someone.

Dr. Collins hesitates.

DR. COLLINS
Was Karen sexually assaulted?

JACOB
They never told us the specifics. We just heard what we could through the walls, even when I was trying to tune them out.
(pause)
Even after they sent her away, they wouldn't stop talking about her. All the things she did. I tried my best to be exactly what Mom wanted me to be, anything not to be sent away like Karen.

DR. COLLINS
That probably wouldn't have happened to--

JACOB
Yeah, but what I have been saying? Someone had to tell me, and no one did.

Jacob stares at the tissue box on the coffee table.

JACOB (CONT'D)
The wrong medication didn't just fuck up Karen, it fucked up our entire family. I'm insecure beyond belief, Melanie's embarrassed by Karen and myself by association, Dad maxed out, and Mom...

Jacob goes quiet. Furrows his brow.

Dr. Collins grabs a piece of paper. Jots down instructions.

DR. COLLINS
Cut the Lexapro in half and stop after a week. The Prozac needs two weeks to wean, half a pill for the first week, a quarter-pill for the second.

Dr. Collins rips the sheet. Holds it out.

Jacob reluctantly takes the paper. Rereads the instructions.

JACOB
That's it?

DR. COLLINS
I wish you the best of luck, Jacob.

Dr. Collins rotates away, putting her glasses back on. Jacob stands by the door.

JACOB
Dr. Collins?

Dr. Collins removes her spectacles. Looks over.

JACOB (CONT'D)
Thank you for everything you've done for me for the past eleven years. I'm sorry it had to end like this. I'm very happy now because of you.

DR. COLLINS
I'm a doctor, Jacob, not a mind reader. The only one who knows what's best for you is you.
(pause)
We both want the same thing.

Jacob shakes her hand with a smile. Opens the door.

MATCH CUT TO:

I/E. STEWIE'S JEEP - DAY

Jacob closes the passenger door. Stewie puts his seatbelt on. Starts the Jeep. "The Way" by Fastball plays through Sirius XM.

STEWIE
(reaches for CD button)
I'll get that for you, Sexy.

JACOB
No.

Stewie looks at Jacob.

STEWIE
You don't want to listen to the Pet Shop Boys?

Jacob keeps listening to "The Way."

JACOB
I like this song.

STEWIE
Do you know it?

JACOB
No.

STEWIE
I never really cared for it when it was out, but I love it now.

Jacob thinks.

JACOB
Why don't you take over the music for a while?

STEWIE
Really?

Jacob nods. Stewie unlatches the emergency break.

STEWIE (CONT'D)
How long did she say it was gonna take?

JACOB
Two weeks total.

STEWIE
Just in time for P-Town, huh?

Jacob nods, distracted.

STEWIE (CONT'D)
You're gonna love it. My friends and I used to go every Summer. The Diva would always bring these confetti shooters and spray them everywhere we went. It would always leave such a mess--

JACOB
Will I be able to look like you one day?

Stewie blinks, startled by the interruption.

STEWIE
What do you mean?

JACOB
The way I look now, is it too late or can I still do it?

Stewie shrugs.

STEWIE
I suppose if you lower your caloric intake and avoid any processed foods with artificial ingredients--

JACOB
Just answer my question.

STEWIE
I am answering your question.

JACOB
I didn't ask how, I'm asking if--

STEWIE
I know what you're asking. Just listen.

Jacob stifles himself.

STEWIE (CONT'D)
If you want to lose weight, you're gonna have to eat less junk, more fruit and vegetables, smaller portions overall, and maintain a steady exercise routine. That's hard enough.

JACOB
So--?

STEWIE
Let me finish.

Jacob nods apologetically.

STEWIE (CONT'D)
Doing all that's hard enough. But if you KEEP doing that, with enough consistency and discipline...
(pause)
Yes.

Jacob hesitates.

JACOB
Okay. I'll do it.

Stewie smiles. Shifts into first. Starts the drive back to Boston.

WHALE

Temptation

Whale looks at himself in the mirror, blue eyes fixed on themselves. He loosens his tie. Unbuttons his shirt. Slips it off. Lifts off the white undershirt. Matted chest hair on his pecs. Tan skin. Shoulder muscles. Triceps. Biceps. Deltoids. Big forearms. He flexes his arms. Pivots his body, his eyes looking over his shoulder. His tummy flatter than his chest. Still flabby as he walks, but a thin layer of fat covering his ab muscles. No lard baby no more. He touches his abdomen. Clenches his ab muscles. Punches it with the soft part of his fist. Harder than it looks down there. He wears Medium shirts now, not XL. He shops around for slim fit, not relaxed.

Whale lifts his eyes to his face. No acne. No dirty pores. No gingivitis. Because he washes his face. Actually gives a crap about his hygiene. He's off processed food, soda, and snacks. His teeth are whiter thanks to him actually brushing them whenever Stewie did. He cuts his hair in a way that actually makes him look hot. He doesn't let it grow out into a sloppy bowl, the look his mom always expected, the one he always hated but never bothered to change. If he saw himself across the bar he'd bang the crap out of him. He'd probably look so hot in the heat of the moment. All those muscles gleaming with sweat. All that energy. Cocky young smirk. A proper bro. But he can't say any of that out loud, can he? Because that's narcissistic. One of those unwritten rules everyone is expected to obey is to never acknowledge your own sex appeal. It backfires into unattractiveness, a sign of vanity. Whale doesn't get it. He knows he's hot. They know he's hot. Everyone's thinking it. Yet he can't say it? Why must he only receive such a compliment? But he can't just receive it, can he? Society expects him to be modest and deny such praise, like how you're supposed to say "Oh, you shouldn't have" when you receive a gift you actually want and need. He didn't lose the weight and bulk up for the health benefits, he did it for those compliments. The only reason he still fights hard to maintain it. And yet not enough people actually compliment him for his attractiveness. Because in their insecure minds, who are they to acknowledge such an elephant in the room?

Whale takes off his pants and underwear. Turns. Studies his ass in the mirror. He really looks like Michelangelo's David now, doesn't he? He never thought that was possible, lusting for all those boys in school, the ones on Disney Channel, all those porn stars. How could he have known when he was staring up at il Davide himself inside the Gallerie dell'Accademia weighing 245lbs with a BMI on the border of Overweight and Obese? He had embraced his plus-size reality. He had to. But it wasn't too late to salvage his body, was it? Much like a push-up, hard as it is to do at the start, making an effort to break a comfort zone is something Whale knows only gets easier with time and consistency. A comfort zone is an echo-chamber of one. Stewie had to come along, coaxing him out with love and logic. Look how much better Whale's life is now. By that logic, it can only get better if he breaks out a second time.

Whale grabs his phone. Taps the number in his texts. Puts the phone to his ear.

"Hello?"

```
                    WHALE
      Hey Theo.
```

"Who is this?" Cashew asks, genuinely confused.

```
                    WHALE
      Jacob.
```

Cashew sighs hard. "What do you want?"

Whale hesitates, checking to see if there was some other instinct, some anxious signal ordering him to stop before it's too late. Of course there was. But what good would that do?

```
                    WHALE
        Alright, I'm in.
```

DREW

Nothing Succeeds Like Succession

Drew lets himself into Theo's office, a folder in his hand. "Theo?"

"Just a second." Theo types the last of an email. Finishes with a sigh. "Okay. What's up?"

Drew tentatively closes the door. "The marketing boys say they're ready with the *Mari and the Babushkas* merch concepts."

"Good. Tell 'em to set aside a 12 o'clock on Friday for the presentation."

"Will do." Drew hesitates. "Can we talk about something?"

"Can it wait? I got a mound of emails to respond to."

"No it can't."

Theo sits back. "What is it?"

Drew holds up the folder. "I want you to look at this with me."

"More reading?" Theo says with a laugh.

"I'm serious."

Theo recognizes that look in Drew's eye. Oh shit.

Drew sits down. Opens the folder. "I've been meeting with Cazden Montgomery over the past week and the two of us drafted a proposal for that new department I told you I wanted."

Theo rolls his eyes. "Not this again."

"Yes, *this again*!" Drew cries. "Are you gonna listen or not?"

"Do I have a choice?"

Drew takes the first page out of the folder. Hands it over. "That's the list of cuts that'll pay for everything."

Theo skims the page. At least fifty items. "What the fuck are you doing?"

"Those productions have been in development hell for the least five years. They're not getting out anytime soon, especially now with *Mari and the Babushkas* taking our immediate attention." Drew hands over the second page. "This is a list of our in-production projects that are overbudget and by how much."

Theo tosses the papers on the desk. "I don't wanna see anymore."

"We're hemorrhaging, Theo. If we cut down on our wasted spending, that'll save us at least $100 million. That's enough for one project at least. That's all I want."

Theo glares at the papers on his desk.

Drew furrows his brow. "You didn't know, did you?"

"I know everything that's going on here."

"No you don't." Drew scoffs. Puts the pages back into the folder. "That's a little disconcerting."

"Get out," Theo snaps.

"Oh come on, it's not that big of a deal. It's better you know now, isn't it?"

"I reject your fucking hypothesis," Theo says with venom. "Get the fuck out of my office."

Drew's face goes numb. "There's no need to be so nasty about it."

"I am the CEO," Theo scolds. "I don't waste money. I don't NOT KNOW the status of my company's financial situation. And I don't appreciate being accused of mismanagement by someone who can't even go five minutes without doing a line! GET! THE FUCK! OUT! OF MY OFFICE! That is a FUCKING order!"

Drew looks away with an uneasy frown.

"What are you, deaf?!" Theo shouts.

"I didn't want it to come to this," Drew murmurs. "But if you don't approve my proposal before the end of the day, I'm withdrawing my half from the company account."

Theo stares, a cold chill pricking the inside of his skin. "What the fuck did you just say?"

"I've been talking to Cheryl as well. Guess I forgot to mention that. She went over our restructuring agreement, and it clearly states, as co-founder, I own 50% of Not That Nutty Productions. Of course I can't actually spend it since you're the CEO, but it's still technically my money. If you want it, you're gonna have to ask me for it and I'll have every right to say no. Cazden says that'll hold up in a court of law. Cheryl too."

"To hell it will," Theo growls. He picks up the phone. Dials a direct number.

"What are you doing?"

"Put Montgomery on," Theo orders Cazden's secretary over the phone.

Drew sits back. Crosses his legs. "He's not gonna answer."

"I'm the CEO, cunt!" Theo yells into the phone. "Put the fag on!"

"That's not very nice."

Theo covers the receiver. "You won't take my fucking money!" he hisses at Drew.

"*Our* money," Drew corrects coldly. "And I already have."

Theo stares. Slowly hangs up the phone.

Drew gives a coy shrug. "Did you really think I was going tell you my master plan if there was even the slightest chance you'd be able to stop it?" He pauses. "I authorized the transfer thirty minutes ago."

Theo's body trembles, his brain exploding from within.

Drew smirks gaily. "Actually it was this morning. I just wanted to misquote *Watchmen*. You know I never get the chance to do that."

Theo's lips flutter. "Why would you do that to me?" he whispers, genuinely hurt.

"You know why." Drew stands. Plops the folder down on Theo's desk. "I never wanted it to get this far. I tried reasoning with you. You wouldn't fucking listen. Time and time again you don't fucking listen. You gave me no choice. Fucking with your money was the only way I could get your attention. That's how serious I am." Drew grimaces. "Jesus, can't you let me have *something* that isn't tangentially beneficial to you? You said yourself I'm the reason this company's what it is today. I think that makes me entitled for something in return."

Theo's breath quickens.

"I've done so much for you!" Drew shouts, his mouth contorting, his cheeks trembling. "I did shit I never wanted to do! For you! Because you wanted me to! I helped you fuck over Peabrain because you wanted me to! I took down The Professor because you WANTED me to! And where the FUCK would you be if I didn't bring you that Paramount deal, huh?! Just another cog in Liu Míng's machine?! YOU OWE ME! YOU OWE ME *EVERYTHING*!" Drew's breath wavers. He points at the file. "Now it's time for you to do what *I* want you to do. I want that department. I'm fucking having it."

Theo blinks. "You're fired."

"Come on, I'm serious."

"So am I. You're fired."

Drew scoffs. Picks up the file. "I'm not fired."

"Yes you are," Theo says sternly. "Clean out your office."

Drew stares. "Stop."

"I don't care. Get the fuck out."

"Wait." Drew holds up both hands. "This is for real?"

Theo picks up the phone. "I'm calling security."

"WAIT!" Drew cries. "Okay! I'll give it back! I'm sorry."

"Too late!" Theo slams the receiver down. "What did you think was gonna happen? I was just gonna keep working alongside the man that tried to muscle me out of my own company?"

"I wasn't muscling you out! I was trying—"

"Exactly, cause I won't let you."

"No, Theo, listen to me—"

"You obviously want to leave so badly. Take your money and get the fuck out of here!"

Drew can't breathe. "Theo, c'mon..."

Theo scowls. Looks away.

Drew takes a step closer, pleading eyes begging for acknowledgment. "I'm sorry, alright?" he whispers. "It'll never happen again."

Theo forces his frown. Keeps himself from looking over, from giving in.

Drew swallows. "You, Larry, Alan... Doris, Simmons, Johnson..." He pauses. "You guys are the only family I got left."

"Then you should've thought twice before fucking us over," Theo scolds. "Get out."

Drew shamefully picks up the folder. Awkwardly puts it back. Silently opens the office door. Leaves.

Theo's face contorts with bitter regret. What the fuck was that? He just signed Nutty's death certificate, that's what he fucking did. It's all over. Theo massages his face with two palms. No. This is just another fixed trial. Drew can't handle too much freedom. He'll cave. He'll come back with the money and apologize. He always does. He'll come back and never think of leaving ever again.

Theo picks up his phone. Presses 1. "Alan, stop what you're doing. I need you to do something for me."

"Just name it."

"It's really drastic. You just gonna have to trust me on this."

Silence. "Of course, Mr. Landreth. What is it?"

"I need you to quit."

Drew locks the handicap stall. Pulls his pants down. Sits on the toilet. He doesn't have to go. He just likes the way it makes him feel, not being so contained, all that fresh air on raw skin. He hunches over. They'll all think he did something to deserve it. Ten years from now the next generation of Not That Nutty employees won't even know Drew Lawrence used to work there, let alone co-founded the damn place. Theo will use Drew to justify their shittiest projects. Drew was the reason *Tequilatown* and *Havremoer* failed. And there'll be tales of the monster that used to roam these halls, the Minotaur in that Sunset Boulevard labyrinth, coked out of his mind, drinking Scotch with no water, sneaking in go-go boys and wannabe interns to fuck them against windows, on Theo's desk, Doris' desk, Larry's desk, the screening room. That's how they'll remember him here.

Unless he goes off and wins Best Picture. Then he'll be one that got away.

Drew struts down the hall toward Larry's office. Turns the handle. Smashes his face into the door. He furrows his brow. Turns the knob again. Locked. The blinds are down but the light is on. KNOCK-KNOCK-KNOCK. "Larry!" Drew shouts. "Come on! Open up!"

Drew's work cell rings. He pulls it out. Swipes. "Larry, where the fuck are you?"

"I can't let you in, Mr. Lawrence," Larry whispers.

"Why not?" Drew desperately tries to peek through the Venetian blinds. "Larry, c'mon. Let me in."

"Alan just quit, Mr. Lawrence."

Drew freezes. "What?"

"Five minutes ago. He heard what Theo did to you and quit out of solidarity."

Drew whips his head. "That literally just happened."

"Theo told me."

"*When*?!"

"Two minutes ago."

Drew scoffs. "God, I go to the bathroom one time and the whole diner's held up. What..." He stops talking. His blood chills. He closes the eyes. "That fucker."

"I'm so sorry Mr. Lawrence."

Drew slides his back down Larry's office door. Plops on the carpet. "He fired Alan and gave you his job, didn't he?"

Silence on the line. "I don't think that's what happened."

"Don't believe him, Larry."

"He's been depressed for a while. I think he really had enough."

"Don't believe it." Drew frowns. "God, you didn't even have to think about it, did you?"

"I've been due for a promotion for over a year now, Mr. Lawrence. You know that."

"I know." Drew sighs. "I'm sorry."

Larry hesitates. "It's okay."

"No." Drew looks up at the fluorescent lighting above him. "I held you down. I didn't think I could do anything without you." His throat tightens. "I still don't."

Soft sigh from Larry.

"Come with me," Drew whispers.

"Mr. Lawrence."

"You don't want to work for Theo. He's a fucking psychopath. He's an immature, weak-willed, manipulative—"

"I don't want to hear any of this!"

"Just come with me."

"I can't." Larry pauses. "I'm sorry, Mr. Lawrence."

Drew closes his eyes. He sits on that.

"Did you really steal half our money?" Larry asks.

Drew hesitates. "Is that what Theo told you?"

"Is it true?"

Drew swallows. "I'm a co-founder. I'm entitled to 50%. I didn't steal shit."

"Forgive me for saying this, Mr. Lawrence, but I hope you realize you just made our jobs so much fucking harder."

Drew grits his teeth. "I wasn't planning on leaving with it. I was just trying to scare him, alright? Theo would've done the same thing in my shoes. I was just trying to impress him. He fired me. He's the one making your jobs harder. My only crime was standing up to him when he was in the wrong. You don't want this, Larry. If you tell him anything he doesn't want to hear, he will fire you on the spot. Please come with me."

Silence. "He didn't tell me you were fired until after I said yes."

"Would you have said no?"

Silence.

Drew nods, disappointment settling in. "I don't know how to do this job without you, Larry."

"You'll find someone."

"There's no one like you out there. Not by a mile."

"Thank you for saying so. You have no idea how much that means to me."

"Of course I do." Drew smiles. "I'm gonna miss you so much."

Larry moves the phone away, squeezing his eyes shut. He puts it back. "I'll miss you too, Mr. Lawrence," he says without emotion.

Drew looks around the hall. No one mulling about. No security yet. "There is something you can do to help me. Now that you're in Theo's inner circle, you'll have access to Alan's computer."

"I don't like how this sounds."

Drew double checks for passersby. "In a few days, Theo's gonna show you how to access the Black List. It's list of his enemies. When he's out of the room, I need you to call me and give me one of the addresses."

"I don't want to be a part of this, Mr. Lawrence."

"Larry, listen to me!"

"I can't lose this job."

"You won't! I swear! It'll never come back to you!" Drew pauses. "You're the only person now who has access to that list. It's just this one last thing. Please. I promise I'll never ask anything from you ever again."

Larry hesitates. "Depends who this person to is Theo."

"The first name he added to the list," Drew whispers.

The next day, the shit hits the headlines:

"DREW LAWRENCE OUT AS NOT THAT NUTTY'S HEAD OF PRODUCTION"
Deadline

"DREW LAWRENCE OUSTED IN 'NUTTY' TRANSITION"
Variety

"LANDRETH VS LAWRENCE: THE 'NUTTY' SCHISM AND WHAT THAT MEANS FOR THE FUTURE OF BLOCKBUSTERS"
The Hollywood Reporter

"'WORSE THAN THE BEATLES': HOLLYWOOD CELEBS TWEET THEIR REACTIONS TO 'NUTTY' PRODUCER FEUD"
Variety

"OPINION: DREW LAWRENCE LEFT NOT THAT NUTTY. COOL. WHO THE F#%! CARES?"
The New York Times

"THE 15 BEST 'NOT THAT NUTTY' MOVIES... AND THE 5 WORST!"
Buzzfeed

"HOLLYWOOD SEEMS TO CARE MORE ABOUT DREW LAWRENCE THAN WHAT THEY'RE PUTTING IN FRONT OF OUR KIDS"
Fox News

"WHO DREW LAWRENCE IS AND WHY HIS DEPARTURE IS ACTUALLY KIND OF A BIG DEAL"
CNN

"OPINION: NOT THAT NUTTY SPLIT IS A SIGN THAT HOLLYWOOD IS DYING... AND IT'S ONLY GONNA GET WORSE"
The New York Times

"OKAY, BUT WHY IS DREW LAWRENCE SO HOT?"
Out

Four days after Drew's departure, Larry knocks on Theo's door. "Cazden can't reverse the transfer."

Theo grimaces out his office window.

Larry sits. "I have a few ideas of who we could ask to be Head of Production."

"Drew's coming back, Larry." Theo turns. "He'll bring back our money if we leave the door open for him."

"But sir, without a Head of Production—"

"Drew Lawrence is our Head of Production." Theo returns to his desk. "I don't want to hear any more on the subject. And before I forget, send out a no-press memo to everyone. No one talks about Drew or the money. If they do, they'll be terminated." Theo thinks. "Matter of fact, anyone talking shit about Drew Lawrence will be fired on the spot. Make that very clear to everyone."

Larry writes all that down. "Yes sir."

Theo stands. "Follow me."

"But what about the—?"

"This is more important." Theo opens the door. Leads Larry into Alan's office next door. "Sit."

Larry sits at Alan's old desk. "Can't I stay in my old office?"

"You're moving here." Theo turns on the monitor and points to a little black square on the desktop. "That's why."

Larry squints at the program. "'The Black List?'"

"Míng got it for me off the Dark Web years ago. It breaks a shit ton of privacy violations, so I'd appreciate you not telling anyone about it." Theo double clicks the program. "When I tell you to add someone's name, you do it. No exceptions. Put in as much as you can. Names. Aliases. Phones numbers. Emails. Addresses. It's an adaptive program. The more you give it, the better it'll do."

Larry looks up. "But what is it?"

Theo smirks. "Do you really wanna know?"

Larry tentatively nods.

Theo closes the office door. "When a person is added to the Black List, all contact is severed between them and my devices. All phone calls are blocked. All emails coming from an address associated with that person are automatically deleted. All social media activity is removed from my feed. If their name is on any documents, memos, web results, however I see it on my end, it gets blurred out. It also has facial recognition, so all photos get redacted too. If they change their phone number, if they make a new email, if they move somewhere else, the Black List updates itself and keeps it going. If I never see them again or hear about them again, I'll never have to think about them again. It's like they don't even exist."

Larry stares. "And that helps you?"

"The only way to sail forward is to jettison the filth, Larry." Theo points to the login box at the top. "Create a good password. Never tell me what it is." He walks away.

"Alan did all this for you?" Larry asks.

"He did a lot of things for me." Theo leaves the office door open.

Larry's blood chills. He remembers what Alan told him that time over the phone. Deporting those undocumented janitors. All those sleepless nights driving him mad. That's gonna be him one day, isn't it? Is that really worth twenty-four vacation days and dental?

Theo pops back in. "Did you do it yet?"

"Oh, sorry. I'll do it now."

Just then Theo's phone rings. "Speak of the devil." Theo swipes. "Alan. What's the update?"

"What the hell's going on, Theo?!" Alan shouts over the phone, loud enough for Larry to overhear. "You said Drew was gonna call me by now!"

Theo furrows his brow, turning away from Larry. "He hasn't called at all?"

"You said I had nothing to worry about!"

"Calm down."

"You said he was gonna take the bait! What the hell's going on?"

Theo's blood curdles. "I don't know. That doesn't..."

"I don't think he's calling me, Theo," Alan says. "Does that mean I'm coming back?"

Theo hesitates. He turns around. Looks at Larry.

"Mr. Landreth?" Alan asks. "I am coming back, righ—?"

Theo hangs up. "Add Alan Lovelace to the Black List." He tosses the phone to Larry. "His info's in the contacts."

Larry looks at the phone in his hands. Mr. Lawrence was right. It was never Alan's idea to leave. But he was wrong about something too. The Black List isn't a list of Theo's enemies. It's a list of his bodies.

"Don't forget about that memo," Theo says, walking out of ~~Alan's~~ Larry's office. "And we got that marketing presentation in twenty minutes. We can't be late for that." He leaves the door open again.

Larry's skin crawls as he creates a password. A list of names and addresses appears. Larry scrolls through the list. He recognizes a few. Sal Kleinberg. Melanie Hapintsky. Gordon Donnelly. Shirley Kerrigan. Jeez, it really doesn't take much, does it?

Larry adds Alan Lovelace to the list. Just as he clicks Enter, Theo's contact app crashes. Larry reopens it. Alan's info is gone. His texts are gone. Even the call that just happened isn't there anymore.

Larry double-checks for Theo returning to get back his phone. He clicks on the search bar. Types the word Drew told him to search. Only one name shows up, just like he said it would. He stares at it for a few moments. If he doesn't call Drew with the info, he won't have a number two to help him spend that $400 million he took. He won't be able to start a new thing. He'll come back, just like Theo said he would. And everything would be just like before, right?

Larry frowns. He can't put Mr. Lawrence through all that. He made a promise.

Drew Lawrence waits in his Marina del Rey condo, personal cell face-up on his coffee table. He studies his fingernails up close, how sturdy and long they are. When did he stop biting them?

The phone buzzes. Drew snatches it up. "Did you get it?"

Muffled sounds on the line.

Drew hesitates. "Larry?"

"Kev Foster," Larry articulates slowly. "4445 Alba Lane, La Brea."

Drew jots everything down on a pad. "Thank you, Larry! Thank you thank you thank you!"

Silence.

Drew furrows his brow. Looks at the screen. Larry hung up. Seventeen years of service and not even a goodbye.

END OF PART THREE

PART FOUR

I Enjoyed It

JACOB

Harold and Maude

INT. STEWIE'S BROWNSTONE APARTMENT - DAY

Jacob is all-fours on a yoga mat in the starting push-up position, exasperated. Stewie stands beside him.

STEWIE
C'mon.

JACOB
Just give me a moment.

STEWIE
It'll only get harder the longer you wait.

JACOB
How many do I have to do?

STEWIE
Just do ten.

Jacob lowers himself. Strains to get back up.

STEWIE (CONT'D)
One.

Jacob hesitates.

STEWIE (CONT'D)
C'mon, that's only one.

Jacob lowers himself again, face straining. He collapses on the ground.

STEWIE (CONT'D)
What happened?

JACOB
(getting up)
I can't do it.

STEWIE
Yes, you can!

JACOB
NO I CAN'T!

STEWIE
Stop yelling at me.

JACOB
I can't! I can't do it.

STEWIE
You didn't even try.

JACOB
I DID! CAN'T YOU SEE THAT I TRIED?! IT'S HARD!

Stewie looks away with a grimace.

STEWIE
I don't like you yelling at me.

JACOB
WELL I DON'T LIKE DOING ANY OF THIS SHIT!

STEWIE
Calm down.

JACOB
I DON'T NEED TO CALM DOWN! I'M CALM!

STEWIE
Really?

Jacob storms into the bedroom.

JACOB
(under his breath)
Fuck this.

He slams the door.

CUT TO:

BEDROOM

Jacob curled up on the bed, listening to Stewie type on his computer. He huffs. Hops out of bed.

CUT TO:

LIVING ROOM

Jacob marches over to Stewie's desk.

JACOB
So what, you just go back to work?

STEWIE
I thought we were done.

JACOB
I wanna get through this before P-Town.

STEWIE
Do the push-ups. It's not that hard.

JACOB
It is for me. I've never done them before.

STEWIE
You were doing fine.

JACOB
No I wasn't. Was my form off?

STEWIE
No.

JACOB
Then why couldn't I do it?

STEWIE
It's hard in the beginning.

JACOB
Can't you give me a straight answer for once?

STEWIE
I thought I was.

JACOB
Just tell me why I couldn't do it.

STEWIE
You didn't want to do it.

JACOB
I do want to do it!

STEWIE
Then do it!

Jacob clenches his lips.

JACOB
I still need help understanding how to do it.

Stewie sighs, annoyed.

STEWIE
Just do five.

JACOB
No. I don't need to cut back. I can do ten.

STEWIE
You've rested too long. It's gonna be harder now.

Jacob's lips flutter.

JACOB
But you said it was gonna get easier after the first few.

STEWIE
Then you rested and now the muscles are rebuilding.

JACOB
WHY DIDN'T YOU TELL ME THAT BEFORE I WENT INTO THE BEDROOM?!

STEWIE
You're really blaming me?

JACOB
I was upset! But you didn't care, did you? You just went right back to work.

STEWIE
You're the one that stormed off.

JACOB
You're the personal trainer! I thought you were good at your job! No wonder you're losing your business.

Stewie laughs sarcastically. Returns to his computer.

JACOB (CONT'D)
Hey!
(pause)
HEY! I'M TALKING TO YOU!

STEWIE
Keep it up.

JACOB
Why won't you listen to me?

STEWIE
I AM listening!

JACOB
Then why won't you help me?

STEWIE
Since when am I not helping you? You're the one that stormed off.

JACOB
And you just let me! And I wait there for you to comfort me and tell me everything's gonna be all right, but you just give up and go to work like I mean nothing!

STEWIE
I'm not gonna coddle you like your mother did.

JACOB
My mom never CODDLED me!

STEWIE
If you expect me to chase after you every time you're having a little tantrum, then you're wasting your time.

Stewie turns away. Jacob cringes.

JACOB
You fucking asshole!

Stewie scoffs.

JACOB (CONT'D)
How can you say you love me when you treat me like this?

STEWIE
Grow up.

Jacob storms into the bedroom.

JACOB (CONT'D)
ENJOY YOUR WORK!

He slams the door.

CUT TO:

BEDROOM

An hour later. Jacob on the bed, a sad frown on his face, replaying his tantrum.

CUT TO:

LIVING ROOM

Stewie hasn't moved from his computer. The bedroom door opens. Jacob meekly walks over.

JACOB
(sad bleating)
AYY BEE.

Stewie doesn't answer.

JACOB (CONT'D)
I'm sorry.

STEWIE
You need to stop cursing at me.

JACOB
I can't help it.

STEWIE
Yes you can. Stop making excuses.

Jacob hesitates.

JACOB
Aren't you gonna apologize?

STEWIE
For what?

JACOB
For being mean to me.

STEWIE
You were the one being mean to me.

JACOB
I apologized to you!

STEWIE
So what?

JACOB
Aren't you sorry for anything?

STEWIE
You wanted me to help you work out. I told you everything you needed.

JACOB
No you didn't! You couldn't even answer any of my questions with a straight answer!

STEWIE
All your questions are complicated!

JACOB
No they're not!

STEWIE
I gotta get payroll done before we head out. You're keeping me away from work.

Jacob frowns. Hesitates.

JACOB
Why can't you just be nice?!

STEWIE
You're the one acting like a seven-year-old.

JACOB
Well maybe I wouldn't be if you made me feel loved more!

STEWIE
I can't believe you're this insecure.

JACOB
I AM NOT INSECURE!

Stewie ignores him. Jacob fumes.

JACOB (CONT'D)
You're always sweet as pie to strangers, but the moment anyone gets to know you, you turn into a bossy jerk. No wonder you were still single.

Jacob storms into the bedroom. Slams the door again.

CUT TO:

I/E. STEWIE'S JEEP - THE NEXT DAY

Stewie drives Jacob down a highway. The atmosphere is awkward. The trunk is stuffed with suitcases, a beach umbrella, towels, a Mets cooler, and a basket of snacks.

The Jeep's Sirius XM plays "Dirty Cash (Money Talks)" by The Adventures of Stevie V.

JACOB
You actually like this crap?

STEWIE
It's freestyle.

JACOB
It sounds like rap.

STEWIE
It's not rap.

JACOB
She's literally rapping.

STEWIE
This is my favorite 90s dance song. You said I could play whatever I wanted.

JACOB
I thought you'd actually play good music. Music I'd like.

The song ends. Stewie changes the channel. "LoveGame" by Lady Gaga plays.

JACOB (CONT'D)
Skip it.

STEWIE
No way, I love this song.

Jacob cringes at Stewie.

STEWIE (CONT'D)
It's her best!

JACOB
You're such a hypocrite.

Stewie sighs at Jacob starting up again.

JACOB (CONT'D)
What happened to you being the non-mainstream rocker?

STEWIE
I still am.

JACOB
But now you're just another 10s pop fag?

STEWIE
I love all dance, especially EDM. There are plenty of songs that I love that never charted on the Hot 100. This one I just happen to like. My brother's the one that hasn't left the 80s.

Jacob sighs.

STEWIE (CONT'D)
Don't you like dance?

JACOB
I never really thought about it.
(pause)
It's not so different from psychedelic rock, I suppose. But I'm sorry, I'm never gonna like a song that uses the words "Disco Stick."

STEWIE
You like "Poker Face?"

JACOB
I've always loved "Poker Face."

STEWIE
There you go.

Jacob takes a deep breath. He starts biting his nails again.

STEWIE (CONT'D)
Stop biting your nails!

JACOB
I can't help it.

STEWIE
Yes you can. Just stop doing it.

JACOB
I don't want to stop doing it. It calms me down.

STEWIE
It's a dirty habit.

JACOB
How is it dirty?

STEWIE
You're putting your fingers in your mouth!

JACOB
I know where they've been.

Jacob self-consciously looks at his nails. Rethinks starting it up again. Puts his hand down.

JACOB (CONT'D)
I'm sorry for how I've been acting these past few weeks.

STEWIE
Just treat me nicely, okay? I don't think I'm asking for that much.

JACOB
I'm trying.

STEWIE
Don't try, just do it. It's not hard.

JACOB
Yes it is! God, why can't you just make it easy for me?

STEWIE
Because if I call you out on it enough, it'll sink in and you'll stop.

JACOB
You're just gonna beat it out of me?

STEWIE
I'm treating you like an adult. Your mother spoiled the heck out of you.

JACOB
She did not!

STEWIE
Yes she did.

JACOB
No, she really didn't. You don't have any clue what it was like in that house! You can't just assume!

Jacob looks away with a sour expression. Neither talk for a while.

JACOB (CONT'D)
I think it's because I've warmed up to you and I feel comfortable enough with you to be unfiltered. You should really take it as a compliment. It's a sign of trust.

STEWIE
That is the stupidest thing you've ever said.

JACOB
I am NOT stupid! Don't you EVER call me stupid!

Jacob turns away, hurt.

STEWIE
I wasn't calling YOU stupid, I was saying you SOUNDED stupid.

JACOB
Same thing.

STEWIE
No it isn't.

"LoveGame" ends. Stewie changes the station. "If You Wanna Sing Out, Sing Out" by Cat Stevens plays. His smooth voice and acoustic guitar calms both of them. The direct lyrics feel especially appropriate to Jacob.

JACOB
Can I drive a bit?

STEWIE
No.

JACOB
I think I can do it now.

STEWIE
I want to drive.

Jacob hunches away.

Stewie looks over at Jacob. Reaches out to pet Jacob's hair. Jacob flinches away. Stewie huffs.

STEWIE (CONT'D)
You make a big deal about me not comforting you, then you pull away.

Jacob hesitates.

JACOB
Try it again.

Stewie reluctantly reaches out again. Pets Jacob's head. Jacob sighs and sits back up.

JACOB (CONT'D)
Thank you.

Stewie gives an exaggerated pout.

STEWIE
(baby talk)
Stop being mean to me.

Jacob frowns, disappointed in himself.

WHALE

Tsunami

Whale pops into Wally McGree's. Cashew's already waiting for him. "His password's a bunch of gibberish," he tells Whale over two slices of pumpkin pie. "I've been watching him every time he logs in, and he logs in a lot. He logs out to use the bathroom."

```
                WHALE
There's no way it's gibberish.
```

"I saw him type it three times now. It's 'gsousbaktar,' I know it."

```
                WHALE
I'm sorry, WHAT?!
```

"'Gsousbaktar!' G-S-O-U-S-B-A-K-T-A-R. Maybe it's a Russian thing. He looks a bit Russian. Who's knows?"

Whale cringes, unconvinced.

"Anyway, I did some tests today. We can't access The Professor's cloud outside work, but we can still log on to any computer and our files will show up, which means I can access Peabrain's cloud from my computer."

```
                WHALE
That's good.
```

"But then I saw Peabrain's desktop this afternoon. It's full of files."

```
                WHALE
So?
```

"He saves it directly to that specific computer. It's not on the cloud."

```
                WHALE
Is that bad?
```

Cashew shrugs. "Yes and no. It's bad because I have to actually sit at the computer he uses all the time, but there's also no backups."

```
                WHALE
Which means once they're gone--
```

"We don't have to wait for the cloud to update itself. It'll take less time to get a complete wipe, but it still leaves me exposed, which is why it's so important that you keep Peabrain distracted for at least five minutes. I have to take my time so Bumps doesn't catch what I'm doing. And I have to check to make sure The Professor or The Secretary aren't wandering about."

```
                WHALE
But you'll be able to wipe everything in five
minutes?
```

"It should be all on the desktop. I'll do some digging if I have time, but my theory is he saves everything to the desktop *because* it's all in one place.

```
                WHALE
Sounds about right.
```

"But what are you gonna do? How are you gonna keep him distracted for five minutes?"

Whale looks down at his plate. Stabs his pie over and over with a fork.

```
                    WHALE
        I know just what to do.
```

"Yeah? How?"

```
                    WHALE
        Experience.
```

The next day, Whale walks into The Classroom a nervous wreck. Peabrain's already at his computer, typing hard and fast like always, blissfully unaware of the shitty day he's about to have. Whale checks his watch. 9:30. He wanders into the coffee room next to the bathroom. Scans the small appliances.

Maybe he should let Peabrain off early to catch Cashew in the act. Then Cashew would be after him, wouldn't he? The last thing he wants is that freak on the other side of a battlefield. Besides, he made a promise. This is just backstage jitters. He's an actor. A five-time non-consecutive award-winning actor. It's just a character. Stall for time. Improvise. He's got this.

Whale checks his watch again. 9:45. Showtime.

Peabrain glances through his coverage of musical black-comedy *The Frightening Predicament of the Superstore Shooter* (just as tasteless as that sounds), checking for spelling errors when Whale approaches him.

```
                    WHALE
        Hey, um... Peabrain?
```

Peabrain turns around in his chair. Whale smiles politely. Thumbs behind him.

```
                    WHALE (CONT'D)
        I can't seem to figure out how to use the Nespresso
        machine. Would you by any chance...?
```

"I-i-i-i-it's v-v-v-v-very easy to operate," Peabrain answers.

```
                    WHALE
        Can you show me? I think I'll understand it better.
```

Peabrain looks back at the computer. He's got fourteen minutes to kill before he sends the email. "S-s-s-s-s-sure, j-j-j-just give me a s-s-s-second, okay?"

```
                    WHALE
        Sure.
```

Peabrain closes the file he was spell-checking. Clicks Log Out. "O-o-o-okay, l-l-l-let's go."

Cashew watches Peabrain lead Whale into the coffee room. He oh-so-causally looks at Bumps sitting at a table, her nose in *Oldest Man Alive*, one of the five books they were assigned. She's never looked prettier. The smallest of smiles creeps onto Cashew's face before he snaps out of it and double-checks the coast is clear.

In the coffee room, Whale grabs a purple Nespresso pod.

```
                    WHALE
        Then I put the pod into this hole here...
```

Whale plops the pod into the Nespresso machine.

```
                    WHALE (CONT'D)
        But then I try to lower the handle...
```

Whale pushes the handle down. It doesn't budge.

```
                    WHALE (CONT'D)
        And it doesn't want to close.
```

Peabrain nods. "I-i-i-it's a v-v-v-v-very common p-p-p-problem, actually."

WHALE
```
I didn't think it'd be this difficult. I use Keurigs
all the time.
```

"Th-th-th-th-th-th-th-th..." Peabrain swallows, his tongue tired.

Whale gives an inviting nod, his eyes intentionally sympathetic and comfortable.

WHALE
```
Take your time.
```

Peabrain relaxes, grateful for Whale's muted understanding. "Th-th-th-the s-s-s-s-same th-th-th-thing happened to my r-r-roommate Tanner b-b-b-back at University of Arizona."

Back in The Classroom, Cashew tiptoes to Peabrain's computer, trying to avoid detection from Bumps in the process. He types Peabrain's username, "Peabrain," and his password: "gsousbaktar." Smacks the enter button.

Incorrect Password
5 Attempts Remaining

Cashew's eyes bulge. He rapidly types "gsousbaktar" again.

Incorrect Password
4 Attempts Remaining

Cashew grabs the sides of his head. Looks around. Bumps hasn't budged. No Peabrain yet. He checks the computer's clock. Holy fuck! Two minutes gone already?!

Back in the coffee room, Peabrain drops a new pod in and lowers the handle. The pod falls into place with a satisfying plastic crunch. "S-s-s-see? No b-b-b-biggie." He presses the Double Shot button.

WHALE
```
You didn't have to flip it?
```

"N-n-n-n-no, you had it right, y-y-y-y-you just d-d-d-didn't p-p-p-p-p-p-push it in d-d-d-d-deep enough."

WHALE
```
I feel like such an idiot now.
```

"Ya-ya-ya-ya-you're n-n-n-n-not an id-id-id-id-id-idiot. It's a l-l-l-lot more complicated than it n-n-n-n-needs to be."

WHALE
```
Thank you for taking the time to show me how to work
it.
```

"I-i-i-it's n-n-n-n-no problem, r-r-r-really." Peabrain smiles gently.

Whale's heart breaks. He's such a freaking sweetheart.

Peabrain looks up at the clock. "I-I-I-I-I r-r-r-really sh-sh-sh-should be getting b-b-b-back. It-it-it-it-it's almost t-t-t-time for The Prof-f-f-f-f-f-f-ffessor's email."

Whale checks his watch. Two minutes left to kill.

WHALE
```
I really, um...
```

Peabrain stops. Looks at Whale, interested.

Whale swallows.

WHALE
```
You really remind me of someone I went to high school
with. He had a pretty bad stuttering problem too.
```

Peabrain nods, half-frowning.

```
                    WHALE (CONT'D)
        I've learned how to... the right way to not be, you
        know...
```

Peabrain nods, completely understanding.

Whale huffs, straining.

```
                    WHALE (CONT'D)
        What I mean to say is, I understand how absolutely
        frustrating it is for you. And I know I'm supposed to
        just let you... you know...
```

Peabrain raises a gentle hand. "Th-th-th-thank you. Y-y-y-y-you don't have t-t-t-t-to say any more. I kn-kn-know you're okay."

Whale smiles, hurting on the inside. This whole thing's been a mistake.

Back in The Classroom, Cashew slowly types "gsousbaktar," checking to see what keys are close to each letter. He starts over. Types "gaoubaktar." Smacks enter.

Incorrect Password
3 Attempts Remaining

"Dammit!" Cashew hisses.

Bumps lifts her eyes in Cashew's direction. Furrows her brow.

Cashew looks left. Peabrain's nowhere to be seen. Whale's doing *his* job. Cashew briefly checks Bumps again. Her head's down. He faces forward. Types "gaoubaltar." Enter.

Incorrect Password
2 Attempts Remaining

Bumps discreetly looks at the computer Cashew was using when she sat down. It's still open to Cashew's email account.

"Wait a minute," Cashew whispers to himself. He types "gaiusbaltar" and hits enter. Peabrain's desktop appears, all his files right there in front of him. Gaius Baltar. Peabrain's a *Battlestar* fan too. How bout that.

Bumps watches Cashew click around Peabrain's computer from across the room, finally understanding. A game of high stakes is being played. Endgame moves. And she almost missed it.

Back in the coffee room, Whale grabs his coffee with unfocused eyes. "It-it-it-it-it's nice to know someone understands," Peabrain tells him. "I f-feel seen."

```
                    WHALE
               (really quiet)
        That's the idea.
```

"Hm?"

```
                    WHALE
        Nothing. Just talking to myself.
```

"G-g-g-g-good luck." Peabrain waves politely and heads back into The Classroom.

Whale stays where he is, standing in silence, a pitiable frown growing.

```
                    WHALE
        You too.
```

Peabrain walks back to his computer. Rapid-types his password. Hits enter. Furrows his brow. Taking longer than usual to load, isn't it? But then he sees the Recycling Bin icon. Chrome. Start. All the toolbar shit. Goosebumps run down his arms. No. Can't be. He looks back up at the Recycling Bin. The logo's transparent. Empty.

Peabrain whips his head around. Cashew casually sighing at his computer, oblivious. Bumps meekly closing her book and taking her time back to hers. How? Who? All the hours of work. All that work shattered. Then the hardest realization of them all. The Professor's email. What he'll think now. Peabrain gapes. Hurt. Powerless. He looks back at Whale strolling through The Classroom, holding that ceramic mug by the tiny handle, looking right at him, facing forward again. Their eye contact was only a millisecond in length, barely even there, but it's so obvious Whale knew just where to look.

Peabrain's jaw clenches. Nostrils flare. Cheeks flush. Rage flows.

DREW

Fredo

Drew parks JEEPGUY 2: Electric Boogaloo outside 4445 Alba Lane. Twenty pounds lighter now that he's off the Tren and Stan. Bright red and black polo. Jet black jeans. Leather boots. Sunglasses. Stewie's red Nike cap for courage. He removes his sunglasses. Stares at Kev Foster's ranch house, a carbon copy of its neighbors. He's not dirt poor, thank God, but he's not really in the position to say no.

Drew rings the doorbell. Looks around at La Brea soaking up the September sun.

The deadbolt unlocks. A forty-year-old man in a light pink Hawaiian shirt opens the door. Papyrus shorts. Flip-flops. Long face. Full head of black hair. Slight wrinkles on the sides of his mouth. He opens his mouth to say something.

"Hi," Drew says with a weak smile. "It's Kev, right? Kev Foster?"

Kev frowns back at him.

Drew sticks his hands in his pockets. Struggles to maintain eye contact. "I don't know if you remember me, but—"

"Of course I remember," Kev interrupts.

Drew blinks. "Alright. Um..." He points inside. "Can I come in?"

Kev reluctantly steps aside. Drew walks in. The air is still. A/C loud but not quite working. Matted carpet. Strange stuffy smell. Clean and organized otherwise.

"How did you find me?" Kev asks.

"Theo has his uses." Drew sits on the couch.

Kev crosses his arms. "Hope you don't plan on staying long."

Drew awkwardly stands. "I just want to talk." He licks his dry mouth. "Actually, do you have any coffee? Or maybe es—?" He stops himself. "You probably just have coffee, don't you?"

Kev stares for a bit. Wanders to the kitchen. "I only have almond milk."

"I take it black. But thank you."

Kev runs the water in the next room. Drew tiptoes around the corner into the kitchen. It's a mess. Kev obviously lives alone.

Kev's standing in front of the bubbling coffee machine as it gurgitates, impatient hand on hip. Drew creeps in, snap-clapping ambiently. "This is nice."

"Thanks."

Drew sits at the square table, a flimsy foldable draped in a yellow kitschy tablecloth. "I was worried you wouldn't recognize me."

"Do you have any idea how public of a figure you are?"

"I don't know why."

"Ditto," Kev says in a loaded tone.

Drew's smile goes away.

Kev juts his head toward the coffee pot. "It'll be a bit."

"That's okay." Drew goes quiet again.

They stand there, just where they are, and don't talk for three uninterrupted minutes.

The coffee machine finally sputters, its water bank fully evaporated. Kev grabs the pot. Fills a white coffee cup. Hands it to Drew.

"Thanks. Smells great." Drew blows steam off the top. "What is this, Columbian?"

"French Roast."

"Uh-huh." Drew nods. "*Hon hon hon, oui oui.*"

Kev hardens his face, refusing to crack a smile for something so stupid.

Drew blows some more, the top of the coffee shimmering. "I've been off coke two months now."

Kev hesitates. "Congratulations."

"Hard part's over, thank God, but I'm so tired all the time." Drew looks at the logo on the mug itself. "News For You." An entertainment company by the look of it. Old mug. Definitely not a current employer.

Kev stays where he is by the coffee pot, staring at Drew. "What is this about?"

Drew takes a micro-sip. A little more. "You sound really good. I can't even tell, you know?"

Kev bobs his head, only just now noticing the stains on the kitchen tile. "Thanks."

"Did you go to a therapist or something?"

"I already did. Ages 4 to 16. It was over. It wasn't a problem anymore. Then I moved here and suddenly I'm a stuttering son of a bitch all over again."

"I was the same way." Drew sees Kev's face and quickly adds, "I have Autism. Back in PA, I had everything. Child psychologist since I was 10, then a psychiatrist. I was on anti-depressants, anti-psychotics. Went to an LD school grades 6 through 12. Lots of group therapy." Drew thinks back. "Then college happened. I did great there too. Living away from home. Bouncing around new places. Trying new things. But then I walked into The Factory and suddenly I'm retarded again."

"Don't say that word," Kev mutters.

Drew deflates. "I'm sorry, I..." He pauses. "I'm just saying I understand how hard it must've been for you to—"

"W-why the f-fuck are you in my house right now?" Kev interrupts. He looks at Drew, pretending it didn't happen.

Drew pretends he didn't notice. Takes a nice sip. Licks his lips. "I wanna start up a production company. It's gonna be just as big as Not That Nutty. Problem is I don't have the business expertise to run anything on that scale, so I'd like a partner to help me manage that side of things."

"I'm supposed to be this person?" Kev asks.

"I want to run it with someone I know. Someone who knows me."

Kev smirks. "Oh, I know you alright."

Drew sighs. "I'm sorry for everything that happened with The Professor. I was under... *We* were under a lot of duress. Things got messy. I listened to the wrong people. But that was a very long time ago."

"Do you have any idea what that internship meant to me? I didn't have another option."

"Neither did I."

"Then why'd you fucking blow it up?" Kev shrugs callously. "Work was more important than ego. That's what The Professor told us Day One, but you didn't do that. When things stopped going your way, instead of working harder or at least taking the L like a man, you went out of your way to ruin it for everyone. Shamed The Professor right out of the business."

"Stop defending him."

"He was our boss!" Kev exclaims. "He was paying us! Why'd you do it? Because he gave us mean nicknames? He was a professional, an industry professional!"

"He had no right to—!"

"Interns don't have rights! He was just doing his job, Drew. We all were."

Drew shakes his head. "He wasn't there to help us. He was pitting us against each other. We can look back on it now and think it was all silly or wrong, but at the time it was fucking war. We were all just trying to survive."

"That's why you published that video?" Kev asks knowingly. "S-survival?"

Drew's lips pout.

"There was no t-tactical advantage to th-that," Kev states, his voice shaking. "That was p-p-personal. You wanted to hurt him. You wanted to fucking bury him. There's a word for that, you know, it's called 'revenge.'"

"He beat the shit out of me!" Drew snaps. "Oh, I'm sorry, did you forget that? Don't you remember why?"

"I don't care how big you are now," Kev snipes. "You're still a crybaby narcissist with your head so far up your ass that you can't even fathom how everything isn't just handed over to you on a silver goddamn platter. I powered through that bullshit. I dealt with it. God forbid we did our fucking jobs."

Drew looks away, his heart spent.

Kev tries not to cry himself. He wanders away. Paces back.

Drew looks back at Kev with puffy eyes. "You're wrong. I tried to stop it, alright? Theo kept pressuring me. No matter how many times I said no, he kept trying to convince me." Drew thinks. "I know The Professor was just a product of his time, scared to death of becoming irrelevant. I get that now. I really do. But he committed a fucking crime, Kev. He was a bad person and he deserved what was coming to him."

Kev furrows his brow. "I don't understand your position. Do you hate the guy or pity him?"

Drew shrugs. "I don't know."

Kev hesitates. "What about Trisha?" he rasps. "Did *she* deserve what was coming to her?"

Drew contorts his face. No tears come out, but not for lack of trying. "I've blamed myself for that every day," he whispers, almost too soft for Kev to hear.

Kev frowns, ashamed he even went there. He slowly pulls out a chair. Sits beside Drew. Retreats to an inner world of his own. "I'm just as responsible as you are," he whispers.

Drew looks over at Kev. Kev looks back. They sigh.

"What bothers me so much is that we'll never the whole story," Drew says, his energy spent. "If it was the right thing or just us..." He shakes his head.

Kev nods imperceptibly. "But we knew her, didn't we? You and I?"

Drew nods. "She really was the best of us."

"Amen."

Drew picks up his coffee. Takes a big sip.

Kev studies Drew's face. "It's been hard, not being able to talk about her."

"I don't have much in my life I'm proud of." Drew looks Kev in the eye. "I just don't want it all to have been a waste of time."

Kev looks down at his hands. "What about what I want? Doesn't that matter?"

"Of course it does."

"What if I don't want to work with you?"

Drew closes his eyes. "Why not?" he asks with the mildest hint of annoyance.

Kev shrugs with a sarcastic smile. "Because this is not about me. I know you gave a shit about Trisha, I believe you there, but you never, ever gave a shit about me."

"That's not true."

"You can pick anyone, 'Drew Lawrence.'" Kev pauses. "Why am I so lucky?"

Drew hesitates. "I deprived you of the career opportunity of a lifetime. I want to give that back to you."

"Right after you were dismissed out of the blue?" Kev asks. "Theo still hates my guts, doesn't he? That's why you want me so bad. You want to team up with me just so you can rub it in his face for firing you."

"No."

"Stop roping me in to your bullshit. I'm too old for that. Leave me fucking be."

Drew frowns. Doesn't talk. Just thinks. "That's not why," he lies. "I was always jealous of you. Of your productivity. The way you were never clouded by emotion or petty... whatever. That's why I did all those things back then. I knew I was never gonna beat you."

Kev softens, surprised by the sincerity of Drew's voice. "You really mean that?"

"Yeah," Drew lies again with unwavering eyes.

Kev turns his head away. Scratches his cheek. Looks at Drew's coffee. "You want a top-off?"

Drew nods. "Please." As Kev stands and makes his way to the coffee pot, a horrible pit grows in Drew's stomach, an old sensation he hasn't felt in years. And no drugs or Theo to blame this time. That was all him.

Kev refills Drew's cup. Replaces the pot. Sits back down. "If I were to say yes," he starts, both hands up. He puts them down. "What would our timeline look like?"

Drew chews on that, ignoring the overwhelming guilt washing over him. "I'm looking into office space now. We've got a lot of freedom as to when, but I still wanna start production as soon as possible."

"You already have a project?"

"I started writing it a few days ago. I'm fast. It should be done in a month."

Kev nods. "What about the release?"

Drew contorts his mouth. "I dunno. I'm thinking Christmas 2037."

Kev stares. "2037."

"Yes."

"Why so far off?"

"I'm anticipating a long post-production."

"CGI?"

"Rotoscoping."

Kev raises his brows. "Rotoscoping?"

Drew nods.

Kev scoffs. "'The gentleman seems to know what he wants,'" he quotes.

Drew lets out a soft chuckle. Makes enigmatic eye contact. "You have no idea."

JACOB

All in the Family

EXT. RACE POINT BEACH - DAY

The beach is mobbed, lots of hot gay guys in speedos mulling about.

Jacob sits on a towel under a beach umbrella, eyes squinting even behind his goofy-looking transition lenses. Stewie lays in the sun beside Jacob on his own towel.

STEWIE
Turn it up, Baby Boy.

Jacob reaches for his iPhone. "You Make Me Feel (Mighty Real)" by Sylvester gets louder.

JACOB
I like this one.

STEWIE
You know it?

JACOB
Not really. I might've heard it in a Vine.

STEWIE
I still don't know what Vine is.

Stewie lifts his head. Sees Jacob in the dumps.

STEWIE (CONT'D)
Did I ever tell you about the time The Diva, Moo-Moo, Wilma, Bam-Bam, and I got really drunk the last time we were here?

JACOB
(unenthused)
And you threw up on the dunes, yeah, you told me.

Jacob hesitates.

JACOB (CONT'D)
I can't believe I said all those things.

STEWIE
You really shouldn't dwell on it.

JACOB
I can't help it. I was real a nasty bitch to you.

Stewie looks out at the ocean.

JACOB (CONT'D)
I have so much clarity now, more than ever now that I'm off the meds. But at the same time, my mind is all over the place. I keep saying everything that comes to my head. I really can't control it.

STEWIE
Don't blame your meds.

JACOB
I'm telling you, I used to be able to. When I first started going to Dr. Collins, I was also going to a child psychologist, Dr. Harrison. I met with him once a week to talk about my Asperger's and my family life

and all the problems I had, and he helped me with QR training and how to filter--

STEWIE
QR?

JACOB
A breathing technique to resettle my brain during sensory overload.

STEWIE
You really need to do start doing that.

JACOB
That's what I'm saying. I used to. I had years of training and now it's like I never did, like a whole section's off my resume. I hate going backwards like this. You probably think I can't do it.

STEWIE
I know you can do it.

Jacob softens.

JACOB
After it's all over, I remember everything I said. I really hate how childish I've been acting, and I don't want you to think I'm a child.
(pause)
I always prided myself for not actually being the one that started fights. Now I'm starting everything.
(pause)
And that scares me because I'm afraid I'm gonna lose you because of it. I'll be the one causing our break-up and not even know it.

Jacob stares at Stewie. His great pecs. Big arms. Childish face.

JACOB (CONT'D)
I love you more than anything, Daddy. I don't want to lose you.

Stewie smiles, squinting into the shade.

STEWIE
I don't think you're a kid, Baby Boy. I think you're a sexy, sexy man.

Jacob grins, a bit vulnerable.

JACOB
You're only saying that because I asked for more compliments.

STEWIE
It's still true.

Stewie pounces Jacob onto the sand, tickling his armpits. Jacob loudly giggles, jostling under Stewie's body weight, trapped. Stewie keeps tickling. He finally relents, kissing Jacob deeply.

STEWIE (CONT'D)
I knew that would cheer you up.

Jacob caresses Stewie's scruff. He's getting hard.

JACOB
"I love you more today than yesterday."

STEWIE
"But not as much as tomorrow."

Jacob kisses Stewie again. Slides out from under him.

JACOB
I wanna play something for you.

Jacob scrolls through his Apple Music. Plays an upbeat dance-pop song, a familiar singer chiming in.

STEWIE
Is that the Pet Shop Boys?

JACOB
Yup. It's called "Love Etc." I found out about it while you were unpacking.

STEWIE
I never heard it.

JACOB
It's from '09.

STEWIE
WHAT?

JACOB
They stopped charting in 1987 over here, but they kept having top 20 hits over in England until 2009. They're like Madonna or Michael Jackson big over there.

STEWIE
I can't believe it. It sounds fantastic!

JACOB
You know why they stopped charting over here?

STEWIE
Why?

JACOB
Neil came out.

CUT TO:

EXT. OCEAN - DAY

Jacob and Stewie splash around, swimming farther from the sand. Lots of other guys are nearby. Jacob dips underwater. Splashes his hair around.

STEWIE
Baby Boy has the wet look!

Stewie wraps his arms around Jacob. Kisses his neck.

JACOB
You weren't kidding about your obsession with hair.

STEWIE
No, I'm not.

JACOB
When I played Vertigo for you, I had no idea that was unironically the most appropriate movie for our first date.

Stewie makes out with Jacob. Jacob wraps his arms and legs around Stewie's muscled body, losing himself in Stewie's passion. He side-eyes the bystanders. Some are looking.

JACOB (CONT'D)
This is so unlike you.

STEWIE
We're in a gay space.

JACOB
So what? Why can't you be like this all the time? This isn't the 80s anymore. We've got nothing to be ashamed of.

STEWIE
I'm just not comfortable.

JACOB
What are you afraid of, a hate crime?

STEWIE
You never know.

A SILVER FOX (49) swims over, flabby with a winkled face and bald spot.

SILVER FOX
You're the guys playing all that 80s music, right?

JACOB
Yup.

SILVER FOX
You guys have great taste.

JACOB
He's expanding my 80s knowledge now I've discovered the Pet Shop Boys.

SILVER FOX
I love the Pet Shop Boys. I saw them in New York City back in '93 just after I finished high school.

STEWIE
Those were the days, huh?

SILVER FOX
Yes they were.

The Silver Fox swims on.

SILVER FOX (CONT'D)
Have a nice one!

JACOB
God, that guy had the Pet Shop Boys in his day, and what do I got? Katy Perry? Maroon 5?

STEWIE
Yuck.

JACOB
I can't relate to anything new nowadays. One of the downsides of being a forty-year-old trapped in a twenty-one-year-old's body.

STEWIE
Oh my God, that guy is FORTY-NINE?!

JACOB
Wow.

STEWIE
Can you believe he looks like that and he's YOUNGER than me?

JACOB
What can I say, you defy all laws.
(pause)
Did he do something to look that old or is time really that indiscriminate?

STEWIE
No one wants to look like that. He probably just got too much sun over the years.

JACOB
What about those guys that stay in all day to avoid skin cancer and end up with a Vitamin D deficiency?

STEWIE
That's a problem too.

JACOB
It's ironic. The opposite of a bad thing's just another bad thing. You touch everything you see, kiss everyone, lick everything, and you end up with a disease that can kill you, but if you avoid germs like the plague, you'll end up with a crappy immune system which makes it easier to catch a disease that wouldn't have killed you if you weren't such a germophobe. It's like God or whatever designed the human anatomy to teach us the virtues of moderation. A scientific Catch-22. Too much of anything can kill us.

STEWIE
George Harrison smoked sixty cigarettes a day because he needed to cope with John and Paul rejecting all his songs. Then he smoked sixty a day to cope with being an ex-Beatle and being forced to play songs from a time in his life he was most ashamed of. Then he kept smoking to cope with his fans hating him for going all Ravi Shankar on them. But even when he came back with <u>Cloud Nine</u> and the Traveling Wilburys, his life back to the way it should've been, he didn't wanna stop smoking. He kept on smoking sixty cigarettes a day until he died of throat cancer at fifty-eight. THAT'S what kills people.

JACOB
He was probably happier. You can't blame him for wanting to make his life a bit better.

STEWIE
He could've worked out or traveled. If he did something that was actually good for him, he'd still be alive. How's that different from having sex without a condom or riding a motorcycle without a helmet?

Jacob's smile is gone. He hides his discomfort.

STEWIE (CONT'D)
It's our vices that get us in the end.

CUT TO:

INT. THE MEWS - NIGHT

Stewie and Jacob sit across from each other, picking at their entrees.

STEWIE
Anyone that found out I was working at Lucent would beg me to get them a job. I thought I was gonna be working there for the rest of my life. But then the stock market crashed in 2000. After that? Forget it.

JACOB
The crash was in '08, Daddy.

STEWIE
I'm talking about the crash of 2000.

JACOB
There wasn't a crash in 2000.

STEWIE
Yes there was!

JACOB
If I go on to Wikipedia right now, it'll tell me the US stock market crashed in the year 2000?

STEWIE
Yes.

JACOB
You're not confusing it with '08?

STEWIE
Look it up.

Jacob pulls out his phone. Searches. Stops. Puts away his phone.

STEWIE (CONT'D)
Well?

Jacob shrugs, embarrassed.

STEWIE (CONT'D)
I got laid off because of it. I'd certainly remember it happening.

JACOB
It must've been really bad losing your dream job like that.

STEWIE
The golden years were never gonna last. People need to remember that nowadays.

JACOB
What do you mean?

STEWIE
The Left wants everyone to think it was so unbelievably bad for the gays before, no happiness at all to be found, to gain sympathy in their fight against the Jerry Falwells and Anita Bryants.

JACOB
The who?

STEWIE
But in doing so, they're killing everything that made gay culture so fun in the first place. It's in their best interest to paint the past as backwards, to justify what they're doing.

JACOB
You're really saying it was better when we couldn't get married?

STEWIE
No, I'm saying the gay bars were actually fun back then, great places to meet people. They were never prisons or big flashy campy palaces with drag shows every night. We hated drag back then. They made us look like freaks.

JACOB
But isn't it better that the world accepts drag now?

STEWIE
How is it better? We've got girls all over Woody's now and Stonewall and everywhere else. And we're supposed to be okay with that?

JACOB
It's not too much to ask.

STEWIE
You're just being a devil's advocate.

JACOB
No, I'm not. I really do believe we should be conscious of the future and how our actions affect others. Isn't that better than stubbornly halting progress and keeping everyone in the dark ages?

STEWIE
Is that what you think Conservatives want?

JACOB

If I was in the South and my whole world revolved around the Bible, I'd believe the same thing. But the truth is that the world's full of people that don't believe in the Bible. That gives them no right to hate everyone that's different from them. They act like a bunch of brainwashed cretins refusing to listen to evidence and filling the airwaves for hours about how Millennials and gays and blacks and feminist women are destroying Middle America.

STEWIE

Which is why you're voting left.

JACOB

I'm not a huge Hillary nut. I'm just against censorship. Democrats are the only ones giving marginalized people a chance to speak. They believe in safe spaces, freedom of the press, science, diversity, education, and they accept everyone from all walks of life.

STEWIE

You're saying the Democrats have never gone backwards on anything?

JACOB

Of course not.

Stewie nods.

STEWIE

Who passed "Don't Ask, Don't Tell?" What President signed it?

JACOB

One of the Bushes?

STEWIE

Clinton.

JACOB

I don't think so.

STEWIE

<u>Obergefell v. Hodges</u> and <u>US v. Windsor</u> overturned the Defense of Marriage Act. Who passed the Defense of Marriage Act in the first place?

Jacob hesitates.

JACOB

Bush?

STEWIE

Clinton. When he ran for office, he promised to be the gays' side to get himself elected, but what did he do? He single-handedly delayed our civil rights progress for another twenty years. And now we're supposed to just trust Hillary because she's deemed the right side of history?

Jacob frowns.

JACOB

You can't hold that against her. It was a different time.

STEWIE

Something you do this year can be considered "backwards" five years from now. I know progressivism sounds great, Baby Boy, I used to be one. It's just not realistic to be on the right side of history about everything. The world is messy. There are so many different views and beliefs that cannot mesh

100% with each other, so naturally we can't be a versatile ally to everyone.

CUT TO:

EXT. COMMERCIAL STREET - NIGHT

Stewie and Jacob race down the road past a group of sitting FRAT BROS (21-22)

STEWIE
Hurry up! They're gonna charge a cover!

JACOB
It's just five bucks! I'll pay!

STEWIE
It's not the money! It's the principle!

JACOB
Don't pretend it's not about the money!

BLOND FRAT BRO
Fucking faggots.

JACOB
(laughing)
That guy just called us faggots.

Stewie halts in his tracks. Turns around.

STEWIE
(to Blond Frat Bro)
What did you call me, shit for brains?

The Frat Bros stand, laughing. Jacob tries to pull Stewie back.

JACOB
Baby, come on!

STEWIE
(to Blond Frat Bro)
Come on, say it again motherfucker. See what happens.

The Frat Bros walk away, waving dismissive hands.

JACOB
Come on! Forget them!

STEWIE
They called us faggots!

JACOB
It's just a word.

STEWIE
I don't care! I'm defending myself. No one gets away with calling me that.

JACOB
So what, you're gonna fight them?

Stewie huffs. Walks away with Jacob.

STEWIE
I have a zero-tolerance policy for that BS.

Jacob looks behind him at the Blond Frat Bro in the distance.

JACOB
That guy was really hot.

STEWIE
I know. It's a shame he's so bigoted.

JACOB
Would you like me better if I dyed my hair blond?

STEWIE
No way. It wouldn't look natural.

Jacob deflates.

JACOB
What about dark red?

STEWIE
Absolutely not.

JACOB
Not the whole head, just a patch in the front. It'll look cool.

STEWIE
You look fine just the way you are.

CUT TO:

INT. A-HOUSE - DANCE FLOOR - NIGHT

Stewie and Jacob dance in a sea of men, the DJ blasting "This is What You Came For" by Calvin Harris feat. Rihanna. They're both shocked at how good the other is at dancing.

CUT TO:

BY THE BAR

Stewie and Jacob hunch over the counter, waiting for the Bartender to get to them.

JACOB
I think it's time we finally talked about the elephant in room.

Stewie raises a brow. Looks around.

STEWIE
Here?

JACOB
How can someone as intelligent as you and so thought-out about everything be a Republican?

STEWIE
I'm not a Republican.

Jacob hesitates.

JACOB
But you're voting for Trump.

STEWIE
(looking around)
SHH!

JACOB
I don't get it. Why?

STEWIE
If it were Bernie vs. Trump, who do you think I'd vote for?

JACOB
Trump?

STEWIE
Bernie.

Jacob grins, relieved.

JACOB
I was gonna vote for him too.
(pause)
So what, it's more of an Anti-Hillary thing than a Pro-Trump thing?

STEWIE
No, I really want Trump. I'm tired of the same old career politicians. I've always said we needed a businessman in the White House.

JACOB
That's what Mom said about Romney in 2012.

STEWIE
God, I hated Romney.

JACOB
Why would you like Trump but hate Romney?

STEWIE
Trump isn't a politician.

JACOB
And that's a good thing?

STEWIE
I think so.

JACOB
What about the fact that he's a racist, sexist blowhard?

STEWIE
I know he puts his foot in his mouth sometimes, but he's no more racist or sexist as everyone else back then.

JACOB
I doubt that.

STEWIE
Have you seen the music videos they used to play back then? That's how it was. That was all normal. No one got offended back then.

JACOB
I'm sure they did, they just didn't have the means to--

STEWIE
No they didn't! And Trump's saying everything I want him to say. Cracking down on illegal immigration. Taking down ISIS. Standing up to China and Putin. He's gonna drain the swamp. And he hates the media just as much as I do.

JACOB
He only hates the media because they tell the truth about him.

STEWIE
You've never heard him speak, have you?

JACOB
You'll never get me to watch Fox News. I've seen enough for one lifetime. Dad was obsessed with O'Reily.

STEWIE
I hate O'Reily. And I hate Hannity more. They're just as bad as Anderson Cooper and Don Lemon. I only watch Fox to hear Trump talk without any commentary. If you just listen to him speak for a few minutes--

JACOB
Don't waste your time. I refuse to be converted.

STEWIE
That's what I thought until Sherry, my next-door neighbor at the condo, put him on one time. I realized I was completely wrong about him.

JACOB
You sound brainwashed.

STEWIE
I can say the same thing about you.

JACOB
What did I say?

STEWIE
You said the media only tells the truth about Trump.

Jacob sighs.

JACOB
I know the media misleads people. I'm a VMA major. I know how long it takes to prepare for a live broadcast. There's no way anyone can realistically fill a 24-hour news cycle without going unscripted and speculating everything to death. But even if Fox News is defending Trump's God-given right to smack a child in the face and CNN's condemning him for cruelly smacking that child in the face, the truth is that Trump smacked a child in the face! They can't just make that part up.

STEWIE
Give me an example of something you've heard about Trump.

Jacob thinks.

JACOB
He denied rent to black people. That's pretty bad.

STEWIE
Who said it was because they were black?

JACOB
Lots of people. Expert witnesses.

STEWIE
Of course they were "experts."
(pause)
But even if he did -- and let's be honest, he probably did -- that was something everyone did in New York in the 1980s.

JACOB
You don't think that's wrong?

STEWIE
Of course it's wrong, but it wasn't like Trump was the only one.

JACOB
What about that disabled reporter he mocked?

Stewie rolls his throat.

STEWIE
I admit, it really looks bad. But if you look further into it, you'll realize he does that jittery, cerebral palsy motion whenever he mocks someone talking bad about him. But no, the media wants you to believe he did that BECAUSE the guy was disabled, because that would help keep him out of office, even though it's not true. Even if they retract the story, which they rarely do, that's what most people will ever hear on the subject, and that narrative will live on in their memory forever, and that'll end up being history. And you can quote Wikipedia to them all you want. That's what they'll go their whole lives believing. The media doesn't know the damage their short-term spinning does in the long-term.

Stripping away the context to make him look bad isn't public service. It's wrong and toxic.

Jacob frowns.

STEWIE (CONT'D)

What's wrong?

Jacob shrugs.

STEWIE (CONT'D)

We were never going to agree on everything, Baby Boy. We're two different people.

JACOB

That's what this keeps highlighting.

STEWIE

I keep telling you, I don't want you to think like me just to make me happy. It won't.

(pause)

Don't let anyone bully you into thinking your perspective doesn't matter. They're just people, and people are stupid. Nine times out of ten their perspective isn't actually theirs, it's someone else's. That someone is in the other 10%.

Jacob smiles a bit, comforted by Stewie's wisdom.

JACOB

There is one thing we can agree on.

STEWIE

What?

JACOB

He's not gonna win.

Stewie takes a deep breath, nodding with a crooked frown.

STEWIE

I know.

WHALE

Fire and Brimstone

Whale opens the black wooden door of The Professor's glass cube.

```
                    WHALE
      You wanted to see me, Professor?
```

The Professor looks up from his computer. "Yes, Whale. Take a seat."

Whale tiptoes across the cube, desperately not looking down at the transparent floor. He sits, grounding himself, preparing himself for another whooping regarding his latest email submission.

The Professor turns off his computer monitor. Stares at Whale with a strange smile. "Good work."

Whale furrows his brow slightly.

```
                    WHALE
      Thank you, sir.
```

The Professor crosses his arms.

```
                    WHALE (CONT'D)
      I wasn't expecting that, to be honest.
```

"Aren't you proud of what you've done?"

Whale hesitates. There's a subtext here. He can't quite place it.

```
                    WHALE
      I think so. Yes.
```

"So everything you've done...?" The Professor shrugs. "You think it's earned you a spot on my staff?"

```
                    WHALE
      I had a bit of a rough start, but I think I've made
      up for it. I understand more of what it is you're
      asking of me.
```

The Professor smirks. "Do you now?"

```
                    WHALE
      I do.
```

"So you think I'd hire someone who'd voluntarily sabotage another member of the team?"

Whale's blood chills.

```
                    WHALE
      What?
```

"Someone who'd set the entire organization back weeks of work?"

```
                    WHALE
      What are you talking about?! I didn't--!
```

"Peabrain already told me you did."

Whale gapes, his mind racing so fast his vision was warping.

```
                    WHALE
      I didn't do anything! I swear!
```

The Professor stands. "Do you think so little of yourself that you'd resort to something as low as deleting his files behind his back?"

```
                    WHALE
      How could I have? I was talking to Peabrain the whole
      time!
```

"The moment I heard Peabrain say your name, I knew it was true." The Professor shakes his head. "You're just so desperate. You'd do anything, wouldn't you?"

```
                    WHALE
      I didn't do it! I swear! That's the truth!
```

"But even I know you couldn't have done it alone." The Professor hardens his face. "So who helped you?"

The little voice inside Whale's head tells him to name-drop Cashew. Let him take the blame. You did nothing wrong.

"Well?!" The Professor shouts.

```
                    WHALE
      I don't know! I don't talk to anybody!
```

The Professor studies Whale's face. "I don't believe you."

```
                    WHALE
      IT'S TRUE! PLEASE! IT WASN'T ME!
```

The Professor sighs, a light airy annoyed kind. "You're done. Go down to one of the computers and log out from the cloud."

```
                    WHALE
      WHAT?!
```

"After that my Secretary will set up your—"

```
                    WHALE
      PLEASE DON'T FIRE ME! PLEASE!
```

"You put this on yourself," The Professor says coldly.

```
                    WHALE
      I told you, I DIDN'T DO IT! How can you believe
      Peabrain? There's no proof! There has to be cameras
      you can check! Please believe me! I didn't do it!
```

"Then tell me who did!"

```
                    WHALE
      I DON'T... KNOW!
```

The Professor shakes his head. "I'm glad you're not coming back. You're a fucking stain on this place. I *seriously* regret not picking a better candidate."

Whale hyperventilates, snot running down his nose.

```
                    WHALE
      Please!
```

"You've been here three months and everything you sent me has been absolute dogshit. You completely missed Locarno. Your Venice coverage is mediocre at best. And you're such a sniveling little baby! I already have a child, I don't need another one."

Whale's head goes all fuzzy. Static brain. Actually kinda stings.

```
                    WHALE
     I don't...
```

"In the real world, you work your way up to a private office. I've been patient about it, but you know what? It's not funny anymore."

```
                    WHALE
               (under breath)
     You should of...
```

"What?"

Whale licks his dry lips.

```
                    WHALE
     You should've told me my work wasn't--
```

"*I* should have told you?" The Professor mocks, a hand to his chest. "YOU SHOULD HAVE KNOWN!"

Whale closes his eyes. Tears dripping down.

"Get the fuck out of here. I never want to see you again." The Professor rotates away in his chair. Whale glares at the back of The Professor's head.

```
                    WHALE
     You get something out of torturing us, don't you?
```

The Professor rotates back with a blank expression.

```
                    WHALE (CONT'D)
     You probably came here from wherever you're from to
     make something for yourself. Perhaps to stand out
     because you never got the attention or love you felt
     you deserved in your home country. But then you found
     out how hard America is. How brutal it is to softies
     like you. It ruined you, didn't it? Sucked the fun
     right out of it.
```

The Professor raises his brow.

```
                    WHALE (CONT'D)
     I mean, c'mon. "The Professor?" Really? What a
     fucking joke. If you're such a fountain of knowledge,
     why don't you tell us shit?
```

The Professor folds his hands. His eyes unmoving. Calm looking. He's hard to read.

```
                    WHALE (CONT'D)
     But then I figured it out. You hit it big with Rant.
     That was an accident, wasn't it? You had no idea what
     you did right, but you didn't wanna fuck it up, so
     you made Alabaster King. Same movie, different
     setting. Every movie's the same thing, isn't it? More
     Rants. You're just like every other washed-up
     writer/director. You did one good thing in the 80s
     and have been milking it ever since.
```

The Professor doesn't react. Whale can't tell if his hits are landing or not.

```
                    WHALE (CONT'D)
     But there was one, wasn't there? Carrie-Anne. That
     was different, wasn't it? And what happened? It
     bombed. Because you didn't have it in you anymore.
     That spark. That intuition. It was all gone. You were
     so busy working your ass off, you didn't even see it
     go. But instead of blaming yourself, you blamed the
     Millennials. You just don't understand them, do you?
     What they like. What they'd watch. If only you did,
     right? You'd be back at the top instead of spiraling
     into obscurity. How sad!
```

The Professor stands. Touches a metal button under his desk. CLICK! The transparent glass cube quickly frosts up.

Whale looks around, stunned. He faces forward just as The Professor punches him across the jaw. Whale falls backwards, the top of his chair jabbing into his back, searing pain racing across his face.

WHALE (CONT'D)
OW! WHAT THE FUCK?!

The Professor pulls Whale up by his shirt. Punches Whale across the jaw again. Once more in the gut. Whale gasps. The Professor lets go. Whale hits the floor hard, coughing, tears stinging his eyes. The Professor kicks Whale in the bicep. Whale shrieks.

The Professor looks down at Whale with a bit of a smirk. "I find it so fascinating that someone as smart as you could be so naive." He kicks Whale in the bicep again.

WHALE
STOP!

The Professor jab-kicks Whale in the gut. Whale covers his face, his eyes wet.

WHALE
(wails through tears)
STO-O-O-OP! PLEEEEAAASE!

"I don't do this because my mommy never loved me, or because it's the only way I can get hard, or because I'm a sympathetic victim of the cruel, cruel system." The Professor nudges Whale's side, rolling him onto his back. Places one shoe on either side of Whale's body. Unbuttons his cuffs. Rolls up his sleeves.

Whale opens his eyes, anticipating, too scared to get hit again.

The Professor drops to his knees, straddling Whale's body, ass pressing down on his abdomen. "You really wanna know why I do this?" The Professor leans in, his entire frame pushing Whale against the hard glass floor, his mouth mere inches from Whale's. "Look at me."

Whale reluctantly holds his gaze, eyelids fluttering.

The Professor stares, his cold eyes unblinking. "Because I can," he whispers.

Whale's body trembles.

"I worked my ass off to get to the point where I can beat the shit out of an intern and get away with it." The Professor grabs Whale by the neck and presses down.

WHALE
(choking)
Please!

The Professor raises his right fist.

Whale struggles to move his arms out from under The Professor's knees.

WHALE (CONT'D)
NO! PLEASE NO--!

The Professor punches Whale across the jaw. Whale bends his head back, trying to get away, screaming. Another punch. Whale screeches with all his might, blood running down his face. Another. Whale's vocal pitch jumps, his head spinning. He stops squirming. Can't do anything but take another. Wail. Pray for the end. Another. Another.

The Professor finally stops. Gets back on his knees, studying his handiwork. Wipes the corners of his mouth.

Whale sobs, his eyes closed, too exhausted to make a sound.

The Professor hocks a loogie. Spits on Whale's face. Wipes his bloody fingers on Whale's shirt. Hoists himself up.

Whale rolls over. Too scared to get up.

The Professor buzzes the intercom. The Secretary pokes her head in. Blood all over the floor. Overturned chair. Whale's bloodied beaten face.

"Get the cleaning crew in here," The Professor tells her. "I've got a conference call at five. I want everything back the way it was."

"What about him?" The Secretary asks. No sympathy in her voice. No sorrow. Just business.

The Professor looks over at Whale, his body curled in the fetal position. "Clean him up. Get him out of here. He's done."

"Entirely?"

"Entirely."

The Secretary nods. "Yes, sir."

The Professor leaves the cube. The Secretary steps gingerly onto the frosted glass, dodging spots of Whale's blood. Unhooks a First Aid kit hiding underneath The Professor's desk. Kneels beside Whale. "Roll over, please," she says softly.

Whale doesn't budge. The Secretary touches his shoulder. Whale flinches, crying out gibberish. Scootches away, dragging blood with him across the floor.

"I need to close your wounds. You're not gonna want them to scar."

Whale sobs into his arms. Chills all over.

The Secretary sits on a dry patch on the floor. "Take your time," she murmurs.

Whale doesn't want to move. Too defeated. Too much pain. His eyes peek open. He stares at the frosted glass. Not even one bit transparent. Just cloudy. Cold.

Opaque.

Nothing beyond.

End of the line.

DREW

Criticism Sandwich

Drew stares out the crystal-clear window wall with a despaired frown. The Hollywood Sign stares back. It's right there, perfectly framed between the dimensions of Ephemeral Pictures' two-story office building on Sunset. This conference room could use a bit of work though. Some soundproofing. A new table. Maybe a whisky bar. Not for him of course, Mr. Ten Weeks Sober. For other people. Future people. People of other people meeting his people. God, this city is weird.

A knock on the door. Kev pops his head in. "Samantha's all done."

Drew sighs. "Guess there's nothing more to do."

"Except get the hell to work."

Drew turns around. "Get everyone together. All hands. Even the interns."

Kev furrows his brow. Looks around the conference room. "Don't think they'll all fit in here."

"I'll meet them down there." Drew unbuttons his suit jacket. Takes it off. Slings it over a chair. "Get Patrick or one of his guys to set up a microphone." He unbuttons his shirt cuffs. Folds back his sleeves at the elbow.

Drew looks over the second floor balcony down at the open floor plan below, rows and rows of glass-enclosed departments, desks, TVs, worktables, a transparent labyrinth winding through the filmmaking process in chronological order, starting with development all the way to marketing. He can't see the color coded floor, the visually pleasing gradient from ruby red to elephant gray to jet black. Instead he sees hundreds of faces looking up at him, their chatty voices easing down to a hush. On the makeshift stage's wings is Kev Foster, Head of Development, Tanner Hennessy, Kev's roommate at University of Arizona and Ephemeral's Head of Post-Production, and Greg Stolliday, Drew's former Head of Marketing at Not That Nut Pictures and Ephemeral's Head of Distribution.

Drew descends the stairs. Walks on stage. Looks out at everyone. "Hello," he says into the mic, a bit too loud. He stands back. Adjusts the stand's height. "Can you hear me? Everyone can hear me?"

Everyone nods back. It's a little weird to behold.

"That's good." Drew chuckles. "Hello everyone. I know it's been a bit hectic these past few weeks with all the formalities, but I just got the okay from Samantha, which means we can finally start pre-production!"

The crowd roars with applause and cheers.

Drew laughs. "Whatever's in the coffee, I want some."

Everyone laughs. It's funny cause he used to be an addict.

"Before we get into the nitty-gritty, I wanted to formally start Ephemeral Pictures on a formal note." Drew pauses. Glances over at Kev standing off-stage. "My favorite thing in the world is movies. Not making movies, movies themselves. Watching them over and over. Most of the content I absorb, most of the stories I experience on a daily basis, come from movies. I've decided to return to that love and commit my full attention and drive toward making the kind of movies you can't stop thinking about. The balls-to-the-wall crazy ones from start to finish. The ones that start normal and evolve into something completely different, different themes, unpredictable twists, with a finale no one saw coming. I'm talking style. Creative directors that combine weird things. Full-on minimalism. Raw slice-of-life. The most bonkers possible. Depth. Satire. Ballsy hot takes challenging the norm. The ones that bring something out of you. The ones that make you feel something, that make you think about your life, your place, the ones that ingrain themselves in you, always there in your brain buzzing around and then and then you see something that speaks to you and you realize this is just like it was in that movie and I know what to do and..." Drew takes a deep breath. "Sorry, I went a little off there, um..."

The crowd listens, intrigued by Drew's passion.

Drew clears his throat. "I want this place to encourage inspiration. I don't want it to be a factory churning out the same old shit. I want you all to bring your best selves to work, just as you are. If something's been fascinating you in your spare time, an intriguing hairstyle you saw someone wear on the street, a fantastic coat you saw in a thrift store, the way the lighting was in the bathroom of your favorite bookstore or nightclub, any emotion you have that takes you out of your day, forcing you to sit by a lake and dwell on it. Bring that in. Do something with it. No judgment. You were all chosen because you are the best in your field. You think outside of the box. You want to do things different because you're different. You're weird. You're provocative. You've seen just as many movies as I have. You're past the boring same-olds. You crave shocking. You crave fucking COOL! Do it here. Be that guy or girl that starts the thing everyone's talking about. This place isn't an office. It's a collaboration. Teamwork. A place for feedback, for transparency. If you have any questions about the job, how it all works, how you're doing, what the schedule is, the newest crisis, the big thing I'm excited about, what I feel about anything, what *you* feel about anything, my office door is always open." Drew points at the balcony above. "Come up. Introduce yourself. I'll see what I can do. I don't want an air of mystery or second guessing. It might waste a workday but it sure as hell won't be a waste of time. This place is one of respect. You don't have to conform here, even a little. Treat each other like professionals. Make partnerships. Make friendships. Ephemeral Pictures is a creative sanctuary, a solace for the creative juices to flow, to inspire. Me, Kev, Tanner, Greg, we are not your bosses. We are not a ruling class. We are open to suggestions. To feedback. Don't be afraid of us. You won't be fired for bearing bad news."

Kev smiles from off-stage.

"Our debut is quite an ambitious project. It's a big one. And to alleviate all confusion about it, I want to tell you all about it." Drew looks off stage. "Tanner, the whiteboard."

Tanner pushes a wheelie whiteboard on stage. Drew picks up a dry erase marker. Uncaps it. Draws big letters. Underlines with a flourish.

<u>*Branson!*</u>

"Has anyone ever heard of Jack Branson?" Drew asks the crowd.

Silence.

Drew caps the marker. Magnets it to the board. "In the late 1880s, there was a pretty nasty sodomy scandal in Victorian England called the Montgomery Street Scandal. A bunch of Victorian aristocrats were revealed to be patrons of an all-male brothel for homosexuals. One of those accused patrons was an MP candidate named Edgar Withers. His opponent, a very prolific politician named Geoffrey Grant, was the one that accused him. Edgar sued Grant for libel, and at the trial a male prostitute took the witness stand, an Irishman named Jack Branson, one of the sex workers at the Montgomery Street Brothel, the man Edgar Withers was accused of sleeping with, and he gave a testimony so shocking and explicit that he actually made headlines. Of course the jury sided with Edgar in the end, but historians now know Jack was telling the truth." Drew shrugs. "How could anyone gay back then have the confidence to do that? That's our story. How an Irish homosexual, exiled from his home, was able to earn that moment in the spotlight. It's a story of loss, fear, courage, and pride." Drew nods. "Really writes itself, doesn't it?

Of course the story itself is great, but that's not enough." Drew uncaps the marker. Writes some more under the title.

Musical

"It's also gonna be a musical," Drew continues. "An overlooked genre in desperate need for a revival. It's a genre I've always loved. Much like *Les Misérables, Branson!* will evoke empathy with the power of song, of rising strings, of raw voices, of pain. But it's not just gonna be a musical." Drew adds another word, leaving a generous gap in the middle.

Animated   Musical

"It will be an *animated* musical. Another favorite genre of mine. It'll be crazy. Definitely NOT for kids. You can create different moods with animation. Unique aesthetics. It's an entire industry that needs more adult applications."

The crowd nods, surprised but still invested.

Drew grins. "So what do we got? A biopic of a historically overlooked gay icon. A transformative character arc culminating in an epic courtroom finale. It's a musical. It's animated. That's okay, right?" Drew shakes his head. "*Hamilton* told a true man's story with masterful pathos. Lin-Manuel Miranda used minimalist staging, pulling a Brecht by constantly reminding the audience they're watching a play. He utilized colorblind casting to bridge the America of then and the America of now. But that's not all. Miranda also utilized his favorite genre of music. Much like how Tarantino combined samurai films, kung-fu pictures, blaxploitation and spaghetti westerns to make *Kill Bill* the unique mash-up that it is, I've decided to go a similar route. *Branson!* is a pastiche of animation, movie-musicals, a marginalized gay man's story of overcoming oppression... and the back catalog of the most criminality overlooked artists of all time." Drew scrawls three words in the gap. Underlines the whole thing.

Animated Pet Shop Boys Musical

"*Branson!* will be an animated Pet Shop Boys musical!" Drew declares, both arms out.

The crowd reacts with mixed emotions. Furrowed brows. Confusion. Eye rolls. Drew looks over at Kev. Kev isn't smiling either.

"Just hear me out," Drew continues, capping the marker. "It's not gonna be like *Mamma Mia.* It will not be just another shitty jukebox musical. And who the fuck are the Pet Shop Boys anyway? I'll tell you. Neil Tennant and Chris Lowe, the Pet Shop Boys, were a synthpop duo from the 1980s. I admit that they only had a few years of hits here in the US: 'It's a Sin,' 'Always on My Mind,' 'Rent,' 'What Have I Done to Deserve This?' 'West End Girls,' 'Opportunities (Let's Make Lots of Money),' but they kept having hits in their native UK until 2009, 'Go West,' 'Absolutely Fabulous,' 'Before,' 'Somewhere,' 'New York City Boy,' 'Home and Dry,' 'Miracles,' 'I'm with Stupid,' 'Love Etc.', but they also had great album tracks, 'I Want a Lover,' 'Shopping,' 'Hit Music,' 'The Theatre,' 'Closer to Heaven,' 'For Your Own Good,' 'Here,' 'Psychological,' 'The Sodom and Gomorrah Show,' 'Luna Park,' 'Integral,' 'Vulnerable,' 'King of Rome,' 'Requiem in Denim and Leopard Skin,' 'Fluorescent,' 'Shouting in the Evening,' 'Burn,' 'Into Thin Air,' AND they also have a shit ton of killer B-sides, many of them far better than the studio tracks, like 'In the Night,' 'That's My Impression,' 'Don Juan,' 'The Sound of the Atom Splitting,' 'Losing My Mind,' 'Decadence,' 'Euroboy,' 'Some Speculation,' 'Forever in Love,' 'The Truck Driver and His Mate,' 'How I Learned to Hate Rock 'n' Roll,' 'Try It (I'm In Love With a Married Man),' 'Somebody Else's Business,' 'No Excuse,' 'Jack and Jill Party,' 'Reunion,' 'Up and Down,' 'After the Event,' 'One Night,' 'Fugitive,' 'Glad All Over,' 'The Way Through the Woods,' 'In His

Imagination,' 'Entschuldigung!,' 'Get It Online,' 'In Bits,' 'One-Hit Wonder,' 'The White Dress,' 'A Cloud in a Box,' 'Widersehen,' 'The Dead Can Dance,' 'No Boundaries,' 'Decide…'" Drew's voice trails off.

The crowd stares back. Silence.

Drew clears his throat. "Just take my word for it. The Pet Shop Boys are unbelievable. Neil Tennant's intelligent, witty, ironic lyrics. Chris Lowe's melodramatic, theatrical, groovy, addicting club beats. They're a pastiche of their own. The sheer variety of their A+ output is astounding. And they haven't been overplayed like Madonna or ABBA or Cher or any of them. *Branson!* will introduce a whole new generation to one of the greatest, if not THE greatest, discography of the last sixty years. And I know exactly what songs will work and when. It'll be unbelievable, an unbelievable true story of an unsung hero that transcends time and place, a postmodern pastiche, combining beautiful visuals and moving songs, the 1880s meets the 1980s, a story just as relevant now as it was back then. In other words, an experience you can only have in the movies."

The crowd still isn't smiling.

Drew nods awkwardly. "You guys are the best of the best, which is why I expect nothing less than for *Branson!* to win Best Picture. Thank you." Drew walks offstage. The crowd gasps, gapes, murmurs, laughs, curses, a sharp mist rising after Drew as he climbs upstairs with a cheeky smile.

About an hour later, Kev knocks on Drew's door to find him typing. "You're still working on it?"

"I'll be done tonight, I swear," Drew murmurs. "I'm on the courtroom scene now. It's flying out like crazy." He stops typing with a sigh. "God, that's a lot."

Kev hesitates. "Does this have to be this project?"

Drew rubs his eyes. "You don't think we can do it?"

"An animated Pet Shop Boys musical about a gay Victorian Irish prostitute with a courtroom finale? That's a bit much right out of the gate, don't you think?"

"When the Beatles broke up, the entire world was devastated except George Harrison. Under the encouragement of his buddy Bob Dylan, George went into a studio with Eric Clapton, Klaus Voormann, Billy Preston, Ringo Starr, the entirety of Badfinger, and famous producer/future murderer Phil Spector to make an album of all the songs George wrote for the Beatles only to get vetoed by Lennon and McCartney. It ended up being a triple LP. When *All Things Must Pass* came out, the music world was flabbergasted. The Quiet Beatle had finally been heard. It went on to sell seven million copies in the US alone. That's more than *Imagine* and *Band on the Run* combined."

Kev stares. "Have you ever directed a musical before?"

"There's a first time for everything."

"What about animation?"

"Can't be that different."

"It is unbelievably different. If you really want to make a Best Picture winner, you need someone else to direct it, someone who knows—"

"This is my project!" Drew sternly interrupts. "I found it. I kept it. I wrote it. I'm directing it. That's final."

Kev nods. "So when you said you were open to feedback, you didn't really mean it."

Drew frowns. Rotates his chair away.

Kev turns to leave. Stops. "I'm not calling you a bad director, you know. You earned the fuck out of that Oscar nom for *Pacé*. I mean it. I cried all three times I saw it."

Drew softens, smiling a bit. "Thanks."

"But as your partner, I'm advising caution. Films of this scope, the ones so obviously vying for the top prize, those are the ones critics want to tear down. They will look for anything that will hurt its chances. The execution has to be flawless. Every performance has to be pitch-perfect. Their *pitch* has to be pitch-perfect. The cast has to be spot-on. There can be no stale jokes, no obtuse metaphors, nothing goofy or unintentionally funny. It can't be too long. It can't be too short. It has to have the right number of endings. Perfect songs choices. Not too many songs. Not too few. Anything even remotely offensive to any minority group. And then there's the historical accuracy hounds."

"They're singing the Pet Shop Boys in Victorian London. No one will care if they're riding a kind of carriage twenty years too early."

"Yes. They. Will. You can't believe what these people end up having a problem with. And I get it, you want *Branson!* to be your *Les Misérables*. But a project like this needs to be in the right hands if you don't want it to end up like *Cats*, and I'm sorry Drew, those hands are not yours."

Drew stares with shock.

Kev half-bows. "Good day." He turns and leaves.

Drew sits on his bed around 3 AM. The balcony door's open, a soft ocean breeze flowing in. Drew's lip quivers as he reaches the final scene of *Branson!*, Jack and Oliver lying on their backs in the empty brothel, smiling up at the dusty rafters just before they head off to Paris together. How sweet. How romantic. So overwhelmingly earned.

Drew presses and holds the Page Up button. Scene by scene flies by. He can't believe all that actually came out of him. Any of it. He finally lands on the title page.

<u>BRANSON!</u>

Written by

Drew Lawrence

Drew reaches for his phone. Taps Kev's number. Puts it to his ear.

"Hey," Kev croaks over the phone, half-asleep. "What are you still doing up?"

"I just finished the final draft."

"Good. Send it over."

Drew scratches his left nipple under his tank top. "It's the best thing I've ever written, Kev. It deserves the best."

Kev hesitates. "Are you saying what I think you're saying?"

"How long will it take to find a director?"

Kev puffs out air. "I've got a few candidates in mind. We'll start shopping tomorrow."

"Kev?"

"Yeah?"

"Thank you for being honest with me and all."

"Just following orders."

Drew smirks. "Have it your way then."

"Don't stay up too late, huh boss?"

"We'll see. Night."

"Night." Kev hangs up.

Drew tosses his phone onto the mattress. Looks out at the balcony. The moon's still out and shining through. Drew moves his laptop aside. Steps out onto the tiled balcony. Cool night air. Moonlight all around. Drew leans over the railing. Gazes out at Venice Beach, the Pacific Ocean shimmering as it rocks along. So quiet out there. No traffic. No pedestrians walking the marina. He can actually hear the ocean waves.

JACOB

Manchester by the Sea

EXT. PROVINCETOWN HOTEL ROOM - BALCONY - NIGHT

Jacob sits naked in their private hot tub. He's looking up at the moon, glasses fogged from the steam, listening to the ocean waves crashing below. A naked Stewie walks over with two cocktails, an Ultimo soda and a screwdriver.

STEWIE
Hope I made it right.

Stewie hands Jacob the screwdriver.

JACOB
You didn't want one?

STEWIE
I never drink spiked OJ. It's my favorite part of the morning. Don't wanna ruin it.

Jacob stares at the screwdriver through the glass. Stewie slides into the hot tub.

STEWIE (CONT'D)
Did a bug get in it?

JACOB
I'm not a devil's advocate.

Stewie furrows his brow.

STEWIE
Alright.

JACOB
I know how I come off. I always seem to give the absolute worst first impressions.

STEWIE
Not to me you didn't.

JACOB
You caught me on a good day. Most times when I'm not in control of my environment or when I'm doing something I really don't wanna do I become insufferable. People end up trying to fill in the blanks with their biases, but they're always wrong about me. I don't blame them though. They can't understand what I mean if I don't make an effort to be understood.
(pause)
The chances of me being unique are infinitesimal so naturally I assume everyone else is the same way. And in my quest to decipher other people, I tend to ask strange questions to tune in to what they really mean. That's why I do it.

STEWIE
Frankly, it comes off as argumentative.

JACOB
I know it does. Which is why I feel the need to explain myself.

Stewie leans back.

STEWIE
Thank you. It actually helps.

Jacob meekly looks at Stewie.

JACOB
Daddy?

STEWIE
Mm?

JACOB
I need to tell you something.

STEWIE
What?

JACOB
It's not good.

Stewie's face goes numb.

JACOB (CONT'D)
I've been wanting to tell you for weeks now, but I just couldn't find the right time.
(pause)
After what you said at the club last night, I feel comfortable telling you, but I know you're not gonna like it.

STEWIE
Is it bad?

Jacob avoids eye contact.

JACOB
Depends who you ask.
(pause)
To you, yes.

Stewie sighs.

DISSOLVE TO:

INT. PROVINCETOWN HOTEL ROOM - NIGHT

Jacob and Stewie sit on their king bed, both of them loosely wrapped in towels. Jacob takes off his glasses. Rubs the bridge of his nose.

JACOB
I didn't know I was gay for a long time. I first started realizing when I was thirteen, but I was in denial for such a long time. I didn't actually come out until June 7, 2014.

STEWIE
You remember the date?

JACOB
Of course I do. It wasn't planned, it just happened. And I'm so happy it did.
(pause)
But one of the reasons I didn't know for so long was because I never really understood what sex was. Mom refused to let me watch rated R movies until I was seventeen. They never gave me The Talk either. Mom said it was Dad's job. Dad expected me to find out from my friends, and I didn't have any friends, none that would actually do that at least. I didn't want to be friends with people like that to look good for Mom.

STEWIE
What about sex ed?

JACOB
Eagle Ridge didn't teach sex ed until 12th grade.

STEWIE
That's ridiculous.

JACOB
It's effed up. You know why? Because even Eagle Ridge infantilizes people with disabilities. They waited until we were eighteen to tell us about pregnancy and STDs and whatever. But of the eighty-five kids in the entire school, only five of them were girls. You know what happens when you refuse to give a gaggle of mentally disabled pubescent boys the sexual education they need? You get a whole bunch of repressed sexual deviants. And I... I had a bit of a problem myself.

Stewie frowns.

JACOB (CONT'D)
I never wanted to be outed by being with a guy, so I waited until I came out to have sex. When I finally did, I wanted to make up for lost time.

STEWIE
How many guys are we talking about?

Jacob pauses to calculate.

JACOB
From Veteran's Day Weekend 2014 until I met I you...
(sighs)
About thirty different guys over an 18-month period. I met them online for the most part. Grindr, Craigslist.

Stewie doesn't react.

JACOB (CONT'D)
About half of those guys were in Florence alone.

Stewie sighs, visibly hurt.

JACOB (CONT'D)
I didn't know most of them. They only had two gay bars in Florence, a Lumber's lookalike called Piccolo and one of those darkroom sex places called Crisco. I went there a lot. Crisco, I mean.

STEWIE
So when we were in the Black Bear bathroom and you said you never did that before--

JACOB
That was a lie.

STEWIE
So you were trying to pick up that troll.

JACOB
No! I already told you. That was the truth.

Stewie nods apologetically.

STEWIE
Did you use condoms at least?

Jacob hesitates.

JACOB
Most of the time no.

Stewie looks away, his lips contorted. He clears his throat and his face returns to normal.

STEWIE
Before we leave tomorrow, I want you to take an HIV test. It won't be hard to find one in this place.

JACOB
I already got one. I'm clean.

STEWIE
I don't care. You're taking another one.
(pause)
So will I.

Jacob lowers his head. Fiddles with his fingers.

JACOB
There's more.

Jacob hesitates. Re-crosses his legs.

JACOB (CONT'D)
In Florence last April I met an American guy named Christopher. I told you about him.

STEWIE
The guy you wrote A Night With Myself about.

JACOB
Yeah. He used to be married to a woman and had a few kids and now they're divorced.

STEWIE
How old did you say he was?

JACOB
Forties. Late forties, I think. He really was exactly like me in every way. Back when I was closeted and in denial, I actually considered marrying a woman one day to pass on the Andrezj name. My dad kept reminding me I was the last male Andrezj. That really got into my head. I was willing to put someone through that, but Christopher did it for me. And it comforted me to know he was able to realign himself in the end, but I felt bad that it took him so long. We were both making up for lost time, I guess.

Jacob takes a deep breath.

JACOB (CONT'D)
We met up several times, just sexual. We always fooled around in his apartment on the other side of the city, right on the Arno. I'd sneak in and we'd do it and I always took a Ridr home. And we never used condoms because he swore he was clean, and I knew he probably was, but I know that's still reckless. But that's why I did it. It was nice being free of Mom's influence for once. Anything I did out there stayed out there.

Jacob licks his cracked lips.

JACOB (CONT'D)
One night he got some cocaine and we did a few lines together.

Stewie closes his eyes, sighing with disappointment.

JACOB (CONT'D)
We got drunk. Went back to his place. Screwed like maniacs. And I wanted to play some music while we did it, and I didn't have my iPhone out there because of how expensive it would be data-wise, so we used his phone. He only had free Spotify. I couldn't pick anything I wanted. And I was really getting into Meat Loaf for the first time, I was playing Bat Out of Hell religiously, just as much as I do now with the Pet Shop Boys, so I looked up Meat Loaf on his phone

and I found three songs to pick from: "Bat Out of Hell," "Paradise By the Dashboard Light," and "Two Out of Three Ain't Bad." I knew "Two Out of Three Ain't Bad" was too slow, and I felt "Paradise By the Dashboard Light" was a bit too cheesy and all over the place for hardcore bareback sex, so I chose "Bat Out of Hell."

(pause)

Once we were done, I called a Ridr to take me home, and he went downstairs with me while I waited, and...

Jacob's heart beats faster.

JACOB (CONT'D)

And it was around three in the morning, so the street was dead. No one's around. No one's on the road. Just a few streetlights and a row of parked cars on my side of the street. And I noticed headlights, or at least I thought they were headlights, and it's three in the morning, so why WOULDN'T it be my Ridr? So I walked a bit into the street, just in line with the park cars, just to poke my hand out and let my Ridr know I was there, right?

(pause)

Well, it wasn't my Ridr, it was a guy on a motorcycle. And just as I realized my mistake, I hear this horrible crash and the bike's flying past me on its side, and sparks are flying everywhere and there was this horrible screeching noise, and...

(pause)

And I remember still being a bit drunk and numb from the coke and it's all happening in front of my eyes with such strange fakeness. Not like a movie with all the cuts and shakeycam, just... happening right there in front of my eyes. The biker's lying on the ground, his helmet still on with the visor cracked open, and when I crouched down to check on him, I could see his eyes were rolled back and he was twitching, and there was a little bit of blood on his nose, and I didn't know what to do. All the neighbors came out and they were all speaking Italian at us, and Christopher and I didn't know what to do, we were panicking, and I think one of the neighbors called the ambulance, but I just kept staring at the biker guy's face, and then he just stops twitching right there and he... died. He died. Right there in front of me.

Jacob's breath wavers.

JACOB (CONT'D)

And Christopher and I just walk away. We're just breaking down crying "Oh God! Oh God!" and I was so scared.

(pause)

And my Ridr finally showed up and I took it home and I went into my room and cried my heart out.

Stewie puts a soothing hand on Jacob's back.

STEWIE

He probably wasn't wearing a helmet.

JACOB

He WAS wearing a helmet!

(pause)

Christopher didn't want to see me again. He was so shook about it days later. I was okay with that, but...

Jacob stares off with cold eyes.

JACOB (CONT'D)

I'm not entirely unconvinced that the guy died because of me.

STEWIE
You can't blame yourself.

JACOB
The first week I was there, I noticed how fast motorcycles sped down those streets. If they hit anyone it's the pedestrian's fault for being in the road. I thought that fact was interesting, so I used that as the titular murder method in Murder in Milan, and that was BEFORE this happened.
(pause)
It was three in the morning, Daddy. He wasn't expecting anyone to be on the street. I popped up from that line of cars. I probably spooked him enough for him to lose balance.

Stewie sighs.

JACOB (CONT'D)
And then I remembered the song. "Bat Out of Hell." I could've picked any song and I picked the one about a man dying in a motorcycle crash after having a one-night stand?
(shakes head)
It was just too freaky. The chances of that. It had to have been a sign. I didn't even believe in God and I knew it had to have been a sign. I was taking too many risks. I was only gonna end up dead if I kept going down that road. And that night I felt so cold and alone and godless, and I actually felt scared.
(pause)
But then the next morning, I felt nothing. No PTSD. No grief. No regret. I watched a man die because of my stupidity and I didn't even feel bad about it. Like it was nothing to me. That's what scared me more than anything. I know you don't want to hear this, I blame my autism. That's a core definition, lack of empathy.
(pause)
And the whole thing just made me scared of how I am if I don't let someone else tell me what to do, because the last time I was just me, I got someone killed. And I just watched and I didn't do anything to save him and I felt absolutely nothing bad the day after.

Stewie holds Jacob close.

STEWIE
My poor baby.

JACOB
I didn't mean what I said yesterday. I always wanted a traditional life. I never had that. I'm just so used to parroting my friends at school. I don't wanna fuck everything up again, so I stick with the crowd.

Jacob moves away from Stewie, sniffing.

JACOB (CONT'D)
But they all keep telling me I should be happy that my family is in shambles because I'm liberated from the oppressive heteronormative blah-blah-blah and they all hate tradition and masculinity and blame nuclear families and neurotypical people and white straight male establishments for all the problems in the world, and there's always someone suffering way more than you and the more minority communities you're a part of, the more "valuable" you are, but I don't want to be proud to be special or odd or be ashamed to be so masculine. I just want to be a normal guy! There's nothing wrong with being normal! A normal life with a normal childhood and a home that

stays there and an actual family! I don't want to be ashamed of thinking like that.

Jacob wipes his eyes, but more tears stream out.

JACOB (CONT'D)
(incredibly emotional)
It's just devastating. Truly, utterly devastating. There's this hole, this big, gaping hole and absolutely no way I can actually fix it. And I go online and I Google things, and all the results are trying to sell me something, but I just want answers, and I don't have anyone to ask because my questions are too big. That's what families are supposed to be for! And I'm not one of those people that gets triggered by the passage of time. I don't binge Disney movies or buy Dunkeroos by the gross or bitch about adulting all the time. I'm not like that. I'm an adult. I've been an adult for a long time. This is not some stupid childhood-is-over reaction. I'm not like that. I know it's just a house and my family really wasn't that great as a unit, but why did it have to be such a hard transition? Why couldn't it just phase out like it was supposed to? Where's my "go back to my hometown to visit Mom" moment? Where's my "We turned your room into a workout center" moment? I loved that house. I wanted to inherit that house. I woulda bought it off of them if I had the chance. But everything was just too damn fast! They didn't even wait until I was done school, they just did it, and I didn't even know it was happening until after it already happened! They took that from me!
(growling)
THEY TOOK THAT FROM ME!

Stewie frowns from afar, overwhelmed, his heart breaking.

JACOB (CONT'D)
If I knew it was all gonna be over, I would've done things differently. I would've said things and done more and appreciated it more, but now I can't. I don't have them anymore. I don't have anything anymore. They don't give two shits about me.

Jacob's face scrunches.

JACOB (CONT'D)
(whimpers)
And I don't blame them because I don't give two shits about them.

Jacob closes his eyes and sobs, his entire body shaking. Stewie opens his arms and holds. Snot dibbles down Stewie's naked torso. He shushes softly.

STEWIE
It's okay. Let it out.

JACOB
I'm so sorry! I'm sorry I'm like this.

STEWIE
I still love you.

JACOB
I love you.
(through tears)
God, I love you so much!

Stewie squeezes Jacob tighter.

JACOB (CONT'D)
I just want to be better for you.

STEWIE
You couldn't be any better.
(smiles)
You're my Baby Boy.

JACOB
But why would you wanna be with someone like me? I'm so fucked up and broken and an absolute mess.

STEWIE
No you're not.

JACOB
Normal people know they're normal, but I don't know what normal is. I don't know if any of this is normal. I don't know how much of this is because of my Asperger's or the fact that I'm young or just...
(pause)
Weak.

Stewie takes a deep breath.

STEWIE
You ever see <u>The Sword in the Stone</u>?

Jacob looks up at Stewie.

JACOB
The stupid Disney King Arthur movie?

STEWIE
It's not stupid. I always thought Arthur was kinda cute.

JACOB
He's a kid!

STEWIE
So was I. He had the blond boyish haircut. And I know I'm not the mythology expert you are, but I do know King Arthur because of that silly, silly musical.

JACOB
You don't like musicals?

STEWIE
I hate musicals.

JACOB
But you like music.

STEWIE
It's the breaking into song and dance I can't stand.
(pause)
Arthur was a prodigy, destined for greatness. But he'd be nothing without Merlin, remember?

JACOB
Of course I remember.

STEWIE
Because Merlin was his role model. Arthur needed him to see the big picture.
(pause)
I know you're smart, Baby Boy. You're so intelligent for your age, so mature to be able to apologize like it's nothing and accept a difference of opinion with grace. I've always known you've had the strength to be a great man. You just need a role model. Arthur did too. Because life is much stranger than you think it is. The world is full of people that have to choose every day between what is right and what is easy. And one day, if they're lucky, they'll know what to do all on their own. I know it's only a matter of time before you get there. I know you can do it. Because I know you.

Stewie wipes away Jacob's tears. Kisses him slow and tender. Jacob breathes deep, regaining his strength.

JACOB
I think we should fool around.

STEWIE
Not until you get tested.

JACOB
You know I don't have it.

STEWIE
I don't want to take the chance. Respect my limits.

Jacob nods, disappointed.

STEWIE (CONT'D)
We can still jerk off.

JACOB
Thank you.

CUT TO:

I/E. STEWIE'S JEEP - DAY

Jacob rides shotgun as Stewie speeds down the highway heading home, a big smile on his face, wind whipping his hair. Stewie smiles too. Turns up the radio. "Jump" by Madonna is on.

JUMP CUT TO:

WHALE

Burning Bush

Whale stands on the concrete edge of the Colorado Street Bridge, staring down at the sparse parkland of the Arroyo Seco. The soft rush of cars on the Ventura Freeway behind him is strangely comforting. He's ready. He wants to. But he can't. He's too scared.

Instead of dwelling on the netherworld and dark nothingness one step ahead of him, Whale recalls his Ridr driver's reaction to his bruised and bandaged face as he slipped into the car outside The Factory. How different it was compared to the same driver's reserved silence when Whale confirmed that, yes, he really is asking to be dropped off in the middle of the night halfway across Pasadena's infamous Suicide Bridge. Almost as if he didn't blame him.

"*Scusa*?"

Whale slowly turns his head.

A man in his forties meekly steps into the lamplight. Black leather jacker. Black beard with scruff running down his neck. Lit cigarette in his hand. "Are you aware that you're standing on the edge of a dangerous drop?" he asks in a clear but prominent Italian accent.

Whale looks back down at the patchy grass one-hundred-fifty feet below him.

```
                    WHALE
     I am aware.
```

The Italian Man takes a drag. "And I take it there's nothing I can say to change your mind?"

```
                    WHALE
     Don't think so.
```

"Alrighty then." The Italian Man turns his back. Walks a bit aways.

Whale takes a deep breath. He's ready again but his legs don't seem to want to move.

The Italian Man blows smoke up at the stars. "You're still there?"

```
                    WHALE
     Temporarily.
```

The Italian Man smiles mysteriously. "Aren't we all."

Whale doesn't move. Just stares down into the darkness.

The Italian Man hunches over the railing beside Whale's shoes. "You're in the entertainment industry, I take it."

```
                    WHALE
     What gave it away? The fact that we're in Los
     Angeles?
```

"Non-Hollywood people have the decency to kill themselves at home. Movie people need an audience, even at the end."

```
                    WHALE
     Don't get your hopes up.
```

"Second thoughts?"

```
                    WHALE
     Nope.
```

The Italian Man flicks ash over the edge. "Then do it already."

```
                        WHALE
        I can't.
```

"Why not?"

Whale hesitates.

```
                        WHALE
        I'm afraid of heights.
```

The Italian Man laughs hard. "That is fucked up!"

```
                        WHALE
        I'm glad you find the irony of my predicament
        hysterical.
```

The Italian Man drags his cigarette, gazing at the Los Angeles skyline in the distance. Flicks ash off the bridge. "Don't you?"

```
                        WHALE
        I find it inconvenient.
```

"One last laugh from God, huh?"

```
                        WHALE
        Something like that.
```

The Italian Man finally notices the bandages on Whale's bruised face. "You're supposed to look like that after you jump."

```
                        WHALE
        Gallows humor.
```

"When in *Roma*." The Italian Man takes one last drag. Throws the cig over the edge. "I read somewhere that people afraid of heights aren't actually afraid of falling to their death. They just don't trust themselves enough not to jump."

Whale hesitates.

```
                        WHALE
                  (murmurs)
        Yeah, I've heard that too.
```

The Italian Man nods. "Tell you what, since I'm most likely the last person you'll ever see, humor me on something." He reaches into his jacket. Pulls a pack of cigarettes. "I'll bet you any amount of money I can get you to step off that ledge with just three questions."

```
                        WHALE
        What good's a bet if I jump?
```

"Like I said, any amount of money." The Italian Man lights up with a smirk. "Seriously though, I can do it in three. If not, I'll let you jump in peace."

Whale hesitates.

"C'mon," the Italian Man whispers with pleasant charm. "What do you have to lose?"

Whale exhales slowly through his nose.

```
                        WHALE
        Three questions.
```

The Italian Man holds out the pack. Whale shakes his head. The Italian Man pockets the pack. "Question one," he says, dragging his cig. "What's your name?"

```
                        WHALE
        My name was Jacob Andrezj.
```

"Nice to meet you, Jacob," the Italian Man says, ignoring Whale's intentional use of past tense. He holds his hand out to shake. "Dario."

Whale side-eyes Dario's open palm.

```
                    WHALE
        The second question?
```

Dario lowers his hand. "What was the last movie you saw?"

```
                    WHALE
        The last movie?
```

"Did I stutter?"

```
                    WHALE
        Is that the third question?
```

Dario laughs. "You're funny!" Takes another drag. "And stalling. C'mon, the last movie you saw."

```
                    WHALE
        Clerks.
```

Dario nods generously. "*Clerks*. Okay. Not bad." He drags again. "And the final question."

Whale avoids eye contact. Keeps staring down into the abyss.

Dario dons a solemn frown. "Jacob. Do you really wanna leave this world—?"

```
                    WHALE
        Yes.
```

"You didn't let me finish." Dario pauses. "Jacob. Do you really wanna leave this world... knowing *Clerks* is the last movie you'll ever see?"

Whale doesn't move, a frown forming.

Dario raises his brows in anticipation.

Whale reluctantly turns around. Steps off the ledge one foot at a time.

Dario grins. "See? I told you."

```
                    WHALE
        How'd you know it was gonna work? What if I watched a
        good one?
```

"To go out on? No such thing. Not to movie people."

Whale sits on the ledge.

```
                    WHALE
        You do this a lot, don't you?
```

Dario shrugs. "When I can."

```
                    WHALE
        There are worse hobbies, I suppose.
```

"Nothing better, actually." Dario sits beside Whale, the two of them watching the cars on the Ventura Freeway like a couple of chums.

```
                    WHALE
        What are you, an EMT or something?
```

"Just some guy." Dario tosses the butt on the ground. Squishes it. "I ride past here all the time on my way home from work. Good place to smoke. Meet new people."

```
                    WHALE
        What do you do?
```

"I run a speakeasy in Los Feliz, Knock Twice."

```
                    WHALE
        Never been.
```

"It's pretty good. You should come by. Courvoisier sidecars half off every Tuesday."

Whale smirks.

```
                    WHALE
        I love sidecars.
```

"They're delicious." Dario studies Whale's facial bandages. "Whoever hit you knew what he was doing."

```
                    WHALE
        I doubt I was his first.
```

"There's no way you were. He aimed for pain, the most he could without sending you to the hospital."

```
                    WHALE
        You sure you're not an EMT?
```

"Pay-per-view at work. Lots of boxing."

Whale looks away, embarrassed.

Dario frowns. "He's somebody isn't he? Someone who can't afford to get caught."

```
                    WHALE
        Yeah.
```

"Wanna tell me who?"

Whale shakes his head.

"Even though he beat you like that?"

```
                    WHALE
        It's none of your business.
```

"Of course. I'm sorry." Dario faces forward, sighing. "He's your boss?"

```
                    WHALE
        Yup.
```

"Do you think you deserved it?"

Whale hesitates.

```
                    WHALE
        I deserved something. Not this.
                 (pause)
        He wanted us to be fighters. I thought he would've at
        least respected me for it. Instead he beats my face
        in.
```

"What do you do for him?"

```
                    WHALE
        I'm just an intern. He hates Millennials.
        Legitimately despises them. I think he just wants to
        hurt us to feel good.
```

"He beats everyone else?

```
                    WHALE
        Just me apparently.
```

Dario nods. "Maybe this is another test."

```
                    WHALE
        I'm done. He fired me.
```

"Did he actually fire you or did he just say you were fired?"

Whale hesitates.

```
                    WHALE
        I don't know. I've never been fired before.
```

"I think you should go back."

```
                    WHALE
        I don't want to go back.
```

"It'll impress him."

```
                    WHALE
        I don't wanna impress him. I don't give a crap about
        him anymore. I just want it to be over.
```

"You don't want it to be over," Dario says softly. "You just want your life to mean something again."

Whale sighs.

```
                    WHALE
        A little over a year ago, I was sitting in some club
        in Boston by myself, debating whether or not to call
        it a day, when a woman sits next to me and starts
        talking. I open up a bit. She convinces me to stay
        out. So I did.
```

Whale looks at Dario.

```
                    WHALE (CONT'D)
        If she didn't do that, I wouldn't have met the man
        that changed my life.
```

Dario frowns sympathetically. Whale faces forward.

```
                    WHALE (CONT'D)
        I used to think she was an angel.
                (pause)
        Now I feel stupid believing in childish things like
        angels and fate. Just me assigning meaning to make me
        feel better about myself.
```

"We all assign meaning. It's only way we can live."

```
                    WHALE
        I don't think The... my boss assigns meaning.
```

"I'd say so." Dario pauses. "Maybe he singles you out more than the others because he sees too much of himself in you. You're making the same mistakes he did. He's really just hitting himself."

```
                    WHALE
        That can't be true.
```

"Why not?"

```
                    WHALE
        It's too simple.
```

"Simple beings tend to be simple. That's a fact."

```
                    WHALE
        It's naive to think like that. The world is just too
        chaotic. And I'm too weak to handle it.
```

"You're not weak. Just innocent."

```
                    WHALE
        That's not good either.
```

Dario smirks. "People always assume innocence is the absence of real-life experience. Something to be ashamed of. But really it's the greatest thing life has to offer. It's also the hardest to maintain. Worse than a bank account. Worse than a child." Dario points to Whale's upper body. "Worse than muscles, which by the way..." He holds up an O.K. sign, clicking his tongue.

Whale beams, blushing a bit.

```
                    WHALE
        Thank you.
```

"Men really need to compliment other men more," Dario says. "Anyway, we're all born innocent. Some of us are lucky enough to carry that innocence into adulthood. But life happens. It hardens people. Makes them vitriol. Some last longer than others."

```
                    WHALE
        But it's inevitable?
```

Dario hesitates. "Some say it is."

```
                    WHALE
        What about you? What do you say?
```

Dario shrugs. "I don't know. Some lose it by the time they're twenty-five, some hold on to it into their fifties. Maybe no one has it their whole life." He pauses. "Maybe they used to a hundred years ago, before the Internet, back when people didn't change so much."

Whale gives a crooked frown.

"Or maybe not, I dunno. Maybe it's supposed to be like this." Dario looks behind him at the LA skyline. "All I know is this place doesn't help. Too many human beings crammed together. A breeding ground of impurity. Naturally produced. Naturally contagious."

```
                    WHALE
        I blame the traffic.
```

Whale smirks. Looks at Dario.

Dario doesn't smile. "Impatience brings out the worst in people." He faces forward again. "The thing about innocence is the moment you lose it, you lose it for life. You can't get it back. No matter how much money you spend, how many hours you pray." He glances at the stretch of ledge to his left. "How many lives you save."

Whale frowns.

"It helps, but..." Dario purses his lips. "It's never quite the same."

```
                    WHALE
        I'm already feeling it. Might even be too late.
```

Dario faces Whale with soft eyes. "It's not. Not for you."

Whale stares back.

"I can hear it in your voice," Dario says. "Gentleness. Hope. Even though you've been through a lot, your soul hasn't been tarnished yet."

```
                    WHALE
        You can't possibly know that.
```

"It's just an intuition I have, seeing so many people at their lowest. Think I'm developing a gauge." Dario smiles. "I've got a feeling you'll be just fine."

Whale's face contorts, emotion flooding in.

Dario looks down at Whale's hand. Takes it. Holds it with both hands, looking Whale dead in the eye. "So I ask you, please, on behalf of all the other poor souls in Los Angeles... Keep going for our sake."

Whale awkwardly nods. Takes his hand away.

```
                    WHALE
      A bit melodramatic, don't you think?
```

"So is jumping off a bridge." Dario looks off with a furrowed brow. "And suicide in general, I suppose."

Whale nods, rubbing the hand Dario touched.

Dario slides off the ledge. Adjusts his jacket. "So, Jacob, what are you going to do?"

```
                    WHALE
      I'll go back on Monday. See what happens.
```

Dario squints, an enigmatic smile on his face. "Go now."

Whale blinks.

```
                    WHALE
      What?
```

"Go there now. Tonight."

```
                    WHALE
      Tonight?
```

"Why not? Get a jump on it."

Whale furrows his brow. The way Dario's looking at him gives him the creeps.

```
                    WHALE
      It's closed. I think they'll consider that
      trespassing.
```

"There's cleaning people, aren't there? Know any good places to hide while you get some work done?"

Whale hesitates.

```
                    WHALE
      Yeah.
```

"He might just fire you again if you go in on Monday. He'll be more likely to let you stay if you have unsubmitted work, won't he?"

Whale tongues his cheek.

```
                    WHALE
      I mean... I guess.
```

"Then do it." Dario holds his shoulders up. "What's the worst that can happen?"

Whale takes a deep breath. He really doesn't want to go home to Alex.

```
                    WHALE
      Sure. Why not.
```

Dario steps backwards. "*Ciao, bello.*" He turns and keeps walking out of the lamplight.

Whale sticks his hands into his pockets. Walks away from the ledge, just far enough to get a good Ridr pickup.

An engine rips the silence of the night, making Whale flinch. A single headlight flicks on a few yards ahead of him. Whale holds up hand to block the light from his eyes, his heart pounding. Another roar as a helmeted Dario kicks off his motorcycle, accelerating past Whale down the length of the Colorado Street Bridge toward the Ventura Freeway junction. Whale watches Dario's bike fade away into the night, disturbed air whipping around him, eyes wide with superstitious terror.

DREW

Groveling for the Public Domain

"You got fire, baby, canya dig it?" says Eli Kerbinger, leaning back in his chair, legs on the conference table, collar popped with aviators on.

Drew and Kev sit across from Eli. "Can you say that again?" Drew asks.

"*Branson!*, my man, *Branson!*. You got yourself hot fire. Hot smoke billowing up. Givin me heartburn. You gotta dig it, baby, you gotta." Eli slurps half his Old Fashioned in one go. "Yow, Drewie boy! Fire in the mind, fire in the glass! Butta! butta! Ya dig?"

Drew nods, taking that as a compliment. "Yeah, I... I dig."

Eli claps. "Okay suckas, let's talk shop. I see bright. I see gay. I see flying twinks through the air. Twinky torpedoes, ya dig? Sweeping crane shots through human pyramids. Heightened reality. Daydream sequences. Wires. All the singin and dancin in the 'magination of its participants. I don't dig all them period deets, ya hear? None of that cholera and dusty sheeeeeeeit, right?"

Drew shrugs with pouted lips. "That sounds okay."

"Who are you, Barbra Billingsley?" Kev whispers.

"Eli, my man," Drew says with a smile, "I get it, I get it, but I think we should talk about what kind of musical *Branson!* will be. You know there's so many kinds."

"No doubt, no doubt!" Eli spits with a grin. "Don't wanna *Les Miz* when we wanna *Moulin Rouge!* and which *West Side*'s the right *Story*, ya feel?"

"I was thinking of avoiding the *Mamma Mia/Moulin Rouge!* route with all the tonal changes. More *Chicago*, *Les Miz*, Spielberg's *West Side*. Serious tone conveyed through music. The story is pretty dark, after all."

"The singin's gonna be diagetic? Less *Rocketman*, more *Bohemian Rhapsody*?"

"No, definitely *Rocketman*. I like the imaginative sequence idea. Gives it more of a postmodern feel without ruining the internal universe. But we should really tweak the lyrics and style of the music to fit the time period. No talk of cell phones or cars. That's too much."

"The words still be like talkin', right?"

"Yes, and I'm picking the songs myself. I have to insist on that. I'm a longtime fan of the Pet Shop Boys. It's gonna be a lot of B-sides and album cuts. Some hits of course. We can't leave 'It's a Sin' or 'Rent' out of a movie like this, you know?"

"We love what you did with *Seven Brides*," Kev says. "Gritty yet theatrical. That's the exact tone we're going for."

"Make 'em cry, I dig, I dig," Eli says. "And I love the rotoscopin. Fits my process betta. Film it live, flips and all."

"Oh goodie," Drew says with a grin. "I was thinking more of a true-to-human-form style of animation than pure Disney cartoon. But there is some Disney Renaissance influence with this, right? Childhood to adulthood. Audiences like that, the 'If Disney were Real' stuff."

"The fuckin' betta gritty," Eli says, pointing. "Don't want nonna dat censa shit in here. Easier to swalla, pardon the pun. Get 'em boys and bitches all hot and bothered."

"It's a rated R story, let it be rated R." Drew shrugs. "Maybe an NC-17 might draw a bigger crowd? Better publicity?"

"Don't wanna gross anyone out now."

Drew chuckles. "R it is, then."

"I use my own DP. Hope you don't mind."

"Use whoever you want."

"I love it, my man," Eli claps their hands one at a time. "Fire. *Branson!* it is!"

Drew and Kev wave goodbye as Eli's limo drives away. "There," Drew says, turning to Kev. "Satisfied?"

"What, that our animated Pet Shop Boys musical about a gay Victorian Irish whore with a courtroom finale is about to be directed by a white guy that speaks jive? I'm *thrilled.*"

"An *Oscar-winning* white guy that speaks jive," Drew corrects. "For a musical no less. Do you have any idea how rare that is?"

"I suppose anyone who'd willingly make a gritty remake of *Seven Brides for Seven* fucking *Brothers* would be of questionable sanity."

"That guy sure made it look easy."

"That he did."

Kev and Drew walk back in just as Trent Bower, chiseled-jawed twunk from Hair & Makeup, rushes over. "Mr. Lawrence! Mr. Foster!" Trent cries in his Ethel Merman voice. "You gotta take a look at this."

Trent escorts Drew and Kev to the crimson-colored Hair and Makeup department. "Timmy and I were planning hairstyles and we wanted to find pictures of the real guys." Trent sits at the computer desk. Clicks through what looks like an old website from the 2000s, stopping on a jpg of a poorly lit pencil sketch on browned paper. "There is it! Look!"

"Zoom in," Kev says.

Trent right-clicks. Blows it up to fill the screen.

The sketch is a profile of a young man with soft bangs and a sharp jaw. There's a sort of toughness in his expression. Black pencil except for his unbelievable cool blue eyes, the only use of color. The amount of detail in his irises is shocking. Sensitive. Looking right at them. On the bottom right hand of the sketch is a signature: "Denny Evans." A modern label in the top left corner with a catalog number and "Jack Branson portrait, 28 Oct 1888" typed.

Chills actually run down Drew's arms. "Oh my God, that's actually him."

"How did you find this?" Kev asks.

"I don't know," Trent says. "The website was on page 7 on Google. I'm lucky to have found it at all."

"Probably one of those old geezers that still doesn't understand the Internet," Drew says.

"Apparently it's in the possession of some guy named Terrance Donahue. It says he's the President of the Jack Branson Society in New York City."

"This is fantastic, Trent, thank you," Kev says.

"Send me the URL," Drew says. He and Kev make their way back upstairs. "Holy shit. Jack Branson has a Society?"

"It's probably a historical organization," Kev says. "Artifact preservation and whatnot. I think we should go out there as soon as possible."

"Why? What's the rush?"

"If we get too involved with the production, we won't be able to make any changes. At the very least, we should get his blessing. The last thing we need is to make a movie about Jack Branson that pisses off the Jack Branson Society. That just might be what costs us Best Picture."

"They can't be that big. You saw that website."

"It still wouldn't look good on paper."

"Didn't fuck it up for *Green Book.*"

"*Branson!*'s no *Green Book.* And who wanted *Green Book* to win anyway?"

"What if they want us do a page-one rewrite?"

"I'm sure we can come to an arrangement to avoid that."

"But what if?"

Kev takes a deep breath. "Guess we won't know until we go out there."

Drew reluctantly nods. "I'll call Donahue and schedule the meeting for Friday."

"I'll get the tickets."

Friday, LAX. Drew and Kev board their 8 AM first-class flight to JFK. They land in New York City at 10:30 AM. They find their driver. Follow him outside. Soft snow falls all around them. "It's fucking freezing!" Kev mutters, wrapping his big coat tighter, shivering his balls off. Drew laughs.

Their driver takes them around the Belt Parkway. Carey Tunnel. Into Greenwich Village. Stops outside a row of businesses on Christopher Street buried in scaffolding. 1101's door is marked with slightly arched lettering:

The Jack Branson Society

"God, we're so late," Kev mutters, scooting to get out of the car.

"Kev, wait," Drew says, gently touching his shoulder.

"What?"

Drew looks at the Society's entrance through the tinted windows. "Do me a favor. This is gonna sound weird, but just trust me."

"What?"

"Don't bring up *Atomic*."

Kev furrows his brow. "Why not?"

"Just don't do it."

"Fine, but..." Kev scoffs. "Drew, you already have a respected biopic under your belt. What if that's what gets this guy to endorse us?"

"It's not relevant."

"Not relevant?! You wrote the fucking thing!"

"No, I..." Drew sighs. "I know, just... When we get to the pitch part, let me do the talking."

"Fine. Whatever. Can we go in now?"

"Yes, please." They step out of the car.

Drew holds the flimsy door for Kev. It slams behind them. Nothing but darkness inside. Kev and Drew stay where they are, intimidated by the quiet pitch black before them. Blinding white light shines in behind them, hurting their eyes. "What's going on?" Kev asks. "Where are we?"

"The Mines of Moria, apparently."

"God, I can't see anything."

"Then knock a skeleton down a well, make a lot of noise and disturb the nest of Goblins. A Balrog will show up in no time. That'll be enough light for you."

Silence.

"What the fuck was that?!" Kev asks.

"What?"

"Holy shit! You really do watch too many movies!"

"Watch too many movies?! We work in fucking Hollywood! That movie's thirty-four years old!"

"You don't hear me quoting shit all the time, do you?"

"I don't know why! Nothing's stopping you!"

"Rosebud," says a third voice.

"AHHH!" Kev and Drew scream.

A single light bulb turns on, revealing a British man in his seventies with snow white hair and a wrinkled face laughing heartily. "Sorry, I couldn't resist," he says with a voice like velvet. "Messrs. Lawrence and Foster, I presume?"

"Mr. Donahue," Drew greets, shaking his hand.

"Terrance, please." Terrance slides a blackout curtain over the door. The daylight vanishes. Kev and Drew's eyes adjust to the dark.

The room isn't really pitch black, just really dimly lit. Musty air. Old book smell. Drew can see a second floor accessible only by rickety ladder with no lighting at all, bookshelves and display cases by the look of it.

"I don't like leaving it open that long," Terrance grumbles. "You boys are late."

"Belt Parkway," Drew says.

"Say no more." Terrance waddles his way between tables of cataloged documents. "I suppose I'll start the tour."

"How long has this place been here?" Drew asks.

"My grandparents founded the Jack Branson Society in 1950. Why I'm not quite sure. Nevertheless, they dedicated their lives to the investigation, conservation, and preservation of all artifacts and documents related to Jack Branson, Oliver Hawkett, Charlie Smith, François Brion, Denny Evans, Andy Baxter, legendary crossdressers Belcher and Kehoe — or Mary and Louise as their contemporaries called them — and all others associated with the infamous Montgomery Street Brothel." Terrance points a wrinkled finger across the room. "That's Mary's wig collection in the corner. Why Mary's and not Louise's I'm also not sure. Maybe Mary got fed up and burned them all out of spite. He does that." Terrance chuckles. "*Did* that, I mean. I've been cooped up in here too long."

Drew beelines toward the wigs. Red curly ones. Short black ones. Drew reaches to touch them. Stops himself. Puts his hand down.

Terrance lifts an old book off a desk. "Here is a book of recipes written François Brion himself."

Kev tenderly holds the book, already open to a recipe for bouillabaisse written in French with a fountain pen.

Terrance places the book gently where it belongs. Waddles on. "And over here is a retrospective recollection of Jack's testimony for the defense during *Withers v Grant*, April 17, 1889."

Drew races over. "Oh my God! I couldn't find that anywhere." Drew and Kev stare at the framed documents hanging on the wall, one page at a time in proper order.

"The original stenographer was just as shocked as the rest of them!" Terrance says, his breath whistling. "When he calmed down he tried his best, but I'm afraid we'll never know how shocking it really was."

Drew recognizes a face with blue eyes hanging on the wall. "There it is! Denny's sketch!"

"Ah yes," Terrance says with understated reverence, approaching the sketch. "October 28, 1888. Notice the isolated use of color in the iris. The soft short strokes along the jaw. Lots of stopping and starting apparently. That's quite unusual for Denny. Not a habit he particularly shows in the rest of his work." Terrance thumbs casually behind him. "We have all that as well, but..." He keeps staring at the portrait, losing himself with amazement. "There's something special about this one. The way it's been preserved so carefully. How clean it is. Not even a corner folded." Terrance sighs. "Denny must've loved this one dearly."

The warm romantic tones of Terrance's Shakespeare voice melts Drew's heart. So much emotion, all for a group of men he's never met. "This is quite a collection, Terrance. You must be very proud."

"I am," Terrance says with a smile. "It's no Coca-Cola, but it's an empire in its own right. And I've lived a good life tending to it. Keeping it safe."

"Are there other members of the Jack Branson Society?" Kev asks.

"Roxane comes in twice a week to clean the place. Mark and Gary come by every now and then to look around, but it's a mailing list mostly. Lots of gays in this neighborhood. Poor boys looking for history, a sense of meaning." Terrance looks at Drew. "I know you're gay."

Drew raises an amused brow.

Terrance turns to Kev. "You're probably not."

"I'm not," Kev says. "I'm sorry."

Terrance smirks at Drew. "He's apologizing for being straight. How funny these times are." He gazes out at all those artifacts. A painful sigh sifts out. "Why the fuck couldn't it have been like that for them?"

Drew frowns. Kev does too. The three men stand in mournful silence.

Drew awkwardly wanders first, studying the detailed minutia around them. "Terrance?"

"Yes, Mr. Lawrence?"

"If the Montgomery Street Brothel was in London, and Jack was born in Dublin—"

"Jack was never from DUBLIN!" Terrance angrily snaps. "He was from Dunderrow!"

Drew halts in his tracks, mouth open. "But I thought he was called Dublin Jack."

"He was called Dublin Jack because stupid Victorian English dandies can't name a fucking Irish town to save their lives!"

"I'm sorry, I... I don't know why I thought that."

Terrance frowns. "Continue."

"I was saying, um..." Drew closes his eyes. "Oh dammit."

"If the Brothel was in London," Kev speaks up, "and Jack was born in Dunderrow, why was the Jack Branson Society established in New York?" Drew sighs with gratitude. Kev nods back.

"That's a very good question," Terrance answers, much calmer now. "Not a very good answer unfortunately. My grandparents lived down the street. That's the reason."

"*When* did you say it was founded?" Drew asks.

"1950. My grandparents were the ones that acquired most of the artifacts here. Homosexuality was still very illegal back then, even in England. The only outlet for them to spread awareness of Jack and his story was through Mattachine Society. They were the first gay liberation organization in the United States. My grandmother felt their radical communist stance would've made Jack proud. Harry Hay in particular was a great admirer of him."

"Who?"

"No, Hay. He was one of Mattachine's founders. But sadly, as time went on, the Mattachine Society was overwhelmed by radically less radical members. To accommodate the new arrivals, the Mattachine founders decided to adopt a non-confrontational policy. Harry Hay got disillusioned by that and left Mattachine in 1953. That really made things difficult for my grandparents."

"How come?" Kev asks.

"The Mattachine Society was very reluctant to allow a platform for heterosexuals, and Hay wasn't around anymore to vouch for them. Then again Hay went on to become a prominent member of the North American Man/Boy Love Association, so what did he know?" Terrance approaches an old photo on the wall, a young blonde woman and a handsome clean-cut young man. "That's them. Beautiful, aren't they?"

"Did you know them well?" Drew asks.

"They passed when I was young. I didn't know what I was then." Terrance frowns. "I could've asked them so much."

Drew's face sags. He misses his mom.

"But this place carried on into the sixties," Terrance continues, waddling ahead. "Steady growth. The Mattachine Society passed out their pamphlets. My grandmother spoke at the meetings. And then Stonewall happened."

"Stonewall?" Kev asks.

Terrance chuckles. "You really aren't gay, are you?"

"It's when all the queeny gays and trans women rioted against the police during a raid at the Stonewall Inn, June 1969," Drew says. "It's the reason we have Pride every year. It's what it commemorates."

Kev bumps his brows. "Okay."

"The Mattachine Society didn't approve of all that riffraff rioting around," Terrance says. "They were non-confrontational now. They wanted gays to assimilate into society. That's something far too gradual and considerate for younger queens to understand. In the days after Stonewall, the Mattachine Society publicly condemned the riots, calling the perpetrators rash, saying they were hurting the cause, but with the establishment of Pride ushering mainstream gay support, the Stonewall Riots started getting looked on more favorably, the Mattachine Society's quick rejection of it making them look backwards and complicit. The first of its kind, backwards and complicit." Terrance shakes his head. "The Jack Branson Society got pummeled by association. They backed the wrong horse, it seemed. My grandparents ended up shutting this place down in shame. Packed everything up. Took their son William to London. There they re-established the Jack Branson Society near 19 Montgomery Street itself, the original address of the Brothel. My father grew up there. He met my mother. They had me. We lived a fairly good life. But when my father took over as President in the mid-70s, he missed a few golden opportunities to expand out there. He wasn't gay. He wasn't in the know. It wasn't until the 90s that most of his contributions materialized here. He's the one that moved us back to New York, to the same building we had before, this one. And his heterosexuality did help the Society acquire recognition through the world of academia. Professors. Historians. Richie Hammond."

"Who?" Drew asks.

"He's a famous playwright in the 90s. Very smart. I actually met him. He was very..." Terrance furrows his brow. "Very *young*."

Kev and Drew look at each other.

Terrance shrugs. "Eh. Anyway. It was around that time that word of Jack Branson finally reached the West Coast. You are not the first producers I've escorted through this place. There were two in fact. The first was 1991. He wanted to change Jack to a girl. The one in '06 wanted to keep everything just as it was... except for the prostitution part." Terrance laughs. "Such fools." He opens his office door. Flicks on a light, making Kev and Drew wince. "When my father retired in '07, I became the first homosexual President of the Jack Branson Society, which ironically is the very thing making me the last Donahue. I made the website, part of my ongoing quest to debunk all that misinformation just floating around out there." Terrance sits, looking at Drew. "Like Jack Branson's hometown, for instance."

Drew smiles apologetically. He and Kev sit too.

"But I'm old," Terrance states with solemn acceptance. "I've been trying for decades to pull that censored version of Jack's book off the market and replace it with a fully authorized edition, but that task turned out to be a lot more difficult than I've anticipated. There's just no demand. I've always felt a feature film would be the perfect substitute." Terrance smiles warmly. "So tell me about yours."

Drew and Kev stare in silence.

"Well?" Terrance asks.

Kev cocks his head at Drew. "He said to let him do all the talking."

Drew glares at Kev.

Kev shrugs back. "What? You did."

Drew sighs. Looks at Terrance. "Mr. Donahue—"

"Terrance, please," Terrance corrects.

Drew takes a deep breath. "It's called *Branson!*"

"Sounds accurate so far."

"Yeahhh," Drew whines. "It's uh..." He swallows. "It's animated."

Terrance stares. "Animated."

"Uh-huh." Drew nods, losing sensation in his face. "And it's a... a musical."

Terrance hesitates. "An animated musical."

Drew's eyes fix forward in terror. "An animated Pet Shop Boys musical."

Terrance blinks. Looks at Kev.

Kev nods back cheerfully.

Terrance crosses his legs. "An animated... Pet Shop Boys... musical."

Drew can feel his stomach rustling.

Kev playfully slaps Drew's knee. "Hey Drew, list all their songs again."

"I'll hit you with a brick," Drew mutters.

Terrance lets out a rough sigh. "Please forgive me, Mr. Lawrence, Mr. Foster, but I think it is incredibly disturbing that two very handsome young men such yourselves should contact me out of the blue from the other side of the country with such aggressive, inconvenient timing, only for you to arrive twenty minutes late, wasting my very valuable time, only to say that you want to turn the very history my family has preserved for three generations... into an intentionally anachronistic jukebox musical revue."

"Don't for-get the roto-scop-ing," Kev sings.

"He doesn't know what rotoscoping is," Drew says.

"Is that supposed to make me feel better?" Terrance asks.

Drew rolls his lips together. "Terrance—"

"Do the whores dance like follies?"

"Please, I—"

"Why not give Denny another leg while you're at it so he can do the splits on Charlie's face?"

"Terrance, I swear to you, *Branson!* is not as sacrilegious as it sounds."

Terrance purses his lips. Looks off.

Drew puts his hands together. "There are people out there that need to know what Jack did, people who won't pay $25 for a documentary. I'm trying keep emotions relevant to a new generation of Jack Branson admirers. They need to feel what he felt. His pain. His success. His failure. They need to cry for him the way they would cry for themselves. That's how they'll remember Jack Branson for the rest of their lives." Drew pauses. "Then people will start paying $25 for a documentary."

Terrance sighs. Twists his mouth in thought.

Kev proudly smiles at Drew.

"I believe you know how to make movies, Mr. Lawrence," Terrance murmurs. "Movies that sell. Movies that make an impact. Those other men, they just wanted an easy story that wrote itself. Jack is not a story. Jack is a person." Terrance sits back in his chair. "And I do not believe you intend to do that person any harm. Like myself, Mr. Lawrence, you seem to be addicted to unnecessarily hard work. Your only crime seems to be ignorance. If given the chance, I believe you have the skills and the drive to mend what once was broken. Not because it would give you a bigger profit. Because then it would be perfect." Terrance smiles slightly. "And I believe Jack would have loved the Pet Shop Boys. As do I."

Drew grins. "Thank you, Terrance."

Terrance rolls his chair over to an old safe under his desk. "How much have you read of Jack's book?"

"Just the summary on Wikipedia. I've always had a lousy attention span."

Terrance sticks in a bronze key. Turns. CLANK! Terrance pulls the door open to reveal a stack of loose papers wrapped in a sealed plastic casing. "This is the Society's crown jewel." Terrance lifts the stack with delicate hands and holds it out. "The original undoctored manuscript of *The Sins of an Irishman in London* by Jack Branson as submitted to the Charlie Smith Publishing House on November 4, 1888."

"Holy fuck!" Drew gushes with wide eyes.

"You have no idea how valuable this is." Terrance gently places the manuscript back in the vault. "After the verdict of *Withers v Grant*, Edgar bought what was left of the Charlie Smith Publishing House in 1890 and sold the novel's rights to a Christian Fundamentalist group. They were the ones that heavily censored the book, the version you can buy now on Amazon. Even before all that, according to documents we found in Charlie Smith's possession, Charlie had altered Jack's draft before publication. *This* copy was written before those alterations. It's because of this manuscript that we now know 'Mr. Drummond,' the purported owner of the Montgomery Street Brothel, was in fact an alias for Charlie Smith himself, and that Marty Williams, the Scotland Yard superintendent who had granted the Brothel immunity, was most likely Morty Blasmyth, future commissioner and longtime speculated homosexual. And there's the matter of the addendum."

"What addendum?" Kev asks.

"The addendum of *The Sins of an Irishman in London*, its ninth chapter, was written two months after the main body. It's a series of origin stories of the men themselves. François Brion. Mary and Louise. Denny Evans. Andy Baxter. Oliver Hawkett. Charlie Smith. Even Jack Branson himself reveals what the Incident was that got him banished from Dunderrow. It is in that addendum that those men are at their most vulnerable. It's their heart and soul. Without it, they're nothing more Victorian stock characters. But because the addendum's epilogue contains a thinly veiled account of Jack and Edgar's encounter, Edgar wanted all copies of it to be destroyed. And he almost succeeded. It's truly amazing. Even after the Brothel was destroyed and Charlie's publishing house dismantled, Edgar was still afraid of a bunch of words on parchment." Terrance smiles. "It was like Jack was living on, terrorizing that man like he did that day in court."

Chills run down Drew's arms. "Can I read it?" he asks.

Terrance looks at Drew with pleasant surprise. "I'll email you the transcript."

"Don't you already know what happens?" Kev asks Drew.

Drew scoffs. "That's like saying there's no difference between *Schindler's List* and Ken Burns' *Holocaust*."

"Precisely, Mr. Lawrence," Terrance says. "*The Sins of an Irishman in London* isn't just a document, Mr. Foster. It's not just a piece of history. Jack Branson lived in a world that wanted to forget men like us. This book isn't just what happened to him. It's everything about him. His family. His employers. His past. His fears. All those unspoken things he did. He knew only he could tell his story and he was one of the few in those days that actually did." Terrance pauses. "This book is his crowning achievement, not his testimony in the Old Bailey. He wouldn't have gone up there if not for the love he had for this book, as a way to undo his request for anonymity brought on by cold feet. Jack wanted everyone to know he wrote it. That he really lived it."

"What ever happened to him?" Kev asks. "After the trial? We couldn't find anything."

"He probably fled the country. Changed his name. There wouldn't be any documentation of that. I don't think we'll ever know for sure."

"Not even a death date?" Drew teases.

Terrance chuckles. "It's been almost 150 years, Mr. Lawrence. I'm sure his book is all that's left of him now." He goes quiet. Looks over at the vault. "And that manuscript is all that's left of that book."

Drew and Kev stare at that plastic bag filled with parchment.

Terrance claps his hands. Kev and Drew flinch. "Okay!" Terrance declares with a triumphant grin. "As President of the Jack Branson Society, I, Terrance Donahue, will allow the production of *Branson!* the animated Pet Shop Boys musical under one condition: that I personally receive a private screening before its official premiere. If I like what I see, the Society will give its official endorsement. If I don't, I will not only condemn it tooth and nail for the rest of my life, I will continue to haunt you both after I'm gone. I think that should be plenty of motivation for you boys."

Kev smiles. "Sounds doable."

"Honestly, Terrance," Drew says, "I didn't think you'd be this compromising."

Terrance nods with sad eyes. "After I'm gone, the role of President of the Jack Branson Society will go to someone with no relation to its founders. No knowledge of its history. No urgency." He lets out a long wavering breath. "It seems in the face of this crushing reality, I find myself quite desperate. Legacy, my dear boys. The people we leave behind. The ones that tell our story. It's so melodramatic to think of these days, but it's real. It's not just an old people thing. It shouldn't be, anyway."

"You never wanted kids?" Drew asks.

Terrance sighs. "I wouldn't have been a good father. Mine was so aloof, you see."

"And it must've been hard finding someone in those days," Kev says.

"But I did find someone," Terrance says. "Liam. I loved him so very much."

"He passed away?"

Terrance nods sadly. "He was twenty-nine years older than I was."

Drew's face goes cold.

"He saved my life," Terrance says. "I thank God every day for sending me that beautiful man, right when I needed him."

Drew's lip stiffens, his heart pounding.

"Sounds like a great guy," Kev says, oblivious.

"It was golden when we were together," Terrance murmurs, a flash of pain in his eyes. "Warm. Easy. Like it all made sense. Life hasn't been the same without him, but he made me strong. I'm happy in the end because I was lucky to have known him. To have been Liam's man. He waited his whole life for me. Of all people, me."

Kev finally looks at Drew. He's catatonic. "Drew?"

Drew exhales, realizing where he is. He wipes his red wet eyes. "I think I need some air."

Terrance points left. "Over there, round the corner."

Drew stands and leaves the office. Kev awkwardly looks at Terrance. "Wanna look at the script?"

"I'd love to." Terrance frowns out his office door, having recognized that despair on Drew's face.

Drew bursts out the side door. Blinding daylight hits him. He's in an alleyway. Snow everywhere, still falling down. Fire escapes above him. Overcast sky. Drew takes in big cold breaths, an overwhelming sadness enveloping him. He sits on the cold concrete. Wraps his arms around his legs. He can feel his nose running. Might even have an angry look on his face. Despair. Snowflakes fall on his hair. He shuts his eyes. Squeezes them tight. His whole body trembles.

JACOB

Cloud Atlas

INT. STEWIE'S BROWNSTONE APARTMENT - DAY

Jacob does fifteen push-ups on a yoga mat with ease, Stewie standing by.

STEWIE
You gotta count them out verbally.

JACOB
No, I'm good.

Jacob stands up. Puts his glasses back on.

JACOB (CONT'D)
Remember I couldn't even do one two weeks ago?

STEWIE
I'm so proud of you, baby!

Jacob grins.

JACOB
You love me?

STEWIE
Uh-huh!

JACOB
How much?

Stewie opens his arms as wide as he can.

STEWIE
THIS much!

CUT TO:

LATER THAT NIGHT

The lights are dim. Two half-drunk French vodka gimlets rest on coasters on the coffee table. Titanic paused on the TV.

Jacob and Stewie roll on the floor, arms around each other's bodies, making out like THEIR ship was going down.

CUT TO:

THE NEXT DAY

Jacob steps onto the electronic scale. Stewie looks at the screen, pen to a paper chart.

STEWIE
Get on again.

Jacob looks down.

JACOB
Oh my God.

STEWIE
Get on again.

Jacob steps off. Steps back on. Tries not to look down.

STEWIE
Okay, 194.7.

JACOB
BABY! I've never been under 200 before!

STEWIE
Now use the scanner.

Jacob inputs his height, weight, and age into the body fat scanner. Stewie steps on the scale.

STEWIE (CONT'D)
Lost a few pounds myself.

Jacobs grips the scanner. It beeps. Jacob shows Stewie the LED screen: "17.0%"

JACOB
It's because I weaned off the meds!

STEWIE
Possibly.

JACOB
No possibly about it.

Jacob grabs his phone. Flips through his photos.

JACOB (CONT'D)
Right before I flew out to Italy, I got Dr. Collins to switch the brands of both of my medications.

Jacob shows Stewie a picture of a much fatter Jacob sitting on a stone wall, Florence's skyline at midday behind him. Stewie widens his eyes, downplaying his disgust.

STEWIE
Oh my God.

JACOB
I was at my all-time high, 245lbs.

STEWIE
Yeesh.

JACOB
What a difference, right? I lost forty pounds over four months just from the brand switch.

STEWIE
Good thing you did. If you looked like that the night we met, I never would've been interested.

Jacob furrows his brow.

JACOB
I thought it didn't matter.

STEWIE
Even I have limits, Baby Boy.

Jacob looks at the photo.

JACOB
I really thought it was a good one at the time. I look like a blob.

STEWIE
<u>The Blob</u>?

JACOB
Funny.
(sighs)
Guess it's a good thing I couldn't cum.

STEWIE
Huh?

JACOB
I had a hard time cumming on my old meds. That's why I switched brands in the first place.

Jacob stares off, realizing something. Stewie uses the body fat scanner. It beeps.

STEWIE
Went down!

Jacob looks around the apartment, brows furrowed.

STEWIE (CONT'D)
(bleating)
AYY BEE!

JACOB
How did your friend tell you about this place?

STEWIE
Who, The Diva?

JACOB
Yeah.

Stewie thinks about it.

STEWIE
Well, I was at his birthday party, and he asked how work was, and I told him about the DDD cracking down on my business and the expensive client moving up here, and that's when he told me about this place.

JACOB
When's his birthday?

Stewie face relaxes with realization.

STEWIE
March 15.

Jacob stares.

JACOB
The Diva's birthday is March 15?

STEWIE
I didn't even realize. That's so weird, you two having the same birthday.

JACOB
So you would've already been here when I got back. If I didn't take the custodial program, I'd still be down in PA right now. We wouldn't have met yet.

Stewie looks off, recollecting.

STEWIE
Actually, I only went to The Diva's birthday party because he texted me out of the blue for the first time in five years.

JACOB
Really?

STEWIE
He never texts first. I felt I had to go.

JACOB
So if he didn't do that, you'd still be in that condo in Marlton?

STEWIE
Yeah.

JACOB
Forty-five minutes from my mom's house in Conshohocken?

Stewie hesitates.

STEWIE
Yeah.

JACOB
And Philly Pride was the same day, June 12.

STEWIE
You would've been up here no matter what.

JACOB
No, I only signed on because Carter emailed me and told me there was an opening. I never would've said yes if Mom hadn't canceled her trip out there.

STEWIE
And when was all this?

JACOB
Two days before my birthday.

Stewie goes quiet.

JACOB (CONT'D)
When did The Diva text you out of the blue?

STEWIE
Two days before his birthday.

Jacob and Stewie stare at each other.

JUMP CUT TO:

MINUTES LATER

Stewie searches his email on his computer. Jacob searches his phone on the couch.

JACOB
Okay, Mom Skyped me on March 12 to tell me that she lost her job and had to cancel the flight out. And then the next day, March 13 at 10:35 AM Eastern time, Carter emailed me about the cancelation. I responded back with a yes at 4:00 PM Eastern time.

STEWIE
The Diva texted me at 11:30 PM on March 13. I said yes five minutes later.

JACOB
Then March 16 at 2:30 PM Eastern time, Carter emailed me again confirming the custodian program was actually happening. When did you actually agree to rent this place?

STEWIE
March 16, 5:00 PM.

JACOB
Holy crap, baby!

STEWIE
I never did something like that. It's so unlike me.

JACOB
Me too. And The Diva too, I guess.

STEWIE
What about your mom?

JACOB
I don't know. I think she could've gone either way.

The two sit in silence, digesting.

JACOB
My mom cancels her trip out to Italy, and then within twenty-four hours I suddenly get an email inviting me personally to stay in Boston for the summer the same day you get a text from a friend you haven't seen in five years who never texts first. And I uncharacteristically say yes to the custodial program, which became official only a few hours before you uncharacteristically decided to relocate your entire business up to Massachusetts.

STEWIE
That's really freaky.

JACOB
If we were both in Philly, we still would've gone out to Pride, right?

STEWIE
Pulse would've happened either way.

JACOB
And yet we both uncharacteristically went out despite that.

Stewie leans forward, thinking.

STEWIE
This is weird.

JACOB
Was the Black Bear the only bar you went to that day?

STEWIE
Yeah. You?

JACOB
No, I didn't know where I was going. I started in City Hall and just hitchhiked with a bunch of guys to Boxer, then I walked over to Lumber's, and then I hitched with a couple guys to Machine.

STEWIE
The guy with the boyfriend.

JACOB
Yeah. In fact, I wanted to go home after that, but someone talked me into staying out. And that's when I met the guys that took me to The Black Bear.

Jacob gasps.

JACOB (CONT'D)
And if I hadn't seen Austin sitting at the bar, I never would've known they had a downstairs.

STEWIE
Which is where I was.

JACOB
If any one of those things happened differently, we never would've met.

STEWIE
And we almost didn't because of your mom.

Jacob hesitates.

JACOB
But maybe we would've met anyway. Maybe I would've done the same in Philly, hitchhiked off some guys in Penn's Landing or something and ended up meeting you along way.

STEWIE
Maybe.

JACOB
Think about it. I had only just turned twenty-one a couple months before. What are the chances that a guy exactly your type, the perfect man you spent fifty-two years looking for, could've crossed paths with you the first day I was ever in an American gay bar?

Stewie smiles, suppressing a heft of emotion.

STEWIE
I knew as soon as I saw you, even without the perfect hair.

JACOB
And you were just standing there.

Jacob looks up at the top of Stewie's head where a hat once stood.

JACOB (CONT'D)
(whispers)
In the perfect red package.

They look at each other, sharing a strange mutual feeling, a deep resonating fulfillment that can't quite describe.

STEWIE
(soft whine)
What took you so long?

JACOB
I had to ripen.

Stewie bursts into laughter. Jacob laughs along. They hug. Hold each other tight.

DISSOLVE TO:

EXT. PARKING LOT - DAY

Stewie steps out of his Jeep. Jacob walks around from the passenger side, stopping next to Stewie. They both stare at the building before them: St. Joan of Arc Catholic Church.

Stewie pats Jacob's back with a smile. Jacob takes a deep breath as Stewie leads the way.

DISSOLVE TO:

INT. ST. JOAN OF ARC CHURCH - DAY

Jacob slides into the pew and sits, Stewie to his left. Jacob studies the cross above the altar. The statues by the confessional. Just like the ones they had back in Phoenixville. He smiles softly.

MATCH CUT TO:

DREW

No Offense, But...

Drew looks left at the empty pew space. Places a hand on the shiny varnished wood. For a second he thought it could've been warm, Stewie just in the bathroom or something. Back in a flash. Drew faces forward. Untunes the old deacon out. He needs to take his religious revival more seriously.

"'...you will be welcomed into eternal dwellings,'" the Deacon continues reading from Luke. "'The person who is trustworthy in very small matters is also trustworthy in great ones, and the person who is dishonest in very small matters is also dishonest in great ones. If, therefore, you are not trustworthy with dishonest wealth, who will trust you with true wealth? If you are not trustworthy with what belongs to another, who will give you what is yours?'"

Drew frowns, a powerful sadness overwhelming him. God knows, doesn't he? Theo. Oscar. Possibly Frankie. Oh no, his mom too. Now that she's gone, she really does know everything.

"'No servant can serve two masters,'" the Deacon reads. "'He will either hate one and love the other or be devoted to one and despise the other. You cannot serve both God and mammon.'" The Deacon pauses for effect. "The Gospel of the Lord."

"Praise to you Lord Jesus Christ," the congregation responds. Drew just stares off, rapt, his lips mouthing along. He doesn't know what mammon means. It'd probably be pretty profound if he did. But he doesn't.

Drew gets into JEEPGUY 2: Electric Boogaloo. Instead of "shifting" into first and peeling out of the church parking lot like every other Catholic, Drew just sits there. Scans the dashboard. It really does look like Stewie's in every way. The amount of time and dedication Theo took to designing it, not to mention all that money he spent. He didn't have to, but he did. For Drew. For his best friend's 40th birthday. Because he knew how special it would be for him to be able to drive it again.

Maybe he was wrong about Theo. He should just be the bigger man and forgive.

Drew's phone rings as he turns onto his Marina Del Rey exit. He sees the caller ID. Taps the button on his steering wheel. "Hey man, what's up?"

"How was it?" Kev asks. "As bad as you thought?"

"No, it was good. Just weird, you know? I used to go all the time."

"As long as you're doing something."

"Yeah."

"I can go with you next time if you want. Keep you company."

Drew smiles. "Maybe. I'll think about it."

"Wanna meet up for lunch? I was really craving Chinese earlier and instantly thought of you."

"Don't tempt me. I've got a lot of work to do."

"Still barreling through the book, huh?"

"As a matter of fact..." Drew hesitates. "Kev, I think I need to page-one rewrite the script."

Silence on the line. "It's that different, huh?"

"No actually, the Wikipedia summary was pretty spot-on, but..." Drew half-frowns. "I can't really explain it. I just feel like my version of Jack's story is all wrong."

"In what way?"

"All the other guys at the brothel, Mary, Louise, Denny, so on... They're really different in the book. I think delineating them as some sort of chorus ensemble instead of fleshing them out as three dimensional members of the starring cast was a mistake."

"I mean, if you think it's worth it..."

"To Jack it would be." Drew pulls into the charging station near his condo. "He's in my head now. I see a lot of myself in him. Like a scary lot. This guy's story has already been butchered and censored and intentionally misunderstood for the past 150 years. I don't feel comfortable going half-ass on this. Charlie Smith really was the mastermind behind everything and he couldn't take credit for the Brothel back then. That's not right. And the Brothel really isn't a brothel at all. I'm getting the sense that they really invented the gar bar but just didn't have the words to call it that. Literally in Chapter Eight, Jack comes up with the idea for what he calls 'a club for homosexuals.' That's a social club, which is what gay bars are, a way for gay people to meet each other, to feel validated. And as a frequent gay bar addict, I have to go that route. It's an homage to my people." Drew unplugs his phone. Puts it to his ear as he starts charging. "It's so hard to explain, Kev. I need to put the pieces back together. All the censored parts, all the trial stuff Jack didn't write about because it hadn't happened yet. I can be the one that finally tells the whole story."

"That sounds like a different movie."

"I think it will be."

"Is it still gonna be a musical?"

"Oh yeah. I got it all figured out. I just gotta pour it out as soon as I get home or else I'll forget."

"Is it gonna be longer?"

"Much longer. I'm thinking three hours plus."

"Jesus."

"Don't gripe. *Titanic*'s only 15 minutes shorter than *The Irishman*. No one's gonna notice if every second's a jaw-dropper." Drew casually looks at the crisp black Dodge Charger two pumps down. Driver's side window down. A young hunk inside wearing sunglasses. The Hunk climbs out. Mid-twenties. Clean shaven. Sharp jawline. Black sleeveless shirt. Black jean shorts, emphasis on short. Tree trunk legs. Sublime ass. Perfect shoulders. Massive biceps and triceps. Hairy forearms. Just enough sweat on his skin to make his body shimmer. And as the Hunk scans his QR code at the pump, Drew can't help but notice a black jockstrap band poking above the rim of his jean shorts. Matter of fact his shirt's armholes reveal a matching bulldog elastic harness strapped across the Hunk's fantastic chest. This boy is ready to play whenever and wherever.

"Before I forget," Kev says over the phone. "Sharon from *Variety* called. There was a scheduling issue, so they had to move up the article to today."

"That's okay," Drew mumbles, not listening at all. "Right?"

"Just keeping you informed."

The Hunk turns his head. Looks Drew up and down.

"So that's good about the book," Kev continues. "I'm just a bit worried about the budget."

Drew snaps his focus away. "Yeah, I was thinking about that. Call Eli. See if he's interested in investing some of his own in exchange for an EP credit. He's the reason it's gonna be a success after all."

"I have to agree with you there. I'll call him in a bit and see what he says."

Drew looks back at the Hunk. He's still looking back, the soft wind tousling his short brown hair. And he's smiling too.

Drew grins back, rock hard. "Kev, I'm gonna have to call you back."

Drew fucks the Hunk on his bed, the frame creaking with every thrust. The Hunk (his real name Heath) takes Drew's cock on all fours, stripped to just his jockstrap and matching black harness, grinning like a madman and moaning like a pornstar. A female pornstar. "Fuck me!" Heath whines like a glitter queen. "Oh my GOD, FUCK me! Fuck my bussy, Daddy! Fuck my BUSSSSSY!"

Drew grits his teeth, his forehead dripping with sweat, furiously grunting as if in pain, slamming into Heath as hard as he can just to shut him up.

"Fuuuuuckkk!" Heath moans, bucking his hips, bouncing back at Drew just as hard. "Don't fucking stop! Oh my GODDD, tear me in HALF!"

Drew grabs Heath's throat with both hands. Heath cackles, his vocal cords vibrating against Drew's palms.

"Oh FUCK yeah," Heath squeals, his eyes rolling back. "Don't stop DADDDDDDDDYYY! Fuck my fucking pink BUSSY!"

"I'm about to cum," Drews breathes, hating himself in the process.

"Yeah?! C'mon Daddy! Breed me! Fill up my fucking HOLE!"

Drew slams his eyes shut. His muscular frame tenses. He holds his breath as finishes. Exhales hard, almost collapsing on top of Heath.

Heath laughs. "God, you're a fucking monster!" he says deeper, his natural masc voice reinstated. Heath pulls Drew in and sloppily kisses him.

Drew slides out, struggling to stand. "No more."

"Get back here. I'm not done."

Drew wipes himself with a towel. "You got three out of me. Isn't that enough?"

"I can keep going if you can." Heath spreads his checks with both hands, flaunting his busted hole.

Drew laughs. "Four months ago maybe. Not now. I gotta get to work."

Heath groans, getting up. "I really wished you let me film that."

"No way," Drew says, slipping a shirt on.

"I know, I know." Heath dresses too. "You got something for me to drink?"

"You like seltzer?"

"That all you got?"

"It's all I got now."

Drew and Heath sip cans of Polar Orange-Vanilla seltzer at the kitchen counter. "This is delicious," Heath says.

"I know. It's a very underrated flavor."

Heath notices the giant whiteboard in Drew's living room, lots of dry erase chaos in grid formation. "Is that your new movie?"

Drew smirks. "Something tells me it's right up your alley."

"Is it about sex?"

Drew bumps his brows. Finishes his can. "You were phenomenal, by the way."

"You too, stud."

"Thanks." Drew crushes the can. Tosses it into the recycling bin.

"Hot." Heath sips his seltzer. "I love sex so much. I can't believe it took me so long to get started."

"You're certainly making up for lost time."

"You're telling me," Heath murmurs. "I didn't lose my virginity until I was twenty-two."

Drew nods. "I was nineteen when I lost mine."

"Oh, that's fun."

"Yeah, well..." Drew hesitates. "You've only been having sex for two years?"

"More like a year and a half." Heath finishes his can.

"How many guys have you been with?"

"Oh, uh..." Heath taps his hands against his thighs. "Around five hundred, I think?"

Drew stares. "You've been with five hundred guys in a year and a half?"

"I don't know. Five-fifty. Five-seventy-five. I don't know. I don't keep track."

Drew takes Heath's empty can. "That's a lot of guys."

"Please. You guys were the ones on OnlyFans. What did you think was gonna happen?"

"That was after my time, actually."

Heath's face contorts into the biggest cringe possible. "God, you're fucking old!"

Drew furrows his brow. "Thanks."

Drew walks Heath to the door. Heath flings himself onto Drew, making out one last time. "Catch you later." Heath smacks Drew's ass. Opens the door. Almost collides with a round-headed midget standing in the hall with a fist in that air ready to knock. "Who the fuck are you?" Heath asks, crossing his arms.

Theo gapes back. Lowers his arm.

Drew's heart stops at the sight of Theo. "I think it's time for you to go, Heath."

"You wanna fuck again later?" Heath asks.

Drew scoffs. Awkwardly looks at Theo. "No, I think that was it."

Heath half-frowns. "Good luck with the movie anyway." He kisses Drew. Shoves past Theo. Races down the stairs, horny as fuck.

Theo watches Heath go, mildly amused. "Who's the dude?"

"Just a hot fuck I picked up at the charging station," Drew murmurs. "I remember when it used to be a gas station. He probably doesn't even know what a gas station is."

"So I guess you can take a man out of the jungle, but you can't—"

"At least he wanted to be with me," Drew interrupts. "I didn't have to pay him or tie him to the bed."

Theo frowns. "Can I..." He gestures into the condo. "Can I come in?"

Drew hesitates. Steps aside. Theo walks in. Drew shuts the door.

Theo approaches the whiteboard. "You're doing the Branson thing after all."

"Of course," Drew says, leaning his back against the door.

Theo looks Drew up-and-down. "You look good."

"I'm clean."

"It shows." Theo points to the sofa. "Is it okay if I sit?"

Drew doesn't react.

Theo awkwardly sits on the edge of the leather. "I come in peace."

Drew walks to a chair. Scoots it closer. Sits across from Theo. Crosses his legs. "What brings this on?"

"I still get *Variety* emails. I saw your name and read a bit."

Drew nods. "You know who I'm working with now?"

"I know it's someone on the Black List. Larry won't tell me who."

"Cause he knows you'd fire him."

Theo looks off. "Who's the lucky guy?" he asks.

Drew takes a slow breath in, savoring the moment he's been looking forward to for months. "Kev Foster."

Theo whips his head back, his mouth hanging open a bit. "*Peabrain*?!"

"His name is Kev Foster."

Theo inhales sharply, a flash of anger he probably doesn't mean to show. "I knew you'd be desperate. I never thought you'd be fucking insane."

"I don't do grudges. That's your thing."

"Forgive me for having my pride. When people fuck me over, I remember. I have standards."

"It's called forgiveness."

"You forgave him for Trisha?"

"Don't pretend you fucking care."

"Of course I care!" Theo says, audibly insulted. "How could you say that?"

Drew crosses his arms. Looks away.

Theo shakes his head. "You didn't snitch on me. I didn't snitch on you. Peabrain was gonna tell The Professor everything."

"We fucked him over first."

"Peabrain's the reason it got bad. He could've joined us and helped take down The Professor, but no. He chose himself. If we didn't do what we did that night, he would've sold you, me, and Trisha down the river for a fucking job. We would've been blacklisted. The Professor would still be there right now, running that same internship, ruining more and more interns just like us. And Peabrain would be there too, in the nice shiny office he earned, letting The Professor get away with it year after year, complicit like every other fuck in this town." Theo pauses. "And you know what, Trisha still would've killed herself."

"Shut up," Drew whispers with a scowl.

"How can you of all people go into work and see that man every day and just *pretend*?" Theo shakes his head. "After what happened to your sister—"

"FUCK YOU!" Drew shouts. "FUCK *YOU!*"

Theo frowns. He looks down at the floor. "That was low. I'm sorry."

Drew glares back.

Theo scratches his toupee. "Forget I said that. That's not why I'm here."

"I don't believe you."

"I don't care." Theo looks up, making reluctant eye contact. "If you see him fit, there's probably something in there I don't know about."

Drew readjusts his posture. "Yeah."

Theo rubs his hands. "I want you back."

"You want your money back."

"No." Theo re-erects his back. "I never should've fired you. I knew I was wrong the moment I said it. I don't know why I did. It's wrong on every level. I thought Larry would've been enough to make up for it, but... Jesus, man, you really made it look easy."

Drew stares blankly.

Theo clears his throat. "I haven't replaced you. I can't." He forces a smile. "I need my buddy back."

Drew hesitates. "I have my own thing going on at the moment."

"I know. I just wanted you to know that I read over the proposal you made and I think I can make it work after all."

"Really."

"If it means absorbing Ephemeral, I'm okay with that. We'll be pooling our money again, of course, but that's not just good for me, that's good for you too. If it benefits us both, what's the harm?" Theo shrugs with an earnest smile. "What's the harm?"

Drew stares.

Theo's smile fades in the silence.

Drew keeps staring. "Why were you really in Beijing for six weeks?"

Theo doesn't react at all. "The UniTopia co-production deal. The contract—"

"It doesn't take six weeks to sign a contract. I've signed three in the last week alone." Drew pauses. "Why were you really there?"

Theo's lips flutter. "I don't know what you mean."

Drew smirks, a hint of pain in his eyes. "You were never going to promote me, were you? You and Míng were probably sitting around, waiting for me to fuck up so you can use it as an excuse *not* to make me equal partners again."

"That's not what happened."

"I may not always be able to tell when you're lying, but I know when you're telling the truth. When you told me you couldn't do your job without me, that was the truth. That's what gave you away. If I didn't break that vase, you would've found some other reason to end the—"

"I'm telling you, dammit, that's not what happened!" Theo interrupts, his voice cracking a bit.

Drew shakes his head imperceptibly.

"Listen," Theo says with an outstretched hand. "I'll tell you, alright, but you can't tell anyone. Not a soul."

Drew purses his lips.

Theo bunches his hands together. "It's true, yes, I never wanted you to share power with you. But I couldn't tell you no. My father told me no and that fucked me up for years. I didn't want to do that to you." He pauses. "I chose six weeks in the summer because I knew you wouldn't make it six weeks in the summer the way you had been carrying on with the coke and the booze. But you didn't want to do it anyway, right? You said it yourself, you would've hated it if you got it. What you're doing now, this is what you really wanted. It's something you actually believe in." Theo pauses again. "And it wasn't my idea to end the trial three weeks early. I promised you six weeks. That was all Míng's idea. He hated me dragging it out with you. If it were up to him…" Theo stops himself again.

Drew keeps staring.

Theo licks his lips. "He wanted me to get rid of you. And I don't mean he wanted me to fire you, I mean *get rid of you.*"

Drew doesn't react.

"Do you understand?" Theo asks in a desperate whisper. "With Míng's capital tied to ours, he saw the way you were acting as a risk to his business. And he really hated that you broke his grandma's vase. I don't give a shit, honestly, but you know how he is with his family. They're all lunatics! Breaking that vase was like... you roasting the family dog and skinning it alive in front of them. He was gonna to do it behind my back, Drew. I had to end it early. To save your life. I stood up to him about it too. What if that means I'm next? He'd actually do it, Drew. Me! It's not even the first time apparently. It'd be over nothing. I'm actually scared! And I can't tell anyone this, not even Larry, just in case he—"

"Do you even know you're lying anymore?" Drew interrupts.

Theo feels faint. "But I'm not lying."

"You don't even know. It just flies off the tongue. You have no control over it."

Theo's breath quickens. "But you just said you could tell when I was—"

"No more bullshit!" Drew stands up. "It's so obvious to me now. Every step, it was all you. You knew just what to say to get me to do just what you wanted me to do, no care if it was gonna fuck up my life. You didn't care how it worked, just so long as it worked!"

"THAT IS NOT TRUE!" Theo screams.

"STOP LYING!"

"I'm not lying!" Theo whines, tears in his eyes. "I'm not!" He wipes his face. "You forgave Kev so easily. Why can't you forgive me?"

"Kev's a good person. You're just a fucking monster."

Theo's lungs evaporate. He's actually dizzy.

Drew shrugs heartlessly. "You fired me for nothing, knowing how that would hurt me. Then you got Alan to quit so you could take Larry from me so I'd be too weak to function and come crawling back to you with your money. That's fucked up."

Theo's lips tremble. "I'm sorry."

"SHUT THE FUCK UP, CASHEW!" Drew hollers.

Theo lowers his head, trying his hardest not to cry.

Drew laughs bitterly. "You'd rather have everyone change around you than admit there's actually something wrong with you. And there is, by the way. Something wrong with you. But you'll never know it, will you? You'd rather everyone be too scared to tell you the truth. Until you start forgiving people, Theo, you'll never be as good as you can be."

"That's why I'm here," Theo whines. "I'm trying to make up for what I did."

"What's your angle?"

"I don't have an angle!"

"YOU ALWAYS HAVE AN ANGLE!" Drew exclaims. "You're a fucking sociopath! Playing on my insecurities?! Gaslighting me?! Getting me hooked on cocaine?! Steroids?! Turning me into a fucking alcoholic?! You just kept on doing it, didn't you? For years and years! No remorse! No regret! No feelings whatsoever!"

"I have feelings!" Theo sobs.

"NO YOU DON'T! YOU DON'T KNOW WHAT FEELINGS ARE! *I* KNOW! *I'M* THE ONE WITH THE FEELINGS!" Drew stops to breathe, his throat getting scratchy. "Frankie even warned me about you! I didn't want to believe it! What am I, stupid or something?! You made me a shittier person, Cashew! You turned me into a fucking mongrel! I gave up God for you! You were never my friend! I know what a friend is now! A friend doesn't make your life a living hell! A friend doesn't keep you down for a fucking profit! Friends support each other! They make sacrifices! You say I have no standards? I HAD PLENTY OF STANDARDS BEFORE I MET YOU!"

Theo's face contorts. "Stop."

"No, you stop. Stop pretending."

"I'M NOT PRETENDING!" Theo wails. "I went too far! I know that now! I'm sorry!"

Drew scoffs, shaking his head.

"Don't you fucking do that!" Theo snarls. "Don't you fucking dismiss me like that!"

"You're a fucking heartless disgusting pig," Drew says simply. "And you're flat-out stupid. You couldn't even tell your own company was bleeding out. And this new waste of time you're putting out? *Mari and the Babushkas*? That's just another *Tequilatown* waiting to happen. I was the brains of the operation, and you know it, don't you? Not That Nutty's heading down the toilet and I'm gonna win Best Picture and you'll be nothing. Because I'm a good person. And Kev is a good person. And you're a heartless disgusting pig."

Theo looks to the floor, both hands gripping the side of his head.

"You're nothing like your father," Drew snarls. "Calvin Landreth had a heart. That's why he was so great. Not just for bumfuck Joseph, Oregon. He could've been great anywhere. Because he knew how to treat people with respect. How to be kind."

"Not to me!" Theo cries, his face all red. "I did everything for that son of a bitch. I stayed out of his way. I smiled and smiled. I obeyed and obeyed. I went months without even seeing my father. He practically lived in that fucking Motor-Mart, giving A+ service to every *other* person in Joseph, but I still loved him. Why wasn't that enough? He loved everyone! Why couldn't he love me?!"

"Because he knew you?"

Theo's mouth hangs open.

Drew shrugs. "Our parents know us a lot better than we think they do. He didn't want to give you Landreth Motors because he knew just what you were like. He was stuck with you. And he'd rather let it die with him than pass it down to his monster of a son."

Theo stares at Drew, simply heartbroken.

Drew callously walks past him. Opens the door. "Get the fuck out of my house."

Theo rises. Doesn't look at Drew. Slowly steps into the hall.

Drew slams the door, echoes shaking the furniture. A picture he had hanging on the wall falls on its face. Drew doesn't move. He just stands in the middle of the room. Everything's dizzy. He feels sick. His urethra burning from three near-consecutive ejaculations. His blood burning from a fit of rage he never knew he had in him. An untouched whiteboard, absolutely zero progress made. No energy left in him to salvage what was left of his day.

Theo stands in the hall on the verge of tears. His feet scrape the landing as he makes his way downstairs.

WHALE

A Nuclear Bomb

Whale creeps up to the front entrance of The Factory. Lights on but dim. A vacuum whirs somewhere. Whale checks behind him. If there was a cleaning van, it must be parked out back. Whale grabs the door handle. Turns it. Unlocked. He flings the door open and darts inside. Presses hand on the closing door. Softens the click.

A pair of cleaning men walk into the lobby, talking in Spanish. Whale stands erect, pretending he belongs there. The cleaning men stop and stare at Whale, all those bandages, the blood stains on his shirt.

Whale's heart pounds. He forces a smile.

```
                    WHALE
      Hola.
```

"*Hola*," says the man holding the clipboard.

"*Hola*," adds the other cleaning man. They look at each other, mumble a bit in Spanish and walk on, avoiding eye contact with Whale.

Whale rushes into The Classroom, a ghost town with no lights on. Rounds the corner. Down the dark hall. Into the copy room. Flips the switch. Too much light. It's seeping into the hall. He flicks it off. Goes into the small office. Flips the light switch in there. Keeps the door open. Lowers the Venetian blinds. Sits at his computer. Types in his username "Whale" and password "StewieHanzJr." Enter. His dashboard appears, his work just as he left it. Whale grins. Peeks out the door to check the hallway. No search party. He closes the side office door. Puts on his PSB YouTube playlist. Picks up where he left off.

After reading his second feature, Whale takes a small break. Checks his watch. Three hours already. He's in quite the groove. He extends his arms behind him, stretching. Notices light coming in the gap between the door and floor. A faint voice. Feet scraping the carpet.

Whale turns off the music. Flicks the light off. The hallway light is on. Whale shuts off his computer monitor. Crouches below the desk. Waits in the dark for whoever it is to pass.

The voice gets closer, a woman. Whatever she's saying, it's in English.

The copy room light turns on, the woman speaking softly as she steps into the room. Whale pokes his head up. Reaches for the blinds. Parts two rungs to get a good look.

It's Bumps. She's loading paper into the copy machine. Probably been doing the same thing he is. Explains why the cleaning guys weren't surprised to see someone walking about after hours. Whale stands, reaching for the doorknob.

"What'cha doing?" The Professor asks, walking into the copy room.

Whale drops to the ground. What's he doing here? If he catches him, he's dead.

"Just copying," Bumps murmurs.

"That's nice," The Professor says.

"What is?"

"What is that?"

"Chanel."

"Mmm." The Professor inhales softly.

Whale furrows his brow.

"You put in on just for me?" The Professor whispers.

"Of course," Bumps says. "Every time I put it on, I think of what you'd do if you caught a whiff." There's something weird about how she sounds. Like she's reading a bad script wrong.

"Is that so?"

"Yes, sir," Bumps says. There it is again. Eager volume but no emotion behind it. What's up with her? Whale hears soft kisses. Brush of fabric. "What are you gonna do to me?" she asks.

"You know what."

"But what if someone catches us?"

"They'll take their turn, now won't they?"

"I got so much work to do. I gotta get these reports in before lunchtime."

Whale scrunches his face. Lunchtime? What the hell is going on? He looks up through the Venetian blinds again. Reaches for the pullcord. Pulls just enough to create a gap. Raises his head. Peeks out the window.

Bumps facing the copy machine, The Professor kissing her neck from behind, hands running up and down her dress. She's thinner than before, almost emaciated. The Professor moans with ecstasy, eyes rolled back, but she stares forward with dead eyes.

"You want it, bitch?" The Professor growls.

"Yeah," Bumps answers, her vocal earnest contrasting her facial disgust.

"Tell me you want it."

"I want it."

"Fuck yeah you do." The Professor spins Bumps around. Kisses her hard. Tongue forcing into her mouth. Bumps doesn't do anything at first, but then she starts kissing him back. Reaches down. Rubs his crotch.

Whale watches, an anger brewing inside him. Cashew couldn't have been right. There's no way. But there she was, right in front of him, earning the frigging job.

The Professor reaches down. Bumps backs her hips away. The Professor tries again to grab it but Bumps gently takes his hand and moves it to her lower back. He roams it down her dress. Pokes his fingers into the fabric, Bumps faking a moan.

Whale grimaces. He hates him. Cheating on his wife. A kid at home. Disgusting degenerate. What a hypocrite. Whale merely helps Cashew cheat and he gets beat up, but Bumps cheats and that's okay? He thought The Professor didn't like her. Just a pair of bumps he said. Was that a lie? Did he change his mind or something? Why?

Bumps' breath quickens, her hands grazing the length of The Professor's erect cock. Big one too.

Whale's lip curls. Why does *she* get to blow her way up?

The Professor chuckles. "You like it, don't you?"

Bumps nods, her eyes empty.

"Tell you like it, whore," The Professor orders.

"I like it."

"Like you mean it."

Bumps looks into The Professor's eyes. "I like it."

The Professor grins. Grabs the back of her head. Kisses her hard, not letting her go.

Whale scowls, his face trembling. Picks his phone off the desk. Opens the camera. Swipes to Video. Turns off the flash. Props the phone against the glass. Hits record. Steps back to watch.

The Professor runs a hand up Bumps' leg, inch by inch on its way to her pussy. Bumps drops to her knees before it does. Unbuckles his belt. Unzips. Whips out The Professor's uncut member. Stares at it, hesitating.

"Come on," The Professor barks. "Show me how much you want it."

Bumps closes her eyes. Puts it in her mouth.

The Professor cocks his head back, gasping with a disgusting grin. "What a good girl!" He puts a hand on the back of her head. Moves it at his rhythm. "I've been wanting this a while. Every time I see you, I just wanna fuck your brains out." Bumps tries to move away. "Uh-uh. Where do you think you're going, bitch?" The Professor presses Bumps' head down. Holds it there. Lets go. Bumps moves away, gagging, spittle dripping down, disoriented. The Professor grabs her shoulders. Ushers her to the copy machine. Lifts the back of her dress.

"What are you doing?" Bumps mumbles, looking behind her. The Professor rips the fabric. "Stop!" Bumps cries, suddenly incredibly emotional. "Wait, what are you doing?!"

Whale's mouth falls open, his blood chilling.

The Professor forces himself in. Bumps tries to move away. "NO!" she screams. "STOP! PLEASE!"

"Keep screaming, bitch!" The Professor jeers. He smacks her ass. Keeps going.

Whale's eyes look around in a panic, Bumps' cries getting more unhinged and desperate. She sounds like she normally does. Out of character. That's all it was, wasn't it? Whale was all wrong. None of this was her idea. She was just being pressured before. That wasn't real, *but this is!* Oh God, he's gotta stop it! He's gotta save her! Whale reaches out to stop the recording.

His fingers stop an inch from the screen. The Professor raping Bumps. How monstrous he looks pulling her hair. All those heartless jeers. Those tears running down Bumps' face as she screams for help. Whale's mind goes numb.

He moves his fingers away. Steps back from the phone, the video uninterrupted, that red light still blinking.

The Professor smacks her shoulders. Slams Bumps down on the copier. He goes faster. Sweat drips down his face. He grunts hard with a sick smile. Bumps pinned down with a wide palm to her scalp. She screams louder, her cheek smushed against the glass.

Whale's eyes widen with horror. He covers his mouth with both hands. Forces himself to look away. Crouches onto to the floor. Covers his ears. But his phone doesn't turn away. It doesn't stop. It just stays right where it is, leaning against the glass, hiding in the dark. It sees everything. It watches.

END OF PART FOUR

PART FIVE

Garlands for the Conqueror

JACOB

Guess Who's Coming to Dinner

INT. WHITMAN UNIVERSITY - LB 710 - JACOB'S ROOM - NIGHT

Stewie helps Jacob load packed boxes into a large cart.

STEWIE
Give me the rundown again.

JACOB
TJ.

STEWIE
Black guy. Rich dad, Directing major, motorhead.

JACOB
Correct. Nich?

STEWIE
Short for Nicholas, Cinematography major, pothead, metalhead.

JACOB
And prog too.

STEWIE
He's the Hasidic, right?

JACOB
No.

STEWIE
Oh that's right, Rian.

JACOB
Ex-Hasidic.

STEWIE
That's what I meant.

JACOB
I wouldn't bring it up if I were you. He did just spend an entire summer with them. He probably wants to forget them while he still can.

STEWIE
That bad, huh?

JACOB
That bad.

CUT TO:

IN THE HALLWAY

Jacob and Stewie push the loaded cart out of the bedroom.

STEWIE
Rian's not much of a Jewish name, even with a Y.

JACOB
It was originally Ezekiel. He legally changed it when he was eighteen, first chance he could.

STEWIE
Yeah, definitely not a conversation for tonight.

JACOB
Though he loves talking S-H-I-T about the Hasidics. He's got stories you wouldn't believe.

STEWIE
Why'd he pick Rian?

JACOB
Rian Johnson, director of the best episodes of Breaking Bad.

STEWIE
That's it?

JACOB
One word: "Ozymandias." Literally the greatest hour of television in history.

STEWIE
Let me know when we're on it.

JACOB
Don't worry, you'll know.

Jacob holds the door open for Stewie.

JACOB (CONT'D)
I never call him Rian anyway. He's always been Frankie to me.

CUT TO:

INT. FILM IMMERSION - CONTINUOUS

Stewie two-hands the cart down the hallway, Jacob pulling the front.

STEWIE
Frankie?

JACOB
Inside joke. Something about Frankie Goes to Hollywood. I don't remember anymore.

STEWIE
I thought you hated 80s music before me.

JACOB
I still knew a bunch. "Relax" is one of the few hits I could stand.

The entire floor is abuzz with new arrivals, an ocean of young bright faces glad to be back, glad to see each other. Clem walks by.

CLEM
Jacob!

JACOB
Hey Clem, how was your summer?

CLEM
Boring. Lots of work, you know.
(to Stewie)
And you must be Jacob's father. I can see the resemblance.

STEWIE
No, I'm his boyfriend.

JACOB
This is Stewie, remember?

CLEM
Oh, I am so sorry!

STEWIE
Happens all the time.

JACOB
Is Kyliee around? I've been meaning to ask her about Comic Con.

CLEM
Kyliee dropped out.

JACOB
What?

Clem's legitimately uncomfortable.

CLEM
She's been going through a lot lately. Personal reasons.

JACOB
Sorry to hear that.

CLEM
It was great seeing you.

JACOB
Seeya.

Clem walks off.

STEWIE
She seems nice.

JACOB
I wonder what happened to Kyliee.

STEWIE
She had her reasons, I'm sure.

JACOB
She was acting weird at our farewell party. Carter talked to her. Maybe he knows something.

STEWIE
What would he know?

Jacob hesitates.

JACOB
I don't know. Maybe you're right.

Jacob and Stewie keep pushing the cart toward Suite 701 at the end of the hall.

JACOB (CONT'D)
God, I hope they like you.

STEWIE
Why wouldn't they like me?

JACOB
I don't know. I've never introduced a partner before.

STEWIE
You just did.

JACOB
I barely know Clem outside Anime Club. Frankie, Nich, and TJ are my best friends. I'm going to LA with these guys. I'd hate for you to end up our Yoko.

STEWIE
(imitating Yoko Ono)
Ya-Ya-Ya! Moto! Moto!

Jacob shushes. Suite 701's door whips open. It's Nich, fuchsia hair shoulder-length wearing a faded Rush 2112 shirt.

NICH
Thought I heard Yoko. How're you doing, man?

Jacob hugs Nich. Nich bro-nods Stewie.

NICH (CONT'D)
Sup. You must be Stewie.

STEWIE
Nich, right?

NICH
That's right.

Nich looks at Jacob as he re-lifts the bags.

NICH (CONT'D)
Damn bro! You been working out?

JACOB
Lost twenty pounds already.

NICH
Fuck. You look great.

JACOB
Thanks.

NICH
(To Stewie)
I'll help you with that.

STEWIE
You sure?

CUT TO:

INT. SUITE 701 - LIVING ROOM - NIGHT

TJ and Rian sit on the sofa playing XBOX. Jacob walks in.

JACOB
Hey guys.

RIAN
Hey!

TJ pauses the game. Rian hugs Jacob. TJ fistbumps.

RIAN (CONT'D)
Dude, you look great!

TJ
Surprised you didn't lose your mind.

JACOB
Almost did.

RIAN
The fitness center hasn't been open, has it?

JACOB
No, this is all Stewie. He's got a home gym.

TJ
Where is he?

Jacob turns. Stewie and Nich are still outside talking.

JACOB
(bleating)
AYY BEE!

STEWIE (O.S.)
Just a second!

RIAN
What was that?

JACOB
What?

RIAN
"AYY BEE?"

JACOB
It's a call-and-response thing. It started as Baby Boy, then Baby, and now it's just Aby.
(bleating)
AYY BEE!

RIAN
Aybe.

JACOB
No-no, more vibrato.
(bleating)
AYY BEE!

RIAN
(bleating)
AYY BEE!

Jacob holds up one finger. Two. Three.

JACOB & RIAN
(discordant bleating)
AYY BEE!

STEWIE (O.S.)
(bleating)
AYY BEE!

Jacob and Rian chuckle.

TJ
I need more black friends.

Stewie and Nich finally push the luggage cart in.

JACOB
What took you guys so long?

STEWIE
We were talking about Rush.

NICH
(to Jacob)
You never told me he saw them live!

JACOB
I never knew.

STEWIE
(to Nich)
You know who stole the show?

NICH
Neil Peart?

STEWIE
Neil Peart!

CUT TO:

INSIDE JACOB'S NEW ROOM

Jacob and Rian hang posters. They can hear Stewie, Nich, and TJ talking excitedly in the next room.

RIAN
Where's the putty?

Jacob doesn't respond, staring out the window at the gorgeous panoramic view of Boston Common.

Rian turns. Sees Jacob's gaze. Gently places his poster down. Shares the view.

JACOB
It's really it, huh?

RIAN
Senior Year.

JACOB
Then LA.

Jacob turns away.

JACOB
Fuck the putty. Let's just thumbtack these bitches.

RIAN
Here here.

Jacob pulls a box of thumbtacks out of the cart. Rian hangs up a <u>Godfather</u> poster. Jacob re-hangs the same <u>Pulp Fiction</u> poster he's had since Freshman Year.

JACOB
Stewie's great, huh?

RIAN
You guys really love each other. I can tell.

JACOB
Didn't think we were doing anything exceptionally different. I'm just being myself.

RIAN
Isn't that what love is? A safe space to be ourselves?

JACOB
You might be right about that.

RIAN
Your family meet him yet?

JACOB
We're driving down for Mom's birthday next month to surprise her.

RIAN
That'll be interesting.

JACOB
With Stewie there I might even see a different side of them.

RIAN
You think so?

JACOB
It's already happening with movies. Why not real life?

Rian opens up a new poster.

RIAN
What's this?

JACOB
All the Pet Shop Boys albums in chronological order. That was a hard one to find too. <u>Super</u> only just came out in April.

RIAN
You're really deep diving into these guys.

JACOB
I'm telling you, Frankie, the Pet Shop Boys are my favorite artist of all time.

RIAN
I'm shocked.

JACOB
Believe me. After I listened to their Greatest Hits I found all their other singles, and then their album tracks, and now I find out their B-Sides are even better. I can't believe it. Neither can Stewie.

RIAN
He didn't know?

JACOB
No way. Until me, he thought they peaked in 1990 like every other 80s group. It's like we're discovering a lost world together.

RIAN
I'm lowkey jealous of you, buddy.

JACOB
God, no one's ever been jealous of me.

STEWIE (O.S.)
(top of his lungs)
STOP! IT'S OKAY! STOP!

Rian flinches.

RIAN
The fuck was that?

JACOB
(unfazed)
It's just his buffalo story.

RIAN
His what?

JACOB
After he got laid off from Lucent, he took his Jeep on a trip cross-country. He almost got charged by a buffalo in Yellowstone and he had to yell at it for it to stop.

RIAN
Wow! That's a hell of a story.

JACOB
It's probably the only good one he has. I've heard it thirty times already. He even said it during his infamous best man speech at his brother's wedding.

RIAN
I kinda wanna hear it now.

JACOB
No you don't. He takes forty-five minutes to say what I've already told you.

Rian hums a bit. Hangs up the Pet Shop Boys poster.

RIAN
You think he has Asperger's?

JACOB
I thought so at first until his brother Ron came up to see deGrom and the Mets at Fenway.

RIAN
Who?

JACOB
Jacob deGrom, Stewie's favorite player. Anyway, Ron acts the same as Stewie. Their sisters too, apparently. That's just how their mother raised them,

I guess.

RIAN
Autistic Lite.

JACOB
Just enough familiarity for me to hold on to with none of the high maintenance.

RIAN
You guys really are perfect for each other.

Jacob grins.

RIAN (CONT'D)
Before I forget, they're showing the roadshow version of The Hateful Eight in 70mm this Saturday at the Somerville. Wanna go? You, me, and Stewie?

JACOB
Sure.

RIAN
You think he'd like it?

JACOB
He won't like the cursing and the gore, but he likes Pulp Fiction. Maybe he will.

RIAN
And maybe we can go out afterwards. Get a few drinks.

JACOB
I don't know about that. We got to get up early for church.

Rian turns.

RIAN
You're going to church?

JACOB
Yeah.

RIAN
When did this happen?

JACOB
Sunday.

RIAN
You're really going every week?

JACOB
That's the idea.

RIAN
Because of Stewie?

JACOB
I want to go.

RIAN
Why?

Jacob shrugs.

JACOB
I believe in God again.

RIAN
Because Stewie wants you to?

Jacob turns to Rian.

JACOB
I believe in a literal God more than he does.

Rian looks away.

JACOB (CONT'D)
What's the big deal?

RIAN
(sarcastic)
There's no big deal. You with the guy three months and suddenly you're Born Again.

JACOB
I'm not Born Again. I was already baptized, remember?

RIAN
I just think it's weird.

JACOB
It's my idea, Frankie.

RIAN
That's what they want you to think. That's what they do. Brainwash people at their most vulnerable.

JACOB
I'm not brainwashed.

RIAN
You can believe whatever you want to believe, I don't care. Just don't pretend you're going to church because of you. You're going because an ancient piece of mistranslated fanfiction is telling you to. Because how else are they gonna make money to raid and pillage and pay off their molestation settlements?

JACOB
Cut it out.

RIAN
I don't get it. How can you be gay and support those people?

JACOB
A lot of religious denominations abuse. I know you've seen quite a bit of that yourself. This is different. It's a lot less political than I remember and way more morally centered. It's about forgiveness and second chances and giving people the benefit of the doubt. I already do that, Frankie. Being there makes me happy. Really happy. Atheism's a hard life. It's dark. I don't want to be like that.

Rian half-frowns.

JACOB (CONT'D)
And I know this sounds cheesy, but when I was in high school I asked God for proof of His existence, something I'd know when I see it.
(shrugs)
So He did. I truly believe that.

RIAN
That could just be a coincidence.

Jacob sighs.

JACOB
Stewie wasn't what I wanted. I wanted a Carter Jackson dreamboat, not a small business owner from New Jersey thirty-one years older than me. I know he can be juvenile and stubborn and even a bit harsh at times, but you know what, that's exactly what I need. He doesn't fall for my manipulative bullshit. He calls me out when I act like a spoiled brat. He values me. He's devoted to me. He loves me more than anyone else in this world. Me. Every day I'm

realizing more and more that the man I'm supposed to be is a man that man would respect.
(pause)
I had no one, Frankie. No one with the time or the patience to fix my fucked up life, let alone the maturity, but he did. For the first time in my life I'm happy. I have hope. All that bullshit I spent my whole life putting up with is suddenly worth it. THAT'S what I wanted. I didn't know it, but God did. He knew me so well. He sent me just what I needed when I needed it.
(pause)
Calling it all a coincidence trivializes the whole thing.

Rian frowns, visibly ashamed.

RIAN
I'm sorry.

JACOB
It's okay.

Jacob resumes his unboxing. Rian doesn't budge.

RIAN
You know you have me too, right?

Jacob looks back at Rian.

RIAN (CONT'D)
Just because I don't agree with you doesn't mean that changes.

JACOB
(smiling)
I know it doesn't.

Rian smiles back with relief.

DISSOLVE TO:

EXT. BEACON HILL - NIGHT

Jacob walks Stewie down a cobblestone street full of brownstones.

STEWIE
TJ's a riot.

JACOB
He is?

STEWIE
You don't think so?

JACOB
I always thought him the lamest of the bunch.

STEWIE
I think they're all great. Your friends are great, Baby Boy.

JACOB
They like you too.

STEWIE
I'm glad.

JACOB
Surprised you didn't mention your political affiliations.

STEWIE
I'm not stupid.

JACOB
Since when is it stupid to talk politics?

STEWIE
It's stupid in an election year, especially among strangers.

JACOB
You weren't strangers for long.

STEWIE
Even still, you should never talk politics. I've had enough experience being a closeted Trump supporter to know it's not worth mentioning.

JACOB
How can you say that?

STEWIE
Because whenever I'm signing a new client and I'm at their house chit-chatting and they start talking S-H-I-T about Trump, assuming I'm voting for Hillary and for no other reason than the fact that I'm polite and cordial, I find that very insulting. I don't bring up my political opinions unannounced like that, why should they?

JACOB
I think you're downplaying their intelligence.

They stop outside Stewie's brownstone apartment building.

STEWIE
You know why I only talk about my friends in past tense? Because when Wilma, Moo-Moo, and Bam-Bam found out I was a Trump supporter, they harassed me mercilessly. And now we're not friends, because they would rather throw away twenty-five years of friendship and Saturday nights and smutty stories and heartache than accept the fact that I have a different opinion from them. I thought THEY were intelligent. Even if they weren't, I thought they'd at least make me an exception.

Jacob frowns, his heart breaking at that.

JACOB
Do you regret it?

STEWIE
What?

JACOB
Fighting so hard for your beliefs?

Stewie takes a deep breath.

STEWIE
Not really.

Jacob nods. He kisses Stewie goodnight. Stewie enters his building.

Jacob stands in silence a moment more, pondering Stewie's words. He sticks his hands in his jacket pockets. Makes his way back to campus.

SLOW FADE TO BLACK.

DREW

Unsubscribers

Sixteen months after he escorted Drew Lawrence and Kev Foster through the Jack Branson Society, Terrance Donahue receives that long awaited email. The final cut is ready. But the title is different. It's not called *Branson!* anymore. It's *The Sins of Jack Branson*.

Terrance drags his rolling suitcase through LAX and onto an escalator. His cotton sweater is making him sweat. The boys weren't joking. February in California is nothing like February in New York. Terrance looks at the ground floor below, trying not to laugh at the two suited men waving their arms over their heads at him.

"Here, let me get that for you," Drew says, grabbing the handle of Terrance's bag.

"You have a good flight, Terrance?" Kev asks, leading the way to the car.

"It was fine," Terrance murmurs.

"You ever been to California before?" Drew asks.

"Can't say I have." Terrance slides in the back seat of a shiny black SUV parked outside.

Kev drives out of the airport zone. Drew looks at the rearview mirror. "You comfortable back there, Mr. Donahue?"

"I told you to call me Terrance."

"Sorry."

"You boys seem pretty confident."

"I think we have a right to be," Kev says.

"I liked what I read. For the most part at least."

Kev and Drew smirk at each other. "Yeah, about that," Drew says.

"I'm glad you came to your senses about the title. I always thought *Branson!* with that silly exclamation point was too campy for such an important story."

"I rewrote the script."

Terrance stares. "Not too much, I hope."

"The *Branson!* draft we walked through?" Kev says. "It's completely obsolete now."

Terrance blinks, too stunned for words. "But it's still an animated Pet Shop Boys musical?"

Drew shrugs. "Kinda."

Terrance furrows his brows. "What?"

"You'll see."

Drew and Kev sit in the back of Ephemeral Pictures' screening room, their eyes fixed on the back of Terrance's bald head in the front row. Very little motion throughout the movie. No guffaws in the wrong place. No laughing at the right place either. The final number ends. The credits roll. The lights rise up. Terrance isn't moving.

"Terrance?" Drew asks.

No response.

Drew looks at Kev. "He didn't fall asleep, did he?"

"Maybe we should've told him it was gonna be three hours." Kev sits up. "Terrance, what did you think of it?"

Terrance doesn't budge.

"Oh God," Drew whispers. "Is he dead?"

"What would we do?" Kev whispers back. "What does anybody do? Do we call the police?"

"If our movie killed him, is that good or bad?"

"You can't kill someone with a movie."

"Ever heard of epilepsy?"

"Old people can't be epileptic."

"It's not just children."

Terrance shifts in his seat.

"Oh thank God," Drew breathes. He and Kev stand up and walk cautiously down the side aisles. Drew sees Terrance first. He's staring at the blank screen with red eyes, face wet with tears. Drew looks uneasily at Kev. Gently sits beside Terrance. "Terrance?"

"I wish my grandparents could have seen this." Terrance closes his eyes and sobs into his hand. Drew places a comforting hand on Terrance's shoulder. Terrance pulls Drew in and hugs the shit out of him, crying into his jacket. "Thank you, Mr. Lawrence. Thank you."

Drew grins, overwhelmed with relief. He hugs Terrance back.

Kev and Drew treat Terrance to dinner at Marcus MacDonald's, gorging their signature meatloaf and shepherd's pie with gusto. "If I had any doubts," Terrance says, lifting his Guinness, "they vanished the moment I saw that opening number."

"'The Sodom and Gomorrah Show,'" Drew says with a nod. "That's Eli's favorite too."

"Was that a real one-take?"

"Technically there are no real one-takes in animated movies. But yes, everything was filmed live. Lots of rehearsals. Stunt rigs. Camera hand-offs. He's quite elaborate."

"The whole thing was beautiful. Moving. And I'm glad you didn't tell me about the live action. My jaw dropped the moment I saw it."

"You're not allowed to tell anyone about that," Kev says. "Not for a long time. We're trying to keep it a secret for Cannes."

"I want it to be *The Wizard of Oz* of the 21st Century," Drew says.

"It fits the structure perfectly," Terrance says. "The animated parts being the book and the live action being everything after. What made you think of that?"

"The book is such a focal part of the scandal," Kev answers. "You can't read an entire book to the audience, so depicting what's actually in the book helps them understand why the scandal's such a big deal from Jack's perspective."

"It's also like how *La La Land* stops being a musical the moment Sebastian and Mia 'grow up,'" Drew says. "Or when *The Artist* becomes a talkie the moment George accepts his new career direction. The animated parts, the world of his memoir, represents Jack's innocent Hollywoodesque interpretation of his early days. His present day hope gives his past color and charm, and he even assigns a three-act structure to his journey. We all do that. We all assign a beginning, middle, and end to our own culminations. He truly feels the worst is behind him when he publishes that book, and when the shit hits the fan and he realizes he's indirectly responsible for his new home being taken away from him, forced to publicly out himself to fight the forces seeking to oppress him, that's the dark and depressing world creeping back it."

"And animated Jack isn't the same as live action Jack," Kev adds.

"Yes, Jack's animated version is the version he wants to be advertised, just like how we put out the version we want everyone to see. The real Jack isn't a Hollywood Hero at all. He's actually a really insecure person. And the real world isn't as simple or predictable or structured. There's no guaranteed finale waiting around the corner unless he makes it happen himself. That's a hard transition a lot of people can relate to, especially if you weren't originally from Los Angeles. I know it was for me."

Terrance nods. "I'm incredibly impressed by your intuition, Mr. Lawrence. I'm particular amazed by the actors themselves. Especially Mr. Munce."

"I know! Wasn't he fantastic?!" Drew exclaims.

"We found that guy in an open casting call," Kev says. "Martin Kennergan. Character actor for forty years. He used to do Life Cereal commercials as a kid."

"I see very big things for him after this," Terrance says.

"He's gonna win Best Supporting Actor," Drew says. "There's no way he's not."

"And the mother!" Terrance exhales with a hand to his heart. "Adding Maggie Branson was the best thing you could've done."

Drew withdraws inward. "Moms are the best."

"What gave you the idea?"

Kev frowns.

Drew hesitates. "My mom passed away almost two years ago."

"I'm so sorry to hear that."

Drew nods. "She tried to call me the day she died and I didn't answer. I still feel awful about that, not getting the chance to say goodbye. But I thought about her when I was writing this, and I thought perhaps my reluctance to reconnect after our falling out was something she felt as well. If only we did. So I gave that to Jack. It's a bit Hollywood, you know, the letter from beyond the grave thing, but it feels right. That's all that matters."

Kev puts a supportive hand on Drew's shoulder. Drew smiles back.

Terrance looks at Drew mysteriously. "How did you know Jack Branson was autistic?"

Kev raises his brows. "You thought so too?"

"My father posited that in the 90s." Terrance looks at Drew. "But how did you know?"

Drew shrugs bashfully. "Takes one to know one, I guess."

Terrance stares. "Really?"

"It's the only explanation for the way he acted. Fixed routines. Dependent on a comfort zone. Brutally stubborn. Bouts of depression. Really intelligent in some ways but brutally dumb in others. C'mon, the way he described his social anxiety when he finally joined the brothel was like something I would write. I didn't really have to think about it. It was just a no-brainer."

Terrance smiles. "It seems to me, Mr. Lawrence, that you were meant to save Jack's story."

Drew melts his seat, moved beyond words.

Terrance checks his watch. "On that somber note, I will retire."

"We can drive you back to your hotel," Kev offers.

"No, no, you two have done enough for an old man like me." Terrance squeezes out of the booth. "Now it's time for a strapping lad young enough to be my grandson to take over." He laughs. "I don't how you boys can get any work done in such a virile town as this." He waddles out the door.

Kev furrows his brow. "Bit of a perv, ain't he?"

Drew points to the bar. "Let's get a drink."

Kev hesitates. "What about your sobriety?"

"I can't give up booze. C'mon, we have to celebrate."

Kev shrugs. "Alright, as long as you're sure."

Kev and Drew sit at the counter. Durrell the bartender gasps. "Drew Lawrence!"

"Durrell," Drew mumbles.

"Your usual, Mr. Lawrence?" Durrell asks, already opening a new bottle of 15yr Domergue Scotch.

Drew looks at Kev. "Sure. Two."

Durrell scoops crushed ice into two rocks glasses.

"We'll take those neat, actually," Drew quickly interjects.

Durrell shrugs. "Whatever you want, Mr. Lawrence." He dumps the ice out. Pours two shots of Scotch. Hands them over. "On the house, of course."

Drew pulls out his wallet. "Please, I insist."

"No, why not?" Kev asks, taking his glass.

Drew awkwardly puts his wallet away. "Thank you Durrell."

Durrell purses his lips at Kev. "Anytime." He walks away.

Kev takes a small sip. "That's good."

Drew doesn't drink his. He just stares off, tracing the rim of his glass. "Remember when I first came to you that time at your house?" he whispers. "You said you didn't want to work with me."

Kev shrugs. "I know man, I..."

"Let me finish." Drew stares at the counter, trying to say it.

Kev's brows come together. "What?"

"I was never jealous of you." Drew looks at Kev. "I hated your guts back then just as much as Theo did."

Kev stares back, unsure what to say.

Drew swallows. "But I needed you to say yes to Ephemeral so I could get back at Theo for firing me." He pauses. "I lied to you. I lied to you so well. I've hated myself every day since then."

Kev frowns, genuinely hurt.

Drew looks away. "I was never gonna tell you." He sips his Scotch. "I might've after the movie came out, when it was too late for you to fuck up the Cannes premiere to get back at me, but..." He shakes his head. "I couldn't do that to you. You've been such an unbelievable friend to me, even though I don't deserve it."

Kev sighs. "I think that was a very shitty thing to do."

"I know it was."

"I'm not a fucking pawn. I told you that."

Drew nods. "If you wanna kick me off and take the writing credit, I don't care. Do it."

Kev sips his Scotch. "I'm not taking credit for your screenplay."

"Why not?"

"I didn't write it. That's just dishonest."

Drew frowns. "So what are we gonna do?"

Kev puts a hand on Drew's shoulder. "If you didn't lie to me, I never would've said yes. If I didn't say yes, I would've gone the rest of my life believing Drew Lawrence was a spoiled brat that only made millions because he spent two decades coasting on the backs of others. But that is so not true. I've seen it myself. You are an unbelievable artist. I can't believe it. I'm actually jealous of *you*."

Drew smiles a bit.

Kev finishes his Scotch. "We've come this far, buddy. We're stuck with each other."

Durrell walks over. "Would you like another drink, sir?"

"Leave the bottle." Kev flicks a miserly finger at Drew. "Give him the check."

Durrell perks up. "Yes sir!" He leaves the open bottle of Domergue 15 on the counter. Wanders off before Kev could change his mind.

Kev gives Drew a shiteating grin. "That's for hurting my feelings."

Drew smiles. "Fair enough." He pours Kev another shot.

Kev sips his second shot. "I can see why you like this so much. It's delicious."

Drew holds up his glass, staring off. "I can't believe you actually forgave me."

"People change."

Drew looks at Kev. "You really are a great person. I can't believe I never saw that before."

Kev goes quiet. "I really wasn't acting like one."

"You're just so direct. Clear. Emotionless 90% of the time." Drew sips his Domergue. "You're a declarative sentence in human form."

Kev nods. "Even I can see that."

"Look right there. Most people would just laugh."

"You would."

"Exactly."

"If I'm a declarative sentence, you're curse words in cursive."

Drew laughs his utter ass off, eyes squeezes shut. "*Oh my God, that's so true!*" he wheezes, squeaking a bit.

Kev grins. "You're a riot."

Drew wipes his eyes, trying to calm down. "Curse words in cursive. More like curse-ive..." He awkwardly stops talking.

Kev stares. "You didn't think that through, did you?"

"I fucked up." Drew downs the rest of his glass.

Kev looks at Drew and suddenly cringes. "Ew! What's wrong with your eyes?!"

"What?"

"They're all bloodshot! What the hell?!"

Drew lifts his butt off the stool, looking at his reflection in the mirror behind the liquor bottles. "Oh yeah," he murmurs. "This happens all the time."

"I never saw it before."

"It happens when I drink."

"Every time?"

"Most times. Or when I snort a line. Or lack of sleep. Fluorescent lighting. Sharp wind."

"Jesus."

"I know. It's just dry eye. Only been like this the past few years. Really freaked me out when I first saw it in the mirror." Drew pours himself another glass. "Help me understand something."

Kev sips his Domergue. "Go ahead."

"You, me, Theo... We all started our Hollywood careers on the same day. How did he end up the megalomaniac narcissist and you ended up so mature and clearheaded?"

Kev thinks. "After the internship I got a job at News For You. It's one of those digital media firms producing content for Conservatives. Facebook political shorts, TikTok, and so on. I loved it there at first. They didn't mock my stuttering, which helped me stop. I actually felt like a respected equal. Then COVID hit. That changed everything. It stopped being news. It was just... fake COVID cure this, vaccine misinformation that, election fraud bullshit. We made everything up ourselves, whatever was getting the most clicks that week. That wasn't what I signed up for. I wanted to teach people, to keep people informed. And our Editor kept justifying it as us setting up the election three cycles down the road, but why? If we were the ones in the right, why couldn't we just tell the truth?"

"God, we're like twins," Drew murmurs.

"One day I said I had enough and went up to the Editor. I told him our new direction was setting a bad precedent against our brand. And he fired me! Five years I was there! He thought *I* was crazy!"

Drew smirks. "I've spent too much of my life observing the world, other people. It's always the same pattern. Everyone blinded by emotion. Acting uncharacteristically stupid. This town is full of 'em. The whole country too. And all those hypocrites out there, the ones preying on decent people, sucking the innocence right out of them, the Theo Landreths, the Professors, the Oscar Blitzes, the two-party system, the media, they're incapable of facing the consequences of their actions. They'd rather stay in their bubbles and throw out honest, intelligent people than admit they're wrong."

"I just wish I jumped off the crazy train sooner. How could I have been so taken up by it?"

"You didn't think enough of yourself. You thought people knew what they were doing, so you let them take control. I was the same way before I met Stewie."

"I'm sure he's proud of you, wherever he is."

Drew shrugs. "I never told him I changed my name. But thank you for saying so."

Kev hunches over the counter. "Do you ever wonder what life would've been like if we never met The Professor?"

"All the time." Drew shakes his head. "It's such a shame. Trisha. And Theo, he's just... If only he wasn't. He's such a great businessman."

"He is?"

"Absolutely, but he has zero self-awareness. He doesn't know how good he is." Drew pauses. "Trisha would've helped him if he only let her."

Kev nods solemnly. "She understood the human side of the business. Accommodations. Trust."

Drew thinks back. "What if we were supposed to work together?"

Kev stares. "What do you mean?"

"You and Theo were strong worker types. Trisha and I were soft thinker types. Trisha and Theo had leadership qualities. You and I were loyal worker bees. What Theo lacked in empathy, Trisha made up for. What I lacked in business savvy, Theo made up for. You followed orders to a fault. I questioned orders to a fault. It's the perfect puzzle." Drew looks at Kev. "We were all so perfectly matched. What were the chances of that?"

Kev purses his lips.

"We were sitting next to each other in that lobby for five minutes," Drew says with disbelief. "None of us said anything. We could've upped and left to start a Factory of our own. Why didn't we think of that?"

"Because of him." Kev sips more Domergue. "Just a promise of something was already enough to corrupt us."

Drew shakes his head. "He hit the jackpot. A new A-team sitting right there in his Classroom." He looks at Kev with a lamentful frown. "Why did he try so hard to keep us away from each other?"

WHALE

Fat Man and Little Boy

Whale bursts into The Factory's lobby. The Secretary widens her eyes in horror and slams the phone down. "What are you doing here?!"

```
                    WHALE
        I'm going to work.
```

"No! No, you can't—!"

```
                    WHALE
        I don't care. I'm going in.
```

Whale storms toward the Classroom door. The Secretary stands. "I still need your cell phone!"

Whale stops. Turns his head to her.

The Secretary stares back, chest rising and falling steady.

```
                    WHALE
        I don't have it.
```

"Really? You forgot your cell phone?"

```
                    WHALE
        I lost it.
```

The Secretary hesitates. "I don't believe you."

```
                    WHALE
        I don't give a fuck what you believe.
```

"How'd you get here without a car?"

```
                    WHALE
        I took a Ridr.
```

"You called a Ridr without a phone?"

```
                    WHALE
        My roommate called it for me.
                  (pause)
        Because I lost my phone.
```

The Secretary stares. "Then you'll have no problem with me patting you down."

Whale reaches into his pants pockets. Pulls out the linings.

```
                    WHALE
        Don't have my phone.
```

"I still have to pat you down."

```
                    WHALE
        Why?
```

"You might have something else."

Whale scoffs.

```
                    WHALE
        You really think I have a gun?
```

"Hold up your arms," The Secretary murmurs.

```
                    WHALE
Why would I go postal? Because your boss beat the
ever-loving shit out of me while you stood by and did
nothing?
               (pause)
I don't know, maybe I should.
```

The Secretary stands there, taking it. "Please raise your arms."

Whale holds out his arms. The Secretary gingerly walks over, stilettos clicking, and reluctantly places her hands on Whale's body. Moves down his torso. Frisks each leg one at a time. His butt. His groin. "Okay. You're good."

Whale pushes into The Classroom. It's quiet. Bumps at her desk, head down, staring at the keyboard. Something's disturbing her alright. And Whale let it happen, didn't he?

A chair scoots hard to Whale's left. He makes eye contact with Peabrain, his mouth agape, eyes bugged.

Whale points at his bruised and battered face.

```
                    WHALE
Thanks.
```

Peabrain looks off, a muted reaction of horror and shame.

A pair of footsteps on Whale's right. The Professor stops in his tracks. "Whale," he says with actual surprise. "What the hell are you doing here?"

Whale discreetly looks at Bumps. She's sitting up, looking back at him, happy to see him but also confused by his face. Not disturbed anymore. Whale furrows his brows slightly. Returns his focus to The Professor.

```
                    WHALE
I work here.
```

"Not anymore you don't."

```
                    WHALE
I can still log in. I have unfinished work. I'm doing
it.
```

The Professor stares back, actually affected by Whale's assertive tone.

```
                    WHALE (CONT'D)
I'd like to get back to work. I suggest you do the
same.
```

The Professor nods slowly. For a split second the edge of his mouth twitches, an unconscious smirk killed in its tracks. Whale maintains his stare as The Professor turns, climbing the staircase back up to his cube.

"Maintaining eye contact to assert dominance?" Bumps quips, walking up with a gentle smile.

Whale flinches, shocked to hear Bumps' levity.

```
                    WHALE
I guess, uh...
```

"God, what happened to you?"

```
                    WHALE
Cut myself shaving.
```

Bumps laughs, an airy giggle. "You do look really banged up though."

```
                    WHALE
It's not as bad as it looks.
```

"You sure?"

```
                    WHALE
      I'm on like three painkillers right now. I'm fine.
```

"Okay." Bumps tentatively points behind her. "I really should get back. Big week."

Whale nods, his face numb.

Bumps wanders a bit. Stops. Looks back. "You sure you're okay?"

Whale walks toward her, meeting her halfway.

```
                    WHALE
      I'm fine, but... Are you okay?
```

Bumps shrugs. "Why wouldn't I be?"

Whale looks down at his feet, unsure what to say.

Bumps touches Whale's shoulder. Walks back to her desk. Whale watches her return to work, bile hitting his throat.

```
                    WHALE
              (to himself)
      I'm losing my fucking mind.
```

Whale notices Peabrain still staring at him from his desk. Sighs. Turns away. Goes into the coffee room. Pops an espresso pod into the Nespresso, just the way Peabrain told him to. Was that the same day? Jesus.

"What the fuck happened to you?" Cashew asks, walking in.

```
                    WHALE
      Don't even know where to start.
```

"Who did that to you?"

Whale looks out into the hallway, checking for shadows.

```
                    WHALE
      Peabrain told The Professor I deleted the files.
```

Cashew gapes. "I don't understand."

```
                    WHALE
      Neither do I. But The Professor believed him and took
      it out on me.
```

Cashew's eyes dart all over Whale's face. "He did that to you?"

```
                    WHALE
      It was a lot worse on Friday.
```

"But why would he do that? Didn't we do what he wanted us to do?"

```
                    WHALE
      I don't think he meant it.
```

Cashew shakes his head. "Does he suspect...?"

```
                    WHALE
      He's not stupid. He knows I couldn't have done it
      alone, but I didn't tell him anything.
```

Cashew looks away, struggling to process.

The Nespresso gurgles. Whale carries his mug to the water cooler and adds hot water on top of the espresso.

"I can't believe you didn't tell on me," Cashew says.

```
                    WHALE
      Why?
```

Cashew doesn't answer, his mind wandering. "It could've been me up there."

```
                    WHALE
      You're welcome.
```

Cashew grimaces. "How dare he?! How FUCKING dare he?!"

```
                    WHALE
      Stop it.
```

"He wants to start a fucking war? This how you start a fucking war."

```
                    WHALE
      Stop!
```

"We can't let him get away with this!"

```
                    WHALE
      It's over.
```

"No, it's not over!"

```
                    WHALE
      Yes it is. We're just gonna move on and pretend
      nothing's happened.
```

"But something *has* happened! Look at your face!"

```
                    WHALE
      It's my face. You got what you wanted. Shut up and
      get back to work.
```

Whale grabs a brown sugar packet. Pours half into his Americano.

Cashew shakes his head. "It's different now."

```
                    WHALE
          (tossing packet into trash)
      Kobe!
```

"He's not playing by the rules!"

```
                    WHALE
      Neither were you.
```

"Yes, I was!" Cashew quick-checks the hallway behind Whale. "You heard him Day One! This was what he wanted. Now it isn't? How are we supposed to trust anything he says now?"

Whale furrows his brow.

```
                    WHALE
      What are you talking about?
```

"You heard what he said."

```
                    WHALE
      The Professor?
```

"Yeah. Who do you think I've been talking about?"

```
                    WHALE
      Peabrain.
```

Cashew cringes his face. "Peabrain?! Who gives a fuck about Peabrain?!"

```
                    WHALE
      You did!
```

"Not now! Now that The Professor beat the crap out of you!"

```
                    WHALE
      You wanna go after THE PROFESSOR now?!
```

"The game's changed," Cashew harshly whispers. "He broke the rules! This isn't about the job anymore."

```
                    WHALE
      What's wrong with you?!
```

"Don't you have any pride? The man beats you up and you're just gonna take it?"

```
                    WHALE
      Stop it!
```

"I'm not just gonna sit and wait for him to smack me around for following his own fucking rules!"

```
                    WHALE
      Well you're gonna have to.
```

"Says who?"

```
                    WHALE
      Says me.
```

Cashew scoffs. "Aren't you scared he's gonna do it again?"

```
                    WHALE
      No.
```

"No?

```
                    WHALE
      No.
```

Whale grabs a spoon. Stirs his coffee. Hesitates.

```
                    WHALE (CONT'D)
      I've got him in check.
```

Cashew looks at Whale. "What does that mean?"

```
                    WHALE
      Don't worry about it.
```

"What's happened?"

```
                    WHALE
      Nothing's happened.
```

"Bullshit."

Whale blows on his coffee.

Cashew blinks, trying desperately to read Whale's expression. "Just tell me if I'm wrong."

Whale takes a deep breath.

```
                    WHALE
      Let's just say I know why The Professor doesn't allow
      phones in the office.
```

"What do you mean?"

```
                    WHALE
      You don't want to know.
```

"You know what, it's better that I don't." Cashew pauses. "But what exactly are you referring to?"

```
                    WHALE
      You don't want to know.
```

"I don't care about the details."

WHALE
Then stop asking.

"Just give me a ballpark."
Whale sighs.

WHALE
Something happened Friday.

"In the cube?"

WHALE
No.

Cashew furrows his brow. "I don't get it."

WHALE
After you left.

"In the office?"

WHALE
Stop asking.

"After we closed?"

WHALE
Yes.

"How do you know?"
Whale exhales hard.

WHALE
Because I saw it. Please stop asking.

"After hours? How'd you get in?"

WHALE
Does it matter?

"Was it Peabrain? Are Peabrain and The Professor in cahoots?"

WHALE
It's not Peabrain!

"Bumps?"
Whale puts down his cup.

WHALE
Stop.

"They were fucking, weren't they?"

WHALE
STOP.

"You saw them?! You saw them fucking?!"

WHALE
I said STOP!

Cashew snickers. "Ohhh myyy Goddd, what a *whore*!"

WHALE
It wasn't like that!

"I fucking told you, didn't I?!"

WHALE
That's not what it was!

"Are you sure about that?"

```
                    WHALE
             (hissing)
      Yes, I'm fucking sure!
```

Cashew's smile fades.

```
                    WHALE (CONT'D)
      Maybe. I don't know. I don't...
```

Cashew's eyes droop. "What?"

```
                    WHALE
      I'm not sure how much was... if any of it was.
      Everything about it was weird. She seems fine now.
```

"He...?" Cashew squints. "You're telling me he—?"

```
                    WHALE
      I don't know. I think so.
```

Cashew covers his mouth.

```
                    WHALE (CONT'D)
      I wouldn't jump to conclusions about it. It's not as
      simple as that. You had to have...
```

Whale stops himself.

Cashew shakes his head. "I can't believe it."

```
                    WHALE
      I...
```

Whale stops himself again.

Cashew looks up with hopeful eyes. "What?"

Whale shakes his head, hating himself all over again.

"What is it? What?"

```
                    WHALE
      I got it on video.
```

Whale wipes the tears from his eyes. Checks the hallway for passersby.

Cashew looks down, processing. "Where?"

```
                    WHALE
      It's on my phone. I hid it in my office.
```

Cashew turns his head in the direction of the copy room.

```
                    WHALE (CONT'D)
      You won't be able to find it.
```

"Can I see it?"

```
                    WHALE
      Why would you want to?
```

"Let me see it."

```
                    WHALE
      It's not for you. It's not for anyone.
```

"Why'd you take it then?"

```
                    WHALE
      I don't know.
                  (pause)
      It's insurance, just in case I need to make a deal.
      Until then, no one sees it.
```

Cashew buttons his lip. "I don't like it."

```
                    WHALE
      It's not your decision to make.
```

"What if I call the cops?"

```
                    WHALE
      Please don't.
```

"It'll never come back to you!"

```
                    WHALE
      That's what you said the last time!
```

"A woman has been raped and you're just gonna let him—?"

```
                    WHALE
      I don't know if it was rape! I'm probably just
      exaggerating. There's definitely nuance to it.
```

"I'm supposed to just take your word on that? What if you're wrong?"

Whale shrugs.

```
                    WHALE
      I don't...
```

"If you want me to understand, I'm gonna have to see it."

Whale rubs the back of his head with both hands.

"If you're downplaying an actual crime, we need to know."

```
                    WHALE
      You can't tell anyone.
```

"I can't promise that."

```
                    WHALE
      I didn't tell The Professor what you did.
```

Cashew stares. "Is that a threat?"

```
                    WHALE
      I'm just reminding you.
```

Cashew sighs. "Fine."

```
                    WHALE
      Fine what?
```

"Fine, I promise I won't tell."

```
                    WHALE
      Either way?
```

Cashew hesitates. "Either way."

Whale grabs his coffee. Leads Cashew down the hall, checking around corners for witnesses. They go into the copy room. Whale locks the door. Hands Cashew his Americano.

```
                    WHALE
      Hold this.
```

Cashew takes the mug with a groan. Whale pulls out the chair in the side office. "I had a feeling it was in the ceiling," Cashew murmurs.

```
                    WHALE
                (stepping up)
      You're still too short.
```

Cashew looks down at Whale's coffee. Considers spitting in it.

Whale pushes up the ceiling panel. Withdraws his iPhone. Wipes dust off the screen. Powers the phone back on. Discreetly types in the password. Taps the Photo app. Whale averts his eyes and hands Cashew the phone, exchanging it for his coffee.

Cashew widens his eyes at the disturbing thumbnail.

```
                    WHALE (CONT'D)
        Keep the volume low.
```

Cashew doesn't tap it. Just stares, the reality of the situation finally hitting home. "Did you re-watch it yet?"

```
                    WHALE
        I couldn't even watch it the first time.
```

"Why not?"

Whale furrows his brow.

```
                    WHALE
        The fuck's wrong with you?
```

"No, I mean... in case you didn't get everything."

Whale steps down.

```
                    WHALE
        You tell me.
```

Cashew pre-adjusts the volume. Taps the video. Watches all twenty-five minutes.

Whale finishes the last of his coffee, tuning out every second of sound. The video mercilessly finished, Whale calmly looks up at Cashew.

```
                    WHALE
        You see what I mean?
```

Cashew clutches Whale's phone tightly. "We fucking got him."

Whale holds out his hand.

```
                    WHALE
        Give me back my phone.
```

"He's dead!" Cashew says with a giddy laugh. "Holy shit, he's fucking dead!"

```
                    WHALE
        Theo! Give me back my fucking phone!
```

Cashew shushes harshly. "You said you wouldn't say it!"

```
                    WHALE
        Give me back my phone! Please!
```

Cashew looks down at the phone. Unconsciously cradles it. Whale snatches Cashew's hand, squeezing hard. Cashew smacks Whale hard in the shoulder as Whale rips the phone away, shoving Cashew out of the side office.

"Fucking asshole!"

```
                    WHALE
        It's my phone!
```

"Keep it. I don't care. I'm gonna tweet some accusations of my own."

```
                    WHALE
        No!
```

"And then everyone's gonna know what he did and he'll never work another day in his life!"

```
                    WHALE
        You said you weren't gonna tell!
```

"I told you she was full of shit! You didn't believe me!"

Whale furrows his brow.

```
                    WHALE
      What?!
```

"She was long conning you from the beginning! That video proves it!"

```
                    WHALE
      Were we watching the same video?
```

"She was there to get the job. If she didn't want to give him the wrong idea, she shouldn't have done it at all."

```
                    WHALE
      What are you talking about?! No one deserves this!
```

"Stop defending her!" Cashew cries. "How do you think she even knew about this place? She's been blowing him here since the beginning."

```
                    WHALE
      You don't know that.
```

"Really? All those trips to the copy room? No one prints that much!"

```
                    WHALE
      Some do! To each their own!
```

"You're in such fucking denial!"

```
                    WHALE
      You just don't want to admit you're wrong!
```

"Ditto!"

```
                    WHALE
      Don't say ditto. It's so fucking stupid.
```

"You know what's stupid? Even if she *was* raped, you still wouldn't publish that video!"

```
                    WHALE
      It's not my place, okay?
```

"You're the one that filmed it."

```
                    WHALE
      And I shouldn't have.
```

"Good thing you did!"

```
                    WHALE
      They didn't know I was there!
```

"Even better!"

```
                    WHALE
               (crying)
      NO! It's not!
```

Whale shakes his head, his rosacea flaring.

```
                    WHALE (CONT'D)
      I should never have told you. I'm just gonna delete
      it.
```

"If anyone saw the video, they'd know what a fucking monster he is!"

```
                    WHALE
      I know!
```

"So?!"

Whale hesitates, his head getting fuzzy.

```
                    WHALE
      It's wrong.
```

Cashew cringes. "WHAT THE FUCK IS WRONG WITH YOU?!"

```
                    WHALE
      Who are we to do that to anybody?
```

"Don't be fucking ridiculous." Cashew beelines for the door.

```
                    WHALE
      You promised not to tell anyone!
```

"I don't care."

```
                    WHALE
      Then you're just like The Professor, aren't you?
```

Cashew stops. Turns around. "How the fuck can you even say that?"

```
                    WHALE
      It's not right and you know it!
```

"How is it not right?"

```
                    WHALE
      We signed NDAs.
```

"So what?"

```
                    WHALE
      We made a promise! He's our boss! We WANTED to be
      here! We can't just do that to him!
```

"He beat the shit out of you for something you didn't even do. Are you really going on about what we shouldn't do to him?!"

```
                    WHALE
      I'm the one he beat up, not you! I say it's not our
      place!
```

"Rape or not, it's still wrong. It is our duty as human beings to report it!"

```
                    WHALE
      To whistleblow?
```

"So what?!"

Whale frowns.

```
                    WHALE
      We have to tell Bumps.
```

Cashew scoffs hard. "Fuck you!"

```
                    WHALE
      WE HAVE TO TELL HER!
```

"She'll warn him and we'll get fucking blacklisted!"

```
                    WHALE
      Then we'll publish the video and take 'em down with
      us!
```

Cashew stares. "What if she says no?"

```
                    WHALE
      Then we don't do it.
```

"And just let him get away with it?"

```
                    WHALE
      She's the one in the video. It's her call. That's
      only fair.
```

Cashew puts hands on his hips, fuming. "Maybe you're right," he says, deliberately calm. "She didn't want this."

```
                    WHALE
      That's what I'm saying.
```

Cashew looks Whale in the eye. "But in order to tell her, you'll have to admit you were there too. You could have saved her and didn't. You just let it happen and got it on video."

Whale's lips contort, his eyes watering.

Cashew shrugs. "There's no other way, is there?"

```
                    WHALE
      I don't know. I don't know what to do.
```

Cashew walks up to Whale. "I'll compromise. I won't tell anyone if you don't delete the video."

```
                    WHALE
      Then what?
```

Cashew hesitates. "We'll sit on it. Until we think of a real plan."

```
                    WHALE
      You promise you won't tell?
```

"I said it, didn't I? We can go to Wally McGree's after work and talk about it there."

```
                    WHALE
      Let's go somewhere else this time.
```

"Wherever you want."

Whale thinks.

```
                    WHALE
      Brique on Sunset. I could use a sidecar. Been really
      craving one lately.
```

"We'll go to a bar on a Monday. Whatever you want."

Whale chuckles.

```
                    WHALE
      I'm sorry.
```

"I'm sorry too," Cashew says. And he actually was.

Peabrain, who had been standing outside the copy room door eavesdropping everything, dashes down the hall. Work doesn't matter anymore. He actually has a chance to get the job now. He better hurry before Whale gets revenge on him for snitching.

Peabrain hops on the closest computer. No Bumps in sight. He rapid-types his username and password. Logs onto his private email account. Starts a new email. Types The Professor's address. No subject. Just starts typing.

> Overheard Whale and Cashew talking about something you did. They have plans. Meet me at Wally McGree's tonight. 8pm.

Peabrain quickly hits send just as Cashew enters The Classroom with Whale's empty coffee cup. "You never use that computer," Cashew says gently.

Peabrain quickly exits the browser and turns around. "Y-y-y-y-yes, I j-j-j-j-just want-t-t-t-t-ted to try something d-d-d-different."

Cashew blinks. "Don't let me stop you."

"Y-y-y-y-y-you didn't," Peabrain stammers, logging out of the computer.

Cashew raises a brow. "Didn't I?"

Peabrain shakes his head. "N-n-n-n-n-no. I was j-j-j-just g-g-g-g-gonna go get some c-coffee." He stands up, faking a smile. "I c-c-c-c-can t-t-t-take that if you w-w-want."

Cashew looks down at Whale's empty cup. Hands it to Peabrain. "Thanks."

Peabrain races to the coffee room, not slowing down or stopping until he's out of sight.

Cashew furrows his brow. Looks at Peabrain's computer. Sits down. Types "Peabrain" and "gaiusbaltar." Hits enter.

Incorrect Password
5 Attempts Remaining

Cashew squints. "Clever girl." He types "karathrace" and hits enter.

Incorrect Password
4 Attempts Remaining

Cashew types "lauraroslin." Enter.

Incorrect Password
3 Attempts Remaining

"karlagathon." Enter.

Incorrect Password
2 Attempts Remaining

Cashew sighs. Which Adama? He types "williamadama." Enter.

Incorrect Password
1 Attempt Remaining

"Goddammit!" Cashew hisses. Maybe it's "billadama"? Or Lee? He slowly types "leeadama." Hits enter.

Peabrain's desktop appears.

"Frak yeah." Cashew opens Chrome. Goes to Peabrain's Browser History. Clicks on the personal mail client Peabrain just had open. The inbox itself appears. "Someone forgot to log out," Cashew says to himself, scanning the inbox. Nothing special. Notices the name at the top: Kev Foster. That's probably it.

Just as he's about to close the browser, a suspicious feeling grows in the back of Cashew's mind. He drags the mouse over to the Sent box. Clicks. Just a second before Cashew walked in, Peabrain had sent an email without a subject to The Professor. He clicks on it.

Reads.

Cashew whips his head around. Closes the browser. Logs out. Races toward the copy room. Goes into the bathroom instead.

Cashew locks the handicap stall and sits on the toilet. If he warns Whale now he might delete the video. But Whale didn't snitch. Cashew can't believe it. Why wouldn't he? Cashew would have. But Whale got beaten so he wouldn't have to. Cashew owes him loyalty, doesn't he? That's what his dad used to say. "If you want to make it in this world, you need to reward your friends and smite your foes."

But what about The Professor? He's his foe, but he can't smite him without betraying his friend.

Cashew once used that axiom on his own father. Long ago. How old was he then? Before the Motor-Mart. Must've been '05. He was ten, wandering around Landreth Motors, bored out of his mind, too young to know how to keep himself busy. His father arguing with Grandpa Martin, Dad planning the Motor-Mart, something Grandpa Martin was always against. He said it went against everything Kerrigan Landreth stood for. That was the first time Cashew heard his dad yell. Screaming at Grandpa Martin over something he did, some vague move against Dad's plans. Dad called him a pathetic wretch. Cashew remembers having to look that up in the dictionary, because whatever it was made Grandpa Martin cry. And that was the last time Cashew ever saw Grandpa Martin. But his father wasn't sad like they always were in the movies. Dad explained he was in the right, Grandpa Martin was trying to stop him from making his business great again. He had to cut Grandpa Martin out in order to save the business. But Cashew couldn't understand why his father would ever yell at *his* father. That's when 10-year-old Cashew quoted Calvin's own axiom back to him: "If you want to make it in this world, you need to reward your friends and smite your foes." He still remembers Dad's smile at how well he recited, and he carried that smile of pride for many years after. But Calvin said Grandpa Martin would realize he was right and forgive him. If not, that would be on him. Cashew asked his father if that'd make him upset. And his father went quiet, something Cashew had never experienced before, saying something so real to make own father go mute. And Cashew never forgot what his father said: "Running a business..." No. Wait. He said: "A *running* business makes up for everything. Smart people understand that."

"Can I have my phone for a moment?" Cashew asks The Secretary.

The Secretary stares suspiciously. "Why?"

"I wanna take a smoke break."

The Secretary reluctantly opens the drawer. "Since when do you smoke?"

"Just started."

The Secretary hands Cashew his phone. Cashew opens the door, cool October air rushing through. Stands on the Avenue of the Arts. Looks both ways. Checks for cameras. Unlocks his phone. Pulls out the business card that funny man in the bejeweled turban gave him at La Cucaracha's. Dials the number on the card. Lets it ring.

"Yes?" a queeny secretary answers.

"I want to speak to Oscar Blitz," Cashew says. "Tell him it's urgent."

JACOB
Bowfinger

INT. SOUTH STREET DINER - NIGHT

Jacob sits in a booth by himself, his once fatty-belly now tight and slim. He's watching YouTube Vine compilations through corded headphones.

Rian walks in. Sits across from Jacob.

RIAN
Hey stranger. Where've you been all week?

Jacob pauses the video. Rolls up his headphones.

JACOB
Recovering.

RIAN
From what?

JACOB
You tell me.

Rian finally notices Jacob's face. Gasps.

RIAN
You're not wearing glasses!

JACOB
Took you long enough.

RIAN
Did you get LASIK?

JACOB
Yup. I've been recovering at Stewie's. He's been very attentive.
(dirty)
VERY attentive.

RIAN
Whore.

JACOB
And the doctor said everything worked out. No side effects.

RIAN
Surprised you did it.

JACOB
I'm sick of seeing the world through a fucking filter I have to clean every five seconds. And I can't stand transition lenses.

RIAN
But you never have to carry sunglasses.

JACOB
They keep changing even if I don't want them to. I look like a blind man in every outdoor picture.

RIAN
"Not that there's anything wrong with it!"

JACOB
"My father's blind!"

They laugh.

RIAN
You tell your mom yet?

JACOB
It'll be another surprise for when we come down. But she wants us to all get LASIK eventually. Swears by it.

RIAN
She got it?

JACOB
Stewie and Ron too.

RIAN
Really?

JACOB
You ever notice how Stewie's eyes get all bloodshot whenever he drinks or walks into Target?

RIAN
God, that's probably gonna happen to you one day.

JACOB
I'm sure it's because they all got it in their forties. I've got a whole lifetime of normal eyes ahead of me.

RIAN
Or it'll compound and you'll end up looking like The Picture of Dorian Gray in twenty years.

JACOB
Thanks for the optimism.

RIAN
Did it hurt?

JACOB
The surgery wasn't bad. The recovery process was a pain though. I had to sleep with goggles on. Three different kinds of eye drops, one every six hours, one two hours, one just twice a day. Stewie had to do it all for me.

RIAN
But it's worth it?

JACOB
Unbelievably so. Best purchase I've ever made.

RIAN
Stewie's not chipping in?

JACOB
Nope. All me.

RIAN
Good for you.

JACOB
As long as I pay it off in two years, I won't be charged any interest.

RIAN
Really good for you.

JACOB
More incentive for me to get a good paying job when we get to LA. Target's fine for now, but we'll see.

RIAN
You didn't get picked for the LA program?

JACOB
I never applied.

RIAN
Oh, I thought that was part of the master plan.

JACOB
It was, but all that bullshit with Mom really left a bad taste in my mouth.
(pause)
Besides, it would've been hard if I got it now that Stewie's in the picture.

RIAN
You guys have such a stable relationship. Maybe it would've worked.

Jacob shrugs, half-frowning.

RIAN (CONT'D)
Any advice?

JACOB
I don't really have any. It was all too easy.

Jacob sighs.

JACOB (CONT'D)
To tell you the truth, though, we still got our moments.

RIAN
It's only been four months. It's still really early.

JACOB
I had a bit of anger problems when I weaned off the meds. It got real bad.

RIAN
Sorry to hear that.

JACOB
We learned from it. It's making our relationship stronger.

RIAN
That's good.

JACOB
But it kept happening over the littlest things. I hated it. I acted like such a jerk.

RIAN
Nothing physical.

JACOB
Of course not. Just yelling. And I knew Stewie was just being tolerant and patient about the whole thing, but he really wasn't a fan of the yelling. It took a long time for me to balance out.

RIAN
It just became a problem all of a sudden?

JACOB
I always had anger problems. The pills just rerouted all that frustration inward.
(pause)
But it was different before. All that constant anger alongside my depression made me easier to sympathize with.

RIAN
Like a starving artist.

JACOB
Once I got off the anti-depressants, all that anger made me look like an asshole.

RIAN
And how's your depression now?

JACOB
Not nearly as bad as before.
(pause)
It's funny though.

RIAN
What?

JACOB
What I said.

RIAN
Which part?

JACOB
If they have the ability to zap depression away with a laser, like LASIK, and some guy with anger problems gets it, he's suddenly an unsympathetic asshole even though nothing's really changed with his personality except his depression's gone.

RIAN
That'd be pretty cool, depression being just as correctable as bad vision.

JACOB
Sounds like a <u>Black Mirror</u> episode.

RIAN
Or <u>Eternal Sunshine</u>.

JACOB
That too.

Rian ponders a bit more.

RIAN
It could make for a good short.

JACOB
Really?

RIAN
Some guy's in a relationship that's in a bit of a rough patch. He gets a surgery to remove his depression, but it leaves his anger behind and now they have to deal with that.

JACOB
He'll probably just assume it's a bad side effect at first. Who wants to admit they have anger issues or that they just spent all that money only to make it worse, especially if they're strapped as it is.

RIAN
That's good.

JACOB
LASIK has some side effects they can correct after a week. What if, rather than dealing with the fact that he's treating his partner like an asshole, he insists it's really not him and THAT'S what ends up ruining their relationship.

RIAN
When he goes to the doctor for the one-week checkup, he finds out he was wrong, he has no side effects.

JACOB
His relationship's destroyed but the surgery's declared a flawless success.

Rian smirks. Jacob chuckles a bit.

RIAN
We gotta write this down.

JUMP CUT TO:

HOURS LATER

Stewie walks into the diner. Looks around.

STEWIE
(bleating)
AYY BEE!

JACOB (O.S.)
(bleating)
AYY BEE!

Stewie approaches Rian and Jacob's table. It's covered in yellow sheets of paper covered in chicken scratch.

STEWIE
You guys weren't kidding.

RIAN
You gotta hear this.

Stewie sits next to Jacob.

JACOB
How'd they do?

STEWIE
(bitter)
They got eliminated.

JACOB
No! With Syndergaard on the mound?

STEWIE
He went seven innings, let up no runs and only two hits and struck out ten batters but Madison Bumgarner had to go and pitch a complete game shutout with only four hits and six strikeouts. No runs on either side for eight innings. No runs! You know what happened? Familia. He let up a three-run homer in the ninth. God, I hate the Mets.

Jacob and Rian look at each other.

RIAN
(to Stewie)
Do you, like, need a minute?

JACOB
He's a Met fan. All Met fans hate the Mets.

Stewie nods with pursed lips. Jacob grabs a piece of paper from the pile.

JACOB (CONT'D)
It's called <u>The Surgery</u>.

STEWIE
<u>The Surgery</u>?

JACOB
Set in the near future where everything's pretty much the same, except there's an elective surgery not

covered by insurance that uses a laser to zap away depression.

STEWIE
Uh-huh.

RIAN
But it's not about the Surgery. The Surgery's a metaphor, like the memory wipe in Eternal Sunshine.

JACOB
(to Rian)
He doesn't know Eternal Sunshine.

STEWIE
Maybe I do. What is it?

JACOB
Eternal Sunshine of the Spotless Mind.

Stewie hesitates.

STEWIE
That's a movie title?

RIAN
The short itself is about people, a waiter named Kevin and his long-term boyfriend Josh.

STEWIE
(smiles at Jacob)
The guys from Who We Are.

JACOB
I knew you'd remember.

RIAN
It follows two timelines, the week before Kevin gets the Surgery--

JACOB
In black and white.

RIAN
And the second following the week after the Surgery.

JACOB
In color.

RIAN
The black and white parts will show Kevin and Josh dealing with the damaging effect of Kevin's depression on their relationship and the sacrifices they make to pay for the Surgery.

JACOB
And all the color parts will depict their relationship's downfall.

STEWIE
Sounds good so far.

JACOB
(to Rian)
Let's start the synopsis.

RIAN
Alternate?

JACOB
Yeah. You start.

Rian and Jacob grab pieces of paper.

RIAN
It'll begin The Day Of, just after the Surgery itself.

JACOB
We never see the Surgery.

RIAN
For cost-cutting reasons and to make it more mysterious.

JACOB
Like the bank robbery in Reservoir Dogs.

STEWIE
And the briefcase in Pulp Fiction.

JACOB
Very good.

RIAN
(points at Jacob's paper)
And then it cuts to...

JACOB
(reading)
"7 Days Before. Kevin's getting a free consultation as to what the Surgery itself will entail. He won't be able to speak for the first two days and won't be able to work for an entire week. Insurance doesn't cover it. It's a lot of money for him. He's just a waiter at a Mexican Restaurant. The doctor assures him that the success rate is 95%, the other 5% being side effects. Nothing that can't be corrected during their one-week follow-up. Kevin is sold and tells the doctor to schedule the appointment seven days from then."

RIAN
"1 Day After. Kevin's boyfriend Josh takes care of a mute Kevin as he's incapacitated." I was thinking part of the recovery process would involve Josh having to assemble a purple paste of some sort.

JACOB
That's good. Write it down.

Rian jots onto a different page.

JACOB (CONT'D)
"6 Days Before. Kevin finds out from his boss he can't get an entire week off on such short notice, and Kevin's pissed. Josh picks Kevin up from work and they argue on the way home."

STEWIE
Kevin can't drive?

JACOB
He doesn't have a car. Josh is a lot wealthier than Kevin and he hates that.

STEWIE
Who does?

JACOB
Kevin. Josh's stance is that Kevin can get the Surgery another time down the line, but Kevin already has his hopes up and he wants it NOW.

RIAN
"2 Days After. Kevin can finally talk after the Surgery, and he only says two words: 'It worked.'" That there's a moment. They hold each other, cry happy tears, it'll be great.

JACOB
Frankie's directing it.

STEWIE
Sounds great so far.

JACOB
"5 Days Before. Kevin and Josh go to visit Kevin's mom who lives nearby. They go and all Kevin's mom can do is point out everything wrong with him, constantly shaming him." That's why he's so depressed, you see. And Josh realizes that in this scene.

RIAN
"3 Days After. Kevin and Josh visit Kevin's mom to tell her about the Surgery. And Kevin and her finally start having a real relationship for the first time, but Kevin starts acting like she did to him but toward Josh."

STEWIE
Oh boy.

RIAN
"On the way home, Josh tells Kevin that he made him feel like shit back there, but Kevin doesn't understand. And he starts yelling at Josh to stop sabotaging his new relationship with his mother. Josh is shocked to hear Kevin treat him like that. Kevin is too."

JACOB
"4 Days Before. Kevin's at work talking to a co-worker about his rocky relationship with Josh. He mentions the Surgery but adds that he doesn't have the money yet, let alone time off. The co-worker suggests he stop obsessing over the Surgery and instead save the money for their future. Kevin reveals he's afraid Josh would leave him if he doesn't do the Surgery."

RIAN
"4 Days After. Kevin and Josh argue about how the Surgery has turned Kevin mean. Kevin insists it's just one of side effects the doctor told him about. It'll be corrected in just three days. Josh doubts anything will change but gives Kevin another chance."

JACOB
"3 Days Before. Kevin and Josh have a romantic night in. Kevin starts to accept the reality of not getting the Surgery and that he was made just the way he's supposed to be."

RIAN
"5 Days After. Kevin and Josh go out with mutual friends to celebrate the Surgery. Kevin is suddenly popular among the friend group. He spends the entire evening ignoring Josh and occasionally throwing him under the bus. Kevin is thrilled to finally be the life of the party. Josh tries to be amenable."

JACOB
"2 Days Before. Kevin's boss texts him to say that he talked to the co-worker Kevin was talking to before and mercifully agrees to let Kevin have the week off to have the Surgery. Kevin is about to text back 'No' when Josh encourages him to say 'Yes' instead. Kevin doesn't want to tell Josh he doesn't have the money yet, so he says yes to the time off.

RIAN
"6 Days After. A day out to the beach shows Kevin at his most assholeish. Josh criticizes him, Kevin blames the side effects again. Josh says Kevin was always angry, that Kevin's depression made his anger almost understandable, but without the depression he

comes off as an asshole. Kevin then scolds Josh for wanting to keep Kevin sad and stupid because it makes Josh feel like a better man himself, and that Josh never really loved Kevin for who he was. Josh is hurt but says nothing the whole ride home. Soon as they get home, Josh packs his things and tells Kevin to move out before he gets back. Kevin's greatest fear playing out before his eyes, he begs Josh to stay, promising to change. Josh says, 'You already did' and leaves."

STEWIE
Wow.

RIAN
Another moment.

JACOB
"1 Day Before. Kevin finally confesses that he doesn't have the money to pay for the Surgery, and with his crappy job he won't be able to pay it off for a while. Josh reveals he's already paid for the procedure in full."

STEWIE
WOW!

JACOB
"Kevin is moved, and Josh tells Kevin he did it to show him how much he loves him and wants him to be happy."

STEWIE
Aww.

JACOB
"And they kiss."

STEWIE
That's so sad. He paid for the Surgery and everything.

RIAN
"7 Days After. Kevin goes to the doctor, desperate to fix the side effects and win Josh back. The doctor says the Surgery was 100% successful, no side effects. Kevin starts feeling genuinely sad for the first time since the Surgery. He closes his eyes in despair at the cost of his own denial."

JACOB
And finally, "The Day Of (Again). Kevin's about to go under. Josh and Kevin share a meaningful farewell, 'See you on the other side' and Kevin is wheeled into the operating room." The End.

Stewie instantly applauds, making Jacob and Rian smile.

RIAN
You liked it, huh?

STEWIE
That's fantastic. It's like a Twilight Zone episode.

RIAN
I want to get Nich and TJ on board. We gotta make it before the end of the year so we can have a great film in our portfolio for LA.

JACOB
You don't think it's too artsy, do you?

RIAN
No way.

JACOB
You really think people will actually want to watch something like this?

STEWIE
I want to watch it.

JACOB
You like non-mainstream stuff. A lot of people don't.

RIAN
It's a great story, Jacob. People like great stories. One day, you and I are gonna see this on the big screen. We'll be in the audience like everyone else and we'll see our names up there. And as soon it ends, everyone in that theater's gonna stand up and applaud all around us.

SMASH CUT TO:

DREW

Light in a Dark Room

Drew and Kev's limo pulls up to the Palais des Festivals et des Congrès on Day Four of the 90th Annual Cannes Film Festival, *The Sins of Jack Branson* the next Palme d'Or contender to be projected inside the Théâtre Lumière. Drew gapes at all the photographers flashing shots of their fantastic ensemble cast in glamorous and exotic outfits, Fergus Connaughton, Jay Blackwell, Martin Kennergan, Marcel Innalls, Bernadette Brewster, Odessa Dykes, Monte Ryans, Prince McAllister, Addison Ryder, all posing in different arrangements with director Eli Kerbinger.

"This is it!" Drew exclaims.

"Come on!" Kev says excitedly, pushing Drew's back. "Let's go!"

Drew opens the door. Everything after is a blur. Drew looks great. Kev looks great. Faces light up everywhere they go. Cameras flash. A few autographs even. It's not fast, just surreal, being the center of that much attention, admiration. Even Drew looking up at the blown-up poster of *The Sins of Jack Branson*, that all-white surreal dreamscape of London iconography and religious symbols surrounding half of Fergus Connaughton's colorless face save for his bold blue eye, gives Drew chills. And the weather's unbelievably perfect. Truly a gift from God.

The lights go down in the packed Théâtre Lumière, all the critics and normies cheering with excitement. Drew's heart is pounding already. "Time to be judged for our *Sins*," Kev whispers with a smirk.

The film is chaotic right off the bat. A young man, his face shadowed, races around his room and haphazardly collects his possessions. The animation is almost incomplete, more a series of rushed lines forming barely discernible shapes, as the young man slams open drawers and throws everything he can into a bag. An older man's hoarse screams distort the soundtrack, and it's suddenly obvious that the young man is crying heavily, almost to the point of incoherence. He screams at the older man as he rushes. Grabs his overfilled bag. Pushes by his father. Sees his silent mother, sitting passively in the corner. He races out of the cottage. Grabs the door. "IF THEY FIND ME DEAD, IT'S YOU FAULT!" the young man screams, truly blood-curdling. He slams the door hard, smashing the screen to black as a rapid beat begins. The title card, white text on black: *The Sins of Jack Branson*.

The beat continues over rotoscoped shots of Victorian London, edited perfectly in time with the song. American runaway Andy Baxter finds a copy of *The North London Press* in the men's restroom at King's Cross. More instruments come into the soundtrack as Andy stops on a full-page advertisement: "Meet the Beautiful Ones on Montgomery Street! Only the Best for Your Needs!" Andy smiles.

Shots of Andy making his way across London flash by the screen, the instrumentation peaking to the full backbeat of the opening number: "The Sodom and Gomorrah Show." Jack Branson greets Andy at the door of the Montgomery Street Brothel, Fergus Connaughton singing live no less. What a fantastic voice. Andy is seduced by Jack's confidence, finding himself swept into the Brothel. François swings from the chandelier. One-legged Denny Evans cheerfully slides down the wooden banister. Mary and Louise literally fly through the air, their gowns fluttering as they hold onto their wigs for dear life. Oliver walks by, distracting Jack momentarily. The opening number reaches its climax with the ensemble getting together for a widescreen money-shot, Jack holding that high note. A jarring match-cut ends the song early,

Jack waking up in his shitty Whitechapel flat draped in gross morning light, the ceiling above him a disgusting Pollack painting of mold and water stains. A title card appears: "Seven Years Earlier..."

The movie rolls along from there. Jack and Mr. Munce start their secret gay prostitution scheme to an upbeat duet of "Opportunities (Let's Make Lots of Money)," culminating in the two of them sitting on the shoulders of human towers of DILFy aristocrats with money raining down from above. Jack sings "Rent" during a montage of aristocratic sexcapades. Oliver Hawkett breaks out into a passionate rendition of *West Side Story*'s "Somewhere," the arrangement the Pet Shop Boys did in the 90s, as he and Jack fly Ghibli style through the unopened brothel house on Montgomery Street. Jack sings "One Night" when he returns to his flat. Jack refuses Oliver's offer to headline the brothel, Jack singing "I Get Along" while Oliver sings "For Your Own Good" back at him. A Greek chorus of sorts sings "Euroboy" during the surreal Collins Affair sequence, returning later when Jack tearfully flees London with a haunting rendition of "Into Thin Air." The Barrington Place chapter features Jack soloing "Invisible." Jack returns to London with a heartfelt boat ride, singing "Indefinite Leave to Remain." Jack and Oliver's reunion turns into another fight, Oliver being the one singing "I Get Along" this time while Jack desperately shout-sings "One More Chance." Denny, François, Mary and Louise are introduced, culminating in the showstopping palate-cleanser "Here." The first day of the brothel features an ensemble mashup of "I Want a Lover" and "Tonight is Forever." The film reaches its midpoint with a somber reunion between Jack and Morty Blasmyth as they duet a slower reprise of "The Sodom and Gomorrah Show."

The second half begins with Jack writing *The Sins of an Irishman in London* as he sings the iconic "It's a Sin." Then the film goes full-on *Chicago* with what Drew calls the "Addendum Medley," François, Denny, Mary, Louise, and Andy monologuing their origin stories one at a time in between choruses from "That's My Impression," "Suburbia," "Psychological," and "New York City Boy" before culminating in a finale group reprise of "That's My Impression." Jack sings "Nervously" to Oliver from afar, possibly Fergus' best performance in the film. Jack and Oliver dance through Dubeau Frères with their toe-tapping duet of "Dreamland." Jack sings "It Always Comes as a Surprise" over voiceover as he admires a sleeping Oliver. And then the Incident, a tragedy within a tragedy, the old-fashioned *Brokeback Mountain*esque melodrama playing out between Jack and Danny O'Brien, the hot DILF next door. Jack duetting with the Dunderrow chorus in an atmospheric performance of "Try It (I'm in Love with a Married Man)." Maggie Branson catching Jack and Danny in bed together. That painful cold open replaying itself. There isn't a dry eye in the house by the end.

But just as Jack and Edgar's piggish Weinsteinesque sex scene is about to take a disgusting turn, the film abruptly switches to live action with Charlie Smith slamming Jack's manuscript onto his desk. The audience goes apeshit at the reveal. Drew and Kev giggle like crazy.

The live action scenes look shockingly different, courtesy of the production designers and costumers bringing their best work every morning. Patches in previously pristine costumes. Dust everywhere. The characters are moodier, more ethically compromised. Jack laments his cowardice with a slower version of "Closer to Heaven." Jack and Oliver race to Dunderrow as they uneasily sing "Reunion." The whores of the brothel comfort Jack with a beautiful performance of "Home and Dry." The Greek chorus returns with a reprise of "Into Thin Air" as Jack runs away again during the All is Lost Moment^{TM}. Jack sings "Numb" alone in his new flat, all in one take, completely a capella. Jack reads his mother's letter aloud as Maggie gives a haunting voiceover performance of "Always on My Mind." Jack makes up with Oliver and they sing "Together." Then the courtroom finale begins. Jack's passionate testimony electrifies both the gallery of the Old Vic and the critics inside the Théâtre Lumière, Jack's *Network*esque monologue turning into a rebellious rendition of "The Theatre." A crestfallen Jack is cheered up by

Oliver with an a cappella duet of "Winner." The whores put on one last talent show for their farewell party, Jack singing the traditional Celtic song "The Water is Wide." And then the grand finale, a group rendition of "Go West."

As Drew watches *The Sins of Jack Branson* with fresh eyes, a bonafide member of the audience instead of creative personnel, a reoccurring thought hits him at various intervals. That looks familiar. That looks familiar. That looks familiar. From the very beginning he felt it, during the scene when Jack and Mr. Munce hatch their scheme as reluctant allies, partners in crime. They knew how each other was, Drew and Theo. They knew where they stood. And it wasn't so bad, was it? And when Jack and Oliver have their first encounter, so intimate with an underlining secret only revealed at the end, that reminds Drew of his first date with Stewie. And Jack refusing Oliver's offer, so final and stubborn, not knowing just how wrong he was, that was Drew at Peet's Coffee fighting with Frankie all those years ago. Frankie tried to warn him about Theo, but Drew knew better, didn't he? So many years pissed away. And the Collins Affair sequence, Jack and those three other telegram boys getting roped into that mansion orgy only to get caught in a police raid, Tucker selling Collins and his brethren out for an immunity deal, that's all what went down at The Factory. And the sequence at Barrington Place, Jack being forced back into the closet to bow and scrape against his grain only to be fired over some bullshit, that's Drew in his Not That Nutty days. And the scene where Jack returns to London to beg for Oliver's forgiveness only for Oliver to deny it because he took too long, there's Drew and Kev only a year and a half ago. And Jack breaking that priceless vase only to get screamed at by someone who wasn't even there to witness the mitigating circumstance, that's him and Theo. And the Incident, Jack getting banished from his idyllic hometown just as he was coming of age, forcing him into premature adulthood, that's Drew with the divorce and the Phoenixville house getting sold. And Charlie the rich benefactor who can't take credit for the biggest contribution to Jack's life, even though Jack felt he deserved to, that's Drew and Oscar Blitz. And the scene where Charlie tricks Jack into meeting Geoffrey Grant, the two-faced politician Drew based on Hillary Clinton, that's Theo ambushing Drew at Brique even though he promised not to tell anyone about the video. And that fight between Jack and Oliver, throwing all that buried resentment at each other, that's Drew and Stewie's last fight in Boston. And Jack meeting Claire in the bookstore, listening to her critique *The Sins of an Irishman in London* without realizing the author's standing right in front of her, that's Drew and the UCLA guy, the waiter, what's his name, Jimmy. Jimmy Lyons. And those Hollywood endings that never happened, Jack getting a letter from his dead mom forgiving him for everything and Jack going west with Oliver to live happily ever after, that's all familiar too. As the last high note of "Go West" holds, Drew finds himself filled with an overwhelming sense of pride. He wouldn't have been able to capture all the small personal nuances of those scenes if all that hadn't already happened to him. Other people might've been able to. Not him.

Fade to black. Credits roll. Drew's heart is pounding. Silence. Seconds upon seconds of silence. Drew looks to Kev to see what's wrong just as blurry motion overwhelms his field of vision. Kev's standing. So are all the people to Drew's right. And the ones in the section below. And in the section above. And then loudest roar Drew's ever heard finally hits his brain, thousands of hands clapping together at different chaotic speeds, cheers rising up. A standing ovation. Overenthusiastic approval. Drew looks up at Kev, too overwhelmed to stand.

"WE DID IT!" Kev screams with a grin.

Drew can barely hear him over the cheers of all the men and women in that theatre. He scans the room. Everyone's smiling. Everyone's looking at him. Applauding. His cheeks flush. His eyes get moist. A little dribble out of the side of his right eye, the first proper tear he's generated in years. He takes a heavy breath, his whole body shaking with emotion, practically sobbing in his seat as the throng of strangers cheer even more because they've just made a grown man cry.

WHALE

Trinity

Whale watches *Carol*'s five-minute Cannes standing ovation while taking a shit. All those Americanos are fucking up his cycle.

The video pauses itself, a call coming in from Cashew.

```
                WHALE
          (into phone)
     What's up?
```

"Where are you?" Cashew asks.

```
                WHALE
     Home.
```

"How far away are you from Brique?"

```
                WHALE
     About fifteen minutes. Why?
```

Cashew doesn't respond. Lots of background noise. "Change of plans. Head over to Brique ASAP."

```
                WHALE
     They're not open till 9.
```

"I'm already in here. Happy hour's almost over. C'mon."

Whale sighs. Tries to shit faster.

Twenty minutes later, Whale gets out of his Ridr. Dimmed lights inside Brique. Strange. But he can see Cashew getting up from the counter with an eager smile on his face.

Cashew holds open the door. "C'mon."

```
                WHALE
     Did I miss it?
```

"No, perfect timing." Cashew leads Whale inside. No customers. No bartenders. No managers.

```
                WHALE
     Where is everyone?
```

A bald man in a yellow pinstriped suit stands, a cell phone to his ear. Whale halts in his tracks. Oscar Blitz's smirk fades away. "Jacob."

Whale glares at Cashew.

```
                WHALE
     You called Oscar Blitz on me?!
```

"I didn't know it was going to be you," Oscar softly interrupts, almost apologetic.

Cashew furrows his brow, looking between the two of them. "You guys already met?"

```
                WHALE
          (to Oscar)
     You knew I worked for The Professor before I told
     you, didn't you?
```

"There are lots of Professors in this town," Oscar explains. "I give my card out to a lot of people."

```
                    WHALE
        You offer him a job too?
```

Cashew's eyes widen. "Job? What job?"

Oscar rolls his eyes. "Of course not."

Cashew whips his head back at Whale. "He offered you a job?" He looks back at Oscar. "Why did you offer *him* a job? I want a job."

"Can we not talk about this now?"

```
                    WHALE
        Fuck you both. I'm leaving.
```

"Wait!" Cashew cries, dashing after Whale. "I told him everything. About the video, about The Professor and Bumps. We're doing this with or without you."

```
                    WHALE
        Without the video? Please.
```

"He knows," Oscar mumbles to Cashew.

Whale marches to the exit. Cashew rushes ahead, blocking his path. "Jacob! Jacob, wait! Please wait!"

```
                    WHALE
        You promised you wouldn't tell anyone!
```

"I know, but—"

```
                    WHALE
        I'm leaving. And I'm deleting that video.
```

Cashew pushes Whale back. "No! Wait!"

```
                    WHALE
        Get out of my way!
```

"Peabrain's gonna tell The Professor about the video!"

Whale stops.

```
                    WHALE
        What are you talking about?
```

Cashew unfolds a piece of paper and hands it over. "This was right after our meeting this morning. He overheard everything!"

Whale unfolds the paper. Reads the email.

Cashew checks his phone. "It's 7:45 now. If we don't publish in the next fifteen minutes, The Professor's gonna know all about the video and it'll be too late!"

Whale re-reads the email. Looks up at Oscar.

Oscar nods solemnly.

Whale steps closer to the light, reading the email a third time.

```
                    WHALE
        This doesn't make any sense. Why wouldn't he just
        tell him over email?
```

"Who cares?!" Cashew asks.

```
                    WHALE
        We don't know what Peabrain heard. Maybe he doesn't
        know anything. He'll get things wrong. Wouldn't be
        the first time. He thought I deleted the files.
```

"Do you really want to take that chance?!"

```
                    WHALE
Considering we don't have all the facts, yes.
```

"Why not?"

```
                    WHALE
I'm not gonna ruin a man's career without knowing
what it is he's actually done!
```

"We don't have time! If we're gonna do this, it's now or never!"

Whale's breath quickens.

```
                    WHALE
You see?! I TOLD YOU! I fucking TOLD YOU this was
gonna blow up in our faces!
```

"Hate to break it to you, Jacob, but Bumps and The Professor STILL would've happened either way! The only difference is we actually know now! How about you stop thinking about how all this will affect the fucking RAPIST and start thinking about how this will help Bumps!"

```
                    WHALE
STOP CALLING HER THAT! HER NAME IS TRISHA!
```

"OH MY GOD, *EXCUUUUSSSE ME* FOR NOT FUCKING KNOWING!" Cashew hollers, a vein popping out of his neck. "She was raped, Jacob! He raped her and will keep doing it if we don't stop him NOW!"

```
                    WHALE
Stop pretending you give a shit! If you really cared
about helping her, you would have told her about this
HOURS AGO!
```

Cashew glares desperately at Oscar. "Hey, you gonna help me out here?!"

Oscar frowns, his arms crossed, eyes to the floor.

```
                    WHALE
You're not doing this for her! You're doing this to
get back at The Professor! And not even him
personally, just what he fucking represents!
```

"Oscar!" Cashew exclaims.

"He knows what he wants," Oscar murmurs. "We should respect his wishes."

Whale softens, moved by the support.

"No!" Cashew points an angry finger at Whale. "You're fucking selfish! It's this kind of complacency that keeps men like The Professor in power! We have a moral duty as human beings to stand up to people like him."

```
                    WHALE
We don't know what's going on in that video. Was it
their first time? Who initiated it? Was it
transactional? Maybe it's just some rapey porn
reenactment. Was there's a safeword neither of them
used? They both verbally consented in the beginning!
Twice! Was that a lie?! Was that the truth and
everything else a lie?! WE DON'T KNOW! All we have is
a candid video, filmed without the consent of either
participant, that we'd be publishing out of context
without the consent of either participant, for no
reason other than revenge and the fact that we can't
seem to get a fucking job from this man.
```

"This is not about the internship anymore!" Cashew cries. "It's about keeping abusive men in power accountable for the actions!"

```
                    WHALE
WHICH IS WHY WE NEED TO TELL TRISHA ABOUT IT!
```

"WE'VE GOT NO TIME NOW!" Cashew yells back. "We don't even have her number. We can't even if we wanted to."

"Theo!" Oscar interrupts. "He doesn't want to do it!"

"Shut up!" Cashew snarls. He glares at Whale, a fire in his eyes. "People like him don't deserve the life they have, discriminating and resenting us and everything we stand for!"

```
                    WHALE
All Boomers do! He has outdated values, but that
doesn't inherently make him a bad person!
```

"He humiliated us, and dehumanized us, and brainwashed us into fucking participating! I cheated Peabrain out of a week's worth of work because of him! Peabrain snitched and got you beaten up because of him! Bumps decided to blow her way to the top because of him! You made that video because of him!"

```
                    WHALE
You can't blame him for everything! We did all that!
That's on us!
```

"He intentionally turned The Factory into a toxic work environment. That's the only reason we did any of that!"

```
                    WHALE
Yeah, you know what that's called? CONTEXT! You
hacked onto another intern's computer and deleted his
files to fuck his chances of getting your job.
Peabrain snitched with no evidence and got the wrong
guy's face smashed in! I broke into an office
building after hours and hid in the dark to film my
boss raping a female work friend of mine! All the
things we did look really fucked up on paper, don't
they? None of that is who we really are! Why should
we treat this any differently? We should be reporting
the truth, and the truth is WE DON'T KNOW THE TRUTH!
There's always another side to the story! If we put
that video out there without even knowing the facts
ourselves, we're just as bad as everyone else!
```

Whale's whole body shakes. His eyes feel like they're popping out.

```
                    WHALE (CONT'D)
He worked his whole life to get where he is, thirty
years of struggle and success and connections,
nowhere near where we are right now, and you want to
just smash that all away?! What about the
internship?! Why should Peabrain and Trisha get
fucked over too?! They've done nothing to deserve it!
What about all the good things The Professor's done,
all those films he made that inspired us. This will
ruin everything about him! That damage will never be
undone. He'll never be given a chance to redeem
himself. I don't care if you believe in a higher
power or not. Doing that is absolutely wrong!
```

"What about all the other interns before us, huh?!" Cashew counters. "All the other doe-eyed Millennials he roped in and ruined?! What happened to them?! They weren't as lucky as you to be in the right place at the right time. And all those other girls he raped?! Those other dreamers he stomped on?! That man has done more damage than we'll ever know, and he'll keep on damaging for years to come if we don't post that video!"

```
                    WHALE
YOU'RE JUST MAKING SHIT UP NOW!
```

"I know his type! That's what they do!"

```
                    WHALE
     You don't know HIM! He thought he knew our type,
     remember? Fragile snowflakes addicted to social
     media, unambitious man-children, spoiled and
     pretentious, and why?! Because of our age?! How is
     this different?! You're acting just like your Grandpa
     Martin! Blinded by emotion! USE YOUR FUCKING BRAIN!
```

"I don't care if The Professor is only a monster part-time or just on weekends, that still makes him a fucking monster! He beat your face in! And he fucked Bumps behind our backs!"

```
                    WHALE
     I know he's a bad person. He deserves something, but
     not this!
```

"If it puts a rapist out of commission, isn't that a good thing?!"

```
                    WHALE
     I DIDN'T SAVE HER!
```

Oscar's face hardens.

Whale shakes his head.

```
                    WHALE (CONT'D)
     I don't know what came over me, I just let it happen!
     That's not me! That's not who I am! I didn't want
     this! I shouldn't profit from this! The Professor
     shouldn't get cancelled because of me. Trisha
     shouldn't be thrown into the limelight because of me.
     I had a moment of weakness. I wish it never happened,
     but it's still my choice, and I want to stop this
     while I still can and undo the damage I'm about to
     create.
```

Cashew glares at Whale. "Well, forgive me for thinking your definition of damage is fucked."

```
                    WHALE
     What we're about to do to Trisha and The Professor's
     careers, their reputations, on a fucking hunch is no
     less wicked and evil as killing a human being!
```

"Why are you being so dramatic about this?!"

```
                    WHALE
     Do you have any idea how damning that video is? We
     are holding too much power for anyone to comprehend!
     Publishing that video won't help anyone. It's only
     gonna hurt more people!
```

"You don't know that!"

```
                    WHALE
     Of course I know that! Every unethical thing the four
     of us have done in the past week has had
     unintentional side effects! You got me to go along
     against Peabrain only for me to take the blame. And
     Bumps may have initiated the sex to get the job, but
     she certainly ended up in a situation she didn't
     want.
```

"I thought you said it could've been consensual."

```
                    WHALE
     The video, you moron! I'm talking about the video!
     The one we're publishing without her knowing it even
     exists! And Peabrain just wanted to punish his
     saboteur. Even if he still believes I did it, he was
     certainly shocked how my face looked this morning. He
     didn't know that was gonna happen. Maybe if he knew
```

```
        he wouldn't have reported it at all. And I thought I
        was trusting a friend with an emotionally sensitive
        and powerful secret. How the hell is this NOT gonna
        end up the same way?! He has a wife! He has a kid!
        Trisha has a family! We're hurting all of them!
```

Oscar frowns, moved by Whale's passion. He grabs his laptop bag off the counter.

"Where are you going?!" Cashew asks him incredulously.

"It's over, Theo."

"No! There's still time!"

"He doesn't want to do it!" Oscar scolds.

"STOP!" Cashew barks. He points at Whale. "You need to grow the fuck up."

Whale laughs bitterly, eyes full of tears.

```
                        WHALE
        Grow up? How am I the only one who thinks this way?!
        When did it suddenly become juvenile to give a fuck
        about right and wrong?
```

Cashew scoffs, looking away.

```
                        WHALE (CONT'D)
        LISTEN TO ME! People have been jumping to conclusions
        about me my whole life. I know how horrible it is to
        be misunderstood. I would not want to be on the
        opposite of a career-ender like this. Why should I go
        along with one now? We're not experts! This is
        vigilante justice at best! Let the professionals
        handle this! That's their job! They know what to do!
        We should've done our jobs! All we had to do was
        follow orders and we couldn't even do that! We lost!
        We have no right to take a man down like this! It's
        too easy and dirty and a low blow! It's unchivalrous
        and it's unfair!
```

"Unfair? He was never gonna give us a job. He rigged the game from the beginning. A nice easy way for him to get four living, breathing Millennial punching bags down here to feel more like a man. He picked us because we were the best, and he made sure to let that go to our heads. But he made us relocate our entire lives out here, gave us a shit ton of work with no instructions, mocked us for asking questions, gave no guidance or feedback, just nicknames. When we fucked up, he called us weak, and when we actually grew balls, he punished us for it. He punished us for shit we even didn't do. He just believes what he wants to believe. Hurts the people he wants to hurt. Fucks the ones he wants to fuck. All those hours, all that stress, all those horrible conditions he created, for what? A job that wasn't real. So think about yourself for a moment, Jacob. All you've done in your life. All those screenplays you wrote. All the movies you watched. All the times you did your homework instead of smoking pot or playing *Pokémon Go!* because you actually gave a fuck about your life, about your career, all those unambitious losers you cut off because they were holding you back, all those trips you gave up and the plans you canceled, everyone you left behind to come out here, that was all for nothing. And he knew it the whole time. From the very beginning he knew, and he didn't tell you. He lied to us. Over and over, he lied to us. And now we finally realize what it was all about, just one giant fuck you from one Boomer to all Millennials. Tell me, is THAT fair?!"

Whale stares. Hollow. Hurt.

Oscar sits on a barstool, his eyes lowered.

Whale presses a tongue against his lower lip.

```
                        WHALE
                   (really quiet)
        I need a moment.
```

"We don't got a moment," Cashew grumbles.

Whale looks at Oscar.

```
                    WHALE
        How much time do we have?
```

Oscar checks his watch. "Six minutes, give or take."

"He's already got the article ready to go," Cashew adds. "His people are down the street waiting for him to give the go-ahead."

```
                    WHALE
        I just want a couple minutes. Alone.
```

Cashew huffs impatiently. "Three max."

"We'll still wait for your approval," Oscar says gently. "But we'd need to start now. I have enough experience to know that extracting a video off a phone will take some time."

Whale hesitates.

```
                    WHALE
        But if I say no, it's a no.
```

Oscar bows honorably, a hand to his chest. "I promise."

Whale looks at Cashew.

"Fine," Cashew says, unenthused. "I also promise."

Whale pulls out his phone. Types the passcode. Places the unlocked iPhone on the bar counter. Walks into the back room and closes the doors behind him.

Oscar pulls out his laptop. "Just gotta get the program up and running,."

Cashew takes Whale's phone. Sits on a stool and watches the video from the beginning.

Oscar lifts his head at the sound of what could possibly be porn. Cringes. "How the fuck can you watch that?"

Cashew stares at the phone, his eyes frozen. The way it lights his face gives Oscar the creeps. "So is this the most fucked up thing you've ever published?"

Oscar types into his software's password encryption. "It's up there."

"He really got everything, didn't he?" Cashew whispers.

"I'm ready," Oscar says, holding out a hand.

Cashew doesn't move, his eyes unable to leave the screen.

"Theo!" Oscar orders.

Cashew gets up. Walks the phone over. "Here." Smacks the phone into Oscar's hand. Oscar plugs in the phone. Starts the rapid data extraction.

Cashew sits back down, his legs fidgeting. "He's gonna say no."

Oscar initiates the extraction. A progress bar appears. Three minutes to go.

Cashew rushes over. "Post it."

Oscar looks up. "What?"

"Just do it. C'mon, before he gets back."

Oscar stares. "We wait for Jacob."

"I don't care!" Cashew hisses angrily. "We'll never get this close again! Just do it, dude! C'mon! We gotta get him! I'll take the heat! We just gotta fucking get him!"

A chill runs down Oscar's spine, a kind he hasn't felt in a long time. "We promised."

"Stop making promises then," Cashews mumbles, plopping on a stool.

Oscar stares at the back of Cashew's head, disturbed beyond comprehension.

Whale sits in the dark, a hard frown stuck on his face, staring into space. Eyes unfocused. Mind rolling back. Autumn wind flying through hair. His fingers tapping on the wheel. ZZ Top floating out of the speakers...

JACOB

Eternal Sunshine of the Spotless Mind

INT. STEWIE'S JEEP - DAY

Jacob drives JEEPGUY down a Connecticut highway, Stewie in the passenger seat. ZZ Top's "Legs" plays over Sirius XM.

JACOB
Don't forget, never under any circumstances call her Helen.

STEWIE
You Andrezjs really have a thing against nicknames.

JACOB
I'm serious. The moment you say or do anything she finds strange, she will remember it and use it against you for the rest of your life.

STEWIE
I'm okay with that.

JACOB
And then she'll tell all her girlfriends and neighbors and co-workers about it and make you seem like such a freak and you'll have no idea she's doing it.

STEWIE
Don't be ridiculous.

JACOB
I've seen it more than you can possibly imagine. It happened to every one of my sisters' boyfriends. And watch out for Karen. She's probably in hot S-H-I-T with finances or employment or school or something.

STEWIE
She's still in school?

JACOB
Community college. She's graduating in June, same as Melanie and me.

STEWIE
That's cool.

JACOB
Three years older than us and graduating the same year with an Associates? Oh yeah, that's a riot.

STEWIE
That's what community college is like. She knows her limits.

JACOB
If she knew her limits, she wouldn't be in community college in the first place.

STEWIE
What does that mean?

Jacob goes quiet.

JACOB
Right after Karen graduated from that equestrian school in Utah, she went to college in Texas.

STEWIE
You never told me that.

Jacob hesitates.

JACOB
Remember what I told you happened to her at Eagle Ridge?

STEWIE
Yeah.

JACOB
Happened there too. Mom had to fly down to Texas and pull her out of school. Karen liked the independence she used to have, so she moved onto campus at Albright. But one week into Orientation she called my mom because her roommates were teasing her too much. She wanted to drop out. Mom was furious. She said if Karen dropped out, she wouldn't be allowed to go to a real college, only community college. But she dropped out anyway, and that was four years ago, and she's still there now.

Stewie nods.

JACOB (CONT'D)
And Melanie's just gonna sit on her phone until she can talk about herself.

STEWIE
I don't like that you're talking this way about your family.

JACOB
Hey, they made their beds.

STEWIE
I get it. I used to not get along with my family.

JACOB
I wish I had your family.

STEWIE
Oh yeah, it's so nice having your brother in Maryland and an older sister down in Florida, and now your mom and kid sister are down there too but nowhere near the other sister.

JACOB
At least they say they love you.

STEWIE
I'm sure your family loves you.

JACOB
They never say it.
(pauses)
When I call Mom during the day, she makes me feel guilty for calling her at work. When I call her at night, she makes me feel guilty for not remembering it's a worknight. And whenever I call her at the perfect time, she doesn't answer. She never calls me back or texts back. And then she complains that I never call her. But Karen can call her three times a day, and when Mom answers she always rolls her eyes and tunes her out the whole time. And then she hangs up and makes a crack about how Karen never stops calling her. And Melanie never calls her, but Mom never complains about that. Melanie could set Mom's Volvo on fire and Mom would take her side. An entire

melodrama has probably been going on since I left for Italy and I have absolutely no idea what because no one thinks to themselves, "How's Jacob doing? Maybe we should keep him in the loop or just call him to see how he's been." Nope. We only call if we need something. We don't love each other. We tolerate each other.

STEWIE

I'm sure you're exaggerating.

JACOB

Really?! When I was in 9th grade, we were getting ready for our Spring Showcase at Eagle Ridge. The play that year was a student-written adaptation of Little Shop of Horrors. We called it "On Our Way" for some reason. I played Audrey's boyfriend, Steve Martin's character. Everyone's talking the whole time about the show and what cool things we could do with it, and someone had the idea that it would be funny if, during the scene in which the good guys stuffed me into a locker, that I'd be tied up with duct tape. And for some reason, while I'm listening to these guys talk about me getting tied up with duct tape, I started getting really hard. I've had erections before, but never like that. So when I got home, I snuck away to my computer in the basement and I did the one thing I never, ever wanted to do out of fear of getting caught.

STEWIE

Porn?

JACOB

It was just softcore photos of men tied up. I only chose men because I was a man. I never even thought for a second I was gay. I didn't even do anything. I didn't even know what masturbation was, no one told me, so I just kept staring at the photos with a massive throbbing erection, horny out of my mind.

(pauses)

So after a few weeks of staring at mildly erotic BDSM pics, I decided to find a way of tying myself up. I wanted it to feel real. Handcuffs weren't enough, I wanted to be BOUND. We didn't have any rope, not that I would've used it, so for a while I used the long sleeves of my pajamas, but they stretched out pretty fast. So I switched to duct tape. I grabbed a massive roll out of the garage no one was gonna miss and hid it in my underwear drawer. And every once in a while, when the coast was clear, I'd sit in my closet and bind my wrists and ankles in duct tape and just sit there in the dark with a massive erection. When I was ready to stop, I'd throw away the evidence and put the roll back in my underwear drawer. Over time, I decided to up the ante by rolling up our dogs' old bandanas into cloth gags.

Stewie stares at Jacob.

STEWIE

You have dogs?

JACOB

Two dachshunds, Marley and Soyer, and a yellow lab named Zoey.

STEWIE

Nice.

JACOB

One day, Melanie was outside on the deck with a friend of hers from softball. No one else was home. Mom and Dad were at work. It might've been Spring

Break. Karen had already been sent away at that point.
(pauses)
I was bored and thought "Why not?" so I grabbed my duct tape from the underwear drawer and the bandanna gags from my sock drawer, I took off my shirt, went into my closet and proceeded to tie myself up as always. And as I'm sitting there at the bottom of my closet in the dark, ripping off sheets of duct tape, I could suddenly hear Melanie racing up the stairs to get something from her room, which I remind you was literally connected to mine, because it's ADORABLE when the twins are six and not fourteen and pubescent and I find her bloody pads in the trash and she walks in on me in my underwear tying myself with duct tape at the bottom of my closet.

STEWIE
She walked in on you?

JACOB
When I heard her footsteps, I stopped pulling the tape. Silence. So she's either standing at the top of the stairs, craning her head like Michael Myers with sonar, wondering where that tearing sound is coming from, or she's back downstairs, so I took the chance and pulled a little bit of tape. Suddenly I hear racing footsteps over to my closet and she opens the door and sees me like that.

Stewie sighs anxiously.

JACOB (CONT'D)
And I'm screaming at her through the doggie bandanas, trying to cover myself up, and she runs away. I was humiliated, having finally been caught. I was paralyzed by anxiety I just wanted to end, so I got dressed and went out on the deck. Pretended nothing happened. But Melanie had already told her friend. The two of them couldn't stop laughing at me. And so I found myself in a horrible situation in which I had to call my mother on a workday to tell her that I had accidentally unlocked a bondage fetish and that Melanie had just walked in on me experimenting with duct tape and that she had already told her friend.

STEWIE
Why would you do that?

JACOB
Melanie was going to tell her sooner or later. I didn't want her getting the story wrong and pass me off as some sort of freak.

Jacob looks at Stewie.

JACOB (CONT'D)
THAT'S what my family is like.

Stewie hesitates.

STEWIE
How'd she take it, your mom?

JACOB
She was so uncomfortable that the duct tape scene of "On Our Way" would give me an erection, so she made me lie to our theatre director that I was not comfortable with being tied up like that. The whole thing made me feel so exposed and weird about my own sexual feelings that I never did anything for years out of fear of how my family would react. And of course, when I finally started jerking off at the healthy age of sixteen, every single one of my family

members ended up walking in on me spanking my monkey multiple times.

STEWIE
Why didn't you just lock the door?

JACOB
(fake cheer)
Ah, because both of my bedroom locks were BROKEN! Just lift the handle from the outside and it opens itself like magic. Oh, and don't knock. You'll miss the show.

STEWIE
Fixing a lock is the easiest thing in the world. You could've done it yourself.

JACOB
No one told me that. Every time I wanted to remind them, I knew that they'd know that the only reason I wanted to fix it was because I wanted to jerk off, and I didn't want to put myself in that position again.

Jacob goes quiet. Realizes something.

JACOB (CONT'D)
Maybe that's why I couldn't come out for so long. That and Karen being such a topic of conversation. Melanie and I got really good at keeping secrets on anything not Mother-approved.

Stewie nods, thinking to himself.

STEWIE
That's why she didn't tell you about the divorce for six months.

Jacob furrows his brow.

JACOB
Huh?

STEWIE
Because of what happened with Karen at Albright. She didn't want that to happen with you, so she kept things from you to avoid that conversation for as long as possible.

JACOB
But I was rocking a 4.0. I was never gonna drop out, let alone pull a Karen after how furious and pissed off it made Mom.

STEWIE
She didn't know that. You intentionally made such a little impact on her. The only point of reference she had for what to do in a similar situation was what happened with Karen.

Jacob withdraws within himself.

JACOB
You think?

STEWIE
You said Karen and Melanie found out about the divorce by accident, right?

JACOB
Right.

STEWIE
She probably hated not being in control of narrative, so she decided to tell you when she felt comfortable,

and she wasn't going to be comfortable until after she knew how you'd react.
(pause)
When did she tell you about the divorce?

JACOB
December 2013.

STEWIE
In the car.

JACOB
Yeah.

STEWIE
And when did you come out to her?

JACOB
June 7, 2014.

STEWIE
In the car.

Jacob hesitates.

JACOB
What are you saying?

STEWIE
If she didn't keep that information from you the way she did, you'd never have realized she didn't know you. SHE broke the status quo, even after everything you did to maintain it. There was no reason for you to keep it up anymore, which is why you had no problem coming out six months later. If she hadn't done that, you'd probably still be closeted to this day.

Jacob takes a soft breath.

JACOB
You might have something there.

STEWIE
And I'll tell you something else. The reason her canceling the Italy trip hurt you so much was probably because you were thriving out there. You weren't living on-campus with the same college friends on the same themed floor where everyone had the same major as you. You were in an actual apartment with six complete strangers. You bought your own groceries. You cooked your own food. You went out. Made friends. Maintained an active, relatively healthy sex life. Kept your grades up anyway. You wanted her to see you like that, being especially NOT Karen.

Jacob frowns.

STEWIE (CONT'D)
If your mom is really just like mine, she's the kind of person that has to see things on her own terms. If someone just tells her it happened, that's not the same as her actually seeing it and coming to her own conclusions about it.

Stewie shrugs.

STEWIE (CONT'D)
It's like it never happened.

Jacob looks at Stewie, flabbergasted.

CUT TO:

I/E. STEWIE'S JEEP - SUNSET

Stewie's in the driver's seat now, speeding JEEPGUY down the Schuylkill Expressway.

JACOB
Slow down, this is our exit.

Stewie doesn't slow down. Doesn't merge out either.

JACOB
What are you doing?! Turn here!

Stewie hits the gas more. Blows past the Conshohocken exit.

JACOB
Great, you just missed our exit.

STEWIE
No I didn't.

JACOB
The sign said Conshohocken.

STEWIE
We're not going to Conshohocken.

JACOB
Yes we are, my mom LIVES there!

Stewie chuckles.

STEWIE
My Baby Boy's so funny.

Jacob hesitates.

JACOB
I don't get it.

STEWIE
Get me directions for 129 Canter Way.

Jacob melts in his seat. Stewie beams.

STEWIE (CONT'D)
Surprise.

DISSOLVE TO:

EXT. SCHUYLKILL EXPRESSWAY - NIGHT

JEEPGUY pulls off on an exit. The sign says:

"Phoenixville"

DISSOLVE TO:

EXT. CANTER WAY - NIGHT

Stewie creeps the Jeep through an upper middle class suburban neighborhood. Jacob looks out the window at the houses.

JACOB
Next one down.

Stewie parks the Jeep in front of an attractive two-story single-family home with a well-manicured lawn. A few lights are on inside.

CUT TO:

INT. STEWIE'S JEEP - CONTINUOUS

Stewie locks the emergency break.

JACOB
What are you doing?

STEWIE
You don't wanna go inside?

```
                    JACOB
      They're not gonna let us walk around their house.

                    STEWIE
      I've done it before with my house in Laurence Harbor.

                    JACOB
      And that's weird.

                    STEWIE
      Okay Helen.

                    JACOB
      Don't even do it, I swear.

                    STEWIE
      I won't.
              (pauses)
      If you're not knocking, I am.

                    JACOB
      Wait.

Jacob looks out at the field behind the house.

                    JACOB (CONT'D)
      I've got a better idea.

                                                  DISSOLVE TO:


EXT. OPEN FIELD - NIGHT

Jacob and Stewie trudge across the grass, stopping at the far edge
of a circular basin approximately six yards in diameter.

Jacob sits. Stewie reluctantly sits beside him. The moon is bright,
illuminating the sight before them.

Ten yards away from the basin is the rear of Jacob's childhood home.
Red stained deck. Black metal fence surrounding the backyard with
generous space. Lights on in the kitchen and a second floor bedroom.

Jacob reaches into his pocket. Pulls out his iPhone. Taps through
his Apple Music library. Selects "You've Got a Way" by Shania Twain.

                    STEWIE
              (side-eyes)
      Is that Shania Twine?

                    JACOB
      My surprise, my soundtrack.

                    STEWIE
      It's country crap.

                    JACOB
      It's Mutt Lange.

                    STEWIE
      Not good Mutt Lange.

                    JACOB
      I harshly disagree.

Jacob wraps his arms around his knees, smiling wistfully. Stewie
folds his hands and watches the house.

                    JACOB (CONT'D)
      Every time we drove to our beach house in Sea Isle,
      Mom would always play two CDs in their entirety: Come
      On Over and Hell Freezes Over.

                    STEWIE
      Eagles?
```

JACOB
Mmm-hmm.

STEWIE
Suppose that makes up for it.

JACOB
Every Thanksgiving, we'd go up to our Aunt's house in Lock Haven. The three of us would sit in the back of the car and watch movies together the whole drive up.
(pause)
Mom and I always watched all the Oscar nominees every year. We'd exchange predictions and have an Oscar night party. We'd watch every minute of the red carpet. The whole ceremony live. Just the two of us.

Jacob smirks.

JACOB (CONT'D)
Mom always took Karen and I up to New York City. We'd see a matinee, go out to dinner somewhere to talk about it, then catch another show before going home. One time the three of us saw Wicked and Avenue Q. You know Avenue Q?

STEWIE
No.

JACOB
It's an off-Broadway musical, like an R-Rated Sesame Street. The puppets have sex and everything. It's hysterical. There's a song in there, "If You Were Gay," between their version of Bert & Ernie. I wasn't expecting that. It was so validating.
(pause)
Mom took me up there the summer I came out, just the two of us. We saw the Metropolitan Museum of Art, the Central Park Zoo, ate at an Italian restaurant with a squid ink pasta special, and the two of us went to see The Book of Mormon. On the drive home in her Volvo, she had the top down and we were blasting Billy Joel and Andrea Bocelli and Led Zeppelin, singing all the way home.
(pause)
That was a good day.

Stewie nods.

JACOB (CONT'D)
And Karen and I always played video games a lot. Before I was a movie nut, I was just as obsessed with video games. Mario Kart, Smash Brothers, Legend of Zelda, Metroid Prime, World of Warcraft. She was too. And we were both huge fans of InuYasha and Studio Ghibli. And we had a huge VHS collection, lots of Disney movies. We watched them all the time.

Jacob points at the house.

JACOB (CONT'D)
Dad built that deck.

STEWIE
Really?

JACOB
We always called him Mr. Fix It.

Jacob chuckles.

JACOB (CONT'D)
I forgot all about that. Mr. Fix It.

Jacob waves a hand across the basin at their feet.

JACOB (CONT'D)
One time this whole thing froze over. Dad took the three of us out here to play on the ice. Mom was in the house having a migraine. About twenty minutes in, Dad slipped and fell face down on the ice. Hit his head. It gave him amnesia. It was only for a few hours, but we had to go to the emergency room and everything. It was a pretty big deal. That was the first time I ever heard of amnesia. If that didn't happen I probably would've assumed it was just a movie thing.
(pause)
And Melanie and I used to have sleepovers in her room. That sounds weird, but we were kids. We never thought it was weird.

Jacob stares at the house, an emotional smile creeping in.

JACOB (CONT'D)
It really wasn't so bad, you know.

STEWIE
There's no reason it can't be like that again.

Jacob takes a slow breath in. Stewie bumps his shoulder into Jacob.

STEWIE (CONT'D)
You like your surprise, Baby Boy?

JACOB
I used to hate surprises, being put on the spot like that. The anxiety of my hand being forced. All those people taking pictures. But after sixteen years of having to share my day with MELANIE of all people, I started wanting surprise parties. All that thought put into something just for me and me alone. Mom never did it though. I never told her, of course, but that wouldn't make it a real surprise, would it?
(pause)
In Florence, I was the only student in the program turning twenty-one. I could tell my suitemates were planning something. Secret meeting in the kitchen. They'd all stop talking when I walked into the room. I let them go on. Didn't wanna ruin it. And so when my birthday came around, they all took me out to dinner. Paid for the whole thing. A bunch of them had to head back early, lots of homework or whatever they said, and two of them stayed behind to take me to my favorite gelato place. I knew what the real reason was, of course. And sure enough, the three of us got back to the apartment, the whole kitchen decorated with penis decals and gay gag gifts. They had a big bottle of Ultimo Vodka in between two Rocky Mountain Oysters. Tons of OJ. They were all drinking screwdrivers in my honor. I hated beer and thought wine was just okay. The only drink I ever ordered was a screwdriver. I only knew it because of Jackie Brown.
(pause)
After they gave me gifts, they suggested we go upstairs to the rooftop terrace for a toast. I love melodramatic stuff like that, so I agreed. But when I opened the door and flicked the lights on... "Surprise!" The terrace was filled with as many students they could wrangle on such short notice. I was so shocked and flattered and... and probably crying.

Jacob laughs.

JACOB (CONT'D)
They even made sure Donny Walker was there, the straight guy my suitemates knew I had a crush on. We

partied for a few hours at a local bar after that. They all bought me anything I wanted.
(pause)
They knew me so well. They actually anticipated me figuring it out and added a second layer to the surprise.

Jacob nods.

JACOB (CONT'D)
That's what made it the best night of my life.

Stewie smiles.

JACOB (CONT'D)
Thank you for this. This means so much to me.

STEWIE
I know it does.

Jacob tries not to cry.

JACOB
(emotional)
I was so lonely!

Jacob shakes his head. Points at the lit window on the second floor.

JACOB (CONT'D)
I always hated having that room. Melanie got the east-facing one out front, every morning waking up to a room glowing with sunshine while I always woke up in the dark. I spent hours looking out that window at the sunset, dreaming. Dreaming of love. Of marriage. Of making it into the history books.

Jacob wipes his puffy eyes.

JACOB (CONT'D)
Do you know what the worst part about autism is? I feel so mentally and physically disconnected from the world around me, like there's an entire movie going on and I'm not even the main character. I'm not a supporting character either. I'm just an audience member. No one's looking at me or touching me...
(pause)
Touching used be a big no-no for me before I was diagnosed, so Mom made sure not to do that, just to make me comfortable. It wasn't until I first started having sex, and kissing and cuddling for the first time, that I finally felt HERE. And it felt weird, someone touching me. And I realized it had been years since someone had touched me. I couldn't even remember the last time--

Stewie touches Jacob's shoulder with his fingertips. Hops them over to his cheek. Hops again on his face. Jacob stares at Stewie. Stewie giggles childishly.

Jacob's lip slowly starts quivering.

STEWIE
(laughing)
Oh Baby! What's wrong?

Jacob's face contorts, tears falling.

STEWIE (CONT'D)
Happy cry or sad cry?

Jacob nods.

STEWIE (CONT'D)
Happy cry?

Jacob nods some more.

Stewie smiles sweetly and puts his arms around Jacob. Stewie's body is warm. Jacob can feel his muscles poking into his back. Jacob looks up to see Stewie already smiling, the moon shining behind his head. Stewie gently lifts Jacob's chin with a finger. Moves in for a kiss.

SMASH BACK TO:

WHALE

Pillar of Salt

Whale's brows droop, lips curled in a warm toothless smile, tears about to fall. He thinks nothing. He feels nothing. Nothing's inside him. Nothing's beside him. Just an empty void of what once was.

Soft knocks behind him. Whale blinks hard, his body jolting a bit. "We're ready to go," Oscar says, his voice muffled by the glass door.

```
                    WHALE
          Coming.
```

Whale wipes his right cheek with a slow palm. Wipes his left. Slow breath in. Presses on his knees and stands. Opens the door, passing Oscar on his way to the bar.

"Well?" Cashew asks, antsy.

Whale stands with hollow eyes. Oscar slowly sits at the computer with a lamentful frown.

"C'mon!" Cashew whispers. "Did you decide?"

```
                    WHALE
          I did.
```

"And?"

Whale nods slightly. "Do it."

Cashew raises his brows. "Do it?"

"Yeah. Do it."

Cashew beams with his entire face. Clasps both arms around Whale. "Yes! Thank you!" Whale doesn't hug back. Just stares at Oscar.

Oscar discreetly looks away. "Yes is a yes," he mumbles, typing away on his computer.

"You've made the right decision, dude!" Cashew lets go. Claps hard. "God, this is really happening!"

"It sure is," Whale says emotionlessly.

Oscar pulls out his cell phone. "Cleo, you got it?" he asks. "Good. Tell Lara and Michael to tweet the video, and make sure to time it with Gary's article. Promote the shit out of both of them. We need to napalm this bitch before he gets a chance to respond." Oscar unconsciously looks up.

Whale's staring back, a hard frown on his face.

Oscar's energy fizzles. "Yes," he answers into his phone. "Gary still has time to spell-check, but it has to be ready in 2, alright?"

Whale wanders toward the back room like a zombie.

Cashew darts into the bathroom and roars as loud and as hard as he can, testosterone ripping through his veins. "LET'S FUCKING GOOOOO!" he screams, high-fiving the tile wall. "FUCK YEAH!" He grins, imagining The Professor's face as he hears the news, that defeated "oh shit" look, the true reality of having been beaten. How the hell did he get Whale to change his mind? His father Calvin was always a brick wall, unreadable, unswayable. And yet Cashew was actually able to persuade someone! Not someone stupid either! Someone smart! Someone moral and steadfast! And Cashew found it all by himself, by accident!

Whale sits in the back room with a sad look in his eyes. Cashew quietly opens the door. "Hey buddy," he says with fragile sympathy. "What's eating you?"

Whale doesn't respond.

Cashew slowly sits beside Whale. "I'm sorry for ambushing you like that. It really wasn't personal, you know."

Whale fiddles his fingers. "'Just some guy,' he said. I'm not so sure now."

Cashew shrugs off Whale's vague nonsense.

"Now that it's actually happened," Whale murmurs, "I don't actually feel bad about it."

Cashew studies Whale's expression. He didn't say it with optimism. Sounded kinda surprised. Sad surprise. Like he was diagnosing himself or something. Who knows. Cashew's already lost interest. "I knew you would. Smart people understand."

Whale looks behind him. Oscar at the counter. "Did he get permission from the manager or something to be in here?" Whale asks.

"I don't think so."

"Figures." Whale checks his watch. "I guess we should be heading out now."

"The openers don't come in until 8:30. Oscar says we don't have to worry about them anyway. Not like they can actually do anything to him."

Whale nods. "'Who watches the Watchmen?'"

"Exactly."

Whale looks at Cashew. "You like *Watchmen*?"

Cashew smirks. "You kidding? I love *Watchmen*."

Whale hesitates. "What's your opinion of musicals?"

"C'mon bro. You're really asking the Classic Hollywood nut if he likes musicals?" Cashew laughs heartily.

Whale smiles. Cashew has a good laugh. Infectious. Just as viral as that video's gonna be.

"I really shouldn't call myself that anymore," Cashew says.

"A Classic Hollywood nut?"

"I don't want to be associated with nuts ever again."

Whale furrows his brow. "But cashews are legumes." He pauses. "Actually, I always thought they were legumes. Turns out they're seeds. Whoever told me 'cashews aren't nuts, they're legumes,' were wrong themselves. Why would they correct a false assumption but not actually do the research to not create another false assumption?"

"Yeah, well, 'not that nut' sounds a whole lot better than 'not that legume' or 'not that seed.'"

"Phonetically of course, but it doesn't change the fact that it's not true. Except literally, because you technically never were named after a nut in the first place, but for the metaphor to work it really should make sense."

Cashew stares. "How about you go fuck yourself? How about that?"

Whale frowns. "Sorry," he whispers, withdrawing into himself.

Cashew claps Whale's shoulder. "I'm heading out. You coming?"

Whale rubs his palms together. "I wanna stay back here a little bit." He looks around. "It's calming."

"Whatever." Cashew opens the door. Reluctantly looks back at Whale. "Hey, um..."

Whale looks up at Cashew.

Cashew smiles weakly. "In case I don't see you." He holds out his hand.

Whale shakes Cashew's hand, tight grip on both sides. They let go.

Cashew nods. "Have a nice life, Jacob."

"You too, Theo."

Cashew slowly shuts the door and walks away. Whale watches Cashew leave through the glass partition. Faces forward. Hangs his head in shame.

Oscar watches Whale from place at the counter, frowning at the sorrowful sight.

Cashew unlocks the door of his Northridge apartment, his roommate Wayne siting on the couch with the TV on. "Dude, you hear about The Professor?! Holy fuck!"

"Yeah, I know," Cashew murmurs. He avoids looking at the TV.

"Twitter's going nuts!"

"I'm sure." Cashew pulls a beer from the fridge. Twists it open.

"So what does that mean for you?" Wayne asks.

Cashew wanders toward his bedroom. "I'm out of a job."

"What are you gonna do now?"

Cashew smirks knowingly. "Get myself a new one." Closes the bedroom door. Locks it. Sits at his desk. Thinks. Looks at his computer. Reluctantly moves the Lubriderm closer. Opens the laptop. Logs onto Twitter. Finds the full uncensored video. Plugs in headphones. Clicks play.

Unbuckles his belt.

DREW

Happier Than Ever

Theo stops, his mouth agape. Suyin's tied to the bed, naked, ass-up, blindfolded, screaming her head off for Theo to let her go, not to do it. Theo looks down at his waist, a belt strap in each hand, a throbbing erection bursting out of his pants. "Peanut brittle," Theo mutters, his breath quickening. His eyes dart around. "Peanut brittle! Peanut brittle!"

Suyin snaps out of character. "What? What's wrong?"

"Nothing, I..." Theo struggles to rebuckle his belt with shaking fingers. "Just remembered something."

Suyin clears her throat, hoarse from all the screaming. "You wanna take a break?"

"Yes." Theo sits on the bed beside her, desperate to calm down. "Yes, yes, yes."

Suyin sighs, quite relaxed despite her wrists bound together with rope and tied to the post, her legs spread with a bar.

Theo looks Suyin in the blindfold. "Suyin?"

"Yeah?"

"Is it possible that...?" Theo hesitates. "Is something wrong with me?"

"No. Take as long as you want."

"I mean me as a person. Do you, Suyin, think something is wrong with me?"

Suyin hesitates. "I don't think I'm the right person to ask. My judgment's been fucked for a while now."

"You can tell me. I want you to."

"No," Suyin lies as sweetly as she can. "There is nothing wrong with you, Theo."

Theo smiles. It fades fast. "If I wasn't paying you, would your answer be different?"

Suyin huffs. "This is about Drew, isn't it?"

"So what if it is?"

"Theo, it's been a year and a half. Who cares what he said? He's a loser."

Theo licks his dry lips. "I fired a bunch of people this week. Doris. Simmons. Johnson."

"I don't know who those people are."

"They were us with before the restructuring."

"Then they must've done something to deserve it."

Theo scratches his exposed bald patch, grateful Suyin's never seen it. "Doris told one of Míng's guys how much she didn't like *Mari and the Babushkas: World Tour*."

Suyin doesn't move. "Okay. Sounds reasonable."

"And Simmons and Johnson asked about Drew, when he was coming back. They were hurting morale obsessing on that. I was the one there, not him. I told them, if they had a problem with that, they were out. They said they didn't. But I had to fire them anyway. To set an example for the others."

"Again, also reasonable."

"I got so upset seeing their faces that I made Larry edit them out of the company photos." Theo pauses. "I just know Drew wouldn't have liked any of that. If he's coming back—"

"He's never coming back, Theo. Move on."

"Maybe I don't want to move on."

"You can run the ship without him. You should be very proud of yourself."

Theo looks down at his beltline. Frowns. "Drew said I didn't actually have feelings, that I just want people to fear me—"

"Not this again!"

"But what if he's right? How would I know, Suyin? No one's gonna tell me. How would I know?"

"He just said that to hurt you."

"But why *that* of all things? He's never lied to me before."

"That you know of."

Theo shakes his head. "I don't want to think of him like that."

Suyin lets out an annoyed breath. "Look, Theo, what you do with me out here doesn't mean you're a bad person."

Theo looks at her. "Doesn't it?"

"Absolutely not," Suyin tells the man paying her $10,000 an hour. "I do all kinds of fucked up things for people. I pretend to be an ex-girlfriend, someone they've lost, their wife, their daughter, some want me to be into it, some don't. I pretend to be asleep, I pretend to be dead. I do everything. That's my thing. You're par for the course. And even if you weren't, I'm in no place to judge anyone. Neither is Drew. You just do whatever you want."

Theo stares at Suyin's face, her smooth skin, the way her mouth moves as she talks, the way her hair falls on her blindfold, the way she grips the rope like a boss, no illusions about anything. He reaches out to caress her cheek. Stops. Retracts his hand. "Suyin?" he asks.

"Yeah?"

Theo grins, a bit bashful. "You know Drew's movie he's got coming out? *The Sins of Jack Branson*?"

"Of course."

Theo takes a silent deep breath. "Do you wanna go see it?" he asks sweetly.

Suyin opens her mouth, unable to hide her shock. "Oh, you mean... With *you*?"

Theo forces a chuckle. "What? No!" His levity fades, his skin stinging. "Fuck no. I-I just wanted to know if *you* wanted to. In general. Like... were you actually planning on seeing it?"

"No."

Theo stares. "Is that the truth or just because I'm paying you?"

Suyin sighs, defeated. "No, I wanna see it. It looks amazing."

Theo frowns. Stares off. "Okay, enough of that." He spanks Suyin's exposed ass as hard as he can.

"Yes sir!"

Theo returns to the foot of his bed. Looks down at his conquest. "Ready?"

"Ready."

"Okay. Three, two, one... Action!"

Suyin screams. "NO! STOP! PLEASE JUST LET ME GO!"

Theo turns off his brain with a savage grin. Unbuckles his belt. Climbs on top of her. Pins down her shackled wrists. She cries her heart out as Theo guiltlessly "rapes" her brains out.

Theo's still thinking about it on Monday, smiling at his desk as Larry walks in with lunch. "They ran out of orange chicken," Larry says. "I got you General Tso's. Hope that's okay."

"Yeah, it's fine," Theo murmurs calmly. He sits up. Makes space on his desk.

Larry unpacks the brown paper bag. Looks up at Theo. "You seem chipper."

"It did me good." Theo cracks open his chicken. Splits his chop sticks. "Any calls?"

"Nothing crazy."

"What about Drew?"

"Still nothing."

Theo sighs. "Suppose I should be used to that by now."

Larry hesitates. "Mr. Landreth, we really need a Head of Production."

"He always apologizes, Larry. He always does."

Larry sits across from Theo with a container of rice. "Maybe he thinks he's on the Black List."

"He's not on the Black List."

"Yeah, but how would he know that? You're always so fast about it."

Theo opens his mouth. Closes it. Rubs his jaw. "He always would've been the exception. He knows that."

Larry shrugs.

Theo's eyes instantly whip up. "What was that?"

"Nothing."

"That shrug."

"It was just a shrug."

"Larry, I mean... He knows I'd never do that, right?"

"Whatever you say." Larry eats his rice.

Theo puts his container down. "The only thing I can think of is that Drew's expecting *me* to apologize, but I didn't do anything wrong, right?"

"Of course not."

"Larry," Theo says sternly. "Tell me the truth. What do you think of me?"

Larry blinks. "What do I think of you?"

"What do you really think of me? You can tell me. It's okay."

"I think you're a great employer and a hard worker," Larry tells the man paying him six figures a year.

"I don't come off as a heartless disgusting pig?"

"You're not a heartless disgusting pig."

"I'm not asking that. I'm asking if I come off as one. I need to know, Larry. I don't think I am. I know I'm not, but I didn't think I was before, so... Was I?" Theo softens with desperate eyes. "Am I?" he whispers.

Larry hesitates. "Not at all," he tells the man that fired Drew for calling him out for being in the wrong.

"So Drew was lying?"

"Probably," Larry tells the man that fired Alan even though he did everything right.

Theo shakes his head. "Should I call him?"

"I don't think he's coming back, but that doesn't mean you shouldn't make up with him. You were a better person with him. You cared more. About everything."

Theo moves his mouth to one side. "I can't help feeling our friendship was better before *Atomic*. We were so busy after that." He pauses. "Maybe that's why Drew lashed out at me the way he did. He was finally free of all that work. He could finally think about us." Theo looks up. "Maybe that was the most honest he's been with me in years."

Larry half-shrugs. "You're doing it too, I guess. This is so unlike you, you know? Thinking back."

Theo nods. "Maybe."

After lunch, Theo Googles "Drew Lawrence" on his desktop. Lots of results. Articles. Pictures. A sponsored header for *The Sins of Jack Branson*, its wide release scheduled for Christmas Day. Theo scrolls through Images. Lots of toothy grins. Drew on the red carpet, *Branson*'s Cannes Premiere two months ago. He looks so fly in that suit! And his face. Sobriety has done wonders for him. And his hair. He just looks so fucking happy! He hasn't looked like that since the early days.

Theo scrolls a bit more. Drew shirtless on the cover of Men's Health. "How I Got Sober." Theo switches to News. A *Variety* interview from July, a profile on Drew's new company. Theo scrolls a bit more. A Cannes critic review raving about *The Sins of Jack Branson*. Theo closes the window, disheartened. He really made his life a living hell, didn't he?

If Drew was right about that, what else was he right about?

Theo drives his vintage '19 Camaro into the mountains, gliding through the San Fernando Valley to the Golden Green in Woodland Hills, a planned community surrounded by fifty-foot steel walls. Only one way in. Only one way out. Theo slows at the security checkpoint. "Who are you here to see?" The Guard asks.

"René Scragg," Theo tells him.

The Guard flips through a manifest. Fingers down the page.

Theo sighs nervously. "I know I'm not on the list, but—"

"No, you're good," the Guard says, not getting paid enough to give a shit. He slams the big red button. The steel doors CLANK and pull apart like the Black Gate of Mordor. Theo eases his car in. Stupid Boomers, paying thousands of dollars a year to keep out the burgling spicks, japs, and coons only to let a stranger waltz his way in.

Theo's Camaro creeps down the drive. Rows and rows of ranch homes, manicured lawns, sprinklers ablowing, hot sun in a hazy sky. On every porch is an old geezer looking at the shiny car with bitter suspicion. They all came of age in a record-shattering economy, born on third base and convinced they hit a triple, hoarding their riches like greedy dwarves, refusing to share with the new "spoiled" generation, the ones born into a world of Wars on Terror and Recessions, the ones that had it so easy. Their grandkids can't afford a car like that. If only they pulled themselves up by their bootstraps.

Theo cringes at all those Hollywood relics, those once-great kings of Los Angeles, too paranoid and fucked up to handle the real world, choosing instead to live in a fantasy land, just like the ones they made millions selling, peddling, perpetuating. He hates them. He should just run them all over and save the world the bother of paying their Social Security and Medicare. But then he remembers Drew, how happier he is now that he left his comfort zone and forgave Peabrain, something he only would've done out of spite, no idea how fulfilled he'd be by doing so. That's what Theo needs to remember. Wherever he ends up will make all this bullshit worth it.

Theo pulls into the driveway of number 58. Steps out. Looks around. A shiver runs down Theo's spine. He knows if it wasn't so bright out he'd see cobwebs everywhere. He's never felt so much like William Holden in his life.

Theo gently raps on René Scragg's screen door. "Hello?" No answer. No movement. Theo pulls the door open. Steps inside. It's musty. Moldy. Too much potpourri. "Anyone home?" He senses movement in the corner of his eye, an old man in his late seventies with white patchy hair on his head waddling over with a cane, his back at a forty-five-degree angle.

"Who are you?" René asks with airy, weak confusion.

Theo softens with pity at the sight of him. "I'm sorry, Professor, the door was open."

René furrows his brow. "Professor?" He waddles closer for a better look. "Have we met before?"

"It's me, Professor," Theo says gently, politely. "Theo Landreth. I was one of your interns at The Factory, remember?" He hesitates. "Cashew."

René smacks his lips. "Cashew."

"I just wanted to, um..." Theo sighs. "I wanted a chance for the two of us to talk."

René stares, panting loudly. "Why?"

"To tell you..." Theo hesitates again. He's physically in pain just being here, let alone having to say it. "I'm sorry for what happened. For everything."

René squints at Theo, not quite getting it. "I'll make you some tea. We can talk."

Theo smiles weakly. "That'll be nice."

René waddles ever so slowly into the kitchen. Theo removes his suit jacket. Hangs it on the rack. Checks the dirty mirror on the wall. Straightens his toupee. He looks around René's home. Old photos in frames. The Professor standing next to Harvey Weinstein, as if he's actually proud of the association. Maybe he missed the memo. They did get busted the same week.

Hanging on the wall is a formal family photo, The Professor as Theo remembered him posing with a gorgeous blonde and a smiling 8- or 9-year old boy.

René carries a mug of hot water from the kitchen. Drops the cup, hot water getting all over the carpet. "WHO ARE YOU?!" René cries, angry and terrified. "WHAT ARE YOU DOING IN MY HOUSE?!"

Theo gapes. "I don't—?"

"I'm calling the police!" René waddles toward the phone.

"Professor, it's me!" Theo says calmly. "Remember? Theo Landreth?"

René freezes, confused. "Theo...?"

"Landreth." Theo huffs. "Cashew. One of your old interns."

René looks at Theo's jacket on the rack. "I was..." He looks back at Theo. "I was making you tea, wasn't I?"

Theo smiles awkwardly. "You only made one."

"I don't drink tea." René thinks hard. "At least I don't think I..." He sighs with embarrassment. "I am so sorry, Mr. Landreth, I..."

"It's okay." Theo crouches. Picks up the ceramic shards.

"The nigger doctor says I have a short-term memory problem. I don't buy it."

Theo lays the shards in a pile on the coffee table. "Please sit down, Professor."

René reluctantly sits, squinting suspiciously at Theo.

Theo sits far enough away. "I was telling you before... I'm sorry, Professor, for what happened. You put us through a lot back then, you made it hell for us, and I hated you for it. So I helped Whale publish that video he took of you and... Bumps."

René stares.

Theo nods. "I was angry. I didn't realize what it was I was doing, but..." He looks up at the Scragg family picture. "But I know now that it was wrong. And I'm sorry."

"Go fuck yourself!" René spits.

"But sir—"

"I don't need your goddamn pity!" René scowls like a proper curmudgeon. "You sniveling little bitch. Get out of my house!" He grabs the pile of mug shards and storms into the kitchen.

Theo doesn't move, shocked. Confused. Hurt. A plastic bag scrapes inside the kitchen, little ceramic pieces chinking. Theo sits tight. Maybe he won't remember when he returns.

René waddles in. Stops at the sight of Theo.

Theo doesn't say anything, a hurt expression still on his face.

"Felipe?!" René breathes. He waddles closer with rapt eyes. "Felipe, is that really you?"

Theo's never seen such emotion on The Professor before. He really is human. "No," Theo says.

René stops walking. "No?"

Theo shakes his head. "I'm not Felipe."

"I'm sorry," René mumbles. He returns to his seat, frowning the whole way. "I thought you were my son."

Theo looks up at the Scragg family photo.

"Who are you?" René asks.

"I'm..." Theo stops himself. Dons a sophisticated expression. "I'm with *The Times*, Mr. Scragg. Remember? I've been interviewing you?"

René nods slowly. "Oh yes, yes, of course. *The Times*."

"Yes, sir. *The Times*."

"Which *Times*? *LA* or *New York*?"

"Yes. I was just asking you about what happened twenty years ago. The video."

"Has it really been that long?"

"It'll be twenty years in October."

René shakes his head. "Fuck."

"Tell me about your son, Mr. Scragg," Theo says, pointing at the family picture.

"Felipe?"

Theo nods.

René shrugs. "What is there to say, really? When that video came out, it was such a mess. Felipe was only ten, but Sophie, my ex-wife that is, she already got him a phone by then. He followed me on Twitter. So when I came home that night, he had already seen the video at least ten times. It was all out there! Sophie was so devastated. And Felipe, he never..." René shakes his head. "I never wanted him to see me like that. It fucked him up. Sophie took him back to Sacramento, and then the divorce happened..." René pauses. "I worked so hard for him. I did so much. Now he won't even visit me."

Theo looks down, his heart breaking.

René swallows. "I just want to explain to him... why. But he doesn't care to know why. He just wants that video to be all he remembers of me." He shrugs helplessly. "Sure I made mistakes, but I'm his father. I love him. Why won't he come home?"

Theo licks his dry lips. "Maybe he felt trapped," he murmurs. "You saw this place as a paradise because everyone loved you here. Maybe he always saw it as a prison, just more people, more adults, monitoring his every move. He'll always be The Professor's kid to them, even after he grew. He was stuck in your shadow. He couldn't make friends even if he tried. He just wanted to be loved, just like you were by everyone. And he wanted to be just like you." Theo stops. "But you were always working, keeping secrets from him. Being such a fucking perfectionist. All he wanted was to make you happy, to make you proud of him. But you shut him out instead. Maybe you didn't have time or maybe you just didn't have it in you, but he needed to hear it. Because he didn't have anyone. Just you."

René stares at Theo.

Theo nods. "And then Felipe saw that horrible side of you, a side of you you'd rather have kept secret, and that scared him." He pauses. "But something is better than nothing, you know. Most people never get anything from their fathers. Maybe it was a good thing it happened this way."

René grimaces. "How can you say that?! None of this was good!"

Theo frowns.

René stands up, pissed. "I'll probably never see my son again. Why? Because I fucked some twat?! A two-faced cunt in tight pants and heels giving me those fuck me eyes? What did she think was gonna happen, flaunting around an office like that? That Jezebel made me cheat on my wife. I'm not a monster. I just did what any man would've done if they only had the balls! And that stuttering fuck Peabrain. What a joke he was. Which is a shame because he worked harder than everyone. I would've given the job if he only talked to me instead of posting that video."

Theo goes numb. "What?"

"The stammering asshole emailed me to meet him that night at Wally's to talk about some scheme Whale had against me. I waited four hours for that son of a bitch! He never showed!"

Theo's lips flutter. "He didn't snitch?"

"Of course he did! Weren't you listening?! He went to Oscar Blitz, him and that Whale! And the Liberal Media witch hunt had to blow it out of proportion!" René scoffs. "Whale. What a retard. What was I thinking? He couldn't have deleted those files. Peabrain must've deleted them himself."

Theo scowls. "What about Cashew?"

"Who?"

"The fourth one."

René squints. Looks off. "There was a fourth one, wasn't there?" He shrugs. "Whoever he was, I forgive him. I forgive all of them."

Theo blinks. "You forgive *them*?"

"They ruined my life."

Theo holds up both hands. "Aren't you sorry?!"

"Yeah I'm sorry. Sorry I didn't cover my blind spots."

"What about what you did to them?"

René furrows his brow. "What did I do to them? I didn't do shit!"

"You didn't beat Whale to a pulp in your office?"

"Nope."

"Or rape Bumps against the copy machine?"

René shakes his head. "That was all Satan."

Theo glares at him. "What."

"I've found God. He's been a guide for me in these dark times."

"You got caught! The whole city hates you now! You used to have fancy offices and floating glass cubes! What do you have now? Nothing!"

"And couldn't be happier!" René declares. "And I don't have nothing. I have my Lord and Savior Jesus Christ."

Theo shakes his head rapidly. "What are you, stupid?! How could you of all people fall for that manipulative horseshit?!"

René squints a bit.

Theo's breath quickens. "You should be fucking suffering for what you did to us! You should be haunted with our faces! Every night and day in constant pain!"

"Who did you say you were again?" René asks slowly.

Theo smiles a bit. "I didn't."

René shakes his head. "I think you should leave," he says, standing up.

"What?" Theo teases. "Did you finally figure it out?" He rips the toupee off his head. "How about now?!" He kicks René's cane away.

René falls to the ground, yelping in pain.

Theo places a dominating foot on René's chest. "*I* deleted Peabrain's files, you stupid fool. And Whale would've deleted the video in a heartbeat if it wasn't for me. I got him to post it. I knew just what to say. That's why you lost everything. Because of me! You're living in shit because of *me*!" Theo removes his foot.

René scoots away, terrified.

Theo follows him, sadistic anger flowing through him. "You'll never see your son again because of ME!"

René's back hits the chair. He tries to stand. He fails.

"I'm smarter that you!" Theo growls. "I'm more powerful than you! You're nothing! No one's afraid of you anymore! No one thinks you're great!"

René frowns up at him, ready to burst into tears. "Please."

"What? What are you gonna do? *Pray*?" Theo cringes at the sniveling old man on the floor. "I hated you. I fucking feared you. How can you be so pathetic?"

René closes his eyes. Tears roll down.

Theo crouches down. Gets right in The Professor's face. "You're fucking scum." He spits on René's face.

"Stop! Please!"

Theo grins. "Yeah. Go on. Beg."

"Stop. Please, please just stop!"

"No way. You're getting me hard."

René shakes his head, sputtering.

"You got off too easy," Theo hisses. "I should've done more. I wish I got the chance to beat the crap out of you, like you would've done to me. Maybe I should. Right now. Why not?"

René tries to back away, his wrinkled face streaked with tears.

Theo grabs a paperweight from the coffee table. "Or I could just kill you."

"No, please!" René cries, holding up weak hands. "Please, no!"

"It'd be easy too. Just smack you in the head with it. Beat your fucking brains in." Theo presses the felt side of the paperweight against René's head. "I think I could do it too," Theo whispers.

René cries desperately.

"Then it'd all be over, wouldn't it?" Theo murmurs. "You'll never see Felipe again." He moves the paperweight back, winding up.

René cowers, eyes slammed shut, wailing on the floor, trapped, his back to a chair.

"You're just vermin now, aren't you?" Theo drops the paperweight, making René jump. "Too weak to walk on your own. Too stupid to remember things. You feel that pain, that pathetic powerlessness? It hurts, doesn't it? But no matter how much it hurts, you're not gonna remember any of it, are you? It's just gonna fade away, like nothing happened. Doesn't that scare you, old man? Having no control over your own mind? You feel it, don't you? Right before you start to forget, you know it's happening. In that brief moment you're scared shitless, aren't you? Knowing everything you know is gonna be gone forever?"

René curls up, terrified.

Theo realizes something. Grins. "I'm gonna go into the next room," he whispers. "I'll wait until you stop crying. You'll forget I'm even here. When you do, I'll walk out and call you Dad. You'll think I'm Felipe, won't you? You'll be so happy your son is home. You'll hug me and tell me how much you missed me. But I'm gonna look you dead in the eye and tell you that I hate you."

René shakes his head.

Theo chuckles. "I love it. I'm telling you everything and you'll still fall for it, won't you? You know you will. You'll forget we even had this conversation. Try and stop it. It might actually stick because it's Felipe. And you'll live the rest of your pathetic life convinced that your son came back just to tell you that he hated you."

René cries some more, shaking his head.

"Where's your God now, old man?" Theo snarls. He grabs his toupee off the floor. "Here I go," he teases. "Try not to forget now." Theo walks into the kitchen. Reattaches his toupee. Waits.

The sobs from the living room fade. Silence. Theo pokes his head in. René is on his feet again, clutching his cane, studying the wet spot on the carpet. Did he piss himself?

"Dad?" Theo greets innocently.

René turns around "Felipe!"

Theo grins. "I'm home, Dad."

René waddles over, about to cry tears of joy. He hugs Theo tightly. "I missed you so much, son!"

Theo reluctantly hugs back, bile hitting his throat, his muscles tense.

"I love you!" René kisses Theo's head. "I'm so sorry, son. I'm sorry for everything."

Theo frowns, ready to cry himself.

René steps back, his hands on Theo's shoulders. "Let me get a good look at you." He smiles. "Such a nice suit! You must be doing so well."

Theo nods weakly. "I am."

"I'm so proud of you!"

Theo looks up at René, that innocent old face, those loving eyes. "I hate you," he rasps.

René's eyes sink.

Theo's face trembles. His eyes tight. Veins popping from his neck. "I've always hated you."

René steps back, not understanding.

"You were a shitty father," Theo snarls, tears in his eyes. "You were a shitty husband. You're nothing. I wish you were dead. I wish there was a Hell so you'd fucking burn in it!"

René's face contorts, ready to cry again.

Theo shakes his head. Grabs his suit jacket. Slips it on.

René stays where he is, body frozen, tears rolling down. He reaches out to Theo. "Son?"

Theo smacks René's hand away. Storms out. Slams the screen door. He steps off to the side, hiding from René's view, desperately trying to stop his own flow of tears. Finally calm, Theo discreetly looks back inside.

René's looking at the picture of Felipe. He wanders over to the couch. Sits. His cane falls to the floor. He hunches over. Sobs mercilessly into his hands. Theo grins wide, overwhelmed with ecstasy, a rush so powerful that he's actually shaking. He carries that smirk all the way back to the car. Speeds out of there a thousand pounds lighter.

"I'm making you my Head of Production," Theo tells his speakerphone over the whipping wind. "How does that sound?"

"Sure!" Larry chuckles. "I mean, I really should talk it over with Aaron first, but I don't think he'd mind at all."

"Good." Theo pauses. "Add Drew Lawrence to the Black List." He hangs up.

JACOB

Lady Bird

EXT. ANDREZJ FAMILY TOWNHOUSE - NIGHT

Jacob knocks on the front door. He and Stewie share nervous smiles.

The door opens and HELENA ANDREZJ (soon to be 58) halts with recognition. Shoulder length hair with highlights. The same resting bitch face as Jacob. The perfect fusion of Sigourney Weaver and Patricia Arquette.

JACOB & STEWIE
Happy birthday!

HELENA
What are you doing here? Did you get kicked out of school?

Jacob exhales, deflating with disappointment.

JACOB
No.

STEWIE
We came down to surprise you.

Helena apologetically holds the door open, stepping aside.

CUT TO:

INT. ANDREZJ FAMILY TOWNHOUSE - CONTINUOUS

Jacob and Stewie walk inside. Two long-haired dachshunds, one black and one blonde, race over, jumping and clawing at Jacob's knees.

JACOB
Hey Soyer! Hey Marley! I missed you!

HELENA
You must be Stewie. I've heard so much about you.

STEWIE
And you're... don't tell me...
(hesitates)
Helen.

JACOB & HELENA
Helena.

Stewie laughs heartily.

STEWIE
Oh my God, I'm so sorry!

HELENA
Don't call me Helen.

STEWIE
I tried not to. I got the one I wasn't supposed to say mixed up.

Jacob recognizes KAREN ANDREZJ (24) sitting at the dining room table. Dark brown ponytail. Pale face full of acne. Big belly bump (not pregnant).

JACOB
Hey.

KAREN
Hey.

STEWIE
You must be Melanie.

JACOB & KAREN
EW!

KAREN
I'm Karen.

STEWIE
Oh, you're...?

JACOB
(to Karen)
This is Stewie.

KAREN
Obviously.

HELENA
Melanie just got off work. She's walking Zoey.

STEWIE
Where does she work?

JACOB, HELENA & KAREN
Best Buy.

Stewie blinks. Why are they all so loud?

JACOB
They all work at the same Best Buy.

KAREN
I'm in Home Theater.

HELENA
Smart Appliances.

JACOB
Melanie's customer service.

KAREN
(laughing)
And Jacob works at Target!

Awkward silence.

JACOB
What's wrong with Target?

KAREN
Nothing. It's just ironic.

JACOB
It's not ironic.

KAREN
Yes it is.

JACOB
That's not irony.

KAREN
Yes it is.

HELENA
Guys! Stop it.

KAREN
But I'm right.

JACOB
Okay Alanis.

STEWIE
(to Helena)
Do you know any good places for takeout around here?

HELENA
You guys didn't eat yet? You must be starving.

STEWIE
We don't eat dinner until 11 anyway.

Jacob softly groans. Helena stares at Stewie.

HELENA
PM?

STEWIE
(hesitant)
Yeah.

HELENA
You don't eat dinner until 11 PM?

Stewie looks at Jacob. Notices his discomfort.

STEWIE
It's not that weird, right?

Helena raises her brows, turning away.

Jacob looks at Karen. Karen HOCKS her throat.

JACOB
(to Helena)
Stewie's been teaching me how to drive.

Helena hands Stewie a stack of takeout menus.

HELENA
That must've been a trip.

Jacob frowns.

HELENA (CONT'D)
I'm just teasing.

STEWIE
He's come a long way.

Karen walks over to the kitchen. Helena joins Jacob at the table.

HELENA
Hey.

JACOB
(unenthused)
Hey.

HELENA
It's been a while.

JACOB
Ten months.

HELENA
Yup.

They sit in silence.

IN THE KITCHEN

Stewie flips through the stack of menus. Slowly looks up. Karen's standing right there with an unopened soda can. Stewie smiles politely.

STEWIE
Hi.

Karen HACKS her throat.

BACK AT THE TABLE

Jacob takes off his shoes.

JACOB
I wanted to stay in Boston. I missed it.

HELENA
It had nothing to do with me canceling my flight?

JACOB
It wasn't the only reason. It just made me realize I wanted to stay up there while I still could.

HELENA
Away from me.

JACOB
That's not what I'm saying at all.

HELENA
I had a lot of things I needed your help with over the summer.

JACOB
Like what?

HELENA
Like cleaning out the storage room. Karen can't lift anything over ten pounds since the accident.

JACOB
What accident?

HELENA
The car accident she got into five months ago. We're suing the driver. How do you not know about this?

JACOB
No one told me!

HELENA
Lower your voice.

Jacob huffs.

JACOB
Stewie and I can help clean while we're down here.

HELENA
No, it's fine.

JACOB
You just said you needed help.

HELENA
No, it's not that big of a deal. Just do your thing.

IN THE KITCHEN

Stewie stares into space with a fuzzy brain. Karen rattles, her soda can still unopened.

KAREN
...and most of the horses were purebreds. Mine was called Lucky because she almost died at birth. The others were Guppy, Honey Pie, Pinkie Pie, Key Lime Pie... A lot of pie names for some reason.

STEWIE
Uh-huh.

KAREM
One of the other girls there had family in Salt Lake City.

STEWIE
Uh-huh.

KAREN
And they came by one with a horse of their own called Starlight and she was a gray...

BACK AT THE TABLE

Jacob sits back.

JACOB
You're not gonna say anything?

HELENA
About what?

JACOB
I lost fifty pounds.

HELENA
Oh. You look good.

Jacob huffs.

HELENA (CONT'D)
What?

JACOB
Nothing.

IN THE KITCHEN

Stewie hunches over the counter, holding his head up, tuning Karen out.

KAREN
(rattling)
...and then it was the N64, and then after that was the GameCube, and that was the first one we had, and then the Wii came out a few years later and we had one of those, and now the new one's a Wii U and we have that too downstairs in my room along with the XBOX 360, but we never had PlayStation growing up...

CUT TO:

LIVING ROOM

Jacob and Stewie sit on the couch, Marley and Soyer in their laps. Helena's upstairs. Karen's in her room downstairs.

STEWIE
Why is there so much dog hair everywhere?

JACOB
It's not that much.

STEWIE
Floating in the air. All over the floor. The couch. Your shirt.
(looks at Jacob's face)
Oh God!

Jacob's face is completely covered with little black and blonde hairs.

JACOB
This is normal.

STEWIE
This is not normal.

JACOB
You never had dogs.

STEWIE
I've had dogs. This is not normal.

JACOB
You're not allergic or anything, are you?

STEWIE
No.

JACOB
Then what's the problem?

Stewie flicks floating blonde hairs away.

STEWIE
They're all girls?

JACOB
Nothing says feminist divorcee like a literal No Boys Allowed policy.

STEWIE
They're so well behaved. I thought dachshunds were supposed to be the most difficult to train.

JACOB
All Mom had to do was use the same parenting techniques she used on us.

STEWIE
At least she didn't hit you guys like my mom did.

JACOB
Oh no, she'd never do that.
(pause)
She'd guilt us long enough until we hit ourselves so she wouldn't have to.

The front door opens, a yellow lab racing in and nearly colliding with Jacob.

JACOB (CONT'D)
Hey Zoey!

Jacob pets the crap out of her, long yellow hairs flying up like dandelion spores. Stewie spits, trying to get hair off his tongue.

MELANIE (O.S.)
Mom, why's there a Jeep parked out--?

MELANIE ANDREZJ (21) stares at Stewie with wide eyes. Long brown hair, blonde highlights, fantastic body. Shorter than all of them. Looks absolutely nothing like Jacob.

STEWIE
You must be Melanie.

Melanie tentatively closes the door.

MELANIE
MOM!

HELENA (O.S.)
I'm in the bedroom.

Melanie heads upstairs, her lime green Crocs squeaking the floorboards.

STEWIE
Friendly.

MELANIE (O.S.)
Zoey!

Zoey dashes upstairs, yellow hair flying up like snow.

CUT TO:

TABLE

Stewie and Jacob hand out boxes to Melanie, Karen, and Helena.

MELANIE
Why aren't you wearing glasses?

JACOB
I got LASIK a couple weeks ago.

HELENA
You didn't tell me you got LASIK!

JACOB
How'd you not notice?

MELANIE
What's with the dark circles around your eyes?

JACOB
I've always had them.

MELANIE
You look like a zombie.

Jacob frowns.

STEWIE
A cute zombie.

KAREN
What's with all the boxes?

JACOB
Italy presents.

HELENA
Oh honey, you didn't have to get us anything.

JACOB
I didn't?

Karen rips her box open, revealing a transparent glass horse, just a bit of green along its back.

KAREN
Wow!

JACOB
It's real Venetian glass. You better not break it. It cost 100 euro.

KAREN
I won't put it in the dishwasher.

Jacob rolls his eyes.

STEWIE
Dishwasher?

JACOB
I bought a Waterford Crystal tumbler when I was in Ireland. Dad put it in the dishwasher and it broke.

HELENA
The one time Dennis actually did anything around the house.

Karen and Jacob frown discreetly. Melanie opens her box, revealing a gold and pink wine glass.

MELANIE
What is it?

JACOB
What do you mean what is it? It's a wine glass.

MELANIE
I don't drink.

JACOB
Then give it to Mom.

MELANIE
Mom gets two presents and I get nothing?

Helena opens a large white box, revealing a brown leather jacket.

HELENA
Oh my God. Jacob!

JACOB
You like it?

Helena rubs the fabric.

HELENA
It's so soft.

JACOB
And real too. They're a dime a dozen over there.

STEWIE
Jacob has a red one just like it.

JACOB
It's a bit more weathered than this one.

STEWIE
It makes him look sexy.

HELENA
Thank you so much, honey.

JACOB
Glad you like it.

HELENA
I love it.

Helena puts the jacket on.

HELENA (CONT'D)
And it fits!

JACOB
Karen sent me your measurements.

HELENA
(to Karen)
You knew about this?

KAREN
Yeah.

HELENA
(to Stewie)
Surprised she didn't tell me anyway. She can't keep a secret to save her life.

KAREN
(insulted)
Yes I can.

HELENA
With Melanie, Karen and Jacob as my kids, I better be designated for sainthood.

Helena laughs, mean-spirited. She's completely oblivious to the fact that Karen, Jacob, and Melanie have their heads bowed with the same self-conscious expression, so retreated inward that they don't recognize they're all feeling the same way. And all four of them are covered in dog hair. If that isn't the Andrezj Family in a nutshell, Stewie doesn't know what is.

JUMP CUT TO:

LATER

Karen scrolls on her phone in the living room. Helena, Stewie, Jacob, and Melanie argue over the dining room table.

MELANIE
They're a bunch of spoiled rotten crybabies that can't stand anyone telling them the truth!

JACOB
Think of it from their perspective. Traditional masculinity is the source of everything they resent. You can't blame them for wanting to double down on being feminine.

MELANIE
I'm worried about the future of this country. Men are being born with significantly less testosterone than previous generations.

JACOB
That is not true!

MELANIE
Yes it is!

JACOB
Even if it was true, which doesn't even make scientific sense, what's so wrong about people choosing to live their lives in a gentler way?

MELANIE
They're not gentle. They're trying to dismantle everything. I don't want guys dressing up like girls being allowed to use my bathroom.

JACOB
You would never be able to tell a woman was trans if you ever saw one.

HELENA
What about all that "they" bullshit?

MELANIE
I have to say my preferred pronouns seven times a day at school.

JACOB
What's the big deal with that? Yours are she/her/hers. How hard is that?

MELANIE
It's the principle of the thing.

HELENA
I couldn't stand the Millennial interns I used to have. They didn't know what they were doing, constantly taking mental health days...

JACOB
We're Millennials.

HELENA
I raised you guys right. You're not real Millennials.

JACOB
Yes we are.

MELANIE
I think all those non-gender binary whatevers are just mentally ill.

JACOB
I suppose you're an expert on mental illness?

MELANIE
Growing up with you and Karen, yes I am.

JACOB
And is me being gay a mental illness?

MELANIE
That's not the same thing. They just want attention.

JACOB
You really think they're making it up?

MELANIE
Of course they're making it up.

HELENA
Careful. You can't say things like that nowadays.

MELANIE
I know. I'm afraid some blue-headed freak's gonna pop out and scream about how triggered they are.

JACOB
You can't cause a confrontation and expect no reaction.

HELENA
But it can be about anything nowadays! They get upset when they see the American flag!

JACOB
There's a lot of problems in this country and they feel ashamed to be American. That's their right, isn't it?

MELANIE
Someone should just wrangle up all those whiny "theys" and drop 'em into the Gaza Strip. Let 'em see what the real world is like.

JACOB
If someone said that about Trump supporters, would you not like that?

MELANIE
They already do!

JACOB
Doesn't that make you upset?

MELANIE
I actually have a thick skin.

JACOB
All they want is to make sure they don't marginalize the way they were marginalized. Sure it gets a bit too PC sometimes, but the Liberals I see every day aren't the whiny stereotype you see highlighted on Fox News. They're smart, forward-thinking, tolerant people. They're not afraid of Trump winning because of some knee-jerk reaction, they're genuinely afraid he won't look out for their interests, and honestly he's shown no clear sign that he will. That's why they're like this right now. But when the dust settles and we're stuck with one or the other, this absolutely stupid election cycle will finally be over and everything will go back to normal.

Jacob looks at Stewie. Stewie nods proudly.

MELANIE
(to Helena)
God, remember the first Thanksgiving after Jacob went off to college?

HELENA
Oh my God, I know. He was the absolute worst.

JACOB
What?

MELANIE
You were spouting all that Liberal bullshit, making everyone uncomfortable.

JACOB
I never did that.

HELENA
Yes you did.

STEWIE
I'm sure he was just doing what every college kid does the first Thanksgiving back.

JACOB
No I didn't! I would've remembered! That did not happen!

MELANIE
It definitely did.

KAREN (O.S.)
(from the living room)
Yup!

JACOB
You never said anything.

HELENA
How could we? You kept chewing our heads off!

JACOB
I did not!

STEWIE
He's certainly not like that anymore.

JACOB
I actually look at both sides, even if you don't.

HELENA
CNN doesn't count as both sides.

JACOB
I don't watch CNN! And you know what, maybe the reason I was so vocal about left-wing issues was because it was the first time I was hearing something different.

HELENA
You were very rude. And clearly you don't care.

JACOB
You guys kept the divorce a secret from me the whole time, oh but MY behavior was the problem?! Give me a fucking break!

STEWIE
Jacob.

HELENA
(to Jacob)
You're still on that?

JACOB
You guys lied to me! You just sat there knowing I was never gonna see the house again, knowing Dad already met someone else. You wanna harp on how I was that Thanksgiving?! I get to harp on you guys! It's only fair!

HELENA
You're being very immature.

JACOB
You and Melanie are ganging up on me and I'M immature?

HELENA
She can control herself.

JACOB
I can control myself too!

HELENA
Well you seem to be doing a real shitty job.

MELANIE
(to Jacob)
Come back in another ten months.

JACOB
Shut up!

HELENA
Stop yelling at your sister.

JACOB
STOP TAKING HER SIDE!

Helena stands angrily.

HELENA
I've had enough of this.

JACOB
I'm sorry, alright? I'll stop.

HELENA
No! No! Clearly you want to go on about how I'm such a bad mother.

STEWIE
We'll change the subject.

HELENA
You really shouldn't have come all the way down here if all you wanted to do was yell at me.

STEWIE
Guys, let's just settle down--

JACOB
You know you really should be thanking me for not applying to LA. Airfare's just so CRAZY these days, I just assumed you'd want to pocket the expense. You obviously need the money.

Helena bows her head with a subdued frown. Jacob's skin feels like it's vibrating. He stands. Storms up the stairs. SLAMS his bedroom door. Silence.

Melanie crosses her arms, intentionally avoiding eye contact with Stewie. Stewie doesn't like the atmosphere in that room. He knows the second he leaves they're gonna start talking about what just happened.

CUT TO:

JACOB'S BEDROOM

Jacob hangs his head with shame. Footsteps creak in the hallway outside. Soft knock. Stewie walks in.

STEWIE
(soft bleating)
AYY BEE.

JACOB
What the heck is wrong with me?

STEWIE
That was way too much.

JACOB
I know it was. You know me. I never get that bad.

STEWIE
Before P-Town you did.

JACOB
Not anymore.
(pause)
You know what it's like? It's like...

Jacob sits up, a bit frustrated.

JACOB
In a video game, there's always a point when you can save your progress up to that point. That way you can reload to a save point and make a different decision if you mess up. But you're stuck with what you had on you when you hit that save point. You revert to that older version of yourself. It's very frustrating, going backwards like that.
(pause)
That's what it feels like around these people. They don't know the version of me you know. They know the old Jacob, the non-assertive Jacob with the black-and-white mentality, and they keep expecting that version of me every time I see them. I know they do because I do the same thing with them. Karen is so NOT what she used to be.

STEWIE
I was shocked you warned me so much about her. You should've warned me about Melanie.

JACOB
She was never like that either. That's what I'm saying.
(sighs)
It's like we're all... off, you know? We're all stuck on our old save points because that's what everyone expects to see. Honestly I don't think I would've noticed if you weren't here. No one ever realizes how stupid and weird they are unless they're in the presence of an outsider.

Stewie sighs.

STEWIE
I'm sure your mom will be fine. She's tough. And she loves you. You can mess up a thousand times and she'll still love you.

JACOB
You think?

STEWIE
I do.

Jacob smiles weakly.

JACOB
Surprised you didn't jump on the Trump brigade.

STEWIE
Why would I? I was on your team.

Jacob exhales with amazement.

JACOB
Wow. I never had that before.

Stewie raises a skeptical brow.

STEWIE
What? Loyalty?

Jacob hesitates.

JACOB
Yeah.

JUMP CUT TO:

THE NEXT MORNING

Jacob snores loudly, drooling onto his pillow. Stewie quietly slides out of bed. Sneaks out of the room.

CUT TO:

FIRST FLOOR

Stewie walks down the stairs. Helena's on the couch, staring off into space the same way Jacob does.

STEWIE
Morning.

Helena snaps back. Forces a hostess smile.

HELENA
You sleep okay?

STEWIE
Not really. I'm not used to sleeping on a foreign bed.

Stewie walks over. Joins her on the couch.

STEWIE (CONT'D)
Jacob's really sorry about last night.

HELENA
I know he is.

STEWIE
He didn't mean any of it. He's just a bit insecure, you know. He really didn't like that you kept taking Melanie's side when she was doing the same thing he was.

Helena softens at Stewie's gentle nature.

HELENA
After so many years trying to fix Karen, I can finally focus on Melanie.
(pause)
I didn't realize until last night that Jacob needs so much more from me too.

Stewie half-frowns.

HELENA (CONT'D)
Promise me you won't tell him this.

STEWIE
I promise.

Helena looks at Stewie.

HELENA
Me going out to Italy... It wasn't just the plane ticket. It was an all-inclusive two-week excursion throughout Italy. Private tour guide with us the whole way. Wine tastings. Cooking classes. Museum tours. Bike rides through Chianti. Everything.

STEWIE
He doesn't know?

HELENA
We planned it together.
(pause)
What he doesn't know is that it would've cost me $20,000.

Stewie whistles.

HELENA (CONT'D)
Don't whistle!

STEWIE
I'm sorry.

HELENA
Jacob's father used to whistle all the time. I can't stand it.

Stewie nods with understanding.

HELENA (CONT'D)
I'm still having a hard time finding a job. It's been ten months. No one wants to hire a middle-aged overqualified woman. Doesn't matter how good I am. How much I've done.
(pause)
I should've gone. I really wanted to. It would've made things better between us. Somehow.

Helena looks at Stewie.

HELENA (CONT'D)
Did he really not apply to the LA program because of what I did?

Stewie hesitates.

STEWIE
I think so. It was a long time ago.

HELENA
He needed to do it. Half of the semester would've been a Hollywood internship. That was a massive career opportunity he'll never have again. He threw that away to get back at me.
(pause)
I'm worried about him more than ever.

Stewie folds his hands.

STEWIE
The Jacob you saw last night, the one that did that with LA, that's not the Jacob I know. He really works hard. He just finished a new feature and he's already on his next one for his Feature Writing class. He's gonna film a short he wrote with his buddy Frankie.
(pauses)
And he goes to church with me every Sunday.

HELENA
No he doesn't.

STEWIE
He does.

Helena looks off.

STEWIE (CONT'D)
He's not just doing it for me either. He really believes in God again. And he's weaned off the meds, which honestly might explain last night. But he's working out too. He's already lost all that weight. He's finally getting his driver's license.

Stewie smiles.

STEWIE (CONT'D)
And he loves you so much. That's one of the things I've always loved about him. No matter what's happened between you two, he still loves his mother.

Helena smiles a bit.

HELENA
He's my buddy.

STEWIE
He just wants to believe that you trust him enough to know what he's doing.

Helena rubs her eyes.

HELENA
He has to keep up with the writing. He can't give that up.

STEWIE
Why would he?

HELENA
To work for you.

Stewie blinks.

STEWIE
What?

HELENA
Jacob's a very emotional person. If he gets to the point where he can't do it anymore, he's gonna try and settle for an easier option. He can't do that. He needs to keep going. That's what he really wants.

Stewie hesitates uneasily.

STEWIE
I think you should be the one to tell him that.

HELENA
He doesn't want to hear it from me.

STEWIE
I think he does.

Helena looks up at the stairs. Hesitates. Stewie flicks dog hair off his thigh.

STEWIE (CONT'D)
Oh, and do you have a lint roller around?

HELENA
Why do you need a lint roller?

STEWIE
There's dog hair EVERYWHERE.

Helena looks around the living room.

HELENA
This is normal.

CUT TO:

JACOB'S BEDROOM

Jacob slides into a pair of pants. Soft knock on the door.

HELENA (O.S.)
Are you covered up? Can I come in?

JACOB
Yeah.

Helena tentatively opens the door.

HELENA
Is it okay if we talk?

Jacob nods nervously. Helena sits on the bed.

HELENA (CONT'D)
You okay?

JACOB
Mm-hmm.

HELENA
Good.

They sit in awkward silence. A truck's backing up outside.

JACOB
What happened to Melanie?

Helena scoffs.

HELENA
I don't know. I don't know what's going on with her anymore.

JACOB
Is she still with Marcus?

HELENA
Oh no. They broke up months ago.

JACOB
Really? Why?

HELENA
He wanted her to settle down with him.

JACOB
So?

HELENA
She didn't want to. I don't blame her.

JACOB
She loved him, didn't she?

HELENA
Not enough to derail her career.

Jacob frowns.

JACOB
I really liked Marcus.

HELENA
I know. Me too.
(pause)
I hate her new guy.

JACOB
She's got a new one already?

HELENA
I don't like him.

JACOB
Why not?

HELENA
She met him online.

JACOB
That's not weird. A lot of people meet online.

HELENA
He's not good enough for her.

JACOB
Unemployed?

HELENA
He paints houses.

JACOB
At least he's not unemployed.

HELENA
He asked her to move in with him, she did. Three weeks later he asked her to move out but they're still together.

Jacob furrows his brow.

JACOB
That's a bit out-of-character for her.

HELENA
I know it is.

JACOB
Does she know you don't like him?

HELENA
No. And don't say anything.

JACOB
I won't.

Jacob hesitates.

JACOB (CONT'D)
You don't have a problem with Stewie, do you?

HELENA
Oh no. He's great.

JACOB
You don't gossip about Stewie behind my back?

HELENA
Why would you say that?

JACOB
You're gossiping about Melanie's guy behind her back.

HELENA
But I don't have a problem with Stewie.

Jacob looks away, unconvinced.

JACOB
I'm sorry about last night.

HELENA
Me too.

Jacob nods.

HELENA (CONT'D)
You really do look great, weight-wise.

Jacob self-consciously covers his body.

JACOB
Thanks.

HELENA
Stewie told me about your writing.

JACOB
He did?

HELENA
Mm-hm.

JACOB
You gotta read the one I just finished. It's called Drive-Thru. It's definitely the best thing I've ever written.

HELENA
My schedule's a bit tight nowadays.

JACOB
You've said that before. And you were working full-time.

HELENA
I've got job interviews lined up.

JACOB
It doesn't take that long. Just read it the next time you read a book.

HELENA
I'm in the middle of the new Jack Reacher at the moment.

Jacob deflates.

HELENA (CONT'D)
But I'll try, okay? I'll try.

Jacob nods.

HELENA (CONT'D)
Stewie's really good for you.

JACOB
I know he is.

HELENA
He kinda reminds me of your father.
(chuckling)
The version he should've been at least.

JACOB
I don't wanna hear you talk shit about Dad anymore.

Helena's taken aback.

HELENA
I thought you wanted the truth.

Jacob keeps staring off.

Helena looks at the door. Thinks about leaving.

HELENA (CONT'D)
Don't lose yourself.

JACOB
What are you talking about?

HELENA
I know he makes you happy, but try not to lose who you are in the--

JACOB
I haven't lost who I am. This is who I am.

Helena hesitates.

HELENA
I understand--

JACOB
The only reason you're saying that is because you can tell I'm not the perfect little copy of you anymore. I don't have to be to get him to love me. I can just be me. The real me.

Helena looks away, suppressing her pain behind pursed lips.

JACOB (CONT'D)
I'm sorry, Mom, but that's the truth.

Helena stands and walks out of the room. Jacob's heart breaks, instantly regretting what he just said.

CUT TO:

EXT. CONSHOHOCKEN STREET - DAY

Leaves fall around as Melanie walks Zoey, Jacob strolling beside them.

JACOB
I don't think it's ever been just the two of us on one of these before.

MELANIE
I guess.

Awkward silence.

JACOB
I'm sorry about last night. I hate talking politics.

Melanie looks away.

JACOB (CONT'D)
Mom told me about your new guy.

Melanie shrugs.

JACOB (CONT'D)
What's his name?

MELANIE
Michael.

JACOB
Is he nice?

MELANIE
I guess.

JACOB
Is he cute?

Melanie doesn't answer.

JACOB (CONT'D)
I know we haven't been very close with what went on with Karen and all, but if it's possible I'd like to start over.

Melanie doesn't look at him. Just stares at the ground.

JACOB (CONT'D)
Stewie's best friends with his twin. Why can't we be like that? We have to have SOMETHING in common, even if our personalities shaped themselves to be the exact opposite of each other. I mean, how much of us was really us in that house?

Melanie frowns. Jacob sticks his hands in his pockets.

JACOB (CONT'D)
I love you, Melanie.

Jacob looks over. No reaction.

JACOB (CONT'D)
Don't you love me?

MELANIE
What is this?

JACOB
Can't you say it?

Melanie hesitates.

MELANIE
I'm not like that.

JACOB
Why not?

MELANIE
I'm just not, okay?

JACOB
But don't you love me?

Melanie doesn't talk. Just stares ahead. Jacob frowns.

JACOB (CONT'D)
What do you think of Stewie?

MELANIE
We get it, you've got Daddy issues. You don't have to shove it in our faces.

JACOB
That's not what it is.

Melanie bumps her brows.

JACOB (CONT'D)
I really resent that. It's insulting to me and it's insulting to him.

MELANIE
He's lying to you, you know.

JACOB
What?

MELANIE
He's not thirty-nine.

JACOB
Who said anything about him being thirty-nine?

MELANIE
Mom did. But there's no way he is.

JACOB
I know he's not.

Melanie doesn't react.

JACOB (CONT'D)
When did she tell you this? In June?

MELANIE
July.

JACOB
July?! Why the hell would she say that? She already knew his real age. Why would she perpetuate it?

MELANIE
How old is he?

Jacob hesitates.

JACOB
He's fifty-two.

Melanie laughs hard and loud. Jacob scowls.

MELANIE
You really are desperate, aren't you?

Jacob opens his mouth. Stops himself.

JACOB (V.O.)
I was gonna tell her what Mom really thought of Michael.

CUT TO:

EXT. ANDREZJ FAMILY TOWNHOUSE - BACKYARD - DAY

Jacob and Stewie wait for Marley and Soyer to pee.

STEWIE
Good thing you didn't.

JACOB
I know. I'm very proud of myself.

STEWIE
I don't see how she can look down on any of you. You're not the ones with the social disorder, she's the one.

JACOB
That's a matter of opinion.

STEWIE
Take my word for it, Baby Boy. She's not gonna make it far if she doesn't grow up one of these days.

Jacob smirks.

JACOB
She's gonna be a doctor.

Stewie stares.

STEWIE
No she's not.

JACOB
By 2023 she'll be Dr. Andrezj and finally put us all in our place.

STEWIE
A DOCTOR?!

Jacob laughs.

JACOB
Isn't that the scariest thing?

CUT TO:

INT. ANDREZJ FAMILY TOWNHOUSE - KAREN'S ROOM - DAY

Jacob steps into Karen's room, adorned to the nines in Disney plushies and anime posters. Karen's playing <u>Mario Kart 8</u> on her Wii U. Jacob watches her curiously, quiet enough for her not to notice.

She's so docile. What happened to the kleptomaniac? The problem sister screaming at him and Melanie, crying her eyes out? Her strained voice piercing the walls and Mom and Dad ganging up on her every three days because of her most recent shenanigan? She's like a deer now. So gentle. All her impulses beaten out of her. He can't imagine her ever living on her own, let alone finding true love or starting a family.

Jacob frowns. How could anyone in their right mind hurt someone like her?

CUT TO:

IN THE STORAGE ROOM

Jacob turns on the lights. Towers and towers of boxes, relics of the Phoenixville house. He cranes his head, checking the top shelf.

He kicks open a stepladder. Tentatively climbs it, vertigo kicking in even then. Reaches. Removes a black camera bag from the top shelf.

JUMP CUT TO:

LATER

Jacob sits on the floor holding an old camcorder. Slides in a tape marked "NEW HOUSE." Hits Play. Pulls out the tiny wing. Watches the square LCD screen.

INSERT - PHOENIXVILLE HOUSE, DECEMBER 2001

YOUNGER HELENA (42), off-screen, records LITTLE KAREN (9) and LITTLE MELANIE (6) running around the empty kitchen. No furniture. No paint on the walls. No damage to the rug. Not even a bit of wear in the finish of the granite countertop.

Coming into frame is LITTLE JACOB (6). Gaunt. Big dark circles around his eyes. Blank gaze. Like he's not even in there.

ON JACOB

Jacob sighs at the sight of Little Jacob. He looks so empty on the outside. So scared. A quiet little observer. Nervous about the new environment, a new house so unlike the last one. Why did it have to change at all? He didn't understand.

Jacob's eyes water at this realization.

BACK ON THE VIDEO

Younger Helena approaches Little Jacob.

YOUNGER HELENA (O.S.)
Hey handsome! Say hi to the camera!

Little Jacob does his best attempt at a smile. He looks real derpy.

YOUNGER HELENA (O.S.)
Say hi to the camera!

Little Jacob waves.

YOUNGER HELENA (O.S.)
(whispers)
I love you, Jacob.

Little Jacob doesn't quite process this. He just keeps smiling awkwardly.

YOUNGER HELENA (O.S.)
Your mother loves you very much.

BACK ON JACOB

Tears fall down Jacob's cheeks. He closes his eyes. Sobs on the cold, dusty storage room floor.

DISSOLVE TO:

INT. ANDREZJ FAMILY TOWNHOUSE - JACOB'S ROOM - NIGHT

Jacob and Stewie lay next to each other, staring up at the ceiling, the lights all on.

STEWIE
What is called?

JACOB
The Help.

STEWIE
And you like it?

JACOB
I've always liked it. In fact it's one of the few movies we all like.

Stewie takes Jacob's hand. Jacob keeps staring at the ceiling, thinking back.

JACOB (CONT'D)
She really did the best she could.

Stewie smiles.

STEWIE
I think so too.

JACOB
They'll come around. Karen, Melanie, Mom... They're all a bit busy with their hero's journeys right now. I'm just the first to reach the finish line.

Jacob looks back at Stewie.

JACOB (CONT'D)
Cause I have you.

Stewie kisses Jacob.

STEWIE
"I love you more today than yesterday."

JACOB
"But not as much as tomorrow."

DISSOLVE TO:

LIVING ROOM

Jacob and Stewie curl up on the couch. Helena sits in a chair, Marley and Soyer on her lap. Karen sits on the floor. Melanie lays beside Zoey. All eyes are on the TV, The Help already in progress.

INSERT - THE HELP

It's the final scene. The evil Ms. Hilly pressures Elizabeth to fire her maid Aibileen out of revenge for Aibileen's involvement in Skeeter's scandalous novel. Aibileen says farewell to Elizabeth's little daughter Mae Mobley, tears streaming down both their cheeks, and leaves.

As Aibileen walks out of the house, Mae Mobley smacks her tiny little hands on the window.

MAE MOBLEY
(trying to say "Aibileen")
AYY BEE!! AYY BEE!!

BACK ON JACOB

Jacob and Stewie gape with shock. Simultaneously look at each other. Mime smacking a glass window with both hands, just like that little white girl.

JACOB & STEWIE
(whispered bleating)
AYY BEE!

They're quiet enough for Karen and Melanie not to notice. But Helena notices. The way Jacob and Stewie look at each other. The way they hold each other. The love radiating off of them. She catches herself frowning. Dennis used to look at her like that. Hold her like that. Love radiating off of them.

Helena snuffs that thought. Sends it to the recycling bin. Right click, delete. Dons a smile instead. Chooses happiness. Happiness that Jacob found the one thing she wasn't able to have herself, and all on his own.

CUT TO:

JACOB'S BEDROOM

It's late. Moon shining through the blinds. Jacob and Stewie sleeping in Jacob's childhood bed.

Jacob's eyes open slightly. Right there next to him is Stewie, his sleeping hunk of a man, probably dreaming of red Jeep rides through cartoon hills, his Baby Boy by his side.

Jacob can't help but smile. A man of his own. Someone he can hold at night to make the bad thoughts go away. A hunky teddy bear just for him. He's not upset with the world anymore. Or afraid. Or confused or bruised. No regrets or shame. Jacob has peace for the first time in a long time. And it just might last this time.

Jacob stares up at his ceiling. Imagines he's making eye contact with something. Probably not someone corporeal, let alone Caucasian, but something nonetheless.

JACOB
(whispers)
Thank you.

Jacob rolls back on his side. Closes his eyes. Dreams Baby Boy dreams.

FADE TO BLACK.

WHALE

The Day After

Whale stares at his empty plate, his bruises now a soft yellow. A fly's landing on his omelet residue. What a nice warm day out. Whale only feels cold inside.

Oscar Blitz sits across from Whale in a shirt (blouse?) made entirely of red and pink beads. His cell's pressed to his ear and he's yelling loud enough for the whole restaurant to hear. That's the point, isn't it? "WE SIGNED A FUCKING CONTRACT! IF SHE WANTS ANYTHING FROM ME AGAIN, TELL HER TO SHOVE IT UP HER TIGHT FUCKING ASS!" Oscar hangs up and throws the phone on the table. "Fuck!"

Whale flashes Oscar judgmental eyes.

"She likes it up the ass," Oscar says. "It's a compliment."

Whale shrugs.

Oscar wipes his mouth. "You have no idea how long I've had a file on Harvey Weinstein. I was right there, but *NOOOOO*! Ronan FUCKING Farrow had to beat me to the FUCKING punch!"

Whale looks off, uninterested.

"I had seventeen girls ready to testify!" Oscar continues. "They all get cold feet at the same time? Bullshit! I'm sorry I don't have Woody Allen money!"

Whale doesn't move.

Oscar sips his mimosa. "What's wrong?"

"You know what's wrong."

"You can't blame yourself for what happened." Oscar brushes crumbs off his pants. "You think it's the first time for me?"

Whale frowns.

Oscar shakes his head. "It's horrible. I know it is. But these things happen. The media needs a Monica, and some people can't handle that."

"I was on the same bridge," Whale whispers, tears forming in his eyes. "Why couldn't it have been me?"

Oscar looks around, embarrassed and a bit vulnerable. "Jacob. Please."

Whale sobs into his hand. "None of this would've happened if I just..."

"You don't know that."

"There wouldn't have been a video."

"Trisha could've jumped for a thousand reasons," Oscar says softly. "Even if it was because of the video, that was her choice."

"She was too gentle. I knew that."

"She was very good to you, but there are many sides to a person. You don't know anything about her, what she's been through, what she's done." Oscar pauses. "I am sorry, of course. I won't pretend to be blasé about young suicide."

Whale wipes his tears.

Oscar sighs. Leans in. "Have you considered the possibility that what happened between The Professor and Trisha was not only 100% consensual but had been going on since the very beginning?"

Whale hesitates. "Of course I've thought of that."

"That could be how she knew about the side office in the first place. They fucked in there one day and she thought it would help you with your work."

"Or maybe she was being raped in the copy room since Day One, and she told me about the office so he wouldn't attack her again. After he fired me, he got her in there as soon as he could and made up for lost time." Whale pauses. "I was supposed to protect her."

"Maybe she was the kind of girl that didn't need protecting," Oscar counters. "Maybe she's just really fucked up and learned to like it. That's how some people deal with it. Who are we to judge?"

Whale doesn't speak.

Oscar smirks. "Little devil's advocate, aren't you?" He looks around for their waiter. "Truth is we're never gonna know what really happened. The Professor will never admit to any wrongdoing now that Trisha's dead." He stares at Whale. Softens. "If it's any consolation…" He smiles warmly. "I'm glad you're still with us."

Whale smiles for the first time in weeks.

Oscar abruptly snaps his fingers. "Excuse me!" he calls after his waiter, his campy demeanor amplified.

The Waiter rushes over. "I'm sorry, Mr. Blitz. I've been running around all day."

"I don't give a fuck if Michael Myers is chasing you with a machete back there. I ordered two Domergue 15s a half-hour ago and we're already done with our food!"

"I-I'm sorry, uh..." The Waiter flips through his flipbook. "I-I-I didn't... You didn't order any, um—"

"I'm sorry, WHAT?"

"I must've been, um... I'll be right back with them, sir." The Waiter runs off, almost colliding with a busboy.

Oscar smirks at Whale. "Surprise."

Whale rolls his eyes as the Busboy collects their dirty plates.

Oscar leans back in chair, arm positioned with utmost pretentiousness. "Theo tells me you're pretty religious."

"Kinda."

"Did you already go to church or are you one of those evening Mass people?"

"I really haven't been since..." Whale furrows brow. "You're talking to Theo now?"

"Yeah," Oscar groans. "He works for me now."

Whale widens his eyes. "As a paparazzo?"

"I really didn't want him." Oscar looks both ways. Leans in. "You know what that son of a bitch did? He called my office every hour for two days straight. Then he camped outside the studio with a megaphone, banging on the door, harassing everyone. We had to call the cops on him."

"You didn't talk to him?"

"I was busy with the... you know."

Whale nods impatiently.

"Anyway, I didn't hear anything from the guy all day Friday, so I just assumed he gave up. But Saturday morning I wake up, I come downstairs in just a purple mink bathrobe and guess who I find in my living room?"

Whale gasps. "No."

"You have to understand, my house is off the grid. If Harvey Weinstein couldn't find it with all his money, how the fuck could Theo Landreth?" Oscar pauses for effect. "And not only did the dead-eyed midget find out where I live — *as terrifying as that is* — he somehow managed to break in without tripping a single alarm. Jacob, I was scared to DEATH!"

Whale chuckles.

"And after all that, you know what that little fucker had the nerve to say to me?" Oscar asks. "'You haven't been answering me. I want a job.'"

"What did you say?"

"What did you think I said?! 'How the FUCK did you get into my house?!'"

Whale laughs.

"And he said to me, 'I'll tell you everything you want to know.'" Oscar pauses. "'If you give me the job.'"

"Holy shit!"

"Who the fuck DOES that?!" Oscar chuckles. Shakes his head with introspective amusement. "That kid's going places, I tell you."

"When can I start?" Whale calmly asks.

Oscar stares at Whale. "What?"

"I want to do it now. For a little while, at least." Whale pauses. "If I wasn't a snob the first time, this wouldn't have happened."

Oscar puts down his napkin, his brow furrowed. "I really think you should reconsider."

"Is it not available anymore?"

"No, it is," Oscar says. "I don't think I was right to offer it to you."

Whale's brows press together. "You don't think I can do it?"

"That's not what I said."

"Then what are you saying?"

Oscar looks off. "When I offered you the job," he says slowly, almost serene, "I thought you were like every other fresh-out-of-college newbie. But that's not who you are. What I saw in Brique last Monday, that was you. That was the real you. You're not a soldier, you're a writer. You see the world as it is. You see the beauty in it. You care about people and feelings and stories. And fairness."

Whale frowns.

Oscar's determination wavers. "The world needs more people like you, Jacob. Hollywood needs more people like you." He shakes his head. "The watchdog world is not the place for you."

"It is now," Whale mumbles.

Oscar's heart skips a beat. "I refuse to believe that."

"I sorry, Mr. Blitz," the Manager interrupts, standing next to Oscar with a bottle of Domergue. "It won't happen again."

"I'm in the middle of something. Shoo."

"But sir—"

"Come back in ten, alright?"

The Manager awkwardly walks away with the Scotch.

"You need to keep writing," Oscar insists to Whale.

"I've got student loans to pay off," Whale says. "Another year of LASIK. Monthly payments on my phone. Data. Health insurance. I'm getting kicked out of the house at the end of the month because Alex wants a 'cooler' roommate. No one in this town's gonna hire me once they find out I was at The Factory when The Professor got busted."

"They'll never know it was you."

"Trisha's dead. That leaves a one in three chance."

"Theo works for me now. That makes him the most likely suspect."

"Who's gonna take that chance? Besides, there are more valuable candidates out there anyway."

"Take a sabbatical then. Write the feature that gets you out of this. Better yet, a short you can make yourself."

"With who? I don't know anyone out here." Whale scratches above his eye. "I don't see what the big deal is. It's not like I'm changing careers. It's just for a few months, just until I have something to build off of."

Oscar hesitates. Whale notices a change on his face, subtle but definitely something he never expected to see on Oscar Blitz. Maybe no one has. He never mentions a girlfriend.

Oscar rubs his jaw. Looks up at Whale. "After the successful bombings of Hiroshima and Nagasaki, the United States decided to make the rapid production of nuclear weapons a top priority. Billions of dollars were spent to out-compete Soviet technology until 1952 when the US military carried out the first full-scale test of the hydrogen bomb. One of the men on that team was a very talented nuclear physicist, ambitious too. In his spare time, he was building a thermonuclear weapon of his own design, a new kind of H-Bomb he codenamed 'The Sodomizer.'"

Whale raises his brows.

Oscar shrugs. "Homophobic, I know. It was the 50s. That was kinda the point. But it was also a double entendre meant to evoke memories of the biblical city of Sodom. It had a blast radius the size of Connecticut and a detonation force powerful enough to change the topography of land. He wanted a bomb that could level mountains, fill valleys, create canyons, not only destroy cities and towns but the entire region, its history, its soil, its agriculture. Like if you bombed Chianti so the world couldn't make Chianti anymore. Total regional genocide." Oscar pauses. "His research took him to a dark place, fueled entirely by his hatred of the enemy and how his superiors would reward him for creating such a devastating weapon. He had only one bright spot in his life, his research partner, a much younger woman named Nancy. He confided in her things he had never told anyone before, and she with him. He trusted her more than anything."

Whale softens.

Oscar shrugs. "He was fucking her too, even though he was married with three kids. That's not really the point. One night, in the lab, the two of them were fooling around when the core of their Sodomizer prototype fell off his desk. The lab crumbled to dust in a single second. He was wearing his lead-lined protection suit at the time, so he survived. Nancy, on the other hand, was killed instantly. He was still holding onto her body when they found him in the rubble, and as they removed her from his clutches, her charred remains turned to dust in his arms. His face had been unprotected, however, shielded only by Nancy's body. His face literally melted off from the explosion. They were able to fix what they could, but he never looked the same. For years he bore the guilt of what happened to his beloved Nancy. At last he finally realized the utter reality of what he was trying to make, how devastating such a weapon would be to his victims."

"What am I listening to?" Whale interrupts. "Is this a parable?"

"Wait! Just listen." Oscar huffs, returning to where he left off. "He left his prestigious position in the US military and instead used every ounce of his energy, every dollar he saved, to make sure nuclear weapons would never be used again. He moved his wife and kids out to California, and throughout the 70s and 80s he was the chief nuclear consultant on dozens of Hollywood films, including his greatest achievement, a little TV movie you may have heard of called *The Day After*. You see, while studying his enemy, he learned a lot about Soviet propaganda techniques, and he used those very strategies *on* the US to make sure the Cold War ended in his lifetime. Chernobyl helped a lot in that regard, but I don't doubt his influence."

Whale nods. "He should've written a book."

"He did," Oscar says plainly. "In the 90s. *Point of No Return: A Nuclear Scientist's Quest to End the Cold War*, but by then the Wall had already come down. There just wasn't a market for it. Now no one even remembers him."

Whale half-frowns, moved by the story.

"His name was Dr. Clark J. Hauser." Oscar pauses. "And he was my grandfather."

The hairs of the back of Whale's neck stand up. "The point emerges."

"My mom never forgave him for cheating on Grandma, but I spent those last few years of his life with him, by his side. He told me everything. He was a soft man at the end. Broken. I felt so bad for him, living alone like that. No matter what he did, he never got the recognition he deserved. He couldn't make it up to his wife, his family, even the world. I wanted to do that for him, to make him a household name." Oscar frowns. "I was a writer, Jacob, just like you, and I came to Hollywood for no other reason than to tell my grandfather's story myself. I didn't want some lazy producer with no idea who he really was to turn him into some cliché action hero or some politically biased figurehead. I wanted to capture just who my grandfather was, the good man I knew, not the military puppet he was in service." Oscar pauses. "But I kept putting it off, waiting until I had enough money to make it on my own, which is why I went into the watchdog business. But even if I could, I don't know how to write anymore. The industry's changed so much. I've made way too many enemies in this town. Any allies I had are long retired. And now this town hates me."

Whale hesitates. "Surprised no one's beat you to it."

"I know, it's such a great story." Oscar pauses. "Which is why I spend thousands of dollars a year keeping Clark Hauser's story out of the public eye. Do you have any idea how hard it is to keep a famous name off Wikipedia? How many shakedowns it takes for the stuffy scientific academia world to pull a crucial chapter of Cold War nuclear history out of every textbook and article in the country? I've never told anyone about my grandfather. I can't. But I'm telling you now. That's how serious I am that you don't do this. I believe in you, Jacob. I've seen it with my own eyes. You're a good person. I know you don't feel like one right now, but you are. You have a gift. You're better man than I am. A better artist."

Whale scratches his leg. "I graduated from one the biggest film schools in the country with six feature-length screenplays, two short scripts, and an episode of *It's Always Sunny in Philadelphia* in my portfolio. But that's it. Screenplays. My best friend Frankie filmed five shorts during his time at Whitman. He's in Savannah right now producing reality TV. One of my suitemates, Nich Holstein, filmed seven shorts from three directors. Now he's a PA for *Last Week Tonight*. Another suitemate of mine, TJ Mason, works for his millionaire father in Cedar Rapids. Our RA, Carter Jackson, literally the most popular guy in the entire class, works for Eddie Passifle personally. If he runs again in 2020 he might actually win, which means Carter would be buddy-buddy with the next President of the United States. And yet *I* was the one The Professor chose for the internship. *I* ended up being the one everyone was jealous of." Whale shakes his head. "I can't go back, Oscar. I'm sorry, but I can't. I refuse to end up like Karen."

"Who?"

"I have to do something real. I can't have a gap on my resume."

Oscars hesitates. "Can you wait until I need to replace one of my writers?"

Whale shakes his head. "The cat's out of the bag with Weinstein. A lot of people are gonna come out of the woodwork with accusations of their own. You're gonna need the extra manpower, let alone someone you can trust to keep Theo at bay. Someone who's not afraid to stand up to him."

Oscar sighs. "You might be right about that," he murmurs.

"It's not like I've never snuck up on someone and took pictures without 'em knowing." Whale deflates, suddenly recollecting. "I've had lots of practice." His lips contort into a horrified frown. He covers his mouth, trying not to cry.

Oscar takes Whale's hand. Looks him in the eye. Smiles sympathetically. They share a touching moment of silence.

Oscar catches the Manager walking over and whips his hand away from Whale. "Thank you so much!" he exclaims, his campy persona returned. "This is so unnecessary."

Whale wipes his eyes, disturbed by Oscar's tonal whiplash.

"I disagree, Mr. Blitz," the Manager says with a smile. "It is our duty to please all of our customers." He snaps his fingers. The Waiter comes over with two tumblers, ice balls already inside. The Manager holds out the bottle of Domergue 15.

"Pour on, *mein* host!" Oscar declares.

The Manager opens the bottle. Pours two glasses, the ice balls cracking hard. He places the bottle on the table. "Enjoy!" The Manager nods at Whale. "Enjoy!"

Whale gives a polite smile back. Stares at his glass of Scotch. He can smell it already.

Oscar looks at Whale briefly. "Put it on my tab."

The Manager furrows his brow. "Sir?"

"It's okay. I insist."

"Whatever you wish, Mr. Blitz." The Manager walks away.

Whale lifts his glass with a smile. "You didn't have to do that."

"I know." Oscar holds his glass out. They click their tumblers.

Whale looks into the glass. Swirls it around. Sniffs. Takes a sip.

DREW

24/7

Midnight. Jimmy Lyons forces down the shittiest vodka he's ever tasted at Elmo's in Lincoln Heights. Finish peeling off the counter. Patches in the booth cushions. A few salty regulars with peeled finish and patches of their own. Billy Joel made a gaggle of losers seem romantic and made millions off of it. It really is anything but.

Jimmy finally feels numb. Orders another shot to feel even number. Hands his credit card to the sleazy bartender covered in face tattoos. Jimmy looks down at his wallet. Digs around the deepest depths of his ID pocket. Pulls out an old relic, his old fake ID, that Washington State driver's license with his stupid teenage face smiling back at him. He and his buddies went all the way up to Seattle to get it. $150 split three ways so Jimmy could buy them all six-packs whenever they wanted. Good times. Jimmy rubs his thumb across his young naive face. What a stupid kid. A fucking fraud. Jimmy slides the ID back into the wallet. Downs his newest refill.

1 AM. Jimmy's blowing an old man in the alleyway behind Elmo's, his knees wet from the rain-soaked asphalt. Smoke billows from a sewer somewhere. Jimmy breathes through his nose, sucking with closed eyes, waiting for the old man to cum already so he can stop. The cock tastes like stale sweat. And the old man is way too into it. Finally his winkled cock pulsates and Jimmy tastes funky cum. He gags, trying to pull away and spit it out, but the old man pushes his head back down with both hands. Jimmy swallows just for a chance to breathe. He might actually throw up.

The old man finally pulls out. Jimmy spits everything he can onto the ground. The geezer pats Jimmy's head like he's a fucking dog. Pulls out two limp, moldy twenties. Awkwardly holds them out. Jimmy stares at them. Reaches out, half-assed. The old man mistimes the handoff, accidentally letting go too early, the twenties falling to the ground like a pair of tissues. He bends forward as if to pick them up. Awkwardly doubles back. Walks away with shame.

"Don't worry, I got it," Jimmy mumbles. He peels the slimy twenties off the wet ground. Dries them on his pant leg. Folds them. Puts them in his empty wallet. He kneels erect, just about to get up. Goes back down instead, his butt resting against heels. He stays where he is, kneeling behind the dumpster, absolutely disgusted with himself.

2 AM. Jimmy sits in the back of an empty bus. Bored. Drunk. Killing time. Anything to avoid going home. He stares out the window, that gross cool-blue fluorescent light glaring off the raindrops clinging to the pane. He thinks about his mother. His bedroom. His brothers. Good cooking. Warmth. Jimmy rests his head against the glass, bumping with every pothole, shaking with every jostle. Maybe he should just go back. Get out of LA while he still can. But a mental flash of his father's face changes his mind again.

3 AM. Jimmy steps into his shitty Chinatown apartment, still reeking of mildew. The fan won't turn off. The water stains aren't drying. Jimmy frowns. The sheer stillness and silence always makes him want to cry.

4 AM. Jimmy watches *The Surgery* on his cheap TV. It never gets old. It'll be twenty years old next year. The credits roll. Jimmy watches the names crawl by. Directed by Rian Hoffman. Written by Jacob Andrezj. Where are they now? In shitty little Chinatown apartments of their own? Back home, wherever they came from? The world doesn't reward artists, after all. Just crooks and liars. Maybe Jacob was another one of Drew's victims. Another sucker.

5 AM. Jimmy scrolls through TrueSwitch on his bed. Empty. Brain turning to mush. His eyes flutter. He slips into unconsciousness, his phone falling over.

6 AM. Jimmy's asleep.

7 AM. Jimmy's still asleep.

8 AM. The sun hits Jimmy's eyes. He wakes up. He must've fallen asleep. He plugs in his phone. Rolls over. Falls back asleep.

9 AM. Jimmy sleeps.

10 AM. Jimmy hits REM sleep. Dreams up something real nice.

11 AM. Jimmy wakes up. Makes a pot of coffee. Checks his email. Nothing. He refreshes again. Still nothing.

Noon. Jimmy hits his vape pen on his windowsill. Blows smoke out his fire escape. A stray cat walks over. Jimmy smiles. Gently pets it.

1 PM. Jimmy paces his apartment, phone pressed to his ear. "I've been a server at Harry 79 for the past three years, and I think I am a very hard worker."

"If we were to consider you, when would you be able to start?" the Interviewer asks.

"As soon as possible. I have complete availability, believe me."

"That is very good to hear." The Interviewer pauses awkwardly. "Okay, I think we have enough. We'll let you know."

Jimmy nods. "Thank you so much. Bye." He hangs up. Angrily sighs. He blew it.

2 PM. Jimmy eats lunch at his favorite cafe down the street. He gives the waiter his credit card. Declined. Jimmy feigns puzzlement. The waiter walks away. Jimmy pulls out those gross twenties. Stares at them. Sticks them back into his wallet. Dashes out instead. Guess he's not coming back here again.

3 PM. Jimmy wanders down Hollywood Boulevard. Passes an old theater. Recognizes the poster with the pale white face and bold blue eye. *The Sins of Jack Branson* is still the number 1 movie in the world. Five weeks in a row now. Jimmy stops to stare at the poster. Something about it hits different this time. It weirds him out. He keeps on walking.

4 PM. Jimmy clocks in at Harry 79. Pulls out his phone. Quick-checks for Gary. Races into his email app.

"Screenplay Contest Notification: *Seattle Kid*"

Jimmy taps it instantly. Skims the first paragraph. His eyes stop on the word "regrettably." He instantly deletes the email. Closes his eyes. His heart rate decelerates hard.

5 PM. Gary yells at Jimmy in front of his table. Jimmy tries to defend himself. Gary's so unfair siding with them on this. But Gary threatens to fire him if he says another word. Jimmy tries his hardest not to speak. Grovels on command like a good little doggie.

6 PM. The dinner rush hits. Jimmy sneaks over to the side nook, just for a breather. He looks around. Dirty floors. Dusty air vents. The mouse they're not supposed to talk about roaming free. They still have their Christmas decorations up. No one cares enough to take them down. Jimmy frowns, zoning out. It finally hits him. He's gonna be there the rest of his life.

7 PM. "How about those Oscar nominations?" Bobby asks Jimmy in the kitchen.

"Oh fuck," Jimmy murmurs. "I missed it."

"Damn. That's not like you."

"Just give me the rundown. I'd look it up myself, but I don't wanna give Gary another reason to fire me."

"*Finnegan's Wake* got a few. *Lamberton* got a bunch. *Jessica* got a bunch."

"What about *The Sins of Jack Branson*?" Jimmy asks timidly. "Did that get anything?"

Bobby laughs hard. "'Did that get anything?' Dude, it's the most nominated movie of the year! How have you not heard?"

"I've had a real shitty day, alright?"

"How come?"

Jimmy frowns. "*Seattle Kid* didn't place."

"Ah, shit." Bobby sighs. "There's always next year, right?"

Jimmy shakes his head. "What did *Branson* get nominated for?"

"Best Picture, obviously. Eli Kerbinger for Best Director. Best Actor for the guy that played Jack."

"Fergus Connaughton."

"Yeah." Bobby starts counting with finger number four. "Martin Kennergan and Marcel Innalls for Supporting Actor. Bernadette Brewster for Supporting Actress. Drew Lawrence for Adapted Screenplay." Bobby hesitates, trying to remember the rest.

Jimmy zones out. Hearing Drew's name still hurts.

"Oh, of course!" Bobby blurts. "Cinematography."

Jimmy raises his brows. "Really?!"

"Also..." Bobby thinks. "Production Design. Editing. Costume Design. Makeup & Hairstyling. Sound." Bobby quickly re-counts. "Yeah. Thirteen."

"Surprised it didn't break the record."

"I'm surprised it didn't tie. Monte Ryans got fucking snubbed for Supporting Actor."

"I know."

"I'm telling you, if he was able-bodied with a CGI stump, they'd have no problem giving him a nomination."

"I don't know about that."

"No, it's true. That's how they are."

Jimmy rolls his eyes. "Whatever."

"But can you believe it?" Bobby continues. "The first time any animated movie was nominated for Best Cinematography?"

"And the first animated Best Picture nominee NOT nominated Best Animated Feature."

"I read something about that. Apparently, it was never eligible because it's 40% live action, which is way below the official threshold."

"It's too live action to be considered animation, but they still gave it a Cinematography nom?"

"The Academy met a few months ago to discuss it. They determined because the animated parts were filmed live and rotoscoped later that it's enough to be considered VFX instead of proper animation."

"That's stupid."

"They can't have it be both. They had to pick one."

"I suppose they're happy either way."

Bobby chuckles. "God, what a weird timeline. Drew Lawrence is actually the favorite to win Best Picture."

Jimmy frowns. "I know just what you mean."

8 PM. Gary went home for the night, which means Jimmy can unmute the tiny TV and watch *Media Man* while he waits for another table to show up.

"The nominations for the 110th Annual Academy Awards were announced this morning," says Garth "Media Man" Davidson, "with *The Sins of Jack Branson* leading the pack with 13 nominations, including Best Picture, Director, and Adapted Screenplay for Drew Lawrence. I'm here with Jenni Putmari, media critic for the *LA Times* and frequent guest on this show. Jenni, what do you feel about *Branson*'s chances?"

"*The Sins of Jack Branson* is the perfect representation of the movie no one asked for," Jenni says, sitting across from Garth. "No one wanted a Pet Shop Boys movie-musical. No one wanted a half-animated adaptation of any novel, let alone an obscure erotic memoir from 1888 by an even obscurer gay prostitute. But you know, that's why *Branson*'s taking the world by storm. Drew Lawrence has defied all industry expectations and has delivered something even *I* haven't seen before, which is why I think *The Sins of Jack Branson* has the best chance to break the single-year win record I've seen in years."

Jimmy rolls his eyes at that.

"That is a bold statement, Jenni!" The Media Man exclaims. "You really think it can win twelve Oscars?"

"Yes, and for three reasons. One: The Academy loves giving the gold to repeat snub cases. Drew Lawrence has been the bridesmaid and never the bride when it comes to wins. Before this he's had five nominations, including two for Best Picture. Much like Scorsese's wins for *The Departed,* Leo DiCaprio for *The Revenant*, and *Return of the King*'s perfect sweep, the odds of a symbolic win only increase with time. Two: Hollywood loves an underdog story. So much has already been said on this show regarding Drew Lawrence's quest for artistic legitimacy after his departure from Not That Nutty, so what I'm about to say won't be anything new, but good God is this a story for the ages! Number one movie in the world for five weeks in a row. 90% Rotten Tomatoes from Critics, 98% from Audiences. I've seen reviews calling it the best musical of all time, the best animated film of all time, the best biopic of all time. I don't agree with any of that, but the fact that so many established voices are reacting like this to a DREW LAWRENCE MOVIE is something no one could have predicted. Three: As good as *The Sins of Jack Branson* is, no sweep is possible in the face of good opposition, and frankly there aren't any other heavy hitters this year. Best Actor, newcomer Fergus Connaughton has been cleaning up this award season. Best Actor at Cannes. Best Actor Musical/Comedy Golden Globe. Best Actor BAFTA. Best Actor Critic's Choice. Audiences love him. Critics love him. He's on fire to win. Best Supporting Actor *will* go to Martin Kennergan as Mr. Munce, guaranteed. Best Supporting Actress, a trans woman is nominated again this year, the fantastic Bernadette Brewster as Mary, but because the other nominees are from films that haven't received any other nominations, that only increases Brewster's odds of finally breaking that pink and blue ceiling. Best Director, Eli Kerbinger has outdone himself again. *Branson* is an original adaptation and far more ambitious in scope than *Seven Brides*, so I say that's a lock. Best Adapted Screenplay, another no-contest win. All the craft awards, Production Design, Cinematography, Sound. Two genres the Academy loves disproportionately are musicals and period pieces. *The Sins of Jack Branson* is both. Honestly, Garth, if I didn't know any better I'd say Drew Lawrence made *The Sins of Jack Branson* Academy-friendly on purpose."

9 PM. Jimmy eats a greasy burger during his federally mandated 30-minute break, zoning out the entire meal. The bell dings. Jimmy stops chewing at the sight of the new arrival's absolutely bizarre outfit. Simple white T-shirt. Eccentric blazer printed with traditional Mexican cantina artwork. Printed slacks with a jarringly different aesthetic, bright bulbed florals like the ones you'd see in Margaritaville, with matching shoes no less. A hat combining a diagonally cocked James Cagney fedora and fake orchids (or perhaps real ones) of assorted colors, its unorthodox brimline cutting across the man's face and blocking his left eye.

Izzy the hostess grabs a menu and walks past Jimmy's booth with the Strange Man in question. The Strange Man's right eye stares at Jimmy the whole way.

Jimmy awkwardly looks away. Resumes his burger.

10 PM. Jimmy serves the earlier than usual late-night stoner crowd. He looks over at the corner booth. The Strange Man from earlier is on a laptop. He stops typing to stretch his fingers. He notices Jimmy staring. Nods with recognition. Jimmy bro-nods in return. Gets back to work.

11 PM. Jimmy watches the tiny TV again. Kat Williams is fixating on *The Sins of Jack Branson* using the same three points Jenni Putmari said earlier. Either Kat watched tonight's *Media*

Man and copied it verbatim, or she came up with the same three points organically. Jimmy doesn't know which is worse.

"Movie guy, huh?" a flamboyant voice asks.

Jimmy turns toward the Strange Man's booth. "I'm sorry. Is it too loud?"

"It's fine," the Strange Man says with a smile. "I like movies too."

Jimmy turns down the volume. Walks over. "I don't really get a chance to watch anything at home. My place doesn't even have cable, can you believe that?"

"Don't let me stop you."

"I think I've heard enough," Jimmy leans his shoulder on the booth. "Only so much to dissect on Oscar nom day apparently."

The Strange Man's right eye looks up. "You like my hat?"

"I don't know," Jimmy murmurs. "Why do you look so familiar?"

The Strange Man smirks enigmatically. "You don't watch Streamer, do you?"

"Like I can afford it." Jimmy hesitates. "How'd you know that?"

"You tell me."

Jimmy scans the Strange Man's face. Shakes his head. "Sorry."

The Strange Man reaches under the brim of his hat. Pulls out a clip. Loosens the strap around his head. Removes the hat. "How about now?" Oscar Blitz asks.

"Oh my God!" Jimmy gushes. "Of course! I am so sorry."

"I understand." Oscar gently places his hat on the table. "You're here all night?"

"Don't get off till 5."

"Eesh!" Oscar says through gritted teeth. "Must be rough."

"The managers don't really give a shit until they do. Then it's hell. But not for a while, thankfully."

"Do they pay well at least?"

"Just enough to keep their slaves fed."

Oscar gestures to the empty seat across from him. "Come. Sit."

Jimmy looks around. Plops down at the table.

"What's your name?" Oscar asks.

"Jimmy. Jimmy Lyons."

"Pleased to meet you, Jimmy Lyons. I'm Oscar Blitz."

"I know. Not that I really watch your show or anything, but I don't think I've ever seen you in that outfit before."

"I never wear anything a second time."

"You must run out of ideas pretty fast."

Oscar smirks. "Quick one, ain't ya?"

"There's only so much of the world to appropriate, don't you think?"

"Very true."

"Even randomness is finite. And the definition of strange varies unpredictably over time, so..." Jimmy nods, mock-impressed. "Good on you for picking such an enduring brand."

Oscar stares. "Thanks for the diagnosis, kid."

"Don't call me 'kid,'" Jimmy snaps.

Oscar hesitates. "Duly noted." He looks up at the small TV playing *Movies Tonight with Kat Williams*. "You see *Branson* yet?"

"I don't have time." Jimmy looks out the window. "It's just so infuriating how everyone's so in love with Drew Lawrence all of a sudden. What happened to him being the elephant guy? Now he's suddenly a criminally overlooked maestro?"

Oscar holds back a smirk.

"And everyone my age is obsessed with the Pet Shop Boys now," Jimmy continues, full-on ranting now, "which they never would've even HEARD OF if it wasn't for that movie. I hear the soundtrack everywhere I go. The original songs are recharting. Even the obscure B-sides no one cared about when they were originally out."

"You sound jealous."

"No," Jimmy states. "I'm not *jealous.*" He pauses. "It's just annoying is all."

Oscar looks at the TV again. Kat Williams talks faintly over a picture of Drew Lawrence, looking hot and fit on the Cannes red carpet.

Jimmy notices Oscar's distracted gaze. Turns around. Scoffs. "Some guy, huh?"

"If only they knew," Oscar whispers, pain in his voice.

Jimmy turns back to Oscar. "What do you mean?"

"He used to work for me back in the day."

"Oh. That's interesting."

Oscar shrugs. Looks back up at the TV.

"You must be happy for him," Jimmy says.

"Hardly," Oscar says with bite. "We have a bit of a history."

Jimmy hesitates. "What did he do?"

"He worked for me a little over a year. We got close." Oscar pauses. "We were good friends, as a matter of fact. Very good friends. And it wasn't even that hard either. He was..." Oscar frowns. "I *thought* he was one of the good ones. So when he needed my help to make his dream come true, I wanted to help him get there. I paid for everything. I called on favors. I pulled all the stops for him. I got him into Tribeca. I got him into the Oscars. I negotiated his first feature deal with Paramount. There wouldn't have been a Not That Nut, let alone a Not That Nutty, if it wasn't for that deal."

Jimmy nods solemnly. "You're saying you made Drew Lawrence what he is today?"

"I wouldn't go that far," Oscar murmurs. "But he wouldn't be 'Drew Lawrence' if it wasn't for me."

Jimmy raises a brow. "Isn't that what I just said?"

"No. Believe it or not, that's not the same thing." Oscar pauses. "And after all I did for him, you know how he repaid me? He tossed me aside like I was nothing. Because that's what Drew does. He gains your trust, he makes you feel important, and he..." Oscar swallows, a scowl forming. "He makes you feel like a better person just by knowing him. The same cannot be said for the reverse. To Drew, you're just a means to an end. The moment he gets what he wants, when you have nothing left you can give him, he rips you off, crumples you up, and tosses you in the trash. He even says 'Kobe" when he does it."

Jimmy's gaze softens. Memories return. "When did you last talk to him?"

"About eighteen years ago or so." Oscar smirks bitterly. "He thinks I'm a fucking joke."

"How can you know that if you haven't spoken in eighteen years?" Jimmy asks. "Maybe he's forgiven you."

Oscar smiles strangely. "Little devil's advocate, aren't you?"

Jimmy tilts his head.

"Nothing." Oscar pauses. "There's a guy at the end of *Branson*, the crooked politician that first uses Jack's memoir to bash his opponent."

"Geoffrey Grant?"

"Thought you said you hadn't seen it."

"Wikipedia." Jimmy pauses. "What about him?"

"He's based on me."

"But he was a real guy."

"Trust me, Drew wrote him to be based on me."

Jimmy hesitates. "Don't you think you're being a little paranoid?"

"Look, the guy is a public figure. He tells the world about Edgar's immorality, right, to get him canceled. But he found out about Edgar and the brothel thanks to his network of spies and blackmailers. He's supportive of Jack and their cause at first, but then Jack figures out that Grant only cares because his seat in the House of Commons is on the line, and Grant's such a good liar that even Charlie the human lie detector couldn't spot it."

"That's supposed to be you?"

"No! That's how Drew thinks of me now! Phony morals! Two-faced eccentricity!"

"But he teams up with Grant to take down Edgar."

"Doesn't matter!" Oscar cries. "Oh my God, I know myself through Drew's eyes when I see it." He shakes his head with a snicker. "He thinks *I'm* phony? If anyone in this town knew the real Drew Lawrence, they'd hate his fucking guts, I'll tell you that."

Jimmy's heart races. "Care to elaborate?" he asks anyway.

Oscar stares at Jimmy. "The only reason I'm telling you this is because it's probably going nowhere, but if you tell anyone about this, I'll know it's you."

"Don't worry about me. What is it?"

Oscar looks around. No one in sight, not even his server. "He's a regular at a club in WeHo. I won't say which one—"

"Sweet Vermouths."

Oscar stares. "How did you know that?"

Jimmy doesn't answer.

Oscar sighs. "Anyway, he has a sort of... arrangement with the managers over there. Whenever they add on a new go-go boy, Drew Lawrence gets first dibs on breaking them in. Like a horse trainer."

"He fucks them?"

"They have no say in the matter. It's not full-on rape, more like a morally gray power dynamic, but my guy on the inside says the manager told him he had to let it happen if he wanted his screenplay to have a ghost of a chance."

Jimmy frowns, suddenly a bit sick. "Sounds pretty damning."

"That's nothing," Oscar mutters. "No, *literally* it's nothing. I haven't been able to get any first-hand evidence. That's what sucks about journalistic fucking integrity."

"But I don't understand, if you know he does it—?"

"I have a reputation to uphold. I never lie. That's my thing. What good are accusations if they don't stick? Then the next time, when I REALLY need to oust a fucker, I'll be stuck in a Boy-Who-Cried-Wolf situation." Oscar pauses. "All I really know is he fucks the boys in the men's room. You would think that would be the perfect place to snag a video midway through, but that's not what the gays do. No way, those Don't-Ask-Don't-Tell fudgepackers form a human wall whenever shit goes down and watch. Complacency must be part of their culture, I guess."

"I'm a fudgepacker, you son of a bitch," Jimmy says with venom.

Oscar hesitates. Raises both hands. "I apologize. I didn't mean to offend."

Jimmy nods respectfully.

"It just pisses me off." Oscar scratches his eyebrow. "My guy, Terry... He graduated *summa cum laude* from UCLA. Philosophy major. Writer in his spare time. And he had good body too. Real athletic." Oscar pauses. "Terry stopped dancing after Drew had his way with him. You know what he's doing now?"

Jimmy shakes his head.

"Heroin." Oscar nods solemnly. "My guys lost track of him a couple weeks ago. Last I heard, he was squatting under a bridge in MacArthur Park." Oscar looks out the window. "He's probably there right now, melting in the dark."

Jimmy rubs a coarse hand along the back of his head and down his neck. "How much do you have on him?" Jimmy asks weakly.

Oscar smirks. "Forgive me if I don't wanna show my hand."

"Just a ballpark then."

Oscar shrugs. "I've been hoarding dirt on Drew Lawrence for almost twenty years, but without anything concrete to form around, it's useless."

"What do you need?" Jimmy asks eagerly.

Oscar stares, his face going numb. "You know something, don't you?"

"Do you really need a video?"

"Ideally, yeah."

"But what if you don't have one? What comes close?"

Oscar shakes his head. "Not much, to be honest."

"What about eyewitness testimony?"

"No way."

"Why?!" Jimmy blurts. "Why not?!"

"In order for a witness to rival an undoctered video in terms of legitimacy, they have to have been there every step of the way. It has to be really bad, what they did. Actually illegal. And even then, they have to go on the show. No aliases. No disguises. No vocal distortions. Stormy fucking Daniels. And they have to be clean. No history of perjury. No mental illness. No reason to lie."

Jimmy hesitates. "That's it?"

"That's asking a lot. Most people don't want to be in front of a camera recounting the whole thing for millions of people. Nine times out of ten, it's ancient history. They've moved on. They got careers now they're trying to maintain."

Jimmy fishes into his pocket. "Well you're in luck, cause I've got nothing to lose." He pulls a California State ID from his wallet. Hands it over.

Oscar holds the bottom edge between his thumb and index finger. "What am I looking at?"

"I had sex with Drew Lawrence," Jimmy declares.

Oscar's eyes flick down at the ID. Back up. "Congratulations."

"Two and a half years ago."

Oscar looks back at the ID. Raises both brows.

Jimmy smiles. "That concrete enough for ya?"

"Jimmy..." Oscar looks up. Smiles. "I think this is the beginning of a beautiful friendship."

END OF PART FIVE

PART SIX

Greedy, Barbarous and Cruel

JACOB

Don't Look Up

INT. STEWIE'S BOSTON APARTMENT - NIGHT

Halloween night. Stewie and Jacob (dressed as Walter White and Jesse Pinkman respectively) lie together on the couch and watch Carrie on the mounted TV.

STEWIE
Pause it!

Jacob grabs the remote and pauses it on Carrie White's smiling face, a Prom Queen tiara on her head, moments before the bullies dump a bucket of pig's blood on her.

STEWIE (CONT'D)
O-kay, that was a good movie, sexy.

JACOB
What?

STEWIE
You can shut it off.

JACOB
Stop. We're finally at the best part.

STEWIE
I thought you haven't seen it.

JACOB
Just because I haven't seen it doesn't mean I don't know what happens. Everybody knows about the pig's blood.

Stewie frowns.

STEWIE
I've always hated this part. It's so sad. Look at her. This is the happiest day of her life.

JACOB
But it's all a lie. And even if we stop the movie now, that doesn't change the fact that we've seen John Travolta and those popular bitches plan the whole thing.

STEWIE
But SHE doesn't know it yet.

Jacob sighs.

JACOB
In the writing world, when the audience knows something the characters don't, it's called dramatic irony. Writers use it to generate suspense, and suspense doesn't mean ANYTHING unless it actually culminates to something.

Stewie stares at the paused screen. Jacob reaches for the remote.

STEWIE
Leave it paused.

JACOB
Why?

STEWIE
Just for a minute. Let her have this.

Jacob looks at the screen. Sissy Spacek's naive face smiles back at them.

JACOB
Just for a minute.

Jacob tosses the remote away. They stare at the screen. How pretty Carrie looks in her prom dress, that tiara. So happy. Jacob rests his head on Stewie's breast. Takes a deep breath. Smiles sweetly.

Stewie rubs Jacob's arms, stopping on a muscle he hadn't noticed before. He kisses Jacob's forehead. Holds him tighter.

Jacob readjusts his posture. Wraps his arms around Stewie. Stares up at Carrie.

Stewie breathes rhythmically. His mind blank. His Baby Boy wrapped around him.

Jacob listens to Stewie's heartbeat. He smiles a bit.

Stewie looks down at Jacob again. Jacob notices Stewie looking and lifts his head. They kiss. Give each other silly smiles.

STEWIE
(reluctant)
Okay.

Jacob grabs the remote and hits play.

SMASH CUT TO:

INT. WHITMAN UNIVERSITY - LITTLE BUILDING - SUITE 701 - NIGHT

Jacob, Rian, TJ, and Nich watch CNN's Election Night coverage with paralyzing shock.

TJ
I can't believe it.

NICH
(freaking out)
Oh fuck!

RIAN
President Donald Trump.

JACOB
This would happen, wouldn't it? Just when we're about to go back to normal, it pulls an <u>American Idol</u>.

TJ
(grins)
I can't believe it.

Nich glares at TJ.

NICH
Why are you smiling?

TJ
What?

NICH
You're smiling.

TJ
No, I'm not.

JACOB
I'm sure he wasn't.

NICH
This isn't funny, TJ.

```
                    JACOB
        He's probably just being ironic. Right TJ?

TJ hesitates.

                    TJ
        I just can't believe she actually lost.

                    JACOB
        See? Just shock. He's still human.

                    NICH
        You'd still be smiling if she won, right?

TJ looks away.

                    TJ
        What's the big deal?

Nich's mouth falls open.

                    NICH
        Please tell me you didn't vote for Trump.

TJ doesn't answer. Jacob and Rian look over.

                    RIAN
        Wait, really?

                    TJ
        Still don't see what the big deal is.

Nich clenches his jaw.

                    JACOB
        I'm surprised.

                    TJ
        Why would that surprise you, Jake?

Jacob hesitates.

                    JACOB
        I just assumed you of all people would vote Democrat.

                    TJ
        Because I'm black?

                    JACOB
        Yeah.

                    TJ
        And Hillary is just a beacon of support in that
        matter?
```

"Trump's got the KKK and Neo-Nazis backing him," Nich blurts. "What the fuck is wrong is you?"

```
Jacob's blood chills.

                    TJ
        Oh, so I just make being black my whole personality,
        right? There ARE more important things, you know.
        Illegal immigration, ISIS, welfare state, the Liberal
        PC police controlling our media.
```

"When they bring back lynching you'll be fucking sorry, won't you?"

```
                    RIAN
        Guys, stop fighting.

                    JACOB
        You didn't vote for Hillary, did you Nich?
```

"Of course I did!" Nich cries, glaring. "What's the matter with you?"

```
                    JACOB
      But you're so anti-establishment. I just assumed you
      voted third party.
```

"Anyone who votes third party is just another Trump supporter."

```
                    JACOB
      If they didn't vote for Trump, that doesn't make them
      a Trump supporter.
```

"They split the vote! They might as well be."

```
                    RIAN
      Well, I voted for her.

                    JACOB
      I just think TJ has a right to opinion without being
      harassed.

                    TJ
      Thank you.
```

"Did you vote for Trump too?" Nich angrily asks Jacob.

```
                    JACOB
      No!
```

"Who'd you vote for?"

```
                    JACOB
      Hillary!
```

"Then you should understand why I'm fucking pissed that anyone would let that fucking orange monster into the White House. He's gonna overturn *Roe v. Wade*, he's gonna abolish gay marriage, he's gonna ban Muslims. He'll deport everyone and make discrimination legal and encourage hate crimes, and everyone's just gonna let it fucking happen."

```
                    JACOB
      Don't you know how absolutely deranged you sound?
```

"Mark my words! He's gonna abolish terms limits and become a fucking dictator. You'll see."

```
                    JACOB
      You don't actually believe that?
```

"Of course I do!"

```
                    TJ
      See what happens when the Left doesn't get their way?
      They act like fucking crybabies.
```

"GET THE FUCK AWAY FROM ME!"

```
                    TJ
      TRUMP! TRUMP! TRUMP! TRUMP!

Nich makes a move at TJ like he's gonna fight him. TJ flinches back.

                    RIAN
      Hey! Cut it out!

                    TJ
      I'm going to bed, asshole. Go fuck yourself.

TJ walks away.
```

"YEAH, GO ON!" Nich shouts after him. "UNCLE TOM!"

```
TJ SLAMS his bedroom door.

                    JACOB
      What the fuck is wrong with you?
```

"I don't wanna fucking hear it! He was harassing me."

```
                    JACOB
      By saying 'Trump?!'
```

"How can a black man vote for the same guy as David Duke?!"

```
                    JACOB
      His dad's a millionaire! Do you really think he'd
      vote for someone who wants to tax the rich?
```

"You're really taking his side?"

```
                    JACOB
      I'm not taking his side! I'm just saying you can't be
      shocked!
```

"I AM shocked!"

```
                    JACOB
      Just because he voted for Trump doesn't mean he
      agrees with him on everything.
```

"Yes it does!"

```
                    JACOB
      Not all Trump supporters wear the hats or attack
      immigrants or gays, you know. Hillary has enough
      haters to get people to vote for him.
```

"They're fucking nutcases. I don't give a shit about them."

```
                    JACOB
      Stewie's not a nutcase!

Nich freezes.

                    RIAN
      Stewie voted for Trump?

                    JACOB
      Yeah.

Rian hesitates.

                    RIAN
      Okay. Alright. I'm sure he has his reasons.
```

"Wait, wait..." Nich laughs bitterly. "So the guy telling me I shouldn't attack a racist—"

```
                    JACOB
      Oh, TJ's a racist now? When the fuck did that happen?
```

"Anyone who votes for a racist is a racist! And you're fucking a racist, Jake! You brought racist into our suite!"

```
                    JACOB
      Stewie's not a racist!
```

"How can you stay with him?"

```
                    JACOB
      I'm not gonna break up with a guy because of
      politics! That's stupid!
```

"No, what's stupid is Trump spouting all that hate speech and alt-right rhetoric and Stewie voting for him anyway! Don't you understand? Racism and sexism aren't fucking dealbreakers for him. God, I knew there was something off about him!"

```
                    JACOB
      What are you talking about?! You liked him!
```

"The age gap always creeped me out. I think it's gross, and that fact that you keep defending him just freaks me out!"

JACOB
When Stewie was here and you had no idea who he was voting for, you liked him! You liked him because he was polite and charming, and you saw the youth and wit that I love so much, and you were FINE! But now you find out he's a Trump supporter, a DEMOCRATIC Trump supporter mind you, and suddenly he's this two-faced old geezer groomer?! He's not a bigot. You're the fucking bigot, asshole!

RIAN
Jacob!

"Talk all you fucking want, I don't care. All I see is a guy who would go to the ends of the earth defending the end of democracy and gay marriage and millions of lives in this piece of shit country so he could have himself a sugar daddy!"

Nich storms away, bumping into Jacob as he goes to his room and SLAMS the door. Jacob's breath wavers, sudden emotion building up.

RIAN
You okay?

JACOB
(crying)
What the fuck just happened?

RIAN
Don't worry about it. It's just Nich.

JACOB
I don't know why he's turning on me. I voted for Hillary. I did my part.

RIAN
He's just upset. Don't take it personally.

Jacob stares off, shaking his head.

JACOB
I shouldn't have said anything.

RIAN
You can't blame yourself.

JACOB
Stewie told me this would happen. What the fuck is wrong with me?

RIAN
He'll get over it. Just give him time.

JACOB
He'd better.

CUT TO:

INSIDE JACOB'S NEW DORM

Jacob curls up on the bed in the dark. He can hear Nich shouting at TJ through the walls. Makes him sick just hearing it. He pulls out his phone and calls Stewie.

STEWIE (V.O.)
(bleating)
AYY BEE!

JACOB
(soft bleating)
Ayy Bee.

STEWIE (V.O.)
Can you believe it? Mom already went to bed thinking Trump lost. She's gonna be so happy when she wakes up tomorrow.
(pause)
You there, Baby Boy?

JACOB
(whispers)
Yeah.

STEWIE (V.O.)
What's wrong?

Jacob closes his eyes and cries.

STEWIE (V.O.)
Oh, Baby... What's wrong?

Jacob keeps crying.

DREW

Sweet Sixteen

"What about making it like *Wolf of Wall Street*?" Drew asks, rotating his chair toward Kev. "Ponzi really was a yuppie ahead of his time. It'd be pretty funny having brag to the future."

"It'll be like he's hijacking the movie and making it his autobiography," Kev says.

"Hubristic, just like he was."

"I love it." Kev jots the idea on a small whiteboard.

KNOCK-KNOCK. Tanner Hennessy pokes his head into Drew's office. "Gary's looking for you guys."

"Tanner, listen to this," Kev says. "Drew and I got a great idea for the next one. An intentionally anachronistic biopic of Charlie Ponzi."

"*The Gilded Age* meets *The Big Short*," Drew chimes in.

"The dude was crazier than we thought. Charming. Deluded lack of awareness of his own villainy."

"He's waiting in the conference room," Tanner meekly tells them. "I think it's important."

Drew and Kev walk into the conference room to see their attorney Gary Green and his associate Thelma Lemmon already sitting at the table. "What's going on?" Drew asks.

"I think you better sit down for this, guys," Gary murmurs.

Drew looks at Kev. They gingerly pull out chairs and sit.

"Drew," Gary starts, hesitant. "Does the name 'Jimmy Lyons' mean anything to you?"

Drew stares blankly. "Why? What about him?"

"Did you have sex with him?"

"Yeah. So what?"

"Who's Jimmy Lyons?" Kev asks.

"Just some guy I met. A waiter. He goes to UCLA."

Gary nods, his brows together. "When exactly did you have sex with Jimmy Lyons?"

"Does it matter?"

"Do you have a timeframe?"

Drew scoffs, thinking back. "Yeah. July 20, 2035."

"You actually remember the date?" Kev asks.

"It was the night my mom died," Drew mumbles. He awkwardly looks at Kev. "I didn't know at the time!"

Gary rubs his mouth with a coarse hand. "You're 100% sure you had sex with a man named Jimmy Lyons in 2035?"

"Yes!" Drew cries. "Jesus, Gary, get to the point! We've got a lot of work to do."

"Yes we do," Gary says coldly. "Jimmy Lyons was sixteen the night you fucked him."

Drew bursts out laughing. "What?!"

"I just got off the phone with an old friend at the Public Defender's office. Jimmy Lyons signed a sworn affidavit accusing you of statutory rape. He's going public in twelve hours, so we need to act fast."

Kev gapes.

"No-no-no!" Drew chuckles, shaking his head. "There's *no way* that guy was sixteen!"

"His passport and State ID already confirmed it," Gary says. "His DOB's June 7, 2019."

"That would put him at sixteen days, one month, and thirteen days old," Thelma adds dryly.

Drew's levity disappears.

"You had sex with a sixteen-year-old?" Kev asks with disgust.

"I didn't know! I didn't..." Drew shakes his head. "It's not my fault! He told me he went to UCLA!"

Gary holds up a gentle hand. "Drew."

"He lied to me!"

"Listen to me. One of my specialties is Crisis PR. The fact that we have a twelve-hour head start is miraculous to say the least."

"Why are you talking to me like I'm a pedophile?!" Drew cries. "I'm not a pedophile."

"He's right," Thelma says. "It's a common misconception. Pedophiles prefer prepubescent victims, under ten for girls, eleven for boys. He'd be considered an ephebophile."

"I didn't rape anyone!" Drew pleads. "I don't do that! I SWEAR!"

"Drew," Gary says, more sternly this time. "I know what works and what doesn't. I'm gonna tell you what works. You're not gonna like it, but you're gonna do it. You understand?"

Drew desperately looks at Kev. Kev refuses to look back.

"Tell me you understand," Gary says.

"I understand," Drew whispers in a daze.

Gary nods. "We're gonna sit here and talk about what happened. Give us all the details you can. Then Thelma here will give your side of the story to the rest of my guys downstairs. They will draft a statement. Once we have vetted that statement, we're gonna put you in front of a camera and you will read it out loud. If we don't spend the next twelve hours fucking around, we'll have control of the narrative before Jimmy gets a chance to accuse you of anything."

Drew shakes his head. "This can't be happening. I didn't know!"

"I know you didn't know. That's what we have to tell people."

"He's just jealous of my Oscar noms! He wants to get back at me for not reading his screenplay! That's all this is! Anyone can see that!"

Gary purses his lips. "Did you approach him?"

"No! He approached me!"

"Did he know who you were when he approached you?"

Drew hesitates. "No."

"Who did he think you were?"

"Brian."

"You're doing the fucking statement."

"I can't!" Drew shouts, his voice cracking. "The Academy starts voting a week from tomorrow!"

"Whatever damage you think a statement is gonna do to your career will be NOTHING compared to the hellfire Jimmy will rain down on you if you don't!"

"But he's a liar!"

"He didn't lie about the stat rape, did he?" Kev asks heartlessly.

Drew's eyes droop. "I'm sorry," he whimpers.

"Why the FUCK didn't you check his ID?!"

"He said he didn't have one on him."

"How old did he tell you he was?" Thelma asks, pen at the ready.

Drew hesitates. "I didn't ask."

"You didn't ask?!" Kev exclaims.

"Why are you writing that down?" Drew asks Thelma. "I didn't agree to that!"

"Where did he approach you?" Gary asks.

"Stop writing!" Drew cries.

"Answer the question!"

"SHUT THE FUCK UP!" Drew screams. "I'm not a rapist! I don't diddle kids! I don't do that! He fucking lied to me! He said he went to UCLA way before he knew who I was! He does this all the time, I'm telling you! He knew what he was doing! I know I wasn't his first! He was a fucking ANIMAL, alright?! He fucking loved it! I didn't ask him for anything! HE came up to ME! I told him, I even told him I wasn't going to! I flat-out told him, 'I'm not fucking you!' But he kept giving me fuck me eyes and he was fucking BEGGING ME for it! How am I the bad guy here?! He's the one who lied! He gets to keep ruining lives all over town?! WHY THE FUCK IS HE COMING AFTER ME?! I DIDN'T DO ANYTHING! I don't go after kids! Look him up on Insta or TrueSwitch or whatever! He doesn't look sixteen! I never would've done it if I knew! I swear!"

Kev closes his eyes, knee deep in embarrassment.

Gary raises an angry finger. "Never... Say that... Again."

"Fuck you." Drew stands. "Fuck all of you. I've got work to do." He beelines for the door.

"Get back here!" Kev barks.

Drew pushes open both conference room doors. Races downstairs.

Kev stands and screams, "DREW!" just as the soundproofed doors shut.

Drew speeds all the way home and races up the stairs to his second floor condo and closes the door and locks it and grabs the bottle of Domergue 15 Eli Kerbinger sent him to commemorate their Best Picture nom (Eli didn't know Drew's sobriety was really-O, ya dig?) and twists off the cap and downs quite a lot in one go and then he remembers why and drinks some more and kicks off his shoes and strips down to a muscle tank and boxer briefs and curls up in the corner with eyes frozen open and every time he thinks about it he drinks, like a fucked up drinking game, take that Jimmy, and that makes him remember again so he drinks some more.

It's dark and Drew's switched to pouring Domergue on the rocks with some *Seinfeld* background noise. He scarfs an entire package of sushi, wasabi and all, and drinks some more to wash it down.

A few hours after that, Drew's not feeling very well. The alcohol isn't settling at all. He imagines *Braveheart*esque Scots fighting little fishy Japs on a giant single malt ocean, a nice big brown *Great Wave off Kanagawa* to boot.

KNOCK-KNOCK-KNOCK-KNOCK. Drew turns his head to the door, his body sliding along the leather. "Who is it?" he slurs.

"Open up, Drew." It's Kev. He sounds pissed.

"Go away!"

KNOCK-KNOCK-KNOCK.

Drew backs away, almost tripping. "Go away!"

"Open the fucking door, Drew!"

"You can't make me, okay?! You can't make me do anything!"

Silence. "Jimmy's on *Oscar Blitz* right now, you scumbag!"

Drew freezes. Races over to the door. Unlocks it. Races back to the couch. Grabs the remote. Switches streaming services. Clicks on *Oscar Blitz.* As it loads, Drew looks at Kev standing next to him with a subdued frown. Kev looks back. Cringes at Drew's bloodshot eyes.

"...in a sort of cutoff red flannel type of shirt," Jimmy tells Oscar on stage inside Studio 1, motioning his hands over his shoulders. "And I admit, I thought he was hot, like most of America when he suddenly hit the headlines. But I *had* heard of Drew Lawrence, and even I didn't know this guy was Drew Lawrence. I just assumed he wore suits as expensive as most cars. The guy looked like a rugged L.L. Bean Daddy type. That always turned me on."

"Who approached who?" Oscar asks.

"He approached me," Jimmy answers. "I was on the phone with a friend of mine when I was passing his Jeep. I had just got off when he walked up to me and started talking."

"That's a lie," Drew murmurs.

"He told me his name was Brian," Jimmy says. "I should say, he was very witty. He complimented my shirt, my hair. What can I say? I was blinded by the flattery."

"Did you try to tell him his age?" Oscar asks.

"Many times. He thought I was joking."

"How did you say it?"

Jimmy hesitates. "Something like, 'I think you should know, just to get it out of the way, I'm sixteen,' and he said something like, 'Sure,' or 'Yeah right.' And multiple times during our conversation, he kept inviting me to a pub down the street, Marcus MacDonald's. I knew it was a restaurant, so I didn't see the harm in it, but he kept mentioning drinks. He didn't seem to believe me that I was underage, so I tried telling him that I didn't have my ID on me. And that's when he promised to get me booze without me having to get carded... which, I'm ashamed to say, won me over."

"You followed him to Marcus MacDonald's?"

"I can't say I followed him. He gripped my shoulder the whole time. Very dominating."

"He was rubbing my fucking ass!" Drew shouts. "What a jerkoff!"

"They didn't card you there?" Oscar asks.

"I think the waiter wanted to," Jimmy says. "Drew must've slipped him a twenty or something."

"I did not!" Drew cries.

"I've since learned that such special treatment is called grooming," Jimmy continues.

"What did he get you?" Oscar asks.

"Vodka. Shots of vodka. Romanoff."

"And what was he drinking?"

"Nothing."

"What did you guys talk about?"

"My job at Harry 79. Also that I wanted to go to UCLA one day."

"And it's around this time that you mentioned your screenplay?"

"Yes. *Seattle Kid.*"

"Couldn't resist a plug, could you?" Drew mumbles.

"And the moment I mentioned it," Jimmy says, "I noticed his eyes light up. That's when he revealed who he really was."

"How did you react to that?" Oscar asks.

"I thought he was lying. But then he showed me his ID. Honestly, I was so thrilled to meet a celebrity, especially one I used to admire so much."

Drew gags with his tongue out.

"Then he drove me back to his place," Jimmy continues. "He gave me more booze. It was at this point that I started getting scared. I was in a famous producer's condo, no idea where I was. And his eyes were all cold. And he was dispassionate. And I got this feeling that I wasn't first boy he lured in." Jimmy inhales, emotions showing. "And that's when he showed lines of coke."

"BULLSHIT!" Drew snarls.

"Why are you shouting?" Kev asks.

"I'll never forget what he said," Jimmy whispers, tears forming in his eyes. "He said, 'You gotta do it, kid. Be like a real producer.'" He covers his mouth, faking tiny sobs into his hand. A producer, Cleo by the looks of her, hands Jimmy a box of tissues. He takes one. "Thank you." Jimmy wipes his eyes. "He tried to initiate sex, but I pushed him off. Tried to get him to watch a movie instead. About an hour later he tried again. But he was much bigger than me, and I was afraid of him hurting me or at least my script not having a chance, so I stiffened up and he took advantage of me. He took me into his room, I let him finish inside me, and then we went to sleep. I woke up many hours later with him already inside me again. I was so scared. I just wanted to go home and see my mom and..." Jimmy contorts his mouth. "I was afraid it was gonna happen again, so I snuck away before he woke up."

Oscar lets that linger. "How did you get home?"

"I called a Ridr." Jimmy shakes his head. "I took a shower as soon as I got home and just burst into tears. He knew where I worked. I had to call out sick for an entire week just to make sure he wouldn't abduct me or anything."

"That must've been horrible."

"I have so many nightmares. I have PTSD. I can't even watch *The Sins of Jack Branson*. I'm the only one in the world it seems that hasn't seen it yet, but I can't tell anyone why. Every time I hear 'It's a Sin' on the radio, I want to throw up."

Oscar lowers his eyes. "I understand you've attempted suicide."

Jimmy nods. "A few times." He pauses. "And I used drugs."

Oscar stares. "Drugs?"

"Heroin. I started shooting up in MacArthur Park."

Oscar's brows furrow a bit. "I'm sorry to hear that."

"The fucker's ad-libbing!" Drew cries. "C'mon! Call him out!"

"And obviously I can't go to the police with this," Jimmy says. "Drew would know it was me. I can't afford to lose this job. I have a shitty apartment. I don't have much. Why should I be the one to uproot my life?"

Oscar hesitates. "People are going to comment on the timing of these accusations."

"I admit, the news of *Branson*'s nominations was the catalyst for me to finally step up and go public with my story. I just can't stand the fact that a monster like that is gonna get rewarded by an industry I love so much. A liar. A manipulative charlatan who plays with people's emotions to get what he wants."

"Thank you so much for your bravery." Oscar looks at the camera. "We'll be right back after this ad break."

Kev turns off the TV. "You goddamn son of a bitch."

"He's a fucking liar!" Drew cries. "Anyone with a brain can see that!"

"No, I believe you," Kev says with angry sarcasm. "No one else will. And now you got forcing coke and vodka onto a minor to apologize for!"

"I didn't buy vodka! I got him room temp Guinness, only because I knew he'd hate it. And I never did coke with him! He wanted to! I had to force him away!"

"Why couldn't you just do what Gary said? Do you have any idea how FUCKED we are now because of you?!"

"I wasn't thinking," Drew whines. "I had just got demoted, and my family wouldn't stop calling, and I didn't have anyone but Theo, and he was in China. And I had a feeling he was young, but I didn't think he was *that* young." Drew shakes his head. "I was so lonely! If asked him his age, the night would have to be over. If I didn't know for sure, he could stay, and we could hang out, and..."

Kev grimaces. "What the fuck?"

"That wasn't me! You have no idea! I was so fucked up back then! That's not who I am! I-can't-I-can't-I-can't-I-can't explain it. I wasn't in my right mind, Kev. I was all over the place. Theo was manipulating me and... You have to believe me, Kev! You have to! You know me!"

Kev looks off with quivering lips. "You're releasing a statement tomorrow."

"I'm not condoning any of that bullshit!" Drew shouts. "He's a fucking liar!"

"You have to debunk it at least!"

"If I leave it be, they won't know what's true and what isn't!"

"THEY'LL BELIEVE EVERYTHING!" Kev hollers. "IT'S OSCAR FUCKING BLITZ!"

Drew paces faster, his face tensing like a pimple about to pop. "I didn't know, okay?! I didn't know it was gonna be him! Of course I would've—"

"Then do the fucking statement!"

"NOOOO!" Drew screams, the veins in his neck popping. "If I do nothing, it'll just go away!"

Kev scoffs. "How can you so fucking irrational?"

"I'm not irrational!" Drew yells, spit flying out. "I worked my ass off making *Branson* and now I have to just throw it all away because I didn't want to read some amateur's piece of shit screenplay?! No fucking way! That was all bullshit! People can smell bullshit! They'll know none of this makes sense!"

"Grow the fuck up," Kev whines. "You fucked a kid, asshole! You fucked a fucking kid! And now you're fucking us over! Own up to it before it gets any worse!"

"I'M NOT A FUCKING CHILD!" Drew screams, his whole body red, muscles popping, veins bulging. "I'M SMART AND HONORABLE AND INTELLIGENT AND MATURE AND BRAVE AND I'M A FUCKING HOT PIECE OF ASS AND JIMMY'S A FUCKING LIAR AND A CUNT AND A FAGGOT AND HE ONLY CARES ABOUT HIMSELF AND HE DOESN'T GET TO GET AWAY WITH THIS!" Drew smacks the side of his head, one hand at a time, alternating, as hard as he can. He lets out a guttural roar.

Kev watches all of this, his heart broken with pity.

"THIS CAN'T BE HAPPENING TO ME!" Drew roars, his face wincing in pain. "WHY IS THIS HAPPENING TO ME?! I DIDN'T..." Drew suddenly stops talking, his face going numb. He wobbles on his feet.

"Drew!" Kev cries.

Drew vomits all over the floor. He falls on all fours and vomits some more. Kev looks away, paralyzed at the sight. Drew's knee slides a bit on the vomit, a loud squeak. He pukes some more, loose wet chunks puddling across the hardwood.

Kev races into the kitchen. Grabs a roll of paper towels.

"Oh God!' Drew sobs in between retches. "I hate this so much!" He vomits more.

"Just lie down." Kev tries fruitlessly to move Drew's sturdy frame. "It's just stress. You have to calm down."

"I gotta clean this up," Drew whispers.

"I'll do that. Just go lie down."

"I'm cleaning it up," Drew angrily slurs. "I'm quite capable of doing things, you know. I'm not a fucking child."

"I know you're not. Just let me clean it up. You go lie down."

Drew looks up at Kev, spittle hanging out of his mouth.

"I'll take care of it," Kev says softly. "Just take care of yourself."

Drew exhales, completely exhausted. "Okay." Drew stumbles to his feet, revealing a vomit trail all the way down the front of his muscle tank. He opens his mouth as if to say something. Waddles over to the bedroom instead. He strips. Slips into bed. Lays on his side.

Kev calmly knocks on the bedroom door an hour later. "How're you doing?"

Drew frowns in bed, his naked lower half covered. "I am so sorry, Kev. That's so unbelievably disgusting on every level."

Kev approaches the bed and sits by Drew's legs. "I shouldn't have riled you up like that."

"It's not your fault. It's the week-old sushi I scarfed down after drinking Scotch on an empty stomach for the past ten hours." Drew laughs at that.

"Even still, I'm sorry," Kev whispers. "As bad as this is for me, I can't imagine how bad this must be for you. I wonder if I'd do the same thing in your shoes."

Drew nods, his eyes hollow. "I'm never drinking again. I swear on my mother's grave, I will never touch a drop of alcohol again. It's gonna be just seltzer from here on out."

"I'm sure you can still drink in moderation."

"No way. I know what Domergue tastes like in reverse now."

Kev nods with a smile.

Drew frowns. "I'm sorry," he whispers.

Kev folds his hands, looking off. "What do we do now?"

Drew hesitates. "I used to work for Oscar."

Kev raises his brows. "Blitz?"

"Right after the internship buckled. I was one of his photographers. We were really good friends too." Drew frowns, his heart breaking with nostalgia. "He's from money. Big money. Nuclear scientist money. It's how he pays for his show. He doesn't care about ratings. He only puts out episodes when he has a story worthy of one. Some years he puts out twenty, some years six, but he can afford to keep working at a loss because that show is the one thing he loves more than anything in the world. And that show wouldn't have the hold it has on this town if it weren't for the fact that he's never made shit up. He loves the fact that everyone believes what he says, that he doesn't have to resort to ratings pushes and sensationalism. It makes him feel like he's better than everyone else. #MeToo was huge for him. He hit green for the first time ever, but since then he hasn't had much to go on. Everyone's more careful at covering their tracks. And now cable's not really a thing anymore so he's switched to Streamer and his views just keep getting worse and worse. He hasn't had a legit studio audience since 2019. I recognized those guys. He's been using the same seat fillers for the past eighteen years. He could've given up and started lying long ago, even if just to get real asses back in the seats, but he hasn't. Why would he start now?"

"Even if there's only ten people watching on average, that's still ten people that believe everything Jimmy just said. All it takes is one."

"That's not what I'm saying, I'm saying Oscar *doesn't know*. He doesn't know because Jimmy's lying to him too, and it's only a matter of time before Oscar and his fact checkers find out Jimmy's story doesn't add up."

Kev furrows his brow slightly. "I don't know..."

"If it's not already buried because no one's watching, Oscar just might pull the episode himself just to save face. He's done it before. George Takei. Jussie Smollett."

"We can't do nothing, Drew."

"But if we release a statement, that will only give the interview more exposure because of the Streisand Effect. It'll become a bigger story *because* we went out of our way to say something. I'm at the center of this. I have the final say, and I don't care. I don't feel like I have to say something just because. I'll get through this just fine. I worked too damn hard on *Branson* to just piss it all away now that we're at the finish line. Call me naive, but I truly believe truth will prevail."

Kev sighs. "Then we'll play it by ear." He stands. "But I should stay here tonight."

"I'll be fine. It's out of my system now."

"Not that." Kev gives him a friendly smile. "I don't think you should be dealing with this alone."

Drew smiles weakly. "Thank you."

Kev nods. "I'll make you some toast." He walks into the other room.

Drew moves his knees to his chest, a horrible frown on his face, his mind drifting back. Before the Not That Nutty days. Before the Nut That Nut days.

The *Oscar Blitz* days.

WHALE

Cockroaches, Twinkies and Cher

Gene the Housekeeper polishes the wooden table, pondering weak and weary as he listens to an audiobook of a quaint and curious volume of forgotten lore, when suddenly there came a tapping, as of someone gently rapping, rapping at George Clooney's foyer door. He pockets his AirPods, puts down the Pledge can and microfiber cloth, and cautiously opens the large mahogany door.

The gentleman caller is wearing a rough and rugged union suit and utility belt of contractor tools. The nametag patch on his breast spells "Carl" in red cursive thread. Carl wears thick black frames on the bridge his nose, like one of those silly Groucho Marx disguises. Gene can see Carl is definitively muscled, his biceps and shoulders pressing into his sleeves like a slim fit. Most curious of all was Carl's hair, a patch of his naturally brown bangs dyed crimson red.

"Hello, I'm Carl Vanderbilt with Roger's Roofs," Whale says cordially. "I spoke to you on the phone about an hour ago."

Gene stares accusingly. "I didn't talk to anyone."

"Maybe it was someone else then."

"I'm the only one here."

Whale half-frowns. "I'm sorry. That must've been Morton Nemechek next door."

"What is it you want?"

"I'm here to do Mr. Clooney's roof inspection."

"He's already had the roof inspected."

"And he scheduled a follow-up appointment."

"I don't know of any appointment."

Whale sighs. "Look, Rog told me to come out here and do a follow-up. I just do what he says."

Gene hesitates. "Rog, huh?"

"I don't wanna start anything, sir. Just let me get through today's appointments. I'm already way behind."

Gene looks off. "I'm gonna have to call Rog and confirm."

Whale nods. "Do your thing."

Gene reluctantly pulls out his cell. "It's not my house, you know?"

"I completely understand."

Gene taps the contact info for Roger's Roofs. The dial tone rings. "Yes, hi, this is Gene Applebaum over at 44 Sycamore. I need to speak to Rog." Gene sighs, lowering the phone. "Bitch put me on hold."

"He's probably at lunch," Whale says. "I can give you his cell if you want. He usually answers right away."

Gene hesitates. Puts the phone to his ear, the distorted version of Vivaldi's Spring hurting his eardrum. He huffs and hangs up. "Okay, go on." Gene hands over the phone. Whale rapid-dials the number. Hits Call. Gene puts the phone back to his ear.

"Rog here," Cashew says over the phone.

"Hey Rog, it's Gene Applebaum at 44 Sycamore."

"Everything okay over there?"

"Yeah."

"Carl make it there alright?"

Gene glances at Whale's nametag. "Yeah."

"That's good. Don't keep him too long, you hear? He's a bit behind for the day."

Gene nods. "I won't."

"What's up?" Cashew asks.

Gene sighs. "Nothing. Just wanted to check in."

"Alright. Have a good one, Gene."

"You too. Enjoy your lunch."

"Thanks man." Cashew hangs up.

Gene pockets his phone. "Sorry for doubting."

"I completely understand," Whale says.

Gene steps aside. Whale walks in, looking around in wonder. "I'm afraid I'm gonna have to be with you the whole time," Gene says reluctantly. "Mr. Clooney is very particularly about who he lets into his home."

"Whatever works for him." Whale starts up the stairs. Gene follows close behind.

Whale beelines to the east facing bedroom and onto the balcony. He marvels the gorgeous Studio City panorama before him, full of trees and equally private multi-million-dollar homes. He casually glances at 42 Sycamore, Morton Nemechek's house, the curtains open.

"You got everything you need?" Gene asks, arms crossed at the doorway with eyes squinting in the sun.

"Just gotta survey first." Whale unclips the tape measure off his utility belt. Measures the gutters just above the balcony door. "Thirty-five," he murmurs, crooking his mouth to the side, faking calculations. He pulls a screwdriver from his pocket. "They swore Kavanaugh in after all. Can you believe that?"

"Thank God."

Whale smirks for a split second. "What a load of bullshit they put him though, huh?"

"You're telling me."

"I'm so sick of the mainstream media, you know? Just let the poor guy go already."

"They only hate him because he's a Trump appointee."

"Hear hear." Whale taps the gutter with the screwdriver. Hollow.

"Why can't they just open their fucking eyes, you know? I've actually seen 'Fuck Donald Trump' bumper stickers. *That's* deplorable!"

"I know."

"He's the fucking President of the United States! Show some fucking respect!"

"And all those people on Twitter asking for someone to assassinate him?"

"It's disgusting." Gene rolls his throat, both annoyed and a bit relieved. "You know what I really can't stand? All that conspiracy bullshit about Russians meddling with the election."

"They're just sore losers."

"They'd rather cry voter fraud than admit Hillary lost fair and square."

"They need to respect their commander-in-chief no matter what," Whale continues. "If they don't like where the country's headed, they should just fucking leave."

"I completely agree." Gene stops a moment to think. "They wouldn't even have a problem if there was a Democrat in office doing the same thing."

"They're all a bunch of crybaby phonies."

"Exactly!" Gene scoffs. "Thank you!"

Whale pockets his screwdriver. "I'm gonna hop up there now. You coming with?"

Gene waves a hand. "Nah, you're good man."

"You sure?"

"Yeah dude. You're fine. Do your thing."

Whale nods. "Thanks."

Gene walks into the hall. Spins around. "Hey, you want a beer or something? What Clooney doesn't know won't kill him."

"Probably on my way out."

"You do you, bro." Gene walks out and races down the stairs.

Whale smirks to himself. "Jacob, you Inglourious Basterd." He pulls a camera out of his hip pocket. Extends the telephoto lens. Leans over the balcony, adjusting the focus.

Through the view finder, he can discern a fully dressed sixty-one-year-old through Morton Nemechek's rear window making out with a nineteen-year-old perfect 10 model, Nemechek's wrinkled hands sliding down into her black lace panties. Whale takes a photo. Flips the shutter. Takes another. Flips the shutter.

Two days later. Cashew flips through a yellow file of photos in a booth at Kathy Wood's in Beverley Hills. First base on the sofa. Anal in the kitchen. Scat play in the master bathroom. "You fucking hit gold, dude."

Whale checks his watch. "You gave him the right address?"

"Stop squirming. He'll be here." Cashew hands the file back to Whale. "How'd you get the housekeeper to leave you unsupervised for so long?"

"I made him think I was a Trump supporter."

"That's it?"

"I'm telling you, you get a Trumper to think you're a Trumper too and that motherfucker will believe ANYTHING." Whale puts the yellow file into his messenger bag.

Cashew notices a green file beside it. "What's that?"

"Last night."

Cashew pulls out the green file. Furrows his brow at the top photo. Morton Nemechek in a fancy French restaurant sitting across from an old woman, staring at her with a soft romantic smile. "Why'd you take these?"

"If breaking the marriage doesn't work, we can guilt the mistress with these. Make her feel like a real homewrecker."

"She doesn't mean anything to him. He'll just get another piece of ass."

"Rejection hurts no matter where it's from."

Cashew hands the green file back. "Whatever." He makes eye contact with a cross-faced Morton Nemechek heading right for them. "I do the talking."

"Of course," Whale murmurs.

Morton stops at their booth. "Why am I not shocked?"

"We were wondering where you were," Cashew says.

"Tell Oscar to go fuck himself." Morton turns to leave.

"I wouldn't do that if I were you."

Morton slowly turns around. "I haven't done anything."

"We're not after you, Morton." Cashew gestures to seat across from them. "Oscar needs a favor."

"He's that desperate?"

"You want to know."

Morton sighs. Reluctantly sits across from Whale and Cashew. "I'm taking my wife to the movies in an hour."

"What are you seeing?"

"Does it matter?" Morton asks. "Come on. What's so urgent?"

"We need two tickets to the *Rigoletto* Gala."

Morton laughs, a dainty chuckle. "Please."

"It's in your best interest."

"It's impossible."

"How'd you get yours?"

Morton hesitates. "I was invited."

Cashew shrugs coldly.

Morton shakes his head. "Even if I wanted to give to them up, I'd never give them to you. I don't respond to threats." Morton stands. "Good day, gentlemen."

"What about your wife?" Cashew asks.

Morton halts. "What are you talking about?"

"She won't like what we got. Are two *Rigoletto* tickets really worth it?"

Morton unconsciously touches his wedding ring with his right hand. Whale sees this. Gasps.

"Sit down," Cashew says softly.

Morton sits. "You wouldn't."

"We've got photos of you and your mistress."

"Fuck you," Morton says with a hint of pain. "She doesn't deserve it."

"Give us the tickets by the end of the day."

Whale discreetly opens his bag and flips through the yellow file. Morton watches, his breath quickening. "You motherfuckers." He shakes his head. "There's no way. You're bluffing."

Cashew grabs the yellow folder. "You tell us."

Whale snatches the folder out of Cashew's hand. "Wait."

"What the fuck are you doing?"

Whale rapidly flips through the green folder. Looks at the pictures.

Morton scoffs. "Intimidating."

"You fucking retard!" Cashew hisses. "You're blowing it."

Whale pulls out the green folder. "Here."

"What are you doing?"

"This is it."

"No it isn't! What the fuck—?!"

"Just do it."

Cashew crosses his arms with a scowl.

Whale huffs. Hands the green folder to Morton himself.

Morton tentatively takes the green folder. Flips through the photos of him and that old woman in the French restaurant, his blood running cold. "Oh my God."

Cashew furrows his brow.

"You want your wife to find out about her?" Whale asks with sinister delight. "I doubt she'd take it well. She's so young. How could she understand?"

Morton's lips tremble. He closes the file. "You're monsters, you know that?"

"It's just a party," Whale eggs. "You'll catch the next one."

Cashew's eyes bounce from one file to the other, confused.

Morton frowns. Looks Whale in the eye. "You're going after Bronski, aren't you?"

Whale smiles. "Do the right thing."

Morton smashes his lips together. "Fine. Just get the son of a bitch."

Whale and Cashew walk backstage at *Oscar Blitz* to the office behind Studio 1. "You got 'em?" Oscar asks through the open door.

Whale hands over Morton Nemechek's Gala tickets. "We got 'em."

Oscar caresses the laminated passes. "My God."

"Clooney turned out to be waste of time."

"He's exaggerating," Cashew interjects.

"The nineteen-year-old was his wife," Whale says. "The old lady was the mistress."

Oscar raises his brows. "How perverse."

"To each their own."

Oscar smirks knowingly. "Indeed." He glances at Cashew. "You didn't know, I take it?"

"Who the fuck could've?" Cashew asks, a bit defensive.

"I did," Whale says.

Cashew pouts, lowering his gaze.

"Good thing," Oscar says. "Who knows when we'd have another chance at Bronski."

"Morton confirmed it too. He'll be there." Whale holds his hands behind his back. "I'll say our chances of catching him on Gala night are around 90%."

Oscars tosses the tickets onto his desk. "Black tie. No rentals. They'll spot it a mile away."

Whale nods. "Yes sir," Cashew says.

Oscar hesitates. "I'm thinking Pete's assisting Jacob on this."

"What?" Cashew asks. Whale awkwardly looks away.

"Pete hasn't had a big one in a while."

"Oscar, what the fuck?"

"You guys aren't joined at the hip. You can have assignments without each other."

"You've still got the Henderson Case," Whale reminds Cashew.

"Doesn't matter!" Cashew snaps. "I can do Bronski too and you know it."

"I've made my decision," Oscar says. "I've got a few calls to make, boys."

Cashew glares at Whale and steps out of the office.

Oscar waves Whale over. "I was thinking Merry's for Sunday."

"Ooh!" Whale whispers back. "I've heard such good things."

Cashew watches the two gab from afar, a bitter frown on his face.

Cashew slouches into his couch at his Northridge apartment, Whale returning from the kitchen with two open beers. "We did good, buddy."

Cashew takes his beer with a mopey frown. "Go fuck yourself."

Whale freezes. "What was that for?"

Cashew sips, facing away.

Whale tentatively sits beside Cashew. "Whatever it is, I'm sorry, alright?"

"You threw me under the fucking bus! You goddamn retard!"

Whale curls away like a wounded animal. "I didn't know."

"No, you never know! You stupid, *stupid* moron!"

"I said I was sorry!" Whale insists, his voice cracking.

Cashew exhales hard. "After all I've done for you."

"I know."

"But no, now you just wanna throw me aside."

Whale swallows. "I've been riding on your charity for almost a year now."

"Charity?" Cashew asks with a mocking scowl. "I didn't take you in because of charity! I did it because we're friends! At least I thought we were friends."

"We're still friends."

"How fucking dare you call that charity! It's what friends do! Friends help each other! They don't throw each other under the bus in front of their boss! They don't just decide one day to move out so they can find better friends!"

"That's not why."

"Sure sounds like it to me."

Whale sighs. "I don't know why he didn't want you on the Bronski Job."

"I know why he wanted you, Mr. Sunday Brunch."

Whale looks away.

Cashew scowls. "Drink your fucking beer already. You're making me nervous."

Whale reluctantly sips. "I don't want special treatment. If that's why he gave me the Bronski Job, I'm turning it down."

Cashew looks over calmly. "Really?"

"You know me. I don't do handouts."

Cashew nods, reinvigorated. "Alright." He holds the bottle to his lips, pausing to think. "I'll ask him tomorrow."

Whale frowns. "Thanks."

Cashew and Whale drink their beers in awkward silence.

JACOB

Mank

INT. WHITMAN UNIVERSITY - LITTLE BUILDING - SUITE 701 - DAY

Jacob walks out of his bedroom, laptop bag slung over his shoulder. He stops at the sight of Nich staring at the TV with the power off.

JACOB
You okay?

Nich doesn't budge, frowning with unblinking eyes.

JACOB (CONT'D)
I'm sorry about last night.

Nich doesn't react. Jacob nods to no one. Turns and leaves.

CUT TO:

INT. FILM IMMERSION - DAY

Students pass Jacob in a daze, worried looks on their faces. It's strangely quiet despite the number of people on the floor. CNN's on in the TV room, a gaggle of morose students watching Hillary giving her concession speech. A few more students sit with their backs on the glass, openly crying. More students sit in silence in the kitchen, uneasy hands clutching their cups of coffee and bowls of ramen.

TJ walks down the hall toward Jacob.

TJ
Hey Jake.

JACOB
Hey.

CUT TO:

INT. WHITMAN UNIVERSITY - LECTURE CLASSROOM - DAY

Jacob walks into his Images of the Disabled class. PROFESSOR WILLIAMS (40) stands by a blank whiteboard with a gloomy expression.

PROFESSOR WILLIAMS
(solemn)
Okay class, we're gonna start now.

Jacob sits, looking around uneasily. The rest of the students are sad too.

PROFESSOR WILLIAMS (CONT'D)
After the events of yesterday, I feel it's necessary to forgo the lesson and talk about what's happened. If doing so would make you uncomfortable in any way, feel free to let me know at any time and I will write a note so you can go recuperate somewhere else. Does anyone want me to do that at this time?

A few students with tears in their eyes gingerly raise their hands. Williams hands them pre-written notes from her pocket. Jacob's weirded out more than anything.

PROFESSOR WILLIAMS (CONT'D)
Anyone want to start?

MARGERIE WHIPSAW (22) raises her hand.

PROFESSOR WILLIAMS (CONT'D)
Yes Margerie?

"I just feel betrayed more than anything," Margerie says. "It's just the worst thing that could ever have happened, you know? It's not even him, per se, it's the fact that so many people support him. I'm already afraid to walk down the street because of catcallers, but now that he's President? They might do something to me because he encourages grabbing women like that."

Jacob leans back in his seat, sighing with a hint of annoyance.

CUT TO:

INT. WHITMAN UNIVERSITY - BIG BUILDING - DINING HALL - DAY

Jacob eats a chicken Caesar salad wrap by himself. The rest of the hall is filled with peak lunch traffic.

A group of activists stand in a clearing with signs with "NOT MY PRESIDENT" on them. Tabitha Maclean holds up a megaphone, preaching loudly at the captive audience:

"THE ELECTORAL COLLEGE WAS DESIGNED BY THE FOUNDING FATHERS AS A COMPROMISE TO GIVE SLAVE-HOLDING STATES IN THE SOUTH AS MUCH VOTING POWER AS THE CITIES IN THE NORTH! IT IS A RACIST, OUTDATED SYSTEM THAT NEEDS TO BE DISMANTLED AND DESTROYED!"

Jacob begrudgingly pulls out his phone, tuning Tabitha out as best he can. Facebook, normally a place to post ugly baby pictures and vacation photos, is now a political mess. Memes involving a weeping Statue of Liberty. Anarchists like Nich posting poorly spellchecked infographs accusing Russia of fixing the election. #NotMyPresident everywhere.

Mixed in between are posts from his sister Melanie and his father Dennis mocking the "snowflakes" using cringy transphobic caricatures with artificially colored hair to mock half of the voting population. And the way they're intercut across his feed, Leftie, Rightie, Leftie, Rightie, makes it look like they're fighting each other.

Jacob opens Reddit. Just five seconds of staring makes him want to vomit, complete strangers perpetuating all that BS.

CUT TO:

INT. WHITMAN UNIVERSITY - CARY GRANT BUILDING - LIBRARY - DAY

Jacob sits with JOYCE BENSON (21) and NORM VICTOR (22), classmates of his from Human Health and Disease, as they work on a group project.

JOYCE
Did you get the link to the Google doc?

JACOB
Let me check. Just one sec.

"NOT MY PRESIDENT! NOT MY PRESIDENT!"

All three of them look out the window.

NORM
Oh God, now what?

Jacob gets up. Looks down at Boylston Street below.

JACOB
There's hundreds of them.

JOYCE
So much for a distraction-free environment.

All three awkwardly look at each other. Jacob leans in.

JACOB
Am I the only one that thinks everyone's overreacting? I voted for Clinton, by the way.

JOYCE
Oh, me too.

NORM
I voted for Johnson, but I'm with you. This is just ridiculous.

JOYCE
What's with all the 9/11 comparisons?

JACOB
I know. If it actually happened on 11/9, I'd kinda understand, but Election Day was 11/8. Immortalizing the day AFTER Election Day just to get a 9/11 metaphor is a bit of a stretch.

NORM
Not to mention incredibly disrespectful.

JOYCE
Especially considering Trump winning is only a bad thing for half the country at most, and not even that.

NORM
I found this hilarious anti-Hillary meme on Twitter, but I'm afraid to share it on Facebook because I don't everyone to think I hate her.

JACOB
The whole campus was Pro-Bernie six months ago. What the fuck is everyone on?

JOYCE
We really should say something.

JACOB
I know.

NORM
We really should.

The three of them sit in silence.

CUT TO:

INT. DISCUSSION CLASSROOM - NIGHT

Jacob walks into his Narrative Ethics class to see all the chairs, normally in rows, lined along the perimeter of the room. Jacob sighs harshly and takes a chair.

PROFESSOR HINKLEY (45) goes one-by-one to each student and gently talks to them. Ten minutes later, Hinkley finally gets around the circle to Jacob.

PROFESSOR HINKLEY
Are you okay, Jacob?

JACOB
I'm fine.

PROFESSOR HINKLEY
Is there anything you need?

JACOB
No.

PROFESSOR HINKLEY
I just want to let you know that if you need to talk to someone, I have a list of on-campus mental health services on my desk. Feel free to take one at any time.

JACOB
Okay.

PROFESSOR HINKLEY
Okay.

Professor Hinkley moves on to the next chair. Jacob eyerolls hard.

JUMP CUT TO:

LATER

Professor Hinkley stands before his class.

PROFESSOR HINKLEY
Instead of discussing The Lobster as originally scheduled, I wanted to spend class today talking about what happened.

Jacob crosses his arms, huffing.

PROFESSOR HINKLEY (CONT'D)
I'm sure everyone is worried and anxious, whether it be about yourself or someone you love, so I feel we should at least acknowledge it. If you are uncomfortable in any way, please ask me for a note at any time and I'll allow you to be dismissed.
(pause)
Who wants to start?

EMILY HYMN (22) raises her hand.

PROFESSOR HINKLEY (CONT'D)
Emily, go ahead.

Emily takes a deep breath.

EMILY
For one of my other classes, I went to a Republican rally last night and... I have to admit, I was surprised at how polite they were and how civil. They were very cooperative and answered all of my questions... And I thought to myself, maybe I was wrong about these guys. They didn't seem racist or cruel or anything like I had imagined. And that made me feel better about being there.

Jacob softens.

"But when they were counting the votes," Emily continues, holding back tears, "and Trump started winning, everyone started getting rowdy and excited and cheering and chanting 'Trump' and 'USA' and I just got so scared. What was going to happen to me? I was a woman in a room full of male Trump supporters and it started getting too..."

She stops talking, too overwhelmed. Jacob discreetly puffs out his lips.

PROFESSOR HINKLEY
It's okay. Would someone else like to say something?

ERROL CAVIL (22) raises his hand.

PROFESSOR HINKLEY
Errol?

"I'm very anxious about Thanksgiving," Errol says. "Seeing my family. They're all Trump supporters and they're already fighting with me on Facebook. I can't imagine what they'll say to me when I'm there. I know they can't help themselves, but I also know I can't stay here, and... It's awful. I-I can't face them. I can't."

PROFESSOR HINKLEY
I'm so sorry to hear that.

JACOB
(raising hand)
Can I say something, Professor?

PROFESSOR HINKLEY
Of course, Jacob. What's on your mind?

JACOB
Before anyone jumps to conclusions, I voted for Hillary. But I have to be honest, and I don't mean any disrespect to anyone by me saying this, but this is my third class today and every single one of them has been just like this and I can't keep quiet about what I feel anymore.

PROFESSOR HINKLEY
Say what you want, Jacob, this is a safe space.

JACOB
That's my point, Professor, I don't really think it is. At least not for my opinion.

Professor Hinkley hesitates.

PROFESSOR HINKLEY
It's okay. Speak your mind.

JACOB
I feel this entire doom and gloom over Trump getting elected is a complete overreaction.

Silence throughout the room.

JACOB (CONT'D)
That's just how I feel. I think anyone who sees Trump's win like the sky is falling is just as bad as the Conservatives freaking out about gay marriage leading to pedophilia or religious types hating rock music and Harry Potter.

"Have you heard the shit he says about women and Muslims?" Darryl Calculus blurts. "People hear that and think it's okay, and it's not okay."

"He didn't win the popular vote," Hannah Wedgwood exclaims. "And there is proof of Russians influencing the outcome of the election."

PROFESSOR HINKLEY
Guys, one at a time.

JACOB
Trump's a blowhard that represents everything Liberals despise. I'm just as disappointed as you are that we have an inexperienced reality TV star playboy in the White House, but I'm sorry, he won fair and square. I'm sure if Trump lost and Hillary had won by the same margin, Fox News would be bitching and moaning right now about election fraud conspiracies and overturning the election in the Supreme Court. Hillary conceded her loss gracefully, so why don't we? Chanting "Not My President" in the street is only making us look like crybaby sore losers.

"The Electoral College is an outdated system based on institutional racism," Celeste Vamoose throws in.

JACOB
I was in the DH too, Celeste. And how's the Electoral College racist all of a sudden? That's how every President got elected, including Obama. But now that Hillary lost it's suddenly outdated?
(to Hannah)
And blaming Russia for fixing the election is moronic. Hillary lost of her own accord. She's a

```
        polarizing figure. A lot of people hate her. "Pokémon
        Go! to the polls," anyone? C'mon. And even if the
        Russians really did buy those political ads, and I'm
        not saying they didn't, that's not fixing an
        election. Voters still voted.

KATIE BEDDING (22) raises a gentle hand.

                          KATIE
        I understand your point, Jacob, and I feel you have
        the right to your own opinion.

                          JACOB
        Thank you.
```

"But considering you're white, cis, and passing for straight," Katie continues, "I don't think you have the right to call other people's fears unsound."

```
                          JACOB
        Gay marriage overturning would affect me very much.
        And I have plenty of trans and POC friends here. I
        don't want them to be hurt if the worst happens. Just
        because I'm advising critical thinking instead of
        treating Trump's win like a giant alien squid just
        crash-landed into Times Square doesn't mean I'd be
        okay with Trump acting like a dictator. I resent your
        implication that I would!

                          PROFESSOR HINKLEY
        Everyone, settle down.

                          JACOB
        I voted for Hillary too, Katie. I did what I had to
        do because you all made me think that'd be enough.
        Now I have to let her loss ruin my day or else I'm a
        Trump supporter? When the fuck did that become a
        rule?
```

"Didn't your boyfriend vote for Trump?" Tracie Sternway asks.

```
Everyone reacts from shock.
```

"There you go," Katie murmurs. "That explains it."

```
                          JACOB
        Leave Stewie out of this. That has nothing to do with
        anything. I'm my own person.
                  (pause)
        But for the record, he is thirty-one years older than
        me. Being a Trumper is typical for his demographic.
        And he's not stupid. He was alive when Trump was
        making headlines in the 80s. He knows who he voted
        for. And he knew Hillary when she was First Lady. He
        has firsthand experience of what they were like. We
        don't. We only know what we know about them from
        history books and memes and John Oliver and SNL and
        CNN and Fox and all that bullshit, not to mention our
        incredibly biased parents.

AUTUMN LINSEED (22) raises their hand, looking at Jacob.

                          AUTUMN
        You ever heard of false balance?

Jacob hesitates.

                          JACOB
        No, what is that?

                          AUTUMN
        It's when someone makes an issue appear more balanced
        than it really is. Journalists use it all the time as
        a way to generate misinformation, but it's also used
        by people in an attempt to be unbiased. A lot of
```

scholars did it after the Holocaust when they dared to ask "What if it was justified?" Or nowadays anytime Climate Change is brought up, "What if it isn't real after all?"

JACOB
I did not know that had a name.

"Trump supporters want white people to be in charge again," Autumn explains. "They want to make it illegal to be a minority and they want Trump to be a dictator for life. I know you just want to be unbiased in this, but adding nuance to something so objectively good and evil is the reason Trump got elected in the first place."

JACOB
How are you in college? None of that is going to happen! None of that has EVER happened in the history of this country!

"Doesn't mean it won't happen."

JACOB
Yes it does! Of course Trump can theoretically start WWIII with a tweet and start bombing Democratic cities if he wanted too and make The Handmaid's Tale and V For Vendetta real life, but he won't! Enough people in the government aren't fucking morons. They will stop him if he tries. It's called checks and balances.

"He'll just rewrite the Constitution and get rid of term limits and the Supreme Court."

JACOB
No he can't! God, do you really think he's the first President that wished checks and balances weren't a thing? If that was even possible, someone would've done it by now!

PROFESSOR HINKLEY
Jacob.

JACOB
He's not even President yet! He's the President-fucking-elect! Why don't we just wait until he's actually President before we start jumping to conclusions!

"Have you been to his rallies? Renita Mole asks.

JACOB
Have you?

Renita doesn't react.

JACOB (CONT'D)
Guys, half the country voted for him! Our parents, our neighbors, my boyfriend, one of my suitemates, they're not stupid. Most people aren't stupid. They picked Trump because they have a different opinion than we do about what this country needs. That's all he is. An opinion. Maybe we need to stop cutting out people that have that opinion and start asking ourselves why. Maybe, just maybe, we're in the wrong here. This is an ethics class, right? Is it ethical for us to cut out anyone with an opinion that isn't blue all the way down the ballot? That's censorship, isn't it? Aren't we the ones that hate censorship?

ANNA FLICK (21) raises her hand.

ANNA
No one's censoring anything.

JACOB
Oh really.

ANNA
Like you said, half the country voted for him. I love my mom more than anything and she voted for him.

Jacob hesitates.

JACOB
Mine too.

"But their opinions and beliefs fundamentally harm people and encourage others to marginalize women and people of color," Anna continues. "Freedom of speech doesn't mean freedom of consequences, and Conservatives shouldn't be allowed to spread hateful rhetoric around people that disagree."

JACOB
But if they really disagree, what's the harm in hearing it? Unless of course you're afraid that'll convince middle-ground voters to flip sides to one they feel better suits them, to which I say you don't actually hate Conservatives, do you? Just as long as they don't act on it.

Anna cringes so hard. Autumn is disgusted. Lots of chatter and dissing all around. Professor Hinkley meekly stands.

PROFESSOR HINKLEY
Jacob, I think you've talked enough. Let someone else have the floor. Courtney?

Katie flashes Jacob a satisfied brow bump. Jacob sinks into his seat.

CUT TO:

INT. STEWIE'S BOSTON APARTMENT - NIGHT

Jacob angrily paces, furiously biting his nails. Stewie sits on the couch.

JACOB
What is wrong with these people?!

STEWIE
Stop biting your nails!

JACOB
Stop telling me what to do!

Jacob keeps biting. Stewie scrolls through his phone.

STEWIE
You can't be that shocked.

JACOB
I'm okay with different views. I can handle different. Different's fine. Believe whatever you wanna believe. Just be consistent! Don't believe one thing and change halfway!

STEWIE
I hear ya.

JACOB
I haven't changed at all. I believe exactly what I did yesterday. But now… what? Everyone changed on me, didn't they? I'm not changing with them, is that it?

STEWIE
They're just bullies.

JACOB
Don't they realize they acting EXACTLY like the Conservatives?! How is it so obvious to me and not to anyone else?

STEWIE
They're all brainwashed.

JACOB
The media was only exaggerating all that about Trump to get him to lose the election, but now that he's won? They gotta keep riding the wave they started in the first place.

STEWIE
And it's the professors too. Colleges are Liberal breeding grounds.

JACOB
Any environment that teaches people to think beyond what they know is inherently Liberal. Conservatives prioritize honor and faith in institutions.

STEWIE
You're telling me your professors aren't teaching you guys to hate Trump?

JACOB
No! In fact, they make sure we don't jump to emotional conclusions, making undercooked judgments and all that. Why do you think I'm so devil's advocate and curious all the time? You know me, I follow the curriculum to a T.

STEWIE
Then why doesn't anyone else?

JACOB
Because the professors spent the whole day coddling everybody. They know the students are misquoting them, they have to, but they can't tell them they're wrong. Whitman's supposed to be a safe space where students think for themselves. Correcting their emotional ramblings would only subvert that philosophy.

STEWIE
So you're saying they're enabling extremism and don't even know it?

JACOB
Exactly. This whole thing's been a ticking time bomb from the start.

Jacob plops next to Stewie on the couch.

JACOB (CONT'D)
It's better I know, right?

Stewie tosses his phone aside with a frown.

JACOB (CONT'D)
What's up, Daddy?

STEWIE
Abby canceled Thanksgiving.

JACOB
What?!

STEWIE
Ron, Gabby, Christine, and Gary have been ganging up on Abby because she's the most vocal Anti-Trumper, and now she's offended and doesn't want anyone coming to her house.

JACOB
The whole "vote the opposite of your parents" thing really gets around, doesn't it?

STEWIE
Not for me, Ron, and Christine. Abby's fifteen years younger, remember. She's a whole other world compared to us.

JACOB
And she's keeping you from seeing your mom.

STEWIE
(emotional)
I really wanted Mom to meet you.

Jacob sidles closer to Stewie. They hold each other.

STEWIE (CONT'D)
I miss my family, Baby Boy. It's bad enough I'm 300 miles away from my brother, but now Abby and Mark took Ma down to Florida and I'm not even allowed to see her because of motherEFFING BULLcrap!

Jacob sighs.

JACOB
I hate seeing you like this.

STEWIE
I hate feeling like this. About my family, no less.

They sit in silence.

JACOB
Does this happen every four years and I was too young notice, or is this really as bad as I think it is?

STEWIE
This isn't good. Not good at all.

WHALE

Mutual Assured Destruction

Oscar waits patiently in Studio 1 for rehearsal to begin, Leon applying makeup for the camera tests. "Can we talk a moment?" Cashew asks, approaching Oscar's chair.

Oscar peeks one eye open. "Can it wait?"

"No it cannot."

"Give us a moment, Leon."

Leon nods. Carries his kit away.

Oscar takes a deep breath and sits up. "Yes, Theo, what is it?"

Cashew hesitates. "How am I doing?"

Oscar blinks. "That wasn't what I was expecting."

"Maybe you've got the wrong opinion of me."

Oscar stares a bit. "You're fine. If you were suddenly shitty, I'd fire you."

"You have no problems with my work?"

"Of course I don't."

"Then why is Jacob on the Bronski Job and not me?"

Oscar scratches his cheek. "Surprised you didn't say, 'Why is *Pete* on the Bronski Job and not me.'"

Cashew looks away.

"So that's what this is about," Oscar realizes. "It was never about you and Jacob working together."

"Just tell me why."

Oscar shrugs. "Jacob actually likes opera."

"So?"

"It's more his scene, don't you think?"

"Isn't it better to have the guy not interested in opera for the opera job?"

"They're not watching the opera."

"No, they're watching Maestro Bronski rape a soloist backstage, and maybe you shouldn't have the gay guy record all that. We're supposed to be objective in the field."

Oscar glares at Cashew. "The fuck are you implying?"

"You know what I mean."

Oscar chuckles.

"What?" Cashew asks, a bit accusatory.

Oscar shakes his head. "I'm just gonna say it."

"Please."

"Jacob's my best guy." Oscar lays calm eyes on Cashew. "By far."

Cashew's blood chills. "You don't have to be so blunt about it."

"You almost fucked up the job of the year. The ones I'm putting on Bronski have to think on their feet in plain view of the most fucked up abuser in classical music and also the wealthy elite who knows not only what he's doing to those boys but do nothing to stop him. They would have to catch a professional who knows how to evade detection *in the act* with only a small window to achieve it. I know my team, I know their limits, and you cannot be trusted with that kind of responsibility."

Cashew tightens his lips. "I'm sorry."

"Stop taking this personally. It could happen to anyone."

Cashew nods.

Oscar waves Leon back over. "Good talk."

Cashew stays put as Leon resumes his application.

Oscar peeks an eye open again. "Yes?"

"I looked up Merry's yesterday. Looks pretty swank."

"That's because it is."

"Can I come with?"

Oscar opens both eyes. Looks at Cashew.

Cashew shrugs meekly. "Just seems like fun is all."

Oscar stands up. "Just wait here, please," he tells Leon. Oscar grabs Cashew by the shoulder, leading him toward the backstage door, a much more private area. "You're not invited. The brunches are for Jacob and I, no one else."

"Every Sunday for the past year? Why does he get special treatment?"

"It has nothing to do with work. We're friends."

"Sounds like a conflict of interest to me. Why do you get to play favorites? That's not fair. And Jacob would agree with me."

Oscar stares at Cashew. "You already work together. You have him all to yourself at home. He only gets two hours a week away from you. Can't you let him have *that*?"

Bile hits Cashew's throat. "What the fuck are you saying?"

Oscar's gaze lingers a moment. He steps away.

"It was your idea for him to move out, wasn't it?" Cashew calls after Oscar. "HEY! I'M TALKING TO YOU!"

Oscar sits back in his chair, a sly smile on his face.

Three days later. Oscar and Whale sit outside at Merry's, Whale in a flattering polo with stretch sleeves hugging his biceps and Oscar in a period-accurate kimono, halfway through their second mimosa pitcher.

"I've never been to the New Beverley before," Whale tells him. "Apparently Quentin himself pops in every once in a while."

"Sounds like a good time."

"You ever watch both *Kill Bills* back-to-back?"

"No."

"It's definitely harder to do with *Volume One*'s epilogue."

"And that's not in this version?"

"No. You don't find out her daughter's still alive until she shows up at the end."

Oscar nods. "It's been so long since I've seen it."

"It was my Tarantino gateway drug." Whale smiles. "I've always wanted to see *The Whole Bloody Affair*. It's not even on Blu-ray. You can only see it at the New Beverley and only once or twice a year."

Brad, a handsome gym bro with Clark Kent hair, approaches their table. "You guys want anything else?"

"No, we're good," Whale says.

"Like the shirt, bro."

Whale looks down. "Thanks. Express."

Brad nods. "How much you curl?"

"45lb dumbbells."

"Not bad."

Oscar looks at both of them, smirking to himself.

"Be right back with your bill, fellas." Brad taps Whale's shoulder as he walks away.

"That's something," Oscar teases.

Whale rolls his eyes. "Think I've had enough fun this week."

Oscar raises his brows. "Oh that's right!"

"Don't bother. It sucked."

"What?! How come?"

Whale covers half of his face. "It was so *weird*."

"Where was it?"

"Battery Park."

"Set the scene. What are you wearing?"

"Red sleeveless hoodie. Tight black jean shorts. Red cap. Red shoes.

"Nice."

"I know, I looked like such a dish. Anyway, a cute blond guy comes up to me. Really short. I like short guys. And young. And that threw me off a bit, you know, cause I always assumed cruising was an old man's game."

"How young we talking?"

"Late twenties, early thirties. And he's really cute, but the whole time he's leading me back there he's very no-nonsense. We kiss for maybe two seconds before he whips it out, so I get on the ground and start sucking him, but I just can't get hard. And then my gums start bleeding."

"Your GUMS start bleeding?!"

Whale laughs, shaking his head. "It was awful! I was just trying to catch up with the guy or get hard or something, and then I'm all worried about my gingivitis and how I must look to him. Anything blood-related is such a buzzkill to gay guys. But then he just cums onto the grass, pulls up his pants and walks away."

Oscar exhales. "Yikes."

"It was so embarrassing." Whale refills their mimosas. "I used to be so carefree about random fucks. I feel like a square now."

"How was it when you were with Stewie?"

"He was always weirded out by anal. All the HIV talk in the news back then really fucked him up. And he's one of those Aught Gay bottomphobes. He never wanted to try it. Never even blew me either."

"Never?"

"He tried once, but he wasn't good at it."

"So all you did was blow him?"

"Yeah, but I liked that." Whale pauses. "You know, until the guy in the woods, I never realized I wasn't really into the physical sensation of sex. It's so messy and high maintenance. Guys use lube for everything back there. The bottom has to spend hours cleaning himself out beforehand. And then there's HIV we still got to worry about. And poppers are just a mess to the brain cells. And then you got all those guys too closeted or virginal to do their hot fantasies justice, or the ones too slutty and promiscuous to really make you feel special. I wanna be adored, obsessed over, lusted for, ogled. That's why I always went for older guys. Even when I was fat, they were easy to snag. I thought being hot now was gonna make it easier for me. Now there's a whole new set of problems. You got ripped six-pack dudes who think I'm still too fat, plus all the swole gym rats that don't want anything to do with me, and everyone else thinks I'm just so out of their league. Even if I meet a guy who's super into me and I'm super into him, they end up being like that guy in the woods that just wants to get off. All I am to him is porn." Whale sighs. "Where's the theatricality these days?"

"Porn."

Whale scoffs. "Guess that's on me then."

"Speaking of getting fucked, how's the apartment search going?"

Whale shrugs. "I did find one. A second-floor condo in Marina Del Rey. Great space. A balcony. Lots of windows. A view of Venice and everything."

"Beachside. Not bad."

"I really like it. And it's only been on the market for a little bit. There's not many offers yet." Whale pauses. "And my credit score's pretty good too, considering. My mom opened a credit line in my name when I was sixteen. She racked up some purchases and kept paying on my behalf."

Oscar stretches his face, shocked. "That's incredibly wise."

"She's a CPA. She knows these things."

Oscar chuckles a bit. "Good thing."

Whale sighs, a glum frown forming. "I don't know. I can put 20% down well enough, but that's really it at the moment."

"Good thing you got that Bronski money coming."

"I've already spent it on the car. I wish I found it before. I might not be able to get a mortgage now."

Oscar hesitates. "I can always co-sign."

Whale stares. "Oscar."

"Give me the papers. I'll do it. I don't care."

"Won't it dent your credit score?"

"Please, I've spent too much money beefing up my home security since Theo got in. I'll never move again for the rest of my life." Oscar gives a paternal smile. "You want the condo. You should have it."

Whale grins, a huge weight off his shoulders. "Well, I just might take you up on that."

Brad returns with the bill. "Have a good day, you two." Whale watches Brad walk away to another table. Muscled ass. Great triceps.

"What about Brad?" Oscar asks with a risqué drag. "Something tells me you want him to co-sign your asshole."

"I still feel like I'm cheating on Stewie." Whale pauses. "He's straight anyway."

"Brad?"

Whale nods.

Oscar squints at Brad talking to the other table. "How can you tell?"

"You see how perpetually uninterested he looks? Like he doesn't give a shit about anything?"

"I guess."

"There you go. He's straight. Heteros fade into the background. Gay guys are always on."

Oscar frowns down at his red and pink kimono. "Good to know."

Whale smiles with encouragement. "I like your aesthetic. It's perpetually non-categorizable."

Oscar smirks, cheering up a bit. "I like that."

"It's criminally underrated to be a human pastiche."

Oscar grins. "See, that's why I like you, Jacob. You always know exactly what to say."

Whale's mirth fades a bit.

Oscar finishes the last of his mimosa. Puts his American Express on the tab.

Whale hesitates. "Oscar, I feel a bit weird about these brunches."

Oscar hands Brad the bill. "Just like that? That's not like you."

"You're my boss. Isn't this like a conflict of interest or something?"

Oscar blood runs cold. It rarely ever does.

"*I* don't think it is," Whale adds, more genuine than his previous utterances. "But some people might. And maybe, I dunno, maybe we should—"

"I'm gonna stop you right there," Oscar interrupts, leaning in. "Don't let anyone else's stupid opinions make you feel bad for having time to yourself. Fuck them. Do what you want to do."

"But if I want to be fair to everyone? If there's a hundred people and I do something that benefits ninety-nine of them at the expense of one, that's still one person who feels slighted. I don't want that for anyone. I've been that guy. It's horrible."

"I commend you for your kindness, Jacob. You're a very trusting person. That's one of the best things about you. Don't let anyone, including me, make you feel bad for that." Oscar sighs. "But there are people in this world that thrive by taking advantage of such humanism."

"No one's taking advantage of me."

"Oh really?" Oscar asks, brows raised. "Do you not remember who you're living with right now?"

Whale nods broadly. "So that's why you want me out of there so badly."

Oscar frowns. Looks the other way.

Whale leans back in his seat. "You really think I'd let myself get Stockholm Syndromed?"

"I think you already have, to be perfectly honest," Oscar blurts.

Whale holds up a finger. "Is it possible that maybe, *just maybe*, you might actually be wrong?"

"I know you're a good person. I'm not wrong about that."

Whale chuckles. "Can't argue with you there.

The next day, Oscar waits in his office. Cashew knocks on the door. "You wanted to see me?"

"Close the door," Oscar says.

Cashew does. "What's up?"

Oscar glares at Cashew. "You'd stop at nothing, wouldn't you?"

Cashew doesn't emote, an inaction more telling than he thinks. "I don't know what you mean."

"After I said no to you yesterday, you went to Jacob and made him feel bad for leaving you out of the brunches, didn't you?"

"Sounds like that's what he wants."

"It's not what he wants."

Cashew takes a soft breath. "It's two against one, Oscar."

"Admit what you did."

Cashew shrugs nonchalantly. "I don't even care about the fucking brunches. It's not about that. It's not even about the Bronski job." He stares Oscar down with cold eyes. "Jacob's the best you got by far, huh? Well I managed to turn him, so what does that make me? I can get him to drop out of the Bronski job and make him think it was his idea. Don't worry, I won't. I wanna get the son of a bitch like everyone else." Cashew pauses for effect. "But I could if I wanted to."

"HE IS NOT A MARK!" Oscar hollers. "You wanna pull that shit, do it on the people that deserve it. You do NOT do that to your friends! If you thought I'd respect for this, you are grossly fucking mistaken!"

Cashew's heart races. He forces a blank expression.

"You don't even know why you did it, do you?" Oscar asks. "You just wanted to see if you could. How far you'd go. You liked him better when he was dependent on you, didn't you? When he didn't know anything about the business, something you knew nothing but. And that made you feel special, didn't it? Being his source of intel. His confidante. But now he's better than you, better than you ever could be, and you know it. He doesn't need you anymore and it makes you feel like shit."

Cashew holds his breath, desperately suppressing a developing frown.

"But at least you know how to control him," Oscar murmurs. "That's the one thing you're still good at. Really good at. And you want me to acknowledge it. Fine. The fact that you're so good at it proves to me that you're no different from Bronski and Henderson and Weinstein or the fucking Professor himself, following every fucking impulse they had until it ruined everything good in their lives. You can say to yourself it's just the one time, just this one specific instance, but I've seen it a thousand times, you won't be able to stop. You'll be doing it to Jacob without even realizing it. And you'll fuck up, just like you almost did with Morton Nemechek, and Jacob will never want to speak to you ever again."

Cashew frowns.

Oscar softens with pity, surprised at such a human reaction. "You're not used to this, are you? Not getting exactly what you want?"

Cashew takes a deep breath.

Oscar half-frowns. "Matter of fact, I don't think you've been observed this long by someone who gives a shit. Jacob was the same way. But he wears his heart on his sleeve with pride. You do too, but you have no control over it. All that information you're unwittingly giving out. That scares you, doesn't it, being just yourself in the eyes of everyone? Not even your preferred version. That awful version too fucked up for you to put into words."

Cashew looks up at Oscar with drooped eyes.

Oscar grabs a Post-It pad and a pen. "One my Chinese contacts is Liu Tāo, CEO of Empire Productions."

"You're friends with Liu Tāo?"

"He's a goddamn commie bastard that hates my guts, but he despises the corrupt Hollywood elite just as much as I do, and when you've lived as long as I have, Theodore Landreth, you'll realize men do not have the luxury of selecting their allies the way they do friends. One must make do with the limited options one has." Oscar jots an address and phone number on a Post-It note. "His son Míng is in town. A bit of a dull spoon if you know what I mean." Oscar peels off the Post-It note and hands it to Cashew. "Here's his cell and hotel address. Pick a nice place nearby and put it on the company card."

Cashew looks down at the Post-It Note. "I don't understand."

"I'm gonna be too busy with Bronski, so I need you to take Liu Míng out to dinner Saturday night. You will let him talk. You will keep him happy. You will laugh at his jokes. Grin and fucking bear it. If you do all these things for me, I'll know I can trust you for the next big job."

"C'mon, this is bullshit."

"It's the human side of the business. Jacob can do it in a heartbeat. Prove to me you can too."

"But I hate millionaire's sons. You can't talk anything real with them."

"Tāo's a billionaire."

"Which makes him a thousand times worse."

"I've learned to make it work. So can you."

Cashew holds the Post-It Note out. "I'll do something else. Anything but this."

Oscar hesitates. "If I recall correctly, you forced Jacob to do something *he* found morally abhorrent. Let's see how you like it." He turns away, head down, back to work.

Cashew frowns at the back of Oscar's bald head. This whole thing's so familiar. He swore he'd never feel like this again. But he has. Cashew reluctantly pockets the Post-It Note and leaves.

Five days later, Whale and Pete use Morton Nemechek's invites to infiltrate the LA Opera's Gala premiere of *Rigoletto*, successfully catching world-renowned Maestro Burto Bronski raping yet another young male soloist. Cashew stays home at their Northridge apartment, a month or two away from it being *his* Northridge apartment, Oscar's ominous words floating around his brain as he frowns in the dark.

Whale steps out of the bedroom the next day, muscles still bulging from his workout, excited to see *Kill Bill: The Whole Bloody Affair* that evening. Cashew's in the bathroom, whispering at his reflection. "You sure?" He pauses. "You're sure?" he tries in a different tone. He hesitates. "Are you sure?" he asks softly.

Cashew walks into the living room. Whale's in a simple black T-shirt with "Written and Directed by Quentin Tarantino" in gold font. "Looking good," Cashew says.

"Thanks."

Cashew plops on the couch with an angry huff.

Whale turns his head. "What's wrong?"

"I have to take Liu Míng to dinner tonight."

"Who?"

"Liu Tāo's son."

"The CEO of Empire Productions?"

"Oscar obviously has a thing against me. I have to do it."

"What do you mean you have to do it?"

"He said if I didn't, I'm fired. If I fuck it up, I'm fired. I'm fucked, Jacob. I don't know this guy. I might just offend him using a goddamn fork!"

Whale blinks. "Why would Oscar do that to you?"

"I don't know! You're the brunch guy! You tell me."

Whale thinks back, recollecting. "He didn't seem to like it when I said..."

"When you said what? What did you say?"

Whale hesitates. "I tried to get him to add you onto the brunches."

Cashew furrows his brow. "What the fuck did you do that for?"

"I felt bad after what you said. I thought you'd want me to."

"No!" Cashew scoffs. "Great, now he probably thinks I put you up to it."

Whale frowns, remembering what Oscar said about letting other people take advantage of him. Cashew's right, that is what Oscar thinks.

"God, I'm so fucked," Cashew whines.

Whale looks down at his shirt. Lets out a lamentful sigh. "I'll go with you tonight if you want."

Cashew looks up at Whale. "You've got the Tarantino thing tonight. You've been looking forward to it."

"You wouldn't be in this position if I hadn't opened my big mouth." Whale looks at the floor with sullen eyes. "If Míng really is unreasonable, I'll vouch for you to Oscar."

Cashew softens. "Are you sure?" he asks gently, just as he rehearsed.

Whale smiles back. "What are friends for?"

"You can always catch the next showing, right?"

"Tonight is the last showing."

Cashew blinks. "I thought it was going for three days."

"It was. Today's the last day."

Cashew hesitates with genuine disappointment. He could've had this conversation all week. He waited till now to capitalize on the urgency. "When's it coming back to the New Beverley?"

Whale shrugs. "This is the first time they're showing *The Whole Bloody Affair* in the past two years, so... Probably 2019, I guess. If that."

Cashew frowns. "Maybe you—"

"Yeah, I should really change," Whale gingerly steps into his bedroom. Cashew closes his eyes, actually ashamed of himself.

DREW

The Ides of February

Oscar and his head producer Cleo wait eagerly by the back entrance. The door opens and a forty-something with long fake blond hair walks in.

"Mr. Holstein!" Oscar greets. "Welcome to Los Angeles."

"I've been here before, you know," Nich responds. "I've been going to Coachella since Beyoncé was a Child."

"Impressive." Oscar and Nich walk-and-talk down the hall. Cleo follows close behind. "Glad you could make it out here on such short notice."

"Any chance to get that antisemitic piece of shit is worth the trip," Nich grumbles.

Oscar awkwardly glances at Cleo. "Alrighty then."

"So what's the gameplan exactly?" Nich asks. "Where are you taking me?"

"Studio 2, over here on the right."

"What's wrong with Studio 1?"

"The A/C's leaking, but that's not important right now. Studio 1 is for live shows. Studio 2 is for pre-recorded interviews."

"I thought I was going to be live."

"It's pronounced 'believe,' and yes, you will eventually be in Studio 1. We work in real time here at *Oscar Blitz*. All guest testimony is pre-recorded in advance in case circumstances arise when live isn't an option. It also helps my fact-checkers cross-check for perjury."

"'When live isn't an option.' What does that mean?"

"Witness intimidation. Suicide. Assassination. Cold feet. Bad traffic. I've seen it all. We can't leave anything to chance."

"What about Drew? What's next with him?"

"Right now we're rallying the players and pre-recording all depositions for tomorrow."

"You're not having everyone on at the same time, are you?"

"Of course not, silly goose. We're spacing everything out to give the public time to digest what we're telling them. Plus the more we stretch it out, the more it appears we have on him.

"We're shooting for a 10-day main wave," Cleo says. "We should have enough call-ins by Saturday to properly start Phase 3, which ideally should carry us into the 19th."

Nich furrows his brow. "I don't understand."

"My apologies for Cleo," Oscar says. "She can get a bit technical. Jimmy's interview last night was Phase 1, something shocking and illegal to shift public perception jarringly against Drew. Phase 2 is the character assassination phase. That's tomorrow. That is where you and Trevor Miller come in."

Nich grins. "You got Trevor around here?!"

"Don't interrupt me. We've got a lot of accusations against Drew that, while not criminal per se, are still social and moral taboos. They might not seem so bad if reported as isolated incidents, but in the aftermath of Phase 1, they'll gain traction and might actually stick. Phase 2 is what turns Phase 1 into a national conversation."

"What's Phase 3?"

"Interrupt me one more goddamn time."

"Sorry."

"That doesn't count. Once Jimmy's allegations hit mainstream, we're expecting a new wave of accusations by people *suddenly inspired* to come forward and join the 'Drew Lawrence Sucks' bandwagon. That's Phase 3. We call it the reaction phase."

"That's when it gets fun," Cleo chimes in with a smile.

Oscar gives Nich a small eye roll. "Yes, that is in fact Cleo's definition of not sounding technical. Forgive her, Nich, she knows not what she's doing."

"Ass."

"No thank you, I already ate." Oscar chuckles like an 18th century French aristocrat.

"When do Trevor and I go on?" Nich asks.

"Cleo will notify you when the time is right for your combined four cents," Oscar answers. "A lot can happen in a day. We often have to rearrange on the fly to compensate for new developments. Thankfully, what Cleo lacks in charm, wit, and empathy she makes up for in cold heartless spontaneity, which is why she is my producer and not my shrink, shawarma carver, or hostage negotiator."

Nich laughs at that.

"Unfortunately my shrink won't return my calls," Oscar adds with utter seriousness. "And I don't know of any shawarma spots in area, which is a shame because I'm actually really hungry right now. That was just a joke before. The hostage negotiator, however, was not a joke. Her name is Capri, she can snap my neck with her legs, and she's single."

"Sir, we need to get moving," Cleo murmurs, pointing at her watch.

"Yes, of course." Oscar nods at Nich. "Lots of people coming in, as you can imagine. Trevor's already inside. Catch up, make yourself comfortable. We'll talk again soon." Oscar and Cleo take one step toward Studio 1.

"You're really gonna take down that Nazi bastard?" Nich asks them.

"Nothing will give me more pleasure," Oscar says with a smile. He pivots on his heels and walks with Cleo around the corner.

Cleo flips through her clipboard. "Tabitha Maclean should be here any minute. CJ Marrow is running late but should be here by 3. Gordy Benson is here. Max Ellis is here. Shayne Parker is here."

"Who's in Studio 2 now?" Oscar asks.

"Dirk, Aarin, and Trenton, the go-go boys from Sweet Vermouths."

"What about Terry? Any word on his whereabouts?"

"Negative on that sir."

Oscar half-frowns. "I guess we're just gonna have to go on without him."

"Considering Drew hasn't made an immediate denial or half-assed apology yet like we anticipated, might I suggest starting off with the Whitman Trumpian block? That just might get the Twitter crowd riled up enough and force a statement out of him."

"What about the Sweet Vermouths 'tradition?'"

"We can bump it to Friday's afternoon block. That'll give us more time to hunt Terry down for the group interview."

"Do it." Oscar looks at Cleo, hesitating. "He *is* gonna release a statement, right?"

"I'm sure he will."

"We don't have anything left over for Monday if he doesn't."

"He'll do it, Oscar. They always do."

Leon races down the hall after Oscar and Cleo. "Oscar, we got a problem."

"We're out of foundation *again*?" Oscar quips. "This is LA. Why's everyone so fucking pale?"

"It's Jimmy."

Oscar halts. "What about Jimmy?"

"He's refusing to leave the Studio 1 dressing room," Leon says.

"Well get him outta there. We've got the 'Why hasn't Drew apologized?' interview at 2."

"He locked the door and won't open it for anyone except you." Leon frowns sympathetically. "I think he's having a meltdown."

Oscar awkwardly looks at Cleo. "I better go see him." He splits from the group. Strides assuredly toward Studio 1. Pounds on the dressing room door. "Jimmy. C'mon. Open up."

Jimmy rushes to the door, his eyes red and full of tears. He unlocks it. Steps back.

Oscar lets himself in. Shuts the door. Hands on hips. "What's the matter?" he asks, soft yet stern.

"'What's the matter?!'" Jimmy repeats, his voice wavering. "I'll tell you what's the MATTER!" He chucks a tissue box at Oscar.

"Ow! What the fuck?!"

"DREW LAWRENCE IS JACOB ANDREZJ?!" Jimmy screams. "DREW LAWRENCE WROTE *THE SURGERY*?!"

Oscar furrows his brow. "That's what this is about?"

"YOU KNEW!" Jimmy cries. "You knew the whole time and you never told me?!"

"It's public info! Why are you making such a big deal about this?! So what if he had a different name? So did I! Why does it matter?!"

Jimmy paces, a rushed hand pulling at his disheveled hair. "I'm out, alright? I'm out. I'm not doing this anymore."

Oscar's heart skips a beat. "Woah. Hold on a minute."

"My lawyer said I can retract at any time!"

"Jimmy. You need to relax. Right now."

"I'm retracting, alright?! I'm retracting!"

"Where the fuck is this coming from?"

Jimmy covers his face and sobs into his palms.

"You're hysterical right now," Oscar whispers. "Take a deep breath. Think about what you're saying."

"This is too much," Jimmy whines, removing his hands. "I thought it was just gonna be the one thing. But now there's all these other guys?! And a whole itinerary?! That's not what I signed up for!" Jimmy shakes his head. "I just wanna stop. I wanna stop. I wanna go home."

"Jimmy." Oscar puts both hands on Jimmy's shoulders. "All these guys are here because of you. You started all of this."

Jimmy smacks Oscar's arms away. "I know! That's why I'm ending it, alright?!"

Oscar bites his lip, incensed.

Jimmy shakes his head. "There has to be more to it. There has to be another side. It doesn't make any sense. How did he end up like this?"

Oscar scoffs. "Don't meet your heroes, kid."

"I'm serious!" Jimmy yells. "I don't want to be a part of this anymore! I don't want to be the reason Jacob Andrezj loses everything!"

"You're just nervous," Oscar says sternly. "Every whistleblower goes through last minute jitters."

"That's not what this is. I shouldn't have said all that. It was wrong." Jimmy stares desperately. "You understand?"

Oscar freezes, suddenly getting it. He takes a deep breath. "I can't say this hasn't happened before."

Jimmy's heart pounds. "Really? It has?"

"More than I care to admit."

Jimmy sighs with relief. "I was just so afraid to say anything in the beginning. I just wanted to help you, you know? I wanted to help you get this guy."

Oscar nods solemnly. "Was it Drew?"

Jimmy furrows his brow. "Huh?"

"Was it Drew or someone else?"

"Was *what* Drew or someone else?"

"Who's threatening you?"

Jimmy gapes. "No one's threatening me! What?!"

"If someone is threatening you, Jimmy, you need to tell me. Lying won't help anyone. It's only gonna make things worse."

"I know it is! That's why I'm trying to stop!"

Oscar sighs. "Jimmy."

"Please listen to me. You're not listening to me."

"No, you listen to me," Oscar says. "Nothing Drew has ever said or done will change what he has done to you. Drew chose to ignore you when you told him your age. Drew chose to slip that waiter a twenty."

Jimmy shakes his head with closed eyes.

"Drew chose to buy you vodka," Oscar continues. "Drew chose to force cocaine into you. Drew chose to seduce you. Drew chose to ignore your discomfort. Why are you shaking your head? This is what you told me."

"I know that's what I *said*, but—!"

"A rational explanation doesn't change the fact that he repeatedly chose to hurt you. The only reason we can stop Drew now is because you came forward. Your testimony is everything we have. Without it, we just have a bunch of uncouth *faux pas*. You did the interview. The hard part's over. But if you retract your statement now, no one will believe anything bad about Drew ever again. So I need you to keep up what you've already been doing. Otherwise Drew's gonna keep hurting people just like he hurt you."

Jimmy looks off, Oscar's words finally sinking in. Jimmy was never hurt by the sex. He loves fucking adults who doesn't know his real age, having the secret ability to ruin a man old enough to be his father if he wanted to. The thrill of it makes him cum like nothing else. What hurt him was what Drew told him beforehand, offering to be his role model, to be a guide whenever he needed him, an easy way to climb the ladder. Drew had no right lying about something so powerful, so tender, so integral, so all-encompassing to a young man's heart. And why? To cover shame? To help someone he loved? Just a misunderstanding? No, he did it to get laid. He did it to all of them. He did it to Terry the go-go boy. Drew doesn't even know what he did to Terry, does he? He doesn't care. He got off. He gets away with it.

Terry isn't there to defend his honor. But Jimmy is. He can do that for him.

"Jimmy?" Oscar asks. "You with me, bud?"

Jimmy nods. "Yeah."

"We got forty-five minutes until we're live. You think you'll be okay in the meantime?"

"I'm sorry."

"It happens." Oscar opens the door. Smiles back at Jimmy. Closes it. Jimmy slowly returns to the makeup chair. Stares at his face in the mirror. Nods to himself. Remember Terry. He's gotta do it for Terry.

Oscar stands outside the dressing room door, puzzled by something Jimmy had said. He didn't hear it before, but it's all coming back to him now. Oscar grabs the door handle.

"Oscar!" Cleo calls down the hallway. "Tabitha Maclean's pulling up now."

"Just a second," Oscar calls back. He steps away from the dressing room door, a cold pit growing in his stomach, the nasty kind.

Does he *really* wanna know?

Oscar's ashamed to even have thought that. So he throws it out. Goes about his day. Does the interview with Jimmy. Drives back home. Makes himself a drink in that empty mansion of his. Lays down to bed, eagerly awaiting Phase 2 the way a kid does for Christmas. And he realizes he forgot all about that cold pit, what it was he needed to ask Jimmy so badly. Oh well. Must not have been that important.

JACOB

The Social Network

INT. 7TH FLOOR RA OFFICE - DAY

Jacob knocks on the open door. Carter looks up from his phone.

JACOB
You wanted to see me?

CARTER
Yes, Jacob. Get the door please?

Jacob shuts the door. Sits across from Carter, handsome as ever.

JACOB
You have a good Thanksgiving?

CARTER
It was alright. You?

JACOB
Eh. What's up?

Carter takes a deep breath.

CARTER
I've heard there's some drama going on in 701.

JACOB
(rolls eyes)
Oh God.

CARTER
Your suitemates are very concerned.

JACOB
It's all over now! It's been settled!

CARTER
Clearly they don't think it's settled.

JACOB
It's just Nich. He needs to get off my fucking ass about it.

CARTER
I'm just a mediator, Jacob. I'm not taking sides.

JACOB
I know. I'm sorry.

CARTER
Can you tell me what this is all about?

JACOB
Don't you already know?

CARTER
All I know is what Nich told me.

JACOB
What did he tell you?

CARTER
I want to hear it from you.

```
                    JACOB
        What did Nich call me?

Carter hesitates.

                    JACOB (CONT'D)
        He called me a Nazi, didn't he?

Carter rolls his lips.

                    CARTER
        A Nazi sympathizer.

Jacob exhales hard.

                    JACOB
        This whole thing has blown out of fucking proportion.
        I'm not a fucking Nazi. I'm not a sympathizer of
        anything. When will this bullshit fucking end?!

                    CARTER
        Tell me what really happened.

Jacob thinks. Looks at Carter. Sexy muscled Carter with his gorgeous
eyes.

                    JACOB
        Fine.

Jacob sits up with a sigh.

                    JACOB (CONT'D)
        It all started on 11/9.

                                                          CUT TO:

INT. FILM IMMERSION - DAY (FLASHBACK)

TJ walks down the hall toward Jacob.

                    TJ
        Hey Jake.

                    JACOB
        Hey.

TJ looks out at all the mourning Liberals out that morning.

                    TJ
        What a bunch of sore losers, huh?

                    JACOB
        You're not making things easier.

                    TJ
        What am I doing?

                    JACOB
        Antagonizing Nich last night.

                    TJ
        I was fucking celebrating.

                    JACOB
        It was rude.

                    TJ
        I don't give a fuck. Everyone's been calling me a
        fucking racist all morning. I'm sick to death of
        bougie white Liberals telling me what I should do to
        better help MY race.

                    JACOB
        That makes them immature. So does egging them on.

TJ looks at the announcement billboard by the elevators.
```

"What if I drew a swastika right there?" TJ asks.

JACOB
That'd be stupid and childish and only make Trumpers look bad.

"They're already making Trumpers look bad."

JACOB
Yeah, by calling them Nazis, which you will only confirm.

"They won't know it's me."

JACOB
Look, I'm late for class. Do whatever the fuck you want, okay? Don't be shocked if this blows up in your face. People tend to have strong reactions when it comes to Third Reich iconography.

Jacob storms toward the elevators.

JACOB (V.O.)
I first saw it a few days later when I was coming home from work.

CUT TO:

INT. FILM IMMERSION - NIGHT (FLASHBACK)

Jacob gets off the elevator in his red leather jacket, a red T-shirt, and khakis. He passes the announcement billboard. Halts. Stares at a small swastika scratched in pencil.

JACOB
Son of a bitch.

JACOB (V.O.)
I had no idea how long it had been there. And it was only the size of a thumb.

Jacob walks on with pursed lips.

JACOB (V.O.)
But who else could it have been?

CUT TO:

INT. FILM IMMERSION - DAY (FLASHBACK)

Jacob walks past the billboard, laptop bag over his shoulder. Slows to check on the swastika.

JACOB (V.O.)
Sure enough, the next day someone scratched it out.

Jacob's eyebrows bump. He walks on.

JACOB (V.O.)
And I just forgot all about it.

CUT TO:

INT. SUITE 701 - LIVING ROOM - NIGHT (FLASHBACK)

Jacob sits on the couch, scrolling through his phone. Rian's playing XBOX. Nich is in the kitchenette nuking homemade nachos.

JACOB (V.O.)
A couple days after that, President Fisher sent out the first email.

JACOB
Holy shit.

RIAN
What?

JACOB
They found a swastika in the Big Building and another in Paramount Way.

"What?" Nich asks.

Jacob shows Rian the phone.

JACOB (CONT'D)
Can you believe someone actually copycatted TJ?

Nich's face goes limp.

"That was TJ?!"

JACOB (V.O.)
I really shouldn't have said anything.

JUMP TO:

INT. 7TH FLOOR RA OFFICE - DAY (PRESENT DAY)

Carter looks off, intrigued.

CARTER
Why did you?

JACOB
I thought he already knew.
(pause)
Of course if I had any brains, I would've realized Nich and TJ had been on thin ice since Election Day.

Carter nods.

CARTER
You don't think TJ did the other two?

JACOB
No way. They were either copycats or just pure serendipity. It's not like it's the most obscure symbol in the world.
(pause)
The timing was weird though.

JUMP BACK TO:

INT. SUITE 701 - LIVING ROOM - NIGHT (FLASHBACK)

Nich's face goes limp.

"That was TJ?!"

JACOB
Yeah. You didn't hear about that?

RIAN
The one in the hallway?

JACOB
Yeah. The only reason I know was because I was there when he came up with the idea.

"When was this?" Nich asks.

JACOB
11/9.

"You've known since 11/9?! And you never reported it?!"

JACOB
I only saw it a few days ago. It was scratched out by morning. What's the big deal?

Nich pulls out his phone. Jacob's blood chills.

```
                    JACOB (CONT'D)
          What are you doing?
```

"I'm calling Campus Police."

```
                    JACOB
          Don't do that.

Jacob stands anxiously.

                    JACOB (CONT'D)
          Nich! Come on. It's just a doodle.
```

"Just a doodle?! It's a symbol of fucking hate is what it is!"

```
                    JACOB
          He didn't mean anything by it.
```

"I don't care! It's a fucking smear on my people!"

```
Jacob hesitates.

                    JACOB
          I didn't know you were Jewish.
```

"I'm getting him fucking expelled."

```
                    JACOB
          What? Why?
```

"Why do you think?!"

```
                    JACOB
          It's just a dumb thing he did. Why are you starting
          shit?
```

"IT'S A SWASTIKA!" Nich screams. "THAT'S A FUCKING HATE CRIME!

```
                    JACOB
          Nich. This is TJ we're talking about. He's not a
          Nazi.
```

"Why are you defending him? Are YOU antisemitic too?!"

```
                    JACOB
          Woah! Where the fuck did that come from?!
```

"Are you?"

```
                    JACOB
          How could you fucking ask me that?

Nich stares, lips tight, eyes squinted.
```

"I wonder about you."

```
                    JACOB
          NICH! I'm not antisemitic! You're blowing this up for
          no reason!
```

"For no reason?! My grandparents were gassed at Auschwitz, you asshole!"

```
                    JACOB
          I'm not saying what TJ did was right. It's not. He's
          a fucking moron. But at the end of the day, that's
          all he is. He was just dicking around, trying to get
          a rise out of people.
```

"Yeah? Well now there's three of them!"

```
                                                  JUMP TO:
```

INT. 7TH FLOOR RA OFFICE - DAY (PRESENT DAY)

Carter silently digests Jacob's story.

CARTER
Why were you defending TJ?

JACOB
I didn't like Nich jumping to conclusions like that without TJ being there to defend himself.
(pause)
I just know if I was in TJ's shoes, I'd want someone sticking up for me. That's all it was.

Carter nods solemnly.

JACOB (CONT'D)
I managed to stop Nich from reporting it, but...
(shakes head)
If I knew it'd make him lose all respect for me, I wouldn't have done it at all.

JUMP BACK TO:

EXT. PUBLIC GARDEN - DAY (FLASHBACK)

Jacob sits by the lake, his back against a tree, 11/22/63 in his lap cracked to page one. He browses through his phone instead.

JACOB (V.O.)
A few days after our fight, President Fisher sent out the second email.

Jacob rubs his face as he reads.

JACOB (V.O.)
A fourth swastika had been found. Campus Police was asking for any information that would help them capture the culprits.

JUMP TO:

INT. 7TH FLOOR RA OFFICE - DAY (PRESENT DAY)

Jacob half-frowns. Carter nods imperceptibly.

CARTER
So what did you do?

JACOB
What do you think I did?

JUMP BACK TO:

EXT. PUBLIC GARDEN - DAY (FLASHBACK)

Jacob talks on the phone.

JACOB
Hi Campus Police? Yeah, I know who did one of the swastikas.

JUMP TO:

INT. 7TH FLOOR RA OFFICE - DAY (PRESENT DAY)

Jacob nods.

JACOB
I went down to Campus PD, filed a report and everything. They brought him in the next day and he confessed immediately.

Carter fiddles with a pen.

CARTER
How do you feel about that?

JACOB
It was the right thing to do.
(pause)
I just thought it would make Nich happy.

JUMP BACK TO:

INT. WHITMAN UNIVERSITY - LB 701 - NIGHT (FLASHBACK)

Jacob returns to the suite with a small duffel bag.

JACOB
Anyone here?

Jacob notices one of the bedrooms open. He approaches it. Stands at the threshold. It's TJ's room. Empty. Stripped clean.

JACOB (V.O.)
After we got back from Thanksgiving, I found out TJ had been kicked out of the suite pending a disciplinary hearing from the Board.

JUMP TO:

INT. 7TH FLOOR RA OFFICE - DAY (PRESENT DAY)

Jacob frowns.

JACOB
Nich volunteered to testify against TJ in favor of expulsion.

Jacob shakes his head, zoning out again.

JACOB (CONT'D)
I can't believe he'd actually do that to him over a fucking doodle.

Carter lowers his head, pleading the fifth.

JACOB (CONT'D)
So I volunteered to testify in his defense.

JUMP BACK TO:

INT. WHITMAN UNIVERSITY - STUDENT AFFAIRS - DAY (FLASHBACK)

Jacob sits on a bench outside a conference room. CLARENCE MASON (49) and LORETTA MASON (47) walk in. Loretta hugs Jacob tight.

LORETTA
Thank you so much for doing this.

JACOB
Let's just hope it works.

LORETTA
Feel free to come over any time. You're always welcome at our house.

Jacob smiles meekly.

JACOB
Thanks.

Clarence makes stern eye contact with Jacob.

CLARENCE
You're the one that reported him as well?

JACOB
Yes sir.

Clarence holds out his hand.

CLARENCE
You're a good man, Jacob.

Jacob reluctantly takes it and shakes it.

JACOB
Thank you, sir.

CUT TO:

A FEW MINUTES LATER

Jacob, Loretta, and Clarence sit on the bench in awkward silence.

JACOB
Mr. Mason, I hear you drink Domergue.

CLARENCE
I do.

JACOB
Does it really taste like shit?

Clarence slowly turns his head, staring blankly at Jacob.

CLARENCE
Would I still be drinking it if it tasted like shit?

JACOB
Possibly.

The doors open, Nich walking out in a suit. He grimaces at Jacob and walks on.

CLARENCE
That's him, huh?

JACOB
That it is.

"Pink-headed faggot," Clarence grumbles.

Jacob tenses up. A SECRETARY (50s) sticks her head into the lobby.

SECRETARY
Mr. Andrezj, we're ready for you.

Jacob stands, too shocked to process what he just heard. Buttons his suit. Follows the Secretary inside. The doors close.

CUT TO:

INT. WHITMAN UNIVERSITY - DISCIPLINARY CHAMBER - DAY (FLASHBACK)

Jacob sits at a desk in the center of the room before a long table with a dozen SCHOOL BOARD MEMBERS (50s-70s) sitting in a row with their own microphones and nametags.

TJ's there too. Jacob nods slightly. TJ nods back with gratitude.

BOARD MEMBER #1
State your name.

Jacob leans into the microphone.

JUMP TO:

INT. 7TH FLOOR RA OFFICE - DAY (PRESENT DAY)

Jacob crosses his legs.

JACOB
The whole thing lasted maybe twenty minutes. I made sure to emphasize that I did not approve of what TJ had done, but I had understood TJ's nature and that he didn't do it with malicious intent.

CARTER
Did they cross-reference you?

JACOB
Just once.

JUMP BACK TO:

INT. WHITMAN UNIVERSITY - DISCIPLINARY CHAMBER - DAY (FLASHBACK)

Board Member #8 leans into the microphone.

BOARD MEMBER #8
Mr. Andrezj, when you first discovered the swastika, why didn't you report it to the Campus Police?

Jacob stares blankly. He thinks. He keeps thinking.

Board Member #8 waits, expectant.

Jacob licks his lips. Swallows a bit.

JACOB
I--

JACOB (V.O.)
--have absolutely no idea what I answered.

JUMP TO:

INT. 7TH FLOOR RA OFFICE - DAY (PRESENT DAY)

Jacob shrugs.

JACOB
I don't even know the hell was going on. Was expulsion even on the table? Did my testimony help? Did it make it worse? I don't know.

Jacob scratches his leg.

JACOB (CONT'D)
Considering what I was giving up, I thought I'd be kept more in the loop. I guess I wasn't that important.

CARTER
What was the verdict?

Jacob takes a deep breath.

JACOB
He didn't get expelled. He's just not allowed to live on campus anymore.

CARTER
Then it worked.

JACOB
Did it?

Jacob shrugs pathetically.

JACOB (CONT'D)
I don't know. I have no idea. Is that good? Is that a victory?

Jacob shakes his head.

JACOB (CONT'D)
I still don't know.

JUMP BACK TO:

INT. WHITMAN UNIVERSITY - LB 701 - NIGHT (FLASHBACK)

Jacob tweaks <u>Drive-Thru</u> in his room, his door wide open. Nich and Trevor walk by with big boxes in their arms.

JACOB (V.O.)
As you know, Nich moved Trevor into TJ's old room.

Nich makes eye contact with Jacob, grimaces, and looks away.

JACOB (V.O.)
Nich locks his bedroom door every night now.

Jacob frowns, about to cry.

JACOB (V.O.)
We haven't spoken since.

JUMP TO:

INT. 7TH FLOOR RA OFFICE - DAY (PRESENT DAY)

Jacob frowns.

JACOB
I shouldn't have spoken at all. To anyone. I should've just kept my fucking mouth shut.

CARTER
Well, I'm glad you talked to me about it.

Jacob smiles warmly.

JACOB
Thanks for listening, man.

CARTER
Any time, bro.

Carter fistbumps Jacob. Jacob blushes. Opens the door.

MATCH CUT TO:

WHALE

Potassium Iodide

Whale and Cashew walk into the dimly lit Ristorante La Riunione on Sunset in attractive blazers. "Fuck, he's not here," Cashew mutters.

"He's probably late too," Whale murmurs, scanning the bar seating.

"Or he fucking left!" Cashew snaps.

"Check with the hostess. Maybe he already sat down."

"Jacob?!" a voice calls behind them.

Whale turns. Spots a familiar face sitting at the bar with a Negroni. "FRANKIE?!"

"Holy shit!" Rian stands with a massive grin. "I can't believe it, dude!"

Cashew watches as Whale and some gastropub-looking motherfucker clap arms around each other. The fuck is this?

Rian steps away, chuckling. "I almost didn't recognize you! Love the hair."

"You look exactly the same."

"Shit, dude, you got yoked!"

Whale chuckles. "Yeah, I've been keeping up with the workouts."

"Why are you wearing glasses again?"

Whale furrows his brow a bit before realizing. "Oh, these aren't real. Look." Whale slides a finger under his frames, poking through the space where lenses would have been.

Rian has a mental spasm. "WHAT?!"

"I know, it's amazing. No one can tell."

Rian sticks his finger through the frames in disbelief, almost poking Whale's eye out. "That's so weird."

"It's like how colorblind people replace red or green with an amorphous gray."

"Aren't you culturally appropriating glasses-wearers?"

"These frames were fucking expensive. I gotta get some use out of them."

Cashew clears his throat. "Jacob?"

"Theo! Come here!" Whale puts a hand on Rian's shoulder. "This is my best friend, Rian Hoffman. We were suitemates at Whitman together." Rian holds his hand out.

Cashew stiffens. Awkwardly waves.

Rian lowers his hand. "This is Theo Landreth," Whale continues, oblivious. "We work together at *Oscar Blitz.*"

"And live together," Cashew adds pointedly.

"Not for much longer." Whale looks at Rian. "You waiting for someone?"

"No, I just popped in for a drink," Rian answers.

"Jacob?" Cashew interjects.

Whale whips his head. "What?!" he snaps.

Cashew stares. "Míng's at the table."

"Okay."

"He's waiting for us."

"He's waiting for you."

"Aren't you coming?"

"Just go on without me. I'll join you in a moment."

Cashew awkwardly looks at Rian. "Jacob—"

"Just let me catch up!" Whale exclaims. "You don't need me. You'll be fine." Whale turns Rian toward the bar. "Sorry about that."

"That was kinda rude of him," Rian whispers.

"I know. He always does that."

Cashew stands where he is, his eyes drooping slightly. He slowly turns away and follows the hostess.

Whale orders a sidecar. "Frankie finally came to Hollywood," he says, raising a toast.

Rian laughs and toasts his Negroni.

"I can't believe it," Whale says. "How long are you out here?"

"For good."

"For good?"

"The show got canceled and Bravo bought out the company."

"Oh, that's too bad."

"Is it? I don't think so."

"When'd you get in?"

"Three days ago."

"Quite a coincidence, huh?"

"I know. I'm staying at the Motel 6 next door, just until my credit check's done for the new apartment."

"Where?"

"La Brea. What about you?"

"I'm living in Northridge right now but I'm moving to Marina Del Rey soon."

"Wow! Fancy shit."

"I'm doing all right." Whale sips his sidecar.

Rian sips his Negroni, humming a bit with recollection. "Crazy what happened to Carter, huh?"

"Carter Jackson? What happened?"

"You don't know?"

Whale smiles a bit. "Know what?"

"Google it." Rian nods eagerly. "Go on, Google it."

Whale reluctantly pulls out his phone. Googles "Carter Jackson." Scrolls through the News results, the hairs on the back of his neck standing up. "Oh my God."

"What the fuck, right?"

Whale's brow furrow as he reads the headlines.

"He was doing some video work with Eddie Passifle a few months ago," Rian says. "He tweeted something about housing inequality stats or something, AOC retweeted it, then suddenly a bunch of girls reply that Carter Jackson raped them when they were at Whitman together. Emily. Margerie. Kyliee."

Whale stares at Rian. "Kyliee?"

Rian nods. "AOC deleted the tweet, apologized for retweeting 'a known abuser,' and that's when everyone picked up the story. Carter's finished. He'll never be able to work again."

Whale locks his phone, stunned. "You think he really did it?"

"I don't know. But since Eddie fired him, he hasn't posted anything on social media. Not even a denial."

Whale stares off.

Rian shakes his head. "Wild, huh?"

Whale licks his dry lips, eyes unblinking. "I don't know how I feel about that," he whispers.

Cashew looks behind him. No Whale in sight. "Am I boring you?" a pale-faced Liu Míng drolls in a flawless Western accent, looking twice Cashew's age despite being two years younger.

Cashew faces forward. "I'm sorry, what were you saying?"

"I'm more interested in knowing what you're thinking." Míng sips his glass of wine. "You're pretty preoccupied."

Cashew sighs. "Don't take this the wrong way, but me being here's a punishment."

"In what way?"

"You know my boss?"

"Oscar Blitz?"

"He wanted me to butter you up, just to see if I could. I dunno."

Míng sips, nodding. "My father hates his guts. He's so fragrant and all over the place."

"Believe me, he's not nearly as unpredictable as he thinks he is."

Míng smirks. "I was a bit wary of tonight myself, to be honest."

"Me too."

"Every time I do this for Dad, it's always with some Boomer or one of those Benedict Arnold Millennials parroting Boomer buzzwords. You seem to have you head on right." Míng grabs a piece of bread and dunks it in oil and vinegar. "I sympathize with your dilemma. I get punished with these things all the time."

Cashew smiles. "I am jealous though."

"Jealous of me?"

"You get to work with your father every day. I'd kill to have that."

"It fucking sucks."

Cashew's glee vanishes. "Oh?"

Míng swallows the bread in one go. "If I wasn't his son, I'd totally love working for him. But I'll always be his son, which means he'll never trust me to do anything real, which means all of my ideas are automatically shit."

Cashew frowns.

"I'm smarter than my father," Míng continues, passion shining through his words. "I was raised to be. But he'll never step down. He'd kill the business before handing the reigns to anyone, least of all me."

Cashew lets out a cold sigh. "My father loves his business more than he loves me."

Míng frowns back. "Sorry to hear that."

Cashew sips his wine. "I never felt I could really say it. Like somehow he'd find out."

"They're not gods, our fathers." Míng pauses. "There is no God. No eternal damnation. Just boring people getting shit done. I think it's very important for us to grow the fuck up and just admit it already."

"Speaking of rapists," Rian segways to Whale back at the bar, "What the hell was all that with The Professor?"

Whale hesitates. "Pretty sure there's nothing left to say that hasn't been said already."

"You know who did it?"

Whale sips his second sidecar with a busy mind. "Course I knew him. There were only four of us."

"Did you know it was happening at the time?"

Whale traces the rim of his coupe glass. "Yup."

Rian places his empty Negroni on the rubber mat. "We don't have to talk about it."

"It was me."

"What was?"

Whale simply looks at Rian.

Rian's eyes don't move, his whole expression shifting.

Cashew eats his squid ink linguine and clams. Míng continues his spiel over untouched (and rapidly cooling) chicken marsala: "Men of that generation, my father's, your father's, Oscar's, they all subscribe to that 'us vs. them' philosophy of business. The only way to out-perform their competition would be to knock them all down, keep secrets from each other, work alone, no care for mental health or treating human beings like limited biological specimens. Our industry pumps out literally the most right-brain product. It's a machine that requires people and personality more than work and action. It simply cannot work with that old model. Maybe in the 50s when films were candy bars instead of emotional commodities. Not nowadays. Not during the golden age of television and the rise of streaming services. Do they really think everything we've fought to achieve will just stay that way forever? Their strength is not from gumption or sheer will, it's from a controlled environment where they're the only ones making the rules. That's not just unrealistic, it's bad business. My father would never allow Western influence into his company. He's trying to keep the CCP golden age alive, but that's impossible thanks to the Internet. Empire could be so much bigger if we only let in capitalist tactics. He's too stubborn in his old Soviet ways. He's killing the company and its future. Oscar too. He's on that judgment shtick of good and evil. It's always moral dogma with these people. How can they lead if they're so dependent on a checklist of what's allowed and not allowed? The world doesn't work that way. We need to cut the fat in order to stay lean."

Cashew wipes his mouth. "The guy I came here with, Jacob, he was one of the interns at The Factory with me."

Míng nods. "That's right, you're the guys that took down The Professor."

"A bad businessman, right?"

"A deplorable businessman."

"He's the one that took the video, but he was such a moral stick-in-the-mud when it came down to it. He felt it wasn't sportsmanlike to do that to the guy."

"It's business. There aren't any rules."

"Thank you!" Cashew exclaims. "Ugh. Finally, someone that gets it."

"How did Jacob change his mind?"

"I got him to. First I tried logic, then I played on his emotions. And it worked. I do it all the time now."

Míng hums a bit. "I think that's fantastic."

Cashew's face lights up. "Really?"

"Manipulation is very difficult to master. If you're able to get a moral man like Jacob to flip like that, you must be very talented."

"I am so sick of feeling bad about it."

"Why should you feel bad about it? It's an incredibly valuable tactic."

Cashew smirks as he lifts his wine glass. "Oscar's trying to make me feel like some sort of monster for thinking outside the box."

"That's because he's threatened by you."

"My father always said to reward your friends and smite your foes."

"That's good advice."

"So why isn't Oscar rewarding me for this? It's what took down The Professor."

"He attributes manipulation to immorality, and in his strictly binary view of the human condition, he can't be friends with immoral people."

"But he does sketchy shit all the time! When I do it, I'm the monster?"

"He's a weak man."

"What's he gonna do? Hold that one night against me the rest of my life?"

"He shouldn't. It's not good for business."

"Thank you!" Cashew drinks his wine. "God, I feel like I'm losing my mind around these people."

Whale finishes his second sidecar. "We sat outside George Clooney's mansion in Studio City and took note of everyone that came into the property. Then a few days later, when we knew he would be out for lunch, I dressed up as the roof inspector and told the housekeeper I was there to do a follow-up. I gave him Theo's burner number and he pretended to be Rog and everything was fine after that."

Rian keeps staring at Whale. "You did all that to get Bronski?"

"No, that was to get the tickets to the Gala where we knew he'd make his next move."

"You broke into George Clooney's mansion to steal his opera tickets?"

"He didn't actually have the tickets. The guy next door did, Morton Nemechek, the hedge fund manager. We had reason to believe he was cheating on his wife with a nineteen-year-old, so we took a bunch of photos of them together to use as blackmail to get Nemechek to give us his opera tickets."

Rian hesitates. "What does that have to do with George Clooney?"

"His roof has the best view of Morton Nemechek's living room."

Rian takes a deep breath. "You pretended to be a roof inspector to break into George Clooney's mansion to gather blackmail on a hedge fund manager that you would use against him to get opera tickets so you could catch a predatory conductor mid-rape with a male soloist?"

Whale lets out a nervous chuckle. "No, turns out the nineteen-year-old *was* his wife. He was cheating on her with a sixty-four-year-old mistress. That's what we ended up using against him."

"So you pretended to be a roof inspector and broke into George Clooney's mansion for nothing."

"We didn't know that at the time."

"That doesn't make it right."

"It's the only way we could've got Bronski."

"That is not normal!" Rian says. "How can you of all people justify all that?"

Whale opens his mouth. Closes it. Opens again. Closes. "It's not easy."

Rian waves over the bartender. "Close my tab."

Whale removes his empty frames. Massages the bridge of his nose. "What the hell happened to me, Frankie?" he whines. "How did I get good at this?"

Rian softens.

"It got so bad!" Whale cries. "It's made me bad." He stops himself. His breath wavers.

"It's okay," Rian whispers.

Whale wipes his eyes. "I haven't written anything in over a year. I haven't been to church. I don't even go to movies anymore."

Rian doesn't speak at first. "What about Stewie?"

Whale shakes his head. "We haven't spoken since I left Boston."

Rian's heart breaks.

Whale follows Rian out, stopping just outside the door. Rian looks at Whale with a disheartened smile, a mere fragment of the bond they used to thrive in. That makes Whale sadder than anything. Never has he felt more tainted than he does at that moment.

"We never made *The Surgery*, did we?" Rian rhetorically asks.

Whale looks off, frowning with disappointment. "I always liked it."

"You wanna?"

Whale hesitates. "I'm so far removed now. You're better off than I am in that world."

"I don't think so."

"The internship was enough. I'm just not cut out for Hollywood."

"According to who? The Professor?"

Whale doesn't answer.

"You're a fantastic writer, Jacob," Rian insists. "You're an amazing filmmaker. What happened with The Professor doesn't change that."

Whale looks at Rian, a bit of strength rebuilding. "Why not? I got Bronski. I think I've earned a few months off."

Rian smiles. "Call me tomorrow. We'll talk."

Whale nods. "Can Theo be a part of it too?"

Rian blinks. "Can't it just be the two of us?"

"He's my friend."

"I don't think he likes me."

"He doesn't know you."

"Which makes it weird that he doesn't like me."

"Please."

Rian hesitates. "I don't like working with guys I don't know."

"Even if I vouch for him?"

Rian sighs.

"Please, Frankie," Whale whispers.

Rian tightens his lips. "I got a really bad vibe from him, Jacob. I'm sorry."

Whale nods slowly. "Count me out then."

"Jacob."

"You can take it. Run with it."

"Jacob, please." Rian sighs. "Fine. Whatever."

"You sure?"

"Yeah, but just as a producer."

"That's fine."

Rian nods. "Call me tomorrow." He walks down the street and turns into the Motel 6.

Thirty minutes later, Whale and Cashew sit in the back of their Ridr. Whale tentatively looks over. "Sorry I bailed on you back there."

"Don't be," Cashew murmurs.

Whale nods. "How bad was he?"

Cashew scoffs. "Who said anything about him being bad?"

"You did."

"I never said that!"

"Why am I here then?"

"You're the one that invited yourself!"

Whale's lips flutter. "You asked me to."

"No I didn't!" Cashew scoffs again. "God, what's up with you lately?"

"No, you said—"

"I was very fucking clear," Cashew interrupts. "I needed to cement Oscar's trust in me, but you didn't think I could! I never, EVER asked for you to come tonight! Then what did you do? You made ME late and you didn't even show up! I had to tell Míng, 'Hey, sorry I'm late *guy I never met*, my autistic roommate is so fucking retarded to pick Ridr Pool on a goddamn Saturday night. Where is he you ask? Hanging out at the bar right now. Yes, he's real. You're just gonna have to believe me!'" Cashew turns away, crossing his arms. "You've got some fucking nerve, you know that?"

"I'm sorry," Whale croaks, hurt and confused.

Cashew sighs. "You just misunderstood. I get it. That's how you are. I just gotta explain things more clearly."

"You didn't fuck up. I fucked up, alright? I'm sorry."

Cashew nods with assurance. "Good."

Whale takes a deep breath. "Frankie and I are making a short film we outlined in college. I got him to add you on as producer."

Cashew looks at Whale, genuinely moved. "You really did that?"

"I felt I owed you one, you know?"

Cashew faces forward, thinking. "Kinda weird how he showed up out of nowhere and offered you that."

Whale hesitates. "I don't think so."

"How long has he been in town?"

"Three days."

Cashew laughs.

"What, you think he wasn't just there by chance?" Whale asks.

"Since when do you believe in coincidences?"

Whale purses his lips.

Cashew smirks a bit. He's got a live one. "What did he say about you adding me on as producer?"

"He wasn't a fan."

"He doesn't know me, but he didn't want me on? That doesn't make sense to me."

"I thought that was weird too."

"We live together. We work together. Why would he hate me if you don't?"

"He's usually way more mature than that."

Cashew nods. "Sounds to me like he wants you to be his meal ticket, an easy way for him to break into Hollywood."

Whale furrows his brow. "We're friends, Theo."

"You haven't spoken to each other in a year and a half and only now, when he needs your script idea, he treats you like a friend?"

Whale zones out. Ponders it over. Thinks back.

JACOB

Chinatown

INT. LIBRARY - NIGHT

Jacob reads the screenplay of The Matrix in serene peace and quiet.

DOC BROWN (V.O.)
GREAT SCOTT!

Jacob looks at his phone's screen. A text from Carter:

"Hey bro. I want to meet with you, Rian, Nich, and Trevor in my room tomorrow night at 8. There's something we gotta discuss as a group."

Jacob frowns, his heart racing. He closes The Matrix, too anxious to get back to it.

CUT TO:

INT. FILM IMMERSION - NIGHT

Jacob gingerly approaches Suite 717. Stops outside the door. Raises a fist to knock.

CUT TO:

INT. SUITE 717 - SAME

KNOCK-KNOCK-KNOCK! Carter stands and opens the door.

CARTER
Jacob.

JACOB
Hey.

Jacob walks in. Freezes at the sight of Nich, Trevor, and Rian on the couch.

JACOB (CONT'D)
Hey everyone.

RIAN
Hey.

TREVOR
Hey.

Nich doesn't answer.

CARTER
Okay. Now that we're all here, I think we just get to it, um...

Jacob takes the empty chair between Carter and the couch.

"Jacob," Carter says in a strangely impersonal tone, "I've met with your suitemates a couple times since we last talked, and it seems there are some things they want talk to you about."

Jacob tenses up. He looks around at everyone.

JACOB
What's going on? What is this?

"Nich?" Carter asks. "Do you want start?"

"I just feel the atmosphere in the suite has been tainted since Jacob's testimony," Nich says. "I'm incredibly offended by what he has done and I do not feel safe in there anymore."

```
                    JACOB
What are you talking about? I haven't done--
```

"Jacob," Carter interrupts, "you'll have a chance to speak after everyone's had their say.

```
                    JACOB
I can't even defend myself?
```

"At the very end. Until then, be respectful without interruptions." Carter looks at Nich. "Continue."

"I just don't think it's fair that WE should have to move out because of what he's done," Nich says.

```
                    JACOB
          (whispers)
What the fuck?
```

"No interruptions," Carter interrupts.

"It's just not fair, you know?" Nich resumes. "If it was only the thing with TJ, I'd understand, but... Jake says a lot of horrible things around the suite and he posts quite a lot of offensive material."

"Like what?" Carter asks.

"I've got one screenshotted here," Nich says, pulling out his phone.

```
                    JACOB
Of course you do.
```

"Jacob," Carter chides.

```
                    JACOB
Fuck off.
```

Nich taps around his phone. "Around this time last year, Jacob posted on Facebook, 'I understand the problem behind minstrel shows. White people doing blackface and acting with exaggerated mannerisms in a stereotypical fashion is definitely problematic, especially considering they were mocking African-Americans for the delight of a predominantly white audience. But how exactly is that different from drag shows? Drag queens are men, not trans women, who wear exaggerated makeup, oversized heels, and dresses, a caricature of women. They speak with stereotypical cattiness and move with feminine mannerisms for the delight of a predominantly cis male audience. Now we can look back and call minstrel shows racist, but how can people nowadays call a minstrel show racist and not call drag shows sexist? Isn't that also being on the right side of history? I'm just curious.'"

```
                    JACOB
          (to Carter)
Can I please say something?
```

"Wait your turn," Carter answers.

```
                    JACOB
Please!
```

"Jacob."

```
Jacob sighs desperately.
```

"It's shit like that that makes Jake impossible to be around," Nich concludes, pocketing his phone. "There. That's all I have to say."

```
Jacob pulls his hair with both hands, shaking his head.
```

"Thank you, Nich," Carter says, sitting up. "Trevor?"

"I mean, I agree with everything he said," Trevor says. "All of it."

```
Jacob sighs harshly.
```

"I can't give many direct examples of my own," Trevor continues, "since I've only just moved in, but... A couple years ago, when they all first moved in together, I was pretty much around all the time. I remember feeling uncomfortable around Jacob because of his, uh... He was a bit vulgar. Really vulgar, actually. A lot. Graphic descriptions of sex and what he does and... And I remember he always had some guy coming over, some stranger he picked up on Grindr or whatever, and... You know, that's a bit much. I've always had a problem with that. And I don't care about them being dudes or anything, I just think he shouldn't be buzzing in all these strangers into the building. And we could hear them fucking. It just made everyone uncomfortable and..."

```
Jacob inhales, trying his darnedest not to cry.
```

"That's it, I guess," Trevor says with a shrug.

"Thank you, Trevor," Carter says with a solemn nod. "Rian?"

```
Rian notices Jacob's pleading eyes staring back at him.

                        RIAN
        I just wanna say that I don't share most of the
        problems Nich and Trevor have with Jacob.

Rian takes a deep breath. Looks at his knees.
```

"But as a Jew," Rian continues, "I'm very offended by how quick Jacob was to defend TJ's right to draw a swastika."

```
Jacob gasps, his eyes watering.
```

"Since then," Rian continues with his head down, "Jacob being in the suite has affected my concentration and my schoolwork, and I feel it would be best for everyone if he were... not."

```
Jacob keeps staring at Rian.
```

"Jacob?" Carter says.

```
Jacob blinks. Looks at Carter.
```

"You can speak now."

```
Jacob swallows his dry throat.

                        JACOB
        If that's how you all feel, why couldn't you just
        tell me yourself instead of sneaking around, meeting
        the RA behind my back?

Nich, Trevor and Rian keep their heads down.

                        JACOB (CONT'D)
        I tried my fucking hardest to keep everyone happy.
        I'm only human. If I'm fucking up, if I make any of
        you uncomfortable, I need to know and I will adjust
        accordingly... which is why I showed TJ that specific
        post before I posted it. He agreed with me. And
        considering I'm the only gay one here, I feel I'm
        more qualified talking about the nuances of gay
        culture than the rest of you hetero bitches.
                  (pause)
        And as for my locker room talk, may I remind you that
        Nich has not only brought women back to the suite on
        multiple occasions, he also goes out of his way to
        describe everything he did to them to us afterwards.
```

If it's a gay thing, which I believe it is, just fucking say it. I'd understand. Straight guys don't like hearing gay shit, no matter how woke they want to appear. Until this very moment, I was under the assumption that I was just being one of the boys. Plus I only came out six months before. I could finally verbalize my sexuality for the first time in my life. Forgive me for not having developed a filter for that yet.

Jacob wipes tears from his eyes.

JACOB (CONT'D)
I don't want to start shit up again, but I repeat that I am not, nor have I ever been, an antisemite. I've already explained my point of view on that subject to everyone here multiple times, but I would like to remind all of you that I was the one who reported TJ to the Campus Police. Not Nich. Me. I made that decision. And I did so because I realized Nich was right, and I wanted to make it up to him. Only when Nich decided to testify against TJ with the hopes of getting him fucking expelled one semester away from graduation did I decide to step in.

Jacob looks at Rian.

JACOB (CONT'D)
Because you were my friends. And I thought, foolishly, you would do the same for me.

Rian closes his eyes.

JACOB (CONT'D)
But thank you for letting your thoughts be known to me. This is the feedback I needed to hear. And if there is any I can do to make it up to you guys, I will. I promise you, I will.

"Okay," Carter says with a nod. "Thank you, Jacob."

JACOB
You're welcome.

"I do have to say that Jacob cannot be forced out of the suite against his will. But Jacob, if you do want to relocate somewhere else, the option is yours."

"I'm okay with that," Nich says.

"Yeah, me too," Trevor adds.

"Rian?"

Rian looks up.

"You okay with that too?" Nich asks.

Rian nods a bit. Jacob glares at him.

"Okay," Carter says, standing up. "You guys can go."

Nich, Trevor, and Rian stand. Jacob stays sitting, looking up at his suitemates as they funnel out of the room. The moment the door closes, Jacob's eyes fill with tears. He bursts into loud sobs, crying loudly into his hands.

Carter moves his chair closer to Jacob, head hanging with pity.

"I'm sorry," Carter whispers.

Jacob wipes the tears and snot from his eyes and nose.

JACOB
I'm not fucking leaving. I'm not. They don't get to fucking win. I'll stay out of spite if I have to.

Jacob closes his eyes and gives into his despair.

Carter frowns, his heart breaking. He reaches out and hugs Jacob. Jacob hugs back, squeezing as tight as he can, sobbing into Carter's shoulder. Carter gently rubs Jacob's back, closing his eyes.

Later, Jacob sits on his bed. He can hear Nich, Trevor and Rian watching a movie, a comedy by the sound of it. Jacob looks around the room. All those posters. That view of Boston Common he waited four years to earn. All those trees covered in Christmas lights. It's dazzling. But Jacob feels no joy.

As his suitemates laugh again, he imagines himself walking out to get something from the living room, their deflated mirth, their angry faces, their vain attempts to ignore the elephant in the room. He's insulted, of course, but he also feels doing so would be disrespectful to them. They'd be so much happier without him. And that just makes him feel broken and unwanted.

Why should he force himself on them like that? What was the point?

The next day, Jacob carries the last box onto the elevator. Floor by floor it descends. The lobby is cold, a chill December breeze flying in from the outside. And as Jacob approaches the blinding midday light coming in from the glass lobby doors, he recognizes the red Jeep parked out front.

Stewie holds the lobby door open, a halfhearted frown on his face. Jacob wears a similar frown as he loads the box into JEEPGUY's trunk along with the rest of them.

STEWIE

You want me to drive?

Jacob plops into the passenger seat, head bowed.

Stewie sits in the driver's seat, shivering from the cold. Starts the engine. Releases the emergency break. Shifts into first. Drives away from the Little Building.

WHALE

Self-Flagellation

Whale sits in the middle of his new Marina Del Rey condo and curls a 45lb dumbbell with his right arm, exhaling on each pump up. He can hear his pulse. He can feel his bicep tighten. No sound in the condo except his breath. After ten reps, Whale lowers the dumbbell, flexes a bit of his right arm, and switches to his left. His eyes glance around his new condo, that blank canvas with Baby Boy all over it.

The walls painted elephant gray with the occasional splattered streak of red. Framed Monet and da Vinci posters on the walls. Impressive home theater setup. A state-of-the-art home media device that can select one of his three hundred Blu-Rays with the touch of a remote.

Whale's computer desk in the bedroom, an all-in-one PC setup complete with a typewriter keyboard, facing his beachside balcony, west-facing, just like he preferred. Pitch black in the morning when he wants to sleep in. Perfect in the evenings for sipping Domergue as the sun sets over Venice Beach.

Whale moves on to pull-ups at his bedroom's threshold. He looks out at the kitchen, big enough for one person to have everything he needs. No Alex lying on the couch smoking pot and cruising him. No Cashew making him feel self-conscious about everything he says, wears or does.

Whale does push-ups in front of his full-length mirror. Imagines Stewie standing next to him, telling him something constructive like "Count each one out loud" or something like that.

Whale downs his unflavored whey protein powder and water, looking out at the sun glistening off the Pacific. His mom had a similar view in their Sea Isle beach house, the one she had the sell to pay for his and Karen's Eagle Ridge tuition. Mostly his. He imagines his mom sitting there with him, her reaction, her amazement, her pride. They haven't talked since graduation. She hasn't tried calling either. He hopes something's not wrong.

Whale switches the inputs of his condo-wide stereo system from the turntable to the CD player. He plops in *Discography: The Complete Singles Collection*. Clicks the track skip button until he gets to 14, "Being Boring." What a fantastic song. Neil's favorite for a reason. The song plays in every room. A speaker in the kitchen, a speaker in the bathroom, a speaker in the bedroom, a small speaker on the balcony. Whale wanders through the condo with nothing on but boxer briefs, his own personal soundtrack surrounding him, kissing his tight body from all sides. He slides open the closet. Stares at the memory lane before him.

His red leather jacket, the one he bought in Florence.

His collection of frames, all the lenses popped.

Stewie's red Nike baseball cap, the one he was wearing in the Black Bear on June 12, 2016, the night they met. Whale's favorite hat.

A thick triangular chunk of asphalt, a piece of Eagle Ridge's driveway he pocketed on his last day of school.

His class rings, one red and platinum from Eagle Ridge Preparatory School, the other purple and silver from Whitman University.

His old graduation cap, its glued-on message written in Santa Monica sand long past legibility, deserty wisdom faded away like Ozymandias' mighty works in that Percy Shelly poem.

His unframed college diploma still in its purple Whitman University cover. Stewie said he didn't know where his was. Mom knows hers burned up in the One Meridian Fire. Whale didn't know which one was worse.

His Eagle Ridge acting awards in a box. Once his whole life, now just a bunch of silly memories. It's how he learned to improvise. To bullshit. To not be embarrassed on stage. To ham it up for applause. For tears. For laughs.

An old T-shirt only worn once, size XL, all-white with two words in big black letters: "LIKES BOYS." Whale touches the fabric and breaks into loose, desperate tears. He wishes Stewie was there. That would make this place a home.

Whale goes down to the parking garage and hops into his hot red (slightly used) 2017 Ferrari 488 GTB and peels off. The gas light is on. He pulls up to the closest gas station, just before the ramp onto the 1.

Whale steps out. Smooths his nice dress shirt in the December sun. Starts filling up with premium. A sky blue Prius pulls up to the pump across from him, a chill-looking guy stepping out. "Nice ride," the Chill Guys tells him.

"Thanks."

The Chill Guy sneaks a peek of Whale's license plate. "'FILMGUY,' huh?"

"Yup."

"What do you do, if you don't mind me asking?"

Whale thinks it over. Smiles. "I film guys."

The Chill Guy stares. "Like gay porn?"

"Wanna find out?"

The Chill Guy furrows his brow.

Whale's cell phone rings. He pulls it out. "Jacob Andrezj."

The Chill Guy resumes pumping gas, weirded out but fascinated nonetheless.

"*Who* is this?" Whale asks, prompting the Chill Guy to look back up. "No, I'm sure we have, I'm just really bad with faces. And names. Faces to names, you..." Whale turns away from the Chill Guy. "Again?"

The Chill Guy stands by, eavesdropping on Whale's conversation with concern.

"Just tell him to do it." Whale pauses. "Tell him I'm telling him to do it." Pause. "Well, I'm not." Whale readjusts his stance. "Look, this is Hollywood. If Rian wants to make it in this town, he has to pay his dues, and that means sucking the producer's dick every once in a while."

The Chill Guy raises both eyebrows.

"I know he is," Whale continues, oblivious to the volume of his voice. "But that's just the way it is."

The Chill Guy looks around for witnesses. No one.

"What did he think was gonna happen? He's living in a Motel 6 for fuck's sake!" Whale rubs the bridge of his nose. "Then make sure he's in a good mood before you tell him." Whale huffs. "Then tell him to loosen up first." Pause. "Yeah, well Theo and I own his ass."

The Chill Guy's mouth opens.

"I don't care how small it is!" Whale exclaims. "The director can fuck the actors all he wants, but the producer fucks the director. That's showbiz. He went to film school. He knows how it works." Whale notices the Chill Guy still standing there. He smiles and nods.

The Chill Guy turns away. He can still hear Whale's voice: "Just tell them I said... Fine, okay? I'm coming. I'm coming, I'm coming, I'm coming." The Chill Guy furrows his brow, too scared to turn around. "Yes, right now." The Chill Guy looks behind him. Whale's just standing there. The Chill Guy sighs relief.

"Well I'm not happy about it either," Whale says into his phone. "They better be on their fucking knees, alright? Both of them."

The Chill Guy scoffs. Who IS this guy?

"And I don't care what Theo wants, I'm not staying an hour this time. Just five minutes and I'm gone. You tell him that. Bye." Whale hangs up. Unhooks the gas pump. Hops into his Ferrari. Whale looks at the Chill Guy standing there with a gas pump in his hand and puckers his lips. He speeds off, laughing his ass off all the way to the 1.

Whale parks outside Sunset Gower Studios. A small thin Asian man, twenty-one years old with that unmistakable fish-out-of-water look, stands outside *The Surgery*'s designated lot. "Mr. Andrezj?"

"Please call me Jacob," Whale says, getting out of the Ferrari.

"I'm sorry sir. Can't help it."

"You're Lloyd, right? The one that called me?"

"Larry."

Whale stomps a foot. "Dammit, I knew that."

Larry awkwardly holds out his hand. "Larry Lin."

Whale smiles apologetically. Shakes his hand. "I'll never call you by the wrong name again."

"It's okay if you do."

"No, it isn't." Whale huffs. "Let's get this over with."

Rian and Cashew stand in the center of the set, a scarily precise recreation of Stewie Hanz's Marlton condo, the crew standing off to the side, desensitized and impatient, actors in chairs looking bored. "I don't care what you say," Rian eggs. "I'm the one that has to direct it."

"I can always fire you," Cashew retorts.

"One month into a three-month shoot? Please."

"I'll do it."

"Who's gonna direct it?"

"I will."

Rian guffaws. "Please!"

"I've directed before."

"*First Murder in Tequilatown*, right?" Rian puffs his lips. "You gotta be kidding me. You actually thought that was good?"

"Frankie!" Whale shouts from across the studio.

Cashew points at Whale walking toward them. "Jacob liked it."

"That's what he told you, huh?" Rian counters. "Well he's the one that showed me. We were up for hours laughing our ass off."

"Frankie!" Whale yells desperately.

"Go on!" Rian yells back, pointing at Cashew. "Tell what you really think of it!"

"Shut up!"

"This one time, tell him how you really feel about him! THIS ONE TIME!"

"I SAID SHUT UP!" Whale hollers, his throat scratching. "It is two o'clock! You've wasted four hours bickering about nonsense. GET A GRIP!"

Cashew raises a hand. "Jacob, he—"

"SHUT THE FUCK UP, BOTH OF YOU!"

Cashew and Rian turn away from each other.

Whale rubs the outside of the throat. "It's always something with you two."

"He won't film the prologue!" Cashew exclaims. "He just won't do it."

Whale looks at the set, his brow furrowing. "You're arguing about a scene you're not even filming today?!"

"I got that big machine prop coming in on Friday."

"Theo had no right to make that decision," Rian interrupts. "This is our project."

"He's the producer," Whale says.

"He's a fucking liar is what he is."

"Jacob gave me the go-ahead!" Cashew looks at Whale. "Tell him."

"The go-ahead?" Whale asks. "What go-ahead?"

"He says you okayed the prologue," Rian grumbles skeptically.

Whale hesitates. "Yeah, I did."

"See?!" Cashew shouts in Rian's face.

"Why would you do that?" Rian asks Whale, embarrassed. "It was always the plan NOT showing the Surgery itself!"

"I know," Whale explains. "But Theo told me his idea for it, and I thought it sounded good now that we have the budget for it."

"But it's more mysterious if it's left unsaid."

"The prop's already on its way," Cashew says. "It's a special order from Míng's cousin in Singapore."

"How many fucking cousins does this Míng guy have?" Rian jeers.

"That is racist, first off!" Cashew counters. "Second off, it's almost half the budget!"

"Fuck the budget!"

"Easy for you to say!"

Whale looks at Cashew. "You never told me it was half the budget."

Cashew hesitates. "Yes I did."

"No you didn't!"

"YES, I DID!"

Whale frowns. Doesn't respond.

"He's a fucking liar, Jacob!" Rian interjects. "I've seen him lie to your face. Don't be fucking stupid!"

"Don't you fucking call him stupid!" Cashew snaps. "He has a disability, you ablest pig!"

"That's not what I meant!"

Cashew looks at Whale. "You should see how he talks shit about you behind your back."

"STOP FUCKING LYING!" Rian screams.

"Shut UP!" Whale yells, hands to his ears, his energy sapped. "It's just a prologue, Frankie. No one's gonna care."

"But it's supposed to be like *Reservoir Dogs*."

"Tarantino didn't show the heist for budgetary reasons, not artistic ones."

"The briefcase in *Pulp Fiction* was artistic."

"It wouldn't make sense having a short about a futuristic surgery without depicting it," Cashew says.

"How stupid do you think audiences are?" Rian asks incredulously.

"Pretty fucking stupid."

"You don't know what you're talking about."

"It'll look low budget without it."

"He's right," Whale adds.

"But what's the alternative?" Rian asks. "Looking too high budget for a split second? The short isn't even about the Surgery. It's twenty minutes of two characters talking. Leaving out the Surgery itself would make it tonally consistent throughout, and it contributes to the mysterious atmosphere I'm trying to convey!"

"You're outnumbered," Cashew whispers to Rian.

"Don't speak for me!" Whale interjects. "You don't know how I feel about this!"

Cashew tenses up, surprised at the outburst.

Whale swallows. "I agree with Frankie. It is better if the Surgery is unfilmed."

"Thank you," Rian says pointedly.

"That being said, Theo has a right to be upset. He is the producer. And as far as he knew, you were aware I approved the purchase." Whale pauses. "I shouldn't have done it without knowing all the facts."

"I told you everything," Cashew lies. "You just didn't listen."

Whale scrunches his lips, thinking. "Can we cancel the order?"

Cashew notices Rian's judgmental look. "No," he lies. "Even if we could, we won't get our money back."

"It's Míng's cousin."

"He already used the money to make it," Cashew lies again. "That's why I asked for your approval. It's too late now."

Whale sighs. "Then we have to film it."

"NO!" Rian shouts.

Cashew smiles at Rian. "Told you."

"Jacob, what the fuck!" Rian cries.

"We can't blow half our budget on a prologue that gets cut!" Whale snaps.

"Why not?"

Whale scoffs.

"No, why not?" Rian asks.

"It's *our* money, Frankie," Whale says. "Not yours."

"You know what?" Rian snarls. "Fuck you! It's bad enough I have to deal with you taking his side on everything. You have no right throwing my financial situation at me anytime you want to exclude me from the decision making process."

Cashew fakes a sneeze. "Motel 6!"

"I'M *SORRRRRY* MY CREDIT GOT DENIED *ONE TIME*!" Rian screams at the top of his lungs. "I'm not a fucking pauper! At least I HAVE fucking credit, Daddy's little bitch boy!"

"Real mature."

"Says the crybaby Cashew, huh?"

Cashew angrily storms at Rian, grabbing his shirt and jabbing punches at him. The two tussle across the stage.

Rian smacks back, trying to land a few of his own. "CASHEW! CASHEW!"

Whale struggles to separate them. "CUT IT OUT!" Whale pushes Cashew away with all his strength.

Cashew stumbles, falling to the ground and intentionally hitting his knee on the stage floor. "OW!" he cries, grabbing his knee with a sharp inhale. "What the fuck?"

"Bullshit!" Rian shouts.

"You could've broken my fucking knee!" Cashew cries at Whale. "What the fuck is wrong with you?!"

Whale gapes. "I'm sorry, I..."

"Don't listen to him!" Rian exclaims. "He's fucking lying!"

"STOP YELLING AT ME!" Whale yells back. He steps off the stage, holding back a wave of emotion in front of all those witnesses. "I'm sorry!" he cries at Rian. "I'm sorry I forced you to work with Theo!" Whale looks at Cashew. "And I'm sorry you had to deal with him at all!"

Cashew uses Larry's eager help to get back on his feet, throwing in a phony wince as he extends his leg. Rian rolls his eyes.

"Just fucking do it!" Whale shouts. "We all need this. Get it done. And get it done right. You'll never have to work with each other ever again." Rian and Cashew awkwardly frown at each other. Whale stands there, wanting to say more. Instead he about-faces and storms away.

Outside Whale sits on the stoop, arms around his knees. Larry sits next to him. "I think it worked."

"Pretty tense in there?"

"Yeah, but it's resolved."

Whale nods. "I hate this, Larry. This isn't fun at all."

"You're only a writer," Larry says sympathetically. "And may I say, I think *The Surgery* is one of the best scripts I've ever read."

Whale looks over. "Really?"

Larry nods. No bullshit in sight.

Whale sighs. "It's good to know I'm a better writer than I am a human being."

"What are you talking about?"

"I fucked up. You saw all that back there."

"You were the only rational one. They were so unreasonable, both of 'em."

Whale looks down at his shoes. "I appreciate your politeness, Larry, but this has been going on for weeks. I brought them together. It's my fault they aren't getting along."

"How was that about you?"

"I approved the purchase, didn't I? I put Rian in that position. I should've just listened to Theo the first time. I don't even remember..."

Larry shakes his head. "I don't think Theo's actually hurt. He's standing on it fine."

Whale hesitates. "Even still, I shouldn't have pushed him."

"He started the fight."

"I still don't know my own strength, I guess."

"I'm sorry, Mr. Andrezj, but I have to insist how wrong you are."

Whale looks at Larry curiously.

"I know it's not my place. I'm just a PA. But I have a nasty family that has a problem with my..." Larry bobs his head. "You know, my orientation. I've seen a lot of argumentative bullshit in my life. You were in the right the whole way back there. So if that's why you were so resistant coming to set, because you'd think you'd only do more harm than good, then you're wrong. Believe me, I know. You just saved a whole day's worth of shooting."

Whale stares at Larry some more. "Do you want a job, Larry?"

Larry chuckles. "I already work for you."

"I want to make you to be my personal assistant."

Larry gapes. "Mr. Andrezj!"

"I told you to call me Jacob."

"Since I'm taking the assistant job, I'm gonna have to insist on 'Mr. Andrezj!'"

Whale laughs sharply. "I just need someone to be with me on set. Someone normal."

"But you're not *not* normal."

"You don't know me, Larry. Don't pretend you do."

"If I don't think you're abnormal, someone who knows nothing about you, I'd say that's a pretty strong case for you being just fine."

Whale nods softly. "I don't seem to know that anymore. I need someone to help me keep a level head. So I'd know what I'm feeling. How much is real or just in my head."

Larry sighs. "I still think you're being a bit too hard on yourself, Mr. Andrezj, but who am I to say otherwise?" He smiles. "I'll do my best."

Whale smiles back. "Thanks Larry."

The two of them stare at the wall of the neighboring studio, their scary futures suddenly not so scary after all.

DREW

Don't Look Down

Larry sits on the edge of his bed of his glorious Malibu home, staring off in deep contemplation. It's the evening of Sunday, February 7th, twenty-four hours before Jimmy's defamatory interview on *Oscar Blitz.*

Aaron Lin, Larry's hunky white boy of a husband, rests a tricep against the bathroom door. He's humming "It's a Sin" as he flosses. What a goofball. "Did you think the guy playing Jack was hot?"

"Yeah," Larry answers, still distracted. "Oliver's way hotter though. I love his voice. He sounded like a rugged Ron Weasley."

Aaron tosses his floss into the bin. Turns off the bathroom light. Slides into bed. Big spoons his husband. "What'cha thinking about?"

"Nothing."

"Don't give me that."

Larry hesitates. "It brought up some memories, that's all."

"No wonder."

"Not that." Larry mind drifts back again. "Drew was all over that movie. It was like I was inside his head looking out. It's very weird when it's someone you know."

Aaron kisses Larry's cheek. "I'm sorry."

"No, I'm glad we saw it," Larry murmurs. "I just wish Theo would."

"Why?"

Larry shrugs.

Aaron caresses Larry's shoulder with a soft touch. "Do you still want Drew to come back?"

"He's thriving over there. I don't want him to leave that."

"Doesn't mean you don't want him to come back."

Larry frowns. "He's family, Aaron. I miss him."

"I still remember the toast he gave at our wedding."

Larry grins. "It really was one of the sweetest things anyone's ever said about me."

"You deserve it, baby." Aaron kisses Larry's cheek again.

"I don't want to be Head of Production anymore."

"You have to now."

"I'm doing Drew's job. It's perverse."

"But think what we have now because of it. We got this house. The girls are in private school."

"I'm not saying I want to quit. I'm just saying I don't like working directly under Theo."

"Why not?"

Larry frowns. "I just wish Drew was here. He could see this life we have. What we built together. You have your mom. I don't have anyone like that."

"Invite him over. I'm sure the girls would love to meet the famous Drew Lawrence they've heard so much about."

Larry goes quiet. "Did I do the right thing, taking Alan's job so quickly?"

"Huh?" Aaron asks, lifting his head. "I'm sorry, what did you say?"

Larry sighs. "Nothing. Go to sleep." They kiss.

Monday, February 8th. Larry catches Theo up to speed. Profits up. Losses down. Schedules unchanged. Pretty standard update. "Aaron and I went to the movies last night," Larry says on his way out.

"That's nice," Theo says, skimming Larry's report. "What did you see?"

"*The Sins of Jack Branson*."

Theo lifts his head. "What did I tell you?!"

"It's the number one movie in the world."

"I don't care. I don't wanna hear anything related to him. You know the rules."

Larry scoffs. "You can't put a movie on the Black List."

"It's not playing in China. If it's not playing in China, it's got nothing to do with business."

"It's number one *despite* not playing in China. That's worth analyzing. And last I checked we're an American company now."

"China's where the money is. Always has been."

"Maybe *Branson*'s a sign of something new, smart, ambitious blockbusters having a market again. We'd really need to reconsider our strategy before the demographic—"

"I don't want to hear anymore. You've made your point. Leave me be."

Larry nods. Leaves Theo's office.

Tuesday, February 9th. Theo steps onto his balcony. What a great spot. George Clooney had no idea when he sold it to him that he'd been there before, talking his way past Gene the housekeeper up to where he was standing just now, leaning over the railing just like he was now to get a good shot of Morton what's-his-name railing his trophy wife. That ex-partner of his almost screwed it up if it wasn't for Theo's quick thinking.

Theo hears the coffee machine sputter. As he turns his head, he stops on Morton what's-his-name's old place, the army commando guy walking around his living room in bodybuilder shorts and a tank top. He could crush Theo between his hands like a PB&J sandwich, but if Theo walked down Sycamore street right now and took an Amazon package off Commando Guy's front step, he wouldn't be able to stop him. He might even thank Theo for it. The thought of that makes Theo smile.

Theo steps onto the 7th Floor of Not That Nutty Productions. His new executive assistant Hector greets him with a smile, a buff chipper redhead just as short as he is. The usual swarm of wannabe applicants stand and beg, resumes in outstretched hands. Theo ignores them as he walks past. Then the producers greet him. Then Larry, his Head of Production. The whole time Theo maintains a corporate aloofness, a stone-faced candor. Inside he's a giggly little boy.

Larry knocks on Theo's door just after lunch. "*Goodbye to You*'s about to hit their budget wall."

Theo stares. "Why wasn't it in the report?"

"Calculation error. Ken just sent over the corrections."

"Come with me." Theo leads Larry into the elevator down to 2, silent as a mouse. They walk out and stop at the blue door. "Wait here," Theo tells Larry.

Larry watches Theo through the blue door's glass window, marching up to Ken Gold's cubicle, knocking a stack of files off of the desk and onto the floor, yelling at Ken, the other producers paralyzed by Theo's presence let alone his behavior, Theo smacking the coffee cup out of Ken's hand, a bit of it splashing on Ken's shirt. Theo storms away and opens the blue door. Larry meekly follows Theo back up to 7.

Theo returns to his office quite content with his speed, his choice of words, his willingness not to soften the blow. Ken's gonna make all the necessary cutbacks to keep his project on budget. Another crack in the hull fixed, just like that.

Wednesday, February 10th. Larry sits at his desk. Munches on a Bavarian cream donut (Cheryl brought in a box). Checks Twitter on his phone. Notices a hashtag with "Branson" in it.

> @drewlawrence is a fucking pig. Do not financially support @jackbransonfilm. #BoycottBranson

Larry stops chewing. Taps the hashtag. Almost 40,000 uses. Larry scrolls through the mass of tweets, skimming each one down the line. Who the fuck is Jimmy Lyons?

Larry logs onto his desktop. Googles "Jimmy Lyons." No major news sites reporting anything. One of the results is from OscarBlitz.com. Larry clicks the link. Plastered all over the *Oscar Blitz* homepage is some eighteen-year-old's face with puffy red eyes, tears, or both.

Larry watches Jimmy's interview with Oscar. By the end of the episode, Larry realizes his heart's been pounding like crazy. He checks the post date: 02/08/38. Monday night? Why is it only gaining traction now?

Larry puts on *Oscar Blitz*'s live feed. Two dudes, one long-haired blond named Nich (pronounced "Niche" for some reason) and a Sk8er Boi named Trevor sitting across from Oscar and telling him something about a swastika and some guy named Carter Jackson. They keep saying his name like he's Hitler or something. They're namedropping Hitler too for some reason.

Larry clicks away, finally understanding. This is bad, not just for Drew. What Jimmy's accusing Drew of allegedly happened while Drew was Acting CEO of Not That Nutty. Black List be damned. Theo needs to hear about this.

Larry opens Theo's office door, knocking. "Sir, something's wrong."

"I gotta get this done before Míng's guys show up tomorrow," Theo murmurs, exhausted. "What is it?"

"It's Drew."

"WHAT DID I TELL YOU?!" Theo yells. "WHAT DID I *FUCKING* TELL YOU?!"

"I'm sorry sir, but—"

"Even after I got Hector, I still wanted you to manage the Black List because I thought I could trust you with it, and yet time and time again I have to keep reminding you how it works! When I put someone on the Black List, I NEVER WANT TO HEAR THEIR NAME AGAIN!"

"But sir—!"

"One more word about that man and I'll fire you on the spot! I swear to God! I'll give the Black List to Hector and tell him to put YOUR name on it! Do you want that?"

Against his better judgment, Larry shakes his head.

"Good," Theo says. "Get the fuck out of here."

Larry can't get back to work. He's too preoccupied by the chaos brewing out there, the danger creeping its way in. #BoycottBranson hits 100,000 tweets by 4 PM. Larry checks again just before bed. 600,000 tweets worldwide.

Thursday, February 11th. Larry wakes up and immediately checks his phone. Number one on Twitter: #BoycottBranson. 1.5 million tweets.

Theo escorts UniTopia ambassadors Lei Dá and Sù Hong into his best conference room for their yearly visit. Larry watches from his office. Theo cannot be disturbed at such a time. Once he's gone, Larry races into kitchen and turns on the TV. Shuffles through the channels. The Jimmy Lyons story has gone mainstream. Associated Press. NBC. ABC. CBS. All the nationwide shebangs. Al Jazeera, Reuters, and BBC too. It's out there. It's everywhere. No Black List can stop it now.

After about forty minutes of actual business, Theo cracks open a few beers. "So Theo," Hong says, sipping on a bottle of Coors Light, "what's all this we hear about Drew Lawrence fucking a teenager?"

Theo laughs a bit. "What?"

"Your former Head of Production? That's his name, right?"

Theo freezes. "What did you say?"

"He fucked a sixteen year old when he was Acting CEO. You didn't know about this?"

"It's all over Twitter," Dá adds, looking at his phone.

Theo hesitates. "You guys are fucking with me, right?"

Dá looks at Hong. "He doesn't know."

"Oscar Blitz," Hong says. "You know Oscar Blitz?"

"Of course I know Oscar Blitz," Theo snaps, panic setting in. "What the fuck did Drew do?"

Theo walks out five minutes later. Bows to Dá and Hong. Rushes his farewells. Beelines past Larry. "OFFICE!" Theo snarls.

Larry jumps from his desk. Discreetly hurries down the hall. Politely waves to Hector. Lets himself into Theo's office.

"WHAT THE FUCK IS GOING ON?!" Theo roars as soon as the door closes.

"I tried to tell you yesterday."

"YOU SHOULD HAVE!"

"You threatened to fire me!"

"I did—!" Theo stops himself. "Do you have any idea how embarrassed I was back there? Míng's guys are asking me how Timothée Chalamet knew about Drew before I did. And who the FUCK asked Timothée Chalamet for a comment in the first place, huh? *Arrakis Weekly*?"

"That's hysterical."

"THIS IS NOT A FUCKING JOKE, LARRY! If they tell Míng I didn't know about this, who knows what he'd do to me?!"

"Why would he do anything to you?"

"I don't know! You can't predict this guy! It could be over anything!"

Larry's blood chills. "You don't mean...?

"I mean *over anything*, Larry! That's what I fucking mean." Theo locks both hands behind his head.

Larry takes a deep breath. "You have to keep the others from saying anything."

"Don't tell me how to do my fucking job." Theo intercoms Hector. "Send out a standard no-press memo to all personnel regarding Drew Lawrence."

"Yes sir," Hector says back.

Theo looks at Larry. "How long have you known about this?"

"Yesterday morning," Larry answers. "Jimmy first went on *Oscar Blitz* Monday night."

"Monday?!"

"It's only gotten worse. NBC, CBS, they're all talking about it now that #BoycottBranson's number one on Twitter, which means CNN and Fox News are gonna have a field day tomorrow."

"CNN? Fox? What do they have to do with it?"

Larry hesitates. "It's not just the stat rape. There's more."

Theo's eyes go wide. "MORE?!"

Oscar Blitz airs more allegations in the afternoon block. Gordy Benson, writer of *Joshua Tree*, rants for thirty uninterrupted minutes how Drew Lawrence ruined his career. Then CJ Marrow, director of Drew's 2024 Sundance hit *You Should Come to California*, calls Drew a "perfectionist asshole" that actively sabotaged his artistic vision.

News of Gordy and CJ's *Oscar Blitz* appearances spread throughout Not That Nutty, their relatable stories hitting close to home to anyone who's ever known Drew at his worst. Larry calls an emergency meeting with all the producers to cool tensions.

"Theo's no-press order still stands!" Larry barks at the discontented gathering. "And that goes for everyone! No one talks, alright?! No one!"

"But Simmons and Johnson were fired for *supporting* Drew!" Gerry Apple speaks up. "Which is it? Theo can't have it both ways!"

"We wanna get in on this!" Damon shouts. "We all have something to say about Drew. Why can't *our* voices be heard?" Everyone shouts in affirmation at this.

"The memo is not optional!" Larry yells over everyone. "It's an order from your CEO. If you want to break it, break it. Don't be shocked if you get fired. You all signed NDAs. You'll also be facing legal action."

The producers deflate, many sighing with disappointment.

Larry scans their faces. "This is Drew we're talking about. *Our* Drew. We've all had problems with him. Of course we have. But nothing he has ever done to you could be worse than what Theo will do to you if you speak out. What you'll be doing to yourselves. To your careers." Larry pauses. "To your conscience. There's no *Oscar Blitz* you can run to to make you feel better about that."

Friday, February 12th. Cable news breaks out the overreaction theater, their 24-hour news cycles filled to the brim with Drew Lawrence's sordid past and how the Jimmy Lyons incident fits into their current issues agenda. CNN discredits Drew as "Trumpian," spending the day nit-picking his rhetoric in college (casually saying "retarded," defending a Trump supporter's right to draw swastikas on billboards, passionately defending Trump on 11/9 after Russia stole the election, Drew's deep admiration for rapist Carter Jackson) in the hopes that it would deter an Alt-Right revival come next election cycle. They also call on their progressive audience to take Jimmy's side 100% if they really didn't want rape to be made legal one day. Fox News on the other hand spends a disconcerting amount of airtime on Drew's right to have sex with a sixteen-year-old if he wants to, using graphs and colored maps to remind their audience that the specific act in question is in fact legal in thirty-one other states, including Drew's native Pennsylvania and Jimmy's native Washington. So what exactly did he do wrong besides use his God-given First Amendment right to trigger those pansy Democrats?

Oscar's guest for Friday's morning block is Drew's former personal trainer Shayne Parker. "Drew didn't want to put in the effort to have a good body," Shayne says. "He just wanted to throw money at the problem. It's an insult to the hard work millions of others put in, vouching for an easy shortcut like that. A purely cosmetic shortcut, mind you. He was never actually gonna gain any strength from it. It's supposed to be used in conjunction with regular exercise. Whoever told him steroids were a good idea forgot to mention that part."

"Did he adjust well to the steroids?" Oscar asks.

"No one really adjusts well. He broke out a lot. He had horrible mood swings. But he *looked* great." Shayne scoffs. "He asked me one time, in all seriousness, if I thought he looked good, if he looked hot. What an absolutely vain person he is. He wasn't doing it for his health or his quality of life, it was purely for him. For sex appeal, I can imagine. When he started realizing the Tren wasn't making him stronger, I told him very plainly what I just told you now, that it wasn't doing the workouts for him. He just didn't listen. In fact he made me add something else on top."

"Another steroid?"

"I told him that was incredibly bad idea, that it was unhealthy, that it could actually kill him, but he just said, 'I don't care.' So I put him on 400mg of androstanolone in addition to the 400mg of trenbolone."

"Was he on both the night he raped Jimmy Lyons?"

"He was."

Oscar furrows his brow a bit. "Don't you think, as a fitness professional, you have a responsibility to deny patients access to illicit Schedule III substances?"

Shayne stares, unsure where that came from. "When Drew Lawrence wants something, he gets it. He doesn't take no for an answer."

Oscar smiles at the camera. "We'll be right back."

Theo frowns out his window at his disgruntled employees. How could this have happened? If he doesn't do something to regain their confidence, he's gonna have an uprising on his hands. He just has to fix the hull. Everything will be just like it was before.

Theo pushes the intercom. "Send out a new memo. All employees from every department are now authorized to go to *Oscar Blitz*, and ONLY *Oscar Blitz*, with any and all allegations they have against Drew Lawrence with no legal repercussions or fear of dismissal."

"Yes, Mr. Landreth," Hector responds.

Theo hesitates. He pushes the intercom again. "And I don't want to know anything. What they're saying about him. What they're accusing him of. Nothing."

"Understood."

Larry reads the new memo, bile forming in his stomach. If he wasn't so afraid of losing his job, he'd punch that son of a bitch in the jaw. But he is. So he doesn't.

Saturday, February 13th. For the first time in its 38-year history, *Oscar Blitz* drops weekend episodes, new developments from Drew's former employees at Not That Nutty Productions. Larry and Aaron anxiously watch *Oscar Blitz* in their living room, their six-year-old Charlotte chasing four-year-old Nina around the kitchen. "Go play in your room, girls," Larry tells them. "Daddy and I got some grownup TV to watch, okay?"

"Okay Dad," Charlotte responds. She ushers Nina upstairs like a good little girl.

Larry looks at Aaron with shame. Aaron holds him close. They force themselves to watch Damon Muller, Janet Gower, and Harold Drayton talk about a violent outburst Drew had during a screening of *Glory*.

Meanwhile at 44 Sycamore in Studio City, paparazzi swarm Theo's home.

"Did Drew ever tell you about Jimmy Lyons?"

"Did you know about cocaine or the steroids?"

"Is it true you recommended Shayne Parker to Drew Lawrence personally?"

"Any comment on Drew's screening room meltdown?"

"Did you know about the Sweet Vermouths tradition when you made Drew Acting CEO of Not That Nutty?"

Theo stays hunched on the floor, hands over his head, elbows blocking his ears, screaming mercilessly.

Sunday, February 14th. Oscar's third interview of the day gains instant nationwide traction: Carlos Gutierrez, a Not That Nutty custodian, reveals on-air that Drew Lawrence routinely smashed up conference rooms in monstrous bursts of fury, causing thousands of dollars of property damage, for Carlos and his team of undocumented workers to clean up the mess and discarded all evidence. Worst of all, every so often and without warning, Carlos would receive a call from "the Gringo" ordering him to pick one of his men to deport back to Mexico. The fear of indiscriminate deportation was meant to keep them silent about what they were doing for Drew Lawrence. This shocking revelation became a new low in the Drew Lawrence saga, a new high for *Oscar Blitz*'s ratings, and a new number-one hashtag: #CarlosChoice.

Larry shuts off the TV. Grabs his keys. Speeds all the way to Studio City. Storms past the paparazzi and flashing cameras. Uses his spare key to let himself in. Races upstairs to Theo's bedroom. Rips the comforter off the bed. "WHAT THE FUCK IS WRONG WITH YOU?!"

Theo glares up at Larry, eyes burning from the daylight. "What are you doing here?"

"It's bad enough he has to deal with all that Jimmy bullshit! Now you're dumping throw YOUR shit on him?!"

"I'm running an ecosystem here. I can't take the chance of a revolution."

"*THAT'S* YOUR PRIORITY?!"

"Of course it is."

Larry cringes. "You're ruining Drew's life, Theo!"

"HE RUINED US FIRST!" Theo hops out of bed. "He stole our money! MY money! I earned it! He doesn't get to get away with that!"

"Do you have any idea what you're doing to him?" Larry asks defiantly. "Of course you don't, because you have that fucking Black List protecting you from ever facing consequences for your actions! What you did to Doris! To Simmons! To Johnson! To *Alan*!"

Theo scowls, a mix of hate and shame.

Larry chuckles harshly. "I know you made him quit, Theo. I'm not stupid. You made me your assistant so Drew would have no choice but to pick Alan up so you could have a man on the inside. But Drew didn't do that, did he? You got rid of Alan for nothing."

Theo's breath wavers.

"He trusted you, Theo!" Larry yells. "He made all those calls to Carlos, not Drew! He did that for you so you'd never have to! He did your dirty work! He dealt with all the grief! He endured those sleepless nights! He even ran your Black List because you couldn't even bear to see the NAMES of the people you fucked over! And what did you do?! You put his job and his future at risk for a fucking chess move YOU fucked up! And then you just tossed him aside! I should've left the moment I found that out. I really wish I did. I know now what a monster you are! How you REALLY reward your friends!"

"GET THE FUCK OUT OF MY HOUSE!"

"Do you wanna know what happened to Alan? What he *did* to himself?"

"SHUT UP!"

"I have the list, Theo! It updates itself! I know where they all are!"

"SHUT UP!"

"How about Rian Hoffman, huh? You wanna know how he's living because of what you did to him?!"

Theo covers both ears. "SHUT UP! SHUT UP! SHUT UP! SHUT UP! SHUT UP! SHUT UP! SHUT UP!"

Larry stops talking, disturbed and disgusted.

Theo points at Larry with shaking hands. "One more fucking word about any of them and you're finished! You're fucking finished, you hear me?! You'll be living just like them! You and your family! Go on! Do it! One more GODDAMN word!"

Larry looks away. Glowers at nothing. At himself. He slowly turns. Walks into the hall.

"Yeah, that's what I thought," Theo rasps. He climbs back into bed.

Larry stops outside the door. Looks back at Theo. "I'm not jeopardizing my girls' futures, Mr. Landreth. But I hope you realize there's an army out there you'll never see coming because of that fucking Black List." Larry grabs the handle. "Sleep on *that*." He slams the door.

Monday, February 15th. Larry looks up from his desk to see Theo walking in the same way he always does, as if everything Larry had said before meant nothing to him, just some steam Larry was blowing off, a bit of heat in the moment.

Larry detaches the TV mounted in the kitchen. Rolls in a couple of amps. Points them at Theo's office. Plugs everything in. Turns on the TV. Selects *Oscar Blitz.* Maxes out the TV's volume. Turns each amp's volume knob to the max. Larry stands back and watches Oscar interview some guy named Artie Henderson, an indie filmmaker from NYC apparently.

Theo curls up on his office floor, hands over his ears, trying and frantically failing to cover Oscar's voice and some douchebag with a New York accent mentioning something about Drew.

"I forgot all about it," Artie says. "It's amazing how people have the time to find these things, you know?"

"For all those watching now who haven't see the video yet," Oscar says, "here's a bit of it now."

"It certainly leaves one with questions to ponder," a decades younger Artie says into a microphone, the amplified voice recorded with a shittier microphone. Must be amateur footage or something. "Okay, so this next question's for all three of you. If there was a Surgery, an elective surgery, to change something about yourself, what would you change?"

"Definitely my hair."

"Nothing." Theo opens his eyes at the sound of his own voice.

"Nothing? You sure?"

"Yeah. Nothing."

Theo's blood chills. He stands up. Listens some more.

"What about you, Jacob?" Young Artie asks.

Silence. "If I'm being honest..." Just the sound of Drew's voice makes Theo's legs wobble. He whips the door open. The TV's right there. Larry's watching it too. In horror, it looks like.

On screen is a vertical video of Artie Henderson sitting across from Whale (looking great with his red dye-job and lensless glasses), Cashew (looking like shit, to be honest) and Rian (ehh) with microphones in their hands. "A little bit louder," Young Artie says into his mic.

"I'd get rid of my autism," Whale states.

Gasps and audience confusion surround the cameraman, an audience member. Young Artie shifts his seat. "Oh, um..."

"It's true," Whale continues. "If they ever made a cure, I'll take it in a heartbeat. They should make a cure. Ask any autistic person. They'll all say the same thing."

The feed cuts back to Oscar and Artie sitting live in Studio 1. "Wow!" Oscar exclaims. "I can't believe he actually said that."

"That was our Tribeca video," Theo murmurs to Larry.

Larry lowers the volume rapidly. "Someone posted it on Twitter. It went viral like crazy, so Oscar brought the guy on to talk about it."

Theo furrows his brow. "But he was there. He was backstage the whole time. Why is he pretending he's never heard it before?"

"To keep his objectivity, I guess," Larry says, just as bewildered. "He knows everyone's gonna believe him at his word. If he's lying about this, what else is he lying about?" Larry looks over at Theo, terrified. "Did *any of this* actually happen?" he whispers.

Theo covers his mouth, eyes frozen open. Oscar isn't playing by the rules anymore. It doesn't matter if he's done anything wrong, does it? Theo can easily be taken down just as quick, just as uncontrollable, and there's nothing he can do about it. Nothing he can do to stop it.

Because there are no rules.

There never were.

WHALE

Golden Calf

"I got you guys into Tribeca," Oscar says, pouring their second round of mimosas.

Whale blinks. "We're not even done filming yet."

"It's not gonna be much longer, right?"

"How can they say yes without even seeing it?"

Oscar shrugs. "I know a guy who owes me a favor. I showed him the script."

Whale frowns, his skin tingling. "You bribed him, didn't you?"

"You got in," Oscar clarifies. "You actually got in. All I did was get him to use a bit of imagination."

Whale covers his nose and mouth with both hands. "Oh my God!" he whimpers excitedly.

"Hey, if I were you, I wouldn't tell Rian or Theo until after you're done shooting."

"You kidding me? I'm not telling them until we get to New York!"

Oscar and Whale laugh hard and loud, their bodies rocking back and forth in their seats.

One month later. Oscar hosts a private screening of *The Surgery* in Studio 1. At the end, during the rapturous of applause of Cashew and Whale's coworkers, Rian leans over and says to Whale, "You know, for a prologue I was forced to film at gunpoint, it really wasn't that bad."

Whale smirks. Puts his arm around Rian and half-hugs, the applause still going at full strength.

Three months later. As Oscar checks them into their Manhattan hotel, Rian watches Whale and Cashew sit by the lobby window, talking quietly to each other. Whale looks upset. He was quiet on the plane, as a matter of fact. Cashew doesn't look like he's helping at all.

That night, Rian knocks on Whale's room with a six-pack of Blue Moon. They sit on Whale's bed and look out at the beautiful lights of New York City. "You haven't been yourself lately," Rian says.

"It's that obvious?"

"Don't you think so?"

Whale shrugs. "It's nothing," he says bitterly. "I'm fine."

Rian shakes his head softly.

"It's not you," Whale adds.

"What is it?"

Whale looks down at his beer. "I had my first beer when I was in Ireland. I'd heard a rumor that Eagle Ridge chaperones let Seniors drink the last night of any trip they did in Europe. Mom somehow found out about it. She was actually okay with it. She told me to get a Guinness. I assumed it was a 'When in Rome' exception with her." Whale sips his beer. Runs his tongue around it. "I didn't complain." He pauses. "So on our last day in Dublin, me and the three other Seniors went to a bar with one of the chaperones. It was right after graduation, probably around the same time Mom and Dad were having that fight in Disney World."

Rian furrows his brow. There's definitely spite in Whale's voice, more than normal.

Whale shrugs. "They serve Guinness room-temp over there."

"Ew."

"I know. It was my first beer too."

Rian cringes. "Not a good introduction."

"Horrible introduction. I couldn't touch beer for three years after that." Whale finishes his Blue Moon. "Which was why Mom told me to do it. She knew I'd hate it. All part of her fucking plan to get me to hate beer and not turn into alcoholic Uncle Bart."

"You don't know that."

"She told me herself. Fucking laughed at me too." Whale stares out the window, zoning out. "How could I have ever let her get away with that?"

"It's just beer, man."

Whale puts the empty bottle on the floor. Opens another one, twisting off the top with a hard *scrunch*. "She has Stage III breast cancer. Lymph nodes." He throws the bottlecap at the window. "Aggressive too. Really big. Really fast."

"Jesus." Rian puts his beer down. "Jacob, I'm—"

"Oh, I'm sorry!" Whale interrupts sarcastically. "I meant she *had* Stage III breast cancer." He drinks half his beer in one go.

Rian hands his head, a deep sadness growing.

"She's not dead," Whale adds pointedly. "She's in remission."

"You got me worried there."

"It was all a year ago." Whale finishes his beer. "Six rounds of chemo. Her *own* surgery last December. As far as Karen knows, they got it all." Whale puts down the empty. Grabs another bottle. *Scrunch.*

"Surprised you didn't tell me," Rian whispers. "I know I've been—"

"I only found out yesterday," Whale says with a laugh. "I wanted to invite her up here to see my short. She didn't answer, so I called Karen and she told me everything." Whale swigs his beer. "She did it again, Frankie. Even after I went out of my way to forgive her for what she did, she went and fucking did it AGAIN." He hurls the bottle cap at the window, much harder this time.

Rian frowns.

"She could've died mid-surgery and I wouldn't have known," Whale says, empty inside. "Not even a phone call. She never even told me she had cancer. I would've just..." He shakes his head. "You know what, if I never talk to that selfish bitch again, that's fine with me."

Rian's stomach drops. "Don't say that."

Whale looks at Rian, both surprised and disappointed. "Since when are you on her side?" He swigs his beer.

Rian doesn't answer. Whale's words actually make him nauseous.

Whale stares at his reflection in the bathroom mirror the next day. Someone knocks on his hotel room door. A chipper man with dyed blond hair struts in carrying a makeup kit. "Morning!" the Chipper Man says, a big smile on his face. "Ready to get started?"

"Leon, right?"

"Yes sir!" Leon pulls a chair over.

Whale sits. "You don't need a mirror or anything?"

"I am the mirror, silly goose!" Leon grabs a brush. Immediately starts applying foundation. "Excited?"

"Kinda."

"What's up?"

Whale doesn't say anything. Leon continues with powder, taking his time on Whale's cheeks.

"Are you happy, Leon?" Whale asks.

"I think so. Why do you ask?"

"I'm not too happy myself."

"How come?"

Whale hesitates. "I don't think there's a real reason. I'm probably just too soft, you know? Too all over the place."

"You're not soft," Leon says sweetly. "You're nice. I love how nice you are."

"That's not necessarily a good thing."

"There you go again."

"I'm sorry. My depression's been acting up lately. It happens." Whale shrugs. "My brain lies to me."

Leon stops applying makeup. Looks Whale right in the eye. "You're a screenwriter now. Not an aspiring screenwriter. An actual screenwriter. You're just about to debut in one of the biggest film festivals in the country. And it wasn't even the film that got you in, it was *your script.* Just look at the big picture. Remember how lucky you are. How good all this is."

Whale smiles a bit.

"There you go!" Leon teases.

Whale smiles some more. Leon chuckles a bit. Resumes applying Whale's makeup.

Whale pushes the down button on the elevator. Looks at his made-up face in the mirror. His attractive blazer. His great haircut. How dashing he looks. How fit. He can't help but smile, rejuvenated by Leon's optimism. The elevator arrives.

Whale steps into the lobby. Cashew and Rian are there waiting for him. "Where's Oscar?" Whale asks.

"Still changing apparently," Rian says. "Won't be long."

"Hope we're not late."

"We got plenty of time."

Whale notices Cashew's unusual introspection. "You okay?"

Cashew glares at Whale and his uncharacteristic cheer. "I'm fucking starving."

"You didn't get breakfast?"

"No!"

"You missed a good one," Rian teases. "Really extra too."

"Reminded me of the brunches Oscar takes me to," Whale says.

Cashew glares at Whale. "You never thought I wanted to go?"

Whale blinks. "It's not my fault you missed it."

"I thought it was gonna be one of those continental kinds."

"In a place like this?"

Cashew scoffs. "Just thought you would've cared, that's all."

Whale's smile drops. "I'm sorry, I didn't know."

"You should've. I would have."

"I'm sorry."

"You keep saying that," Cashew mumbles bitterly.

"Cut it out," Rian says.

"Stay out of it, Frankie," Whale snaps. "God. Let me fight my own fucking battles."

Rian furrows his brow. Whale walks to the other side of the lobby, his self-disgust revived. He was sitting with Rian for hours. He even noticed Cashew hadn't come down. How selfish he was. How careless. One of the greatest days of their lives and now Cashew's starving his ass off.

A few hours later, *The Surgery* makes its world premiere at the 2019 Tribeca Film Festival. After several minutes of rapturous applause, Whale, Rian, and Cashew take the stage for a Q&A moderated by local indie filmmaker Artie Henderson.

"So Jacob, tell us about the process," Artie starts. "How did the idea come about?"

"Well..." Whale starts, glancing a bit at Rian sitting next to him. "A few years ago, I was in a transitionary period of my life. I had my first serious boyfriend. I did a semester in Florence. I weaned off my medication for the first time ever. I lost a significant amount of weight."

"How much weight?"

"Around eighty pounds."

"Oh, congratulation."

A few audience members applaud. Whale shifts in his seat, smiling but unsure how to react. "I also got LASIK around that time. Pretty much a lot of changes at the same time, you know. And I thought it was interesting how relatively small additions and changes affected a lot of things. Like my boyfriend at the time, Stewie. He was just a guy, you know? Just another person I could hang out with, but..." Whale pauses. "But somehow he was so much more than that. And what makes Florence so exotic of a locale? I went to school in Boston, which was another world to me compared to my native Phoenixville, Pennsylvania, so what makes one more special than the other? That's what I used to explore the nature of change. And I think this story appeals to a lot of people. We all deal with change in one way or another. And I don't mean the normal kind of change, the hetero narrative of growing up, career, marriage, kids, so on. I mean the kind of change no one expects, like finding your soulmate only for them to pass away two years later. Having a child come out stillborn. Or maybe you have everything you could possibly want but there's something still missing. What if there was a way to go in and just take out only the bad parts of your life. Would that really make it all better? Or is it the addiction to change that's the real problem, that perpetual unsatisfaction?"

"That's absolutely right," Artie says into the microphone. "It's such a simple story in a way, but there's still so much to unpack about us as human beings. Failure to take responsibility for one's actions. Selective memory. Historical revisionism. The ethics of such a Surgery in the first place."

"It's also a dig at the medical industry," Rian adds. "From the practitioner's perspective, it was another successful surgery with no side effects, but from Kevin's point of view, it ruined his relationship. Begs the question of how many other patients had the same tragic result as Kevin. They'd conveniently leave that out of their free consultation, wouldn't they?"

"It certainly leaves one with questions to ponder." Artie checks his notecards. "Okay, so this next question's for all three of you. If there was a Surgery, an elective surgery, to change something about yourself, what would you change?"

"Definitely my hair," Rian says. Everyone laughs.

Cashew shrugs. "Nothing."

Rian looks at Cashew. "Nothing? You sure?"

Cashew stares back. "Yeah. Nothing."

"What about you, Jacob?" Artie asks.

Whale zones out, tracing the arm of his chair with a finger. "If I'm being honest..."

"A little bit louder."

Whale clears his throat. "I'd get rid of my autism."

The audience murmurs uncomfortably. Artie is taken aback. "Oh, um..."

"It's true," Whale insists. "If they ever made a cure, I'll take it in a heartbeat. They should make a cure. Ask any autistic person. They'll all say the same thing."

Rian and Cashew exchange awkward glances.

Artie clears his throat. "I think we should move on to the next question."

"It's not just a series of social quirks," Whale interrupts. "That I could live with, but it affects everything about me. My dependence on others. My black-and-white worldview. My dependence on place, on a familiar state of mind, on comfort zones. Realistically that's impossible, so most times I just end up feeling broken, trapped in a perpetual state of doubt. In myself. In my abilities. What I can do. It's never going away. No matter where I go, what I do, it just won't end. There's nothing I can do about it. And I know this isn't something everyone goes through, just me. Because I'm the autistic one. I can be happy for a week then I'm anxious out of nowhere.

Then I overthink everything to death. Then I'm sad, so fucking sad. Then it fades away and I'm happy again. I want it to stop. You'd think me being aware of it would allow me to adapt, you know, to predict it, to base my whole life around it, but my mind, my consciousness, believes it every time. That's what's so fucking scary about it. I genuinely believe everything I feel at the time. It's not until later that I look back and realize how stupid I was. That's something children do, not adults. I'm stuck being a fake grown-up. A wannabe. It's just so depressing thinking of my life as a waste. I want it to be just delusions, but to a lot of people it's reality. A lot of people like me."

Rian stares at Whale, horrified.

"About a year and a half ago, I was caught in a very messy situation." Whale goes quiet for a moment. "I thought I was handling everything so rationally at the time, but I was so wrong. That's just how fucked up I can be. If I didn't let my friends beat sense into me, it could've fucked a whole lot of things up."

Rian looks at Cashew, catching an unconscious smile before it vanishes. "What?" Cashew asks.

Rian faces forward, retreating inward. The Q&A quickly moves on to far less controversial subject matter, but Rian can't stop thinking about that smile.

After the Q&A, that autism *faux pas* longed buried by many minutes of pleasant conversation, Rian, Cashew, and Whale join Oscar backstage. "What's next?" Rian asks.

"Now we celebrate!" Oscar says, masking his own concern in Whale's demeanor. "I've got a car coming in just a moment."

"Can I use the bathroom?" Whale asks.

"Of course."

Whale pops into the men's room. Oscar heads outside with his cell phone. "Can I talk to you for a moment?" Rian forces himself to ask Cashew.

Cashew shrugs. "Sure. Why not."

"You heard what Jacob said back there?"

"The man knows his limits."

"He's never talked that way about his Asperger's before."

Cashew blinks. "It's been a long time since you two were friends."

"I know him, Theo. That man wasn't Jacob."

"What are you saying?"

Rian takes a slow breath, letting his reluctance show. "I don't think you realize how impressionable he can be."

"Oh, I do."

Rian hesitates. "I thought I did too but... I know how little comments here and there can add up with someone like him. You can't just say whatever comes to your mind. Believe me, I know."

"What are you saying?"

"I don't think you realize what you're doing to him."

Cashew scoffs. "What I'm doing to him?"

"I'm not saying intentionally, but—"

"Why not?"

Rian furrows his brow. There's that smile again. "What?"

"It was 100% intentional," Cashew says calmly.

"What was?"

Cashew gets really close to Rian. "Do you have any idea how fucking lucky we are to have someone as passionate as Jacob be so emotionally malleable?"

Rian studies Cashew's face up close. "I don't think we're talking about the same thing."

"Yes we are," Cashew teases. "I'm gaslighting him. I've been gaslighting him for over a year now. I'm very proud of myself. It's all in the beginning, you know. You gotta be patient. Dial the flame up just a little bit at a time." Cashew puts on a devious smirk. "I had a huge breakfast this morning. But he believed me, didn't he?"

Rian's heart races, disgust creeping throughout his body. "What the fuck is wrong with you?" he hisses.

"Nothing, man!" Cashew declares. "I'm on cloud nine. I've got myself a clone who wants everything I want, who's capable of doing everything I can do. Don't you know how valuable that is? How much higher we can go with twice the equally motivated manpower?"

"I can't believe what I'm hearing."

"You should be fucking THANKING me!" Cashew says, jabbing a finger into Rian's chest. "We wouldn't even be here if it wasn't for me."

Rian's brows press together. "Jacob's script got us in."

"Exactly! He's the one they wanted, not us. If he couldn't make here, I doubt we'd even get the screening."

"That's not how it works."

"Even still, would you really want to take that chance? He was going to leave if I didn't stop him."

Rian stares. "What are you talking about?"

"His mom, dude. When he found out she had cancer, he wanted to bail. Said he was gonna tell Oscar to let him go to PA instead to see her. He would've let him too, that son of a bitch."

"That's not how he felt last night."

"Yeah," Cashew says. "You're welcome."

Rian's blood chills. "That's his fucking mother!" he snarls. "He loves her!"

Cashew laughs. "Not anyone he doesn't."

"You destroyed the last familial relationship he has left so you could get into Tribeca?"

"So WE could get into Tribeca!" Cashew corrects. "Besides, she didn't want to tell him because she knew he'd do something stupid exactly like that. I'm just following her lead on this."

"She doesn't want him to hate her!"

"Well that's what happens when you're an impulsive, emotionally unstable cunt that loves keeping secrets from your kids. He's better off without her and you know it."

"THAT'S NOT YOUR DECISION TO MAKE!" Rian hollers.

"It's my career at stake, so... Yeah, I think it is."

Rian points at the bathroom door. "I'm telling him."

"Go ahead," Cashew says casually. "He won't believe you."

"I'm still his friend."

"I'm the one that got him to publish that video," Cashew declares. "I'm the one that comforted him afterwards. I took him in. I let him cry all over my furniture. For this. For us to be here. To finally make it. The Professor would still be out there raping and abusing if I hadn't done that. I'd still be bowing and scraping for Oscar 'The Faggot' Blitz if I hadn't done that. I'm not gonna let conventional morality deprive me of a fucking future. What good has anything conventional done for anyone, huh?"

Rian shakes his head rapidly. "You're a fucking monster!"

Cashew rolls his eyes. "Oh please."

"You sadistic heartless FREAK!"

"I know all about you, Rian Hoffman. Don't pretend you haven't been manipulating him yourself."

"No, I have not!"

Cashew blinks with genuine surprise. "Really?"

"Yes!"

"Why the hell not?"

"Because any decent person with any care for another living soul wouldn't do any of that shit!"

"But that's why it works so well, isn't it?"

Rian squints at Cashew. "How are you real?! How do you not see how fucking wrong this is?!"

Cashew laughs heartily. "You really think what I'm doing to Jacob is wrong? What is it you went to school for again? Directing. Getting people to believe what they're seeing is real. Making them cry when you want them to. Making their pulse go up and down, up and down just when you want it to. Getting the guys hard and the bitches wet. Giving them nightmares. Making them laugh at fairy dust. You get people talking at dinner parties about how they felt, how you made them feel, and they praise you for it. You make millions. And you learn how to be even better for next time, how to fuck with their bodies and brains even more."

Rian frowns, his eyes frozen.

"But it was never about the money for you," Cashew adds with a squint. "That's right, you're an *artist*. You only care about the craft. The thousand little ways you can control people. So many people. They'll think what you want them to think. Hate who you want them to hate. Like the medical industry! Who's gonna be your next target, huh? The Hasidics?" Cashew pauses. "Tell me, *Frankie*, how is that any different?"

Rian lowers his eyes.

Cashew scowls. "Call me a monster all you want. You're the one that wants to do it for a living."

Whale pops out of the bathroom to see Cashew and Rian standing close together. "What's up?"

"Nothing," Cashew says. "Just chatting."

Whale looks at Rian. "You okay?"

Rian swallows bitterly, feeling Cashew's eyes on him. "I'm fine."

Whale furrows his brow, looking between the two. Cashew walks over and puts an arm around him. "So what do you say? Show? Bar? How do we celebrate?"

Rian stares at the two of them, the way Whale lets Cashew grip him in such a friendly yet possessive way behind the neck. "I just want to go back to the hotel if that's okay."

Whale frowns at Rian. "Why?"

"He's just being a stick-in-the-mud," Cashew says.

Rian doesn't say anything. How can he? What good will it do?

Oscar pokes his head in. "Okay! It's here."

"Let's go," Cashew says, turning Whale toward the exit. Whale looks back at Rian. He's just standing there. How disappointing. Cashew pushes the door open.

JACOB

San Junipero

Jacob pushes through Fenway Target's employee exit, stepping out into the snow. Soft flakes drift down, quite a bit of accumulation on the ground. Warm streetlights. It's so quiet.

STEWIE (O.S.)
(bleating)
AYY BEE!

Jacob looks left. Looks right.

STEWIE (O.S.)
(bleating)
AYY BEE!

Jacob turns around. Recognizes the red blaze of JEEPGUY parked under one of the streetlights, Stewie leaning against the driverside door. Black trenchcoat. Pearly white smile.

STEWIE
Your chariot awaits.

Jacob practically melts right there. He walks over, boots crunching the snow.

JACOB
You didn't have to do this.

STEWIE
I wanted to, Sexy. It's Christmas Eve.

JACOB
Merry Clayton, Daddy.

STEWIE
Merry Clayton, Baby Boy.

Jacob's ears perk with recognition at Celine Dion's "O Holy Night" playing inside JEEPGUY.

JACOB
Turn it up.

STEWIE
Just get in.

JACOB
No, turn it up.

Stewie smiles. Reluctantly cracks open the Jeep door. Unrolls the window. Flicks the volume knob a bit. Shuts the door. Celine Dion's angelic voice fills the empty Boston street.

Jacob steps closer to Stewie. Takes his hand. Puts a hand on his waist.

STEWIE
Silly Beatle.

Jacob leads Stewie into a slow-dance, flakes falling gracefully around them, the lamplight shining on them like a spotlight. Jacob rests his head on Stewie shoulder as they dance, warmth radiating off out of his coat. He can't help but close his eyes.

STEWIE (CONT'D)
Oh Charlie.

JACOB
Just enjoy it, Sexy.

Stewie closes his eyes, relenting to the melodramatic gesture. He rests his cheek against Jacob's hair. They dance nice and slow to Celine's heavenly French-Canadian voice.

Jacob turns off his brain. Just him and Stewie dancing in the snow, black sky above filled with billions of stars. And he's getting hard.

Stewie kisses Jacob's temple, holding his lips there longer than usual. He's getting hard too.

Celine's crescendo gives both of them chills. Jacob looks up at Stewie. Stewie smiles down at him. And they kiss under the snow, their noses cold and runny.

The next morning, Stewie and Jacob go to the 11 AM mass at St. Joan of Arc. The Priest's homily in particular affects Jacob, a call for the congregation to remember respect and tolerance during these particularly divisive times. Jacob smiles at that. He was so wrong about them.

During the Our Father, the only segment untouched by Pope Benedict's invasive 2011 translation overhaul, Jacob and Stewie hold hands and recite The Lord's Prayer along with the larger-than-most congregation, the Christmas Catholics out of their caves.

PRIEST
The peace of the Lord be with you always.

JACOB & STEWIE
And with your spirit.

DEACON
Let us offer each other a sign of peace.

Jacob leans in to kiss Stewie. Stewie sharply backs away. Offers a chaste handshake instead.

Jacob looks down at Stewie's hand, deflating with crushing disappointment. He reluctantly shakes Stewie's hand. Politely waves to the family sitting behind them. The elderly married couple in front of them.

Jacob drives JEEPGUY home, shifting from second to third. He looks at Stewie smiling back from the passenger seat. Elton John's "Step into Christmas" plays via AUX cord.

JACOB
I really like how church is still the one place politics hasn't ruined.

STEWIE
I know. It's nice.

JACOB
That's what's so great about it. Even with all the messy BS going on in the world, for one hour a week it's the same safe serene place it was the week before.

STEWIE
Yup.

JACOB
It's like the ones that watch the news every day. Big whoop, the icebergs are melting or there's a shooting in Philly. If it's something you can't change, why let it ruin your day?

STEWIE
I don't think they want it to ruin their day. It just does. I don't know a single person who uses Facebook that actually enjoys it.

JACOB
I'm so glad I deleted mine.

STEWIE
I never saw the point. It's just more work. More things to complain about. It's not healthy.

JACOB
And yet they can't just stop. Why do something you hate because everyone tells you to?

STEWIE
It's easier living life on autopilot. Why make decisions or take the time researching fields of interest when you can just do what others tell you to do?

Jacob thinks.

JACOB
You've got to admit, as fulfilling as a niche lifestyle is, it's pretty darn lonely by definition.

STEWIE
We're not lonely. We have each other.

JACOB
Imagine if we didn't.

Stewie looks at Jacob. Handsome face. Great haircut. Sharp jawline. Big muscled arms. Driving JEEPGUY like a pro. He can't help but smile with pure amazement.

Back at their Beacon Hill apartment, Stewie makes a nice batch of blueberry pancakes. Jacob empties the trash and carries the bag outside.

On his way back inside, Jacob notices a glint of metal buried in the snow. He approaches it curiously. He reaches down. Pulls out a STAINLESS STEEL SPOON. Jacob brushes the snow off, inspecting it. Deep head. Hammered handle. Attractive curve to it. He smiles and brings it inside.

JACOB
Hey, look what I found in the snow.

STEWIE
Ew. Put that back.

JACOB
Why? You have a special spoon. I can have one too.

STEWIE
You don't where that's been! A landscaper probably dropped it.

JACOB
If I wash it, it's fine, right?

STEWIE
If you use that spoon, don't even kiss me.

JACOB
WHY?! If it's clean, it's clean. What's the problem?

STEWIE
You're really gonna take the chance of getting yourself sick? Getting ME sick?

JACOB
I'm not taking the chance! I'm using soap!

Jacob washes the snow off the spoon. Squirts dish soap. Rubs it around. Stewie shakes his head with disapproval.

JACOB (CONT'D)
This is what soap is for, you know. If you don't think it works, buy something else.

Stewie purses his lips.

JACOB (CONT'D)
I didn't know you were so germophobic.

STEWIE
I'm not germophobic.

JACOB
Diseasephobic then.

Stewie hesitates.

STEWIE
If it lets me live twenty years longer, I think it's worth it. What's the big deal?

JACOB
I'm not judging. I'm just stating a fact.

Jacob turns his head and smiles. Stewie smiles back.

Stewie and Jacob sit on the sofa, eating pancakes off TV trays. Jacob admires their tree, a white artificial covered in pink LED lights, pink glittery ornaments, and topped with a pink glittery star. Gayest Christmas tree ever. And look at all those presents underneath too!

Stewie watches Jacob eating with a spoon he found in the snow.

STEWIE
You are stark-staring nuts, Baby Boy.

JACOB
(mouth full)
Oh Charlie.

After breakfast, Stewie and Jacob stand shoulder-to-shoulder, peeing into the toilet bowl. Stewie checks out Jacob's cock. Jacob checks out Stewie's cock.

Not long after, Jacob chases Stewie around the apartment. Stewie is almost trapped in a corner but manages to outmaneuver Jacob and race away. Jacob dashes after him, laughing as he frantically tries to trap Stewie.

Just before lunchtime (THEIR lunchtime, 5 PM), Jacob and Stewie cuddle together on the couch and scroll through their phones. "It Doesn't Often Snow at Christmas" by the Pet Shop Boys (Yes, they have a Christmas song) plays on Jacob's phone.

JACOB
George Michael died.

Stewie looks up.

STEWIE
Oh my God. How old was he?

JACOB
Fifty-three.

Stewie furrows his brow.

STEWIE
I can't believe it.

JACOB
The guy famous for "Last Christmas" literally dies on Christmas. His last Christmas. How does that happen?

STEWIE
This whole year's been weird.

JACOB
No, I'm sick to death of the whole "2016 is cursed" BS. It's bad enough they're lumping Trump into the mix. It's all just a media-fueled self-fulfilling prophecy that only happened because David Bowie and Alan Rickman both died of undisclosed cancer four days apart back in January. Ever since then, everyone's all, "Ooh, the celebrities are dying! Ooh look, another one! Add 'em add to the list! I wonder who's gonna die next!" It's a societal placebo effect, not supernatural.

STEWIE
You have to admit, a lot of famous people died this year. Glenn Fry. Prince. Muhammad Ali. Nancy Reagan. George Martin. Emerson, Lake, and Arnold Palmer.

JACOB
Harper Lee. Abe Vigoda.

STEWIE
Frank Sinatra Jr.

JACOB
Oh yeah, I forgot about him.

STEWIE
Gene Wilder.

JACOB
Kenny Baker, the guy who played R2.

STEWIE
John Glenn. Pete Burns.

JACOB
Leonard Cohen.

STEWIE
Fidel Castro. Zsa Zsa Gabor...
(pause)
And now George Michael. And we still got a week left.

JACOB
Please. George Michael's the last one.

STEWIE
You know what they say, death comes in threes.

JACOB
We've listed way more than three. And what about the non-celebrities?

Stewie nods.

STEWIE
It's still quite a lot. A lot of young ones too. It might not be supernatural, Baby Boy, but it's still worth commenting on.

Stewie makes the two of them delicious turkey sammiches and put on his Christmas movie pick, the 1971 TV movie The Homecoming: A Christmas Story. Jacob had heard of The Waltons before and was expecting to absolutely hate The Homecoming, but he was quite shocked by how spectacular it actually was. And relatable, the protagonist John Boy being an aspiring writer with daddy issues. And of course, no one (not even his mother) talks about how good it is.

After the movie, Stewie and Jacob play Sorry on the glass coffee table.

JACOB
You know what's funny? Because this game uses cards and not dice, we can play against inanimate objects and legitimately lose.

Stewie stares at the board, surprised. He looks at Jacob. Jacob looks back at him.

Jacob pulls his red leather jacket out of the coat closet.

Stewie picks up the little red Jeep wrangler Matchbox car he keeps on his desk, a surrogate for JEEPGUY himself.

Thirty minutes later, Stewie, Jacob, the red leather jacket, and JEEPGUY finish their game of Sorry. Stewie and Jacob accept the fact that they've lost fair and square to a vehicle, let alone a 1998 Jeep Wrangler with over 250,000 miles, but Jacob's red leather jacket is still quite hung up about it.

Hours later, well after dark, Stewie and Jacob finally, FINALLY, give into temptation and exchange gifts. Jacob carries two coupe glasses into the living room, being sure not to spill their contents.

STEWIE
What's this?

JACOB
A sidecar.

STEWIE
What's a sidecar?

JACOB
Just try it.

Stewie takes a nervous sip. Smacks his tongue around.

STEWIE
That's dangerous.

JACOB
You like it?

STEWIE
I love it. Oh my God.

Stewie sips some more.

STEWIE (CONT'D)
You gonna tell me what's in it?

JACOB
Courvoisier.

STEWIE
(amazed)
REALLY? No wonder you didn't wanna tell me.

JACOB
It's good though, right?

STEWIE
What else?

JACOB
Cointreau and lemon juice.

STEWIE
Cointreau?

JACOB
Orange liqueur. It's like a rich orange-lemon flavor, right?

STEWIE
Yeah. How'd you find out about it?

JACOB
It's from the Roaring Twenties. I know you don't like mixing booze and OJ, so I wanted to find an orange cocktail that doesn't use OJ. Something we can drink together.

Stewie raises his glass.

STEWIE
Merry Clayton, Baby Boy.

JACOB
Merry Clayton, Daddy.

They toast their glasses. Stewie hands Jacob a present.

STEWIE
Here you go.

Jacob puts his glass down and gets up.

JACOB
Oh! Just a second!

STEWIE
(bleating)
AYY BEE!

JACOB
(ala Jerry Seinfeld)
Just a SECOND!

STEWIE
(desperate bleating)
AYYY BEEE!

Jacob plays "Underneath the Tree" by Kelly Clarkson from his phone. Returns to his spot.

JACOB
Suck it, Mariah.

Jacob studies his first present's shape, that perfectly recognizable LP square.

JACOB (CONT'D)
I know what this is.

STEWIE
There's a whole bunch of 'em.

JACOB
Ooh!

Jacob rips off the paper and reveals <u>Super</u> by the Pet Shop Boys.

JACOB (CONT'D)
(childlike)
Yay, their new one!

Stewie hands another wrapped record.

STEWIE
Keep going.

Jacob unwraps it and reveals <u>Very</u> by the Pet Shop Boys.

JACOB
Another Pet Shop Boys?!

STEWIE
That might be my favorite by them.

JACOB
It came out after <u>Discography</u> too.

STEWIE
I was so wrong about them, Baby Boy. All thanks to you.

Jacob grins. Opens the next present: If You Can Believe Your Eyes and Ears by The Mammas and the Papas.

JACOB
Alright.

STEWIE
That's the one with "California Dreamin'" on it. You know that one?

JACOB
Only because of Chungking Express.

Stewie stares.

STEWIE
I'm sorry, because of...?

JACOB
Chungking Express, the 1994 Hong Kong film by Wong Kar-Wai.

STEWIE
Oh, of course. That's what I thought you said.

JACOB
It's a good film. They play "California Dreamin'" in full, like, twenty times. I'm not even exaggerating.

Stewie hands over the next present. Jacob opens it, startled by the phantasmagorical Boschesque cover art.

JACOB (CONT'D)
Captain Fantastic and the Brown Dirt Cowboy?

STEWIE
Elton's best by far. There's only one single on it, "Someone Saved My Life Tonight." You know that one?

JACOB
Stephen King used the lyrics in The Dark Tower V: Wolves of the Calla.

STEWIE
You know a song from a BOOK?

JACOB
Hey, you asked.

STEWIE
Your fount of knowledge is absurdly diverse.

JACOB
I try.

STEWIE
The rest of the songs are great too. They're all about Elton and Bernie in their early days.

JACOB
A secret autobiography.

STEWIE
It's not that secret. Though given Bernie's songwriting MO, it's probably not obvious at all. Who'd ever guess "Daniel" was about Vietnam?

Jacob notices Stewie holding something behind his back.

JACOB
What are you hiding?

Stewie reveals a thicker square present.

STEWIE
Last one.

JACOB
A box set?

STEWIE
Open and find out.

Jacob eagerly rips open the present. Gasps.

JACOB
Hamilton?!

STEWIE
It won the Tony for Best Musical the night we met, remember?

Jacob turns over the 4-LP box set.

JACOB
I'm shocked. You hate musicals. AND black people!

STEWIE
(laughing)
Hey, that is not funny! Don't even say that!

JACOB
Remember that time I called you a racist?

STEWIE
Of course.

JACOB
Yeah, turns out it really sucks getting called a racist when you're especially NOT acting remotely racist, not even a little bit. And that fact I experienced it myself firsthand is both ironic and incredibly sobering.

STEWIE
I believe that is, verbatim, one of the reviews for Hamilton.

Jacob chuckles. Opens the box set's lid.

JACOB
Usually I don't like listening to the soundtrack without seeing the--

Jacob stares at the piece of paper lying on top of the discs: HAMILTON TICKETS, Orchestra level.

STEWIE
I know.

Jacob looks at Stewie, tears forming in his eyes.

STEWIE (CONT'D)
What's the matter?

JACOB
Are you insane?! These must've cost a fortune!

STEWIE
Yeah, they kinda did. It's also your birthday gift.
(pointing to the date on the ticket)
And your anniversary present.

Jacob hugs Stewie tightly.

JACOB
Oh my God, baby! I love you so so much!

They kiss.

STEWIE
I want you to pick an evening show. We can do a double feature, just like your mom used to do.

JACOB
Do you wanna see Avenue Q? I don't mind seeing it again.

STEWIE
Sure.

JACOB
It'll be my treat.

STEWIE
You don't have to.

JACOB
It's off-Broadway. I can afford it.

Jacob hands over a small box.

JACOB (CONT'D)
But now I feel bad. Mine's not nearly as expensive.

STEWIE
It's the thought that counts, Sexy.

Stewie rips the wrapping paper. Opens the box. Inside is a DOG TAG with a date laser-engraved on the front:

"June 12, 2016"

JACOB
Turn it over.

Stewie flips the tag over. His heart stops. Laser-engraved on the back:

"I Knew You Were Waiting for Me"

Jacob smiles. Stewie keeps staring, downright moved, quite unusually so.

STEWIE
(whispers)
Like the song.

JACOB
Of course George Michael had to die the same day.

Jacob chuckles a bit. Looks at Stewie curiously.

JACOB (CONT'D)
You okay?

Stewie takes a deep breath.

STEWIE
I never got anything personalized before.

JACOB
Really? Never?

Stewie shakes his head, re-reading the back of the tag.

STEWIE
This is so beautiful, Baby, thank you.

Jacob hugs Stewie tightly.

JACOB
You're beautiful.

Stewie grins wide. Holds Jacob as hard as he can.

Just before dinnertime (THEIR dinnertime, 11 PM) Stewie talks to his mom on speakerphone, the new dog tag already around his neck. Jacob sits nearby.

STEWIE
(into phone)
No, but we're just about to.

CATHERINE (V.O.)
Okay, then I'll leave you to it. Goodnight Stewie. Goodnight Jacob.

STEWIE
Goodnight Mom.

JACOB
Goodnight Catherine. Merry Christmas.

CATHERINE (V.O.)
You're so sweet.

STEWIE
Yes he is.

Jacob beams.

CATHERINE (V.O.)
Merry Christmas to you both.

STEWIE
Night, Mom.

CATHERINE (V.O.)
You too dear.

Stewie cooks salmon in bourbon and brown sugar while Jacob shakes up another round of sidecars.

STEWIE
What are you putting on for dinner?

JACOB
I have a Christmas tradition I've never been able to share with anyone.

STEWIE
Even your mother?

JACOB
I've tried and tried. She flat-out refuses.

STEWIE
What is it?

JACOB
Two words: <u>Downton</u>. <u>Abbey</u>.

STEWIE
"<u>Downton</u>" <u>Abbey</u>?

JACOB
Yeah, <u>Downton</u>. Downtown without the W. Very common mistake.

STEWIE
Is it a movie?

JACOB
A British TV show. On PBS.

STEWIE
You actually watch a show made by PBS?

JACOB
It's made by ITV, one of BBC's competition, and they air it on PBS over here, but for some reason they edit down the episodes for the stupid American

audience. Anyway, when it was originally out, they released each new season on Blu-Ray two weeks before it started airing in America, so for the last four Christmases, I asked my family for that year's <u>Downton Abbey</u> season so I could watch all the unedited UK versions before they aired over here.

STEWIE
I already hate it.

JACOB
You don't even know what it's about!

STEWIE
What is it about?

JACOB
The 5th Earl of Grantham, Robert Crawley, and his family of aristocrats live at Downton Abbey, a really big house in Downton, England, as well as their servants, butlers, maids, and cooks as they deal with the effects of the First World War and the slow decline of the British aristocracy in the postwar era.

Stewie slack-jaw stares at Jacob.

STEWIE
You LIKE that?

JACOB
Trust me, YOU DON'T KNOW HOW GOOD IT IS.

STEWIE
You really think I'm gonna like it?

Thirty minutes later, Stewie's on the couch laughing his ass off. Jacob grins.

JACOB
I told you.

STEWIE
The whole show is everyone insulting each other. This is hysterical!

JACOB
Strangely addicting, right? These guys are my family.

STEWIE
We're gonna keep going after this, right?

JACOB
Of course!

Three episodes later, Stewie and Jacob cuddle on the couch.

STEWIE
That one's cute.

JACOB
Thomas?

STEWIE
No, that guy, the one on the left by Mr. Carson. Who's he?

JACOB
No one. He's just an extra.

STEWIE
He's hot!

JACOB
I can't believe I found me a guy that likes <u>Downton</u> as much as I do.

STEWIE
If your mom doesn't watch this, she's out of her mind.

JACOB
That's what I keep telling her.

STEWIE
Mary reminds me of Melanie.

JACOB
I know.

STEWIE
And Edith reminds me of Karen.

JACOB
Yup.

Stewie looks at Jacob.

STEWIE
That's why you like it, isn't it? They're your family.

JACOB
I literally called them my family.

STEWIE
(points)
Who is THAT?!

Stewie growls suggestively.

JACOB
Daddy, for the last time, STOP CRUISING THE EXTRAS!

At bedtime (THEIR bedtime, 3 AM) Jacob lays face-up under the covers. Stewie gets on top of him. Kisses Jacob's left cheek three times.

STEWIE
Turn over.

Jacob tilts his head. Stewie kisses his right cheek three times. Jacob returns his head to starting position and Stewie plants a big one on Jacob's lips.

STEWIE (CONT'D)
You've been officially SUCKED IN!

Jacob giggles, kicking his feet under the covers.

JACOB
I'm excited to see Hamilton.

STEWIE
I didn't know what your plans were for after graduation. I didn't want to ask and spoil the surprise.

JACOB
Graduation's in May, so you're fine. I'm sure I'll be free by our anniversary.

Stewie strokes Jacob's cheek with a finger.

STEWIE
What ARE you doing after graduation?

JACOB
I was gonna go to LA and start something with the guys, remember? That's obviously not happening.

STEWIE
But you're still going to LA, right?

JACOB
For what?

Stewie hesitates.

STEWIE
For an internship or something.

JACOB
They don't do internships after college. That's how they get away with it. Work for credits.

STEWIE
They have paid internships, don't they?

JACOB
Not many. If they do, they're really hard to get.

STEWIE
You're gonna still apply to a few, aren't you?

JACOB
I don't know. Maybe.

STEWIE
They have writing jobs too, right? What are your options?

Jacob sighs.

JACOB
I don't know. I really don't want to talk about all that right now.

STEWIE
When do you wanna talk about it?

JACOB
Later.

STEWIE
How much later?

JACOB
Jeez, can't you let me graduate first?
(pause)
I've still got another semester. We've got plenty of time. Don't worry.

Stewie sighs. Nods.

STEWIE
Okay. Go to sleep.

Stewie kisses Jacob again. Stands.

JACOB
I love you, Daddy.

Stewie looks back at Jacob. Smiles.

STEWIE
I love you.

JACOB
Goodnight.

Jacob turns off the lamp. Rolls over. Stewie watches a bit more. Closes the door.

Stewie stays up for another hour getting some work done on his computer. He touches the dog tag around his neck. Rereads the inscription on the back:

"I Knew You Were Waiting For Me"

Stewie lifts his eyes and looks toward the bedroom door, suddenly worried.

DREW

Nose Goes

It's Friday, February 12th. Ephemeral's been shut down for the past two days due to the Jimmy business interfering with work. Every day Gary calls Drew asking to release a statement. Every day Drew says no.

Kev passive-aggressively plays *Oscar Blitz* in Drew's Marina Del Rey condo. Drew listens but refuses to look. Oscar's interviewing three go-go boys now from Sweet Vermouths. Dirk, Aarin, and Trenton describe how the management of their establishment pressured them into having degrading sex with Drew Lawrence as a matter of routine, insisting they wouldn't be able to make it in this town if they don't let him have his way with them. Drew figured it was only a matter of time before Oscar found out about Sweet Vermouths, but he always made sure to ask their consent first. They all said yes. If they didn't mean it, then that's on them. Drew did nothing wrong.

Drew's phone rings. He mutes the TV. Kev hands the phone over. "It's Gary."

Drew answers the phone and puts it to his ear. "Yes?"

"You seeing this?" Gary Green asks.

"Of course."

"It's not stopping."

"I know it's not."

"It's only getting worse."

"That's debatable."

"Come in right now and release a statement."

Drew hesitates. "I never made a deal with management."

"You routinely fucked dancers in a seedy nightclub bathroom."

"And I'd be the first Hollywood producer to ever fuck strippers in a bathroom."

"They're go-go boys."

"They're the closest we've got."

"I don't care how you justify it, Drew. To a rational human being, it looks really really shitty. We need to throw out some mitigating circumstances before it all turns to cement."

"Anything I say they'll use to legitimize Jimmy's narrative."

"Your silence is already doing that. Do you have any idea how bad you look right now because you haven't released a statement?"

Drew has to think about that. Carter went off the grid after his allegations. Not even a countersuit. Didn't take long for Drew of all people to assume his guilt, didn't it? Drew takes a deep breath. "Tell me what to say and I'll say it."

Drew and Kev meet Gary at Ephemeral Pictures around 6 PM, its first floor already converted into a temporary studio. Drew waits backstage, his head bowed, eyes closed, spotlights shining through the swaying black curtain. The camera crew shuffles and mutters. Some clicks and flits. Some coughs and claps. Never loud, of course. Just soft white noise tickling the sensitive situation about. Don't poke the bear. Don't wake Daddy. Don't touch the sides. Don't stop me now. Don't let the sun go down on me. Don't cry for me Argentina. Don't dream it's over. Don't stop believin'. Don't go breaking my heart. Don't stand so close to me.

"Mr. Lawrence," Kelly the producer tells him, "We're all set."

Drew pushes the curtain aside. Strong light hits his eyes. His shoes clank on the wooden stage. He sits behind the desk. The leather chair squeaks. Drew stares ahead.

The black camera lens inches from his face. A dozen crew members behind the camera. Gary in the corner with crossed arms. Kev just close enough to see. He gives Drew a supportive thumbs up.

Drew closes his eyes to center himself. He exhales lightly. Opens his eyes. Nods to the Director.

"We're on in five," the Director calls out, holding up five fingers. "Four. Three." Two fingers. One finger. Points.

CLICK.

Red light goes on.

"'Hello everyone,'" Drew reads from the teleprompter. "'The purpose of this statement is to clarify my recollection of the events pertaining to my encounter with Jimmy Lyons on the night of Friday, July 20, 2035.'" Drew pauses, his intense eyes looking right at the camera. "'I did, in fact, have sexual relations with Jimmy Lyons. However, I did not know Jimmy was sixteen until four days ago. The reason I didn't know was because Jimmy deliberately and repeatedly lied to me throughout the evening, just like he's been lying to you.'"

Drew drinks from a glass of water. "'I had my Jeep parked outside Sweet Vermouths before it opened. Jimmy was walking down the street and approached me first. I naturally assumed he was over eighteen, though I did suspect he was under twenty-one. When he asked me my name, I made the conscious decision to give him an alias because I know people treated me differently because of who I am and what I could do for them. At some point after that, Jimmy asked me how old I was and I said, "Forty." Jimmy never volunteered his age. He said his ID was in the car, but not only did he not have a car, he didn't even have a driver's license, just a California State ID. He wanted to go into Sweet Vermouths with me, which would be the only way he could get in there, but instead I suggested going to a restaurant down the street called Marcus MacDonald's that I was sure would card him. My intentions were for friendly conversation only, though I had reason to believe he wanted to sleep with me the moment he saw me. Inside Marcus MacDonald's, I ordered two room temp bottles of Guinness, not vodka like Jimmy had said. I did so for two reasons. First, I expected the server to card Jimmy. He did not. Second, in the unlikely event that Jimmy wouldn't get carded, I wanted to deter Jimmy from future beer drinking by ordering literally the worst beer for an unseasoned drinker to have. My mom pulled the same shit on me when I was eighteen. It deterred me from drinking beer for many years. Jimmy took one sip and refused to drink any more. Later on in our conversation, Jimmy told me he was currently enrolled at UCLA online, knowingly implying he was at least eighteen. The bartender then delivered an unsolicited Scotch on the rocks I did not order, and I felt forced to mix beer and Scotch, triggering my alcoholism, and said celebrity treatment was enough for Jimmy to suspect my true identity. He hadn't mentioned *Seattle Kid* at this point. In fact I never knew what its title was until a few days ago.'"

Drew stops to drink more water. "'At this point I was very drunk and Jimmy was completely sober. I asked Jimmy to drive me home in my 2036 electric Jeep Wrangler, the only one of its kind. It's perhaps my most prized possession. And before you jump to any conclusions, cable media hivemind, it was a gift.'" Drew finishes the glass. "'I'm going through this stuff like water,'" he quips. He clears his throat. "'Jimmy managed to get us back to my condo safely. I took him upstairs and offered an IPA, knowing very well he would say no. When he asked for vodka instead, I refused. Jimmy wanted to snort lines of cocaine with me and I refused. After some more conversation, and two more IPAs for me, Jimmy persistently asked to have sex with me. Having been led up to this point to believe he was eighteen, I felt no reason not to pursue. We fell asleep afterwards. I woke before him the next day and asked him to leave. He took a Ridr home and I never saw him again.'"

Drew pauses for effect. "'I hope my debunking of Jimmy's story casts enough reasonable doubt on the allegations made against me. I acknowledge my behavior was problematic, but I insist that it was quite uncharacteristic for me and not nearly as criminal as Jimmy has claimed. I hope you will understand why he chose to air his grievances on television instead of pursuing legal action against me. This entire situation has been nothing more than an over-exaggerated, over-politicized misunderstanding. I do not have sex with minors. Since the night in question, I have been completely sober of all illicit substances as well as alcohol, and I have rehabilitated my personal and professional reputation among my industry peers. My own personal take is that Jimmy wanted to get revenge for me not reading his screenplay and seeks to damage *The Sins of Jack Branson*'s chances of winning the Academy Awards it deserves. I plead all of you to understand the complexity of this situation and for you all to avoid jumping to rash conclusions. Thank you.'"

"And we're clear!" the Director calls. The crew applauds. Gary and Kev too.

Drew smiles nervously as he stands. Kev walks over. Pats Drew on the back. "I think you killed it, dude," Kev says.

"Really?" Drew asks.

"Absolutely," Gary says. "We'll take care of the rest. Just go home. Rest. Don't watch the news."

"I won't, don't worry."

"We'll call you after it drops and let you know."

"Can't we just drop it tomorrow?"

"With no one reporting on it?" Gary scoffs. "Give me some credit, surely."

Drew looks at Kev. "Monday at Noon?"

"Monday at Noon," Kev parrots with assurance.

"Enjoy yourself," Gary tells Drew. "Take a break. You've earned it."

Drew keeps replaying that last line on the drive home. You've earned it. You've earned it. Even hours later when he slides into bed, he's still thinking about it. You've earned it. He smiles. You're right, he has earned it. That really was a hell of a statement reading. Everything's gonna be okay now. All they have to do is watch the video on Monday and they'll understand. People might be irrational in the face of fear and the absence of facts, but they're also rational in the face of truth. And they hate finding out they've been conned. Jimmy sure conned the hell out of them.

Saturday, February 13th, is fun and relaxing, a proper vacation. Drew's favorite movies on the big screen. His favorite meals. Lots of music in between. A full workout. He looks hot. He feels hot. He's thrilled. Every three hours or so, he remembers the real world and all that bullshit about him on Twitter, all those calls to boycott *Branson*, and he tells himself not to get all anxious and worked up again and puts on another movie and forgets the real world by the First Act Break.

Sunday, February 14th. A quiet day in. Drew sits and thinks. When's the last time he's had a good long contemplation? Thank God *Oscar Blitz* doesn't air on weekends.

Monday, February 15th. Drew wakes up late. Bright sun. Open balcony door drifting in the warm midday breeze. He makes coffee and a great breakfast to the sweet sounds of the Mamas and the Papas' *If You Can Believe Your Eyes and Ears*, with such great songs like "Monday, Monday," "California Dreamin'," and his personal favorite "Straight Shooter." What an interesting song. Not just a sonic bop, its lyrics are a rollercoaster. First you think it's about a guy asking his girlfriend if she's cheating on him, then you realize he's threatening to hit her, THEN you find out it's not about his girl cheating at all, it's about her running off with his half of the drugs.

Funny enough, its sheet music was found at 10050 Cielo Drive the night the Manson guys slaughtered Sharon Tate, her unborn son, Jay Sebring, Abigail Folger and Wojciech Frykowski. Pretty fucked up backstory for a happy song written by a guy that drugged and raped his own daughter for ten years until she conceived a child that might or might not have been his so he paid for her to get an abortion, huh?

Drew switches to *Physical Graffiti*. At the end of Side 3, as Drew walks over to flip the disc over, he realizes he hasn't heard from Kev or Gary at all. The video dropped two hours ago. They still haven't called. That's strange. Drew reluctantly turns off the record player. Sits on the couch. Pulls out his phone. Taps Kev's name atop his favorites list.

"Hey," Kev says.

"Any word?" Drew asks.

Silence on the line. "Any word on what?"

"C'mon, I'm climbing the walls here."

Kev hesitates again. "Yeah, can I call you back?"

Drew furrows his brow. "What's going on? What aren't you telling me?"

"Gary doesn't want me saying anything until we have a better hold of the situation."

"What the fuck does that mean?" Drew asks quickly.

Silence.

"Kev!" Drew exclaims. "You better fucking tell me!"

"It was flat-out rejected by pretty much everyone."

Drew's blood races. "How?!"

"The Academy starts voting tomorrow. It's all around Twitter that you only apologized to win Oscars."

Drew gapes. "I didn't even think about that!"

"Not to mention no one actually believes you're sober because of how totally bloodshot your eyes were by the end of the video."

"Why didn't you say anything?!"

"I didn't notice."

"It's those stupid fluorescent lights. I told them they were too fucking bright. They don't fucking listen to me."

"Believe me, Gary wishes he did now."

Drew huffs angrily. "Jimmy can say whatever the fuck he wants and everyone believes him. Why can't they do that to me?"

"I guess people already got it in the minds that you weren't sorry, just sorry you got caught."

"How could I have been sorry *before* if I didn't know he was sixteen until *after*?! Jesus! Do any of these people have brains?!"

"And they didn't like you not mentioning any of new developments."

Drew sits right up. "What new developments?"

"*Oscar Blitz* had weekend episodes."

Drew's head starts hurting. "What did he say?"

"I kept telling Gary to call you. He didn't want you flying off the handle like you did the last time."

"Oh my God, Kev, what did Oscar say?!"

"It's not what he said, it's what they said."

"Who?"

"Your former employees at Not That Nutty."

Drew closes his eyes. "You gotta be fucking kidding me."

"It's pretty bad stuff too. Meltdowns in front of producers, demolishing your conference rooms—"

"FUCK!" Drew lays back, shaking his head. "Why did I throw out all the booze?" he whines. "I could really use a drink right now."

A Molotov cocktail flies in through the window and crashes onto the hardwood floor, bursting into flames. Drew screams. Drops his phone. Scurries down the couch. A second Molotov flies in. Crashes close to the first one. A third one crashes in his bedroom from the open balcony door. Drew picks up his phone and runs into the kitchen.

"DREW!" Kev keeps screaming over the phone. "WHAT'S GOING ON?!"

"FIRE!" Drew screams, tears in his eyes as he backs up against the kitchen sink. "THERE'S FIRE EVERYWHERE! MOLOTOVS THROUGH THE WINDOW AND—" Glass shatters behind him. Large thump. Hard pain at the back of his head. Drew goes dizzy. Falls face-first onto the kitchen floor. A brick bounces beside him. It's all fuzzy from there.

Drew knows he's lying on the ground. He's aware of the fire spreading throughout his condo. He can feel the heat rising, all that the smoking floating up. He can hear the fire alarms. Glass shattering, more Molotovs, or maybe more windows breaking. But he can't move. He really needs to get out of there, he can't help but dwell on a dark memory from his childhood.

At his Catholic elementary school back in Phoenixville, Jacob and the rest of his second grade class were funneled into the library for a fire safety awareness VHS. Part of the video had real firefighters go through the remains of a real burned down suburban home. The firefighters told the film crew about a seven-year-old boy in that house that got so scared that he ran into his closet to hide. The firefighters opened the charred remains of that seven-year-old's closet to reveal a black carpet stain, the spot where the seven-year-old got burned alive. Seeing that fucked Jacob up royally. For years he woke up in the middle of the night, screaming from a flame-drenched nightmare, waking his mother, in tears, scared to death of dying in a fire. Reading *A Series of Unfortunate Events* even made him nervous, the idea of becoming an orphan because of his parents perishing in a fire that destroyed the entire home being the absolute worst thing in the world for little Jacob Andrezj. But now it's really happening. He's gonna die. And he's terrified. And his mom isn't around anymore to help.

This must've been how she felt, Drew realizes. Her worst fear finally coming to pass.

Drew wakes himself up coughing. Blood in his hair and down his face. Lots of light everywhere. Lots of heat. Hazy smoke. He's still alive. Couldn't have been that long. He peeks his eyes open. Fire. Everything on fire. The whole condo. It really doesn't look real. It can't be real. Drew gets up on all-fours, his eyes burning from the smoke. He crawls slowly, little by little, toward the front door, keeping himself as low as possible. An inferno's billowing out of his bedroom, far worse than everywhere else. The balcony door being more obvious from the ground? The assumption that the uber-rich rapist fatcat must still be in bed? Who knows.

Front door. Drew removes a sock from his foot. Puts it on his hand. Grabs the metal handle. Tries to turn. Barely any friction. He squeezes tighter. Tries again. Pulls the door open. Hallway air rushing in and smoke billowing out. Drew crawls out. Gets as far away from the door as he can. Sits there on the landing, finally able to breathe, coughing up a storm. He looks down at himself. Pants and a white T-shirt. No shoes. One sock on his hand covered in soot, another still on his foot. That's all he has. No suits. No cutoff shirts. No Rolexes. No special spoon. No Pet Shop Boys CD. No records. No Blu-Rays. No "Like Boys" shirt. No red leather jacket. No class rings. No diplomas. No acting awards. No red Nike baseball cap. No Jeep keys. It's all gone. Fucking gone. Drew slams his eyes shut. Passes out.

"C'mon," he dreams Kev saying. "Help me out here, buddy." Imaginary Kev puts Drew's arm around his shoulder. "They're all over the front. We gotta go out the backway, okay? Just hold on. Hold on to me, okay?" Drew watches his dream the way one experiences Soarin' at Disney World. Obviously no movement. Obviously all visual. Obviously fake. Just go along with it. Slowly down the stairs they go, trying to make as little noise as possible. Then Drew starts feeling numbness in his legs. Stopping and starting whenever Kev abruptly halts or rushes past a clearing. This isn't a dream, is it? Kev's really there. He's really saving him. He's not gonna remember any of this, is he? He sure hopes he does. He needs to retain this trauma. It's gonna make him a better writer. It can't all be for nothing.

Drew's laying on the backseat of Kev's car, realizing he barely remembers how he got there, just a vague sense that they made it. He's jostling with no seat belt. He sits up. Looks out the window. "Keep your head down," he hears Kev say. Drew ducks on command. Peeks out anyway. Twenty or so men in black ski masks and camo gear chucking Molotovs at Drew's second floor condo. Drew notices light coming from inside the parking garage: JEEPGUY 2: Electric Boogaloo, flames billowing out from all orifices, surrounded by a half-dozen more masked men livestreaming in front of it, some posing with exposed penises and asses, some pissing on it, some just dancing. Fools. All that toxic smoke pouring out of a burning electric battery. Kill, JEEPGUY 2: Electric Boogaloo, kill. Good boy. Give 'em cancer. Take those fuckers with you to hell. Drew collapses onto the back seat and passes out.

A doctor shines light into his eyeballs. "Can you hear me, Mr. Lawrence? Blink if you can hear me." Drew blinks. The Doctor asks some more things. The ceiling behind him is moving. It lulls Drew back to sleep.

Drew wakes up in a hospital bed with an IV in his arm and a plastic oxygen tube plugging his nose, lots of wires everywhere. He peers to his right. Kev's sitting beside the bed, asleep. No sounds but heart monitors. Drew looks ahead of him. A small TV on the wall in front of him. Drew grabs the remote. Turns it on. "What happened was a travesty!" a Fox News commentator rants over aerial footage of Drew's burning condo. "Like him or not, no one deserves this!"

Kev jolts awake. Sees the TV. Sees Drew. "You're awake."

Drew hits shuffle on the remote. "The men that attacked his condo do not represent us," a CNN commentator commentates. "They're a pack of lone wolves that went too far and should not be condoned in any way shape or form for their behavior." Drew smirks. He's never heard both sides agree on something before.

Kev takes the remote from Drew's hand. "Just rest." He turns off the TV. Places the remote out of Drew's reach. Heads for the door.

"Where—?" Drew croaks. Coughs a bit.

"You're not supposed to talk," Kev says softly. "I'm coming right back. I'm just getting a doctor." He leaves the room.

Drew looks at the remote Kev placed far away. He tries to reach. No can do. He stares at the blank TV.

"Mr. Lawrence!" a Doctor greets, walking in with Kev. "I'm Dr. Kapoor. How are you feeling?"

Drew swallows. "Fine," he rasps.

Kapoor flips through Drew's chart. "Yes, I see... It appears you've inhaled a lot of smoke. There's a bit of damage to your esophagus, nothing critical but a bit too much for our comfort. We're gonna give you some inhalants every few hours or so to help the healing process. Otherwise there's no brain damage or sign of concussion, so I don't see any reason why you can't go home Wednesday, Thursday at the latest."

"My home burned down," Drew whispers.

Kapoor gapes. Double-checks the chart. "Oh yes, that's right. Uh-huh. Well, we'll figure that out." Kapoor smiles. Bolts out of there.

Drew scoffs. Looks at Kev. "It really happened, huh?" he breathes.

Kev leans in to hear better.

"It wasn't a dream?" Drew whispers.

Kev shakes his head.

"It's really all gone?"

Kev steps away. Nods.

Drew frowns. He points at the remote. Snaps his fingers.

Kev reluctantly hands it over. "You really shouldn't be watching the news."

"What am I gonna do?" Drew rasps.

"Huh?"

Drew waves his hand. "Forget it."

"What?"

"Forget—!" Drew winces. Grabs his throat.

"It's okay, I understand."

A Nurse comes in. "I'm gonna check his vitals now," she tells Kev. "Can you leave the room for just a second?"

"Sure." Kev smiles at Drew. "I'll be right back, buddy."

"No," Drew whispers. "Go home. Sleep."

"You sure?"

Drew nods.

Kev smiles a bit. Makes his way past the Nurse.

Drew snaps his fingers at Kev. Waves him over. Kev gets up close. Drew waves over some more. Kev puts his ear to Drew's lips. "You saved my life," Drew whispers, taking Kev's hand, squeezing it tight. "Thank you."

Kev squeezes back. "See you tomorrow, man." He waves and leaves.

Tuesday, February 16th. Drew meets with Agent Howard and Agent Gonzalez from the FBI. Kev sits beside him. "We're characterizing it as domestic terrorism," Agent Howard tells them. "The motivation seems to be closer to intimidation than actual murder. They probably just assumed you weren't home."

"It seems to have been barely planned," Agent Gonzalez says. "An hour or two at most."

Drew shakes his head. "Jesus."

"Who were they?" Kev asks. "Were they affiliated with anyone?"

"Just a bunch of disgruntled Redditors," Agent Howard responds. "We're still hunting them down. It seems the attack was in response to the video of Mr. Lawrence, so we have no reason to suspect a repeat in the future."

"He doesn't know about the video."

Drew furrows his brow. "Yes I do."

Kev hesitates. "Not that video."

Drew stares at Kev.

"Nevertheless, we've traced the origins of the attack to a Ridr administrator who had access to Jimmy's receipt," Agent Howard says. "He's the one that doxxed your address on Reddit."

Drew's still staring at Kev. "What other video?" he asks, getting angry.

Kev frowns back. "Can we have some privacy for a moment?" he asks the FBI Agents.

"I think we've covered it all," Agent Howard says. They leave.

Kev closes the door behind them. Returns beside the bed. Rubs his face. "Around the same time Oscar was having his weekend shows, an old video resurfaced of you, Theo, and some other guy getting interviewed at the Tribeca Film Festival."

"So?"

"You were saying there should be a cure for autism."

Drew blows his lips. "I never said that."

Kev pulls out his phone. "It's pretty clear you did."

"I think I'd remember saying something like that."

"See for yourself." Kev holds out his phone, the video already queued. Drew recognizes his own face in the thumbnail. He looks away. Kev pockets the phone. "It went viral over the weekend, even more so after Oscar had the interviewer on his Monday show."

"He was there, you know."

Kev blinks. "Oscar?"

"Standing just backstage." Drew furrows his brow. "When on Monday?"

"The morning block."

"Before my statement, you mean?"

Kev nods. "Yeah."

"He probably came into work, saw I didn't release a statement yet and got scared. Started breaking his own rules. He's graduated to half-lying."

"I think he started half-lying with Jimmy."

"There's no way he knows the truth about Jimmy. He might suspect something, but he's never gonna ask. It's easier that way. Everything stays the same. I would know. I used to do the same thing. With Jimmy no less. That's how this whole thing started in the first place."

Kev looks at the blank TV.

Drew shakes his head. "A long time ago, an Italian man on a bridge told me impatience brought the worst out of people. I think that's what's happening. Oscar waited and waited to get something else on me and he got impatient and now he's put blinders on."

Kev nods solemnly. "Gary did say he felt Oscar was rushing out the Not That Nutty interviews out to provoke a reaction, so… yes, I think you might be right about that."

"How long did he talk about the video?"

Kev shrugs. "Four hours."

Drew glares at Kev. "He spent four hours amplifying a story that wasn't even his? On a Monday?"

Kev looks away.

Drew scoffs. "He didn't have anything else, did he?"

Kev reluctantly shakes his head.

"And I'm assuming the fact that I didn't mention the autism cure stuff in my statement is what pissed off the Redditors in the first place?"

"It certainly appears..." Kev whispers. "To some... Yes, it looked like you didn't care."

"We could've changed the statement if Gary told me about the video."

"I know."

Drew mock nods. "And if we hadn't released a statement at all, *like I wanted to*, I'd still be sitting in my condo right now." He pauses. "Is that what you're telling me?"

Kev tightens his lips. "In every other scenario it would've worked."

"Good to know," Drew grumbles, turning away.

Kev frowns desperately.

Drew doesn't budge.

Kev stands up. "Can I get you anything?"

"I want my fucking house back, that's what I want. How about my Jeep? Can you get me that?"

Kev's eyes droop. "I'm sorry, okay?"

Drew doesn't answer.

Kev hangs his head. Turns to leave.

"Wait," Drew says.

Kev looks back.

Drew hesitates. "Polar Orange-Vanilla seltzer. Get a ton of cases. Eight. Ten. Whatever they have. I'll pay you back. Just get them."

"You really like it, huh?"

"I used to eat orange-vanilla softserve every time my family took us to Wildwood. I forgot all about it until I found that flavor in the seltzer aisle right after I got clean. I could drink a case a day of that shit. It's the best flavor in the world."

Kev nods. "Then I'll be back." He leaves.

Drew calms down in the silence. Takes a nap. Wakes up about an hour later. No Kev. He looks for his phone. Oh yeah. That's right. He reluctantly picks up the remote. Against his better judgment, he turns on the TV. Hits shuffle.

Local news. "...released a statement today in response Drew Lawrence's unapologetic statement: 'Myself and rest of the Whitman University community are deeply ashamed to have Mr. Lawrence among our esteemed graduates. We have revoked his Honorary Diploma and removed his name from the alumni wall and all promotional—'" Shuffle.

CNN. "...Democratic Party has publicly apologized for accepting political contributions from Drew Lawrence over the past twenty—" Shuffle.

Fox News. "...Ridge Preparatory School has decided to rename their Jacob Andrezj Theatre in response to Drew Lawrence's autism comments. This is what I'm talking about people. The Left just wants to censor history and prevent people, *their* people, from having a safe space to utilize the First Amend—" Shuffle.

E! Network. "...Blitz has had his greatest string of ratings in years—" Shuffle.

NBC. "...other news, the LA LGBT Alliance has revoked Drew Lawrence's Lifetime Achievement award in response to Lawrence's controversial statement yesterday afternoon. This comes right after the Aspies for Autism Awareness revoked their Aspie of the Year Award, saying—" Shuffle.

CBS. "The North American Man/Boy Love Association has released a statement today *supporting* Drew Lawrence—" Shuffle.

MSNBC. "The bidding war over Jimmy Lyons' *Seattle Kid* has concluded today with Netflix buying the feature for a *whopping*—" Shuffle.

ABC. "I'm hear with Melanie An—" Shuffle. Drew rapid-taps undo. His sister in an interview chair. "...'s twin sister, and she's been very outright about her brother's sordid past." The Interviewer turns to Melanie. "Thank you so much for taking the time to speak to us this evening, Ms. Andrezj."

"You're very welcome," Melanie responds, cold as always.

"What happened to *Dr.* Andrezj?" Drew muses.

Kev walks down the hallway with three cases of Polar Orange-Vanilla seltzer. He slows outside Drew's room at the sound of the TV.

"When was the last time you spoke to your brother?" the Interviewer asks.

"A year or so before Mom died," Melanie answers. "She was having health problems and couldn't afford to live on her own anymore, and... He was really insistent on her moving in with me. I don't know why they hadn't spoken for as long as they did. I just thought it was really presumptuous of him to force me into that position."

"Oh, I'm sorry!" Drew yells at the TV. "I thought it wouldn't make any difference since you're a FUCKING *DOCTOR*!"

Dr. Kapoor races over. Kev stops him at the door. "He's alright. He does that."

"When her cancer came back, she tried to make it up with him," Melanie continues. "She was always deathly afraid of anesthesia, not waking up after surgery, and so she tried calling my brother. He kept sending it to voicemail. For so long I couldn't understand why he would do that, but now I do. He was too busy screwing a kid."

"Fucking cunt," Drew whispers.

"Do the accusations against your brother surprise you?" the Interviewer asks.

"Not really," Melanie says. "He was always a sexual deviant, you know, ever since we were kids. I remember walking in on him one time. He was tying himself up with duct tape at the bottom of his—"

Drew shuts off the TV. Throws the remote away. Slams his fists down on the bed, screaming with a whiny throat, his face beet red.

Kev can't bear to look. It's too horrible just listening to it. He lowers himself to the floor, seltzer in his lap. Patiently waits for Drew to mellow out.

Wednesday, February 17th. Kev comes by with a care package of new clothes. They don't fit Drew very well, but they're better than nothing. Drew brushes his teeth for the first time in days. "Everything good?" he asks Kev.

"Everything's set up." Kev pauses. "You sure you don't want a hotel instead?"

Drew spits in the sink. "Not secure enough. I want my office anyway. It's not a foreign place, you know?"

Kev shrugs, half-assed.

Drew slides back into bed. "What's wrong?"

"Nothing."

"Don't give me that. I know something's wrong."

Kev hesitates. "The Academy is seriously considering disqualifying *The Sins of Jack Branson* across the board."

Drew stares. "Because of the statement? The autism video?"

"Everything. It just added up, I guess."

Drew looks off. "They've never done that before."

"You would know more than I would."

"They haven't."

Kev folds his hands. Stares off.

Drew lays back in defeat. "You know what the worst part of all this is? I just wrote this! I'm literally living out *Branson*! High profile sex scandal. Bestselling, thinly veiled autobiography. I did it again! I wrote my own future again! What the fuck?!"

Kev smirks.

"How does this keep happening to me?" Drew asks rhetorically. "Is it a self-fulfilling prophecy or something, or am I'm just so in-tune with my own unconscious mind that I end up predicting my own behavior before it happens?"

"I don't know."

Drew scoffs. "Or is God just punishing me in ways He knows I'll recognize. Familiar situations I feel in my bones. Or maybe I'm just addicted to assigning meaning to everything. I don't know." Drew pauses. "It's still kinda freaky though."

"You know who I feel really bad for?" Kev asks.

"Hm?"

"Terrance."

Drew nods. "Surprised he hasn't said anything."

"He has," Kev says instantly. "He left a voicemail for you at work. You don't want to hear it."

"I can imagine."

"Poor guy. His grandparents backed the wrong horse out of necessity only to end up on the wrong side of history because of their association with an organization founded by a guy who thinks it's okay to diddle kids. Now he's gone and done the same thing."

"I don't diddle kids."

"You know what I mean."

Drew hesitates. "Why's everyone so moral all of a sudden?" he asks softly. "Like they haven't spent the last twenty-two years saying uncouth things, justifying shady shit, bringing actually decent people down to their level. Suddenly all eyes are on them and they turn into zero-tolerance Puritans?" Drew frowns. "I just wish…" He shakes his head, looking down at his lap.

"What?" Kev asks.

Drew smirks. Looks back up at Kev with despaired eyes. "Why couldn't they have been like this *before*?" he whispers.

Kev's heart breaks at that. "It took all this for everyone to realize the culture we've made for ourselves. If they can just blame you for what's otherwise an institutional matter, they can keep their hands clean. Feel better about themselves."

"But I'm one of the good ones. I've always done the right thing. Sure I've made mistakes, but I've always had the best intentions." Drew pulls his knees in. Wraps his arms around them. His feet are cold. "Why do I get punished while other people, people way worse than I am, get to keep everything they have?"

"I don't have the answers to that."

"Maybe that Priest was right," Drew tells himself. "Maybe God doesn't have the power he used to. Or maybe He left because we're too fucking weird."

"I wouldn't say that."

Drew sighs. "I feel like I'm just a character in a story. My God is just some perverted author inflicting misery on a series of loosely defined versions of Himself." Drew looks at Kev. "He technically is, right? That's what a God ultimately is?"

Kev furrows his brow. "Is that a Depeche Mode song?"

Drew bursts out laughing, loud out-of-control cackles. "It really sounds like one, doesn't it?"

"Maybe He's doing this to you..." Kev awkwardly matches eyes with Drew. "Maybe He's doing this because you *haven't* been doing the right things. There's still hope for you, not everyone else."

Drew frowns, unsure how to respond.

Kev shrugs. "How else would you've have known?"

"Could that be it?" Drew murmurs.

"It's either that or there really is no God. Who wants to think that?"

Drew withdraws into himself. His eyes unfocus.

Kev stands. "I'm gonna pick up some food before we go."

"I've done something." Drew looks up. "A long time ago. Something bad."

Kev hesitates. Drew's expression looks pretty intense. "Worse than Jimmy?"

"Way worse. The worst thing I've ever done. It's the only thing I'd ever call…" Drew's voice fizzles on the last word. He tries again: "Evil."

Kev's heart races. "What is it?"

"I can't tell you."

"Why the hell not?"

"Because it wasn't just me."

Kev purses his lips. "Theo."

"I made a promise, Kev," Drew insists. "I want to tell you, I really do, but I can't."

"You know you can trust me."

"I know you'll never use it against him, but it's still a promise. I'm sick to death of justifying my broken promises."

Kev nods. "I take it Oscar doesn't know about it yet."

"Oh no, he knows everything," Drew says definitively. "He won't use it though. He would've ages ago."

"Then it can't be that bad."

"But it is. It's the reason he's so hell-bent against me. It's revenge." Drew pauses. "I wouldn't be surprised if he's trying to make a point by especially *not* using it, because that would be too easy or something. Too dirty. A low blow." Drew pauses. "Like an out-of-context video of a producer raping an intern."

Kev's stomach hardens.

Drew frowns, memories flying back. "Maybe you're right, Kev. Maybe I'm not one of the good ones. This whole thing is just a wake-up call for me to start doing the right things, so I'm gonna start doing the right thing, and the right thing is letting you jump ship while you still can."

Kev stares.

Drew nods. "It was good, Ephemeral. What you do next will be even better, but I will not drag you down with me. I've been in that position. I know what that feels like. I will not do that to you." Drew pauses. "Because you're a good person."

Kev looks at the blank TV, thinking.

Drew licks his dry lips. "I know this has been hard, all this coming out now. I wouldn't blame you. You still have a future in this town, Kev Foster." Drew nods, his face taut with emotion. "You deserve one."

Kev points at the TV. "All this coming out now?" He shakes his head. "That's not the man I started Ephemeral with."

Drew's face slacks.

Kev shrugs. "Whatever it is you and Theo did, I'd be just as bad if I abandoned you now."

Drew smiles slowly, moved beyond comprehension.

Kev pulls a cold Orange-Vanilla seltzer from the mini-fridge. Cracks it open. "Back in a flash." He hands the can to Drew. Heads out to grab a couple of those delicious looking burgers to-go.

END OF PART SIX

PART SEVEN

Riding the Whirlwind

WHALE

Ascension

"C'mon, Oscar, tell us!" Whale says eagerly over their candlelight dinner at the Russian Tea Room.

Oscar inhales wistfully. He looks at Whale's face shining in the candlelight. At Rian sitting next to him. Even Cashew is smiling. Oscar scratches his cheek. "IFC wants to buy *The Surgery* for $10,000."

Whale gasps.

"Holy fuck!" Rian exclaims, covering his mouth with both hands.

"Is that good?" Cashew asks.

"Very good, considering you guys are nobodies," Oscar tells them. "And since no one else is offering anything more than five grand, I think you should take it. They'll get you guys into so many more festivals, at least twelve before award season starts. They want to create as much buzz as they can."

"Not for the Oscars?" Whale asks.

"That's the idea. I'll keep running your campaign out west while you hop around and get your names out there."

"I can't believe it," Whale says.

"There's more," Oscar adds.

Rian widens his eyes. "More?!"

"I wanted to keep it a surprise."

"C'mon, what is it?" Cashew asks with a laugh.

Oscar makes eye contact with Cashew. His glee wavers a bit. Cashew notices. "An old friend of mine was in town," Oscar says slowly. "Serge Lamoule. He's a producer over at Paramount. Tribeca isn't usually his scene, but I got him to sit-in for *The Surgery* and he was very impressed. He's offering Rian and Jacob a first-look distribution deal for a feature."

Cashew's smile fades, brows furrowed in confusion.

"A feature?!" Whale exclaims.

"Yes, a feature."

"But we have to make it first," Rian clarifies.

"Correct," Oscar says. "Use the time on the road to network yourselves with a production studio. If you can bring Serge a feature, Paramount will distribute it."

"And it can be anything we want?" Whale asks.

"Paramount has to approve the idea, but I don't see why they wouldn't."

Rian laughs heartily. "Oh my God!" Whale hugs Rian tightly, growling excitedly. They bounce in their seats. Cashew frowns, staring at the spoon in his hand, rubbing its head.

"Fuck it, I'm getting a vodka flight!" Whale says excitedly.

"Me too!" Rian exclaims.

They scoot out of the booth. "We'll be right back," Whale calls behind him.

"Take your time!" Oscar says with a smile. Rian and Whale race out of sight, laughing their way upstairs to the vodka bar. Cashew stays where he is, avoiding eye contact with Oscar.

Oscar sits in silence with an unusually somber frown. "I tried, Theo. I really did. That was the best I could get."

"So you say," Cashew mumbles.

"I say it because it's true." Oscar shakes his head subtly. "I'm so sorry."

Cashew drinks some more water. "I don't care. I didn't wanna work with Rian again anyway."

"I figured that."

Cashew keeps glaring down at the table.

Oscar swallows, anxious eyes waiting for a reaction. "Does this mean you're coming back to work?"

Cashew doesn't say anything.

Rian and Whale buy two flights of top shelf vodka at the upstairs bar. "I can't believe it, buddy," Rian says. "This is really happening. This is real."

"We did it, man," Whale says, raising the first sample. They click their glasses and sip. "Really smooth."

"Yeah."

"So what's next?"

"We gotta make a movie," Rian answers. "Pretty much exactly what we did with *The Surgery* except with a bigger budget and no Cashew fucking it up."

"Don't call him that."

"He's not here."

Whale sighs. "I'm sorry. You're right."

Rian finishes his first sample. "Don't worry about the networking, I'll do all that. Just write the feature. You're already so good at that." Rian thinks a bit. "Wanna use one of your old scripts?"

"Don't think so," Whale murmurs. "They're nowhere near the caliber of real Hollywood."

"Just think, dude. This time next year we could be entering production on our first feature together."

"If this works, we might be able to open up a studio of our own. Be the Medicis after all."

"Exactly! We can make anything we want. Badass films, great films, films that fucking matter. Every aspect curated to be the best they can be."

Whale stares into the rest of his first vodka sample. "Maybe we can take submissions from outside writers, the ones that want to push the envelope and try something different, you know? Give 'em a real boost."

Rian smiles. "I like that. A place for art to thrive for everyone."

"Why should we waste our lives making films everyone already wants to see?" Whale murmurs. "Algorithms already ruin society."

"Absolutely."

"We should just make what we like and put it out there. Hope someone likes it too." Whale sighs. "It might be easier to change to fit into the world around you, but it's not nearly as fulfilling as living the life we're made for."

"Life's too damn short for that."

Whale grabs his second vodka sample. "It's like this... We all want something, even if we don't know it's out there. We feel it every day, floating around. It's there for a moment until we blink and it's gone."

"Ephemeral."

Whale nods. "I like that. Ephemeral Pictures."

Rian raises his second sample. "To Ephemeral Pictures."

They drink. Whale beams widely. "God, I haven't felt this good in years."

"About what?"

"The future." Whale looks at Rian. "I've been treating you like shit, haven't I?"

"It's okay, buddy. I know it's been rough."

"Please forgive me."

"You know I forgive you, buddy." Rian smiles a bit. "I'm just glad we're still friends."

"Always."

Rian raises the third vodka in his flight. "To the future."

"You know, we really should be slowing down on these."

"We just sold our Hollywood debut to IFC and Paramount's itching to sell a feature we haven't even written yet. We deserve to fuck our brains up on expensive-ass vodka."

Whale lifts his third vodka. "Eh, what the hell." They toast and down it.

Two weeks later, Cashew sits in his Northridge apartment fantasizing about Trisha. He's just about to pull up that old video for a quick wank when he hears a knock on his door. Cashew opens the door to reveal Whale standing with meek eyes. "Hey."

"Hey," Cashew says.

Whale steps in. "Been a while."

"Yeah." Cashew sits on the couch.

Whale puts a hand in his pocket, thinking of what to say. "How've you been?"

"Back to work. It's been fine."

"Just fine?"

"What do you want me to say?"

Whale frowns a bit. "We just got back from Savannah."

"Isn't that where Rian's from?"

"We avoided his folks of course. It was fun. We won Best Short."

Cashew nods. "Congratulations." He pauses. "What's next on the tour?"

Whale puffs out his cheeks. "St. Louis. Nashville. Rhode Island. Palm Springs."

"I'm happy for you, dude."

Whale smiles.

Cashew takes a deep breath. "Any leads on a production company for that feature?"

Whale shakes his head. "Nothing yet. I'm starting to get antsy. I'm worried if we take too long, Paramount might change their mind."

Cashew scratches his cheek. "I'm sure you would've found something by now if Rian had let you network with him."

Whale furrows his brow. "You think?"

"He probably thinks you'll fuck it up or something. I know the type, believe me."

Whale pulls an envelope out of his pocket and holds it out.

Cashew furrows his brow. Opens the envelope, revealing a check for $10,000. "What is this?"

"Your end of the IFC deal, plus the prize money from Tribeca and Savannah."

"That doesn't make sense."

Whale hesitates. "I threw my share in too."

"Jacob..."

"I don't want to hear it."

Cashew hands the check back. "I told you guys I didn't want the money."

"It's your short too."

"I'm just the producer."

"You're the only one that's supposed to make money."

"You're the one not working right now. You need this more than I do."

Whale's face sinks. He takes the check back. "I just feel bad that you got shafted out of the Paramount deal."

Cashew sighs audibly. "What can you do?"

"I'm sure Oscar didn't do it on purpose."

"You just want us to get along," Cashew says solemnly. "Truth is Oscar could've gotten any deal he wanted, and he wanted to shut me out."

"I don't think so."

"He's just proving a point as always." Cashew stands up. "I don't think he'll ever forgive me for muscling my way into the job."

"You did break into his house."

"I was desperate." Cashew pulls a beer from the fridge and cracks it open. "It's like he's saying, 'You wanted to work here so bad, why would you wanna leave?'" Cashew sips his beer. "But I'm not like that anymore. How long is he gonna hold that old version against me?"

Whale hesitates. "Oscar made me promise not to tell you this, but..."

Cashew stares at Whale curiously.

Whale looks back at Cashew. "Yesterday he told me he thinks he was wrong about you."

Cashew doesn't emote. "And you believe him? *Him*?"

Whale opens his mouth, unsure of what Cashew means. Or maybe he does.

Cashew drinks his beer. Returns to the couch. "Maybe it was for the best anyway."

"What do you mean?"

Cashew looks up at Whale with childlike glee. "Oh, I have to tell someone!"

"What?" Whale asks, sitting beside Cashew on the couch. "What is it?"

"I'm not supposed to say anything. You can't tell Oscar."

"I won't."

"I mean it. It'll ruin everything."

"I promise."

Cashew nods. "Liu Míng reached out to me last week. Remember Liu Míng?"

"Of course."

"Apparently a lot of people at Empire aren't happy with the way his dad's running things. Míng says there's gonna be a coup in six months."

"Not literally?"

"No, not literally," Cashew says. "Míng's creating his own company and taking Empire's top brass with him. He's calling it UniTopia Pictures. It's gonna incorporate Western capitalism into Empire's business model. One of the ways he's gonna do that is by having multiple studios under his banner in different markets. India. France. England. South Korea. Japan—"

"But why is Míng telling you all this?"

Cashew struggles to hide his smile. "He wants me to run his LA satellite!"

Whale's jaw drops. "THEO!"

"I know!" Cashew hugs Whale hard, beaming wide, literally shaking with joy.

"Why? Because of that dinner?"

"Yeah!" Cashew sits back, trying to catch his breath. "We have a lot in common. He doesn't have many people he can trust out here. Worst case scenario I blow it and he replaces me, but... Dude, I'm actually gonna have my own studio!"

"That's unbelievable!"

"He wants me to name it myself so it isn't obviously connected to UniTopia. I'm thinking 'Not That Nut Pictures.' What do you think?"

Whale hesitates. "You know cashews—"

"I know they're not nuts!" Cashew snaps. "Jesus fucking Christ! You don't fucking stop, do you?!"

Whale frowns. "Sorry."

"No, it's fine. I'll just change the name."

"Please, no, I like it." Whale forces a smile. "Not That Nut's a good name."

Cashew nods. "I know it is."

Whale turns his head away. Sighs. "Guess you're gonna be Louis B. Mayer after all."

"Don't knock yourself down. You'll be an auteur soon. I know you will."

"Yeah, but yours is guaranteed," Whale murmurs with self-deprecation. "I still have to write mine."

JACOB

~~La La Land~~

Moonlight

"Can I see your ID?" the Waiter asks.

JACOB
You sure can!

Jacob hands over his brand-spanking-new Pennsylvania Driver's License. Grins at Stewie sitting across from him, his face flicking in the candlelight.

"Okay," the Waiter says. "Two Courvoisier sidecars coming up."

The Waiter walks away. Jacob pockets his wallet.

JACOB
Happy Valentine's Day, Daddy!

STEWIE
Happy Valentine's Day, Baby Boy!

Jacob grins. Looks through the menu.

JACOB
God, can you believe we've only been living together for two months?

STEWIE
I know! I can't believe it.

JACOB
It's so much better, right?

STEWIE
Oh yeah.

JACOB
Screw you, Gus.

Stewie lifts his glass of water with a shrug.

STEWIE
So what are the Whitty's again?

JACOB
Whitman's Oscars. They have this big ceremony every year before graduation.

STEWIE
Like Eagle Ridge.

JACOB
They really go all-out with the Whitty's. Camera crews, stage lighting, formal attire. It's really a legit production, just like a real award show.

STEWIE
How do you get nominated?

JACOB
You submit whatever it is you made that year, a short film, screenplay, theatre clip, radio reel, and

Whitman alumni go through the submissions and pick the nominees in every category.

STEWIE
They pick the winners too?

JACOB
I think so.

STEWIE
Is that how the Oscars do it?

JACOB
Pretty much. And it's not just for bragging rights. The Whitty Awards are pretty famous. Just a nomination will look good on my resume.

Jacob takes another sip of his sidecar.

STEWIE
You've never submitted before?

JACOB
I've thought about it. When I wrote Who We Are and Daddy I wasn't quite sure I was any good as a writer, and then I was in Florence when I finished Through the Red Door. Murder in Milan and A Night with Myself aren't as good as everything else.

STEWIE
You submitted Drive-Thru?

JACOB
I submitted Drive-Thru and Waiting for Me.

STEWIE
Is there a category for features?

JACOB
No, they just lump it into Outstanding Writing for Film. It can be short, long, filmed, unfilmed.

STEWIE
I'm surprised you didn't submit The Surgery.

JACOB
It's just a treatment. It's not even a script yet.

Stewie frowns, remembering.

STEWIE
It's a shame.

JACOB
I know.

Jacob sighs. Dons a smile.

The Waiter returns with two sidecars with sugar rims. Jacob furrows his brow.

JACOB (CONT'D)
Oh.

"Enjoy," the Waiter says.

JACOB
Thanks.

The Waiter walks off. Jacob lifts the coupe glass, staring at the sugar rim.

STEWIE
Send it back.

JACOB
No, it's okay.

STEWIE
You should get it the way you want it.

JACOB
No, it's fine. He's in the weeds.

STEWIE
I'm gonna call him over if you don't.

JACOB
It's Valentine's Day. Just let him be.

Stewie purses his lips. They toast their glasses and sip. Jacob rolls his tongue around the sugar.

JACOB (CONT'D)
It's not bad.

STEWIE
I don't like it.

JACOB
Just rub it off.

STEWIE
I shouldn't have to. Send them back. They'll make new ones.

JACOB
We already drank out of them.

STEWIE
So what?

JACOB
Change the subject.

Stewie scratches his nose.

STEWIE
What were we talking about?

JACOB
Ooh! Speaking of award shows, the Oscars are on the 27th.

Stewie scrunches his face.

STEWIE
I really don't wanna.

JACOB
Why not?

STEWIE
They're just gonna bash Trump the whole time.

JACOB
They bash everyone.

STEWIE
Not the way they bash Trump. It's awful. I can't stand it.

Jacob nods reluctantly.

JACOB
It's okay. I'm not gonna force you.

STEWIE
Who do you think is gonna win?

JACOB
Well, I think it's really a toss-up between <u>Moonlight</u>, <u>La La Land</u>, and <u>Manchester by the Sea</u>.

STEWIE
Who do you want to win?

JACOB

For me it's a tie between Moonlight and La La Land. They're not even that similar, they're complete opposites in every way. On one hand you got Moonlight, a small indie epic about a black gay man across three stages of his life, changing himself to fit in to appease his intense mom and toxic masculine environment, and on the other hand you got La La Land the big-budget throwback movie-musical about dreamers trying to make it in LA while trying to stay together, culminating in probably the most devastating ending ever made. I just can't pick.

STEWIE

You certainly ruled the third one out pretty fast.

JACOB

I love Manchester by the Sea. It's unbelievable. Casey Affleck gives one of the best acting performances I've ever seen. The other two are just more relatable to me at this time in my life. If either of them wins I'll be happy.

Stewie rubs some sugar off the rim of his glass. Sips.

JACOB (CONT'D)

Since you're not really interested in seeing it, I'll just go to Film Immersion and watch it there.

STEWIE

What?

JACOB

It's my Super Bowl. I want to be around as many movie lovers as I can.

STEWIE

Aren't you gonna bump into Frankie and Nich?

JACOB

Nich won't be there. He's always hated the Oscars. TJ too.

(pause)

And I want to make up with Frankie.

STEWIE

(disgusted)

Why?

Jacob blinks at Stewie's acidic tone.

JACOB

He's still my best friend.

STEWIE

He threw you under the bus. Who needs him?

Jacob hesitates.

JACOB

I know him. I understand why he did it.

(pause)

And I don't believe in holding grudges.

Jacob steps off the elevator onto the 7th Floor of the Little Building. Tentatively approaches the crowd gathered around the common room. He recognizes lots of faces. Clem. Carter. Max. Tabitha. They recognize him too. Some look away with disgust. Some awkwardly nod or wave.

Jacob feels a bit too exposed. Looks to his left. Rian's approaching him with a somber apologetic grin.

"I was hoping you'd show up," Rian says softly.

Jacob half-frowns.

"I'm so sorry. It was so shitty of me to do that. I really wish I didn't."

```
Jacob sighs.

                    JACOB
        It's okay.
```

"No, it's not."

```
                    JACOB
        Don't worry about it. I forgive you.
```

Rian softens. "Really?"

```
                    JACOB
        It really fucking hurt.
                 (pause)
        But it was for the best. I'm just happy to be out of
        there, you know.

Rian smiles. Jacob brings him in for a nice quick hug. They make
their way into the TV room, the Red Carpet already in progress.
```

"How's Stewie doing?"

```
                    JACOB
        We're better than ever.
```

"Glad to hear it, buddy."

```
The two of them sit at one of the high-top tables set up for the
event. Norm Victor walks by.

                    JACOB
        Hey Norm!

                    NORM
        Hey Jake, how's it going?

                    JACOB
        Frankie, this is Norm Victor. He was in my Human
        Health and Disease class last semester.
```

"Nice to meet you," Rian says.

```
                    JACOB
                (to Norm)
        Didn't know you were on this floor.

                    NORM
        I'm not. This is just where the party is, you know?
```

"Carter did a good job."

```
                    NORM
        You guys fill out the predictions?

                    JACOB
        Predictions?

                    NORM
        $100 Amazon gift card to the one that gets the most
        right.

                    JACOB
        Oh damn! I'm getting in on that.

Norm brings Jacob and Rian two forms and watches then select their
predictions.
```

"Jeez, what a stacked year," Rian says.

JACOB
I know. Lion, Arrival, Hell or High Water. Hidden Figures sucks ass though.

"Yeah, I'm not a fan of it either."

NORM
I'm probably the only one that put Arrival for Best Picture. I'm such a Villeneuve fan.

JACOB
That's how you pronounce his name?

"You hear he's doing a *Blade Runner* sequel next year?" Rian asks.

JACOB
Please. Has Harrison Ford learned nothing from Kingdom of the Crystal Skull?

NORM
Hey, in Villeneuve We Trust.

JACOB
The last thing anyone wants right now is a sequel to Blade Runner. It's gonna suck. Mark my words.

"What did you pick for Best Picture, Jacob?"

JACOB
La La Land. You?

"Same."

JACOB
It's so good, right?

NORM
I don't know. Don't you think it's a little racist?

Jacob and Rian share eye contact.

JACOB
No?

"Since when is not having a racial angle racist?" Rian asks Norm.

NORM
The white guy's the only one saving traditional jazz? Sounds like a racial angle to me.

JACOB
That's not what the movie's saying at all. That's just the Whitman Girls finding something to hate about it.

NORM
The what?

JACOB
That's what I call the uber-PC progressive types. The Tumblr crowd, you know. The ones that subscribe to the majority to save face.

"That's fucking sexist," Norm mutters.

JACOB
How is that sexist?! 60% of campus are women! They're literally the majority!

"Calling out their gender like it's a bad thing is literally chauvinistic."

JACOB
Whitman Girls can be men too. You know, the ones that apologize for being men. Male guilt. The ones that

grovel and go "I come in peace" so they don't end up getting canceled one day.

Norm points off.

"I'm sitting over there."

Norm walks off. Jacob blinks, flabbergasted. Rian's equally shocked.

JACOB
Case and point.

The room goes quiet as the 89th Academy Awards begin on schedule.

"If we were at the LA campus right now," Rian whispers to Jacob, "We'd be only a few blocks away."

Jacob's predictions start failing as the night goes on. By the time the ceremony gets down to the Big Four, La La Land only has four wins out of its all-time record tying fourteen nominations. Jacob and Rian both thought La La Land would win Best Original Screenplay but it went to Manchester by the Sea instead.

But then HALLE BERRY (50) opens the envelope for Best Director.

HALLE BERRY
And the Oscar goes to...
(pause)
Damien Chazelle! La La Land!

All the Whitman Girls in the TV room react with angry cries and disgusted expressions. Jacob furrows his brow.

"They really wanted Barry Jenkins to win, huh?" Rian murmurs.

JACOB
I think they're finally realizing La La Land's gonna win Best Picture.

"That's no guarantee. I was so sure *The Revenant* was winning last year."

JACOB
You got a point there. I'm pretty sure I'm the only person in the world that knew Spotlight was gonna win.

"I wouldn't mind if *Moonlight* ends up winning."

JACOB
That's what I told Stewie.

Jacob scans the tense faces around him.

JACOB (CONT'D)
Though a little part of me wants La La Land to win just to piss these guys off.

"It's probably gonna win."

JACOB
The whole racist thing is such bullshit. It's a fucking movie. Why do they have to paint it like some sort of wrong-side-of-history, ethically backwards minstrel show?

"They always pick on the frontrunner for something stupid. Happens every year. The moment Oscar season ends, no one remembers what was so wrong with them."

JACOB
I know. It just feels different this year.

"How so?"

JACOB
Because calling <u>La La Land</u> racist makes people like me look bad.

"People like you?"

JACOB
The ones who actually like the movie!

"Oh! Shh! Best Actor."

Jacob eagerly sits up with a grin.

BRIE LARSON (27), last year's well-deserved Best Actress winner for <u>Room</u>, presents this year's Academy Award for Best Actor. The nominees are Casey Affleck for <u>Manchester by the Sea</u>, Andrew Garfield for <u>Hacksaw Ridge</u>, Ryan Gosling for <u>La La Land</u>, Viggo Mortensen for <u>Captain Fantastic</u>, and Denzel Washington for <u>Fences</u>.

"It's not even close!" Rian says with a chuckle.

JACOB
C'mon Casey Affleck!

Jacob's unconsciously loud voice draws attention from Tabitha, Max, and Norm sitting nearby.

Brie Larson opens the envelope.

BRIE LARSON
And the Oscar goes to...
(pause)
Casey Affleck.

Jacob and Rian cheer with hearty applause, drowned out by a louder onslaught of boos, hisses, and groans.

"How the fuck could you cheer for him?" Tabitha asks them with seething disgust.

JACOB
It was one of the best performances of all time. What, am I supposed to forget that?

"Look!" Norm calls out, pointing at the TV. "She's not clapping!"

Jacob looks up. Brie Larson really isn't clapping for Casey.

"Just because he was accused doesn't mean he actually did it," Rian chimes in. "Whatever happened to innocent until proven guilty?"

"You're supposed to believe the victims," Max retorts.

JACOB
What happened is irrelevant! It was years ago. People change.

"Why do you keep making excuses for him?" Norm claps back. "Because he was in a movie you like?"

JACOB
I'm not making excuses for anything! I'm just happy he won!

"Lower your voice," Rian says calmly.

JACOB
They're attacking ME here!

"You're making a scene."

Jacob huffs angrily. Looks away.

Leonardo DiCaprio presents Best Actress to Emma Stone for La La Land. Soon after FAYE DUNAWAY (76) and WARREN BEATTY (79) walk on stage to present Best Picture.

WARREN BEATTY
(opening envelope)
And the Oscar goes to...

Warren Beatty stares at the envelope, hesitating.

"God, he's really blowing it," Rian murmurs.

JACOB
The dude's almost eighty.

"He looks it."

Faye Dunaway impatiently takes one look at the envelope.

FAYE DUNAWAY
(blurts)
La La Land!

Rian and Jacob cheer loudly, the only ones in the room.

JACOB
Thank you!

As the cast and crew of La La Land take the stage, Jacob and Rian go through their predictions.

JACOB (CONT'D)
I got Visual Effects, Production Design, Original Score, Animated Short, Documentary Feature, Animated Feature, Supporting Actress, Supporting Actor, Actress, Actor, Director, and Picture. That's what? One-two-three-four-five... twelve out of twenty-four. Damn.

"It's your fault for giving Sound Mixing and Film Editing to *La La Land.* War films always win those."

JACOB
And musicals. No, what really did me in was giving Best Original Song to "Audition" instead of "City of Stars." What a dummy move that was.

"You fucked up Adapted Screenplay too, huh?"

JACOB
Arrival's not a bad choice.

"I know, but *Moonlight*'s got the scope. That's why it won."

"What's going on?" Max asks, looking at the TV.

Jacob notices a lot more people on the Oscar stage than normal. Lots of muttering during La La Land producer FRED BERGER'S (35) speech.

FRED BERGER
(quick; deadpan)
We lost by the way.

"Wait," Norm blurts.

"WHAT?!" Tabitha cries.

La La Land producer JORDAN HOROWITZ (36) steps up to the microphone.

JORDAN HOROWITZ
There's been a mistake.
(gestures off-stage)
Moonlight, you guys won Best Picture.

Jacob's blood runs cold as the Whitman Girls scream simultaneously. "This is not a joke," Jordan Horowitz adds, but Jacob can't hear the TV amid the tonal whiplash on Film Immersion. He can't look at the screen from social anxiety alone. And a lot of those cheers, those jeers, are directed at him and Rian. The bad guys. They lost! They lost! Thank God they lost!

Jacob feels sick to his stomach. He can feel the symbolic egg on his face, tomatoes being thrown up at him from the pit. He's seen every Oscars ceremony since he was twelve. He knows what happens and what simply doesn't happen. John Travolta inexplicably mispronouncing "Idina Menzel" as "Adele Dazeem" happens. Ellen taking the world's most famous selfie happens. One of the nominees being read over and over every time as *Precious: Based on the Novel 'Push' by Sapphire* happens. Fucking up Best Picture DOES NOT HAPPEN! This is not the Grammy's with their bullshit popularity bias! This is not the Emmy's with their bullshit recency bias, or the Golden Globes with their shameless corruption and laughably awarding Best Comedy to *The Martian*, nor is it the People's/Teen's/Kid's Choice Awards giving Marvel or *Star Wars* or fucking *Twilight* Film of the Year, or the VMAs with Madonna kissing Britney and Christina or Miley grinding against Robin Thicke's dick and teaching middle-class white moms what twerking is. This is the Oscars! The goddamn Academy motherfucking Awards! They've all borne witness to by far the most embarrassing moment of Hollywood's longest lasting and most revered artistic institution and they're fucking CELEBRATING?!

Stewie drives Jacob home in his Jeep.

JACOB

The one night a year I look forward to more than anything and they had to effing ruin it.

STEWIE

They're the worst.

JACOB

They make me feel like S-H-I-T for even liking the Oscars. Why were they even there? Do they even LIKE movies? They've already been giving the Academy crap for all that Oscars So White BS, but when they break records for black nominees this year, suddenly there's not enough Latino and Asian representation? They gave them exactly what they asked for and it's still not enough!

STEWIE

They'll never be satisfied.

JACOB

Not saying the N-word? Fine, that's easy. Taking the side of the victim every time and hating the police every time they choke out a black guy? Okay, that's a bit much, but what's the harm, right? But me wanting Best Actor to go to the best actor is a problem? Me liking a movie-musical that I actually connect to on a deep profound level is a problem? Me not wanting to cheer for the worst Oscar's gaffe in history, that makes me part of the problem? I'm not just gonna throw aside what I love because they tell me to! That's not unrealistic, right? Am I crazy?

STEWIE

You're not crazy.

JACOB

After all those years defending them, taking their side on abortion, gay marriage, police brutality, they're just gonna lump me in with the same braindead morons in those godawful red hats? I DID EVERYTHING THEY ASKED ME TO DO! I voted for Hillary! I gave them the benefit of the doubt time and time again! But now they're just gonna toss me aside because I'm not drinking their mother-effing Kool Aid?! What is wrong with these people?!

Stewie shrugs. Jacob goes quiet. Leans against the door.

STEWIE
What's going on with the internship?

JACOB
I don't know.

STEWIE
Have you started looking yet?

JACOB
No.

STEWIE
You gonna start looking tomorrow?

JACOB
I've got class.

STEWIE
After class then.

JACOB
It's an evening class.

STEWIE
So what? We can look together.

JACOB
What's the rush?

STEWIE
You're running out of time for the summer internships, aren't you?

JACOB
Can't we just talk about this tomorrow?

STEWIE
Do you NOT want to do an internship all of a sudden?

Jacob hesitates.

JACOB
No, I do.

STEWIE
Then you better find something before all the good ones are gone.

Jacob frowns a bit. Scratches his cheek.

JACOB
There is something.

STEWIE
An internship?

JACOB
My Writing the Short Subject professor sends out a jobs blast to a hundred or so of his former students once or twice week, and not anything you'd find on Indeed or LinkedIn. Stuff he'd only hear about working part-time at Whitman's LA campus.

STEWIE
Really? Anything good?

JACOB
The only one I'd actually consider is a paid internship with The Professor.

STEWIE
He has an internship too? In LA?

JACOB
No, not that professor. THE Professor. That's his name.

STEWIE
Who's name?

JACOB
Just some French guy that calls himself "The Professor." You ever see Rant? Or hear about it?

STEWIE
I think I remember seeing the trailer actually. In the 80s, right?

JACOB
That was him.

STEWIE
Really?

JACOB
He's switched to producing since.
(pause)
You'd like him, he's a Trump Supporter.

STEWIE
REALLY?

JACOB
Trump's number one private donor.

STEWIE
I don't believe it.

JACOB
There's a lot of Conservatives in Hollywood.

STEWIE
And you'd be working for him at his production company?

JACOB
I'd be AUDITIONING for the real job, and no, it'd be for his development company. I'd be reading screenplay submissions, summarizing them, determining what makes the cut and what doesn't. It's called "coverage."

STEWIE
That sounds perfect.

JACOB
It sounds perfect to any screenwriting major with no set experience, which is why it's an incredibly hard internship to get.

STEWIE
How hard are we talking?

JACOB
He gets around 15,000 applications a year apparently.

STEWIE
That's not that much, Baby Boy.

JACOB
It's a very exclusive internship. You need a recommendation from someone in the industry, which in this case would be Jim my Writing the Short Subject professor, and you can only be a recent grad from one of the top twenty film schools in the country, and even then you have to send in an application with

something from your portfolio, something to prove you're not just book smart.

STEWIE
You can do THAT.

JACOB
I don't know.

STEWIE
What's the harm in applying?

JACOB
It's a lot of work.

STEWIE
How much time do you have?

JACOB
I think March 31 is the cutoff.

STEWIE
Alright then. Get on that.

JACOB
I'm kinda pissed off at the moment.

STEWIE
I know. You can start tomorrow.

Jacob eyerolls.

JACOB
Fine. Tomorrow.

Stewie hesitates.

STEWIE
You promise?

JACOB
Yes! I promise! Stop bugging me about it, okay?! God!

Jacob glares off, wind buffeting his hair around. Stewie frowns.

DREW
Making Up

Drew does pushups on the floor of his office, the corporate carpet burning his palms. No shirt. Muscles shining with sweat. Cock hard from the bloodflow. Kev opens the door, halting at the sweaty beast before him. "You made a full recovery."

Drew laughs, resting on his knees. He flops his sweaty hair about. "You get it?" he asks, breathing heavily.

"I sure did." Kev hangs the suit holder on the door. Unzips down, revealing a beautiful black Armani suit, an elephant gray Brooks Brothers dress shirt, red and black tie, and a red pocket square still in its plastic packaging.

"Oh yeah," Drew breathes, standing up. "That's the fucker."

"Your measurements are incredibly complicated."

"But it's ready to go, right?"

"Yeah, but why? What's it for?"

Drew tosses a scoop of unflavored whey protein powder into a blender bottle. Fills it with water. Kev waits with anticipation as Drew shakes, rattles, and rolls the protein down his throat in a single go. "I'm going on *Oscar Blitz* tonight." Drew says, burping a bit.

Kev's smile drops hard. "What."

"8 PM. Live and all. The son of a bitch couldn't resist."

"You already called him?!"

"Yeah. I want the full Friday promotion push. The bigger the ratings, the better."

Kev shakes his head. "This is such a stupid idea, Drew."

"I disagree."

"Why couldn't you fly it by me and Gary first?"

"One, you would've said no. Two, I've already listened to Gary. He had his chance. And three, I'm not gonna sit on my ass and wait for the Academy to take the one thing I got left."

Kev frowns. "Talk to Gary before you head over there."

"I'm doing this myself." Drew slips on a black T-Shirt.

"Be wise about this, dude."

"I need to do this," Drew says sternly. "I need to know how to clean my own fucking mess."

"You don't think it's too soon? You only just got out of the hospital."

"It's been two days. I'm fine."

"Alright." Kev watches Drew rip open a protein bar, smirking at his renewed determinism. "You know you're not gonna change everyone's mind overnight."

"I don't need to change everyone's mind." Drew rips off a chunk of protein bar and chomps. "Just Oscar's."

Drew sits in the *Oscar Blitz* Studio 1 dressing room around 5:30 with absolutely no idea what he's doing, scared out of his wits. The door opens, Leon slowly walking in, making eye contact with a somber frown. He approaches the back of Drew's head. An awkward atmosphere's already brewing.

"Hey Leon," Drew says.

"Jacob." Leon walks around Drew's chair. Opens his makeup kit. Starts applying powder on Drew's face.

Drew looks up at Leon. Leon isn't looking back. "How's it been?" Drew asks.

"You know what's going on."

Drew nods, just enough not to disturb Leon's application.

"Your skin's turned to shit," Leon says.

"It's the steroids. Four months was all it took, I guess."

"Nah, it's the coke. It fucks up a lot of people that come in here."

"You're probably right."

Leon puts down the brush. Hesitates picking up another one.

"How's Oscar been?" Drew asks. "The real Oscar, not the one he plays on TV?"

Leon can't even look at Drew's reflection. "Do you have any idea how hard this is for me right now? Being in the same room with you?"

"I know."

"What the fuck is wrong with you?" Leon scolds, looking Drew in the eye. "How the fuck could you do all those things?"

"Actually Carlos Gutierrez retracted his testimony when he found out people were assuming I made the deportation call."

"Big deal. That's one thing."

Drew frowns. "I don't know why."

"You could've had a great career, Jacob. You could've been just fine, just the way you were." Leon shakes his head, gesturing to Drew's body, his face, his bloodshot eyes. "What was wrong with *you*?"

Drew exhales through his nose, his deviated septum whistling. "I don't know." He pauses. "But I want to fix it, Leon. I want to fix everything."

"But why?" Leon asks. "For people to like you again?"

Drew hesitates.

Leon frowns. "I don't know what's wrong with Oscar. He went too fucking far bringing that Tribeca guy on, pretending he wasn't backstage with me. And he's not asking enough questions, or the right questions, or whatever he's not doing. This isn't the *Oscar Blitz* I signed up for. I don't know what the fuck you guys did to him, but he's throwing everything away just to get back at you for it."

Drew scoffs. "I can't believe it."

"I can."

"I actually..." Drew shakes his head, smiling. "I actually figured that one out on my own."

Leon recognizes that smile. That relief. That softie's still in there somewhere. That nice boy.

"I think I can fix this, Leon," Drew insists. "Just trust me."

Leon takes a deep breath. "A bit of drama's gone down since the attack on your home."

Drew sits up. "Behind the scenes?"

Leon hesitates. "Oscar's been looking for this guy... Terry. He was one of the go-go boys you had your way with at Sweet Vermouths. He was supposed to be with Dirk, Aarin, and Trenton on Friday but he's been off the grid for the last two months or so."

"I think I remember him," Drew whispers. "Blond, right?"

"And crazy smart. A *summa cum laude* laureate."

"Damn."

"After you and him... he said he gave up dancing at Sweet Vermouths and got into heroin because of it."

Drew's blood goes cold. He leans back. "I didn't..."

"I know," Leon says solemnly. "How could you have?"

Drew's face tightens. He feels sick.

Leon sees this. Clears his throat. "Don't worry, he's been in rehab. That's why Cleo and the guys couldn't find him in time. He only called back yesterday to tell her. They only let him have phone privileges once a week or something."

Drew nods, still harrowed.

"But he said something else," Leon continues. "He told Cleo Jimmy was a liar."

Drew lifts his eyes. "He did?"

"He watched your YouTube video after he heard about the attack. That put the bug in his ear. He snuck a stream of Jimmy's testimony and said that the way he talked, the way he acted, that there was no way he's ever done a drug in his life, not to mention he had no track marks or anything."

"And he told Cleo this?"

"That's how I know. He wanted to give her a heads up. Said you didn't deserve to be ganged up like this."

Drew smiles. "That's nice at least."

"Oscar didn't believe her though."

"What Terry said?"

"That she even talked to Terry. He actually accused her of making up the phone call to make up for not being able to find him. He's been sending guys to crack dens and under bridges in MacArthur Park. As if a heroin user wouldn't want to clean themselves up one day, let alone a smart guy like Terry."

"Where's Cleo? I wanna talk to her."

"Oscar fired her."

Drew gapes. "He fired CLEO?!"

"Thirty seconds after she told him about the call."

Drew shakes his head. "He really has lost his mind."

"And now that you're here, shit's really hit the fan."

"What did I do?"

Leon hesitates. "About twenty minutes before you got here, there was a..." He rotates his hands. "I guess you can call it a schism."

"A schism?"

"Cleo's firing scared the shit out of a lot of people. The fact checkers. Some sound guys. Pete. They were already weirded out by how Oscar's been since he met Jimmy, but the Tribeca thing happened, and your condo. And now Cleo? That was it. Half the team walked out."

"Half?"

"They don't want to be a part of Oscar's mad crusade anymore. They have their pride, even if he doesn't."

"I can't believe it." Drew looks at Leon. Realizes. "You're still here."

Leon nods apologetically.

Drew hesitates. "What does that mean?"

Leon takes a deep breath. "It means I don't want to lose my job." He pauses. "Don't think because I'm still here that I agree with Oscar in any way. I hate Jimmy, that conniving little shit. His lies only hurt real stat rape victims."

"He wasn't always like that," Drew murmurs. "He was actually a lot like Terry. And me."

"What changed?"

Drew goes quiet. Looks off.

Leon looks at his makeup kit. "I need to go get more foundation. Be back in five." He heads for the door.

"Is there anything Oscar doesn't want me to know about?" Drew asks, turning around. "About tonight?"

Leon stops at the door. Sighs.

"Just give me something," Drew says. "Some intel I can use against him. To put him in his place for what he did to Cleo."

Leon swallows. Looks back at Drew with soft eyes.

"Do what you feel is right," Drew tells him. "You'll only regret it if you don't."

Leon nods. "He's gonna bring Jimmy out. To try and trip you up."

Drew smiles. "Thank you, Leon."

Leon nods. Leaves the room.

Drew faces forward. Replays that conversation in his mind. Thinks of Terry. Theo. Kev. Jimmy. Oscar. Trisha. All those guys from Whitman that held a grudge for so long. All those Not That Nutty guys forced into silence like he was under Theo, finally able to speak up without fear. He thinks of Frankie, wherever he is. His mom, wherever she is. Stewie, wherever he is. And it dawns on him, what he needs to do, the only thing that can make everything right. Drew closes his eyes. He really doesn't wanna do it. But he has to. It's the right thing.

Drew pulls out his cell phone. Goes through his email. Finds the number. Makes the hardest call of his life.

Leon returns five minutes later to find Drew still talking on the phone. "Yes, I am. And don't make the announcement until I do, okay?" Drew listens. "Thank you, sir. Have a good night." He hangs up. It's done. Emotional phase over. Time to execute. Drew looks up at Leon, already in damage control mode. "How much time do I have?"

"Two hours," Leon says.

"Do you have something I can type on? Something I can bring out?"

Leon looks around. "Is an iPad okay?"

"Perfect."

Leon grabs an iPad from the shelf. Hands it to Drew. Drew flips the cover. Taps on the Notes app. Creates a new doc. Types away with both hands.

WHALE
Second Coming

Whale slouches on his couch, watching *Downton Abbey* for the fiftieth time, zoning out with boredom. It's been three weeks since he got back from Savannah and he hasn't come up with a single decent idea for the Paramount feature. How's he supposed to recreate *The Surgery*'s success? He can't adapt it into a feature. That would ruin its small-scale charm. Besides, did he really wanna be the small-scale *Black Mirror* guy? Where's the fun in that?

Whale's not living a creative life anymore, meeting new people, traveling to new lands. What's actually happened that he could draw from? Being a bystander to an ethically ambiguous rape whistleblow scenario? Almost jumping off a bridge? It all screams amateur feature debut.

One of his best friends from Eagle Ridge, Abby Millhouse, one of the two people in the car with him when he first said the words "I'm gay," had a stepfather named Dr. Kaufman who made a secret living selling drugs out of his New Jersey practice. When Dr. Kaufman's first wife April discovered his scheme, he hired a Mexican biker to assassinate her in their home and make it look like a random junkie break-in, and since the assassin OD'd a few years later Kaufman got away with it. And then Kaufman married his high school sweetheart, Mrs. Millhouse, Abby's mother. But then April's daughter from a previous marriage, who had always suspected her stepfather of murdering her mother, worked with the authorities to charge Kaufman with murder-for-hire. And when they finally had enough to arrest, Kaufman locked himself in his practice with a gun and there was a standoff with the police until they finally caught him alive. Mrs. Millhouse apparently had no idea what Kaufman had done, and she was thrust into a pretty bad media spotlight because of her vapid complacency. Then as soon as Kaufman was charged with murder, he hung himself in prison. Something like that actually happened to someone Whale knows very well. But if he turned it into a movie? *Cliché.*

What if *The Surgery* is only successful *because* they're nobodies? Anyone can succeed with such low expectations. What if Whale isn't a good writer, just good for what he is? He doesn't have a brand. *The Surgery* is admittedly good story, but that's all he's known for at the moment, the guy who wrote *The Surgery*. The moment he releases something else, he's Jacob Andrezj. What if the world doesn't like Jacob Andrezj the writer? One-hit wonders face this problem all the time. "She Blinded Me With Science" was a zany song, but did anyone care about Thomas fucking Dolby because of it?

What if he writes a really good follow-up ala *Pulp Fiction* and Paramount butchers it with lazy rewrites? What if Rian doesn't want to deviate from the narrow vision in his head like he did with *The Surgery*'s prologue? Was Whale willing to fight for stupid stuff like that? What if everything's planned great and the cast fucks it up? What if it's flawless in every way but poorly marketed?

Whale tries to tune out such questions with *Downton* or *The Americans* or *Six Feet Under* or *Battlestar* or *Breaking Bad*, but then he feels like he's procrastinating. He's limited to these shows as creative influences. What if he accidentally writes a knockoff and THAT'S what ends up being his undoing? How uninteresting his life is. Why didn't he spend all those years of college learning more exotic things?

On Sunday, Whale gets the lobster omelet at Merry's while Oscar gets the strawberry ricotta pancakes. His garb-of-the-day is a very bland-looking leather Navajo poncho.

"You look like a fucking moccasin," Whale quips.

"So do you."

Whale looks away.

Oscar laughs. "Oh come on, that was funny."

"I'm really not in the mood."

"No progress on the Paramount feature, I take it?"

Whale shakes his head.

Oscar shrugs. "Everyone gets writer's block from time to time."

"It's not even writer's block. It's outliner's block. It's even worse."

"Just take your time with it. If you fuck it up, no one's gonna wanna see the next one."

Whale glares. "Thanks for the reminder, asshole!"

Oscar looks at Whale, startled. "I wasn't insulting you. That's good advice."

"'Don't fuck up' is good advice?"

"There's no rush," Oscar says deliberately. "I'm trying to help you here."

"You're not fucking helping."

"Excuse me, Mr. Blitz," their Waiter interrupts, a small dish in his hand. "The extra strawberries you requested—"

"Took too long." Oscar dumps the dish over the balcony. Strawberries and gummy juice rain onto the tables below. Chairs screech on concrete. Irate customers cry out. "Better get to that," Oscar mumbles, not looking at the Waiter.

The Waiter races away. Gallops down the stairs.

Oscar flicks his hand over the balcony. "Goddammit," he mutters. He stands sharply, looking down at the strawberry spatter across his thigh. "It's gonna get fucking ruined if it settles."

"What is that, real buffalo skin?" Whale asks.

"No, just baboon ass." Oscar looks behind him, holding out his dripping hand. "I gotta run to the little boy's room. Do me a favor. Get out my laptop and email Pete the proofs I've got saved on the desktop. I told him he'd have 'em by noon."

Whale tentatively opens Oscar's computer bag. "Where do I email from?"

"Just use the client I've got pinned to the taskbar. Send them to Pete's usual."

Whale opens the laptop. "Password?"

Oscar leans in. "'CapybaraKid64.' Don't ask."

"One word?"

"All one word, capital C, capital K." Oscar scoots his chair aside with a foot. Slowly walks to the bathroom, both hands raised like a surgeon.

Whale opens Oscar's email client. Sends Pete the PDFs. Notices all the subject lines in Oscar's inbox. Scrolls a bit. Lots of newsletters. No signs of girlfriends or secret admirers. Whale double-checks for Oscar's return. Clicks on the search bar.

Three days later. Whale waits in a booth at Harry 79 in Los Feliz, the lunch crowd busy, mostly tourists. Whale checks his watch. A family of four comes in, a cross-looking man in his thirties, a pregnant woman, and two hyper boys around five and three.

Whale looks at his half-empty booth, all that generous space. "Excuse me!" Whale calls over to family, scooting out.

"Oh, thank you!" the Mother says with an exhausted sigh.

"I'm just waiting for one more," Whale says with a chivalrous smile. "I'm sure he won't mind the counter."

"Daddy!" the oldest boy whines. "I gotta pee!"

"Yeah, me too!" adds the younger boy.

The Father sighs. Looks to his wife.

"Take them, I'll be fine." The Mother slides back-first into booth, both feet hanging off the side. The Father reluctantly leads the two boys into the men's room.

"I can move the table over if you want," Whale offers.

"Oh, no, I'm fine like this." The Mother stretches out her legs. "We've been on a bus all day, all the way from Seattle."

"I used to take the bus to school. First one on, last one off every time. An hour and a half each way. It was one of the worst experiences of my life." Whale touches the bridge of his nose. "Pretty sure I deviated my own septum sleeping against on the window."

The Mother chuckles sympathetically.

"First time in LA?" Whale asks.

"Yeah." The Mother caresses her bump. "We couldn't fly, obviously."

"When's he due?"

"June 10."

Whale nods ambiently. "Did you pick a name out yet?"

"James. Jimmy for short, after my father."

"I like that." Whale crouches down. "Hi Jimmy," he coos with a childish wave.

The Mother beams with pride.

Whale smiles, picturing a little baby boy waving back at him. "Hard to believe we were all like this at one time, huh?"

"I know."

Whale stares at the bump, his expression hardening. "Just make sure he never feels the need to leave home. LA has enough waiters."

The Mother softens with equal parts confusion and sympathy.

Whale nods. Stands. Relocates to the counter.

An hour later, Whale hears a bell ding. He turns. "About time."

"There was an accident on the 5," Cashew mutters, sitting beside Whale. "Why'd you pick the counter?"

"Is everyone okay?"

"Where?"

"The accident on the 5."

"I don't know."

"You didn't check?"

"No." Cashew grabs a menu. "By the time I got up to it, I lost interest."

Whale sighs. "Did you read what I sent you?"

"I did."

"What'd you think?"

Cashew dismissively closes the menu. "What does Rian think about it?"

"I haven't told him yet."

Cashew raises a subtle brow. "Why not?"

Whale shrugs. "Just wanted to see what you thought first."

Cashew thinks. "Honestly, I just don't see it working."

Whale huffs hard. "Really?!"

"How'd you come up with that one?" Cashew asks with palpable judgment.

"What's so wrong with it?"

"C'mon, a gay Victorian brothel? That's way too smutty for a first feature."

"Not in this day and age, with Pornhub and OnlyFans and whatnot."

"Sex doesn't shock like it did in the 70s. It just comes off as lazy or bawdy. You need something impactful. Something with class."

"What about that trial? You're telling me that wouldn't be a badass finale?"

"If they won. No one wants to watch an entire movie leading up to a trial only for them to lose."

"But that's what really happened!"

"Audiences don't want real. They want happy."

Whale scoffs. "Theo, it wouldn't make sense for Jack to win a libel trial in those days. It's more realistic this way. It's not about the end result, it's the fact that they gave it all they got. It might not be happy, but it's still hopeful. So is life. Why should I pretend it isn't just because people don't wanna hear it?"

Cashew folds his hands. "Jacob, people *need* happy endings. Life's already hard enough with politics everywhere and taxes and North Korea and Notre Dame burning down and social media shoving war crimes and slaughterhouses in our faces. We can't get away even if we wanted to. That's why people go to the movies. They want two hours of flashy superheroes beating up thinly veiled Republican caricatures because that's two hours of not looking at your phone, two hours of not having to worry about the future, two hours of good whooping evil's ass for once. All those downer pictures are powerful and artsy and all, but they're textbooks. No one wants that nowadays."

"Isn't there already enough of that out there? Can't I just do my own thing for the people that want it?"

"This feature has to launch your career. Selling tickets now is what's gonna lead up to the artsy ones. Why do think debuts are always boring? They're good writers. They're just playing it safe at the start. Easing their brand into the pool, not cannonballing in."

"So you think I should change the ending of the Jack Branson story?"

Cashew hesitates. "I don't think you should make it at all. You need something China will approve of."

"China?"

"You want box office, don't you? That's how you do it. Something nice and simple. Nothing too American or complicated. Something you can easily translate with subtitles." Cashew pauses. "And definitely nothing gay."

Whale stares. "I only want to write gay stories."

"Then don't be shocked if you don't hit mainstream."

"That's why I wanted to be a writer in the first place," Whale whispers harshly. "That's why I fucking came here to begin with. To tell gay stories. Autistic stories. We need more fucking representation."

"You still can. Later."

Whale shakes his head.

"Hey, I'm sorry if that's not what you wanted to hear, but it's true," Cashew says. "C'mon Jacob, don't be a Whitman Girl. You're never gonna change the world to fit your specifications. If you wanna make it, you gotta play the game."

The family of four slides out of the booth behind them. The Mother waves at Whale on her way out. Whale waves back. Cashew's confused.

"I was just asking advice," Whale murmurs, facing Cashew. "You gave it. Duly noted."

"You have a real stubbornness problem."

"No I don't."

"Yeah you do. You fell in love with this story and you wanted me to like it. But now that I don't, you'd rather discredit my opinion than admit that I might actually be right."

Whale doesn't answer. Sighs instead.

"This is the business we've chosen," Cashew tells him. "We all gotta do things we don't want to do. One for us, one for them. You really think you'd be the exception?"

"It's not in my programming to grovel."

"Then don't look at it like groveling. It's like..." Cashew pauses. "It's taking a risk. You gotta make a movie that isn't a pet project. That might feel like work, but it doesn't mean it's gotta be a shitty movie. There *are* blockbusters that are great movies, you know. Make the most fascinating commercial film you can. If you can do that, that's gonna impress everyone."

Whale hesitates. "I really feel Jack Branson—"

"Forget about him. He's a nobody for a reason."

"Yeah, institutional homophobia."

Cashew rolls his eyes. "You're being unnecessarily dramatic about this."

"If I let China tell me I can't write gay stories, I'm just as bad as everyone else."

"Just for the first one."

Whale rests his chin on the counter with a frown. "That's what they all say, isn't it?"

"You can do it, you know."

Whale looks over. "Do what?"

"Write a movie that isn't secretly about you."

Whale doesn't talk. Cashew's words strike a chord.

Cashew nods sympathetically. "I've seen you in action, man. You can do anything. I know it."

Whale smiles.

Cashew picks up the menu. "When's the last time Rian told you that?"

DREW

Truth or Dare

Drew sits across from Oscar Blitz in Studio 1. All those eyes on him. Real people. A full house. Lights down. Cameras off. Leon's powdering Oscar's face. The man himself. The two of them surrounded by bystanders, just like old times.

"You really haven't aged, have you?" Drew asks.

Oscar doesn't answer. Leon finishes his job. Throws Drew a discreet look. Retreats from the multi-camera setup's splash zone. Drew readjusts his butt. iPad still back there, stuffed in his waistband like the Man With No Name's secret gun in those Sergio Leone standoffs. It's gonna get *The Good, The Bad, and The Ugly* very soon, isn't it?

Drew looks out at the crowd. The shuffled feet. The hushed whispers. The fascination in their eyes, the eagerness. He turns his head back toward Oscar, accidentally making eye contact. He's been staring for a while, Drew can tell. They hold their gaze, the connection still there after so much time, picking up right where they left off. And overall it's just sad. Sad everything had to happen the way it did. Sad it took so long to be in the same room, and under such shitty circumstances.

The Director starts counting down from ten.

"I'm sorry about the condo," Oscar murmurs sincerely. "I never wanted it to go that far."

"Didn't you?" Drew asks.

Oscar furrows his brow. "How could you ask me that?"

The Director holds up two fingers. One. Points.

Lights on.

Red light above all cameras.

"Good evening everyone!" Oscar tells Camera 1, his pearly white smile wide as ever. "We've been talking about him all week, and now the moment you've all been waiting for has arrived. Drew Lawrence is in the studio with me tonight, four days after that horrifying attack on his home in the wake of his controversial autism cure comments." Oscar faces Drew. "I want to start off, Mr. Lawrence, by expressing my sincerest condolences over what happened to your home."

Drew keeps watching Oscar. Says nothing.

"That being said," Oscar continues, switching tones on a dime, "one can't help but understand the effect your behavior has had over so many people, people who have loved your movies over the years. This show, of course, does not condone domestic terrorism in any way, but... Are you really that shocked by such a passionate response to your statement?"

Drew smiles enigmatically. "That's how."

Oscar's face slacks.

"Jimmy's backstage, isn't he?" Drew asks, pointing. The audience shifts around the stage, whispering.

Oscar sticks his tongue in his cheek, unamused. "I don't know what you mean."

"Yeah you do." Drew shrugs. "Go on. Bring him out."

Oscar's eyes narrow slightly. "Alright." He nods to the Director. The Director signals a guy.

Jimmy Lyons walks out on stage, suddenly self-conscious and awkward. The audience reacts predictably, lots of gabbing and gasps, as he sits on a third chair brought out just now. Oscar and Drew angle theirs, the three facing each other like corners of a triangle. Jimmy keeps his head down. Oscar's posture is solid, his mind is obviously ablaze with anger and paranoia. Drew is truly calm and confident.

Oscar clears his throat. Looks at Drew. "So Drew, walk us through what happened the night you two met. Were you so blinded by sex that you unconsciously sent your dying mother's calls to voicemail, or were you fully aware of the situation?"

Drew stares Jimmy down. Judgy eyes on Jimmy.

Jimmy half-peeks back with equal parts embarrassment and regret.

"Drew?" Oscar asks, pretending not to notice the atmospheric showdown. "Do you have anything to say regarding the accusations from your sister regarding your past dabblings in BDSM and anonymous Grindr—?"

"I'm not here to answer questions," Drew interrupts, looking at Oscar. "I have a prepared statement I'd like to read to everybody."

Oscar chuckles. "I believe you already tried—"

"Yes or no?"

Oscar awkwardly looks out at the audience. The cameras. "I'm sure you can summarize what you—"

"You know very well I have problems speaking on the spot," Drew says. "My brain makes it difficult for me to verbalize my own thoughts without messing up somehow. I don't want to leave the wrong things up for interpretation, so I wrote what I wanted to say down. Can you give me that at least?"

Oscar softens. After a moment of dead air, he inhales and says, "Okay."

"Excuse me while I whip this out." Drew pulls an iPad from his back waistband. He smirks at his cheeky reference. He opens the lid. Goes to the Notes app.

Oscar recognizes the pastel pink lid. Glares at Leon standing just behind Camera 2. Leon salutes back.

Drew looks at Jimmy. Looks at Oscar. Takes a deep breath. "'I want to start off by expressing my gratitude,'" he reads in a deliberate audiobook-like pace, "'to all those who have stood up for me in the last couple of weeks. In particular, I want to show my thanks to the cast and crew of *The Sins of Jack Branson* who have stood by my side throughout this ordeal and have not resorted to sneaky weekend testimonies like those at my previous place of employment. Loyalty should always be commended. I would also like to thank Carlos Gutierrez for retracting his testimony, as well as the Latin community on Twitter for pointing out the horrible mistranslation made by members of this show.'" Drew makes pointed eye contact with Oscar. "'And I would like to thank Terry, wherever you are.'"

Jimmy lifts his head, confused.

"'I'm sorry, Terry,'" Drew reads, "'for what I did to you. And I want to thank you for having the bravery to voice your concern in the face of blatant public dishonesty. And from one recovering addict to another, I wish you the best of luck with your sobriety.'"

Jimmy looks off. Disturbed.

Drew reads the next paragraph silently. His heart grows heavy. "'When I first came to Los Angeles in 2017, I still went by my birth name, Jacob Andrezj. I was very fortunate to have been recruited for The Professor's internship at The Factory. I tried to do the right things there, but I soon discovered doing right thing was too fucking hard. No one else was doing the right thing, so I gave in and instead started acting on impulse.'" Drew goes quiet again. "'I was the one that recorded The Professor raping Trisha Robins. I was there. It was me. I let it happen.'" Drew rolls his lips. "'I took down a career professional with limited intel and publicly shamed a woman I had so much respect for, and I made the choice to post that video without asking for the facts nor her consent.'" Drew pauses. "'Trisha killed herself a few days after that, which I hold myself entirely responsible for.'"

Oscar frowns, the wound resurfacing.

"'So what if I played devil's advocate on 11/9?'" Drew reads with bite. "'So what if I fucked a few go-go boys in a bar bathroom? Those weren't crimes. What I did to The Professor, what I did to Trisha, those were crimes, so stop splitting hairs on my uncouth bullshit and really judge me on what I've actually done, why don't you?'" Drew pauses to regain his strength. "'That's what started it all. Because of that decision, I gave up. I stopped thinking about how my actions affected others. I just did what I wanted to do. I became an alcoholic. I developed a cocaine addiction. I got myself hooked on steroids for a few months. I started using during work hours. I smashed up conference rooms. I embarrassed my colleagues. I guilted people into agreeing with me on everything, to consenting to everything. I couldn't control myself.'" Drew looks at Jimmy. "'When I met Jimmy, I only saw that boy I was before, that good person with so much potential, and it was that encounter that inspired me to break free from that prison, to start caring, to take better care of myself. And how did I repay such inspiration? With selfishness. I cast you out. I'm sorry, Jimmy. You met me at very horrible time in my life. I was so moved that you'd approach me despite not recognizing me. And the way we befriended each other...'" Drew smiles a bit. "'And the way we befriended each other reminded me of one of the greatest nights of my life, and I tried to recreate that with you. That was a mistake. I should've been a responsible adult instead. But I think I understand you now. You find yourself buried in your own impulsive actions, caught in a lie you can't undo if you tried. And call my naive for thinking so, but I like to believe you've already tried.'"

Oscar furrows his brow at Jimmy. Recognizes guilt on his face.

"'And the reason we're here today,'" Drew reads, "'the reason you felt the need to mislead Oscar Blitz and his loyal trusting audience, wasn't because of the sex. It wasn't to get back at me for my success at the behest of yours. It was because I did something that night no mentor should ever do lightly. I promised you the world. I promised guidance. A source of knowledge. A source of safety. Companionship.'" Drew makes eye contact with Jimmy. "'When morning came, I reneged on that promise. I know now it was wrong of me to do that to you, to break your spirit. Your hope. Your sense of adventure. Your trust. Again, I am very sorry."

Oscar looks at Drew, horror finally creeping its way in.

Drew takes a deep breath. "'That being said, I condemn your selfishness in recent weeks. It's that very behavior that turned Jacob Andrezj into Drew Lawrence. You should be very ashamed of yourself for what you've done. People have lost jobs because of you. People have committed felonies, violent felonies, because of you. People have spread hate because of you. You have shown cowardice by not coming to me personally after all these years. You have shown dishonor by lying to a once-great watchdog journalist who has debased himself to that of a tabloid peddler because of you. One day, when the damage of your actions has finally become clear, you will regret your decision the same way I've regretted mine.'"

Jimmy frowns, on the verge of tears.

Drew returns to his iPad. "'At the same time, however, I acknowledge said decision spawned directly from the damage I inflicted on you first. In lieu of proper atonement, I humbly ask for you to stop this crusade while you still can and just leave it at that. Let me be the only one that gets punished. If you continue, you will only hurt yourself as well.'"

Jimmy doesn't react, even though his heart is racing.

Drew shakes his head. "'I thought if I could just cut out my toxic friends and go sober I could be Jacob Andrezj again. I liked believing Drew Lawrence was just a phase, a persona I was forced into by twisted people abusing my trust for selfish motives.'" He goes quiet again. Retreats inward. "'But I have since realized that I cannot use that as an excuse anymore. I'll never be Jacob Andrezj again. My choices were my choices. My *irrational* behavior was in fact in-character after all. I really did cut my mother out of my life and wasted all those years refusing to make up. I really did inflict pain on my collegiate peers during a very uncomfortable time in our lives. I really was an abusive boss, a perfectionist asshole, an insecure nut. Even if I didn't make Carlos pick a person to deport, I still trashed those rooms knowing other people would clean them up for me, people without the language to complain nor the power to refuse." Drew swallows. "'I want to believe, even now, that all these men and women coming forward are lying, or at the very least exaggerating, but I do not know their side of the story enough to say that definitively. I've always made an effort to trust people, to believe people, because I know how easily misunderstood I am, how difficult it is for me to verbalize what I know and believe, even in written form, so I assume everyone else is too. I've always made a conscious effort not to judge people without having all the facts.'" Drew pauses. "'So I acknowledge the grain of truth in everything they've said about me, and I apologize for how I have offended all of you.'"

Oscar smiles a bit. Very faint.

Drew looks at Jimmy. "'I apologize again, Jimmy Lyons, and to you, Oscar Blitz, and to all those I have wronged in this city, this place I've called home for more than half my life. I hope future generations so far removed from this brouhaha will heed my words now and understand how wrong it is to trivialize and condemn, to deny forgiveness, to not give a concrete path to redemption for those who seek it. I know I am not free from sin. I've hurt people. I've taken advantage of trust and kindness and continuously repaid it wrongly. A mere apology and a promise to change is not enough. I need to prove how serious I am in redeeming myself in the eyes of my fans and this industry that I love, which means I have to make a s-sacrifice.'"

Oscar's heart breaks.

Drew struggles to read on. "'I was informed two days ago that the Academy of Motion Picture Arts & Sciences is seriously discussing the possibility of renouncing all thirteen of *The Sins of Jack Branson*'s nominations this year. To relieve the Academy of making such a difficult, unprecedented decision, and because my dishonorable actions have left me undeserving to be an honoree of such a prestigious institution I have spent my life admiring, I hereby...'" Drew stops at the sight of those words. Those horrible words. "'I hereby voluntarily renounce the following Academy Award nominations: Best Picture for *The Sins of...*'" Drew's lip trembles. He covers his mouth. Closes his eyes. Holds back tears with the strength of a thousand winds. "'Best Picture for *The Sins of Jack Branson*, Best Adapted Screenplay for *The Sins of Jack Branson*, Best Picture for *Pacé*, Best Director for *Pacé*, Best Picture for *Onio*, Best Adapted Screenplay for *Onio...*" Drew looks right at Oscar. "'Best Adapted Screenplay for *Atomic...*'"

Oscar simply stares back.

"'...Best Picture for *Atomic...*'" Drew looks over at Jimmy. "'...and Best Live Action Short Film for *The Surgery*, which I received under the name "Jacob Andrezj."'"

Jimmy makes brief eye contact. Looks back down.

Drew takes a deep breath, snot in his nose rustling. "'I feel the need to emphasize that I am only renouncing MY Academy Award nominations. The other nominees for *The Sins of Jack Branson* deserve an unbesmirched chance to achieve the acclaim and praise they deserve, including my co-producers Kev Foster and Eli Kerbinger for Best Picture. The same goes for the cast and crew of every film I've put my name on. I discourage all boycotts of *The Sins of Jack Branson*. The brilliant artists at Ephemeral Pictures have given their best work on every level. They do not deserve to be punished for my actions.'" Drew makes eye contact with Camera 1. "'And I vow hereon in to continue doing what is right in the future with the hopes that I will earn forgiveness for my crimes, all of them, big and small, and I hope doing so will set a precedent for future men in power to know what it takes to redeem themselves in the eyes of society. Jimmy, Oscar, I entrust my fate entirely in your hands, and I trust that you will also do right thing here as well.'" Drew locks the iPad. Closes the lid. Sits back. Stares off with unfocused eyes.

Silence. Slowly, the audience of Studio 1 breaks into shocked, awed applause. No cheers or cries. Just claps.

Jimmy awkwardly looks at Oscar. Oscar frowns back with cruel disappointment.

The clapping eventually does stop. All eyes on Oscar.

Oscar hears the pinging of room tone, his left hand fiddling with itself. He hesitates, trying to pick the proper tone to open with. "That was an incredible speech, Drew," he says with monotone acceptance. "Incredibly sobering, and might I say, quite valid."

"I'm straight," Jimmy blurts.

The audience gasps. Drew sits up hard. "What?"

"I'm straight!" Jimmy says louder. "I love girls! I love pussy!"

Oscar stares in horror at the bold-faced liar sitting next to him.

"He came up to me in Marcus MacDonald's!" Jimmy cries, pointing at Drew. "He gave me a drink! I passed out!"

"Oscar!" Drew snarls over the confused crowd. "Say something!"

"When I woke up, he was already on top of me—!" Jimmy says with fake waterworks brewing.

"Oscar!" Drew cries.

"He forced himself in!"

The audience gets louder as the chaos increases.

"He fed me booze!" Jimmy whines. "He spat coke in my mouth!"

"That doesn't make any sense!" Drew hisses. "Oscar!"

Oscar stares at Jimmy, the real Jimmy, scared out of his wits.

"I cried and cried!" Jimmy cries. "I tried to fight him off!"

Oscar shakes his head. "Jimmy, what the fuck are you—"

"He doesn't get to win!" Jimmy hisses back through gritted teeth.

Oscar doesn't respond. It's so outlandish it defies logic. After so many weeks telling the same story, how could anyone possibly believe them now? Oscar has to say something, even if just save himself, if he had any hope of being taken seriously ever again. And he's just about to, willing to endure an embarrassing week of apologies in the name of a future the way it used to be, when he looks at Drew's wide eyes and open mouth.

That look Drew's giving him right now, that desperate pleading, that total fear of what will happen if Oscar doesn't speak up, that changes everything. Oscar's never seen Drew that vulnerable before, that terrified. Recognizing that weakness, something snaps in Oscar's brain, that last tether he's been holding onto for so long. It all comes boiling up again. The fire. The acid. All that pain Drew inflicted all those years ago, all those nights Oscar endured aching with betrayal. He can finally inflict all that back to him.

Drew's expression changes from *please* to *oh shit*. That alone was worth the price of admission.

Oscar crosses his legs. "Well?" he asks Drew pointedly. "What do you have to say to that?"

Drew pants pathetically. "Oscar."

"He's straight." Oscar shrugs. "How do you explain that?"

Drew freezes, not even knowing how to begin. The audience is confused, not buying it. Or are they and they're interested in the shocking new development?

Oscar raises his brows impatiently.

Jimmy stares plainly at Drew. He'll never have to admit he lied. He won't lose the Netflix deal. He'll never have to work at Harry 79 ever again. He can finally move out of that shithole apartment.

Drew lowers his head in defeat. Oscar starts his closing remarks five seconds later, but it's those five seconds of silence that the audience remembers the most. No applause. No laughs. No cheers. Just a cold realization that something just died in front of them, even if they don't know exactly what it was. And they take that five second moment home with them. They dwell on it. They carry it their whole lives and they tell no one. Because words couldn't even do it justice. It's just five seconds of nothing, even though they all felt the same thing, all four hundred of them. No one else would ever be able to understand.

You really had to have been there.

JACOB

And I Am Telling You...

Jacob turns off the TV. Stewie's on the couch beside him.

JACOB
It's such a perfect movie, isn't it?

STEWIE
You still love the second one better?

JACOB
It's not even close.

Jacob collects their dinner plates off their TV trays.

JACOB (CONT'D)
Frank Pentangeli, Hyman Roth, FREDO. All the Cuba stuff. The Senate hearing. The flashbacks to young Vito in New York. Michael smacking Kay. And of course the final flashback to Sonny, Fredo, Carlo, and Tessio all coming back, revealing that Fredo was the only one on Michael's side after he dropped out of college to join the Marines, and yet Michael had him killed anyway. It's unbelievable. Best movie ever made.

Jacob rinses the dishes. Stewie walks over.

STEWIE
I don't know, you can't beat the original. The horse head. Apollonia. Moe Green. Fredo banging cocktail waitresses two at a time.

JACOB
(imitating Fredo)
"C'mon! SCRAAM!"

Stewie smacks his hand on the countertop.

STEWIE
(imitating Michael)
"ENOUGH!"

JACOB
(imitating Fredo)
"I can handle things! I'm SMAAT!"

STEWIE
(imitating Fredo)
"Not like everyone says! That I'm dumb!"

JACOB
(imitating Fredo)
"I want RESPECT!"

STEWIE
I do love that part.

JACOB
That's <u>Part II</u>.

STEWIE
It is?

JACOB
We JUST finished Part I.

STEWIE
I know.

Jacob rolls his eyes. Stewie sits at his desk.

JACOB
Watching all the Sicily scenes again really made me want to go back.

STEWIE
I bet.

JACOB
Would you be up for it?

Stewie looks over at Jacob.

STEWIE
What, going to Italy?

JACOB
Yeah. We can stay at the same Airbnb I stayed at in Taormina. It's gorgeous. We can go to Florence too. I can show you around.

Stewie sits back, uneasy.

JACOB (CONT'D)
We should really go in the Fall. That's the best time to avoid all the tourist traps. And if we sign up for one of those credit cards, we can get a ton of miles. It won't cost us much.

STEWIE
You're not doing the internship then?

Jacob hesitates.

JACOB
When can always go next Fall. Doesn't have to be this year.

STEWIE
So you are doing the internship?

JACOB
I'm probably not gonna get one.

STEWIE
Did you apply yet?

JACOB
No.

STEWIE
Why not?

JACOB
I've been busy! Why are you pressuring me?

STEWIE
Pressuring you? We haven't talked about it for four weeks!

JACOB
It hasn't been a month.

STEWIE
Almost four weeks.

JACOB
It's my last semester. School's been rough.

STEWIE
It's Spring Break. You have nothing else to do.

JACOB
I'm still at Target.

STEWIE
Two shifts a week.

JACOB
Double shifts.

STEWIE
Just get it out of the way. I don't see you procrastinating like this when you're writing.

JACOB
It's a mail-in application. I have to print out whatever it is I'm submitting on good paper with all the proper margins and studs for the three-hole punches and fill out the application and get the recommendation letter from Jim. That takes time.

STEWIE
You have six days.

JACOB
He picks four people out of 15,000. The odds just aren't in my favor.

STEWIE
Then pick another internship.

JACOB
ANOTHER internship?

STEWIE
From Jim's email blast.

JACOB
They're all set-related. I'll never get picked for them.

STEWIE
Then look somewhere else. You don't want to put all your eggs in one basket.

JACOB
That's what I did for Whitman. It was the only school I applied for.

STEWIE
What's the problem with going with The Professor's internship?

Jacob sits on the couch, looking across the living room at Stewie.

JACOB
What's the endgame here? I get an internship in LA and best-case scenario get a job away from you? Worst-case scenario I end up wasting six months of my life and thousands of dollars on housing and overpriced food and probably a car?

STEWIE
We'll make it work.

JACOB
What, long distance?

STEWIE
Why not?

JACOB
I don't want to leave you behind. I love you.

STEWIE
(giddy)
Of course!

Jacob hesitates.

JACOB
Don't you love me?

STEWIE
Of course, Baby. How could you ask me that?

Jacob doesn't answer. Looks off.

JACOB
Can't you move out there?

STEWIE
To California?

JACOB
Why not?

STEWIE
I'm still transitioning the company. I can't just hop around.

JACOB
You already did. You work remotely anyway. What's the big deal?

STEWIE
I only moved the business because a very expensive client moved up here. I have no one out there.

JACOB
Find someone. They're all health nuts out there.

STEWIE
Does their DDD use the Medicaid system like Jersey does?

JACOB
Can't you find that out?

STEWIE
Baby, I've got clients that need me. My family's on this coast. My mom's almost eighty.

JACOB
They're all in Florida.

STEWIE
Ron's not.

JACOB
You barely see him anyway. And you fly to Florida as it is.

STEWIE
A flight from Boston to Fort Myers is a hell of a lot cheaper than flying across the country.

JACOB
You got the money.

STEWIE
I'm trying to buy a house.

JACOB
Why haven't you already?

STEWIE
I told you, I'm waiting for the business to settle down first.

JACOB
How long will that take?

STEWIE
I don't know. A while. Maybe another year.

Jacob stands with a groan. He grabs a bottle of water from the fridge.

STEWIE (CONT'D)
Why can't you just find an internship on the East Coast?

JACOB
There are no film jobs outside of Los Angeles.

STEWIE
You don't know that.

JACOB
(snarky)
YES, I DO know that, thank you very much.

Jacob cracks the water bottle open. Drinks the whole thing in a single gulp. Crushes the plastic.

JACOB (CONT'D)
That's just the way it is.

STEWIE
You can write anywhere. You've got all those screenplays.

JACOB
And send them to who? Who do I know in Los Angeles?

STEWIE
Jim.

JACOB
Oh yeah, I'm gonna ask a film professor who's only in LA part-time, in the middle of his workload, to go around town pimping out my scripts on my behalf. Don't be ridiculous.

STEWIE
Make them out here.

JACOB
The scripts?! Even if I had the money, which I don't, who would I make 'em with? Nich? TJ?

STEWIE
You got Frankie.

JACOB
He's from Savannah. He doesn't live up here.

STEWIE
Isn't he going to LA ultimately?

JACOB
We can't make a feature just the two of us.

STEWIE
Why not?

JACOB
Because it's not that simple! Films cost millions of dollars! I'll never find enough people to make it happen.

STEWIE
You don't know that.

JACOB
You ever hear of "Development Hell?" The vast majority of film productions never result in a final product, whether it be from lack of money or investors pulling out or scheduling delays. I'm just the screenplay guy, Daddy. I don't know that world. Neither does Frankie.

STEWIE
What about networking?

JACOB
That's all in LA. Anybody who's anybody is in LA right now, and I won't be able to get in the room with any of them unless I have an entry-level job at least.

STEWIE
Like what?

JACOB
Like an internship.

STEWIE
Then find another internship.

JACOB
I can't just go to LA and look for work. Who knows how long that would take? I'd have to live there. Ninety percent of them are just gonna tell me to apply online.

STEWIE
Then apply online now.

JACOB
I can't just Google Hollywood paid internships.

STEWIE
Why not?

JACOB
Because any jobs I can see on my end are either oversaturated with applications or too old to even still be open. This isn't the seventies anymore. I can't just walk in and drop off my resume and get a job with a firm handshake. Jobs are a pain in the ass to get nowadays, especially for Millennials. Too many of us have college degrees.

STEWIE
How many Whitman students right now have six features under their belt?

JACOB
I don't know.

STEWIE
With a resume like yours, you can get any position you want.

JACOB
They're just scripts! They're not films! I can write a hundred features and it'll all mean nothing because it's all just paper. No one reads features anyway. It takes too long.

STEWIE
This guy reads features, The Professor.

JACOB
Even if he did go through the applications himself, which chances are he doesn't, he's not gonna read a feature!

```
                    STEWIE
How could you say that?

                    JACOB
If he can read features himself, he wouldn't be
hiring interns to read for him!

                    STEWIE
What's the harm in just applying?

                    JACOB
I'm not gonna get it.

                    STEWIE
You might. You just might.
```

Jacob sighs uneasily.

```
                    JACOB
Maybe I don't want to.

                    STEWIE
What do you mean? Do what?

                    JACOB
Screenwriting, Hollywood...
          (shrugs)
I don't want to do this anymore. This isn't fun.
Hollywood people are hard. They can handle
themselves. I'm not like that. I'm not. I'm too
dependent and territorial and...
```

Jacob frowns, tears in his eyes.

```
                    JACOB (CONT'D)
I've got this great brain that can see everything,
all the stupidity going on around me, all the
patterns no one seems to care about, and I'm actually
curious about people and what they've been through
and I'm such a great listener and I'm not limited by
emotional triggers like politics or gore or really
really dark S-H-I-T, none of that bothers me, it
doesn't make me squeamish, I can see it all, and I
know what people like and what's predictable and
what's not predictable and what people absolutely
love to see in a movie and what they NEED to see, I
get it, I really do get it, but I'm cursed with
this... this THING, this awful thing jumbling up my
brain and making me talk all weird and not know when
it's wrong or out of place or too loud and I can't
put my thoughts and wisdom into words that people can
understand and I friggin HATE IT! I'm just fooling
myself. I'm making it work because I feel like I have
to, because my mom drilled it into my brain that I'm
a failure if I don't make money or get into the
history--

                    STEWIE
Stop talking about your mother like that!

                    JACOB
STOP INTERRUPTING ME!

                    STEWIE
Lower your voice!

                    JACOB
Are you listening to me at all?

                    STEWIE
I understand.

                    JACOB
No you don't! You don't!
```

STEWIE
You're just overwhelmed with everything that's been going on at Whitman lately.

JACOB
That's not it at all! GOD, why don't just listen to me?!

STEWIE
All I'm hearing are excuses. I know you really want to go, Baby Boy. I know you can do it. You just gotta do it.

JACOB
You want to break up with me, don't you?

Stewie furrows his brow hard.

STEWIE
What?!

JACOB
You want me to go off to LA without you so this ends and it ends up being my idea so you'll never have to actually break up with me.

STEWIE
Where do you come up with this stuff?

JACOB
You didn't say you love me!

STEWIE
When?

JACOB
Before, when I said "I love you," you said "of course!" Why couldn't you just say "I love you too?!"

STEWIE
I did.

JACOB
No, you said "Of course."

STEWIE
You asked if I love you and I said "of course."

JACOB
No, before that! That was a different "of course." The second "of course" was with quite a hint of judgment.

STEWIE
I didn't say "of course" a second time.

JACOB
YES YOU DID!

STEWIE
Lower your voice!

JACOB
I know what I heard! You said, "Of course," and I said, "Don't you love me?" and YOU SAID, "Of course, how could you ask me that?"

STEWIE
I did not!

JACOB
YES YOU DID! I heard you!

STEWIE
I don't want to talk about this anymore.

JACOB
We need to talk about it. You never ever tell me you love me first. I always have to get it out of you. Why is that? What's wrong with me?

STEWIE
Nothing's wrong with you!

JACOB
You never compliment my muscles.

STEWIE
So?

JACOB
So what am I doing it for?

STEWIE
I just don't find muscles attractive. I only care about the neck up. You know that.

JACOB
I'm supposed to just go on without any praise or compliments?

STEWIE
I don't have to compliment you. You know I love you just the way you are.

JACOB
I give you all the compliments in the world. Why don't you do that with me?

STEWIE
I'm sorry. I'm just not like that.

JACOB
Why not?

STEWIE
I don't know. I'm just not.

JACOB
It's because of my hair, isn't it?

STEWIE
Your hair's fine.

JACOB
Stop saying that! I know what that means! You don't like it, but you don't want to tell me you don't like it.

STEWIE
I say it's fine because it's fine. That's all. You're the one doing linguistic gymnastics and having a thousand little meanings to every word you utter.

JACOB
Just give me compliments! I don't think I'm asking for that much!

STEWIE
Is that the only thing keeping us together? Are you that insecure?

JACOB
You know I am! Why can't you just make things easier for me?

STEWIE
You have it easy enough! When I was your age, I had to work my ass off to have everything I had. I wasn't spoiled or lazy. Or crazy!

JACOB
(screaming)
I AM NOT CRAZY! HOW DARE YOU CALL ME CRAZY!

STEWIE
You look pretty freaking crazy to me!

Jacob's face gets all red.

STEWIE (CONT'D)
Look at you! You're having a freaking tantrum again!

JACOB
(exhausted)
Stop.

STEWIE
Grow up.

JACOB
WHY DO I HAVE KEEP CHANGING?!

STEWIE
Lower your voice!

JACOB
SHUT UP!

STEWIE
Stop telling me to shut up!

JACOB
NO, YOU LISTEN TO ME GODDAMMIT!

Jacob's breath wavers, veins popping out of his neck.

JACOB (CONT'D)
You keep telling me I have to grow up, to stop biting my nails, to lower my voice, stop doing this, stop being like that, but you never meet me halfway. That's not fair. You need to change too. Stop bullying me and treating me like crap.

STEWIE
I'm not listening to this.

JACOB
Please listen to this!

STEWIE
I'm not gonna be your punching bag. Talk like an actual adult if you want to talk.

JACOB
I've already tried that! Nothing's changed!

STEWIE
Oh, but acting like an a-hole will?

JACOB
I'M NOT AN A-HOLE! HOW DARE YOU!

STEWIE
I never said that!

JACOB
YES YOU DID! You just called me an a-hole!

STEWIE
No, I said you were ACTING like an a-hole! You are! I never actually called you an a-hole.

JACOB
Stop using semantics and getting anal over what freaking words I use, okay? That's literally the

worst possible way to interact with someone with a MASSIVE COMMUNICATION PROBLEM!

STEWIE
Your voice is cracking! Drink some water for God's sake!

JACOB
Stop focusing on that! Can't you just listen to what I'm saying?

STEWIE
You're not saying anything!

JACOB
YES I AM!

STEWIE
There you go! Acting like a lunatic again!

JACOB
STOP CALLING ME A LUNATIC!

STEWIE
I didn't! You're acting like one!

JACOB
I'M FOLLOWING YOUR LEAD HERE! Maybe I don't want to be a punching bag either, huh? Maybe I want to stand up for myself and not just stay silent about how you are and what parts of you need to change!

STEWIE
How can you say you love me when you treat me like this?

Jacob suddenly bursts into tears.

STEWIE (CONT'D)
Really? You're crying now?!

JACOB
WHAT DO YOU WANT?! Do you want me to be tough or do you want me to be a pussy?! Just tell me what you want and I'll do it! I'll fucking do it, okay?!

Stewie widens his eyes hard.

STEWIE
You're REALLY using the f-word?

JACOB
Did you not hear anything I've just said?

STEWIE
You say so many things! Stop cursing and I'll listen!

JACOB
I HAVE STOPPED CURSING!

STEWIE
Apparently not.

JACOB
I HAVE! HOW HAVE YOU NOT NOTICED?!

STEWIE
Lower your voice!

JACOB
Stop yelling at me!

STEWIE
You're the one yelling at me! Everyone outside can hear you. They all know we fight now. Thanks for that.

Jacob's eyes dart around, his breath quickening.

```
                        JACOB
        Stop.

                        STEWIE
        Stop what?

                        JACOB
        Stop being mean to me.

                        STEWIE
        You started it.

                        JACOB
        I did not!

                        STEWIE
        Yes you did!

                        JACOB
        I DID NOT! SHUT UP! SHUT UP!

                        STEWIE
        Why the hell would I want to be someone that keeps
        acting like a freaking child all the time?!
```

Jacob's face contorts, tears streaming down.

```
                        JACOB
        SHUT UP! SHUT UP!
```

Stewie grimaces. Turns away.

Jacob darts into the bedroom and slams the door. Faceplants on the bed. Hopes Stewie doesn't follow him in. He just needs to calm down in the dark. It's soft on the bed, his long body laying diagonally on top of the comforter. Jacob closes his eyes, his brain in pain., whatever that means.

After a few minutes, he just feels numb. Cold. He doesn't want to crawl under the covers. He'd fall asleep, and he doesn't get to go to sleep. He can't stand thinking about how Stewie must think of him now. He pulls out his phone for some distraction. There's no more Vine, no more Facebook to go to anymore. But he can't just sit there. He's got no Stewie to help him through this. How little else he has outside of Stewie Hanz. No friends. Barely a family.

No wait, he does have a friend. Let's hope he's up.

Jacob texts Rian: "You still up?" Send. Jacob waits. Gray dots appear.

"hey buddy what's up"

Jacob types away. "Just got into a bit fight with Stewie." Send.

"what about"

"LA. And a bunch of other things too, I guess." Send.

"bad?"

"Yeah." Send.

Gray dots appear for a long time. "its ok man. it happens to everyone. the best thing to do is not to dwell on it."

Jacob half-frowns. "It's really hard not to." Send.

"wanna talk about it then"

"No," Jacob types. "It's so stupid, not even worth rehashing." Send.

Gray dots again. "i've seen how you two are together. he adores you. i don't think what you two have is something you can destroy in a single fight."

"I'm not so sure about that," Jacob types. Rereads it. Backspace. Types, "It just pisses me off, you know? I couldn't just verbalize what I meant better. It's so obvious to me now, but why can I have this clarity at the time, you know? In the moment?" Send.

Gray dots. "you seem pretty lucid now."

"Cause I'm not talking." Send.

"so type it out for him. while it's still fresh."

Jacob hesitates. "You think?" Send.

"why not?"

Jacob hesitates.

Gray dots reappear. "you two deserve each other. he knows that. he's fifty-three. he's not stupid. neither are you."

Jacob smiles. "Then I will. Thanks." Send.

"no problem dude :)"

WHALE

The Purge

Whale sips an Americano outside Peet's Coffee. "How does the name change process work exactly?"

Rian hesitates, surprised by the question. "A lot of paperwork at first. Birth certificate, social security card, *et cetera*." He slurps his Frappuccino through a paper straw. "The real bitch of it's the snail-slow processing. You can't update the name on your credit cards and health insurance until you get the new license, but you can't apply for the new license until you've got the new social card, and you can't get that for a few months at least. Then there's getting a new passport, that's a pain in the ass. You can't believe how many things have your name on it until you have to change it."

"You didn't actually get a new social security number, did you?"

"No."

Whale nods, thinking it over. "So when did you first start going by 'Rian Hoffman?' After the new social card or when you first applied?"

"The day I first got approved for the name change. It's all retroactive to the day you first applied anyway, so... Who's changing their name?"

"I am."

Rian raises his brows. "Really?" he asks softly. "Why?"

"I don't wanna be an Andrezj anymore. I never felt like one. And I'm sick of having such a high-maintenance last name no one can spell right or pronounce correctly. So ethnically ambiguous too. I don't have a heritage or culture or anything." Whale pauses. "I hate Jacob too."

"Why?"

Whale sips his Americano.

Rian frowns. "It's cause your mom picked it out, isn't it?"

"I want something that actually represents me. Who I really am. She's the last person that fucking knows that."

Rian buttons his lip. "You decide on a name yet?"

"I don't know. I'll think about it."

Rian sits up. "Let's talk about the feature."

"Yes, please."

Rian pulls out his phone. "I think Jack Branson's the best one by far."

Whale stares. "Really?"

"I couldn't stop reading his Wikipedia over breakfast. It's perfect. It really writes itself. Plus there's still some room for stylistic choices."

"Like what?"

"Genre bending. Who wants a same-old period biopic when we can do something really interesting?"

"What, like make it a comedy?"

"Actually I was thinking of a musical. Victorian literature on Broadway worked well for *Les Misérables*. Hell, why not make it animated?!"

Whale scoffs. "An animated musical… about a gay prostitute?"

"Why not?" Rian asks with a grin. "You know how much I love anime. You love graphic novels. When we first we met, the first thing we ever talked about was how adult animation needs more respect from the mainstream."

"I doubt we can do it Ghibli style."

"What about rotoscoping? You ever see *A Scanner Darkly*? A period drama would be perfect in that style, especially a musical. The singing would look so cool."

Whale scrunches his face. "Isn't that a bit much?"

"We need it to be a bit much, dude! This is our debut. We need to make a mark on the world."

"We need box office, Frankie. An animated musical of some historical nobody, let alone a gay whore, is gonna end up being too much for people, especially in China and the Middle East."

Rian furrows his brow. "What's up with you? You're sounding like Theo."

Whale hesitates. "I met with him yesterday."

Rian doesn't move. "You talked to him about this?"

"Yeah."

"Before you talked to me?"

Whale holds his shoulders up. "What do you want me to say?"

"Why the fuck would you do that?" Rian asks, his panic showing. "His opinion's not relevant here. This is our feature. Our Paramount deal."

"I can have a friend, can't I?"

"He's not your friend."

Whale scoffs. "I can actually do things now, you know. I've done a whole lot on my own out here. Theo actually knows that."

"So do I."

"No you don't. You coddle me. You tell me all the time not to push myself too hard, to take it easy and all."

"Because I know you need that, man."

"You're not my fucking mother!" Whale snaps. "I'm not some beached whale, Frankie! I can actually do shit!"

Rian's blood chills. "What are you talking about?"

"I get it, you don't like Theo for some reason. I don't care. Just stop shitting on him all the time! Deep down it makes me wonder if you think someone's wrong with me!"

"Nothing's wrong with you!" Rian says, raising his voice. "God, where is this all coming from?"

"It's been two months and we still don't have a production company!"

"That takes time."

"It'll go faster if you let me network with you."

"You have to write the feature!"

"I can do both! You ever think of that?"

"Far as I can tell you can't even do the one!"

Whale angrily gapes.

"What?!" Rian asks. "It's true! You haven't even STARTED writing yet!"

"This is what I'm fucking talking about!" Whale yells, an angry finger pointed. "Do you even LIKE me?!"

"Of course I do!"

"No, you just tolerate me because I'm the only way for you to get a fucking career."

"First of all," Rian says with a laugh, "you're not the only way I can have a career out here. I *want* to work with you. We're friends!"

"Then why won't you treat me like an equal?!"

"I have been treating you like an equal! This is all in your head!"

"I know what being a friend is."

Rian laughs bitterly. "I'm the only person out here that actually gives a shit about you! Why are you lashing at ME?!"

"You have no idea how wrong you are," Whale says, snarling a bit.

Rian rolls his lips. Looks off, his heart pounding. "Theo's gaslighting you."

Whale's expression goes blank. "What's wrong with you?"

"He told me he was. After the Tribeca Q&A, when you were in the bathroom."

Whale hesitates. "That's ridiculous."

"You wanted to fly down to Conshy when you found out your mom had cancer, right? But Theo talked you out of it?"

Whale's face goes numb. "How do you know about that?"

"He told me! He was fucking bragging to me that he got you to hate her! That was INTENTIONAL!"

Whale shakes his head, grasping at straws. "You don't like him. You don't even know him."

"He told me it was! He thought we wouldn't get a screening at Tribeca without you being there since they liked your script so much."

"Of course they would've screened it without me."

"But that's what he believed! He didn't want to take the chance!"

"I can hate my own mother, you know! I don't need someone else to tell me how to think!"

"That's not what I'm saying."

"I don't appreciate you slandering Theo like this!"

"He actually said that! Ask him!"

"What's the point?!" Whale cries. "You've won! You already have me!"

"You're still going to him behind my back!" Rian cries, his throat hurting. "You're letting his STUPID opinions affect your own!"

"Am I not allowed to have a second opinion? Who's the real gaslighter here?"

"He's not your friend, Jacob." Rian shakes his head. "He never was."

"Stop telling me how to think!"

"Listen to me!" Rian begs. "Theo is not your friend!"

"WHY DO YOU KEEP SAYING THAT?!"

"BECAUSE HE'S NOT! He only cares about himself! Once he gets everything out of you, he'll drop you like a piece of garbage, and you'll realize how stupid you were to believe him at all!"

"LOOK WHO'S TALKING!" Whale hollers.

Rian stops breathing.

Whale shakes his head. "You were always my best friend, Frankie. Was I ever yours?"

A frown forms on Rian's face.

Whale scoffs. "I was just one of many to you. I had to fight to even get you to notice me. And sure, I wasn't particularly fascinating company in those days, but I was loyal." He scowls. "But when the chips were down and I needed someone on *my* side, you decided to be a Jew for the first time in your fucking life."

"You don't mean that," Rian whimpers. "You forgave me."

"I was a fucking lying," Whale says coldly. "I was so pathetic, clinging on to scraps like that. I saw the real you that day, the kind of a man you really are. But I thought so little of myself. I just looked the other way. Pretended it didn't happen. But I don't need you anymore. I have a new best friend now, and he doesn't have a whole back catalog of bullshit to use against me whenever he wants."

"Can't you hear yourself?!" Rian asks. "This is not you! This is him! How can you not see that?!"

"I wanted to stay behind!" Whale whines. "I could've had Stewie! I could've had a normal, stable, happy fucking life, but you had to go out of your way to convince me, didn't you?! You said if I didn't take the internship, I'd regret it for the rest of my life! It's all your fucking fault!"

Rian's face contorts, his lips fluttering. "I was just..." he whispers. "I was just talking out loud. I wasn't trying to—"

"I trusted you! I trusted your word, Frankie, and you fucking abused it!"

"I didn't make you get on that plane!"

"Yes, you fucking did!" Whale growls. "With TJ out of the way and Nich in New York, you had no way to get into Hollywood yourself. You needed me to follow through with it just in case you ended up out here."

Rian furrows his brow. "What are you TALKING about?!"

"You knew I was gonna be at the restaurant that night, didn't you?"

"What?!"

"THE RESTAURANT!"

"No! That was a coincidence!"

"Bullshit! You suddenly found yourself on your ass and sought me out, didn't you? You found out from Oscar or tracked me down or I don't know how, but Theo saw through it instantly. And you know what, I guess I did too."

Rian shakes his head. "What the fuck is wrong with you? Why are you saying these things?"

"I've always felt like this!"

"No you haven't!"

"YES I HAVE!" Whale yells. "I've always felt like this! You never cared! You were never gonna listen to me! The only time you ever gave a shit about me was when I was suddenly valuable to you. Otherwise, I was just a retarded little embarrassment to you."

Rian tries to hold back tears. "I'm sorry," he whines. "If that's what you took from it, if that's what I gave off, I didn't know. That wasn't my intention. I'm sorry. I was wrong, just..." Rian voice sputters. He covers his mouth and closes his eyes. Whimpers in his seat.

Whale looks away, disappointed more than anything.

Rian inhales hard. "I'm sorry!" He swallows his dry throat. "Please forgive me! I'm sorry!"

Whale silently stands. Walks away.

"Jacob!" Rian calls desperately, tears streaming down. "Please! I'm sorry!"

Whale keeps walking, head down, hands in his pockets, face hard as stone.

JACOB

525,600 Minutes

Stewie doesn't type at his desk. He can't focus. He's too sad. Has he gone too far this time? What the heck happened? Was it his fault? Was it Baby Boy's? Is doing nothing not working? He actually envies Helena. He can't imagine dealing with a pubescent Jacob plus Karen times a thousand and Melanie too with no assistance, not even from her husband, while also working as a full-time executive bitch in the boardroom.

Just then, his printer whirs up. Stewie looks behind him. An 8.5-by-11 spits out, words on it. Another one. And one more. The printer settles down. Stewie takes the document and reads it.

> Dear Daddy,
>
> Please read this without jumping to conclusions. I come in peace. But I'm laying here, dwelling on what just occurred, and I can't help but feel I was right in what I was saying but wrong in how I said it. I realize now that the volume of my speech and the jadedness of my tone come off a lot harsher than I had anticipated. Believe it or not, such loudness and coarseness was not meant to be loud nor coarse. It's just how I get when I'm excited. Much like how I am when I zone out, retreating inward with a stupid and/or bitchy expression, or how I get sometimes when I walk, transfixed by the movement of my own feet without realizing my head is craned toward the floor like a Neanderthal. I'm not consciously aware of how I appear or sound on the outside when I'm "in the zone," so to speak. That's why I kept telling you to listen to what I was saying, why you harping on my accidental cursing or the dryness of my throat only made me angrier, and why you highlighting the neighbors overhearing me made me self-conscious, and thus embarrassed, and thus more upset.
>
> But I'm not trying to blame my autism. That was the one thing they taught us at Eagle Ridge, never to use our disabilities as an excuse. When I met you I was. Then I wasn't. Now I'm back to it again. And I apologize. You know I'm better than this, which is why I'm not too upset. But I do want to explain something physiological that cannot go away, no matter how much conditioning I get.
>
> I have a problem with something called sensory overload. It's when too much stimuli overwhelms my brain and I end up acting out to try and stop it, which nine times out of ten causes more stimuli and thus more acting out. A big contributor is me no longer being on the pills. I know you don't like hearing that, but I can't help but feel the timing is a bit too perfect for it to be anything but. They were mood influencers, you know, not placebos. I'm dealing with big-boy emotions for the first time without a pharmaceutical cushion like before. And while I'm thrilled to finally be able to see the world as it really is, to feel stimuli the same way normal people do without some rose-colored filter, hitting that overload threshold is a lot easier than ever. My mom, being the freaking Autism whiz she made herself to be, knew enough about Asperger's to stop the cycle at once. While I appreciate you doing the contrary, treating me like a neurotypical individual in the hopes of me feeling like one and thus no longer getting stuck in the autism excuse cycle, I

admit I find myself grasping for a vine that isn't there. All I ask is for patience on this. I'll only even out with time, especially in the secure presence of someone that loves me as much as you do.

I'm sorry for yelling. I'm sorry for accusing you of not loving me and sneakily trying to break up with me. That was beyond stupid. I'm embarrassed just typing it out. To be honest, most of my bottled up emotion that just got dumped on you isn't even you, it's everything that's been going on with me lately. Ever since I've lost the weight and started gaining muscle I've felt like a different person. When I was medicated I was numb but nice, and now that I'm not, now that I'm feeling strong and confident for the first time ever, I find myself losing that niceness. One of the best things you ever told me was how mature I was for my age, how sweet, and I'm starting to worry that I'm losing that maturity, that sweetness, that gentle boyishness you first fell in love with. It's amazing how something so small as an exterior appearance can change an entire personality. I actually feel like a bro now that I'm swole and jock passing. And honestly that scares me. I'm afraid I'm changing away from your Mr. Preference archetype too much and that it's only a matter of time before you see a different Jacob, the way Mom saw a different Dennis Andrezj one day and realized she had made a big mistake. Ever since the beginning, the fact that you were with Gus for five years and broke up after a single fight has been weighing on my mind.

Since Trump got elected I find myself in a world I no longer recognize, my former friends and collegiate peers revealing their true colors in ways I never saw coming. Getting forced out of my comfort zone makes me feel powerless, as you very well know. I'm glad to be given the bitter truth over sweet lies, but as a consequence I find myself walking on eggshells with you. (This is my anxiety talking.) I don't want to be one of those Wendy Torrances that let themselves get taken advantage of. Not that I'm saying you ever will. Like I said, that's just my anxiety talking.

Maybe deep down I find it so hard to believe that someone would actually like me as I am, completely unfiltered, no veils or delusions between them and the real me. I've never exposed myself like this to anyone before. It's more naked than literal nudity, which you very much know I have no problem with. And I second guess myself, thinking that you'd be too nice to break up with me the way my dad was too nice to initiate the divorce. Maybe one day you'd want to and never tell me. And I think to myself that that's why you're so insistent that I go off to LA. You'd be losing me. Why would you want to lose me? Because who'd want to be in a relationship with a high-maintenance retard like me? I know I wouldn't. That's all I can go off of, what I would do. And I would hate having myself as a boyfriend.

So if I'm wrong, I need to hear it. I really hope I'm wrong. But I don't wanna hear what I wanna hear. I wanna hear the truth.

Love,
Baby Boy

Jacob puts away his laptop and returns to bed, listening intently. After a few minutes, he hears Stewie walking up to the door. A stream of light hits the pillow. Jacob doesn't move. He just lays on his belly, eyes obviously open.

Stewie approaches the bed with a calculator in his hand and lays on top of Jacob, his body pressing down like a weighted blanket. He sighs.

Jacob sighs too, his Daddy laying on top of him.

JACOB
You read my letter?

He can feel Stewie nod his head.

JACOB (CONT'D)
Well?

Stewie shows Jacob the calculator. Jacob reaches for the bedside lamp. Flicks it on. Light stings Jacob's eyes. He sees a number on the calculator: 19,389.

JACOB (CONT'D)
What am I looking at?

Stewie rolls off Jacob. Sits beside him.

STEWIE
That's the number of days I've been alive.

JACOB
Seems like it should be more.

STEWIE
Subtract 287.

Jacob hits minus. Types 287. Hits equal: 19,102.

STEWIE (CONT'D)
Those are the days between February 24, 1964 and June 12, 2016.

Stewie looks at the dog tag hanging around his neck.

STEWIE (CONT'D)
In those 19,102 days, I've witnessed the birth of my sister Abby when I was fifteen. Me, Ron, and couple of our cousins walked out onto Raritan Bay when it froze over in the winter of 1979, by far the stupidest and most dangerous thing I ever did. In those 19,102 days, me and Ron became the first of our family, as big as it is, Mom's twelve siblings, Dad's eleven, all those cousins, we were the first ones to go to college. I sold videotapes in a call center. Worked at Red Lobster. GFDL. Lucent. Got laid off at Lucent. Took my trip cross-country. Almost got killed by a buffalo. Moved to Marlton. Worked at Bally's. Started my own business, which is now serving two states, at the moment anyway. In those 19,102 days, I finally came out to my brother at twenty-seven, the rest of my family in my thirties. I found gay friends of my own. The Diva. Wilma. Moo-Moo. Bam-Bam. Lost most of them because of politics. And then Gus. I watched all my siblings get married and my father die of lung cancer. I've had a full life. No regrets whatsoever.

Stewie adds 287 back in.

STEWIE (CONT'D)
But the past 287 days have been the best days of my life.

Jacob can already feel tears coming on.

STEWIE (CONT'D)
Because of you. I finally have someone to talk to. Someone to do things with. And you're just getting better and better every day. And I'm so proud of you. You're such a great writer and you've lost all that weight and... I didn't think you'd get this far with the workouts, honestly. It's really hard for anyone.

JACOB
If there's one thing Asperger's people do best, it's relentless repetition with no desire to deviate.

Stewie smiles warmly.

STEWIE
I don't want to lose you, Baby Boy. It took so long for me to find you.

Stewie sighs, his face blank.

STEWIE (CONT'D)
But I'm torn. I want you to be the big successful screenwriter you've always wanted to be. I know how much it means to you to actually finish what you've started. But at the same time I want you to stay for selfish reasons.

Stewie pets the back of Jacob's head.

STEWIE (CONT'D)
I don't want to be the reason you can't be the next Tarantino.

Jacob takes a deep breath.

JACOB
I don't know how to do anything else.

Jacob and Stewie hold eye contact. Blank stares. Blank expressions.

STEWIE
What do we do?

Jacob hesitates.

JACOB
Let's leave it up to fate. I'll submit Drive-Thru to The Professor. It's the best I've got. If I don't get it, I'll stay here with you and start my career some other way.

STEWIE
Not in film?

JACOB
There are other things I can write. Books. Plays. Poetry. I'll figure it out.

STEWIE
But you'll go to California if you get the internship?

Jacob nods solemnly.

JACOB
It has to be worth it.

They kiss. Jacob rests his head on Stewie's chest. They hold each other with closed eyes.

DREW

Irreconcilable Differences

Drew leaves first, bolting out of Studio 1 as soon as the cameras go cut. Then the audience files out. Then the crew, what's left of them at least, one by one until it's just Oscar and Jimmy left on stage. They don't say anything to each other. In time, Jimmy gets up and leaves. Then it's just Oscar. It's so much colder without all those people around.

Oscar holes himself in his office, playing Solitaire on his computer for an hour or two, until at last it's time for him to go home too. He turns off the light, wanders slowly down the empty halls of that once-great program, shuts off the rest of the power, and takes the alleyway exit behind Studio 2.

It's humid out. Dark. Just a few streetlights. Oscar locks up with a sigh. Stuffs his keys into his pocket.

"You must proud of yourself," Drew says, wandering out of the dark with a calm face.

Oscar half-frowns back. "No," he states plainly. "When I wake up tomorrow morning, I'm gonna realize what I've done and I'll bitterly regret it. And again the day after that, and the next, and every day for the rest of my life. And it's so stupid. So small. And yet I'll never get it back." Oscar shakes his head. "But not tonight. Tonight I'm going to Brique to fucking celebrate. I'm patting myself on the back. I'm fucking laughing." Pain flashes across Oscar's face. "Because I finally got you. I can fucking revel in the fact that you'll never have a box office smash again, you'll never get back into the Oscars, because there will always be someone out there that doubts your word. It'll come back up on Twitter every time there's a new movie with your name on it. You'll never escape it. You'll never be able to bullshit your way out of anything ever again." Oscar pauses, his face tight. "Because this will always haunt you. Just like it'll always haunt me."

Drew frowns with harrowed eyes. "What more could I have done?"

"I don't owe you an explanation." Oscar turns to leave.

"This didn't have to happen, you know," Drew blurts.

Oscar halts. He turns.

"You never needed Jimmy. You coulda got me and kept your reputation. That's all on you." Drew shrugs. "Nich. Trevor. The Go-Go boys. Shayne. Carlos. All those stories from all those people, all except one." He smirks. "I guess when push came to shove, you couldn't throw your hat in the ring?"

"I didn't have to," Oscar says sternly. "You're such a bad person, Drew Lawrence. You made such a mess. You spent your entire career ruining lives. You gave me plenty to pick from." He pauses. "Besides, how could I prove it? You got everything."

"I don't believe that."

"It's true."

"You *never* printed it out?"

"To leave it around for Theo to steal?" Oscar shakes his head. "No. It was all on the laptop. You got it all."

"What about those linguistic forensics we used on Sanchez? You could've used them." Drew shrugs with a ruined smile. "They could've proved beyond a shadow of a doubt that I never wrote *Atomic*."

Oscar lowers his head.

Drew chuckles suddenly. "God, it's so weird saying it out loud." He holds the back of his neck, his eyes getting puffy. "I actually forget. I've said the same thing so many times. I can actually remember writing it."

Oscar looks off, the wound still sore.

"Tell me I'm wrong," Drew says. "Please."

Oscar takes a deep breath. "That guy you're with now. Kev. He doesn't know, doesn't he?"

"No. He doesn't know."

"I'm surprised you didn't confess it tonight."

Drew hesitates. "Would that have made a difference?"

Oscar shakes his head. "Probably not."

Drew nods. "That's all I needed to know." He stuffs his hands in his pockets and walks away.

"Is that why you didn't?" Oscar calls after him.

Drew stops. Turns around. Reluctantly walks back.

"Because Kev would've disowned you if he found out?" Oscar asks.

"He already knows you were after me for something. He knows it's bad. But he's used to it. In your zealousness to end me, you've oversaturated the market with 'Drew Lawrence Bad.' He's already blanket forgave me for my past sins. One more wouldn't have made a difference."

"Then why didn't you?"

Drew smiles. Braces for the worst. "Because I promised Theo not to."

Oscar snickers. "You promised...?" He laughs bitterly. "You promised *Theo*? Oh, that's rich."

Drew looks away.

"He promised Theo!" Oscar declares to the night. "Just like he promised you he wouldn't tell me about the video? Just like he promised to wait for your consent before publishing it? As soon as you left the room, he begged me to do it before you got back. Did you know that?"

Drew furrows his brow. "What?"

"Yeah. He's broken so many promises to you over the years. You probably know of a few others I don't know about. But I gave you everything, Jacob. I was always there for you. You told me so many things on those brunches. Didn't you notice I never used any of that against you? I never told a soul. But after all the shit he's put you through, you'd still keep his secret? Why couldn't you keep mine?"

Drew's blood chills. His face goes numb. "What are you talking about?"

"Hauser. How did he get it out of you? Tell me."

Drew stares. "Oh my God."

"Did he beat it out of you?" Oscar asks, desperation showing through. "Is that what did it? Did he bribe you? It couldn't have been much. I know how much I paid him." He laughs.

"Oscar."

"Look!" Oscar lifts his shirt, exposing his flabby chest. "See? I don't care!" He drops his shirt, arms outstretched. "I really don't care anymore! It's over! I know it's over! Just tell me! He threatened you, didn't he? Did he threaten Stewie? Oh God, did he?! He couldn't have threatened Stewie!"

"He didn't threaten anyone."

"Was it me?" Oscar scoffs. "No, it couldn't have been me."

"You really don't know?" Drew whispers. "After all this time?"

Oscar readjusts his posture. "What? Know what?"

Drew's heart pounds hard in his chest. He feels faint. "Theo didn't convince me to do anything." He hesitates. "I was the one that convinced him."

Oscar furrows his brow.

Drew's eyes droop. "Stealing *Atomic* was my idea."

Oscar exhales hard, his back giving way. "No..."

"He never even heard the name Clark Hauser until after I got it off your computer. By then I already pitched it to Paramount and got the green light from Serge—"

"OH GOD!" Oscar screams, covering his eyes with both hands. He sobs loud and mercilessly, his throat making a squeaky friction sound.

Drew stands in horror, appalled by that awful display of grief before him. He looks around, not really for witnesses as much as for help. His bones ache with every guttural moan, every wet inhale, every drawn-out cry. He just wants to vomit.

Oscar wipes his face, sad eyes begging Drew for something. "STOP LYING FOR HIM!"

"I'm not," Drew says softly. "I really wish I was. But I'm not."

Oscar's breath wavers as he looks away.

Drew swallows. "Isn't it better that you know?"

"Fuck you," Oscar spits, glaring. "Do you have any idea what you've just done to me?"

"Oh, I'm supposed to feel sympathy for you now?!" Drew whines. "You ruined my career, Oscar, and for what? Because you thought Theo *tricked me* into telling him about Clark Hauser? How is that even remotely just?!"

"I never told anyone about my grandfather! I trusted you!"

"You trusted me?"

"Yeah!"

"Then why didn't you tell me you already wrote the fucking thing, huh?! Why didn't you tell me that?!"

Oscar frowns.

Drew glowers, ancient hate flowing. "When we were making *The Surgery*, I thought, 'Why is he helping us? What does he get out of this?' But I didn't say anything. I just let you keep going, the same way I let Theo run my life for me, because it was easier that way. Because at the end of the day I was getting something out of it. But you were too, weren't you? I watched you lie to a bartender the night we met over and over to get yourself a free bottle of Domergue, so what was it this time? I couldn't figure it out until I saw *Point of No Return* on your laptop and then it ALLLL made sense. You needed me to rise up, to get into festivals, to network on your behalf, because no Hollywood anybody would ever go near you with a ten-foot pole! With me in the room you'd be able to sit with them and talk with them and show them you came in peace. That way you'd know who the big players were, which ones you could threaten so you could make *Point of No Return* on your own. Go ahead justify it all you want, but don't lie and say that isn't true."

Oscar furrows his brow. "You thought the reason I co-signed your condo and got you that space at Sunset Gower, the reason I gave *The Surgery* my full undivided attention instead of putting that energy into my show — a decision which, by the way, forever slashed my ratings and got me dropped by the network — was because I was secretly thinking of *myself*?"

Drew stares.

Oscar grimaces. "I'm sorry I lied, but goddamn there was no reason! No fucking reason! None at all! So if that's what you told yourself to justify plagiarizing my script, the script I spent twenty years of my life pouring my heart and soul into, then you don't deserve forgiveness! You don't deserve joy or love! You deserve fucking pain and suffering! Just OD already and let us move on with our fucking lives!"

Drew looks down at the ground, taking it all in.

Oscar instantly regrets saying that. He rests one hand on the brick alleyway. Calms himself down.

Drew shakes his head, confused, overwhelmed.

"Is it really that surprising?" Oscar asks.

Drew breathes deeper, rubbing the back of his head with both hands.

Oscar's face relaxes. "You don't know me at all, do you? After everything I've done, everything I've given you, you still just don't know me at all."

"How could I have?" Drew exclaims. "Wasn't that the point? So no one could ever hurt you? What did you think was gonna happen? I was never gonna see you as a human being if all you did was act like a goddamn caricature!"

Oscar scoffs. "Oh wow." He looks off. "Jesus."

Drew puts hands on his hips, too frazzled for words.

Oscar shakes his head, amused. "That would be the reason, wouldn't it?"

Drew frowns. They look at each other from across the alley. Oscar's face is softer. Clearer. And he can see Drew's is the same. It's all out there now. Nothing more to interpret. No magic. Just disappointment.

"We both got what we deserved, huh?" Oscar murmurs.

Drew nods.

Oscar shrugs. "And on that anticlimactic note…" He regally bows. "Zounds."

Drew smirks.

Oscar half-turns. Stops. Hesitates. Keeps walking out of the alleyway. He crosses the street and disappears into the night.

WHALE

The Devil You Know

"Oscar and I were at Merry's again a few weeks ago," Whale says sitting at the counter in Brique. "He threw some strawberries over the balcony and got juice all over his baboon ass skin poncho."

Cashew stares from the next stool over. "I'm sorry, his *what*?"

"But before he ran to the bathroom to go clean it, he told me he needed to send Pete proofs for that Gutierrez thing you two were working on." Whale sips his Courvoisier sidecar. "So he gave me his laptop password so I could send it before the deadline."

Cashew raises his brows. "Oscar gave you his laptop password?"

"Yeah."

"Why?"

Whale hesitates. "Because he trusts me."

Cashew nods.

Whale takes a deep breath. "After I was done, I did a bit of snooping around his inbox before he came back. I found an old email from Valley Ridge Press regarding Clark Hauser's book."

Cashew's brows furrow slightly.

Whale holds up both hands. "I just told you."

"Oh, the nuclear guy."

"Yes. The nuclear guy." Whale rotates his coupe glass by its stem. "Apparently Valley Ridge Press was a shitty operation. They were emailing Oscar to tell him, due to a clerical error, that *Point of No Return* was improperly filed with the Library of Congress."

"It's public domain," Cashew realizes.

"Which explains why Oscar fought so hard to hide Dr. Hauser's story from the general public. If anyone got wind of it, they'd beat him to the punch in a heartbeat and it'd be completely legal."

Cashew nods. "Good find."

"I really didn't want to. I knew how much it meant to him, and..." Whale stops himself. "So I kept trying to move on to something else. The Jack Branson story for example." He finishes his drink. "But I kept coming back to *Point of No Return*. I can't help it. It's too good. Nothing was gonna come close."

"Another sidecar?" The Bartender asks.

"Yes please." Whale looks back at Cashew. "I tried looking for the book but I couldn't find it anywhere. It's out of print, no doubt thanks to Oscar."

The Bartender drops off a new sidecar. "There you go."

"Thanks." Whale instantly takes a sip. "I figured there's no way Oscar destroyed every copy, there had to have been one on his laptop, so when I called Oscar last Saturday to finalize our brunch plans, I made sure to bring up North Korea, all that progress Trump was making with Kim Jong Un, Putin, China. We talked about it for an hour. I had a feeling all that nuclear talk would get Oscar nostalgic for his grandfather's book and that he'd do some midnight memory lane walking."

"And did he?"

"He did." Whale takes another sip. "I 'accidentally' knocked our mimosa pitcher all over his priceless Peruvian parrot feather dress. I logged onto his computer when he was in the bathroom trying to get dry. Guess what I found in his Recents list."

"*Point of No Return.*"

Whale shakes his head. "Not the book."

"What?"

"The feature," Whale whispers with sad eyes. "He already wrote it. He told me he didn't, but he did." He laughs tastelessly. "His real name's Willie Gumption. Isn't that stupidest *fucking* name you've ever heard?"

Cashew doesn't laugh. Doesn't know what to say.

"I copied the PDF and emailed myself." Whale shakes his head. "It's the best screenplay I've ever read in my entire life. There are so many fucking details, so many parallels, and yet it's so streamlined. It must've taken him years."

Cashew lowers his head.

"He knows how hard this has been for me," Whale says with a grimace. "He knows I've been struggling. And he's been sitting on it the whole time. That's not fucking right." He drinks a bigger sip than usual. "So I'm taking it. I'm putting my name on it. It's gonna be my debut."

Cashew hesitates. "And Rian's okay with this?"

"I don't want him. I want you." Whale lifts his drink. "What do you say?"

Cashew stares, actually disturbed.

Whale looks off. "You were right about Rian. He's not my friend."

Cashew's eyes droop a bit.

Whale forces a smile. "I need someone strong to help me through it. Someone I can trust to speak for me."

Cashew smiles, his face red with flattery. He's never felt this way before. It's actually quite profound. "What about Paramount?"

"I've already pitched it to Serge. He said it's fine if Rian can't do it." Whale drinks some more. "What about China? What would they think of Dr. Hauser?"

Cashew takes a deep breath. "Considering it praises Soviet propaganda methods and paints the U.S. high command in a bad light, I don't see why not."

"That's what I figured."

Cashew clears his throat. "If you're really serious about this, we gotta make sure Oscar can't stop us. He'll end our careers before they even begin."

"The book's public domain, isn't it?"

"The screenplay's still considered his intellectual property."

Whale's lips form a puzzled frown. "What do we have to do?"

"Make changes. Drastic ones. Entire scenes."

Whale shakes his head slowly. "It's too perfect."

"Then we're gonna have to extract the original files off his laptop. The master Final Draft doc, all PDFs, original outlines, ancillary .txt files, everything. We can't leave anything behind for him to use against us to prove his authorship."

Whale hesitates. "Isn't my copy of the PDF enough?"

"If you have the original files, you can say you found an old out-of-print copy of Clark's book in Boston somewhere and wrote it when you were at Whitman. Oscar can't claim plagiarism because you didn't know him back then. And he can't say you couldn't have had an old copy of the book because it's so detailed. How else could you have written it? He pulled all traces of the story everywhere else."

"He'll still know it's his screenplay, no matter what we say."

Cashew adjusts his posture. "UniTopia's membership contract includes an intellectual property protection clause. Liu Tāo has a lot of allies all over the world. Míng doesn't want his father to slander UniTopia's satellites as a way to regain control of his former Empire, pardon the pun. I talked Míng's lawyers a few months ago about turning *Tequilatown* into a feature that I'd direct myself, that I was still worried about Oscar sabotaging me down the road, but they assured me UniTopia's legal team was vastly stronger than Oscar's, especially in the realm of international business law. So even if Oscar knows we stole it, because I work for Míng, he can hit Oscar so hard that Oscar would have to mortgage his mansion to pay for it. He might even lose the show. You know he loves that thing more than anything."

Whale lowers his eyes. "Am I gonna have to sneak on again?"

"Twice is already suspicious enough, I think."

"If Oscar has any idea it's happening, we're screwed."

"Don't I know it." Cashew thinks some more. "Which is why we need to distract him while we do it."

"Rian too. He'd snitch if he found out. He's always been weird like that."

"So the four of us need to be in a place where no one will suspect a thing."

"A place where Oscar would bring his laptop."

Cashew smiles. "Míng would be there too, with plenty of video evidence proving we were nowhere near him the entire time."

"You've got an idea?"

"Oscar night. Míng's got a cousin in the Dolby Theatre's body scanner detail. Oscar gets press passes every year. He always brings his laptop. They can pull it during security, and you have the password. They won't even be breaking in."

Whale nods. "This contract you're signing with UniTopia. It only protects *you*, doesn't it?"

Cashew hesitates. "It protects the founding CEOs of Not That Nut Pictures." He smiles slightly. "Wanna join me, bro?"

Whale's eyes light up. "My own production studio?"

"We can make anything we want, just the two of us."

Whale grins. "Now I really hope *The Surgery* gets nominated! That would just be too good!"

"With Oscar managing the campaign? Of course we're getting nominated."

Whale's smile fades. "It's got to be harder than that."

Cashew scoffs. "Please."

Whale frowns a bit. "Okay. I'll keep going to brunch with Oscar in the meantime. And I'll make up with Rian. That way they'll never suspect anything until it's too late."

Cashew smiles slightly. He holds out his hand. "Partners?"

"Partners." Whale takes Cashew's hand, warm skin on skin, and shakes it.

DREW

Forgive and Forget

Drew frowns at the mini-poster of *Atomic* hanging in the upper corner of his office. He reluctantly pulls out his phone. Makes the fucking call.

Larry types away in his office. The phone rings. Larry picks up the receiver. "Not That Nutty Productions, Larry Lin speaking."

"Hi Larry," Drew says meekly.

Larry stops typing. Looks around for Theo. "Mr. Lawrence?"

"I need to talk to Theo."

"I can't help you, Mr. Lawrence. I'm sorry. I'm in hot water as it is with him."

"I know," Drew says softly. "This is the last thing I'll ever ask you for."

"You've already used that one."

"Listen to me, Larry." Drew struggles to speak. "Just tell him it's Rodney Unger from Sony. They used to work together on a few projects back in the day. His voice sounds a lot like mine."

"I can't do that, Mr. Lawrence. You're on the Black List."

"I want to come back, Larry."

Larry freezes. "What?"

"That's what I want to talk to Theo about. Me coming back. What I'd have to do."

Larry hesitates. "Really?"

"He wanted me to, last we talked.

"That was almost three years ago."

"I know just what to say. He'll do it, Larry. I promise. Just patch me through."

Larry closes his eyes. "Mr. Lawrence."

"Please."

Larry smashes his lips together. "Then I'm telling him you threatened my family. In a way you kinda are. They need me in this job."

Drew hesitates. "Alright."

"Rodney Unger from Sony."

"That's right." Drew pauses. "Oh, and Larry?"

"Yes, Mr. Lawrence?"

"Thank you for everything you've done for me."

Larry struggles to talk. "Just get your ass back here, Mr. Lawrence."

"I will."

Larry puts Drew on hold. Stares at the buttons. Seriously considers bumping Drew. But he taps Theo's intercom anyway. "Mr. Landreth, Rodney Unger from Sony on Line 1."

Theo sits up. Picks up the receiver with a big smile. "Rodney! My man! What's up?"

"Please don't hang up."

Theo's heart races. "Son of a bitch."

"Just listen."

Theo grimaces, his hands shaking. "I'm listening."

"I threatened Larry. It's not his fault."

"I don't believe that for a single second."

"Please." Drew takes a deep breath. "I've been thinking a lot about us. What we did. All you've done for me. Apologizing for me. Making excuses for me. And I repaid that loyalty with extortion and lies and betrayal."

Theo's face hardens.

"I'm sorry for ending it like I did," Drew murmurs. "I shouldn't have tossed our friendship aside so lightly. It wasn't nothing. It was real. I can spin the last twenty years all I want as some sort of prison I was trapped in, but at the end of the day you and I were everything to each other. We were partners. I had no right blaming you for everything bad that ever happened to me. That was wrong."

"What do you want, Drew?" Theo asks, weakening. "I'm busy."

Drew looks back up at the *Atomic* poster. "I want to be partners again. Let me come back. I'll bring back the money I stole. It'll be just like before."

Theo hesitates. "And what do you get out of that?" he reluctantly asks.

Drew struggles to say it. "A pardon."

Theo closes his eyes with crushing disappointment.

"You're the only one in this town who can do it," Drew says. "You have the clout. Everyone's afraid of you. I'll be in your debt. I'll do everything I did before. I'll be Thalberg again and Not That Nutty will be bigger and better than ever. You'll see." Drew pauses. "I don't know how to do anything else. My life is here. My life is this. It's movies. And all this... I can't live without it. I'll do it. I'll come back. And that'll fuck Kev over big time. You'd like that, wouldn't—"

"You *actually* expect me to take you back after all that shit you said to me?" Theo asks.

Drew goes cold. "Theo."

"Bringing up my father like that? Calling me a heartless disgusting pig?"

"Theo. Please."

"I kept you off the Black List for over a year. You could've called and apologized. Oh, but now the Oscar vote's about to close and that's when I get the call out of the blue?"

"Theo, please! I didn't—"

"I don't need you anymore, Drew. I'm making waves. I'm kicking ass. All you ever did for me was make me feel guilty and slow me down. I can't believe I actually made excuses for you. I've wasted so much money on your retarded ass. I've lost clients and partners because of you. And now you're a fucking embarrassment to the City of Los Angeles. I wish I never met you, faggot. Sayonara."

"WAIT!" Drew begs, his voice straining. "I'M SORRY!"

"I'm hanging up."

"WAIT-WAIT-WAIT-WAIT!" Drew stammers. "What about your father? Remember what he told you?! You're supposed to *reward* your friends and smite your foes!"

"I am." Theo hangs up.

Drew can't move, the phone still on his ear, lips trembling.

Theo replays what Drew just said, squinting. He picks up his phone. Dials 2. "Larry, get in here." He hangs up.

A terrified Larry walks into the office. "Yes, Mr. Landreth?"

"You let that happen," Theo scolds.

"He threatened me, sir. He threatened Aaron."

"He's never threatened anyone in his life. Tell me the truth."

Larry reluctantly nods. "I'm sorry sir."

Theo stares. "I'm just fucking with you."

Larry freezes. "What?"

"He tried to say that at first, but he told me everything. Don't worry, he's coming back."

Larry sighs with relief. "He is?"

"I'm gonna pardon him and make him Head of Production again. Unfortunately, that means I'm demoting you."

"That's okay, sir. Really, I don't care."

"But I'll keep your salary just as it was," Theo says with a cheeky grin. "I'll take it out of Drew's paycheck. That's what he gets for taking his sweet-ass time."

Larry laughs. "That's fine. Wow. Thank you sir."

"See, I do know how to reward my friends." Theo leans back with a wistful sigh. "You know what, I wouldn't have been able to take that call if the Black List rules were followed, so... Maybe you're right. Maybe I should just end it."

"The Black List?"

"I think it's time. Don't you?"

Larry nods proudly. "Absolutely, sir."

Theo pulls out a pad and a pen. "Just tell me your password. I'll do it myself."

"I can do it."

"No, I'd rather do it. It's better that way. Psychologically."

Larry shrugs. "Yeah, I guess you're right."

Theo clicks his pen. "Go ahead."

"'AaronLin25.' One word, caps at the beginning of each name."

Theo writes it down. Shows Larry. "Like that?"

"Yeah."

Theo looks at the pad. "Your anniversary year."

Larry beams. "Yeah."

Theo plops the pad down. "I'll get to it in a bit."

"Okay." Larry opens the office door.

"Oh, Lar?"

"Yeah?"

Theo chuckles a bit. "I was updating Drew on the phone with what's going on with you and..." He blows through his lips. "I completely blanked on your kids' names. I'm so sorry."

"Charlotte and Nina."

"That's right." Theo jots their names on the pad. "Charlotte and Nina Lin."

"Yup."

Theo shows Larry the pad. "Now I won't forget them."

"You can always just ask me. I don't mind."

Theo shrugs. "What if you weren't here?"

Larry nods. "I'm gonna go then."

"Go on."

Larry leaves with a smile. Closes the door.

Theo's face instantly hardens. Larry snuck Drew past the Black List. He's still loyal to him. How long has that been going on? What else has he done for him? Have they been talking this whole time? About what? When's it gonna happen? Theo picks up the phone. Dials a number by hand. Dial tone.

"*Wéi*?"

"Míng. Theo."

"Hey."

"Don't worry, it's a private line."

Silence. "Is this the call I think it is?"

Theo looks out his office window at Larry exchanging pleasantries with Heath. "Think it's time I met that friend of yours."

Drew can't even watch the 110th Academy Awards. He holes himself in his office instead. A text from Kev confirms the worst. A complete snub. Not a single win for *Branson*. That and the fact that it's plummeting out of the worldwide box office. It's really over. Finished. Dead in the water.

Drew wanders down Sunset Boulevard, both hands in his jeans, staring forward. He walks up to a guy. Buys a vial. Retreats to a dark little alley. Pops the top. Leans his head back. Slides the coke right into his nose. Snorts it all up. Bad coke. Lots of junk in it. Not even that great of a high. But it's enough. Drew curls up on the ground. Two-and-a-half years of sobriety down the drain.

END OF PART SEVEN

PART EIGHT

Only the Desert for You

JACOB

California Dreamin'

Jacob sits beside the lake at the Public Garden, listening to "Tomorrow Never Knows" with a contemplative look. No clouds in the sky. Finally warm enough to wear short sleeves. Green grass. Colorful flowers in bloom. Happy people and kids and dogs roaming around in the late April sun.

"No Stephen King?" Rian asks, walking over with a laptop bag.

Jacob removes an earbud.

```
                    JACOB
      I'm probably never going to finish that book. It's a
      shame because I actually really like the premise.
```

Jacob stops the music as Rian sits beside him on the grass. "What were you listening to? The Pet Shop Boys?"

```
                    JACOB
      The Beatles actually.
```

"Oh. That's a nice change of pace."

Jacob nods. Wraps his arms around his folded legs.

Rian leans back in the sun, propped up by both arms like a cornhole plank. "When's the last time you listened to them?"

```
                    JACOB
      A while.
               (pause)
      They were the first discography I ever deep dove
      into. I think it's that way for a lot of music fans.
      It's why they've stood the test of time. They're so
      accessible compared to Pink Floyd or Led Zeppelin,
      like a gateway drug for people to start caring about
      music.
```

"The marijuana of music."

Jacob chuckles.

```
                    JACOB
      In a thousand ways.
               (pause)
      Most people get sick of 'em and move on to someone
      else, but I make sure to keep them in rotation. I
      wouldn't have sonic taste or lyrical nuance if it
      wasn't for them. Wouldn't be right for me to toss
      them aside just because I outgrew them.
```

"Which album were you listening to?"

```
                    JACOB
      Revolver.
```

"That's a good one."

Jacob smirks.

```
                    JACOB
      The same night I met Stewie, I was talking to a girl
      at Machine, a woman named Sandy, and we were talking
      about my "Likes Boys" T-shirt. She said something I
```

```
still think about. She said when people first see
something, their mind goes straight to the gutter.
Like how Revolver isn't a gun, it's an LP literally
revolving on a turntable. And the Beatles have
nothing to do with real beetles, it's just a pun on
"beat," like beats-per-minute.
          (pause)
That's just so true, you know?
```

They share a silence. Nothing to hear but the soft breeze. A dog barking somewhere. A street performer. Some bass-heavy hip-hop blasting out of a car behind them as it drives down Boylston.

```
                    JACOB (CONT'D)
You really don't think you'll change your mind?
```

Rian shakes his head. "LA's a spent force, my guy."

```
                    JACOB
Hollywood's the reason we wanted to be filmmakers in
the first place.
```

"Hollywood of the 70s maybe, back when there were Robert Evanses running the studios and Coppolas, Scorseses, Spielbergs, and Kubricks in every corner drugstore, but that's not the way it is anymore. It's all about China now. They've gone and outsourced the entire demographic. Everything's all Disneyfied and Marvelfied and *Star Wars*ed."

```
                    JACOB
It can still go back to the way it used to be.
```

"Nah man. I'm only thinking about the future."

```
                    JACOB
You were all gung-ho for LA when TJ was in the
picture.
```

"Good thing he isn't. I've had a chance to really think over what it is I want, and this is what I want."

```
                    JACOB
Filming reality TV in Savannah?
```

"It's real experience. And the pay is great. That's what I need right now. It's the right move."

Jacob sighs.

Rian looks over. "Almost forgot. Congrats on the Whitty nomination."

Jacob smiles.

```
                    JACOB
My family's going nuts about it. Funny how it took me
getting nominated for them to suddenly give a shit
about my work.
```

"That must be fun."

```
                    JACOB
It's unusual, that's for sure.
          (pause)
They're all coming up here for the ceremony. Mom.
Karen. Melanie. Even Dad and his girlfriend. They
haven't even met Stewie yet.
```

"That's great man."

Jacob shrugs.

"Have they ever been up here before?"

```
                    JACOB
      Just my parents the one time. Parents' Weekend
      Freshman Year. Pretending to still be together. What
      a disaster that was.
```

Jacob frowns.

```
                    JACOB (CONT'D)
      But I forgive them.
```

Rian smiles. "*Drive-Thru*'s the one you sent The Professor?"

Jacob nods emotionlessly.

"Good sign. Maybe you'll get it."

```
                    JACOB
      I already did.
```

Rian blinks, suddenly sitting up. "What?"

```
                    JACOB
      I got the internship.
```

Rian scoffs, a stunned grin curling the edges of his mouth. "Dude!" he cries, super pumped. "Holy SHIT, dude!" He hugs Jacob hard. "Why didn't you tell me?! Oh my God!"

Jacob forces a smile, amused by Rian's sudden mirth.

"When did you find out?!"

```
                    JACOB
      Yesterday.
```

"Stewie must be thrilled, huh?"

```
                    JACOB
      I haven't told him yet.
```

Rian softens. "Why not?"

Jacob tightens his grip around his knees. Stares between his legs at the shaded grass beneath.

```
                    JACOB
      If he never finds out, I'll never have to go.
```

Rian looks out at the lake, flabbergasted. "You have to tell him."

```
                    JACOB
      No I don't.
              (pause)
      If I have to lie for the rest of my life, I'll do it.
```

"This is *The Professor* we're talking about! You've got a 1 in 4 chance of getting a job with a fucking Oscar winner! Or maybe it's more like a 50% chance! You don't know what he's like! You don't know!"

```
                    JACOB
      What I don't know is if I'll ever find someone like
      Stewie again. If I CAN find someone else.
```

Rian sighs. "I don't know, man."

```
                    JACOB
      If I want to be a career writer, I need a good
      support system. People who believed in me before the
      awards and nominations. Before I was famous. Or thin.
      Or hot.
```

Rian scratches the back of his head. "Look, I don't wanna guilt you or anything, you should only do what you're comfortable with, but if I were in your situation right now, I'd take the job." He looks out at the serene water. "I know Stewie's age doesn't matter to you now, but it will.

Realistically speaking, how many years do you think you guys got? Twenty-five? Thirty? Thirty years from now he'll be eighty-three."

Jacob frowns, a chord striking.

Rian shrugs. "I'm sorry, but that's just facts. Chances are he's going before you and you'll be single in your fifties, just like he was, and you might not be so lucky in the looks department. Most guys don't look good in their fifties. Plus you're such an old soul. Maybe instead of a forty-year-old in a twenty-year-old's body, you'll be a seventy-year-old in a fifty-year-old's body. Who wants that?" Rian pauses. "Old people have it rough. I know it's sad, but it's true."

Jacob exhales slowly through his nose, listening intently.

Rian half-frowns. "Do you really wanna be an adult this fast, dealing with taxes and mortgages and insurance for everything? C'mon man, you're twenty-two. You're a fucking stud now. Wouldn't you rather get it out of your system before you start thinking about settling down? Who knows, maybe monogamy doesn't work. Look at your parents." He pauses. "Or maybe it's different for gay guys. I don't know."

Jacob keeps staring off.

Rian huffs. "Don't listen to me. I don't know what I'm talking about." He looks back at Jacob. Senses him dwelling on it. "I don't mean to be such a devil's advocate here, I'm just saying... What if one day you're house-husbanding Stewie in the country somewhere with only his Boomer friends to talk to, listening to them reminisce the glory days of their twenties and thirties with none of your own? Miles away from everyone else your age." He looks softly at Jacob. "And you'll look back and wish you hadn't turned down the internship because of a little stage fright."

Jacob lowers his eyes.

Rian digs a finger into his ear canal. Flicks some wax dust off. "At the very least, you have to tell Stewie the truth. A promise is a promise. Don't be like your mom."

Jacob extends his legs, his eyes still looking off.

"It's the right thing," Rian murmurs with reluctant honesty. "The fair thing."

Jacob nods weakly.

```
                    JACOB
      I'll tell him.
```

Jacob looks out at the murky water shimmering in the sunlight.

```
                    JACOB (CONT'D)
      I'll tell him, and we'll talk.
```

WHALE

Baptism

Larry buttons Whale's top button in the Studio 1 dressing room. "No phony glasses tonight, Mr. Andrezj?" Larry murmurs pointedly. Whale frowns back with shame.

"How does it look?" Rian asks obliviously, craning his head. He's in a Joseph Abboud of his own, looking quite dashing.

Whale about-faces and holds up his arms. It fits perfectly, tastefully showing off his muscles.

"Fuck, dude!" Rian exclaims. "You look hot as shit."

Whale smiles bashfully at Larry. "He says that a lot. He's not gay."

"Bitch I might be now." Rian smirks. "Must be the tuxes."

"Oscar really went all-out on you guys," Larry says, flashing serious eyes at Whale.

Rian scrolls though his phone. "God, this is unreal. My family is actually texting me, wishing me luck and all."

Larry brushes Whale with a lint roller. "That's good."

"Took 'em long enough, but... you know, I'm happy to hear it."

Larry ties Whale's bowtie. Looks knowingly at Whale. "Please stop," Whale whispers back.

"Huh?" Rian asks, looking up. "What?"

"Nothing."

Rian furrows his brow. "You okay, buddy? You've been quiet all night."

"Just nervous."

"What do you have to be nervous about?" Larry mumbles.

Rian pockets his phone. "I don't want to jinx it by asking, but who's gonna speak if we win?"

"I think you should," Whale answers.

"You're still gonna throw out some names at the end, right?"

"Really, Frankie, who am I gonna thank?"

Rian looks at his watch. "I'm gonna go check on Oscar." He stands up, buttoning his jacket. "See you at the afterparty, Lar."

"Bye, Rian!" Larry says with a smile. "Good luck!"

Rian looks at Whale's reflection. Nods. Closes the door.

Larry's levity fades. "You're really not gonna tell him, huh?"

Whale plops into a makeup chair. He can't even look at his own reflection.

Larry grimaces at the back of Whale's head. "How the fuck can you this to—?"

"It's out of my hands now, alright?!" Whale snaps with a dry throat. "We're paying you to go along and not ask any questions, so stop fucking asking!"

"No, you're *paying me* to let you know when you're out of your head, Mr. Andrezj. And I'm sorry, you're out of your fucking head."

Whale stares off. Cross his arms around his tummy.

KNOCK KNOCK. "How's it going?" Cashew asks with a grin, dressed to the nines. Not even Joseph Abboud can make the guy look fuckable.

"He's all set," Larry says.

Cashew looks at Whale's reflection. "Can you give us a moment, Larry? I want to ask Jacob something."

Larry gives Whale a solemn frown. "Good luck."

Whale nods apologetically. He knows Larry's not talking about the Oscars. Larry moves past Cashew and closes the door behind him.

Cashew steps up to the back of Whale's chair. Whale sighs, registering Cashew's presence only in the peripherals of his downcast eyes. "Míng's contracts are in the men's room on Mezzanine," Cashew ominously reports. "Last stall, in a waterproof case behind the tank. Green's for me, red's for you."

Whale nods.

Cashew tilts his head. "Everything okay?"

"Yeah."

Cashew hesitates. "If you wanna switch seats, I can switch seats."

"I'm sitting with Frankie and that's that," Whale says with stern eyes.

Cashew stares back hard. "You're calling him Frankie again, I see."

Whale doesn't answer. Cashew half-turns to leave. "Theo?"

"Hm?"

"Did you...?" Whale stops himself, chickening out.

Cashew blinks. "Did I what?"

Whale forces a smile. "Nothing. Just something stupid Frankie said."

"What did he say?"

Whale shrugs a bit. "Just..." He chuckles nervously. "He said you were gaslighting me. That you were bragging about it when I was in the bathroom at Tribeca." Whale makes eye contact with Cashew's reflection. He's not laughing. Why isn't he laughing?

Cashew bites his lip. Looks off. "Sign the fucking papers, Jacob," he mumbles.

"What?" Whale's skin crawls. "Theo, did—?"

"This was your idea. Don't punish me for it." Cashew opens the dressing room door and closes it hard. Whale can't move, his mouth wide open.

"You don't look so good, dude," Rian tells him.

Whale blinks out of his trance. Sees Rian standing next to him. Remembers where they are, the security line outside the Dolby Theatre, handsome men in suits and gorgeous women in dresses in front and behind in the perfect weather. "I guess don't feel very good," Whale says.

"I'm sorry to hear that." Rian takes a step closer to the metal detectors. "How's the new feature coming along?"

"Fantastic."

"You gonna tell me anything about it?"

"Nope."

Rian smirks. "This is so unlike you, dude. Usually you're telling me every scene out of order just from the sheer excitement of it all."

"Guess I'm growing up."

Rian hesitates for a beat. "I *am* going to see it sometime, right? I've got a few production leads that want to read it before committing."

"Just leads, huh?"

"It's pretty fucking hard to sell a project without a script, dude. When's it gonna be finished?"

Whale hesitates. "Tomorrow."

Rian nods broadly. "I see. That's why you're so preoccupied tonight."

Whale blinks. "Sure. Why not."

"Can't wait to read it."

A few spots behind them, Oscar and Cashew wait impatiently to enter the Dolby Theater with press passes around their necks. Oscar's in an Indiana Jones cosplay, whip on hip, satchel slung over his shoulder. "You look absolutely ridiculous," Cashew tells him with utmost disdain.

"You think this is bad, you should've seen me five years ago. I went as the Blob."

Cashew looks at Oscar curiously. "The Blob? Really?"

"The Steve McQueen one, not that Chuck Russell bullshit."

Cashew nods. "They shot the original *Blob* in Jacob's hometown."

Oscar stops in his tracks. "Jacob's from Phoenixville?"

Cashew furrows his brow. "I don't know which is more disconcerting, the fact that you've gone to brunch with him every week for the past two and a half years and never once asked him about his hometown, or the fact that you actually know the name of the town where they filmed *The Blob*."

"Of course I know Phoenixville. I've been there many times."

"Really?"

"My grandfather lived there the last years of his life. It's where he grew up."

Cashew hesitates. Looks at Oscar funny.

Oscar smirks. "What's up with you?"

"Which grandfather?"

Oscar stares. "What do you mean 'which grandfather?'"

"Just curious," Cashew quickly adds.

Oscar keeps staring. "What a strange question."

"Get a move on, Dr. Jones," some schmuck behind Oscar whines. Oscar paces up to the metal detector, his mind still replaying that strange question.

"What's in the bag, sir?" the Security Guard asks in an Americanized droll despite him being Asian, Chinese by the look of him.

"Just my laptop and few other things," Oscar responds.

"We gonna have to look through it." The Security Guard waves over another guard.

"I always bring my laptop here. You've never had to screen it before."

"New security measures, sir. Please comply."

Oscar begrudgingly removes his satchel. "I'm proficient with a whip, you know."

The Security Guard takes the satchel and immediately hands it over to the other guard who... Oh wait, a SECOND Chinaman?! Two in one detail?! No way, something's up. "Where's he taking it?" Oscar asks, the Other Guard taking the satchel into a side office. "What the fuck is going on here?"

"There's been an alert," the Security Guard says calmly. "Just let us investigate."

"This is incredibly unnecessary. I want to speak to your supervisor."

"What's going on?" Cashew asks from the other side, feigning ignorance.

"I am the supervisor," the Security Guard tells Oscar.

"Well *I'm* Oscar Blitz! So if you want to work in this town again, buster, you better bring my satchel back right now!"

"If you're gonna cause a scene right now, I'm throwing you out and we're keeping the bag."

Oscar stifles himself. "Can I go through at least?" The Security Guard steps aside. Oscar steps through the scanner unscathed. "This is bullshit!" Oscar hisses at Cashew. "Fucker's probably one of Míng's cousins busting my balls."

"Little racist, ain't it?"

"Wouldn't put it past him!" Oscar stares at the side office door. "God, they're probably hacking my computer right now."

Cashew laughs way too conspicuously. "Don't be ridiculous."

"They don't need to go into another room to pilfer through my things. What the fuck's taking them so long?!"

"What's the big deal?"

Oscar takes a deep breath. "I don't like this. I don't like not knowing what's going on in there."

"I know what's going on."

Oscar looks at Cashew. "You do?"

"They're planting coke on you." Cashew throws in an eyeroll.

The Other Guard opens the side office door and carries the satchel back to Oscar. "Here you go, sir."

"Oh, I'm good all of a sudden?" Oscar snaps.

"Enjoy the show." The Other Guard makes split-second eye contact with Cashew and returns to his post. So smooth. Cashew can't help but smirk.

Oscar immediately opens his laptop and types his login. He scans the desktop. Everything's all there. Unless...

"What are you doing now?" Cashew whines, hiding his utter terror.

"Just a second." Oscar's heart races, his fingers unsure where to move. There's no way. He couldn't have.

"Come on, we're gonna miss the monologue."

"Alright, just..." Oscar sighs uneasily. Closes the laptop. Stuffs it away.

Whale and Rian sit down in their assigned Mezzanine seats. Whale doesn't say anything. Just watches the camera crew and roadies mulling about. "We're really here," Rian declares in a soft whisper. He looks over the Mezzanine's edge. Quickly plops down. "I just saw Rian Johnson!"

"Wow."

"Look! Third row!"

"I'll take your word for it."

"Dude!"

"Please," Whale says with emphasis, avoiding eye contact with Rian.

Rian looks at the railing. "Oh shit, I forgot. Sorry."

Whale furrows his brow. "What?"

"You're afraid of heights."

Whale hesitates. "I'm okay. It's fine."

"You sure? We can move somewhere else."

"I'm fine. Thanks." Whale checks behind him. The only seats Cashew and Oscar can take are two rows back at least. "I don't wanna move."

Rian pats Whale's shoulder with a soft smile. Whale maintains his blank stare, trying his hardest not to look at Frankie, not to let it in. But he can't stop feeling like shit. Like a piece of shit, actually.

The 92nd Academy Awards begin with an over-the-top musical performance by Janelle Monáe and Billy Porter, followed by a monologue from Chris Rock and Steve Martin, concluding their spiel by introducing Regina King (2018's Best Supporting Actress winner) to present the Academy Award for Best Supporting Actor. Only in 2019 can Tom Hanks, Anthony Hopkins, Al Pacino, Joe Pesci, and Brad Pitt be vying for the same award. *Once Upon a Time in Hollywood. The Irishman. Joker. 1917. Jojo Rabbit. Little Women. Parasite. Marriage Story. Midsommar. The Lighthouse. Rocketman. Doctor Sleep. Knives Out. El Camino.* The *Downton Abbey* movie. Even *Avengers: Endgame* and *Star Wars: The Rise of Skywalker*. Easily the greatest year in movie history BY FAR.

Brad predictably wins (He's been cleaning up everywhere all season), and as he kisses his mom and takes the stage to accept his first ever Oscar, Whale feels a twinge in his throat. It finally hits him. He's breathing the same poorly-ventilated air as Brad Pitt, Tom Hanks, Anthony Hopkins, Al Pacino, Joe Pesci, Janelle Monáe, Billy Porter, Chris Rock, Steve Martin, Regina King, Joaquin Phoenix, Adam Driver, Robert De Niro, Leonardo DiCaprio, Renée Zellweger, Scarlett Johansson, Saoirse Ronan, Charlize Theron, Laura Dern, Kathy Bates, Florence Pugh, Margot Robbie, Rian Johnson, Taika Waititi, John Williams, Randy Newman,

Thomas Newman, Alexandre Desplat, Elton John, Billie Eilish, Finneas, Diane Warren, Idina Menzel, Shia LaBeouf, Roger Deakens, Thelma Schoonmaker, Diane Keaton, Timothée Chalamet, Natalie Portman, Lin-Manuel Miranda, Julia Louis-Dreyfus, Brie Larson, Olivia Colman, Sigourney Weaver, Jane Fonda, Spike Lee, Sam Mendes, Steven Spielberg, Todd Phillips, Greta Gerwig, Bong Joon-ho, Martin Scorsese, and Quentin Tarantino. Whale does not belong in that room, among such class.

Oscar Blitz and Cashew pop into the bathroom to tinkle during the first commercial break, Cashew using a stall like a little sissy boy. Oscar washes his hands, adjusts his Indy fedora in the mirror, and waits outside the bathroom for Cashew to finish, hands on hips and scoping the area for a good Nazi to punch. "Short Round!" Oscar cries, approaching Liu Míng with open arms and a patronizing smile. "Step on it!"

Míng sighs harshly. "Oscar."

"Remember I used to say that to you?" Oscar says, holding back a snicker. "And you'd say, 'Okie dokie Docta Jone! Hold on to your potato!'" He laughs hard.

Míng glares at Oscar's ridiculous costume. "My father always said you had method to your madness."

"Just for you, Short Round."

"Stop calling me that."

"I can call you whatever the fuck I want." Oscar looks at all the people mulling about them. "How'd you get in here anyway? You're not a nominee or press."

"I have my ways."

"Weaseling your way around, just like your father. All this Hollywood glitterati all in one place? Perfectly way for you to spread the word about Empire 2.0."

"UniTopia."

"You handing out business cards? I'll take one."

Míng buttons his suit. "Good day." He walks away.

"My condolences, of course," Oscar says, pivoting.

Míng turns around. "I'm sorry?"

"Your father."

Míng nods respectfully. "Thank you."

"He will be missed."

"Yes he will."

"Heard you were in the room when it happened."

"I was."

"Must've been awful to watch, huh?"

Míng hesitates. "Life goes on, doesn't it?"

Oscar rubs his chin. "Pretty interesting timing, don't you think, your father ousted like that only to have a heart attack at fifty-eight? He wasn't really in bad shape, was he?"

"I have somewhere to be, Oscar."

"Tell me, Short Round, now that you have everything you've ever wanted and no one left alive to stop you, do you like what you see in the mirror?"

"I love what I see in the mirror," Míng responds. "Do you?"

"Look at how I'm dressed right now and tell me I don't love the face staring back at me."

"I think you dress this way *because* you hate the face staring back at you," Míng whispers. "Under all those absurd costumes and that miasma of mystery is just… *Willie*."

Oscar stares. "We do what we can to survive, don't we? The ones who survive are the ones that think about their place in the world. They don't just do whatever they please."

"But doesn't all that thinking make you tired?" Míng asks enigmatically. "All that honesty, showmanship, temperance? What does that get you? Brownie points? Shouldn't we all get exactly what we want when we want it? How else can we appreciate our short godless lives?"

"Tantalus."

Míng blinks. "Come again?"

"Don't you know about Tantalus?"

"Of course I know Tantalus. He stole ambrosia from the Gods. Gave it to mortal men. As punishment, he was forced to spend an eternity standing in a pool of water he can't drink and under a tree with delicious fruit he can't reach."

"Wrong," Oscar says. "That wasn't Tantalus' punishment."

"Yes it was."

"No it wasn't."

"I know it was. It's how you got the word 'tantalize.'"

"That's not a punishment," Oscar states. "That's something we humans deal with every day, wanting something we can't have. But Tantalus wasn't a human, was he? He was a son of Zeus. His punishment was *mortality*. There's nothing worse to a demigod, is there?"

Míng stares blankly at Oscar.

Oscar shrugs. "No water in the world would taste nearly as good as the version of that water in Tantalus' imagination, being so close to it, so thirsty. You see, Short Round, it's the myth of that water, the myth of that fruit hanging above his head, where poetry comes from, and music, and art, dreams, desire, drive, ambition. That's where life happens, in that Tantalus Zone. No reality can ever compete with that." Oscar smirks. "And now that you've got the Holy Grail in your hands, it's only a matter of time before you realize you just threw away the only father you'll ever have for a dusty… old… cup." Oscar tips his hat and walks away.

"My father couldn't accept reality either," Míng speaks up.

Oscar stops. Looks back.

"He was addicted to the chase, you see," Míng continues. "The drama. The day-to-day. But it was gonna end sooner or later. All he had to do was accept it. That there was nothing left to do but let go and walk away. But he couldn't do that. He refused to." Míng shrugs. "And he gave himself a heart attack."

"Will you be able to let go when it's your turn?"

"If that day ever comes, of course I will."

Oscar laughs. "'If that day ever comes.' You weren't even joking were you?"

Míng doesn't respond.

Cashew comes out of the bathroom. "What took you so long?" Oscar asks.

"Had to shit," Cashew lies.

"C'mon." Oscar and Cashew return to their seats in the press section, just in time to catch the tail-end of *Frozen II*'s "Into the Unknown," headed by the *Wicked*ly talented Adele Dazeem. Oscar can see the backs of Rian and Whale's heads a few rows ahead of them, just by the balcony's edge. A sharp ping of sadness makes Oscar's legs ache. How handsome Whale looks in that tux. What a beautiful man he's grown up to be. Oscar daydreams for a few seconds, a smile creeping in.

The lights go up for another commercial break. Whale reluctantly stands. "Where are you going?" Rian asks.

"I'll be quick, I promise." Whale shuffles down the row and strolls into the Mezzanine bathroom. His heart pounds fast. His legs vibrate. His arms too. He opens the last stall, the barriers blocking the mirror's marquee lights. Whale reaches behind the toilet tank. Nothing. He waves his hand further down, straining. His fingers finally find it halfway down the toilet's porcelain spine. Whale hears the bathroom door open and sits down. Slowly unzips the waterproof case.

Pages through the moldy inspection paperwork. Finds the UniTopia contracts, Cashew's already filled out and signed. Whale flips to the back page of his. Takes the pen inside the case. Presses it to the blank dotted line. Stares into space.

It's already off Oscar's computer. He already stole it. The crime had occurred. The rest is just protection. A legal formality he'd only benefit from. But he can't seem to get his fingers to move.

At that moment, the man soon to be officially formally known as Jacob Andrezj decides he wants to call the whole thing off.

But he can't, can he? The events he so emotionally initiated were already in motion. He can't stop it, even if he wanted to. And he wanted to. Just sitting with Rian made him realize that. And poor Oscar.

There's no way to stop it. He can only follow through with it. He'll learn to accept what he's done one day. And he can't trust himself right now anyway. He's just nervous is all.

Whale signs the papers. Re-tapes the plastic case to the back of the toilet. Steps out of the stall to wash his hands. Casually looks over at the man that walked in, a tall guy in his fifties with short black hair peeing at the urinal and *HOLY SHIT IT'S QUENTIN TARANTINO!*

Whale turns off the water, dumbfounded. He's actually real. An actual human. And he's peeing right in front of him. Quentin notices Whale staring and smiles. "Hey man, how's it going?"

Whale smiles back. "Good."

"You one of the nominees?" Quentin asks, zipping his fly. He takes the sink next to Whale and washes his hands, looking up for a response.

Whale nods. "Yeah."

"That's great, dude. What are you up for?"

Whale blinks, trying to remember. "Live Action Short Film."

"*The Surgery*?"

Whale freezes. "Uh…"

"It's only one I've seen so far. Sorry."

"No, that's it!" Whale chuckles a bit. "That's me. I wrote it."

"Wow! Great!" Quentin marvels. "I loved it, man. It's fantastic."

"Really? You think so?"

"DUDE," Quentin says with giddy emphasis. "You're at the motherfucking OSCARS right now. You are a fucking rockstar."

Whale can't breathe. "Thanks."

Quentin turns off the faucet. "What's your name, man?" he asks, drying his hands.

"Jacob. Jacob Andrezj."

Quentin tosses the paper towel into the trash. "Good luck, Jacob. I'm rooting for you."

Whale might be grinning. "I'm rooting for you too."

Quentin waves a dismissive hand. "Eh. We'll see." He whips the bathroom door open and walks out.

Whale just stands there, his body aching with despair, utterly sick to his stomach. As the silence sets in, a rush of tears stream down his face.

Whale makes his distracted return to his seat. He can hear Diane Keaton and Keanu Reeves declare Bong Joon-ho and Han Jin-won the Best Original Screenplay winners. Everyone stands and claps, making it easier for Whale to walk down the row.

"What took you so long?" Rian asks over the enthusiastic cheer of the crowd.

"I was talking to Quentin Tarantino in the bathroom," Whale says.

Rian's jaw drops. "The fuck?!"

"Believe me, I know."

"Dude!" Rian scoffs. "Well? How was he?"

"Fucking perfect of course. Humble as hell."

The crowd dies down to hear the adorable Sharon Choi translate Bong Joon-ho's speech. Rian and Whale lean close together. "You must've been talking for a while," Rian whispers.

"Not really. A minute tops."

"What kept you then?"

Whale hesitates. "I needed a moment."

Rian looks out at the podium. "Can't believe *Parasite* beat *Hollywood* for Original."

"It's probably gonna win."

"It should," Rian concurs. "All of them should. God, what an amazing year."

"I was thinking that earlier."

"Who wouldn't?"

"Theo probably."

"Pfft." Rian rolls his eyes.

"His favorite year is probably something stupid like 1951," Whale says with a smirk. "Back in the good old days of predictable musicals and repackaged westerns with all those phony movie stars popping barbiturates and having secret gay sex and back-alley abortions."

Rian doesn't laugh. "I can't stop thinking about that fight."

Whale looks at Rian, alarmed and a bit unsure of what to say. "It's okay, dude."

"I know we've moved past it, but…" Rian idly scratches his armrest with a finger. "I still feel it lingering between us." He gives Whale a soft vulnerable gaze. "It feels so wrong not to acknowledge it. I just wanted to say it again, that I'm sorry for everything."

Whale frowns. For the first time in his life, he realizes what it must be like to have a brother.

Rian sits up suddenly. "Ooh! Adapted Screenplay!" Whale, in a daze, watches the prerecorded montage of Natalie Portman and Timothée Chalamet reading off the nominees. "My money's on *Jojo Rabbit*," Rian says.

Whale nods. "Me too."

Taika Waititi wins, just as they predicted. Whale and Rian stand and clap, quickly sitting back down with the rest.

"Next one's us!" Rian sings with a gleeful squeal.

Whale studies Rian's cheer. "You know what I was thinking in there?"

"Where?"

"The bathroom, after Quentin left."

"What?"

Whale hesitates. "What a killer year for endings."

"Oh yeah. *Once Upon a Time in Hollywood. Parasite. Jojo Rabbit.*"

"*Little Women. Joker. Midsommar. The Lighthouse.*"

"*1917*, I guess. The run counts as the ending, doesn't it?"

"I'd say so." Whale pauses. "*The Irishman.*"

"Oh yeah."

Whale nods. "But *Once Upon a Time in Hollywood*'s gotta be the best ending in history."

"You could write a fucking dissertation on that ending."

"It's not just another historically inaccurate bait-and-switch like *Inglourious Basterds*. It really is a satire on Hollywood endings."

"All those payoffs converging at the end there. The acid cigarette. The clicky thing Cliff does with his mouth. The dog food can."

"Don't forget the flamethrower."

"The fucking FLAMETHROWER!"

"I was thinking about that in there, how appealing it is to just…" Whale sighs softly. "The 10s were such a decade of change, weren't they? In politics. Minority relations. Digital overhaul. Social media. Everyone suddenly re-analyzing the past. Judging everything out of context. And all that uncertainty, as a society, as a country. *Hollywood*'s ending is everything anyone could want. The perfect wish fulfillment scenario. No matter what ideology or political affiliation you subscribe to, we all want the same thing." Whale looks at Rian. "For change to stop. To keep right now just like it is forever. Is it healthy to want that? Is it bad? Who knows. It feels right. And why shouldn't it?"

Rian softens at Whale's words. "But life goes on. A golden age ends, another comes along."

"That it does."

"You either stick around and watch the good times die a slow, silent death, or you decide you've had enough and move on. There are no happy endings."

"Unless you kill it yourself," Whale states a bit too plainly. "Then you'll never have to watch it rot."

Rian furrows his brow.

"You'll always wonder what could've been, of course," Whale murmurs. "But isn't it better not knowing it was all gonna end in disappointment, with everyone glad to be rid of it?" Whale gives Rian a strange reassuring smile.

Rian stares back, alarmed by Whale's tone.

Whale suddenly gasps at the sight of *The Peanut Butter Falcon*'s Shia LaBeouf and Zack Gottsagen walking on stage. "It's time! Holy fuck!"

Shia LaBeouf leans down to the microphone. "Short films allow new voices to be seen and heard without the constraints of budget or permission. I've seen these films and they are beautiful."

Zack Gottsagen, the first ever Academy Award presenter with Down Syndrome, leans in. "And..." he reads from the teleprompter with generous pauses. "If you haven't seen it... Come see it."

"Thank you," Shia says quickly. "Here are the nominees for Best Live Action Short Film."

The montage starts, Shia LaBeouf reading off the nominees. "*Brotherhood*. Meryam Joobeur and Maria Gracia Turgeon." Light applause. "*Nefta Football Club*. Yves Piat and Damien Megherbi." Applause. "*The Neighbors' Window*. Marshall Curry." Applause and some cheers. "*A Sister*. Delphine Girard." Applause. "*The Surgery*. Jacob Andrezj and Rian Hoffman." Applause and cheers. Whale and Rian grin. Not only did Actual Cannibal Shia LaBeouf actually read their names aloud to an international audience of millions, he did so with flawless pronunciation.

Zack struggles to open the envelope. Shia points to the bottom, letting Zack open it by himself. Zack stares at the camera a bit longer than usual, envelope open, mouth struggling for words. Shia smiles, obviously embarrassed by the delay.

Rian and Whale's hearts pound furiously in anticipation. Rian mentally yells at the poor Down Syndrome guy to just spit it out already. Whale asks God to lose.

"The..." Zack says, lengthy pause again. "Oscars goes to..."

"*The Neighbors' Widow*," Shia LaBeouf reads impatiently, bungling the title in the process.

Rian falls back in his seat. "Fuck!"

Whale muscles relax. Wonders if he anything he's done, said, or thought tonight actually affected the outcome, as silly as that sounds.

As Marshall Curry eagerly accepts his Oscar, his wife by his side, Rian runs a hand through his hair. "I really thought we had it."

Whale retreats inward. Stays on autopilot for the rest of the ceremony. Except for the In Memoriam montage, that is. Billie Eilish's performance of "Yesterday" reminds him of Stewie. That alone almost brings Whale to tears.

Parasite ultimately wins Best Picture, the first non-English film to do so. Whale finally looks at his phone. A text from Cashew two minutes earlier: "Sorry, had to bail early. Cleo needed Oscar back at the studio. Something afterparty related. Oscar's sending back the car now."

Rian and Whale descend the stairs of the Dolby Theatre just as their limo pulls up. Rian opens the door, looking back to see Whale standing a few steps back with glazed eyes. "I think I'm just gonna go home," Whale murmurs. "I don't feel very good."

Rian frowns. "I'm sorry, man."

"Go on without me. I'll take a Ridr back."

"You can just tell the guy to drop you off at home."

"No, I'm kinda nauseous," Whale says, only half-lying. "Don't wanna hurl on the leather or anything."

Rian deflates. "Text me when you get home, alright?"

"Give my regards to Oscar."

"I'm sure he'll understand." Rian waits a moment more. Reluctantly steps into the limo.

"Frankie!" Whale blurts.

Rian stands back up, awaiting Whale's words with gentle eyes.

Whale opens his mouth, both lips trembling, voice stuck. He lets out a guttural wheeze and whines the only incriminating words he can bring himself to utter: "I'm so sorry."

"Don't sweat it, buddy. Just get some rest." Rian smiles. Gets back in the limo. Closes the door.

Whale watches the limo drive off with a hard frown. He sticks his hands in his pockets and walks down Hollywood Boulevard.

DREW

Green Light

Drew frowns behind folded hands. Kev rubs his jaw. "How many times?" Kev asks.

Drew hesitates. "The one on Oscar night. A couple more the next day. Another three on Friday, one at breakfast, two after dinner." He swallows. "Oh, and another on Friday night after you left. Almost forgot that one."

Kev nods, his face intense yet receptive.

"Saturday was bad," Drew continues humbly. "About five, I think. Before noon." He shakes his head. "And I got really scared, so I stopped for about four days or so. But then I did another four on Thursday, another six on Friday, and another ten on Saturday."

"Ten lines?"

"Not all at once. Spread throughout the day."

"How does that compare to you before?"

"At Not That Nutty, my worst was about three times that."

"Every day?"

"Every day."

"Jesus." Kev looks at Drew, the shame in his eyes. "You haven't touched any since Saturday, right?"

"Yeah, I can't," Drew murmurs.

Kev nods. "Then this is just something we're gonna have to monitor."

"Yeah."

"Let me know if you need professional help."

"I don't think so." Drew smirks, letting out an airy scoff. "But what do I know? I can't predict shit."

Kev nods, numb.

"I'm sorry," Drew mumbles. "About Theo, I mean. I'm sorry about this too, but..."

"It's okay," Kev says with an encouraging glance. "I understand. I just think Theo's a fucking moron if he thinks you wouldn't be the greatest help to him."

Drew smiles warmly. "That is so sweet, man. Thank you."

Kev shrugs. "Hey, it's the truth."

Drew looks out the window. "I really need to get out of here. Being on Sunset, so close to everything, it's just making everything worse."

Kev awkwardly looks away. "We'll talk about it tomorrow."

"What's wrong with today?"

"It's your birthday, dude."

Drew squints. "What are you planning?"

"Something."

"I knew it."

"It's just a little get together with everyone at the office. It was supposed to be a surprise. I'm sorry for spoiling it."

"Hey," Drew says with a laugh, "I think I've had enough surprises for one year."

Kev chuckles. "It's nothing crazy, I just..." He pauses. "You've had too many bad days lately. I think it's about time you had a really good one."

"Couldn't agree more."

"We're gonna go in about an hour or so." Kev stands up. "I just gotta add a few things to *Ponzi* before we head out."

"Don't tell me any more about tonight."

"Who says I have?" The phone on the desk rings. Kev picks it up. "What's up, Suze?"

Drew stretches his arms, leaning back on Kev's couch. He can hear Suze talking to Kev but not about what.

"No, he's not supposed to come here. I told him to meet us over at..." Kev furrows his brow. "Wait, *who* is it?"

Drew looks up at Kev, a bit tired. He hasn't been getting good sleep in his office.

"Oh my God!" Kev exclaims. "Oh my God. No-no, that's not him, that's someone else. Send him up. Yes! Really! We're waiting for him." Kev hangs up, laughing subtly.

"What was that about?" Drew asks.

"You've got yourself a visitor, my friend."

Drew narrows his eyes. "Is this part of the surprise?"

"No, it's actually not!"

Drew hears footsteps climbing the stairs. "It's not another reporter, is it? Not on my birthday."

"It's not a reporter." Kev opens the office door. "He's all yours."

"Thank you," an older man responds, walking in as Kev walks out.

Drew stands with a huff. Then nothing. No breath. No thought. He can't hear anything, not even Kev closing the door. All he feels is his pounding heart and a sharp sensation clawing up his arms.

Stewie stands there with a suitcase, smiling back with a hint of sadness. "Ayy bee."

Drew's entire body shakes. His lips quiver. His face tightens. He feels the foreign sensation of cold moisture soaking into his dried-out veins, once barren tear ducts suddenly alive and free-flowing. He's actually crying on his feet, a grown man with tears streaming down, pathetically yet shamelessly. Stewie drops his bag. Rushes over to Drew. Holds him tight. Drew hugs back too, trying to talk but too pent-up to speak. He buries his head in Stewie's breast, tears and snot soaking in.

"It's okay," Stewie whispers, placing a hand on the back of Drew's head. "It's okay. I'm here."

Drew sobs harder, his echoes absorbed by Stewie's soft chest, still quite a lot of muscle for a man in his seventies. "I'm sorry," Drew whines. "I'm so sorry."

Stewie shushes, petting Drew's hair. "It's okay. Let it out. Let it out."

Drew's lungs cough, his throat wailing as hard as he can into Stewie Hanz. He's real. He's really here. He's really holding him again.

Kev pops in a half-hour later with two ice-cold bottles of water, Stewie and Drew still sitting on the sofa in happy, eager conversation. "Thought you guys could use these," Kev says.

"That's so nice of you," Stewie says, grabbing a bottle. "Thank you."

"I'm sorry about hogging your office," Drew says. "We can move."

"I'll just use your computer," Kev says with a dismissive wave. "I know your password."

"Don't delete anything while you're in there."

Kev sighs with a grin. "Memories."

"You wanna join us, Kev?" Stewie asks.

"Nah, you catch up." Kev smiles. Leaves them be.

Stewie cracks open his water. "I like him."

"You two really didn't plan this?" Drew asks.

"No, I just came out here for your birthday. I didn't actually think you were gonna be here. I just knew you worked here. I'm glad I caught you before you went back to your hotel or wherever it is you're staying now."

"I've been staying here," Drew says, thumbing behind him. "I got a bed in my office. Some food. Movies. Books. It's been alright. Not the same, obviously."

"I take it your boss is fine with all that?"

"Kev? No, he's not my boss, he's my partner."

Stewie nods. "Oh."

"My business partner. I don't have a boyfriend."

Stewie hesitates. "This is *your* company?"

"Kev and I founded it together."

"I guess I never really thought of it like that."

"How's business with you?" Drew takes a gulp of water.

"Smalltown? Great. Everything's great."

"Still running itself?"

"For the most part."

"How did the transition from New Jersey worked out?"

"Actually, I decided to keep the Jersey side of the business after all."

Drew raises his brows. "You're doing both?"

"Physical Therapy down there, Personal Training up in Mass."

"It's still called Smalltown Trainers?"

"We changed the name to Smalltown Health & Fitness actually."

"That's a mouthful."

"You should see our email address."

"So moving up to Boston wasn't a waste of time?"

Stewie smiles. "Of course it wasn't."

"Besides me."

"If I was just doing Physical Therapy in Jersey, it would've been really bad. There was a bit of a nasty hiring drought after COVID ended."

"Why?"

"There just weren't enough Physical Therapists. The Personal Training in Mass helped a lot income-wise."

"That's great." Drew looks down a bit. "I was in Boston a few years ago." Eyes slowly back up.

Stewie stares. "When?"

"Four summers ago, right after I turned thirty-nine. Pride was on June 11, so I stopped into the Black Bear to look for you."

"I didn't know that," Stewie murmurs. "I don't really go into Boston anymore."

"You're not still in that brownstone apartment?"

"I bought a house right after you left."

Drew gapes. "Oh my God! That's great!"

"Within a year, actually."

"Where?"

"Danvers."

Drew's brow furrows. "Where's that in relation to Boston?"

"Twenty-five miles north. It's really nice. Big yard. Used to be bank owned. Got a really good deal on it."

"That explains it then." Drew takes a deep breath. "So does...?" He hesitates. "Does anybody know you're here? With me?"

Stewie's face softens. "What do you mean?"

"Are you with someone?" Drew reluctantly asks.

Stewie nods. "Yeah," he says sadly.

Drew feels faint. "Okay. Cool."

Stewie takes a deep breath.

Drew scratches the back of his head. "What's his name?"

Stewie furrows his brow. "His name?"

"Yeah."

"Don't you know your own name?" Stewie laughs childishly, high pitch giggles.

"What?"

"Of course I'm with *someone*! I'm sitting with you, aren't I?"

Drew slaps Stewie's shoulder. "You jerk!"

"I knew what you meant!" Stewie teases. "Silly Beatle."

Drew props his head with a hand. "I can't believe you're actually here. I was so worried you moved or found someone else."

"Why would I? You're my Baby Boy."

"Hate to break it to you, Daddy, but I'm forty-three now."

"I don't care. You'll always be Baby Boy."

"I'm not even Jacob Andrezj anymore."

Stewie nods, suddenly remembering. "Oh yes. I have to get used to calling you Drew."

"You can call me Jacob."

"You sure?"

Drew takes Stewie's hand. "Of course I'm sure."

Stewie caresses Drew's cheeks. "You really look better than ever."

"You look pretty darn good yourself. Jeez."

"I certainly don't pass for thirty-nine anymore."

"Only around the eyes. You're still freaking hot for seventy-four."

"God, don't remind me!"

"How long did it take you to find out I changed my name?"

"I saw the trailer for *Onio* during a Met game. That's your novella, right? Your Senior Project at Eagle Ridge?"

"I'm surprised you remembered all that."

"Of course I remembered. Ohio with an N."

Drew smiles. "Did you see it?"

"I did," Stewie says with a proud nod. "I've seen everything you made. A lot of it really wasn't my thing if I'm being honest."

"Wasn't mine either, believe me."

"Except for *Branson*."

"You liked it, huh?"

"It was FANTASTIC," Stewie says with slow emphasis.

"Even though it's a musical?"

"It's a Pet Shop Boys musical. What's not to love?"

Drew beams. "I got you watching movies. You."

"I still haven't seen *Atomic* though," Stewie adds regrettably. "I just keep putting it off. I'll get around to it one of these days."

"Don't bother, I didn't write it."

"You didn't?"

"Nope."

Stewie shrugs. "Alright. Forget it then."

Drew bursts out laughing.

"What?" Stewie asks, amused. "What's so funny?"

Drew wipes his eyes. "It is such a long story. You'll hate me by the end of it."

Stewie smiles. "I could never hate you."

Drew's eyes droop. He melts in his seat.

KNOCK-KNOCK. Kev pokes his head in. "All set. Ready to go, Birthday Boy?"

"Is it okay if we take Stewie along?" Drew asks meekly, standing up.

Kev scoffs. "What do you mean 'is it okay?' I've already phoned it in. Of course he's coming."

Drew and Stewie slide into the back of a limo. "Where are we going?" Stewie asks.

"I have absolutely no idea," Drew responds.

"Is Kev coming too?"

"In his own car, apparently."

"Was this always the plan, you taking a limo by yourself?"

"I don't know what the plan is." Drew pauses. "Probably not. He probably just wants us to have alone time."

Stewie looks out the window. All those palm trees going by. The Hollywood Sign. Blue sky. Grauman's Chinese Theatre. "This really is amazing." He looks at Drew. "You live here, Baby Boy."

"I know." Drew takes Stewie's hand. "This is already the best birthday ever."

Stewie smiles.

Drew kisses the back of Stewie's hand. Grins widely. "What did you get me, Daddy?"

"You'll see!" Stewie teases.

"You're not gonna tell me now?"

"Not until after dinner."

Drew stares into Stewie's beautiful eyes, nice cool pools he could swim in. Stewie stares into Drew's. Drew leans in and they kiss, soft and sweet. "This really wasn't part of the plan?" Drew asks.

"I really had no idea."

"I can't believe it, you showing up at the exact same time."

"I can't believe it either."

Drew rests his cheek against Stewie's shirt. "It's just so perfect."

"Yes, you are." Stewie kisses Drew on the forehead.

Kev waits outside the limo. Drew climbs out, followed by Stewie. He recognizes the building they're standing in front of. A chill runs through Drew's body.

His Marina Del Rey condo covered in tarps flapping in the breeze. No cars in the garage. No people mulling about. Evacuated due to reconstruction. It's so quiet.

Stewie frowns. Puts an arm around Drew.

"California homeowner's insurance doesn't cover much when it comes to fires," Kev says solemnly. "Lots of Jewish lightning in LA, apparently. But the one thing it does cover is terrorism." He looks up at the condo. "In a few weeks, it'll be just like it was before."

"It'll never be like it was before," Drew murmurs.

"I know." Kev sighs. "It was supposed to be done by now. We were planning a dinner party up there and everything."

"I'm not shocked." Drew half-smiles at Kev. "Thanks anyway."

Kev furrows his brow. "For what?"

"For the surprise."

Kev takes Drew by the shoulder. "That's not the surprise." He turns Drew around.

"SURPRISE!!!" screams a crowd of four hundred people standing on the beach. They break into a mass of cheers and rapturous applause. Everyone's there. Tanner Hennessy, Greg Stolliday, Gary Green, Thelma Lemmon, Suze the secretary, Samantha Maycock, Trent Bower, and every other employee at Ephemeral Pictures, as well as Eli Kerbinger, Fergus Connaughton, Jay Blackwell, Martin Kennergan, Marcel Innalls, Bernadette Brewster, Odessa Dykes, Monte Ryans, Prince McAllister, Addison Ryder, and the rest of the cast and crew of *The Sins of Jack Branson*.

Drew looks at Kev and that shit-eating grin on his face. "Just a little get together, huh?" Drew teases.

Kev shrugs.

Stewie's completely shocked, his mouth hanging open, brows put together. He's never had stage fright, but he assumes this is pretty close. But Drew's not fazed at all. He's grinning wide. He's running in. Shaking hands. High-fiving. Cracking inside jokes. He knows all of them. He's dragging Stewie along and suddenly he's shaking hands too. They're all thanking Drew for passionately defending their nominations and careers and whatnot. And Drew's going one by one and introducing Stewie to every single one of them. Stewie can't remember the last time he's been around this many people, let alone with all eyes directly on him.

Down the beach are three gigantic family-style tables in parallel with the ocean completely decked out with gold-painted branches and berries. At the end of the middle table is a beautiful golden throne. As the mass of people make their way across the sand toward their assigned seats, Drew and Stewie coming up from the rear (giggity!), Kev splits off and races back to the parking garage. Drew turns his head and recognizes the man getting out of the Ridr that just pulled up. "No way!" he cries taking Stewie's hand and leading him back to the concrete.

Kev helps Terrance Donahue out of the car. "Sorry I'm late," Terrance says. "Damn traffic sucks ass in this town."

Kev smiles at Drew. "Look who's here."

"I don't understand," Drew says with a confused smile, hand-in-hand with Stewie.

"I don't blame you." Terrance looks Drew in the eye. "Forgive me for that voicemail. I didn't mean to say such horrible things."

"Don't worry, I never actually listened it."

"I did," Kev says on his way back to the beach. "He ain't kidding."

Terrance shoos Kev off. "If you don't mind," he tells Drew, "I'd very much prefer you never listening to it."

"I won't." Drew remembers Stewie standing next to him. "Oh, Stewie, this is Terrance Donahue. He's the president of the Jack Branson Society in New York."

"Oh!" Stewie eagerly shakes Terrance's hand. "I didn't know he had a Society. I'd very much like to see it."

Terrance smiles. "My door is always open, Mr…?"

"Hanz."

"Terrance, this is Stewie Hanz." Drew puts a hand on Stewie's shoulder. "The best thing that ever happened to me." That hits Stewie harder than he thought it would. He smiles, moved beyond words.

"I can see that," Terrance says proudly.

Drew beams. Hugs Stewie tightly.

Terrance puts a hand on Drew's shoulder. "Drew, what you did on that show..." He scoffs. "Jack would've been so proud of you."

Drew nods. "Thank you, Terrance. I can't tell you how much that means to me."

"I know it does."

"I just feel like shit for how I've repaid you."

"*Please*," Terrance whines. "If there's one thing the President of the Jack Branson Society knows more than anything, there's no such thing as bad publicity." He raises a stern finger. "Just stop fucking kids!"

"I don't!"

Terrance claps Drew's shoulder with a teasing grin. Walks on without them.

Stewie half-frowns at Drew. "He wasn't actually sixteen, was he?"

"He was," Drew murmurs.

"You didn't know, right?"

"Of course I didn't know." Drew hesitates. "Why? Is it still bothering you?"

"Let's just not talk about it."

"Okay." Drew and Stewie walk back onto the beach, feet pressing loose sand, the sun setting over the Pacific. "Can I ask you something?" Drew asks.

"Anything."

Drew hesitates. All this talk of voicemails unheard got him thinking about that Schrödinger's cat scenario he put himself in all those years ago. Was it Stewie's number after all? Was he really calling Drew back that day? Did Stewie ever listen to that lie of a voicemail, the one that started it all?

"What?" Stewie asks.

Drew shakes his head with a smile. "Doesn't matter." He puts his arm around Stewie as they walk back to the beach banquet.

WHALE

Judas

Rian angrily paces his Chinatown apartment, phone to his ear. On a TV tray rests his laptop, a *Variety* email still onscreen:

"Paramount to Distribute Cold War Biopic 'Atomic' from Oscar-Nominated 'Surgery' Team's Not That Nut Pictures (EXCLUSIVE)"

"Goddammit!" Rian mutters, hanging up. Swipes to his favorites. Tries Whale again. Instant voicemail. BEEP. "Jacob, what the fuck is going on?!" Rian yells into the phone. "Pick up the fucking phone! Why is Paramount giving me the reach around?! Call me back, you son of a bitch!" Rian hangs up. Dials Paramount again.

"Serge Lamoule's office," a female voice answers.

"It's Rian Hoffman again. I *really* need to speak to Mr. Lamoule."

"Please hold."

"Don't you put me on hold! I..." Rian squeezes the bridge of his nose. "I really need to talk to someone. Can't you just bring the phone to him?"

"Mr. Lamoule's in a very important meeting at the moment," The Secretary answers, the same secretary The Professor had at The Factory. "I still have your message from before. I'll give it to him when he's finished."

"No, I'll just come in. Where's your office located?"

"Sir, you can't—"

"I know! I just..." Rian's face contorts, emotion creeping its way in. "I just wanna know what's going on," he whimpers.

"I'm sorry," The Secretary says softly. "I don't know how to help you here."

"You know that studio you're doing *Atomic* with, Not That Nut Pictures? I just need their phone number. I can't reach them on their cell phones."

"I'm not allowed to give out that information."

"It was supposed to be my deal!" Rian shouts, his voice straining. "I'm getting fucking Shanghaied here! I need to speak to Jacob Andrezj immediately! Please!"

The Secretary sighs with reluctance. "Just give me a second. I'll look it up."

Rian closes his eyes. "Thank you. Thank you thank you thank you."

Nine miles away, a desk phone rings in a Sunset Boulevard production office. Larry picks up the receiver. "Not That Nut Pictures."

"Put him on, Lar."

Larry's heart skips a beat. "Mr. Hoffman."

"Put him on right fucking now."

Larry licks his dry mouth. "Mr. Andrezj is in a meeting at the moment."

"The day after the Oscars? Bullshit. I know he's there. Hand him the phone."

"I'm serious, Rian." Larry matches eyes with Whale sitting behind the desk. "He's in the conference room right now in an important meeting."

"Really? With who?"

Whale mouths *Serge*.

"Mr. Lamoule," Larry says.

Rian hesitates. "Serge Lamoule?"

"Yeah."

Whale motions a phone next to his face, mouths *Call Back*.

"He'll call you back as soon as he's done," Larry tells Rian. "I promise."

Whale holds up an OK sign.

Rian sighs. "Good. As soon as he can."

"Of course. Bye bye." Larry hangs up.

"Block him," Whale orders.

Larry nods. Taps the office phone's touchscreen and blocks Rian's cell. Whale watches with an uneasy frown.

Cashew walks into the office with a preppy young man. "And this is Jacob's office." Cashew smiles at Larry and Whale. "Guys, this is Alan Lovelace, my new personal assistant."

"Hey everyone!" Alan greets with a nervous wave.

"Welcome aboard," Larry says. Whale contributes a distracted nod.

"Eeyore over there is Jacob," Cashew mumbles dismissively. "Who was that on the phone?"

"Rian Hoffman," Larry murmurs.

"Who's Rian Hoffman?" Alan asks.

"Nobody," Cashew answers proudly. "He's nobody."

Whale stares into space, morose.

"How did he know what number to call, I wonder," Larry muses.

"He must've gotten it from Lamoule's secretary," Cashew says.

"You don't know that," Whale mutters.

Cashew stares at Whale. "Considering the only people that know your extension exists are Míng and Serge, and since Rian doesn't know Míng and I was just on the phone with Serge, I think *yeah*, I do know that."

Whale looks away.

Cashew rolls his eyes. Looks at Alan. "Call Serge back."

"Just forget it," Whale says. "He probably just persuaded her or nagged her to death or something."

Cashew looks at Whale pointedly. "You don't know that."

Whale's face tightens.

Cashew opens his mouth. Thinks. "Fine. I'll drop it."

"You promise?"

Cashew hesitates. "Yeah. Whatever." He leads Alan out of Whale's office. Closes the door. "Alright, first order of business, call Serge back and tell him to fire that bitch."

Alan's eyes drift back toward Whale's office.

"You're *my* guy," Cashew emphasizes, pointing at himself. "Okay? Remember that."

Alan nods reluctantly. "Alright."

"Good lad." Cashew playfully smacks Alan in the tricep.

BANG! Alan and Cashew flinch, whipping their heads toward Reception. "What the FUCK was that?!" Alan cries.

Cashew can hear muffled voices. Raised voices. One far cattier than the other. "Change of plans," Cashew murmurs pseudo-calmly. "Call security, *then* call Serge."

"Got it." Alan dashes down the hall to Cashew's office.

Cashew races back into Whale's office and shuts the door. "Oscar's in the build-ing!" he sings.

Larry jumps to his feet. "I'll get security."

"Alan's already on that."

"You can't go in there!" a muffled voice cries from behind the door. Whale tenses in his seat.

The door whips open. Oscar bursts in the room, eyes blazing with fury, quite an intimidating presence for a man in a white leotard covered in neon feathers on tiny hooks. "You fuckers! You goddamned motherfucking cocksucking cuntsuckers! Burn in Hell, you curs! Burn in fucking Hell!"

Whale slouches in his chair, scared to death.

A cross woman in her forties with long brown hair walks in behind Oscar. "I'm sorry, Mr. Andrezj. He just stormed in."

"It's okay, Doris," Cashew interjects. "We'll take it from here." Doris nods. Returns to Reception.

"How'd you do it?" Oscar snarls. "It was the chinky guard, wasn't it?"

Cashew awkwardly looks at Larry. "Gives us a moment, won't you Larry?"

Larry nods and walks out. "Get the door," Whale mumbles after him. Larry frowns sympathetically at his boss. Shuts the door.

Cashew sighs calmly. "What can I do you for, Oscar?"

"You fucking asshole!" Oscar growls, pointing a finger at Cashew. "You can't do this to me! That was my screenplay! My grandfather!"

"I have no idea what you're talking about."

"You really think you can just steal from me and get away with it?" Oscar cackles. "NEWSFLASH, RETARDS, I *OWN* THE POLICE! I AM THE COURTS! I AM THE JURIES! I'M THE CEO OF PUBLIC FUCKING OPINION IN THIS TOWN! YOU THINK YOU'VE WON, BITCHES?! *OHHH NOOO*! I'LL MANUFACTURE AN OUTRAGE SO COLOSSAL, YOU'LL BE BEGGING ON THE STREET BY DINNERTIME! I CAN GET AN ANGRY MOB DOWN HERE IN THIRTY MINUTES THAT'LL RAPE YOUR HOLES SO WIDE THAT TOURISTS WILL THINK IT'S THE SAN ANDREAS FUCKING FAULT! PEGGY ENTWISTLE WANNABES CAN TO SWAN DIVE INTO YOUR GODDAMNED *COLORECTAL TRACT!*"

Whale grips his armrests. He's never seen Oscar so deranged.

Cashew crosses his arms. "You finished?"

"OH, I'M JUST GETTING STARTED, YOU BEAST!"

"I don't know what it is you think we did, but if it's regarding *Atomic*, that has nothing to do with you."

"You stole it from me!"

"I don't know how you could say that. Jacob's had that screenplay for years."

Oscar laughs hard. "Oh please!"

"He wrote it Senior Year of high school about a hometown hero of his."

Whale freezes. "What?"

"Clark Hauser *was* from Phoenixville, wasn't he?" Cashew asks Oscar.

Oscar grimaces hard.

Whale's lips flutter with confusion.

"He found a copy of his book in a local bookstore," Cashew lies with complete confidence. "It's public domain. How exactly could he have stolen it?"

Oscar's face goes blank from shock. "How did you…?"

"If you *did* write a script yourself, I'm sure it's not the same one. Unless you could prove that, but… I guess you can't." Cashew smiles. "Are we really worth breaking that 'no speculation' streak of yours?"

The door bursts open. A big black man with a security polo storms in. "You called, Boss?" he asks in deep baritone.

"Yes, Bubba. Perfect timing." Cashew points to Oscar. "Hold him back."

Bubba grabs Oscar's arms one at a time, pulling them back and locking his shoulders. "Get the fuck off me!" Oscar snaps.

"Theo, what are you doing?" Whale cries.

Cashew reaches for the collar of Oscar's leotard. "Don't you fucking touch me!" Oscar snaps, kicking at Cashew. Bubba pulls Oscar's arms further apart, making Oscar cry in pain.

"THEO!" Whale shouts.

Cashew grabs Oscar by the collar and rips open his leotard, revealing a running tape recorder duct taped to his pale flabby chest. Whale gapes. Cashew laughs. "I fucking knew it!" He grips the recorder and slowly peels it off of Oscar, tearing up hair and bits of skin.

Oscar screams bloody murder.

Cashew finally rips the band aid off with a twisted smile. Throws the recorder on the ground. Stomp it to bits. "WHAT DID YOU THINK WAS GONNA HAPPEN?!" Cashew taunts, completely unhinged. "YOU REALLY THINK WE'RE THAT STUPID?! DON'T YOU KNOW WHO YOU'RE DEALING WITH?!" Cashew snaps his fingers.

Bubba throws Oscar on the ground. Cashew curb-stomps Oscar in the back. Oscar yelps.

"Oh my God, stop!" Whale cries desperately.

"Wearing a wire?" Cashew taunts down at Oscar. "How pathetic!" He kicks Oscar in the side. "You're so stupid, aren't you?!" Kick. "Stupid!" Kick. "STUPID!"

"CUT IT OUT!" Whale screams.

"I'll call Paramount," Oscar threatens, lifting his head off the floor. "I'll tell 'em everything. Serge doesn't deal with dirty shit. You'll be on your fucking ass in no time."

"Good luck getting to him now he's got no secretary," Cashew says.

Whale's lungs evaporate. "What?"

"We've got Míng's finest lawyers on our side," Cashew continues. "One word from you and we'll take everything. Your show. Your pretty mansion. And for what? An old script collecting dust on your hard drive? In the grand scheme of things, are we really worth it?"

Oscar chuckles. "A digital file can't collect dust on a hard drive, Cashew."

"IT'S A METAPHOR, ASSHOLE!" Cashew screams. Kicks Oscar in the gut, knocking the wind out of him.

"C'MON!" Whale cries.

Cashew admires Oscar Blitz curled up on the floor, shriveling like a sponge. Hocks a loogie. Spits on Oscar's face. "I'd piss on you if you wouldn't enjoy it so much." Cashew grabs a paper cup from Whale's water dispenser. "Throw him to the fucking curb," he tells Bubba.

"Don't fucking touch me," Oscar croaks, smacking Bubba's hand away. He props his arms up. Stands on his own two feet, panting heavily. "I refuse to be thrown out." Oscar looks at Whale. Shrugs. "Have you nothing to say for yourself?"

Whale tightens his lips, only making them tremble more.

Oscar sighs with a lamentful frown. He wanders into the hall. Bubba follows, closing the door behind him.

Whale stands. "What the fuck is wrong with you?!" he shouts at Cashew, on the verge of tears. "Why would you do that?!"

"Why the fuck not?" Cashew retorts. He pours himself a cup. Gulps it down.

Whale looks down at the crushed tape recorder. The office phone on his desk. Cashew's totally unfazed and remorseless posture. A sharp pain stings him in the gut. He collapses onto the chair. "What did just we do?" he whispers.

"I'll tell you what we did." Cashew crumples the paper cup. "We grew up." He tosses the paper ball on the floor. Blows out of Whale's office.

Many hours later, Whale cracks open Míng's Welcome Aboard present, a 30-pack case of 15yr Domergue. Pours a generous helping. Sips his Scotch in silence, staring out at that nighttime view of Downtown LA.

A soft knock behind him. "I'm heading out now," Cashew says softly. "You coming?"

Whale doesn't rotate his chair. Simply glances at Cashew's distorted reflection. "I'm gonna stick around if that's okay. I'll lock up."

Cashew stands at the threshold of Whale's office a bit more. "Let's go to Brique and celebrate."

"No." Whale sips some more.

Cashew sighs. "*The Whole Bloody Affair*'s back at the New Beverley tonight. Wanna go see it?

Whale doesn't say anything. Just looks off.

Cashew deflates. He takes a step into the hallway.

"I was thinking about Oscar earlier," Whale says.

Cashew awkwardly leans against the doorframe. "Oh?"

"And Frankie." Whale pauses. "*Rian*, I mean."

"What about?"

Whale sips a big swig. "That program Míng used on Oscar's laptop…"

"The Claw Machine.

"Yeah. He got it off the Dark Web, right?"

"Probably."

"You think he can get us something we can use to prevent Rian and Oscar from contacting us, even after we blocked them?"

Cashew thinks. "I can ask." He pauses. "That's a good idea."

Whale frowns. Sips some more.

"Oh, hey!" Cashew says with forced cheer. "Larry told me you picked out a new name."

"I sent out my application just after Oscar left."

"What'd you settle on?"

Whale raises the glass with unfocused eyes. "Drew."

"Drew?"

"Andrezj is the Polish form of Andrew. Drew sounds snappier. No nicknames."

Cashew hesitates. "I thought you hated Andrezj."

Whale grabs the Domergue bottle. Refills his glass.

Cashew licks his lips. "Drew what?"

Whale grabs the glass with two hands. "Lawrence," he whispers.

"*Lawrence*?" Cashew parrots with a cringe. "Why the hell did you pick that?"

Whale licks Scotch off his lips, his brain getting fuzzier by the second. "Inside joke."

"Inside joke with who?"

Whale keeps drinking. Anything to feel numb.

"You know what, fuck you. Why do I even bother?" Cashew storms off. Slams the hallway light off. Leaves the office.

Whale doesn't budge. Just sits in the dark, mind wandering off, unfocused eyes blurring the Downtown Los Angeles skyline as he slowly fades to black.

DREW

Quid Pro Quo

Theo stares out his office window at Downton Los Angeles "Everyone's so agreeable and understanding now. Maybe it's just fear keeping it all together, but that doesn't make it any less real. This is real. This is the real LA. We've all done bad shit. We know where the line is. How unrealistic American legal standards and Judeo-Christian morals are. That's why this city is the greatest nation in the world." Theo pauses for effect. "But the outside world doesn't understand that. To the customers, this is the City of Angels. It's La La Land. A world of sunshine. Where dreams come true. Every so often, we have to play naive. Everyone gets all self-conscious. So they pick their worst, the one whose demise they'd profit most from, and they all turn into black-and-white lunatics. You can't stop it once it's started. You can't see when it's coming. When it's someone else, you'd do anything to be there at the kill. But when it's your turn?" Theo shakes his head, scanning the little ant cars for little ant backstabbers inside. "You'll never know until it's too late. So you gotta cover your bases while you still can, Frankie." Theo turns around to face the man with a bald spot and five o'clock shadow. "How else can a man get any sleep in this town?"

Frankie raises a brow, his eyes bloodshot from a botched LASIK even cheaper than Drew's. "You're calling me Frankie now?"

"Of course." Theo paces toward Frankie's chair. "Drew seems humbled now, sure, but you know just as well as I do how he can get when he's properly motivated. He's already got a traitor on his side, Kev Foster. We used to call him Peabrain back at The Factory. He hates my guts just as much as you do."

"I doubt that very much."

"But I never hated you, Frankie. I think it's very unfair that you keep thinking of me how I used to be. An older version, a weaker version I'd very much like to forget. You had a bit of a problem with that yourself, didn't you? Drew told me about that fight you had that time at Peet's Coffee. How terrible that must've been for you, him misremembering the past like that, bringing it up just to hurt you, not even allowing you a chance to redeem yourself."

Frankie crosses his arms.

Theo sighs. "I was always against what Drew did to you. You know how he is. When he wants something, he gets it. He wanted poor Oscar's screenplay, so he took it. Passed it off as his own. Threw you out of the deal. That must've stung, huh? Getting bumped for script he didn't even write?"

"I don't believe you."

"I tried to stop him, Frankie. I really did. The moment he told me what he was going to do, I tried to talk him out of it, but he threatened to cut me out of the deal. I couldn't allow that. I'm sorry I was forced into complacency at your detriment, but I had no choice. I was legitimately afraid of him."

"Bullshit!" Frankie cries. "There's no way he plagiarized *Atomic*."

"It's true."

"Don't waste your breath, Cashew. I'm not falling for the same manipulations Jacob did."

"I never manipulated him, Frankie. I didn't even know what happened between you two back at Whitman. He didn't tell me until much later. What happened at Peet's Coffee, that was all him."

"Really?" Frankie challenges. "You don't think I know what's going on here? You call me up out of the blue for the first time in eighteen years and I'm supposed to believe you've had a change of heart? You want Jacob dead. The only reason you need me to do it is because you're too pathetic to do it yourself."

"That is not true, Frankie," Theo lies effortlessly. "The reason it took eighteen years was because Drew had his thumb over me. Now thanks to his hubris, the pendulum has swung the other way and I can finally get out from under him and stand up for myself."

"I hate the way you're talking right now. Pick an idiom and stick with it."

"If I come at him, he'll see me coming. He's already tried to muscle his way back into my company."

"Why would he want to come back here?"

"Because doing so would pardon him. Or at least he'd be in a better position to make me pardon him. But I refused. It's only a matter of time before Drew comes at me first. I'm not gonna let that happen, Frankie. It's him or me. I'm not letting it be me."

"Why would I possibly want to interfere with that?"

Theo fakes shame. "I was always jealous of you, Frankie. That's why I was so angry at you. So mean to you."

Frankie softens. He's actually serious.

Theo returns to the window. Stares out of it. "Larry's no longer with us."

"Really?" Frankie looks out the office window behind him. "That's too bad. I kinda wanted to see him again."

"You will," Theo says enigmatically. "Soon. Ideally."

"I always liked him."

"Wish I could say the same," Theo mumbles. "He and his family went on a little trip together. Very last minute. Very inconvenient."

"Inconvenient how?"

"He's left me with a vacancy." Theo turns back to Frankie. "Head of Production is an incredibly important role in my company. I cannot have someone in that position I can't trust. If you do this for me, I'll know I can trust you."

"What do you mean?"

"Do what I ask and I will make you Head of Production."

Frankie furrows his brow. "You're not serious."

"I'm absolutely serious," Theo says with unblinking eyes. "That's the one thing Drew never did for you. Ephemeral's whole concept was your idea. Making *Jack Branson* an animated musical was your idea. He's plagiarized you twice now. You really think stealing *Atomic* is so out of character for him? Ask him yourself."

Frankie hesitates. "I will."

"I can only imagine how these last two decades have been for you. Waiting for an answer. For a call. For an apology. No friends. No contacts. Just every day in a shitty little apartment, your golden days of productivity fading away little by little. You felt shame being unemployed at first, but then you got used to it, didn't you? And then you realized you got used to it, which isn't the same thing, is it? That came much later, when it was already too late to do anything about it. It just compounds, more and more, that shame, that pressure. And it just paralyzes you into that chair, those stains on your shirt, your youth fading away each year, all that energy.

Frankie zones out, his face growing heavier, the pain cracking through.

"You even think you look like your father once in a while," Theo continues, "when that beard gets a little too long. But you don't want to tell him what's been going on. You were at the fucking Oscars. Your whole family suddenly saw the artist in you they never saw before, the one their faith actively suppressed, but it's been twenty years and *bupkis*, eh *meshugganah*?"

Frankie frowns, his eyes drooping.

"But that didn't happen to Drew, did it?" Theo murmurs. "He never slowed down. Never stopped getting richer. More successful. But now he's burnt out. He's nothing. You're the man on top, the one that conserved his energy. You're the one that's gonna get rewarded for his patience. You'll never have to apply for a job ever again. It's already here, waiting for you."

Frankie looks to the floor. "I don't want to kill anybody," he whispers.

"Why not? We used to kill people all the time. It's called survival."

"It's just the principle of it, is all."

Theo stares Frankie down. "What are you afraid of?"

"Nothing. It's just a silly old rule."

"There are no rules, Frankie. No one's gonna reward you for following rules. No one will punish you for breaking rules. There is no God. No eternal damnation. Just boring people getting shit done. I think it's very important for us to grow the fuck up and just admit it already."

Frankie frowns. "Maybe I don't want to see it. Just cause I eat burgers doesn't mean I wanna watch a cow get slaughtered, you know?"

"I already thought of that." Theo sits behind his desk. "My man already has the stuff on hand. If he puts it in a bottle of Domergue, it'll pass a toxicology check. It's potent too. A splash on the tongue is all takes. One sip and he's a dead man. Ask to use the bathroom. Wait ten minutes and leave. It'll already be done."

Frankie rubs his jaw. "Will it hurt?"

Theo blinks, studying his tone. "No," he lies. "He won't even feel a thing."

Frankie nods with relief.

"Do we have a deal?" Theo holds out his hand.

Frankie looks at Theo's palm. No sweat. He matches eyes. "Can I pick the year?"

"Of the Domergue?"

"Make it a 22 and I'll do it."

"Do you have any idea how expensive that is?!" Theo cries, taking his hand back. "You're not drinking it, you know. We're poisoning every drop."

"Don't pretend you can't afford it." Frankie pauses. "He'll more likely to drink it without question, won't he? That alone makes it worth the investment."

Theo stares.

"The way I see it," Frankie says, holding out his hand, "why take the chance?"

Theo hesitates. "Will you do it if it's a 22?"

"Absolutely."

Theo takes Frankie's hand and shakes it. "Get it done by Friday and you can start on Monday." They stand. Theo escorts Frankie to the door. "My guy will drop the package off at your place as soon as it comes in."

"Can I ask you something?" Frankie asks, stopping at the threshold.

Theo hesitates. "Anything."

"If your father were here right now, what would he think of you?" Frankie asks knowingly. "What you're doing? Calvin Landreth, the pride of Joseph, the great businessman everyone loved, especially you. He'd never let personal shit interfere with anything, would he?"

Theo doesn't talk.

Frankie cracks a smirk.

Theo blinks calmly. "My father died a pathetic man on an empire of dirt. I can buy what he took his whole life to achieve and it'll be nothing more to me than lunch money."

Frankie's smile fades. He slowly walks on. Theo watches him go with a studious gaze.

During lunch with Hector, Theo sits at his desk and stares off. "That guy earlier," Hector says in between lo mien slurps. "Ree-an Hoffman?"

"Rian," Theo corrects, distracted.

"Rian, right." Hector wipes his mouth. "Him coming in and all, does that mean I'm taking him off the Black List?"

"You don't take anyone off the Black List unless I say so," Theo scolds with alarming clarity. "You understand me?"

Hector nods. "Of course."

Theo returns to that mental zone. Where was he? Ugh, he's gonna have to start over. Larry and the Lins are gone. Drew on Friday. Frankie after that. Then what? Alan? He's definitely gotta kill Alan. And Suyin cause she knows too much. Sooner or later he's gonna have to kill Míng's friend for getting the poison in the first place, and Míng before he kills him first, and Oscar too while he's at it, and all those guys he used to work with like Harry and Pete and Cleo and Leon and Peabrain and The Professor and that Secretary of his and Carlos and all his guys and all those traitors who talked like Gerry Apple and Damon Muller and Janet Gower and Harold Drayton and Shayne Parker and Gordy Benson and CJ Marrow and Cazden Montgomery and Ken Gold for going overbudget that time and Hector just to be safe and…

JACOB

The Graduate

Pacific seafoam flutters through the air, shimmering like glitter. Seagulls cry overhead. Cheap flip flops clip-clop along the Santa Monica pier and stop at the wooden railing. Jacob frowns at the ocean waves, an unopened bottle of water in his hand. Stewie sidles up and holds him from behind. He feels Jacob's fantastic biceps, getting bigger and bigger every month, his skin warm from the California sun.

STEWIE
What's wrong?

JACOB
Just thinking.

STEWIE
The place didn't seem so bad. Good neighborhood.

Jacob nods.

STEWIE (CONT'D)
And the guy... What's his name?

JACOB
Alex.

STEWIE
Yeah. He's not so bad either. By Craigslist standards at least.

JACOB
He went to Yale.

STEWIE
Which finally explains why the rent is so low. He obviously doesn't need the money.

JACOB
He's probably just lonely.
(pause)
He was watching Wolf of Wall Street. Good to know he's got good taste.

Stewie smiles. Sun on his face. Ocean waves nearby. Jacob turns around, his butt pressed against the railing. All those California tourists mulling about. People on bikes. Ripped guys and big bosomed babes.

JACOB (CONT'D)
If I don't get the job, that's it for me. I've got nothing else.

Jacob takes a deep breath.

JACOB (CONT'D)
Jeez, I don't even want to say it.

Stewie waits patiently.

JACOB (CONT'D)
I know myself. The only way this is going to work is if it's the only thing in my life. If I know I can

```
just come back and be with you, I'm gonna end up
taking the dive.
          (pause)
I can't fail, Daddy. I can't. I'll regret it for the
rest of my life.
```

Stewie frowns.

```
                    STEWIE
You don't want to come back?

                    JACOB
If I have a cop-out, no matter how small, I'm gonna
end up using it.
          (pause)
Chekhov's cop-out.

                    STEWIE
I don't know what that means.
```

Jacob screws open the disposable water bottle.

```
                    JACOB
It's a writer thing.
```

Jacob downs the water, gulping the entire thing without stopping. Stewie watches uneasily.

```
                    STEWIE
So you're saying... when you get on that plane, it's
over?

                    JACOB
It has to be.
```

Jacob screws the top back onto the empty bottle.

```
                    JACOB (CONT'D)
No calling or texting either. I'm only gonna thank
myself later.
```

Stewie lets out a soft sigh.

```
                    STEWIE
          (reluctant)
I think you're right.
```

Jacob frowns at Stewie. Stewie frowns back. They hold their gaze. Jacob walks away from the railing, the empty water bottle still in his hand.

```
                    STEWIE (CONT'D)
Where're you going?
```

Jacob keeps walking. Diverts onto the sand. Beelines toward the light, dustier part of the beach. Jacob screws off the bottle cap. Crouches. Scoops up sand.

Stewie walks along the sand, watching Jacob curiously.

```
                    JACOB
Hope this is enough.

                    STEWIE
For what?
```

Jacob caps the bottle. Smiles at Stewie.

```
                    JACOB
You'll see.
```

One week later, Jacob sits on the floor of Stewie's brownstone apartment and carves a hot glue message onto his graduation cap. He uncaps the bottle. Pours the Santa Monica sand onto a paper plate. Sprinkles it onto the wet glue. Jacob smiles with pride as his creation.

STEWIE
They just pulled up.

JACOB
Look.

Jacob turns the cap. Stewie reads the message.

JACOB (CONT'D)
You remember where it's from?

STEWIE
Of course.

Jacob gently places the graduation cap on the coffee table.

JACOB
Gotta let it dry.

STEWIE
Are you the only one decorating?

JACOB
You kidding me? Everyone decorates their caps.

STEWIE
Not when I graduated they didn't.

JACOB
Hate to break it to you, Daddy, but a lot's happened in the past thirty-one years.

STEWIE
Don't I know it.

KNOCK-KNOCK-KNOCK.

JACOB
(ala Poltergeist)
"They're here!"

STEWIE
How do I look?

Jacob studies at Stewie's suit.

JACOB
You look good.

STEWIE
What about my hair?

JACOB
Your hair's fine.

KNOCK-KNOCK-KNOCK-KNOCK.

STEWIE
Jeez.

JACOB
Twenty bucks says it's Melanie and she's starving.

Jacob opens the door, revealing Melanie in a sleeveless black cocktail dress. "Will you hurry up? I'm starving!"

JACOB
Where's Mom?

"In the car. C'mon!" Melanie rushes downstairs. Jacob flashes Stewie a sly smirk. Locks the door behind them.

They step onto the street to see Helena and Karen Andrezj in a Volvo convertible, both dressed to the nines. "Should we park here or at the restaurant?" Helena asks.

```
                    STEWIE
        It's only down Tremont. Just park here.
```

"Get out, Karen." Helena holds down a button, the top automatically rising from inside the trunk like a Transformer. Karen opens the passenger door. "Watch your head!" Helena yells at her.

"I'm already out!" Karen gripes.

"Just making sure." The top seals. Helena gets out. Locks the car.

```
                    JACOB
               (to Melanie)
        Where's Dad and Daphne?
```

"They're running a bit late," Melanie answers.

```
                    STEWIE
        Just tell them to meet us there.
```

"What's this place called again?" Helena asks, stepping onto the curb. "Is it really called 'The Dumpling Cafe?'"

```
                    JACOB
        It's a Chinese restaurant.
```

Helena scoffs. "I KNOW it's Chinese!"

"Okay! Okay!" Melanie claps her hands like a camp counselor. "Let's go! Someone lead the way!"

Stewie walks down the street first, Melanie eagerly following. Karen waddles at half-pace. Jacob and Helena stroll in the rear. "It's beautiful out," Helena says.

```
                    JACOB
        I know. Perfect weather.
```

Helena notices Jacob's black Armani suit. Elephant gray Brooks Brothers shirt. Red and black tie. Red pocket square. "My little man's all grown up."

```
                    JACOB
        Please don't tell me you're gonna be one of those
        gushing moms tomorrow.
```

"All my kids are graduating three weeks apart. It's not supposed to be this fast. Let me enjoy it."

```
                    JACOB
        Melanie's wasn't so bad, huh?
```

"No, it was good."

```
                    JACOB
        I liked her speaker. That black preacher lady. She
        was fun.
```

"Who's yours?"

```
                    JACOB
        Dennis Lehane. He wrote Mystic River.
```

"What a coincidence, considering your father's gonna be there."

```
                    JACOB
        No, the coincidence is Dad's middle name.
```

Helena furrows her brow. "Stewart? What about it?" Jacob points at Stewie. Helena nods, suddenly getting it. "Oh, that is weird."

JACOB
You ever get around to reading Drive-Thru?

"I did. I can see why it got nominated."

JACOB
It's my best one, right?

"Absolutely." Helena pauses. "The other nominees, are they features too?"

JACOB
Just shorts.

"And were they all filmed or just screenplays?"

JACOB
A mix of both.

"You know what you're gonna say if you get up there?"

JACOB
I might have something written down already.

"Nothing embarrassing, I hope."

JACOB
You'll definitely hear whatever I say. That power might just go to my head.

"We're your family, Jacob."

JACOB
I know. Don't worry, I'm not throwing you guys under the bus.

"When you get nominated for an Oscar, I better be your date. Brad Pitt brings his mom every time."

JACOB
Oh, so that's why he's never won.

Helena slaps him on the shoulder. "Oh, you're bad!"

JACOB
Of course you'll be my date.

Helena wraps her arm around Jacob. "Good."

As they enter Chinatown, they make eye contact with a man and a woman standing outside the Dumpling Cafe, Dennis Andrezj and his girlfriend Daphne Erins. Dennis is in his low sixties. Light gray suit. Bit of a gut. Gray hair combed back like Gordon Gecko. Bushy Keith Hernandez mustache. Daphne's the same age. Shoulder-length brown hair. Wide smile. Grace Kelly dress and shawl.

"THERE HE IS!" Daphne cries, racing over to Jacob in high heels. "Oh my God, I'M SO EXCITED FOR YOU!"

JACOB
Thanks.

Daphne gasps at Stewie. "And you must be Stewie!" She hugs him tight. "I'm a hugger." Stewie chuckles and hugs back.

STEWIE
That's okay. I love huggers.

"I've heard so much about you!" Daphne growls, shaking Stewie excitedly.

Dennis sidles up to Melanie. "How old is he?"

"Don't ask," Melanie murmurs.

```
                    STEWIE
       Dennis, right? It's nice to finally meet you.
```

"Nice to meet you," Dennis says, shaking Stewie's hand. "Welcome to the family."

Jacob watches this with a heavy heart.

Dennis finally makes eye contact with Jacob. Smiles. "Hey Jake!"

Jacob purses his lips.

"Can we talk inside?" Melanie asks. "I wanna get a table."

Dennis chuckles. "'Five, ten minutes!'"

```
                    JACOB
       "Seinfeld, FOUR!"
```

Dennis laughs heartily. Looks at Stewie. "It's amazing how much he can remember from that show."

```
                    JACOB
       It's not that hard.

                    STEWIE
       What show?
```

"SEINFELD!" Dennis, Melanie, Karen, Daphne, Helena, and Jacob all answer at once. Stewie almost has an aneurysm.

"C'mon," Helena says, holding the door open. "We're blocking traffic."

Everyone sits at seven-man table inside. Lin walks over. "Can I get everyone something to drink?"

"Coke," Karen blurts.

"Please," Helena corrects.

"Coke, *please*."

"Diet coke," Dennis says.

"Unsweetened iced tea," Daphne says.

```
                    JACOB
       Club soda with lime. Thank you.
```

"You didn't say please," Helena tells him.

```
                    JACOB
       I said it gently with a thank you at the end.
```

"Water," Melanie orders. "And a couple orders of spring rolls while you're at it."

Jacob looks at Helena. Nothing. Nothing at all.

Lin jots everything down. Looks at Stewie. "And for you, sir?"

```
                    STEWIE
       Do you have any wine?
```

"We have a house red."

```
                    STEWIE
       A glass of that for me.

                    JACOB
       Ooh, change mine to a house red actually. Please.
```

"I think a lot of us are gonna have wine," Helena says. "My son's graduating from Whitman tomorrow."

"Ooh, congratulations," Lin says to Jacob, not recognizing him without all that excess body fat.

"And he's nominated for an award," Karen adds.

"A screenwriting award!" Daphne declares enthusiastically. "He's going to LA to intern for a famous Hollywood producer!"

"Let's get wine for the table," Helena says.

Lin nods, already losing steam. "Who's having wine?"

```
                    JACOB
             (points to Stewie)
      Wine, obviously.
             (points to Melanie)
      No wine.
```

"Fuck no," Melanie mumbles.

```
                    JACOB (CONT'D)
             (points to Dennis)
      No wine.
             (points to Karen)
      Half a glass of wine.
```

Karen hocks her throat.

```
                    JACOB (CONT'D)
             (points to Helena)
      Wine.
             (points to himself)
      Wine.
             (points to Daphne)
      Rest of the bottle for her.
```

Daphne applauds enthusiastically. "Bravo!"

Lin jots everything down. "Okay, so wine for your dad, no wine for your girlfriend, no wine for your uncle, half a glass for your sister, wine for your mom, wine for you, and the rest of the bottle for your aunt."

Jacob holds up a finger.

```
                    JACOB
      That is not what I said.
```

"We're his parents." Dennis says, gesturing between him and Helena.

"I'm his girlfriend," Daphne adds.

"*HIS* girlfriend," Melanie corrects, pointing at Dennis. "That's my dad." She points at Jacob. "That's my twin brother."

```
                    STEWIE
      I also have a twin.

                    JACOB
      Don't confuse him.
```

Helena points at Dennis. "That's my ex." She points at Stewie. "That's my son's boyfriend. I'm not with either of them."

"At least he got me right!" Karen says with a laugh.

Lin stares, way too tired for this shit. "I'll be back." He dashes away.

For the next forty-five minutes, the five Andrezjs and two honorary ones gobble up food and talk multiple conversations at once. Much to Jacob's surprise, most of the conversation is about him. His college. His GPA. Stories of his from his four years in Boston and four months in Florence. His new living situation in North Hollywood. The internship at The Factory. The Professor and his filmography. The Whitty Awards. The other nominees. Daphne absolutely RAVING about *Drive-Thru* (she read it twice) and how excited he must be for tonight. Jacob can't believe it. He looks at everyone sitting there. Civil. Friendly. Like the divorce never happened. Like they were out in Phoenixville somewhere.

At the end of the dinner, Daphne goes to the bathroom, Melanie and Helena talk to Stewie, and Karen stares at her phone. Dennis and Jacob awkwardly look at each other. "Hey son."

```
                    JACOB
        Dad.
```

"You look great."

```
                    JACOB
        Thank you.
```

"Nominated for an award. Going off to Hollywood." Dennis grins. "I can't believe it. You're really going places."

```
                    JACOB
        You sound surprised.
```

Dennis chuckles, his smile unwavering. "I am."

Jacob frowns. Looks away just as Daphne returns from the bathroom.

Jacob, Stewie, Helena, Karen, Melanie, Dennis, and Daphne file into the Glamour Prix Theatre, marveling in wonder at the handpainted ceiling, the professional lighting, the camera crews and stagehands all about, almost every seat filled with eager, excited people.

"Nominees and plus ones through here," an Usher tells Jacob in front of a red velvet barrier.

```
                    JACOB
        What about everyone else?
```

The Usher points behind them. "First come first serve in Mezzanine."

```
                    JACOB
              (to the others)
        Okay, so I guess Stewie can take everyone up to
        Mezzanine and I'll go up front with Mom.

                    STEWIE
        Fine by me.
```

Stewie kisses Jacob for luck. Dennis awkwardly looks away. Stewie glances at Dennis.

```
                    STEWIE (CONT'D)
        "Not that there's anything wrong with it."
```

Dennis laughs hysterically, actually wheezing. "I can't believe it! You said the line!"

```
                    STEWIE
        I've seen the show. I just don't find it funny.
```

"How can you not find it funny?!"

Jacob and Helena stand where they are, watching the others climb, their loud voices fading off and yet still discernible above all the others. "You don't have to have me with you if you don't want to," Helena says.

```
                    JACOB
        When you read Onio for the first time, you came
        downstairs and told me I was an amazing writer. I
        wouldn't be here tonight if you hadn't said that.
```

Jacob holds out his elbow. Helena wraps her arm. The usher removes the velvet rope, Jacob escorting his mom down the Orchestra section toward their assigned seats.

Stewie, Melanie, Dennis, Daphne, and Karen all sit next to each other in Mezzanine. Stewie can see Jacob and Helena three rows from the stage. He waves at Jacob.

Jacob waves back with a silly grin. Notices Helena watching with a smile. Jacob smiles back, a bit embarrassed. The lights go down, applause rising.

The hosts, two Whitman students, come out and give probably the silliest, least funny monologue Jacob's ever heard, almost like they were too afraid to go ballsy in front of their parents. Oh wait, they probably were. But before the 2017 Whitty's could officially begin, the hosts introduce a performance art piece from a local high school.

"RACISM!" the kids hiss in unison, strutting around the stage. "INJUSTICE! INEQUALITY!" Loud gun shots. Disorienting strobe lights. "Violence."

Jacob and Helena furrow their brows with extreme discomfort.

"Evil!" the kids hiss, swastika banners hanging above them. A kid (a black kid, not that it matters) dressed as Hitler in center stage. Two others remove his brown suit, revealing a blue jacket, red tie, white shirt. He removes his mustache just as someone puts an orange wig on him. "Let's make American great again!" Black-Hitler-turned-Black-Trump declares.

A series of uncomfortable hushes fill the Glamour Prix. "BULLSHIT!" someone yells from the Mezzanine.

"Boo!" someone else yells, a woman perhaps.

Jacob grips the armrests. What the fuck are they doing?! How could Whitman allow this?!

Stewie shifts awkwardly. Dennis and Daphne are flustered. Melanie's pissed. Karen doesn't react, just bored. Stewie frowns. Poor Jacob must be so embarrassed.

The performance mercifully ends to mixed applause. Jacob lets out a hefty sigh, praying to God that no one remembers this by the end.

"That was so uncalled for," Helena mumbles angrily.

```
                    JACOB
        I had no idea they were going to do that.
```

Helena doesn't respond. Jacob stares at the back of the seat in front of him, instantly choosing to forget what he just witnessed.

An hour later, "Outstanding Writing for Film" appears on the screens. Jacob nearly squeals. "Here we go!" Helena says, clutching Jacob's hand. Jacob clutches back, relieved that Mom isn't upset anymore by that cringy anti-Trump propaganda at the beginning.

"And the nominees are..." the presenter reads.

The screens show a silent clip of a black couple arguing. "*Groceries*," the voice says over the speakers. "Written by Jamalina Anders." The audience applauds.

The screens switch to a pan-and-scan of a screenplay page. "*Drive-Thru.*" Jacob can hear Stewie and Daphne walloping from the Mezzanine. Helena cheers too. Jacob grins. "Written by Jacob Andrezj."

"*Scurry*," the voice continues over another screenplay pan-and-scan. It's so much quieter without Helena, Daphne, and Stewie's cheers. "Written by Donna Hagerty."

Last one, another actual short film, a mockumentary of sorts. "*Belevedere: Making of a Moment*," the voice says. "Written by Gareth Sapperstein." Applause.

Lights go back on the presenter. "And the Whitty goes to..." She opens the envelope. "*Groceries*!"

Jacob deflates in his seat. Helena looks at her son. "Sorry, bud."

Jacob shrugs. Looks up at where Stewie's sitting. He's already looking back with a halfhearted *What can you do?* look. Jacob frowns and faces forward. The rest of the ceremony crawls.

Helena and Jacob wait in the lobby, disappointment in the air. Or maybe that's just old popcorn.

```
                    STEWIE (O.S.)
               (bleating)
        AYY BEE!
```

Jacob instantly turns his head toward the sound. Smiles at Stewie coming down the stairs with the others.

```
                    JACOB
              (bleating)
        AYY BEE!
```

Melanie huffs with an annoyed glare. "That was stupid."

```
                    JACOB
        Oh c'mon, it's cute.
```

"Not *that*. The awful pre-show with those high school kids."

"Oh I know," Helena instantly adds, making Jacob's stomach turn. "So fucking inappropriate."

"I'm sure they wouldn't say anything bad if Obama was still President," Dennis chimes in.

"Sorry you lost, Jacob," Karen says, in her usual deadpan.

```
                    JACOB
        Thanks.
```

"The one that won's about black people," Melanie says. "No wonder you lost."

```
                    JACOB
        Maybe it's a better film.
```

"No honey," Helena tells him with soft assurance. "I'm sure that's the reason."

"Being a minority is the only way to win nowadays," Melanie says. "They were never gonna give it to you."

```
                    JACOB
        But I am a minority.
```

"Not the one that's in right now."

"I'm sure they didn't even read it," Dennis says.

```
                    JACOB
        I don't want to think of it like that!
```

"This certainly explains a lot," Karen adds, looking around at the Whitman University iconography.

"Oh yeah," Helena concurs. "No wonder Jacob's so woke."

Jacob sighs with defeat. Stewie notices this.

The five others unconsciously drift toward the open lobby doors, leaving Stewie and Jacob where they are. "I'm glad this is the last time we have to come up here," Melanie says with a laugh. "This place gives me the creeps."

```
                    STEWIE
        Guys?
```

"I was the one that booed," Daphne says.

"That was you?!" Helena asks excitedly. "I heard that all the way down there!"

"Yeah!"

"Good for you!"

"How dare they force us to watch that," Melanie says. "So uncivilized."

"I wanted to shout something too," Dennis says.

"You should've! Trigger the shit out of 'em. They don't care about us."

```
                    STEWIE
        Guys.
```

"Hurry up, you two!" Helena calls behind her. "We're getting cannolis!"

Stewie gapes, brows furrowed.

```
                    STEWIE
      What's wrong with these people?

                    JACOB
      They're comfortable with you now. That's the real
      them.
```

Jacob heads for the door, shaking his head with amusement.

```
                    JACOB (CONT'D)
      You can finally see 'em.
```

Stewie still doesn't budge, dumbfounded.

```
                    STEWIE
      I don't understand. You gave them the benefit of the
      doubt in Conshy. Why couldn't they do the same for
      you?
```

Jacob grins back at Stewie.

```
                    JACOB
      I can't believe I'm actually quoting my father, but
      "welcome to the family."
```

Stewie sighs with disappointment. They rejoin the others outside.

The next morning, Jacob sits in his mother's Airbnb. Melanie's in the shower. Mom's applying makeup in her room. Stewie's grabbing Jacob's graduation gown, honors sash, and customized cap from the apartment. Nothing for Jacob to do now but wait.

Karen looks up from the official Whitman University Class of 2017 program. "Why did you pick Phoenixville for your hometown?"

```
                    JACOB
      I started college when we were still in the
      Phoenixville house.
```

Karen laughs. "Your legal address is Conshohocken. You were only a resident of Phoenixville for, what, half a semester?"

Jacob sighs.

```
                    JACOB
      It's funny how we're all graduating at the same time,
      huh?
```

"Yeah, well you two are twins and I got held back because of all the college switching."

```
                    JACOB
      I know that. I was just making a comment.
```

"I'm getting my Bachelor's in motion capture. They've got a school in New Zealand founded by the guys that made *Lord of the Rings*."

```
                    JACOB
      You're gonna go to school in New Zealand?
```

"Mom's trying to talk me out of it. I don't care. I just want to make animated movies. Disney. DreamWorks. Or video games."

```
                    JACOB
      That's a lot of work. It's not gonna be nearly as fun
      as you think it is.
```

Karen rolls her throat. "Let me put it this way..." she says just before plummeting Jacob into a long-winded, barely coherent narrative about animation and motion capture and video games and Disney, Disney World, and for some reason the list of upcoming Disney films over the next five years. As Jacob tunes out Karen's autistic ramblings, thankful that she can't read facial expressions and realize how utterly uninterested he is, he suddenly realizes something. Karen's "master plan" is something he's heard many times from his neurodiverse peers at Eagle Ridge, all of them full of dreams but no actual skills, too fixed in their routines, diagnosed too late perhaps or misdiagnosed like Karen was, with parents far worse off than Dennis and Helena Andrezj. Most people with Asperger's never make their dreams come true, ending up living with their parents, bagging groceries or working retail, never getting their driver's license. Jacob's really lucky, isn't he? Lucky to be able to handle living out of state, out of the country. Lucky to have the confidence to put himself in real situations and not juvenile made-up ones. He has what's probably the greatest possible job for ANY screenwriting major right out of college. He'll never have a chance like this again, a chance not to end up like Karen and all those other unambitious Aspies. He's actually gonna make his dreams come true. And then he'll be a role model for other Aspies so they'll know how to do what he did. Maybe they'll have an easier life because of him. That'd be nice.

It was at that moment, tuning out his sister's autistic ramblings in that Boston Airbnb, that Jacob Andrezj first got excited about going to Hollywood.

```
                    JACOB (V.O.)
      The Wikipedia article for "Daddy (Slang)" is as
      follows.
```

Jacob zips up his graduation gown. Gently places his custom cap on his head, careful not disturb the glued-on sand on top. Lays his yellow honors rope around his neck. Studies himself in the mirror.

```
                    JACOB (V.O.)
      "A daddy in gay culture is a slang term meaning an
      (typically) older man sexually involved in a
      relationship or wanting sex with a younger male."
```

Jacob smiles for pictures taken by an excited Helena Andrezj. Jacob glances at Stewie standing next to her. They smile the moment their eyes make contact.

```
                    JACOB (V.O.)
      "In the homonormative sense, a dad (or daddy) is a
      gay man who applies a state of mind that encompasses
      care, consideration, mentorship and leadership to a
      gay junior male."
```

Jacob wanders into what appears to be a gymnasium, filled to the brim with hundreds of other students wearing similar gowns. Talking excitedly to each other. Hugging each other. Making jokes. All their caps customized. Some with memes mocking student loans or adulting. Others are political, either Anti-Trump or incredibly woke. Jacob takes it all in with a smile.

```
                    JACOB (V.O.)
      "The dad has the welfare of a younger man at heart,
      and his natural impulse is benevolent guardianship."
```

Jacob spots Carter from across the gym. They walk up to each other. Give each other a big hug, Carter clapping Jacob on the back.

```
                    JACOB (V.O.)
      "In the heteronormative sense, the father/son,
      teacher/student, coach/protege relationship is
      assumed to be finite and not questioned, but an
      ongoing relationship is looked at askance."
```

Jacob turns his head. Sees TJ standing on the sidelines. Jacob crosses the floor, waving awkwardly. TJ smiles a bit with recognition. Hugs Jacob with palpable gratitude.

JACOB (V.O.)
"Dad-son relationships are a form of mentoring, and the shared homosexuality of the partners is a personal extension of societal gender norms and expectations about masculinities."

Jacob accidentally makes eye contact with Nich, hot pink hair poking out the sides of his cap. Jacob's body tenses, but he keeps his gaze. Nich glares back. Coldly turns away first. Walks on.

JACOB (V.O.)
"Most partners in dad-son relationships subscribe to common values: masculinity is praised and therefore celebrated between them."

Jacob sees Rian smiling back at him. God, he looks all grown up. Jacob grins back. They pace toward each other. Clapsarms around. Big tight hug. They shake their heads in disbelief, trying to hold back laughter.

JACOB (V.O.)
"Age difference may be the initial attraction, but it is more of a mutual attitude that makes the dad-son relationship work and thrive."

Jacob files into the massive auditorium, quite a shock considering Whitman University barely has a sports program. Who the heck is this stadium for? So many people here! He's never gonna find Stewie in a crowd like this.

Jacob sits and listens to Dennis Lehane's commencement speech.

JACOB (V.O.)
"There is a resonance between both dad and son based on essential personal values: recognition of different levels of experience, honesty and clarity in communication, a lack of selfishness and a capacity for giving, the need for mutual emotional expression, guidance and learning, and an acute awareness of respect and boundaries."

Jacob readjusts his cap, filing slowly toward the stage to accept his diploma. His heart races. The stage lights look so much brighter on the receiving end. He looks out at the audience behind where he was sitting before. Thanks to his new LASIK-granted 20/20 vision, he can tell with complete certainty that they are NOT sitting all the way back there.

"Jacob Andrezj!" the presenter reads into the microphone. "*Manga cum laude*!"

Applause throughout. Jacob makes his way on stage toward President Fisher, looking around one last time.

JACOB (V.O.)
"Additionally, the negotiation between dad and son can galvanize right-minded behaviors and resolve inner conflicts in both parties."

Facing forward, Jacob's eyes finally land on the familiar faces he was searching for. He smiles.

JACOB (V.O.)
"Both will be better men for it."

Directly ahead of him, standing just off the Stage Right, is Dennis Andrezj, Helena Andrezj, Melanie Andrezj, Karen Andrezj, Daphne Erins, and of course Stewie Hanz Jr. Stewie's cheering harder and louder than everyone else combined, an emblem of pride and love, close enough to throw a baseball to.

JACOB (V.O.)
"This resonance dictates that the relationship is negotiable but based on mutual organization and complementary self-discipline and restraint."

Jacob grins so hard at Stewie. He knows he's blushing.

```
                    JACOB (V.O.)
      "In a healthy relationship, there is genuine and
      mutual admiration."
```

President Fisher hands Jacob his diploma and shakes his hand. Jacob blows Stewie a kiss, the spotlight hitting his graduation cap one last time, its three word adage written in Santa Monica sand and bookended with lines meant to represent the dusty desert dunes of Arabia:

~Nothing is Written~

DREW

Meant to Be

Drew sits on his golden throne, Stewie to his right, Kev to his left, all four hundred plus members of Ephemeral Pictures and/or *The Sins of Jack Branson* either at his table or the two others lit with warm yellow strands. The sun has set. Everyone has a chalice filled with Polar Orange-Vanilla seltzer, Drew's favorite, and they had just finished his favorite meal, salmon in bourbon and brown sugar ("Booze cooked off, of course!" Kev quipped to much amusement). Drew can still taste the deliciousness in his mouth. But everyone's looking at him now. Drew looks down at all forty-three candles. The gorgeous three-tiered strawberry shortcake. "Happy Birthday Drew!" in thin red icing.

"Make a wish!" someone shouts. Several others nod and chatter in agreement.

"Just a second," Kev says into the microphone, standing up. "I wanna say a few words."

Drew smiles. Stewie holds his hand under the table.

Kev swallows nervously. "Matter of fact, I have a bit of a confession to make." He looks down. "As you all know, Drew here's been in a bit of a bind lately. A lot of people assumed the worst about him, myself included. And we gather here in the shadow of a horrible event that we're all pretending not to notice." He pauses. "But I have to come clean about something."

Drew's face goes numb.

Kev makes eye contact. "I hired those guys to Molotov your condo."

Drew's blood chills. Everyone reacts in shock. Stewie's heart pounds hard.

"When all that shit came out, I was really hurt," Kev continues shamefully. "I was just mad that you would put us through all that. I just hope that... you'll be able to forgive me."

Drew stares at Kev.

Kev stares back.

Drew points. "That's fucked up!"

"DAMMIT!" Kev stomps his foot with a grin. "I almost got you!"

Everyone laughs heartily. Stewie's more confused than ever.

"I almost got you!" Kev declares, pointing back at Drew. "Come on, I almost got you!"

"You son of a bitch!" Drew jumps up and mock-wrestles Kev on their feet. Everyone laughs. A smile finally cracks on Stewie's face.

"Alright, it was me!" Gary shouts from across the table. Everyone laughs harder, especially Drew.

Everyone settles back down. "But in all seriousness," Kev says, "Drew, you've had a really rough month. I'm very proud of how you've handled it, and I'm very proud to call you my friend."

Drew smiles.

Kev raises his glass of orange-vanilla seltzer. "To Drew."

Everyone raises theirs "TO DREW!"

"To Baby Boy," Stewie says softly.

Everyone drinks. Kev pulls a rolled up cloth out of his pocket. "But before you blow out the candles, I wanted to give you this."

Drew unrolls the cloth. A steel spoon flops out. Deep head. Hammered handle. Drew's smile drops.

"Everything didn't get destroyed after all," Kev says into the mic. "And we have another surprise. Everyone?" He pulls a strange spoon out of his pocket and holds it up.

Drew looks out at every single man and woman smiling back at him with special spoons of their own raised up. Different heads on each. Different handles. Different sizes. Some curved, some not. Some steel, some not. But each one completely different. Stewie quickly holds up the catering company's dinner spoon. Still unique. It counts.

Drew's stunned by all those supportive faces. He holds his spoon up and smiles.

"Alright, now you can make your wish." Kev hands the sound guy the microphone. Sits back down.

Drew looks down at the shimmering cake. Sneaks a glance at his special spoon. At Stewie too. Takes a deep breath. Blows out all forty-three candles. Applause, applause, applause.

Drew discreetly rushes across the beach in the dark. Sits on the cold sand. Folds his legs. Marvels at the moon hanging over the shimmering Pacific. What a sight. Drew caresses his special spoon with both hands, the one he pulled out of the snow all those years ago.

"I knew I'd find you out here."

Drew looks behind him. Stewie's walking over with a smile.

"I can only handle so much apparently," Drew murmurs. "As you very well know."

Stewie sits next to Drew in the sand. "You gonna put on a song?"

"I was thinking about it." Drew looks at Stewie. "Wanna pick?"

Stewie shakes his head. "Your surprise, your soundtrack."

Drew pulls out his phone. Goes through his Apple Music library. "You know, for the parallel to be complete we have to be facing my former home." He thumbs behind him at the tarp-drenched condo hiding in the dark. "West-facing side no less."

"I was actually going for a *Moonlight* moment."

Drew raises his brows. "Can't believe you finally saw *Moonlight*."

"It's the first gay Best Picture winner. It's a requirement now to get a new fag visa."

"I'm about to get a handjob, aren't I?"

Stewie chuckles. "Still the exhibitionist."

"A tiger can't change his stripes." Drew softens. "Actually, turns out, he can." He finally picks a song: "Make You Feel My Love" by Adele.

"I like this song," Stewie murmurs.

Drew folds his arms around his knees. Looks up at the moon. "You wanna know what I wished for?"

"It won't come true if you say it out loud."

"It can't come true. It's one of those impossible wishes."

"You don't know that. Maybe it will. Anything's poss—"

"I wished that I never got on that plane." Drew looks Stewie in the eye.

Stewie stares back.

Drew nods. Stares out at that dark ocean water. "I should've taken your out. Stayed in Boston instead. Or Danvers, I guess."

Stewie hesitates. "I don't understand."

"This isn't me. This was never me. This is the guy Jacob Andrezj wanted to be when he grew up." Drew shakes his head. "But this isn't who I was meant to be."

Stewie furrows his brow.

Drew studies the special spoon. Rotates it between two fingers. "When I was in Budapest shooting *Onio*, there was a whole lot of BS going on with the production. So much they made a whole documentary out of it. First week, we got hit with a bad storm. Our sets got totaled. We had to stop filming for a week to get everything rebuilt. On the third day in the hotel, I started having this strange feeling around six in the morning. I don't really know how to describe it, it's like..." Drew strains to formulate. "Like everything was wrong. Where I was. What I looked like. What I was doing. The air I was breathing. Like when you realize you forgot something, like your keys or wallet, and you know you really should be getting back, but before you know what it is you're supposed to get. That middle feeling." Drew pauses. "It just wore me out. I couldn't stay up very late, I just felt... I actually went to bed around 8 or something."

Stewie stares out at the waves crashing in the dark, listening intently to Drew's words.

"And I had this dream," Drew says in a soft pleading voice. "It was you and I in this big house on a golf course, right by the hole. It looked like my Phoenixville house, but it was smaller, more geometrically unusual. And really long, for some reason. And the living room was just windows, almost like a glass house, and the room itself was filled with sunshine, and it was you, but... it *wasn't* you, you know? You looked the same and sounded the same and *were* the same, but you weren't the same, you were different, but only just a little bit. And same with me, I wasn't... Anyway, we were lying together on the couch, and we were writing down songs, names of songs, on a list, and we were going back and forth over what order they should be in, and there was a baby elephant sitting on the coffee table."

"A baby elephant?" Stewie asks, chuckling.

"A stuffed baby elephant. He could talk. No, actually, he couldn't talk. We were talking for him. But he *was* talking, even though we knew he wasn't actually talking. I think."

Stewie hesitates. "Did he have a name?"

"Corey."

"Corey?"

"Corey Zander."

"Corey *Zander*?"

"Yeah," Drew confirms with a smile, "Corey Zander."

Stewie shakes his head. "You've always had weird dreams."

"This was different. I lucid dream all the time, I can always tell when I'm dreaming, and this wasn't... It felt too real. Like those guys you see on *20/20* who went to sleep one time and ended up dreaming a whole other lifetime somewhere that lasted decades, and then they wake up and don't believe it wasn't real and they go crazy and end up in therapy. It's like one of those." Drew pauses. "When I woke up, that funny feeling was gone. I looked at the clock and saw it had just turned 6:01 AM. Twenty-four hours long that feeling was, 6 AM to 6 AM in Budapest, midnight to midnight on the East Coast." Drew looks at Stewie. "The entirety of June 12, 2021."

Stewie hesitates. "What is that?"

Drew furrows his brow. "Five years to the day we met."

Stewie nods suddenly. "Oh yeah."

"How could you forget? It's on the dog tag I gave you."

"I haven't worn that in years."

Drew frowns.

Stewie swallows. "I know where it is. I just haven't worn it."

Drew nods a bit. "Ever since I got here, I felt something was off. And as time went on, it just kept getting worse and worse, and now I know why that is. Everything went bad because me coming out here was never supposed to happen. It was never part of the plan." Drew stops himself, on the verge of tears. "There's a reason so many people aren't meant for this town. It wears them down. I knew Day One that this was the wrong life for me. I didn't want to be a producer or run a business. I just wanted to write. I didn't know being a producer was the only way anyone could make money, or that it's the only way to write. And now I'm somebody I don't even like, which is EXACTLY the kind of person I was before I met you. I never wanted anything when we were together. I never wanted drugs or sex. I never needed other people to like me. I wasn't insecure. I wasn't vain or weak. I was nice. I was satisfied and happy with everything, with life. I was fulfilled. I only wanted to come here because who wouldn't, growing up in the Andrezj household? Always ignored. Always underestimated. I didn't have anything. Nothing was just mine, not even my birthday. And I couldn't keep friends no matter how hard I tried. I don't know, I was just too weird. Too aggressive. Too much work. To understand, to maintain, just... too much. So I told myself I was gonna be a storyteller so I could finally show the world what it was that I found so interesting, and for a price of an admission ticket, they could finally get inside my mind and see what I saw and feel what I felt and just understand me for a couple hours without having to be fluent in Asperger's or require years of sensitivity training to not go haywire every time I opened my mouth. And I needed a sense of place. A home. A hometown. Something for me to root into. And I loved cities. I loved being around tons of people, always having something to do. I loved being HERE. Being alive, being noticed, being admired, by as many people as possible, even people I couldn't see, especially people I couldn't see. I thought coming here was the only way. Another coast. Another world. I could finally start over and become Drew Lawrence and put them all in their place, but that was just a reaction to how I was before I met you. I wasn't me before I met you. I didn't even KNOW I wasn't me until I met you. That's how deep I was against my grain. I was meant to find you exactly when I did because I was never meant to be Drew Lawrence. I was never meant to stay Jacob Andrezj." Drew's eyes droop. "I was meant to be Jacob *Hanz*."

Stewie frowns down at the sand.

"I knew as soon as I woke from that dream," Drew continues. "It felt so right, in a way this place never felt to me. I never needed thousands and thousands of people to love me, to listen to me, to care for me, to fix me. One would've been enough. It could've been anyone. It could've been a father. Or a brother. Or lover. Or a guardian angel. You were all those things. All these years, it could've been just the two of us against the world, in the middle of nowhere, sitting back and saying, 'Screw you, world' while we ate dinner at 11 and watched movies together and binged 70s sitcoms together, talking about music all night, going on adventures to new places together, making fun of everyone. Being there for each other. Having someone. That was all I really wanted."

Stewie keeps looking into the sand, withdrawn.

"I know we were never gonna grow old together," Drew whispers. "But you knew I was out there your whole life and you found me. And when you're gone, I'm going to go the rest of my life knowing you were out there and that I found you, and that's..." Drew shakes his head. "So much more than most people get."

Stewie doesn't respond.

Drew tilts his head, smiling desperately. "So what do you say? Let's pick up where we left off while we still can. Come save me. Fly me out of here."

Stewie readjusts his legs. "I'm sorry to disappoint."

Drew deflates, his body sinking into the sand.

Stewie shrugs. "It's not like I've been living half a life since you left. How could I? I had it all. I always wanted to have my own business and a house. All I needed to do was find Mr. Preference." He smiles. "And after all those years going to the bars, sifting through all those losers and dregs and trolls, breathing in all that secondhand smoke, I found Mr. Perfect."

Drew can't smile back. "But you lost me."

"I never lost you. I just didn't have you anymore. I knew where you were. You were out here, making your own dreams come true. I see that now. What a life you have out here! I'm so proud of you! You have no idea!"

Drew hesitates. "Was I so bad?"

"That's not what I'm saying at all." Stewie takes a deep breath. "My whole life I was worried that it was impossible, or at least unrealistic, for a guy like me to have it all. But I did." He pauses for effect. "Just not all at the same time."

Drew furrows his brow.

"You had a great love." Stewie takes Drew's hand. "*We* had a great love. And you managed to turn your one chance at success, that internship, into an actual Hollywood career. And now you're living a life of decency and fairness, all on your own terms. When you really think about it, Baby Boy, you really had it all too." Stewie half-shrugs. "Just not all at the same time."

Drew softens.

"I know you," Stewie continues sweetly. "If you stayed in Mass with me, you would've found something wrong with it. You'd feel like you were missing out on LA, or you'd feel like a failure because you didn't have a film career, the one you always wanted, the one you went to school for, settling for second best the way I settled for Gus. You'd feel too domesticated. You love being around guys your own age. Even when we were together you loved having sex and partying and drinking in bars. You'd feel trapped mowing a lawn or going on grocery runs. You'd be stuck at home during COVID collecting unemployment like your Uncle Bart, just like you told me you never wanted to end up. Instead you were off in Budapest adapting your own novella. You'd wish something was different no matter where you were. Because you're not a squatter, Baby Boy. You're a doer, just like your mom was. If you never came out here and tried it for yourself, you'd never believe you had it in you."

Drew sighs.

Stewie smiles, his heart breaking. "Don't get me wrong. You would've been a fantastic husband. And if you went on to write books instead, or plays, I know you'd be the absolute best because you always give everything everything you've got. But you're still an amazing screenwriter. And you're only forty-three. You've got so much ahead of you." Stewie juts his chin down the beach. "And now you got Kev and those guys. I'd kill to have friends like those. They don't just want you on their terms. They can see the man I fell in love with, and they love you for it. They listen to you. They trust you. They'll stand by you. You're gonna make more great films, more *Jack Bransons*. This just might be the beginning of your greatest golden age yet." Stewie nods. "You're the King Arthur of your story now. With a Round Table of your own."

"What good's a movie career if no one's watching?"

"Fuck them," Stewie blurts. "You did the right thing. If they can't see that, that's their problem. You never needed their approval before. And it was never about the money for you, was it?"

Drew smiles a bit, his strength returning. "You know Arthur gets killed at the end, right?"

"No he doesn't."

"In the real legend, Daddy. The big-boy story for adults."

Stewie blinks. "Does he still have good hair?"

"Arthur is killed by his bastard son Mordred, who he conceived through incest with his half-sister Morgan le Fay, an evil sorceress who raises Mordred to hate his father until she sics him on Camelot right when it's at its most vulnerable."

Stewie stares. "So is that a yes?"

Drew chuckles. "You keep comparing me to King Arthur when the reality is a lot less romantic than Disney makes it seem."

"I might not be the writer here," Stewie teases, "but even I know all stories, romantic or not, end in the main character's death. Everything before, all the details, *that's* what we're paying for."

Drew hugs Stewie as tight as he can. Stewie closes his eyes and enjoys it.

"Hey you two!" Kev calls, halfway between the banquet and the ocean. "It's time for the gift! C'mon!"

Stewie stands. "We gotta go."

"Just give me a moment," Drew says from the ground.

"Alright." Stewie makes his way back toward Kev.

Drew gets up. Stares out at the water. Looks at the spoon in his hand. Rotates it. Kisses the convex side. Winds up. Chucks it into the Pacific. The flying steel shines in the moonlight until it plops into the water. Drew stands a bit more, relieved and unburdened. He turns and walks across the sand toward the banquet.

The dance floor is empty. All the tables are cleared. For some reason everyone's over by the condo's parking garage. "What's going on?" Drew asks Tanner. "Where's Kev?"

ROAR! An engine revs, a pair of round headlights lighting up the dark. Kev inches a bright red Jeep Wrangler out of the garage. "Well?" he asks out the driver's side window. "What do you think?"

Drew gapes. "Oh my God!"

Kev locks the emergency break. Hops out. "Happy Birthday, dude!"

Drew sniffs. "Is that gasoline?!"

"Yeah!" Kev says with an eager nod. "It's gonna be a pain in the ass to fill around here, but with all this pre-EV nostalgia going around, it's only a matter of time before they bring 'em all back."

Drew caresses the hood of the car. "This a '98!"

Kev lifts himself by his heels. "Is it though? With all the parts Frankensteined in from older Wranglers, and not a single one from '98, can it still be considered a '98 Wrangler? Quite the Ship of Theseus conundrum you got there."

"They're all still the best quality parts, considering their age," Tanner says, stepping forward. "Kev and I hunted them down ourselves all over Cali."

"We all chipped in though," Kev adds. "Every one of us."

Drew looks out at the hundreds of people surrounding him. He finally finds Stewie beaming back at him with pride. "Wow guys," Drew says with a wavering pitch. "You're amazing. All of you."

Tanner claps. "Okay everyone! Show's over! Back to the dance floor!" Everyone laughs and races back to the beach. Drew and Kev stay behind to look at the Jeep.

"It's not quite the '36 electric concept car you lost," Kev says softly. "But it's still technically the original, so... Suck it, Theo."

Drew chuckles.

Kev looks down at the temporary California license plate. "What are you gonna call it? JEEPGUY the Third perhaps?"

Drew smiles. "I'm thinking BRANSON."

Kev nods. "BRANSON it is."

Drew and Kev return to the dance floor just as the vastly superior Felix Da Housecat's Devin Dazzle Edit of Madonna's "American Life" comes on, and after that comes "Some Speculation" by the Pet Shop Boys, by far their best song ever, and then "Junk" by Bronski Beat, and then "Generate" by Eric Prydz, and so on. All obscure songs by popular artists, exactly Drew's taste. And he's dancing on Venice Beach with Stewie and all his friends and coworkers on the best motherfucking birthday he's ever had.

Many hours later, the party finally dissolves, Drew says goodbye to Kev and Terrance and Tanner and all the other guests still hanging around. He hops into the driver's seat of BRANSON. Looks to his right. Stewie smiles back at him. Drew starts the Jeep. Shifts into first. Speeds off, shifting as he goes. It drives great. The mileage number's high, but who knows if that can even be trusted. Who knows how long it'll be able to drive for. But the top's down. The satellite radio's on, "L'amour Toujours" by Gigi D'Agostino surrounding them. And he's got Stewie by his side. And the lamplights of Route 1 flutter across their faces one by one, just like a heartbeat, and suddenly it's 2016 again, Stewie driving Jacob back to campus in JEEPGUY. Jacob grins. Stewie whispers, "So cute," and pets his head sweetly. Jacob closes his eyes and opens then outside Ephemeral Pictures. They're in BRANSON. It's parked on the street. Drew sighs. Looks at Stewie sitting beside him. Stewie half-frowns back. He was there too.

Drew reluctantly opens the door. Walks around. Opens Stewie's. "I can take you in and show you around if you want."

Stewie hops out. "Actually, I gotta catch a red-eye."

Drew softens. "Tonight?"

Stewie nods.

Drew pockets his hands. "You still got time?"

"Only if I go now."

Drew hesitates. "I can drive you if you want."

Stewie smiles. "I think you've done enough driving tonight."

Drew nods weakly. "I can get you a car. It'll only take a few minutes."

Stewie thinks it over. "Sure."

Drew retrieves Stewie's bag from Kev's office. They stand on the curb, waiting patiently for the driver to pull up. Sunset Boulevard's eerily quiet. The whole world to themselves. Drew admires BRANSON again. "Did you chip in too?" he asks Stewie.

"No, I didn't know."

Drew looks at Stewie. "Then what did you get me?"

"Huh?"

"You said you got me a present. What did you get me?"

Stewie hesitates. "You asked what I got you and I said you'll see."

"So you don't actually have a present?"

Stewie shakes his head.

Drew bobs his. "I understand. You didn't want to disappoint me."

Stewie doesn't say anything. Just stares off.

Drew smirks. "A lie began it all and a lie ends it all, huh?"

"Something like that," Stewie murmurs.

"You're my present," Drew says proudly. "That's all that matters."

Stewie nods, unenthused. The car pulls up. The Driver puts his bag in the trunk. Holds the door open for him. Stewie presses down the window. Smiles out at Drew.

"I love you," Drew tells him. "I always will."

"Of course!" Stewie says childishly with a juvenile shrug.

Drew chuckles. The car drives on, Stewie's face disappearing into the dark. Drew keeps standing there, his joy fading away with every half-mile.

Stewie looks out the back window at Drew standing there, getting smaller and smaller. His heart gets heavier with every half-mile. He faces forward. "LAX, right?" the Driver asks.

"Yeah."

"What terminal?"

"5." Stewie doesn't speak for the rest of the drive.

Stewie carries his bag into LAX. He stops at the American Airlines counter. "Excuse me? Is it too late for me to refund a ticket?"

"Let me check for you," the Clerk says, clicking her mouse. "The name on the reservation?"

"Stewart, S-T-E-W-A-R-T. Hanz, H-A-N-Z."

The Clerk furrows her brow. "I don't see a..."

"Try 'Hanz Jr.'"

The Clerk types. Click. "Ah, there it is. Flight 425 to Boston..." She frowns. "Oh, I'm sorry, Mr. Hanz. Unfortunately we cannot refund a round-trip already in progress."

"Not mine. The other ticket."

"Oh." The Clerk clicks. "Oh yes, I see a one-way ticket for the same flight, number 425 to Boston, for Drew Lawrence."

Stewie nods solemnly. "That's it."

"Reason for cancellation?"

Stewie doesn't answer.

The Clerk looks up. "Sir?"

Stewie blinks. "I'm sorry?"

"I need a reason for cancellation."

Stewie shrugs. "Change of plans."

"Okay." The Clerk clicks about. "I'm sorry, that reason for cancellation is not one we give a full refund for. We can only give you half."

Stewie sighs. "Is there any way you can waive the other half?"

"I'm sorry, sir. Airline policy." The Clerk looks behind her. "I can call my supervisor over if you'd like."

Stewie hesitates. "No, just cancel it. I'll take half."

"You sure?"

"It's only money," Stewie says somberly. "What's the point if you don't spend it?"

The Clerk clicks a bunch. "Okay Mr. Hanz, you should receive the partial refund in about 8-10 business days. Is there anything else I can help you with this evening?"

Stewie looks behind him at the empty seats. "My flight's not boarding for another two hours. Is it okay if I sit and wait?"

"Of course."

"Thank you." Stewie lifts his bag and relocates. Thinks back. He slips a hand under his collar and pulls out a dog tag. Stares at it.

June 12, 2016

He flips it.

I Knew You Were Waiting for Me

Stewie rubs the tag slowly, a frown forming. He's never lied to Jacob before, except that one time. But this was different. Far worse. A real lie.

Nineteen days ago, Stewie Hanz Jr. turned seventy-four years old, making him officially older than his father ever was, a man who smoked three packs a day for thirty-five years, quit for fifteen years, and still died of Stage IV lung cancer three weeks after his diagnosis. And thinking about his father reminded Stewie Jr. of late 2022, when he went for a calcium heart scan because his identical twin Ron had one and found 11% blockage in one artery. Fortunately Stewie's came back completely clean... except for a strange shape the doctors found in his lung. A nodule they called it. 98% chance of it being benign. A CT Scan with contrast revealed it was actually a malignant tumor, and way too many weeks later a PET scan revealed it had spread to a local lymph node. During the biopsy, the idiot doctors watched their naive residents accidentally puncture Stewie's lung, and after a few extra days recovering, Stewie Hanz Jr., a man who never smoked a day in his life, who kept working out into his fifties and made sure to check every ingredient on every box of food he ever bought, who made sure never to do drugs or fall into bad habits, who isolated himself from human contact for two long years of COVID to make sure he never got it, not even once, was officially diagnosed with Stage IIb lung cancer. Five-year survival rate of 50%. A coin flip. He did everything right and got cancer anyway. That scared him to his core. He wouldn't find out his cancer was actually Stage Ia for another month, 97% survival rate, that the larger-than-usual lymph node was only severely irritated, not cancerous, but that month was worse than Hell could ever be. Stewie felt so helpless, convinced he was going to die just as fast as Stewie Sr., and he wished more than anything for Jacob to have been there to help him through it, to beat rationality into him from time to time, to hold him at night when he got scared, to kiss him, to talk about movies on and on for hours so he'd be so distracted he'd actually forget.

Life's been hard without Jacob. Stewie had gotten used to being a bachelor for the first fifty-two years of his life, but now he actually knows what he's missing. And he thought he almost lost his Baby Boy when those thugs attacked his home. That's why he flew out to LA, to bring Jacob back east with him and finally make that big Danvers house a home.

Stewie releases the dog tag. It plops against his chest. Jacob's happier now that he believes the life he chose wasn't a waste of time. Stewie should be happy for him too. And he should feel the same way about his own life.

Back at Ephemeral Pictures, Drew unbuttons his shit for bed. "Can't believe Stewie actually showed up like that," Kev marvels. "Weird."

Drew doesn't remove the shirt. Just stares into space. "He really made it the perfect day."

"Glad to hear it, man." Kev claps Drew on the shoulder. Walks into the hallway.

"Why can't it be like this every day?" Drew wonders aloud.

Kev pokes his head back in. "People do."

Drew looks up.

Kev smirks. "In the movies."

Drew nods, still withdrawn. He looks out the window. Stares at his new Jeep parked out front.

Stewie readjusts his legs in that uncomfortable metal chair. Not many people mulling about the lobby. He looks over at the door. He gasps. Jacob?! Stewie sits up. Jacob! What the hell is he…? Oh wait, no, it's just some other brown-haired guy walking in with his father. Or maybe not. Who is he of all people to assume that? The young man and the older man stop walking to talk up close. They're saying goodbye. A big hug.

Stewie watches from his vantage point, pain setting in. It's all too familiar. He wears "June 12, 2016" around his neck, the greatest night of his life on a royal medallion he publicly bears with pride, literal Pride, Boston Pride, because even on a day of tragedy and gun violence, so many young men's lives destroyed in an instant, there was still hope and new life to come. But if he were ever to get a tattoo, he'd get "June 30, 2017" branded around the fleshy rim of his rectum or scalded on the inside tip of his dickhole because that's where you put the worst day of your life.

JACOB

Casablanca

2 AM. Jacob packs his backpack in complete silence by yellow lamplight. He lays his laptop and charging cord into the middle pocket. Unplugs his iPhone charging cord from the wall. Stands idly, staring at the backpack sitting on the bed. The large red suitcase on the floor. All toiletries packed. The clothes on his person. He hasn't forgotten anything, has he?

Jacob lifts his head to Stewie's closet. Slides the hanging door just enough not to make any noise. Looks up at Stewie's clothes. Polos. Pants. Long-sleeved shirts. Concert tees. Shoes. Hats. He slides open a drawer. Undies. Jacob lifts one. Puts the inside crotchal part to his nose. Big inhale. Jacobs sighs, staring at the cotton briefs in his hands. Puts it back. Closes the drawer. Looks at the hats next. Delicately lifts the top cap, a Mets plastic adjustable, then the next one, going through the stack like sheets of paper. He stops on a red one. Takes it out. Studies it in the lamplight. The white Nike swoosh. The Velcro strap. The one that started it all.

Jacob slides his backpack over. Throws in the hat. Zips it shut.

4 AM. Stewie drives JEEPGUY down the pitch-black freeway, Jacob in the passenger seat. Neither say anything. They just stare forward and listen to *Hamilton*'s soundtrack. They can't get enough of it now. Two years late to the party, no hype in sight, all on their own terms, just the way it should be.

"Satisfied" comes on. Track 11 already? Jacob checks his new wristwatch, a handsome thick-band Fossil with a large clockface.

```
                    JACOB
I swear, if I miss my flight because you took two
hours to write a freaking email, you're paying for
it.

                    STEWIE
You're not gonna miss it.
```

Twenty minutes later, Stewie and Jacob dash into Logan International. Jacob's backpack thumps with each step, his red case rolling behind him.

```
                    JACOB
WHAT DID I TELL YOU?!

                    STEWIE
Look, there's no line.
```

Stewie and Jacob stop at the American Airlines desk. A cross older woman with a 60s 'do raises an eyebrow. Her nametag says Eunice.

```
                    STEWIE (CONT'D)
He's checking a bag.
```

Eunice simply looks at Jacob. How dare they talk to her before her morning coffee. "Name?"

```
                    JACOB
Jacob Andrezj, A-N-D-R-E-Z-J.
```

Eunice takes her time typing. Jacob looks behind him at the kiosk next to the entrance. Crucifixes hanging on a board. Stars of David. Prayer mats. Rosaries on a holder. A cross pole standing straight in a holder right by the door, Eastern Orthodox by the look of it. A bored Polish man standing behind the counter. The sign says "Chekhov's Religious Artifacts."

Jacob taps Stewie on the shoulder.

```
                    JACOB (CONT'D)
      Check that out.
```

Stewie looks at the kiosk.

```
                    STEWIE
      That's weird.
```

"It's too late to check your bag," Eunice drolls.

```
                    JACOB
      Oh come on!
```

"It's too close to your boarding time. It'll never make it on."

```
                    JACOB
      I have full size shampoo and conditioner in there!
      Moisturizers. Cologne. They're gonna confiscate
      everything.
```

```
                    STEWIE
      There has to be something you can do.
```

"I'm sorry," Eunice mumbles. "You should've got here sooner."

```
                    STEWIE
      He has to get it checked. Look at it. There's no way
      that's gonna fit in the overhead.
```

"Peyton?" Eunice calls.

A flamboyant baggage handler with a blond gel-soaked curlicue on his head steps over. "What's the problem here?" he asks with catty sass.

```
                    JACOB
      I just wanna make my flight.
```

"Yeah," Peyton whines at the sight of the heavy bag. "It's not gonna make it."

```
                    STEWIE
      Of course it can make it!
```

"You can always check it at the gate."

Jacob sighs.

```
                    JACOB
      If that's what it is, that's what it is.
```

```
                    STEWIE
      That doesn't make any sense. How is it okay to check
      it at the gate but not here? It takes just as long to
      load it on there than it does now.
```

"We don't make the rules," Peyton retorts.

```
                    STEWIE
      You're really not gonna check his bag?
```

Eunice shrugs. "I'm sorry, it's too late."

```
                    JACOB
      Let's just go.
```

```
                    STEWIE
      You guys are just being lazy. I want to speak to your
      supervisor.
```

```
                    JACOB
        We don't have time for that.
```

Stewie looks at Jacob. Jacob juts his head toward the terminal entrance.

```
                    JACOB (CONT'D)
        Let's go.
```

Stewie follows Jacob. Glares back at Eunice and Peyton.

```
                    STEWIE
        You shouldn't just take that.

                    JACOB
        I don't wanna miss my flight.

                    STEWIE
        You won't miss it! It takes thirty minutes to board
        and you know you'll be held on the ground for a
        while.

                    JACOB
        I just wanna make it through security, okay?
```

Jacob quickens the pace to a jog, his red case rolling behind him. Stewie follows around the corner.

```
                    JACOB (CONT'D)
        Thanks for sticking up for me though.

                    STEWIE
        Of course!
```

The two of them follow the signs. Turn left. Turn right. Up the escalator. Down the steps. Left. Left. Right. Right. Quite the maze. Finally the TSA checkpoint emerges. Jacob and Stewie slow down, desperately catching their breath. Jacob notices a bored Persian man sitting at a kiosk full of plastic water bottles. Sign says "Last Chance Water."

```
                    JACOB
        I'm gonna get some water. You want any?

                    STEWIE
        Just buy one on the other side.

                    JACOB
        I'm thirsty now. What's the difference?

                    STEWIE
              (to Vendor)
        How much is it?
```

"$6.23," the Vendor mumbles.

```
                    JACOB
              (handing over a $20)
        Sold.

                    STEWIE
        That's a such rip-off! He knows people can't bring
        water through security so he's gouged the prices.
```

"That's America, my friend." The Vendor hands Jacob a bottle of water and $13.77 in change.

```
                    STEWIE (CONT'D)
        Why not $6.25? That's such a strange choice.
```

Jacob slowly opens the water. Stewie watches as Jacob takes the tiniest of sips.

STEWIE (CONT'D)
That's the first time I've ever seen you drink a bottle of water like a normal person.

Jacob sighs.

JACOB
This is really happening, isn't it?

STEWIE
You're gonna be okay. Think of LA.

JACOB
I don't want to lose you.

STEWIE
You haven't lost me.

Jacob's breath quickens, panic settling in.

JACOB
I stole your Nike hat!

STEWIE
What?

JACOB
The red one. The one you had on in the Black Bear. I stole it.

STEWIE
(smiling)
That's alright.

JACOB
No it's not. It's stealing.

STEWIE
I forgive you.

JACOB
You shouldn't. Stealing is wrong.

Stewie nods.

STEWIE
Where is it?

JACOB
Main compartment.

Stewie walks around. Unzips Jacob's backpack.

JACOB (CONT'D)
No, the MAIN compartment. The big one, all the way up.

Stewie unzips the big part. Pulls out the red Nike hat. Walks back around. Holds it out.

STEWIE
There. Now it's not stealing.

Jacob looks into Stewie's eyes. Stewie holds it out more. Jacob reluctantly takes the hat. Puts it on.

JACOB
Well? How do I look?

Stewie beams at the handsome man with the clear blue eyes smiling back at him, a bit of brown bangs hanging over his forehead.

STEWIE
I could kiss you right now.

Jacob looks at all the people waiting in the TSA line.

JACOB
Well then maybe you should go get some--

Stewie plants one on him, holding Jacob's cheeks with both hands, their lips smacking slowly, warm tongues gliding in, tender yet passionate. They separate with spittle hanging between their lips, both of them rock hard.

JACOB (CONT'D)
You know there's people behind me, right?

STEWIE
The swoosh told me to.

Jacob laughs.

JACOB
Yeah. Same reason I stole it.

They stare in silence. Thirty seconds of uninterrupted eye contact, their mouths still warm. Stewie pulls a wrapped square present from his waistband.

STEWIE
Your graduation present.

Jacob stares at the package. He thinks he knows what it is.

STEWIE (CONT'D)
Open it.

JACOB
Now?

STEWIE
Why not?

Jacob rips the paper from behind. *Discography: The Complete Singles Collection*, the Pet Shop Boys' greatest hits album from 1991. It's not shrink-wrapped.

JACOB
This is your CD.

Stewie shakes his head.

STEWIE
It's always been yours.

Jacob studies the cover. Neil and Chris' faded faces. The once-white booklet yellow from years of sun exposure.

STEWIE (CONT'D)
You wouldn't even give 'em a chance, remember?

Jacob shakes his head, tears forming.

JACOB
Oh God, this doesn't feel right at all.

Stewie hesitates.

STEWIE
Did you change your mind?

JACOB
It's too late for that.

STEWIE
No it isn't.

```
                    JACOB
      My bags are already on their way to Alex's. I've
      already paid my rent.

                    STEWIE
      You're not on the plane yet.
               (pause)
      It's never too late to make different choices.
```

Jacob looks up at Stewie's sweet face.

```
                    JACOB
      Choose for me.

                    STEWIE
      That's not how it works. You make your own choices
      and stand by the consequences.
```

Jacob sighs. Looks off, his lips tight.

```
                    STEWIE (CONT'D)
      Do you want to get on that plane?
```

Jacob exhales softly, thinking it all over. Looks back up at Stewie.

```
                    JACOB
      I do.
```

Stewie stares back. A slow smile creeps in.

```
                    JACOB (CONT'D)
      What's wrong?
```

"Nothing." Stewie shakes his head. "Just looking at you."

Jacob sticks the PSB CD into his backpack's side pocket.

```
                    JACOB
      I don't think I can write anything nearly as special
      as you.
```

Stewie takes Jacob's hands. Grips them tight. "You are the greatest screenwriter ever, Baby Boy. Everyone's gonna love you. The Professor. The critics. The audiences. Rotten Tomatoes. You're gonna be a big star. I'll be able to tell everyone I knew Jacob Andrezj before he was famous. I'm so unbelievably proud of you." Stewie grins. "I love you so much."

Jacob hugs Stewie nice and tight. Kisses him more, one last time. Smiles.

```
                    JACOB
      I love you.
```

Stewie smiles. "Go on! 'SCRAM!'"

Jacob chuckles. Grabs his red bag's handle. Turns around. Enters the TSA line. He looks back. Stewie's gone, already heading back to his Jeep. Jacob sighs. Maybe it's better that way.

"Sir!" a TSA Agent scolds, a big black woman. "You better finish that water."

Jacob remembers the almost full water bottle in his hand. Tosses it in the trash.

```
                    JACOB
      I'm not thirsty.
```

Jacob empties his pockets. Kicks off his shoes. Removes his belt. Drops off his bags. Walks through the body scanner. A team of TSA agents remove all his oversized body care products, some of them very expensive. Jacob ties his shoes with an eyeroll. It's not like he's going overseas. He'll just buy 'em all back when he lands.

The TSA Agent, the one that scolded him before, rolls the bag over. "Here you go, honey."

```
                    JACOB
      Thanks.
```

Jacob lifts it. Its lightness startles him. As he juts his left shoulder down, the Pet Shop Boys CD slips out of his backpack's side pocket. Jacob instantly snatches the falling CD before it hits the ground. He grins wide. Instantly looks around.

"I saw it," a bookish black man says, walking by.

Jacob chuckles. Repockets the CD. Grabs his suitcase. Walks toward his gate.

Jacob waits patiently for his group number to be called. His phone buzzes. He pulls it out. A text from Stewie: "Leaving on a Jet Plane came on soon as I started the Jeep. :("

Jacob frowns, his heart panging much harder than he thought it would. He goes into his Favorites lists. Swipes away Stewie's name at the top. Goes into his contacts. Deletes "Stewie Hanz Jr." Goes into his texts. Deletes the entire thread. Goes into his Recent Calls list. Deletes every number he sees. Then his voicemails, every one. Only after it's all gone does he realize he forgot to block the number itself.

Jacob pockets the phone. He can't remember Stewie's cell number. What's the harm in leaving it like that? Then he remembers the numbers from his Missed Calls list. Stewie's number is definitely in there. But Jacob doesn't pull out his phone. He doesn't go in to delete the Missed Calls. He's gonna leave it there. Just in case he's really desperate.

Stewie leans against the hood of JEEPGUY, no longer in the parking garage, parked out front instead. No cars coming or going. An American Airlines plane soars off the tarmac. That's the one. That's Baby Boy's. As the plane moves farther and farther away, Stewie feels a strange draining sensation, something getting sucked out of him little by little until he's nothing but a cold shell. The sun's rising and he's cold. In June. Awful.

A whiff of cigarette smoke hits his nostrils. Stewie instantly holds his breath. Fans the air in front of his face. It's Eunice and Peyton on their smoke break. "Sorry," Eunice drones.

"It's fine," Stewie says.

"Did your son make it on the plane alright?"

Stewie stares at her, no energy left. "He's not my son."

Eunice raises her brows. "Shit. My mistake."

"Mistake's all mine." Stewie opens the Jeep door, slides in, starts it up, and drives back home.

30,000 feet above Boston, Jacob plugs his headphones into his iPhone. Scrolls through his Apple Music downloads. Picks his overall playlist. Hits shuffle. "Stay" by Jackson Browne instantly comes on. No "Load-Out" before? No way. Jacob taps shuffle again. "Don't Go" by Yaz comes on. After a few seconds of grooving to the beat, Jacob realizes the name of the song. Taps shuffle again. "Get Back" by The Beatles. Jacob furrows his brow. One more time. "Baby Don't Go," by Sonny & Cher. One more. "So Far Away" by Carole King. Last one. "Don't Change" by INXS.

Jacob pauses the music, weirded out. Goes into the playlist itself. Scrolls down a bit. Handpicks "Go Where You Wanna Go" by the Mamas and the Papas. Looks out at the window. Sun's rising. And because he's going west, much faster than the sun itself, he's technically traveling back in time. Like Superman.

Jacob lands in LAX. Takes a Ridr to North Hollywood. Alex greets him at the door. Lights up a joint. Jacob doesn't mind. He's not anti-reefer like Stewie. He's cool. And it's California, he can't be that shocked. Jacob unpacks in his room, the rest of his bags already there. He hangs his favorite poster, *Pulp Fiction*, above his bed with a smile.

The next day, Jacob walks around Hollywood for the first time. A few guys check him out. Jacob realizes he's single again. With better goods this time. A part of him likes the freedom. He actually gets a bit excited.

A week later, Jacob walks through a department store to shop for work clothes. As he's changing, "Come Back" by the J. Geils Band plays through the fitting room's speakers. Quite an obscure choice. Normally people play their incredibly overrated "Centerfold," but not this. A chill goes down Jacob's spine. That's really weird.

The night before his internship, Jacob goes into Target to buy a jar of American Crew Molding Clay, the same kind Carter Jackson used. Changes his mind. Buys the Forming Cream instead. Less hold, same shine. Much more his style. Jacob smiles, kinda glad the TSA confiscated his stuff. But as he slides his RedCard into the scanner, he hears a familiar song over the speakers: "It's Too Late" by Carole King. Jacob looks up. What the hell is going on?

Jacob lays in bed. Alarm set. Lights off. Nothing to do but get up and go to work, his career about to begin. He smiles. Closes his eyes. Tries to go to sleep.

Fantasizes about his future instead.

WHALE

Inferno

Stripper ass SMACK. Loud pulsating music. Hot pink underlighting. Gross squeaky couch varnished in back sweat. Cashew's shitty laugh as he SMACKS Crystal's ass grinding against his crotch, Tiffany licking his neck with a randy grin. A tall black one named Lola approaches Whale. "Hey there."

"I'm gay," Whale says again, his voice slurring from his third glass of Domergue.

Lola nods rapidly and moves on. Twenty seconds later, another stripper comes by, a slender blonde named Brandi. "Hey handsome. All by yourself?"

"I'm gay," Whale groans. The cycle goes on. And Cashew doesn't even notice, sitting next to him but in a hedonistic world of his own.

A tall Asian one struts by. Cashew snaps his fingers at her. "Hey! HEY!"

The Asian, a three year veteran at Oh LàLà named Kitty, forces a smile and approaches the asshole in VIP. "Yes?"

"Make out with her!" Cashew points down at Crystal.

Kitty kneels beside Crystal and kisses her, Crystal's ass still gyrating against Cashew's groin.

"No, over there!" Cashew barks. "Eyes on me, chink!"

Kitty repositions herself. Makes eye contact with Cashew and she tenderly kisses Crystal's lips.

"Use your fucking tongue!" Cashew screams. "Fucking *KISS HER* Goddammit!"

Kitty eats Crystal's face.

Cashew grins, pressing the back of Tiffany's head against his neck. "That's right, bitch," he breathes. "C'mon, more. MORE!"

A red head named Ginger approaches Whale. "How are you tonight?"

"I'm gay," Whale says, audibly annoyed.

"Touch yourself," Cashew tells Tiffany. She rubs her breasts. "Slower." Tiffany slows down. "No, like *this*!" Cashew grabs her hands, roughly forcing them down her abdomen. "Like that! C'mon, cunt, try a little! C'mon!"

"Cool it!" Whale says.

"Shut up!" Cashew throws Tiffany's hands back at her. "Do it, slut!"

Tiffany forces a smile and does the motion Cashew demonstrated.

"Nice and slow. Yeah, that's right." Cashew unbuckles his belt.

"Dude, what the fuck?" Whale yells.

"STOP RUINING THIS FOR ME!" Cashew snaps, unzipping his fly. "Keep kissing, whores!"

"I just want to go home."

"We're staying here!" Cashew rubs his cock over his boxers. "Stop talking. And don't be a faggot, alright? Look away. Get another drink."

"I don't want another drink."

"I'M PAYING, ASSHOLE!" Cashew bellows. "God, why can't you just be fucking grateful?!"

Whale scoots down the couch just as a barmaid named Amber walks by. "Another Domergue, please."

"You guys have a tab?" Amber asks.

"He does," Whale says, thumbing back at Cashew. "It's either under Theo or Not That Nut."

"You're the producers, right?"

"Yeah."

Amber chuckles a bit at the action Cashew's getting. "That's the birthday boy?"

"I am," Whale says with a sarcastic grin. "And I'm gay."

Amber half-frowns. "This wasn't your idea?"

Whale shakes his head.

Amber sighs. "Be right back with that Domergue." She walks away.

Whale glances over at Cashew. Kitty and Crystal on their knees making out, their faces between Cashew's legs this time, Cashew smacking them with some... *wait*, WHAT?! His cock is huge! At least seven inches, maybe eight. Girthy. Bigger than Whale's. Why's he always so butthurt anytime someone calls him Cashew?

Amber returns with a Domergue. "Made it myself. I used a clear ice ball. It's much colder that way. Really makes the Scotch pop."

Whale lifts the glass, marveling at how transparent the ice is. "That's amazing."

"And it's on the house." Amber smiles. "Happy birthday, handsome."

Whale actually smiles back.

"Wait, what?!" Cashew pockets his pecker and swats the girls away. "Put it on the fucking tab."

"No, it's okay," Amber says cautiously. "It's fine."

"Put it on the fucking tab, bitch!"

Amber scowls. "No!"

"It's on the house!" Whale exclaims. "What's the big deal?"

"We're fucking PRODUCERS, toots!" Cashew snaps at Amber. "You think you too good for our money, you cum-guzzling cooze?"

Amber storms off with a scoff.

Cashew stands. Whips out a thick wad of singles. "Hey, you want a tip, don't you?!"

Amber stops. Reluctantly turns around.

Cashew frowns at her. "Get over here."

Amber reluctantly approaches Cashew, legitimately scared.

"On your fucking knees," Cashew growls.

"Theo!" Whale cries.

Amber lowers herself to the floor. Looks up at Cashew.

Cashew grins down at her. "Here's your tip, bitch." He smacks Amber across the face with the wad of bills.

"THEO!" Whale jumps to his feet. Pulls Cashew back. "WHAT THE FUCK IS WRONG WITH YOU!"

"SHE'S FINE!" Cashew shouts. "LOOK! LOOK!" He points at Amber eagerly scooping the money off the ground with a shameful frown. "SEE?"

Whale sighs hard. "I should just go."

Cashew pulls a vial from his pocket. "Here! Surprise!"

Whale looks at it. "What is this?"

"What do you think?" Cashew shakes his head in disbelief. "I don't know what the fuck is up with you tonight. You gotta unwind man."

Whale rubs the vial of coke between his fingers, unsure.

An hour later, Whale snorts his third line of coke, washing it down with his sixth glass of Domergue. Cashew's got a new girl on his lap, an anorexic brunette named Cherry in pink lace lingerie. "Míng thinks the Coronavirus is gonna hit us any day now," Cashew shouts over the music. "He's got a couple cousins down in Wuhan. They say it's pretty bad. Really contagious. Not that fatal though. But you know who it does kill? Old people. *Old people*, Drew!" Cashew laughs heartily. "Can you believe it? A fucking virus that only kills Boomers! Maybe there really is a God!" Cashew laughs even harder. Cherry forces out a laugh too.

Whale frowns. Cashew's levity makes him sick.

Cashew snaps his fingers at Amber walking by. "Three Coronas please!" He and Cherry laugh hard. "Come on!" Cashew yells at Whale. "Laugh goddammit! Laugh!"

"I don't wanna mix!" Whale slurs, wiping coke off his nose.

"Too bad!"

Amber drops off three Corona Extras and limes. "Good girl!" Cashew exclaims, smacking her ass. He and Cherry pop their limes in and chug their Coronas. Cashew momma-birds his into Cherry's mouth. Cherry gives it back. They make out, Corona drool rolling down their chins. Cashew pulls away. "I just thought of something!" he tells Whale. "You know what they should really be calling the Coronavirus? BOOMER REMOVER!" Cherry and Cashew both laugh at that.

Whale stares at the fourth line on the tray. He snorts it. Downs the Corona anyway. The rest of the conversation is a blur, Cashew going off on Cherry about how the country's probably gonna get shut down any day now, and with all the older CEO establishment types getting wiped out by the Coronavirus, it's gonna absolutely destroy Not That Nut's future competition and only help them in the long term.

Whale feels Cashew poking his chest. "Hey man! You feeling okay?"

"Can we go home now?" Whale murmurs.

"What?! No!" Cashew points to a brunette with large breasts. "This is Candy. Say hi, Candy."

Candy waves. "Hi, Candy."

"She's a pretty little puss, ain't she?" Cashew side-eyes Whale. "Take my word for it. Anyway, she's gonna give you a lapdance. Happy 25th, my dude."

"I don't want a lapdance," Whale says.

"I already paid her."

"I don't care. I don't want it." Whale stares at Cashew. "I don't want it!"

Cashew leans into Whale's ear, his breath reeking. "I DON'T CARE!"

Whale smacks Cashew away. "OW!"

"What's your fucking problem?! C'mon, you're embarrassing me!"

"I'M embarrassing YOU?!" Whale shouts back. "You've been acting like an asshole all night! I'm shocked they haven't thrown us out by now! This place keeps getting worse and worse!"

"Quit being so fucking pious! Enjoy it!"

"I don't want to be here! Why couldn't we just go someplace gay?!"

"Those places make me uncomfortable!"

"This place makes ME uncomfortable!"

"Not the same thing."

"Why? Because you think they'd treat you the same way you treat women? Don't flatter yourself, Cashew, you're not that hot. Like, at all."

Cashew stares. "Why do you keep insulting me?"

"It's my birthday, Theo. What the fuck?"

"STOP BEING SO FUCKING SELFISH!" Cashew hollers. "I'M PAYING FOR EVERYTHING! STOP WHINING! YOU'RE RUINING THE NIGHT FOR BOTH OF US!"

Whale frowns. "Fine, alright, I'll do it," he croaks. "But she has to know I'm gay beforehand."

"I don't fucking care."

"Evidently."

"What?!" Cashew leans closer. "What did you say?!"

Whale gets up. Follows Candy to one of the circular pink velvet backrooms, fully lit with a curved couch perimeter that puts the cum in circumference. "I'm gay by the way," Whale loudly tells her, his eardrums blown.

"Oh." Candy awkwardly looks around. "Do you still want me to do it, or...?"

"I'd like to talk if that's okay."

Candy bites her lip. Thinks. "I don't think I can unless I dance."

"Whatever make you comfortable." Whale leans back on the couch. "I can actually hear myself think back here."

Candy starts dancing on Whale's lap, hips grazing his crotch. She pops off her brazier, revealing a pair of tits with hot pink nipples. Whale studies her body the way he'd admire a tropical fish in an aquarium. "You're very hot."

"Thank you."

"I like your body. It's... It's nice."

"Thanks."

Whale bobs his head. Soft as mashed potatoes down there. "Can I, uh...?" He points up at her exposed areolas. "Can I touch your boobs? I've never touched boobs before."

Candy smirks. "Of course."

"I'm sorry, is that not allowed?"

"No, it's just so funny you asked."

Whale chuckles. Tenderly reaches up. Softly grabs a breast in each hand. Squeezes. "Oh."

"You like?"

"I don't know. I wasn't expecting them to feel like memory foam pillows."

Candy laughs some more. "Okay?"

Whale squeezes a bit more. Lowers his hands.

"Well? What's your verdict?"

"Still gay," Whale says with a shrug. "But you know what, honestly, I can see the appeal."

"You ever see a vagina?"

"No."

"Do you wanna?"

Whale laughs. "Maybe another time."

Candy smiles. "Alright then."

Whale looks up at Candy's face. That smart look in her eye. "Why do you do this?"

Candy doesn't slow down at all. "You're not one of those guys that's gonna try and save me, are you?"

"No. You just..." Whale's smile fades a little. "I'm just jealous, you know?"

"What is there to be jealous of?"

"All these men wanting you. Lusting after you. All that attention. And yet you're the one in control."

Candy hesitates. "I wouldn't say that."

"What do you mean?"

Candy turns away from Whale, her body still keeping the rhythm. "Before this I was working at a firm downtown, Evelyn Marketing Solutions."

"You have a Marketing degree?"

"From UCLA."

"Is that a B.S. or a B.A.?"

"B.S."

Whale raises his brows. "Damn."

"It was a really good job too. Very stressful." Candy goes quiet. "I'm from Nebraska originally. Very strict family. No sex ed. I never got a chance to go through my slut phase. Too busy being responsible."

"I know what that's like."

"After a few years I was really burning out at Evelyn, so a friend of mine suggested I go to a club called Palace in Ventura. You ever been there?"

"No."

"No, I guess you wouldn't have. It's one of those seedy dungeon sex places. Lots of young girls and older guys fucking. It's pretty hot if you're into that."

"I bet."

"I didn't wanna go at first, but my friend kept insisting I try it out. So one day I went out and did it. Got drunk. Fucked a few guys. I just wanted to get it out of my system. One night off from my life. It was so much fun. Holy shit. And I know I told myself it was just gonna be that one time, but I was so nervous in the beginning, so I decided to go back the following weekend to try again without the first-time jitters. That was even better. Getting used like that. Degraded. Touched all over the place. Being treated like trash. All those old guys cumming and sweating all over me. I just wanted more, you know? Just a way to let off steam after work. I knew I was gonna be okay. I only did what I was comfortable with. I was in control. The way I saw it, it was just like a hobby. I felt attractive. I made friends. I was actually happy for the first time in my life. So after a while I thought, 'I'm already at Palace ten hours a week. Why not get paid for it?' So one of my Palace friends got me a job here. It was just gonna be a side gig, only Monday and Wednesday nights, but I was always so tired by the time I had to go in for work, I actually changed my availability at Evelyn. I thought why not just work four days a week and dance the other three. Then this place took over. Then Evelyn let me go. But that's when I realized. Most of my clothes I bought for this place. I ate different things. My body was different. My hair was different. My Palace friends were my only friends. This place stopped being an escape from my life. From the sheer number of hours alone, somewhere along the line, it became my life."

Whale frowns. Her total indifference, the way she's perpetually dancing throughout, disturbs him more than the story itself. "Candy?" he whispers.

"What?" Candy looks back. Notices Whale staring down at his chewed-up fingernails. She stops dancing. "What's wrong?"

Whale looks up with wet eyes, trying not to cry. "I think I've made a big mistake."

Cashew suddenly bursts in with a loud parade of strippers shouting and laughing and before Whale could react he's lifted off the couch and dragged by his arm and pushed from behind and handed another glass of Domergue that Whale can't even look at and drops off on some shelf on the way up a flight of rickety wooden stares in a weird dark closet area up to a large green door Cashew pushes open and its suddenly very cold very fast and Whale realizes he's on the roof of Oh LàLà and Hollywood Boulevard below. "What's going on?" he asks Cashew. He sees the strippers are all in their underwear, freezing with desperate tip-seeking grins and Cashew's climbing a small metal ladder up up up to some lofty rooftop way up there.

"It's almost midnight!" Cashew calls down over the wind, climbing one rung at a time with a drink in his hand. "We gotta have a rooftop toast!"

"I'm not climbing up there!"

"Why not?"

"We'll get in trouble!"

"Live a little!" Cashew keeps climbing. The strippers follow one by one until Whale's the only one left. He shivers. Looks around at all those people in their cars and on the street. "GET UP HERE, FAGGOT!" Cashew screams from the second roof above. "COME ON! MOVE YOUR FUCKING ASS!"

"Okay!" Whale cries. He reluctantly grabs the top rung. Slowly ascends. Up and up. Closes his eyes. The wind's so strong. He opens his eyes and looks up to see he's halfway to the top, but then a spotlight hits his eye and he looks left and sees the pitch-black sky and the illuminated Hollywood Sign and he realizes how far up and he is and he looks down and stops and can't move and clings onto the ladder for dear life.

"HURRY UP!" Cashew screeches down at him.

"I CAN'T!"

Cashew's face turns red, his insults and slurs incomprehensible over the wind thank God and the metal rungs are wet making Whale more nervous and the feeling of vertigo fills his body and he can't breathe and the wind stings his eyes and tears streak down and he just wants to go home and he's scared and he misses Frankie and his mom and Stewie and he's cold and scared and way too drunk and high to feel sturdy and stable and strong and a gust of wind could just blow him away and he make him fall his body hitting the ground his soul smashing to smithereens and he can't even let go to readjust his hands and he can't climb up because Cashew's a fucking monster that hates him for this and his stupidity and probably wishes he had someone normal and dependable like Míng instead of a retarded consolation prize like him and he just wants to step down but he can't do that either because he's too scared of falling so he closes his eyes to tune Cashew out and he doesn't want to fall and he doesn't want keep climbing either and he can't even tell anymore which one's worse.

DREW

Cold Open, On the Rocks

Frankie sits on his musty sofa in a sweat-drenched gray wifebeater. His hands fidget. Goosebumps run up and down his arms. It's dark in his Chinatown apartment. Red neon shines in. He's cold. He can taste the mold on the air. Dust breezing past his nose hairs. But he doesn't want to move. He just sits there. Waiting.

KNOCK-KNOCK-KNOCK. Frankie flinches, his eyes widening at the door. Footsteps in the hall dash away. Frankie's legs wobble as he stands. He gingerly goes to the door, remembering "The Monkey's Paw" from high school. He turns the knob. Opens the door.

Nothing. Just yellow lights in the hallway. No one in sight. Frankie pokes his head left. Right. Looks down. Standing resolute is a brown paper bag with a red wax seal poking out. Frankie grabs the bottle. Slams the door.

Frankie pulls down the paper, revealing a 750mL bottle of 22yr Domergue Single Malt Whisky. Frankie studies the seal up close. Perfect. Like it had never been opened. He holds the glass up to the light. No sediment. No strange color. It is in there, right? Frankie places the bottle on his coffee table. Sits on the couch. Studies it from afar. Ten minutes, Theo said. Just one sip. It won't even hurt him. Frankie closes his eyes. Reminds himself what it's all for. How much better his life will be. He can start on Monday if he does it before the night is through. That's what he said. All Frankie has to do is find a way to get in a room with Drew Lawrence. That might not be so easy after his condo attack. He's probably hiding in a bunker somewhere like Hitler in Berlin, afraid of anyone getting in, knowing a hit is coming. It can come from anywhere. Even if he can somehow talk his way in, Drew's gonna suspect something's amiss and bring someone into the room just in case. How far is Frankie willing to go with this? Oh God, what if he doesn't drink it? It's not gonna work. There's no way he gonna be able to—

"Lone Digger" by Caravan Palace blasts out of nowhere. Frankie flinches. That's his ringtone. His phone's ringing. A California number not in his contacts. Frankie swipes. Doesn't say anything at first. "Hello?" he murmurs cautiously.

Pages turn over speakerphone. "Hey."

Frankie freezes, his stomach hardening.

"Frankie? You there?"

Frankie licks his lips. "Hey buddy, uh..." He furrows his brow. "Jacob, I mean. Or I guess you go by Drew now."

Drew laughs over the phone. "It's okay, man. Don't worry about it." Pause. "Been a while, huh?"

"Yeah."

"How you been?"

"Fine, I guess. You?"

Drew's sitting in Ephemeral Pictures' newly refurbished conference room, a view of the illuminated Hollywood sign behind him, a dozen scripts laid out before him, his iPhone flat on the table. "Can't complain," he says with a self-deprecating chuckle. "Under the circumstances at least."

"I heard."

"I was going through a bunch of old scripts just now. I saw your number on *The Surgery*'s title page and I thought, you know, why not?"

Frankie sighs. "Yeah."

"You doing anything right now?"

Frankie peers over at the Domergue bottle smirking back at him. "No."

"Come on over. I want to talk to you about something."

Frankie hesitates.

"Is that okay?" Drew asks.

Frankie clears his throat. "Alright."

"I'm at 2700 Sunset Boulevard. Let me know when you're out front. I'll buzz you in."

Frankie nods nervously. "Yeah. Sounds good."

"You okay?"

"Yeah. I'll see you there."

"Seeya." Drew hangs up.

Frankie puts his phone away. His muscles tense up. He presses his head with both hands.

Drew adjusts his red and black tie before the full length mirror in his office. His only suit. His only shirt. His only tie. But the best of each. He checks his teeth. His breath. Messes with his hair. Throws in a bit more American Crew Pomade for good measure. Maybe too much. Oh well. He spritzes on another hit of Unpredictable Pour Homme by Glenn Perri, literally the only cologne he's ever worn. Nice. He buttons his black Armani jacket. Turns left. Frowns. Unbuttons the jacket. Takes off the tie. Undoes the collar button. Oh yeah. Much better.

Frankie paces outside Ephemeral Pictures, nervously clutching the Domergue with two hands. He looks down at the ground. The dark patches. But what if a wino finds it? Or a kid? Frankie forces his eyes closed.

Drew passes the time re-reading *The Surgery*. Remembers South Street Diner. They were so great then. And then again at Ristorante La Riunione. A year and a half apart but still just like before. And it's not like it just happened. Eighteen years ago. Old enough to fuck. Tensions had to have cooled.

Drew's phone blips. A text. Showtime.

Frankie looks around the sparse street, the traffic lights switching for no one. BUZZZZZZ! CLACK! Frankie pulls the door open. Walks right in.

The office is dark. Empty chairs. Empty desks. Big open concept ground floor. Frankie imagines the place full of people, of artists, all working at full strength. Frankie lets out a sigh, making him realize how quiet it is in there. No one's around, the only light coming from upstairs. He hears footsteps on the balcony. Instinctively hides the bottle behind his back. Looks up.

Drew's smiling down at him. He's jacked. Handsome as shit. Great hair. Clean face. "Hey."

"Hey."

Drew juts his head. "C'mon. Let me get a good look at you."

Frankie ambles up the stairs, letting the Domergue fall to his side. Half his body hits the light. How common he must look. Rushed shave. Combed back hair. Flab along his belly. Stained Whitman hoodie. And Drew's in a suit. A goddamn Armani suit. He probably had a thousand of those fuckers before the fire. How convenient that was. Now he can claim to be Buddhist if he wanted to.

"Don't think I've ever seen you without a beard," Drew says. "And no glasses. Wow."

"Do you have any body fat left at all?"

Drew chuckles, eyes down, flattered grin. God, even with a baseball grand-slammer's build he's still the same old Jacob. This is gonna be harder than Frankie thought.

Drew puts an arm around him, meaning to walk him into the conference room, but he finds himself giving a hug instead. Frankie's body's softer now. It's nicer that way. And warm.

Frankie frowns. He hugs Drew back, still holding onto the Domergue bottle. He squeezes. Closes his eyes. What the fuck is wrong with him? He can't do it.

Drew steps back, laughing at the heavy thing in Frankie's hand. "What'cha got there?"

"Nothing."

"What is it?"

Frankie moves the bottle behind him. "Nothing, it's just..."

"What?" Drew asks eagerly.

Frankie reluctantly hands it over. "A peace offering, I guess."

Drew takes the bottle. "Thanks man. That's so sweet of..." He reads the label. "Frankie, holy shit! This is a..." Drew shakes his head. "This must've cost you a fortune! I can't accept this."

Frankie furrows his brow. Drew could probably afford a whole case of Domergue 22s. How dare he rub his salary in like that. The salary he gives himself. "I wanted to go all out," Frankie says cordially.

"But can you really afford this?"

There he goes again. "It doesn't matter. It's for you." Frankie suddenly remembers what day he met with Theo. What a coincidence. "Happy Birthday."

Drew smiles. "I can't believe you remembered."

"The Ides of March. How could I forget? It's the most metal birthday ever."

Drew looks at the label again. "It's a shame. I never had a 22 before."

"I never had a normal one." Frankie realizes. "What do you mean 'it's a shame?'"

Drew hesitates. "I'm kinda sober now."

"What do you mean kinda?"

"I'm trying to be sober now. I haven't had booze in weeks."

Frankie doesn't react. "Well if you're not gonna drink it, I'm just gonna return it."

"No." Drew looks at the label. "I don't know."

"I picked the year myself. Remember when you first got back from Italy, the four of us in King of Siam's looking up at that $1,200 bottle of Domergue?"

"The one you hoped tasted like shit?"

Frankie hesitates. "Well that's when this Scotch began. It was made in a batch with hundreds of others, poured into a cask, and stashed away in a moldy old cellar. Inside the cask the whisky stewed, trapped in its own air, in the dark. Year after year it changed, its composition altering a little bit at a time. All the other barrels get drained, but not that one. That's the one they keep in oppressive conditions longer than the rest. The men who filled it probably don't even remember doing it anymore, but someone remembered it was there, hiding in the dark. And they poured every drop of that barrel into the bottle you're holding right now. It's the one time forgot and yet, because of that, it's more valuable than all the others combined. And it's all right there, in your hands. All for you. Every single drop from that forgotten barrel."

Drew softens at Frankie's words. "I don't think I deserve this."

Frankie smirks. "Yeah you do."

Drew takes a reluctant breath. "Well, what the hell, right?" He chuckles. "C'mon, I wanna show you something."

Frankie follows Drew inside the conference room, the overhead lights actually hurting his eyes. Mahogany conference table. Twenty chairs of Florentine leather. An entire window wall showing the motherfucking Hollywood sign. A small sink along the wall. Shelf of Waterford crystal tumblers and decanters. Mini-fridge underneath.

Drew returns to his seat at the far end of the table. Gestures at the scripts in front of him. "Recognize these?"

Frankie places the poisoned Domergue bottle at the center of the table. He sits in the next chair over from Jacob — *Drew*, the next chair over from *Drew* — and scoots it over for a better look. "*Who We Are*," Frankie reads. "*Through the Red Door. Daddy. Waiting for Me.* Wow, it's really all of them. *Drive-Thru.*"

"I had Kev pull 'em all from the archives."

Frankie looks at Drew curiously. "Kev's your partner?"

"Yeah," Drew says, a hint of guilt shining through. He picks up *The Surgery*. Shows Frankie. "Look."

Frankie smiles with genuine nostalgia. "What started all this?"

"Stewie was here." Drew puts the script down. "LA. He was here."

Frankie's face goes numb. "Stewie? Really?"

"First time I saw him since I got on the plane." Drew beams warmly. "He looked really good. I missed him."

Frankie shifts uneasily. "That's good."

Drew notices minute discomfort in Frankie's expression. "I think it's time we talked about the elephant in the room."

"Let's have a drink first."

"No, I..." Drew bobs his head. "In a second. I just want to say what..." He sighs.

Frankie stares at the wooden table. Not even a scuff mark. The bastard.

Drew rubs his eyes. "I should never have cut you out of the Paramount deal. I'm sorry."

Frankie looks at Drew with no sympathy at all.

"You were right about Theo," Drew continues anyway. "He was manipulating me, just like you said he was. Always for himself. And I fell for it hook line and sinker."

Frankie blinks. Looks away.

"I only gave him the deal because..." Drew murmurs, picking at his fingernails. "It was so stupid, I felt like I needed to, like I owed him something. But it was just a trick. He was jealous of us since Day One, the way the two of us were together. That's when he decided to turn me against you."

Frankie furrows his brow. What a liar.

Drew makes tender eye contact. "I know it's been hard for me to... you know, keep going after all that's happened. But I wanna make amends, Frankie. I realize now I need to be a better man, and that means mending my bridges." He pauses. "I need to be more aware of the consequences of my actions."

"What are you gonna do about that?"

Drew shrugs. "What can I do? I've already tried making up with Theo. That didn't work out. I'm just gonna have to move on. Redeem myself in his eyes some other way."

Frankie can't breathe. "You're not gonna get back at him or anything?

Drew chuckles. "That's just not my thing, man. You know that."

Frankie looks off, confused.

Drew points at the whisky. "C'mon, let's crack that open."

"Just a second," Frankie says quickly. He rubs his face. "Is that why I'm here? Because you wanted to make up with me?"

Drew's brows lower a bit. "You make it sound like it's not mutual."

"Who said it was mutual?"

Drew points at the Domergue. "You brought the peace offering, my guy."

Frankie nervously chuckles. "No, I mean... What was it you had in mind? Not just an apology eighteen years late, I hope."

"Of course not." Drew sits back. This isn't going as well as he hoped. "I want us to be friends again."

Frankie hesitates. Not good enough. "Can I join you here?"

"As what?" Drew instantly asks.

Bile hits Frankie's throat. He wasn't expecting that at all. "Whatever... you could need me for."

Drew scratches his scalp with a crooked frown. "It's kinda complicated at the moment."

Relief flows down Frankie's arms. "Oh really?"

"Our next project's a Charles Ponzi biopic stylized like *Wolf of Wall Street*, but Kev's spearheading that one. I'm just helping out here and there. We might not credit my contributions if all the Jimmy stuff's still lingering by the time it comes out."

"So the answer's no."

"No, the answer is not no."

"I'm hearing a no."

"It's a maybe. I have to talk with Kev first."

Frankie leans back with disappointment.

Drew shrugs. "I'll see what I can do. I just can't make any promises."

Frankie contorts his lips, thinking it over. "Yeah, let's open the whisky now."

"Yes. Let's." Drew stands. Tosses two coasters onto the wooden table. Moves to the bar. Grabs two octagonal tumblers made of genuine Waterford crystal. "You excited for your first taste of Domergue?" Drew asks, crouching down to the mini-fridge.

Frankie rotates his chair. "What's in there?"

"Clear ice balls." Drew removes two perfectly translucent spheres with tiny tongs and drops them into the tumblers. "The coldest ice can get."

"Is that good for Scotch?"

"Yeah. Really makes the flavor pop. Helps you smell every inch."

Frankie nods uneasily. "Really."

"And the older the Scotch, the more detailed the smell." Drew places the two tumblers on the coasters. Grabs the bottle. Undoes the wax seal. Frankie watches Drew uncork the bottle, suddenly nervous.

Drew pours a generous serving in Frankie's. A generous serving in his own. Drew places the bottle back on the table. Recorks it. Grabs his glass. Raises it. "To the future."

Frankie doesn't budge. He can already feel his hands shaking.

Drew grins. "C'mon man, hurry up."

Frankie tenderly takes the glass. Raises it. "The future."

Drew taps his glass. Brings it toward himself. "Now you gotta shake it around." Drew moves his tumbler in a circular motion. "The scent is, like, 95% of the fun. That's why you don't shoot whisky. You really need to swirl it around until you can smell it. Take a whiff..." Drew lifts the glass to his nose and inhales. "And then you..." He abruptly stops, looking down at the glass.

Frankie's heart pounds. He just might shit his pants.

Drew furrows his brow. Swirls the Scotch around again. Sniff. A bigger sniff. Drew slowly looks at Frankie with dead eyes.

Frankie stares back, too scared to move.

Drew puts the glass back on the coaster. "What's in this?" he asks slowly.

Frankie shrugs. "Drink it and find out."

A long gasp floats out of Drew's lungs. His lower lip trembles in horror. And Frankie's unchanged expression, that knowing look, just makes it all worse. "I don't understand."

Frankie slams his glass onto the table. "You never asked me once this entire time what the hell it is I've been doing for the past eighteen years."

Drew opens his mouth, no sound coming out. "Okay, what have you been—?"

"Don't fucking start now!" Frankie snaps. "Did you really throw me over for a stolen script?"

Drew can't move. The bottle. The glasses. This isn't a joke. This is really happening. "Oscar told you?"

Frankie's blood races. "So it's true? You never wrote *Atomic*?"

Drew hesitates. Nods a bit.

Frankie hacks with disgust. "You fucker."

"It was a mistake!" Drew cries, his eyes filling with tears. "It was all wrong! I was wrong about everything! I only just found out how wrong I was about the whole thing! And everything after—"

"You took my career from me! The Paramount deal! I earned it just as much as you did and you fucking STOLE IT FROM ME!" Frankie chuckles, his face getting red. "Because of a script you DIDN'T EVEN WRITE?!"

"Believe me, I wish to God I didn't do it!" Drew cries back. "I couldn't tell anyone! I was living a fucking lie! I built my entire career on a fucking lie! Everyone was expecting me to be this amazing prodigy because of it! I hated it! You have no idea how hard it is living up to that!" Drew inhales, snot rattling. "That's why I left Not That Nutty! I was trying to make up for it!"

"Bullshit!" Frankie snarls, jumping to his feet. "You were fired!"

"Because I didn't want to do it anymore!" Drew sobs. "I needed to know I could still do it! Now I know I can! I know Oscar must've been upset when he told you, but he knows my side of it now! It's all settled now! I can finally be free of it!"

"You really expect me to feel sympathy for a man in an expensive suit sitting in a leather chair at a mahogany table with a crystal tumbler and the goddamn HOLLYWOOD SIGN OUT THE WINDOW?!"

"I DIDN'T PUT IT THERE!" Drew screams back.

Frankie bursts out laughing, deep bass-heavy chortles, lots of air.

Drew wipes his cheeks. "I didn't want you to be part of it, okay? I knew it was wrong. Of course it was wrong. I tried to keep you out of it. Why should I drag you down with me the way Theo dragged me down with that video?"

"Don't fucking lie to me!" Frankie snaps. "You didn't want me to talk you out of it, that's why!"

"What part of any of this could I possibly be lying about?!" Drew asks angrily. "I'm confessing to pretty damning stuff here! You can't just decide what parts are true or not based on what you feel—!"

"SHUT THE FUCK UP!" Frankie hollers.

Drew sinks in his seat.

Frankie rubs his neck. Clears his throat. "I know what really happened. I know all about Theo trying to talk you out of it, you threatening to cut him out of it if he didn't go along with it. I know all about that, so don't pretend you were doing me any favors."

Drew's face hardens.

"I know that's how you are," Frankie eggs. "When you want something, you take it. You don't let anyone else talk you out of it."

"Oh my God," Drew says with alarming clarity. "Theo put you up to this, didn't he?"

"No-no-no, it was my fucking idea!" Frankie shouts, a finger jabbing his chest. "I'm the one here right now! I'm the one who's had enough! I'm the one trying to kill..." His voice fizzles.

Drew smirks bitterly. "You can't even say it, can you?"

"Shut up!"

"If that's what Theo told you, Frankie, that's a lie. That's a fucking lie. He was on board instantly. It was his idea to get Míng's cousins involved. He didn't give a shit about you at all. He was thrilled."

Frankie struggles to breathe. "I don't believe you!"

"Oh, but you believe him?" Drew retorts. "Theo the liar? Theo the gaslighter? What, are you fucking stupid?!"

Frankie's head gets all fuzzy. "He said…" He sits back down. "He said he had to kill you before you killed him first."

"Of course he did." Drew softens with disappointment. "But that's not why you agreed, is it?"

Frankie hesitates, his poker face breaking. "It is."

"What's the reason, Frankie?"

"That was the reason!"

"This is Theo we're talking about, dude." Drew nods. "Just tell me the reason."

Frankie frowns with immense shame. "He said he was gonna make me Head of Production."

Drew scowls. "A job?! You were gonna kill me for a fucking job?! THAT'S what convinced you?!"

"Of course it was!" Frankie cries. "You already got everything, Drew! You got everything you fucking wanted! Money! Drugs! Sluts in a club! Oscar noms! So many films! All that clout! And even after all that, you STILL got to go and make whatever you wanted?! Haven't you had enough? If you died now, what could you said you haven't done? I did everything right. I trusted you, even after everything. I didn't STEAL my breakthrough feature. Everything I made was mine. You can't even say that. Not even now. *Branson*'s premise was my idea. Ephemeral's mission statement was my idea. You couldn't even think of your own. It's my turn in the spotlight. You might never have deserved it, but I sure as hell fucking do."

"You fucking idiot, don't you realize he's gonna kill you after you kill me? Or he'll find some other way not to deliver on his promise? That's what he does! That's what Theo Landreth fucking does! We promised each other we weren't gonna tell anyone about *Atomic*. I never told Kev because of that. I couldn't even tell Stewie." Drew shakes his head. "But Theo's the one that told you, didn't he? Oscar never told anyone. I know he didn't. As soon as you said it, I knew it didn't make any sense."

Frankie looks away.

Drew scoffs. "How is it so obvious to me now and so hard for you of a sudden?"

"I don't understand why..." Frankie shakes his head. "Why does it matter?"

"You don't want to kill me, Frankie," Drew begs with a soft whisper. "He's the one that wants to kill me. The only reason you're here right now is because he's too much of a coward to do it himself or too paranoid that it'll come back to him and he'll end up going down like The Professor." Drew shakes his head. "Why the hell would you ever want to work for a man like that?"

"I wanted to work for YOU!" Frankie yells, painful anger rushing through him like a deluge. "I knew it was only a matter of time before you came to your senses about that goddamned midget little fucking SHIT! Anyone with a brain could see it! One day you'd wake up and leave Theo behind, AND YOU DID! You actually fucking did! It took you a long fucking time, a lot more than I thought it would, but YOU DID!" Frankie moves a finger back and forth between them, too hurt to speak. "But I never got that call," he croaks. "The apology call. The 'Come Start This Thing With Me' call."

A frown forms on Drew's face.

"This could've been mine," Frankie says, pointing all around. "I didn't want to go through with it when I first walked down here, but then I saw this place, THIS PLACE, and suddenly I wanted to do it again. This was supposed to be for us, Jacob. We could've made *Branson* together. It could've been just like it should've been, just like the way we wanted it to. We could've been the fucking Medicis, just like we always talked about!" Frankie's eyes get all red. "But you didn't, you called... Kev? Who the fuck is Kev? One of the interns you fucked over at

The Factory? He hated your guts as far as you knew, didn't he? Why the fuck would you call him if he hated your guts?"

Drew's eyes droop.

Frankie scoffs. "You didn't even know his real name, did you?"

Drew looks up with shame.

Frankie scrunches his face. "You're fucking awful."

"You don't understand," Drew whispers. "I was... I wasn't..." He takes a wavering breath. "It wasn't even personal."

"Yeah, no shit!"

"It was just to get back at Theo!" Drew cries. "I really genuinely thought I couldn't do anything without him, so I tried to make my own Ephemeral in-house. and the fucker just fires me! I wanted to get back at him by teaming up with someone he hated, just to piss him off!"

"And you getting back with me wouldn't have pissed him off?"

Drew stares.

"I don't know anything about Kev," Frankie says, "I don't know why Theo hates him so much, but I got a feeling I would've pissed him off more. SO much more."

Drew frowns.

Frankie clenches his jaw. "You're just like him, you know? Just like him. A goddamn. Fucking. Coward. You couldn't face me after what you did to me, and you knew EXACTLY what you did to me, but you couldn't even do it because you thought if you just left me alone, you could imagine a whole other happy version of the last eighteen years of my life instead of the truth, and truth is that I've spent the last eighteen years hating the only real friend I ever had." Frankie sighs pathetically. "And I never would've hated you if you hadn't done that to me."

Drew feels hollow. Cold. "I'm sorry," he murmurs. "What can I do?"

"You can fucking die, that's what you can fucking do."

"I wanna fix this, Frankie." Drew sits up. "I know now. You were right. Just let me fix this."

"You're a coward!" Frankie declares. "You were a coward in Boston, you were coward when you first came here, and you're a coward right now. Do you really think you can say or do anything that can possibly change that? To change the damage you've already done? Every single person in this town hates you. If you died tonight, everyone would cheer! Twitter would go ballistic. They'd be happy justice was served for once. 'Thank God! Drew Lawrence is dead!' Do you really think you have it in you to undo all that? You ruined my life! You've ruined so many lives! You spent the last eighteen years making so many other Jacob Andrezjs cynical and backwards!"

"I spent the last eighteen years working my ass off," Drew growls. "I worked my ass off on film sets, in studios, in writer's rooms. Standing up to my friends, who I thought were my friends. Apologizing to people who fucking hated me. Telling the truth to people who spent years thinking I was actually LESS responsible than I really was. And I lost a lot. That was hard. That was so fucking hard. But it was all worth it because at the end of the day I can say I did something and failed. I didn't just sit on my ass for eighteen years expecting the world to hand me my future!"

Frankie's nostrils flare.

Drew angrily stands. "You could've started your own thing, but you didn't. You could've come up to me or tried to get in touch with me somehow. I know I made that pretty difficult, but if it really mattered to you, you would've found a way. But you didn't, did you? You just wanted to sit back like a Hasidic fucking Jew and follow all the rules and honors and say all the right things and just hope and pray that somehow the universe rewards you for your strict adherence. But that's not the world, Frankie. There are no rules. No one has the answers. If you really wanted to be a Hollywood producer, you would've fought for it every day with no results in sight, on faith alone that what you're making is not only what you want but also something that's gonna work. Yes, when I left Not That Nutty to make this place I should have picked you to run it with me." Drew slips into a scowl. "But thank fucking God I didn't because THAT would've been the biggest mistake of my life!"

Frankie's cheeks tremble with fury.

Drew flicks a dismissive hand. "Why the fuck would I want *this*? A man with no drive. A man with no balls. So easily manipulated. A fucking quitter. Stop waiting for a solution to show up, Frankie, and just solve it yourself, why don't—"

Frankie lunges at Drew with both hands, Drew's chair going down with them. Drew scrambles on the floor, panting, trying to push Frankie off of him. Frankie clutches Drew's shirt. Rips it just under his right arm. Elbows Drew in the gut, knocking the wind out of him. Drew gasps. Frankie straddles on top of him. Grips Drew's neck with both hands. Squeezes as tight as he can. Pushes Drew down onto the floor. Chokes the life out of him.

"I want that job!" Frankie hiss-snarls with bulging bloodshot eyes. "Give me that fucking job!"

Drew's face turns blue, his vision blurring. His legs flop. His left knee jabs Frankie in ballsack. Frankie yelps. Lets go. Slides off. Falls on his side. Gasps in pain.

Drew crawls away, recatching his breath. Looks back. Kicks Frankie right in the face, knocking him back, drawing blood. Drew struggles to stand, using Frankie's old chair for support.

Frankie's adrenaline revived, he waddles on his knees over to the table. Grabs his tumbler of Domergue. Flicks the glass up at Drew.

Drew dodges the poisoned Scotch just in time, falling over Frankie's chair. The whisky lands on the screenplays, soaking *Drive-Thru* to the bone. The clear ice ball bounces on the wood, rolling down the length of the table onto the carpet.

Drew gets up. Knocks Frankie on his back. Curbstomps the crystal tumbler in Frankie's hand, glass shattering, tiny bones breaking with a crunch. Frankie screeches in pain, his palm covered in blood. He whips his hand away, flicks it, blood flinging across the carpet, desperate to prevent stray poison from entering his bloodstream.

Drew stops at the sight of *Drive-Thru* soaked with whisky, the other scripts absorbing the brown like old sponges. His heart breaks. The originals.

BAM! Frankie suckerpuches Drew across his left cheek, Drew slamming hard against the wooden table. Frankie picks him up by the jacket. Punches him straight in the face, a knuckle bouncing off Drew's gumlime. Drew instantly tastes blood. His lip's cut too.

Frankie winds back for another punch. Drew two-hand shoves him onto the floor with all his strength. Jumps on top of Frankie. Straddles his body with both knees on the carpet. Presses his ass down on Frankie's abdomen. Drew grabs Frankie's throat with his left hand. Raises his right fist.

"Don't!" Frankie croaks. "Please!"

Drew punches Frankie across the jaw. Again. Frankie struggles to get his arms out from under Drew's knees. Punch. Drew's face tight with hate. Punch. Entire body trembling with adrenaline. Punch. Straining bloodshot eyes. He winds up for another punch.

And stops.

Drew looks at his raised fist. Blood. Covered in blood. He gasps, suddenly able to hear Frankie's sobs. He looks down. Covers his mouth in horror. Desperately slides off Frankie. Scurries away as fast as he can. The back of his head bumps the edge of the table. He stays there, panting with terror at what he just did. Who he was just emulating.

Frankie coughs. Lifts his bruised head, desperately trying to regain his breath, unable to move the rest of his body. He sees Drew lying on the floor too, just across from him. He sits up. Makes eye contact. They stare at each other, both of them panting.

Drew tries not to cry. "Get out of here," he whispers.

Frankie's bloody brows draw together.

Drew wipes blood off his lips. "You hear me?! Get out!"

Frankie blinks. Looks around in a daze. Slowly stands.

Drew jumps to his feet, anticipating another suckerpunch. Frankie takes his time toward the conference room door. He stops.

"Get out!" Drew cries, his throat hurting.

"My hand..." Frankie murmurs, inspecting his right palm.

"I said GET OUT!" Drew clutches the practically full 750mL bottle of Domergue by its slender neck and chucks it across the conference room. Upon deafening impact the glass shatters into a million microscopic pieces, a razor-sharp mist floating down the air like a cloud of gnats. Poisoned Scotch spatters across the slamming door and ricochets onto the carpet. Vibrations of the collision echo throughout the room, shaking the overturned chairs, shimmying across the carpet, crawling up Drew's legs and rattling his bones.

The metaphorical smoke clears from Drew's elongated 80 proof baseball. A single unsmeared handprint reveals itself on the conference room door, a beautiful, seemingly phosphorescent scarlet stinging Drew's eyes. Frankie was gone, racing down the stairs if not already outside. But did he really leave that room? Even if he had pushed the door with his left hand, the one covered in sweat instead of blood, could Drew really forget what just happened? What Frankie said? What he tried to do?

Nevertheless, Drew was alone.

Truly, utterly alone.

This is where we came in. Drew finds his Domergue tumbler undisturbed. Doesn't dump it out. Thinks about drinking it anyway. And after four hours of staring out at the Hollywood sign, he determines it's all too fucking much, the acceptance of death creeping in like the sun is behind Griffith Park right now. He should've just jumped off the Colorado Street Bridge when he had the chance. He'd end up at the same place without all those ruined lives in his wake. Heh. It's funny because wake means funeral.

"Excuse me, sir? Sir?" Drew looks to his left at the grinning twenty-two-year-old with the big nose and the red Nike baseball cap. "Is this seat taken?" Jacob asks, rolling a leather chair over.

"Oh you've got to be fucking kidding me," Drew mumbles.

"Thanks!" Jacob plops down with a contented sigh. "If I fall asleep and you need to use the bathroom, just go ahead and wake me. I wouldn't mind."

Drew rolls his eyes. "Let me guess. This will be your first time in LA?"

"How did you know?!" Jacob asks with a bouncy grin. "I'm about to have my big break. In Hollywood. I'm gonna be a big star." He holds up jazz hands. "A *screen writer*."

Drew cringes at Jacob using two words. He looks down at the glass of Domergue in his hand.

"My name's Jacob Andrezj." Jacob holds up a hand. "What's yours?"

"You know what my name is."

Jacob's brow furrows. He holds his hovering hand higher. "No I don't."

"Shut up."

Jacob drops his hand. "Just say your name."

"Drew Lawrence, okay? Drew Lawrence."

"Wow!" Jacob props his head up with a hand. "Are you in the industry?"

Drew glares. "I'm not playing along with this."

"Someone's grumpy."

"Yeah, no shit."

"Uh-oh!" Jacob cries like a Teletubbie. "Someone used a curse word! I don't use curse words because that makes me better than you."

"If you don't shut the fuck up, I'm drinking this whole thing right now."

"Alright!" Jacob snaps, breaking character. "Fine. Jeez."

Drew purses his lips. Looks away.

Jacob side-eyes Drew's muscles. "God, I get so fucking hot."

"Stop being such a fucking narcissist."

"Says the guy literally talking himself down from suicide." Jacob pauses. "It's that bad, huh?"

Drew nods.

"Remember what Dario said. What was the last movie you saw?"

"*Cloud Atlas*."

Jacob furrows his brow. "That's a great fucking movie to go out on."

"I know!" Drew whines. "That's the problem!"

"It always reminded me of Stewie."

"Which is why I watched it."

"God, I miss him already."

"Yeah, well, he stops missing you fast." Drew frowns instantly after saying it.

Jacob hesitates. "Is that why you're so grumpy?"

Drew shakes his head. "No. I didn't mean that."

"I know you didn't."

"Then why'd you ask?"

"I just did," Jacob says. "Tell me what's wrong."

"You want the list?"

"We got a long flight. Might as well."

Drew groans. "Fine." Finger number one. "Theo's trying to kill me."

"Hey, at least you're somebody worth assassinating."

Drew glares at Jacob.

Jacob scoffs. "Number two. Go on."

"You wanna hear number two?! I'll tell you number two! Not only was Frankie so easily turned against me, he actually hates me for a legitimate reason!"

"Don't blame yourself."

"Did I not ruin his life? He's right. I should've picked him. It would've made up for everything. Choosing Theo. Stealing the Paramount deal. Everything would've been fine."

"Except Kev," Jacob reminds him. "If he hadn't joined the team, he'd still be hating your guts for publishing that video of Trisha."

"That's not why I picked him."

"Lord Grantham married Cora against the Dowager's wishes for her money. They didn't have problems admitting they loved each other. Wrong reason or not, you picked the right man, and because you picked Kev, he learned to realize he was wrong about you. Isn't that better than another evil memory of Whale lingering around out there?"

Drew shakes his head. "Kev would've spent the past eighteen years resenting me for destroying the internship. That alone would put him on the top of Theo's assassin list." Drew thumbs behind him. "If I picked Frankie, that'd be Kev's blood on my door right now."

Jacob looks at the red handprint. Frowns at the thought.

Drew swirls the whisky around. "Is Kev a better person? Sure. But Frankie had dibs. How am I supposed to do the right thing if the right thing for somebody is the wrong thing for somebody else?" Drew sighs helplessly. "There's no use trying to rationalize with emotional beings."

"Kev's not irrational. He stuck by you after all that with Jimmy. Frankie could never have done that."

"He doesn't know about Frankie," Drew counters. "When he comes in tomorrow to check up on me, he's gonna see all this and ask what happened. That means I have to lie to him again or tell him the truth. That just might be what ends it all, you know? The last straw. It's not in the past anymore. It's something Kev's currently profiting off of, and I knew it very well and never told him."

Jacob folds his hands. "I say tell him everything."

"I'm not gonna lie."

"No, I mean everything. This. Theo. *Atomic*. What just happened with Stewie. Everything."

Drew stares at the younger version of himself sitting next to him. "Are you out of your fucking mind?"

"Just listen. If you tell Kev all that there is to tell, if he really is a true friend, he'll understand."

Drew shrugs. "What if there's a limit to forgiveness? A total number of crimes, accidental or not, intentional or not, emotional or not, that makes a person too far gone to pardon? There has to be, right?"

Jacob gives a crooked frown. "I'm just speaking from my point of view, but I wish I had a friend like Kev."

"We did. We had Stewie."

"Stewie was delivered to us a silver platter. Just another handout. A handout from God. You earned Kev fair and square. You forged the best friend you always wanted. Maybe you were meant to cross paths with Kev. Your friendship's been proven to endure, and it's only getting better. Maybe he's the Garfunkel to your Simon and you don't even know it yet."

"Fate's not real," Drew says. "It's just a word people use to take the blame off themselves."

Jacob shakes his head. "You made your dreams come true despite all those doubts you had about whether or not you could. Look at you. If you knew for a fact you were gonna be Drew Lawrence one day, of course you would've made different choices. You would've started working out in high school. You would've come out earlier. You wouldn't have wasted all those years being exactly what your mom wanted you to be, being exactly what Theo wanted you to be, or all those Whitman girls, what they wanted you to be. You definitely wouldn't have cried the first day of your internship, that's for sure. Think how much would've changed if that hadn't happened. How much harder you would've worked. How much confidence you would've had. But life didn't work out that way. You did cry that first day. And The Professor told you it was over for you, didn't he? But here you are. How is this any different from that?"

Drew rolls his lips.

Jacob smiles. "The key is to remember that there are still good people in the world, people who'd hear everything you've ever done and love you anyway and still want to help you, even if you can't see them." He stands. Heads for the door.

"You're not even real!" Drew calls after Jacob, rotating his chair. "Who cares what you think?"

Jacob stops halfway out the door. "No one."

Drew softens.

Jacob shrugs sadly. "No one at all." He closes the door.

Drew snaps out of his daydream, glass of poisoned whisky still in his hand. There's color in the sky now. The sun's about to rise. He thinks back on how much he's grown, all that character development he's too distracted by life to notice. He thinks of Kev, of all those men and women that work for him, the ones sleeping at home, dreaming of new ways to change costume design and production design and screenwriting and cinematography, etc. All because of him. They're gonna become masters of their field and teach others what skills they've learned. Because of him.

Drew lifts the octagonal tumbler like Yorick's skull. Stares through the amber fog. That dark brown abyss obfuscating his view of Griffith Park. If the sun was rising, he wouldn't have known. He takes a deep breath. Closes his eyes. Makes his choice. He lets the unsipped glass of

Domergue slip out of his fingers. The crystal tumbler falls to the floor. Bounces away, ice and poisoned Domergue flying everywhere.

A sudden tremble races down Drew's body. For the grimmest of moments he regrets not drinking the poison, and now he can't go back. He can't change his mind now. He just has to wait. Prepare. Endure.

Dawn's first light blazes across his eyes. Drew looks up at the sun-soaked City of Angels before him, Debbie Reynolds singing "Good Morning, Good Morning!" in his head. Drew finds himself smiling. A massive wave of euphoria hits him. He made the right choice. The sun is what convinced him. There's something so magical about it, the web that lured all those flies. So warm and pure. So beautiful. Everyone always takes it for granted. As Drew Lawrence watches the morning light stroll down Sunset Boulevard frame-by-frame, he suddenly remembers what's next on the docket: breaking the news to Kev. That scares him shitless. Best case scenario, he'll still have his friend and a bond stronger than ever. Worst case... well, he'll cross that bridge when he comes to it.

But he won't jump off. No sir, he will not. Not anymore.

END OF PART EIGHT

EPILOGUE

Nothing is Written

"I'm sorry, it's too late."

```
                    JACOB
       Let's just go.

                    STEWIE
       You guys are just being lazy. I want to speak to your
       supervisor.

                    JACOB
       We don't have time for that.
```

Stewie looks at Jacob. Jacob juts his head toward the terminal entrance.

```
                    JACOB (CONT'D)
       Let's go.
```

Stewie follows Jacob. Glares back at Eunice and Peyton.

```
                    STEWIE
       You shouldn't just take that.

                    JACOB
       I don't wanna miss my flight.

                    STEWIE
       You won't miss it! It takes thirty minutes to board
       and you know you'll be held on the ground for a
       while.

                    JACOB
       I just wanna make it through security, okay?
```

Jacob quickens the pace to a jog, his red case rolling behind him. Stewie follows around the corner.

```
                    JACOB (CONT'D)
       Thanks for sticking up for me though.

                    STEWIE
       Of course!
```

The two of them follow the signs. Turn left. Turn right. Up the escalator. Down the steps. Left. Left. Right. Right. Quite the maze. Finally the TSA checkpoint emerges. Jacob and Stewie slow down, desperately catching their breath. Jacob notices a bored Persian man sitting at a kiosk full of plastic water bottles. Sign says "Last Chance Water."

```
                    JACOB
       I'm gonna get some water. You want any?

                    STEWIE
       Just buy one on the other side.

                    JACOB
       I'm thirsty now. What's the difference?

                    STEWIE
              (to Vendor)
       How much is it?
```

"$6.23," the Vendor mumbles.

```
                    JACOB
          (handing over a $20)
Sold.

                    STEWIE
That's a such rip-off! He knows people can't bring
water through security so he's gouged the prices.
```

"That's America, my friend." The Vendor hands Jacob a bottle of water and $13.77 in change.

```
                    STEWIE (CONT'D)
Why not $6.25? That's such a strange choice.
```

Jacob slowly opens the water. Stewie watches as Jacob takes the tiniest of sips.

```
                    STEWIE (CONT'D)
That's the first time I've ever seen you drink a
bottle of water like a normal person.
```

Jacob sighs.

```
                    JACOB
This is really happening, isn't it?

                    STEWIE
You're gonna be okay. Think of LA.

                    JACOB
I don't want to lose you.

                    STEWIE
You haven't lost me.
```

Jacob's breath quickens, panic settling in.

```
                    JACOB
I stole your Nike hat!

                    STEWIE
What?

                    JACOB
The red one. The one you had on in the Black Bear. I
stole it.

                    STEWIE
          (smiling)
That's alright.

                    JACOB
No it's not. It's stealing.

                    STEWIE
I forgive you.

                    JACOB
You shouldn't. Stealing is wrong.
```

Stewie nods.

```
                    STEWIE
Where is it?

                    JACOB
Main compartment.
```

Stewie walks around. Unzips Jacob's backpack.

```
                    JACOB (CONT'D)
No, the MAIN compartment. The big one, all the way
up.
```

Stewie unzips the big part. Pulls out the red Nike hat. Walks back around. Holds it out.

STEWIE
There. Now it's not stealing.

Jacob looks into Stewie's eyes. Stewie holds it out more. Jacob reluctantly takes the hat. Puts it on.

JACOB
Well? How do I look?

Stewie beams at the handsome man with the clear blue eyes smiling back at him, a bit of brown bangs hanging over his forehead.

STEWIE
I could kiss you right now.

Jacob looks at all the people waiting in the TSA line.

JACOB
Well then maybe you should go get some--

Stewie plants one on him, holding Jacob's cheeks with both hands, their lips smacking slowly, warm tongues gliding in, tender yet passionate. They separate with spittle hanging between their lips, both of them rock hard.

JACOB (CONT'D)
You know there's people behind me, right?

STEWIE
The swoosh told me to.

Jacob laughs.

JACOB
Yeah. Same reason I stole it.

They stare in silence. Thirty seconds of uninterrupted eye contact, their mouths still warm. Stewie pulls a wrapped square present from his waistband.

STEWIE
Your graduation present.

Jacob stares at the package. He thinks he knows what it is.

STEWIE (CONT'D)
Open it.

JACOB
Now?

STEWIE
Why not?

Jacob rips the paper from behind. *Discography: The Complete Singles Collection*, the Pet Shop Boys' greatest hits album from 1991. It's not shrink-wrapped.

JACOB
This is your CD.

Stewie shakes his head.

STEWIE
It's always been yours.

Jacob studies the cover. Neil and Chris' faded faces. The once-white booklet yellow from years of sun exposure.

STEWIE (CONT'D)
You wouldn't even give 'em a chance, remember?

Jacob shakes his head, tears forming.

JACOB
Oh God, this doesn't feel right at all.

Stewie hesitates.

STEWIE
Did you change your mind?

JACOB
It's too late for that.

STEWIE
No it isn't.

JACOB
My bags are already on their way to Alex's. I've already paid my rent.

STEWIE
You're not on the plane yet.
(pause)
It's never too late to make different choices.

Jacob looks up at Stewie's sweet face.

JACOB
Choose for me.

STEWIE
That's not how it works. You make your own choices and stand by the consequences.

Jacob sighs. Looks off, his lips tight.

STEWIE (CONT'D)
Do you want to get on that plane?

Jacob exhales softly, thinking it all over. Looks back up at Stewie.

JACOB
I do.

Stewie stares back. A slow smile creeps in.

JACOB (CONT'D)
What's wrong?

"Nothing." Stewie shakes his head. "Just looking at you."

Jacob sticks the PSB CD into his backpack's side pocket.

JACOB
I don't think I can write anything nearly as special as you.

Stewie takes Jacob's hands. Grips them tight. "You are the greatest screenwriter ever, Baby Boy. Everyone's gonna love you. The Professor. The critics. The audiences. Rotten Tomatoes. You're gonna be a big star. I'll be able to tell everyone I knew Jacob Andrezj before he was famous. I'm so unbelievably proud of you." Stewie grins. "I love you so much."

Jacob hugs Stewie nice and tight. Kisses him more, one last time. Smiles.

JACOB
I love you.

Stewie smiles. "Go on! 'SCRAM!'"

Jacob chuckles. Grabs his red bag's handle. Turns around. Enters the TSA line. He looks back. Stewie's gone, already heading back to his Jeep. Jacob sighs. Maybe it's better that way.

"Sir!" a TSA Agent scolds, a big black woman. "You better finish that water."

Jacob remembers the almost full water bottle in his hand. Tosses it in the trash.

```
                    JACOB
        I'm not thirsty.
```

Jacob empties his pockets. Kicks off his shoes. Removes his belt. Drops off his bags. Walks through the body scanner. A team of TSA agents remove all his oversized body care products, some of them very expensive. Jacob ties his shoes with an eyeroll. It's not like he's going overseas. He'll just buy 'em all back when he lands.

The TSA Agent, the one that scolded him before, rolls the bag over. "Here you go, honey."

```
                    JACOB
        Thanks.
```

Jacob lifts it. Its lightness startles him. As he juts his left shoulder down, the Pet Shop Boys CD slips out of his backpack's side pocket. Jacob instantly reaches down. The CD clips his fingers, spinning in midair and crashing onto the ground, lid detaching, disc flopping out.

Jacob furrows his brow. He had it. He was sure he had it. All those decades of video games gave him quite spectacular hand-eye coordination, something he's always prided himself for because of how notorious Aspies were with basic motor function. And yet he missed it by that much.

Jacob crouches, delicately rebuilding the CD case, nudging himself away from the bookish black man walking by. He finds himself staring at the CD's cover art again. He remembers his first date with Stewie. His smile, all that love radiating already. How proud Jacob was showing off his floor. How lonely he had been before. What a magical night it was. *Vertigo* in the TV room. Pasta in the kitchen. Botched intercourse thanks to Jacob's medication. And then all that followed. Hot chocolate in July. That trip to P-Town. Dancing in the snow. Christmas at home. Always that same smile when Jacob walked in, even after a long day working on his business.

```
                    JACOB (CONT'D)
        What am I doing?
```

Jacob throws the CD into his backpack and marches toward the scanner he had just passed through. The TSA Agent that scolded him before, the big black woman, bugs her eyes instantly. "Excuse me!" she cries, holding out a stopping hand just before Jacob and his giant red bag can cross.

```
                    JACOB
        I want to go back through.
```

"You can't come through this way."

```
                    JACOB
        I was just through here. Let me go back.
```

"You have to go around."

```
                    JACOB
        That'll take too long! I have to get through NOW!
```

"If you don't go around right now, I'm calling security."

```
                    JACOB
        Please.
```

"Turn around. Follow the signs." The TSA Agent moves to touch his shoulder. Jacob dodges out of the way.

```
                    JACOB
      What's your name?
```

"I beg your pardon?"

```
                    JACOB
      Your name. What is it?
```

The TSA Agent hesitates. "Sharonda."

```
                    JACOB
      Hello Sharonda. I'm Jacob. Jacob Andrezj.
```

"Nice to meet you. Now can you please—?"

```
                    JACOB
      Have you ever been in love?
```

Sharonda blinks. "I don't believe that is any of your business."

```
                    JACOB
      I found my soulmate, Sharonda. Do you know what that
      means? That means he loves me more than anyone else
      in the world. Even more than his own mother, and you
      have NO IDEA how impressive that is. I'm never gonna
      find someone that likes Downton Abbey as much as I
      do, let alone psychedelic rock AND grunge AND dance
      AND new wave AND prog AND still wants to listen to
      the new stuff. I'm never gonna find someone who knows
      every bit of me, just the way I am, and wants to
      spend every night with me.
```

A crowd forms around them, other agents and passengers listening to Jacob's passion with dumbstruck grins. A few hold hands to their hearts in romantic wonder.

```
                    JACOB (CONT'D)
      He's everything to me. He's been looking for me his
      whole life. I love him. I love him so much. I can't
      even describe how much and I'm a goddamn writer! It's
      my job to describe shit like this and I can't even do
      it. I can only tell you just how bad my life will be
      without him. All those nights alone, working in a job
      I can't stand, dealing with horrible, awful, stupid
      idiots every day until I end up just like them. Do
      you know what that's like, Sharonda? Don't you just
      wish someone could hold you when you got sad? Don't
      you wish someone was there for you, a special man all
      of your own, through good times and bad?
```

Sharonda softens, moved.

```
                    JACOB (CONT'D)
              (tears in his eyes)
      Well I do. His name Stewie. Stewie Hanz Jr. He's the
      best thing that ever happened to me, and he's RIGHT
      DOWN THERE, Sharonda! He is GETTING AWAY! I need to
      go after him! Just let me through. I need to be with
      him. That is where I belong. With him. With the man I
      love, the man who loves me. He loves me enough to
      sacrifice his own happiness to make my dreams come
      true, but he is my dream come true, Sharonda. He is
      my dream come true.
              (shakes head)
      You just gotta let me through.
```

"Come on!" a female bystander begs. "Let him through!"

The rest of the crowd affirmatively nods with eager grins, their voices trampling over each other, a Wall of Sound of romantic glory.

Sharonda sighs. Looks up at Jacob. Smiles.

SHARONDA
Go get him, child!

THE WHOLE CONGREGATION CHEERS! Jacob kisses Sharonda on the cheek and races through the checkpoint. Sharonda turns her head with a smile, a single tear rolling down her cheek.

CUT TO:

INT. AIRPORT HALLWAY - NIGHT

Jacob dashes past pedestrians, his backpack thumping, his massive suitcase rolling behind him. Pedestrians stop conversations, interactions and scoldings to cheer Jacob on as he walks by. Crowds of people voluntarily move aside for him, rooting him on with applause, fist pumps and whistles.

RANDOM BYSTANDER #1
C'mon Jacob!

RANDOM BYSTANDER #2
We believe in you!

RANDOM BYSTANDER #3
Yeah! Do it for Stewie!

Jacob feels the energy. Runs just a bit faster.

JACOB
(breaking fourth wall)
If it wasn't already established that I did cross-country at Eagle Ridge, this wouldn't be believable at all!

CUT TO:

INT. CONNECTOR - NIGHT

Jacob turns the corner and halts. A BLOCKADE OF TSA AGENTS ARE WAITING FOR HIM.

TSA AGENT #1
(placing hand on gun)
You were supposed to get on that plane.

Jacob charges the blockade, YELLING as he does. He heaves his rolling suitcase by the handle ahead of him, KNOCKING OVER THREE TSA AGENTS. He races through the blockade.

The other two agents unholster their guns and point them at Jacob's back.

TSA AGENT #2
SHOOT HIM!

The TSA Agents unload their entire clips. Each bullet misses to Jacob's left and right.

TSA AGENT #3
(into a walkie)
He's headed for the escalators.

CUT TO:

INT. TERMINAL CENTER - NIGHT

Both escalators are full of BYSTANDERS. As Jacob stops to catch his breath, he notices A MILITIA OF TSA AGENTS running into the open space below.

TSA AGENT #4
(pointing up)
There he is! Get the doors!

A TSA Agent PULLS A STEEL LEVER. All steel hallway gates on the ground floor start lowering inch by inch. The TSA Militia waits at the bottom of the escalators, guns drawn.

Jacob gasps. Looks at how full the escalators are. Readjusts his hat. Hoists his big red bag onto the steel divider between the up and down escalators. Hops on top. Kicks off a pillar, shoving off.

Jacob rides his big red bag all the way down the steel divider, SPARKS FLYING IN BOTH DIRECTIONS onto screaming bystanders. Just as the divider levels off, Jacob rolls off the bag and lands feet-first on the ground. THE RED SUITCASE FLIES OFF THE DIVIDER AT MISSILE SPEED

The TSA Agents SCREAM as the massive suitcase CRASHES INTO THEM, landing on its tiny wheels just long enough for Jacob to catch up and clutch the handle. He keeps running, dragging the suitcase as fast as he can toward the descending steel gate.

RANDOM BYSTANDER #4

Look out!

A HUNDRED TSA AGENTS COME OUT OF NOWHERE, an angry mob on Jacob's tail. Jacob strains, the steel gate's gap now shorter than he is.

RANDOM BYSTANDER #5

He'll never make it!

Jacob throws his suitcase ahead of him. It slides under the gate just before it would've otherwise crushed it. Jacob drops to the floor and slides under, the gate knocking off his Nike hat. He reaches back and grabs the hat just as the steel gate closes with a CHUNG.

The TSA Agents collide into the steel, bouncing off, falling to the floor.

CUT TO:

INT. AIRPORT HALLWAY - CONTINUOUS

Jacob puts his hat back on, desperately trying to catch his breath. He turns and sees A BAGGAGE CART parked on the side, its DRIVER (29) eating an apple.

JACOB

Sir! Sir! My bag's slowing me down!

DRIVER

I'm on break.

JACOB

Please! These TSAs, they're trying to murder me!

THE TSA AGENTS CARVE A BUZZ SAW THROUGH THE STEEL GATE.

JACOB (CONT'D)

Look, they're coming through!

DRIVER

(shrugs)

Don't know what to tell you, kid.

JACOB

There has to be something that'll change your mind.

The Driver thinks.

DRIVER

I'll do it for $13.77, not a penny more.

Jacob reaches into his pocket. Smacks $13.77 in bills and coins into the Driver's hand. The Driver bugs his eyes.

JACOB

(breaking fourth wall)

Good thing I bought that water, huh?

A TSA Agent kicks a vertical rectangular hole out of the grate. CRASH!

JACOB (CONT'D)

Oh no!

The Driver winds up and pitches his apple through the hole, HITTING THE TSA AGENT IN THE FACE and knocking him back. Jacob looks at the Driver in wonder.

JACOB (CONT'D)

That was 100 mph! How did you do that?

DRIVER

What, you don't recognize me?

The Driver pulls out a New York Mets hat and puts it on. Jacob instantly gasps.

JACOB

JACOB DEGROM?!

DEGROM

That's right, kid! Now let's go get Stewie!

DeGrom lifts the oversized red suitcase with one hand and drops it onto the cart like it's nothing.

Jacob's phone buzzes. He pulls it out. It's a text from Stewie:

"Leaving on a Jet Plane came on soon as I started the Jeep :("

DEGROM (CONT'D)

C'mon kid, let's go!

JACOB

It's Stewie! I gotta text him back!

DEGROM

We don't have time!

An ARROW whips by Jacob's nose. Jacob gasps at a TSA archer reloading his bow.

JACOB

They shoot arrows now?!

DeGrom bobs his head to the side.

DEGROM

They shoot arrows now.

Jacob hops onto the passenger side of the baggage cart. DeGrom slams on the gas, racing down the hallway. TWO GOLF CARTS OF TSA AGENTS AND ARCHERS CRASH THROUGH THE GATE, GAINING ON THEM.

JACOB

(looking back)

We've got company!

Multiple arrows whiz by deGrom's cart.

DEGROM

Time for evasive maneuvers.

DeGrom pops the lid of his gearshift, revealing a little red button.

JACOB

What is that?!

DEGROM

You better hold on to something, kid.

Jacob grabs onto the cart's roof, tight as he can. DeGrom stares at his rearview mirror. The carts are getting closer.

DEGROM (CONT'D)

Come on...

JACOB
They're almost on us!

DEGROM
Just a bit more...

The carts are right on their tail. An archer winds up an arrow. Points it right at Jacob's face. Jacob squeezes his eyes shut.

DEGROM (CONT'D)
Eat shit, Sox fans!

DeGrom pushes the little red button. FLAMES BURST OUT THE BACK OF THE CART, LAUNCHING THEM FORWARD AT NOS SPEED, "Mrs. Robinson" by Simon and Garfunkel playing over the soundtrack.

The carts behind them catch fire, agents jumping off. The carts crash into the wall and INSTANTLY EXPLODE.

DeGrom zips down the hallway, dodging pedestrians like a pro. Jacob's grooving to "Mrs. Robinson" on the soundtrack. He suddenly furrows his brow. Look at the backseat.

PAUL SIMON (26) and ART GARFUNKEL (26) stop strumming their acoustic guitars, awkwardly looking back.

JACOB
What are you guys doing here?

SIMON
What are WE doing here? What are YOU doing here?

JACOB
New York Mets all-star Jacob deGrom's helping me evade the TSA in his suped up baggage cart. What does it look like?

SIMON
That's what you get for breaking protocol.

JACOB
Going the other way breaks TSA protocol?! Really?!

SIMON
Do you want another 9/11?! Cause this is how you get another 9/11!

JACOB
Of course I don't want another 9/11, Paul Simon. I just don't understand why they're shooting at ME. I'm an unarmed WHITE man running through an airport.

GARFUNKEL
Based.

SIMON
What'd you think was gonna happen? You're really going off-script here, man.

JACOB
I DON'T GIVE A SHIT! I WANT STEWIE, GODDAMMIT!

GARFUNKEL
You know you guys missed your turn, right?

JACOB
Huh?

GARFUNKEL
You're going the wrong way!

JACOB
(hand to his ear)
WHAT?!

SIMON & GARFUNKEL
YOU'RE GOING THE WRONG WAY!

Jacob bugs his eyes.

JACOB
STOP THE CART!

Jacob deGrom slams on the brakes, the tires screeching to a halt. Jacob hops out, grabs his bag, and races back from whence they came.

JACOB (CONT'D)
(calling behind him)
Thank you Paul Simon and Art Garfunkel circa 1967!

SIMON
No problem, kid!
(to Garfunkel)
Five, six, seven, eight.

Simon and Garfunkel strum away to "Mrs. Robinson." Jacob deGrom drives on.

DEGROM
You guys can skip the DiMaggio part.

CUT TO:

INT. GLASS HALLWAY - NIGHT

Jacob rolls his suitcase around the corner toward Terminal B. Stops to catch his breath. He notices a pair of RED BRAKE LIGHTS outside, A JEEP WRANGLER crawling over a speed bump on its way out of the complex.

JACOB
Oh, Jesus God. No.

Jacob repeatedly smacks the glass window with his hands.

JACOB (CONT'D)
(bleating)
AYY BEE! AYY BEE! AYY BEE!

CUT TO:

EXT. LOGAN INTERNATIONAL AIRPORT - SAME

Eunice and Peyton, still on their smoke break, hear a smacking sound. They look up to see Jacob banging on the glass with flat palms.

JACOB
(muffled by glass)
AYY BEE! AYY BEE! AYY BEE!

Peyton throws his cig away, pissed.

PEYTON
I'll take care of him.

EUNICE
(stopping him; menacing)
He's too late.

CUT TO:

INT. GLASS HALLWAY - SAME

Jacob keeps smacking, tears forming in his eyes.

JACOB
(bleating)
AYY BEE! AYY BEE! AYY BEE!

The Jeep doesn't stop. It keeps on driving into the night.

JACOB (CONT'D)
(desperate bleating)
AYYYYY BEEEEE! AYYYYY BEEEEE!

```
THE JEEP SCREECHES TO A HALT. The driver's side door whips open.
Stewie hops out.

                         STEWIE
                    (screams)
          AYYYYYYYYYYYYYYYYYY BEEEEEEEEEEEE!

Jacob widens his eyes. Bolts down the stairs with his bag.

                                                       CUT TO:

INT. TERMINAL B LOBBY - CONTINUOUS

Jacob finds Peyton waiting for him at the bottom of the stairs,
fists up.

                         PEYTON
          You crazy punk!

Peyton lunges for him. Jacob drops his bag. Hops over the railing.
Punches Peyton. Hits him with the back of his elbow. Knocks him to
the ground. Jacob goes back up the stairs for his bag. Clip-clops it
down the stairs.

A security door kicks open, A SWARM OF TSA AGENTS POUR OUT. Stewie
comes out of nowhere and torpedoes into them, knocking them down
like dominoes.

Eunice races after Jacob. Grabs his arm. Spins him around.

                         EUNICE
          Jacob! It's too late!

                         JACOB
          NOT FOR ME!

Eunice smacks the shit out of Jacob. Twice.

Stewie races over to Chekhov's Religious Artifacts. Lifts the cross
pole out of its stand. Waves it at the mob like a lion tamer.

                         STEWIE
          MOVE! MOVE!

The angry TSA mob stays back. Jacob breaks free from Eunice,
sneaking through with his suitcase.

                         STEWIE (CONT'D)
          Hey, some of these guys are pretty cute.

                         JACOB
          Stop cruising the extras!

JACOB KICKS THE DOOR OPEN. Stewie follows out. Jacob holds the doors
closed while Stewie slides the cross pole through the door handles.

                                                       CUT TO:

EXT. LOGAN INTERNATIONAL AIRPORT - CONTINUOUS

The trapped mob slam their hands against the doors as Jacob and
Stewie run away, laughing hand in hand all the way back to the Jeep.

                                                       CUT TO:

I/E. STEWIE'S JEEP - DAWN

Stewie speeds JEEPGUY down an empty highway, the sun rising ahead of
them.

                         JACOB
                    (into his phone)
          Just request the Venmo and I'll send it over.
                    (pause)
          Alright man. Thank you so much. Bye-bye.

Jacob hangs up.

                         JACOB (CONT'D)
          Alex said he'll ship everything back tomorrow.
```

STEWIE
He's not upset?

JACOB
No, he's actually pretty chill about it.

Jacob turns on the satellite radio. "Isn't It a Pity" by George Harrison is playing. Jacob turns it up. Looks out at the sunrise with a smile.

JACOB (CONT'D)
It was never gonna work out.

STEWIE
What?

JACOB
LA.

Stewie hesitates.

STEWIE
Not necessarily.

JACOB
Let's be real, if I actually got the job at The Factory and became a famous screenwriter, it probably would've ruined my life.

STEWIE
How can you say that?

JACOB
I don't know. What if someone offered me coke?

STEWIE
You'd just say no, wouldn't you?

Jacob thinks about it.

JACOB
I guess.
(pause)
I'd still turn into a huge a-hole though.

STEWIE
You don't know that.

JACOB
I know how I am, Daddy. I always go for the route that makes me the most comfortable, and the most comfortable route tends to be the one with the least disruption, and typically that ends up with me melding into my environment. If I'm surrounded only by nasty people, sooner or later I'm gonna end up nasty.

STEWIE
You didn't turn into a Whitman Girl.

Jacob's taken aback by that one.

JACOB
Maybe without you I would've found myself stuck against my grain like I was in Phoenixville. Too afraid to speak up. Dependent on selfish people taking advantage of my good nature.

STEWIE
You watch WAY too many movies, Baby Boy. I'm sure LA is just a really boring corporate office of a city.

JACOB
And you don't think I'd find that disappointing?

STEWIE
Only if you ended up settling for less.

Jacob barely shrugs.

JACOB
Maybe I would have.

STEWIE
I doubt it.

JACOB
Isn't that what I just did?

Stewie looks at Jacob. Back on the road.

STEWIE
I don't think so.

JACOB
Let's just say for the sake of argument that I am right, that Hollywood really is the amoral Shakespearean hellscape I think it is. Do you really think I'd make it through with all my morals intact?

STEWIE
Of course.

Jacob frowns. Looks away.

STEWIE (CONT'D)
Don't you?

Jacob keeps staring out the window with glum eyes. Stewie softens. Reaches over and pets Jacob's hair with a childish smile.

Jacob smiles back for a little bit before turning away and reverting back to that same blank stare. Morose. Introspective.

Stewie's smile melts away. He faces forward with that same uncertain look.

The Jeep drives off toward the rising sun. The profound soundwaves of "Isn't It a Pity" float off its tailwind, the once silent morning air filled with beautiful music for the briefest and most wonderful of moments before fading away and returning once more to nothing.

FADE OUT.

POSTSCRIPT

1. While Jacob Andrezj as a character is largely autobiographical, his story is set in a slightly altered timeline from my own. My mom really did fly out to Italy for an expensive vacation despite her abrupt unemployment. Our relationship has never been stronger thanks to that trip. *Andrezj of Hollywood* posits how our lives would've been greatly affected had she simply canceled the trip and pocketed the money instead.
2. Whale's story is what easily could've happened had I relocated to LA after graduation like I originally planned. Drew's story is a continuation of that timeline.
3. Despite the altered timeline, Jacob and Stewie meet in Boston on June 12, 2016 under the exact same strange circumstances that brought me and Howie together in Philadelphia on June 12, 2016. Some things really are meant to be.
4. Jacob Andrezj is me if I only knew Howie Schulze for a year. Theo Landreth is me if I never met Howie at all.
5. Carter Jackson is based on a real person. I don't think I can go into too many details, but safe to say I really did know him and I really did have a crush on him.
6. The swastika incident really happened, albeit two years before I met Howie.
7. The motorcycle crash was tweaked to include cocaine use, but otherwise it really did happen as described, "Bat Out of Hell" and all.
8. The private Facebook post Jacob reads to his psychiatrist in "(Wish I Could Fly Like) Superman" is 100% real, Jacob's name swapped in for my own.
9. The red Nike cap, the special spoon Jacob finds in the snow, the "Likes Boys" T-Shirt, the Italian red leather jacket, the stuffed baby elephant (Corey Zander), the "I Knew You Were Waiting for Me" dog tag, the Pet Shop Boys CD, and the sandy "Nothing is Written" graduation cap are all real. The only object I slightly altered is JEEPGUY. In reality, Howie alternated between two manual Jeep Wranglers, a red 1998 named JEEPBOY and a blue 2006 named JEEPGUY.
10. Howie and I got married June 12, 2021, exactly five years from the day we met. Some things really are meant to be.

ACKNOWLEDGEMENTS

Andrezj of Hollywood was first conceived in January of 2018. In the five and a half years this novel has been in development, I've received vital help from several people that I would like to thank personally.

Thank you Nicholas Passell, my very good friend, for your expertise in Los Angeles geography. You have been a very crucial help in a thousand little ways.

Thank you Tory Hunter for reading *The Sins of Jack Branson* and *Andrezj of Hollywood* before everyone else. Your enthusiasm has affected me in so many ways. I cannot even begin to describe how much you've impacted my career. Thank you so much for what you do for so many budding writers.

Thank you Lisa Tinianow for being there for me whenever I need you, for being my best man at my wedding, for aiding me as a writer and as a person.

Thank you Michael Star and shommy, my cover artists for *The Sins of Jack Branson* and *Andrezj of Hollywood*. An author is only as good as his covers, and my career would be nothing if it weren't for you guys.

Thank you Middleton Media Group for ruining LA for me before it was all too late.

Thank you Stehman family, John and Jane, Deb, Rachel, Michelle, Joan, Beth and Mark, as well as the Stepnowskis, Lyn, Martine, Mike and Jess, Candice and Sam, Joy, for your faith in me and continued support.

Thank you Schulze family, Jeannie, Ray and Chrissy, Jeannine and Matt, Lorraine and Mike, for being the best in-laws anyone could ever ask for.

And thanks most of all to Howie, my beautiful husband. Not only was a novel-writing career your idea, you also continue to inspire me every day. I really couldn't have come this far without you. And I know I just wrote an 800+ page book saying pretty much the same thing, but I really want to emphasize again that I have never been happier or as fulfilled as I have been being your man. You make me feel like everything is possible. I love you so much. Happy Anniversary.

— David Schulze
June 12, 2023

FROM THE PUBLISHER

Thank you so much for reading *Andrezj of Hollywood*. This is by far my most personal project yet, and I'm incredibly proud of how it turned out. I really hope you enjoyed it too.

I believe the most interesting stories are those with personality, intelligence, and just a bit of strange. That can only be possible with a singular creative voice. I chose to self-publish my novels through David Schulze Books so I could tell my stories without compromising my final cut privileges.

All I ask in return is an **honest** review on Amazon, Goodreads, B&N.com, or the social media platform of your choice. Doing so not only provides feedback I can use on future projects, it also directly supports my growth as a career author.

If you want to mention this book on Facebook, Twitter, or Instagram, don't forget to add #AndrezjOfHollywood or #DavidSchulze.

Thanks again, and I hope you read more of my work.

— David Schulze

COMING SOON

Their grandparents created the Internet.

Their parents weaponized it.

They want to be the generation that destroys it.

ABOUT THE AUTHOR

David Schulze (né Stehman) was born and raised in Phoenixville, Pennsylvania. A lifelong admirer of movies, mythology, and classic literature, David loves stories across all mediums.

In 2017, David graduated from Emerson College with a B.A. in Writing for Film and Television and a Minor in Literature. He has written nine feature screenplays and four shorts, many of them placing in screenwriting competitions. His bestselling debut novel *The Sins of Jack Branson*, adapted from the screenplay of the same name, was published in 2021.

David lives in Marlton, New Jersey with his husband Howie.

Want exclusive stories, in-depth analyses, and updates on future projects? Go to davidschulzebooks.com

---

CPSIA information can be obtained
at www.ICGtesting.com
Printed in the USA
BVHW051805150523
664198BV00008B/115

9 781737 037835